ADVANCE PRAISE FOR
THE PASSION OF MARY MAGDALEN

"Magdalen fans are in for more surprises in Cunningham's classy, sexy novel."

Patricia Monaghan, *Booklist*

"I found it thrilling and inspiring to read Elizabeth Cunningham's retelling of the old familiar Gospel stories from a radically new and fresh perspective. Listening to her Magdalen remember the joys and sorrows of her life with Jesus moves all of us to search our souls deeply for what it means to love a person, an idea, or a God."

Tom Cowan, Author of *Yearning for the Wind: Celtic Reflections on Nature and the Soul*

"*The Passion of Mary Magdalen* searches out, savors, and celebrates Mary's place in the religious and cultural imagination of the West. Elizabeth Cunningham's novel offers us a way to understand the relationship between the feminine and the divine, and points toward healing what has typically been the dichotomy between the two."

Bruce Chilton, Author of *Mary Magdalene: A Biography* and *Rabbi Jesus*

"We have seen quite a bit about Mary Magdalen recently, but very little that can match the living woman that Elizabeth Cunningham invokes. She does not drain Mary of her life by making her pious, or an intellectual symbol. In this Mary we get a woman we can believe in, a woman we celebrate, a woman we want to know. *The Passion of Mary Magdalen* is aptly named, on all levels."

Rachel Pollack, Author of *Godmother Night*

"A profound meditation on the alchemical significance of the union between Jesus and Mary Magdalen. But don't let that scare you off. Cunningham's mouthy heroine, raucous wit, and astonishing plot turns make The Maeve Chronicles a treat. At once hilarious and deeply moving, this *tour de force* is guaranteed to keep you up well past your bedtime."

Catherine MacCoun, Author of *Beyond the Abbey Gates*

PRAISE FOR ELIZABETH CUNNINGHAM'S PREVIOUS WORKS

DAUGHTER OF THE SHINING ISLES
(prequel to THE PASSION OF MARY MAGDALEN)

"... long and rich and the epitome of the storyteller's art. It has characters you care about, enough history to magnetize the fantasies in place and time, and a little magic....It matters little what [the author] calls it as long as she gets on with writing the next volume." ~**St. Louis Post-Dispatch**

"From the beginning we are caught up in a cocky irreverence that is captivating ....Wrestling with destiny and the sense of conflict as all true heroines must, Maeve searches for the land of Mona and its famous Druid university. Once she is there, prophecies begin to fulfill themselves and we are swept into an adventure that tugs at our hearts and minds. This amazing book could well become a classic of women's literature." ~**Booklist**

"High adventure; magic; a detailed look at the world of the ancient Druids; and the most engaging heroine of recent Goddess fiction come together to make *Daughter of the Shining Isles* a must-have for any lover of historical or Goddess-oriented fantasy." ~**SageWoman**

"If you're interested in Celtic or Christian lore, here are both, seamlessly interwoven, told in such a delightful narrative that it was difficult to put the book down." ~**The Beltane Papers**

THE RETURN OF THE GODDESS: A DIVINE COMEDY

"This captivating novel measures the relationship between pagan rites and modern Christianity....With solid characterizations and a fluid narrative, Cunningham gracefully crosses the borders of plausibility into a luminous metaphysical realm." ~**Publishers Weekly**

THE WILD MOTHER

"Captivating archetypal characters dramatize the everyday magic of self-discovery in a work as intriguing as Cunningham's previous novels. ...a beguiling tour de force." ~**Publishers Weekly**

HOW TO SPIN GOLD

"...pure poetic magic...." ~**The Beltane Papers**

THE
PASSION
OF
MARY
MAGDALEN

THE MAEVE CHRONICLES

THE
PASSION
OF
MARY
MAGDALEN

A NOVEL

ELIZABETH CUNNINGHAM

Monkfish Book Publishing Company
Rhinebeck, New York

Printed in the United States of America
Book and cover design by Georgia Dent
Cover art used with permission: *Mary Magdalen in a Grotto*, LeFevre, Jules Joseph, c. 1876. Oil on Canvas. The State Hermitage Museum, St. Petersburg.
The poems Poem for May 15, Egyptian prayer to Isis, and Poem for November 12, Egyptian coffin texts, have been reprinted with kind permission from the publisher from *The Goddess Companion: Daily Meditations on the Feminine Spirit* by Patrician Monaghan © 1999. Llewellyn Worldwide, 2143 Wooddale Drive, Woodbury, MN 55125-2989. All rights reserved.

Library of Congress Cataloging-in-Publication Data

Cunningham, Elizabeth, 1953-
  The passion of Mary Magdalen : a novel / Elizabeth Cunningham.
    p. cm. -- (The Maeve chronicles ; 1)
  ISBN 0-9766843-0-6
1. Mary Magdalene, Saint--Fiction. 2. Bible. N.T. Gospels--History of Biblical events--Fiction. 3. Christian women saints--Fiction. 4. Women in the Bible--Fiction. 5. Jesus Christ--Fiction. I. Title.
  PS3553.U473P37 2006
  813'.54--dc22
                       2005027344

Bulk purchase discounts for educational or promotional purposes are available.

First Edition

First Impression

10 9 8 7 6 5 4 3 2 1

Monkfish Book Publishing Company
27 Lamoree Road
Rhinebeck, New York 12572
www.monkfishpublishing.com

In loving memory of my father, Raymond Cunningham

PROLOGUE

IN THE NIGHT

This story begins in the night. There will be a dawn, I promise. I will also tell of mornings when I didn't want to wake and noons full of harsh light and judgment. Sometimes there will be shade and ease in the afternoons, camaraderie and rest, even pleasure.

There will be passion, I promise. Morning, noon, and night, season after season. Passion that breaks time open wide so that you can taste the mystery inside.

This story begins in the night. It begins in the middle of the story. In the middle of the night. When the thief comes, when the bridegroom comes. When the bride has long since given up hope. When the foolish virgins are snoring. When only a whore is awake.

The last stranger has gone home. That's what we call the men who seek the priestess-whores at Temple of Isis Magdala—Temple Magdalen for short a.k.a. the hottest holy whorehouse in the Galilee. Magdala is the place for nightlife on Lake Gennesaret, The Lake of the Harp, as it's called because of its shape. Many of the towns along the shore are fishing towns, but Magdala, sitting pretty under the cliffs of Mount Arbel, is right between two opposing worlds—the swanky new Roman spa city Tiberias and Capernaum, a Jewish stronghold. Romans come to Magdala to slum; Jews come to get out from under the noses of upright neighbors. Native gentiles from the region of the Gerasenes across the lake find their way here, too. Magdala is the place where all the clashing elements in this country of crossroads mix it up. A honky-tonk town full of juke joints, bars, and street brawls. Where else will you find Roman soldiers and Jewish guerilla fighters gaming together?

At Temple Magdalen, on the outskirts of town, we welcome them all, because we remember what most religions teach but people prefer to forget—the stranger could be a god or an angel.

Now the last stranger is gone for the night. Reginus has barred the gate. We need time to rest in these times of unrest. The priestess-whores are heading for bed. There's a storm rising on the lake. I decide to go to the roof of what I call the tower. I lived so many years inside high narrow walls, I love the roof and sleep there every night I can. It's too wild tonight to stay out, but I will watch for a while. The huge living darkness of the lake moves below me. Mount Arbel has my back. Even through the wind I can just hear the sound of our spring rising and flowing through the Temple towards the lake—the spring that called me to this place so far from the tiny island where I was born.

"Red!" Reginus calls up the stairs. "There's someone at the gate. I told him we were closed for the night, but he won't go away."

"Is he a suppliant?" our other term for the stranger who comes seeking the goddess (even when he thinks he's just looking for a whore).

"No." Reginus climbs the rest of the way up. "He says he has a sick man with him. That's what makes me suspicious. It could be a trick. They might be robbers. It could be even an ambush. It's so dark tonight I can't tell if the thing slung across his donkey is a man or a sack of grain."

"I'll go speak to him," I say.

"*Domina,*" says the man at the portal, using the Latin word for lady, but he is no Roman. "I have a sick man. Near death."

The man is a Samaritan, I am guessing by his accent.

"Why do you seek help at Temple Magdalen?" I ask in Aramaic.

"Please, there is nowhere else. I found the man naked and bleeding on the Jerusalem-Jericho road. He'd been beaten and left for dead. What was I to do? I couldn't leave him there. I've been traveling for two days now, but no one will take him in. They don't know who he is—a Jew, a Samaritan, an outlaw, a demoniac? I can't keep caring for him myself. I don't have the skill or the time. I'm just a merchant on my way to Tyre to meet a shipment. I've heard you welcome the stranger here. I've heard there are healers here."

"If it's a trick, it's a trick," I say to Reginus. "We'll have to risk it. What you have heard is true," I say through the portal. "In the name of Isis who welcomes all, I welcome you."

Reginus and I open the gates, and the merchant leads his burdened donkey inside. It is a man and not a sack. That much is clear by the torch in the wall.

"Help me, both of you. The rain hasn't started yet. I want to examine him first by the spring, and wash his wounds there. The water has healing properties," I explain to the Samaritan. "I'll get a lamp while you move him. Carefully."

Even though I am a seasoned healer, I am taken aback by what I see. This man hasn't just been beaten. He's starving. I can count all his ribs. He is covered with sores; his hair is matted and thick with dust. The Samaritan has done his best to bind the man's wounds, but he has bled through the bandages. I kneel down and place the lamp at his head, so I can get a better look at his face.

His face. My heart knows before my eyes; my eyes know before my mind. All I know is I am lost. There are lines here that go on for miles, for years. I am looking at his face, and what I see are his feet, brown as earth, beautiful, lost. I see the sun wheeling out of control, and the stars trying to find him. The moon flinging the ocean after him. And he is lost. No, I am. We are. From each other.

"Maeve, we are lovers," he pleaded on another shore in a terrible dawn after a long night long ago.

"You are lovers," said the old woman, "but not just of each other, you are the lovers of the world."

"We can't love if we're apart," he said.

"We can't love unless we part," I answered him.

I didn't know then what I meant. But now here I am, here we are in this moment, and all the loss is lifting, changing, like leaves turned by the wind before the storm.

"Red, honey," says Reginus. "Why are you crying? What's wrong?"

"Whore's tears," I say. "Cure anything."

I soak them up with the hem of my garment, and begin to wash his wounds.

And my own wounds.

By our wounds we are healed.

Here is the story, of my lost years and what I found, of our found years and what we lost. Stories unfold in time, backwards, forwards, every moment changing the meaning of all the others. This is a passion story—my passion, his, ours, yours. Passion breaks time open.

Come. Taste the mystery.

THE VINE

AND

THE FIG TREE

CHAPTER ONE

RED

"What am I bid for Red here?" the pug-faced slave dealer harangued the thinning crowd. "Last lot of the day. Who bids for Red?"

"My name," I said one more time, "is Maeve Rhuad." I wasn't sure if I was speaking in Celtic or Latin or Greek or even if I was speaking out loud. But that didn't stop me. "I am the daughter of the Warrior Witches of Tir na mBan, daughters of the Cailleach, daughter of the goddess Bride, daughter of—"

"Put a sock in it, Red," muttered Pug Face (or the first century street Latin equivalent). "How many times I gotta tell you, you ain't got no lineage now. You're property. Mine. Until I unload you. If you know what's good for you, you'll keep your mouth shut and look pretty."

Immediately I opened my mouth again. Then I thought better of it. Confrontation and defiance hadn't gotten me anywhere—except shackled and displayed on a slave block at the southwest corner of the Temple of Castor and Pollux in the heart of the Roman Forum.

Not that I knew the exact address then; I wasn't even certain I was in Rome, but I had strong suspicions. All my life I had been taught to hate all things Roman. Only Rome could be as hellish as this place appeared to me. You must understand; I had never, ever been in a city before, unless you count the port at Ostia where I was captured. Until now my knowledge of architecture was limited to round wattle and daub huts. You may think I'm an ignorant barbarian. The Romans certainly did. In fact, I had been kicked out of one of the finest schools in the world, the druid college on the Isle of Mona, where I had been studying literature, medicine, and law. So there. Not that I appreciated the opportunity when I had it. Not that I could ever go back. Not only had I been expelled and exiled—sent beyond the ninth wave as the druids so poetically put it—they were also mighty particular about their students bearing no taint of slavery.

Now here I was in the heart of the first century's Evil Empire—on sale.

"A fine female specimen, no more than fourteen years old." In fact I was closer to nineteen, but false advertising is nothing new. "In prime condition. Good breeder, would make an excellent wet nurse." Here he slipped his hand into my rag of a tunic and whipped out a breast, aiming it at the crowd as if about to demonstrate. "What is more, the merchandise in question is a *novica*." Translation: a first-time slave, a desirable commodity especially when young. "Fresh from Sardinia," he added for good measure. Everyone there but me knew that Sardinia was a penal colony; to be a slave in Rome was definitely a step up.

"Or so you'd have us believe," said a balding man, swathed in complicated folds of white fringed with purple that I would later come to know as a toga worn only by men of senatorial rank. "Along with all the other lies you've written on that plaque around her lovely neck."

I had wondered about that. Though I speak five languages, I read only *ogham*, the sacred druid alphabet.

"I've a good mind to set the *aedile* on you for misrepresenting your wares," the man continued wagging a threatening finger. "If that girl has ever seen Sardinia it was only on the way from Gaul—or worse. I know a Celt when I see one. They are useless as slaves, untrainable and some of them are downright treacherous."

I considered loosing one of the battle cries for which my people are famous—the kind that make Roman knees rattle and Roman testicles retract, but then I thought better of it. Anything would be preferable to the holding tank, a lightless back room of a fish shop where I had woken bound and gagged after having been raped, beaten (carefully so as to leave no marks) and drugged into a reasonable facsimile of submission.

"Now, now, now, there's no cause for that. You got no right to drive away a man's custom, sir. Red here is no savage. Why she speaks Latin like a senator. Go on, Red, say something for the gentleman."

He smiled for the benefit of the crowd and yanked my chain hard enough to remind me who was shackled and who wasn't. Like I didn't know. Still, I found, I couldn't resist. I turned to him.

"Your father," I said in my sweetest, clearest voice, "fucked a sheep, and your mother did it with a donkey."

The crowd, growing now, roared and applauded. It was a good show—as long I wasn't *their* slave. Pug Face jerked my chain so hard I nearly fell to my knees; then he lifted his hand to strike me.

"No," someone shouted. "Let her say on! She's only proving your point."

His face had turned an unbecoming shade of puce, but pleasing the crowd came first. He lowered his fist, which I took as a signal to continue.

"Which explains your face," I said. "Though it is hard to say which coupling resulted in your unfortunate conception. Take your pick of lineage. And as Bride is my witness, I do not intend to insult a worthy animal who gives wool or one that is of use in bearing burdens. It is not the sheep's fault that you fart in your sleep or the donkey's that your breath stinks of rancid meat and sour wine or that the fleas desert the rats in preference for your smelly hide—"

If he didn't drop dead of a stroke—and I had some hope he might—or if I didn't get sold to someone quickly, I might not live to enjoy another night among the fish guts. Oh well, death was more honorable than slavery, and now that I was on a roll I couldn't stop to save my life. I might be speaking Latin, but I was a Celt. In other words: impossible to shut up as long as I was breathing.

"One thing is certain," I went on, "you are a slave and the son of slaves. You are a coward and the son of cowards. When the sun rises in the morning it turns red with shame that it must shine on you—"

Then I felt the lash of the whip; I stopped for a moment to breathe. "And the moon hides its face and weeps," I improvised wildly, anticipating the next stroke, knowing that watching a slave being beaten to death would be considered a mild entertainment for people who regularly watched men slaughter each other.

But the next stroke never fell. I turned and was rendered temporarily speechless by the sight of the tall, handsome woman who had mounted the block and grabbed Pug Face's arm, knocking the whip out of his hand.

"Don't mar your wares before I get a good look." The woman's voice was brisk.

More swiftly than I would have imagined possible, Pug Face recovered himself and shifted smoothly into his most obsequious gear.

"Delighted to see you, *domina*. Always a pleasure to do business with you. Delighted to be of service. Would you like me to remove her garment?"

"If you can call that sack a garment. Yes, strip her. And don't even think about telling me she's a virgin with that mouth on her. You're lucky I didn't go to the *aedile* about that last piece of baggage you passed off as pure. Next time you say you have a virgin for sale I'm inspecting her hymen right here. As for this one, there's no need for me to get a crick in my neck. She's already whelped at least once. See?" She pointed. "Stretch marks. What happened to the brat?" she addressed me. "Dead, exposed, or sold?"

Never mind that I was naked, far from any place I could call home or any people I could call mine in front of a leering Roman crowd. There are things you recover from—like being raped by a man who turned out to be my father, which is why being raped by my captor was a mere outrage. And there are things you never get over. Having a child stolen from your arms is one. I stared at the woman. I saw how hard her face was, hard as the street stones pounded into the innocent earth, smooth as the marble slabs the Romans like to pile into huge, ugly buildings. I stared till my eyes were dry and I could no longer see the brightness I'd once held against my breast. The woman made the mistake of staring back. Her face did not soften exactly, but something strained it for an instant.

"Never mind," she said. "As far as I'm concerned, you have no past as long as it doesn't interfere with present purposes. Mine. Now, open your mouth."

"A fine set of choppers if I do say so myself." Pug Face inanely took credit.

What could he or anyone in this world know of the source of my strong teeth and bones, the sixteen lactating breasts of my mothers and the magical orchard on Tir na mBan that blossomed and bore fruit the year round.

After she inspected my teeth, she searched my head for lice. "He's gotten better about cleaning them up," she spoke to herself. "Or maybe this one kept herself clean. Would have been a shame to shave this head. And as red below as above. That could be popular."

"I'll come around if you set her out," said one man. "I like them picante."

"I haven't quite made up my mind. You there," she said to Pug Face, "show us how clean you think she is. Wait, let me have a look at you first."

To the crowd's delight, she inspected his mouth as thoroughly as she had mine. Then she gestured for him to lift his tunic and with an apparently practiced eye she appraised his prick. Pug Face bore it all with an ingratiating grin. He wanted a sale. Badly.

"I just need to be sure, because I've no doubt you've sampled her. All right. Now put your mouth where your money is." To me she said, "Bend over."

I gave her another blank stare, but this time she wasn't playing. She grabbed my hair and forced my head down. I lost my balance and ended up on all fours. Before I knew it, his snout was buried in me. Given my position, nose to the ground, ankles bound, there was only one path of resistance open to me. I took it.

It was long; it was loud, both redolent and resonant. The crowd applauded, and Pug Face surfaced sputtering, holding his nose with one hand while he felt around for his whip with the other.

"There are men in this town who will pay good money to be humiliated like that," mused the woman. "O.K., I'll take her."

"An excellent choice, *Domina*." Pug Face recovered instantly. "A girl with rare talents. Because you are such a good customer, I'll let you have her for one hundred and fifty *denarii*."

"One hundred and ten, take it or leave it."

"*Domina*, you would not make a pauper of me, take food out of my children's mouths. One hundred and forty."

They went on with their obligatory haggling. The morning market was closing up. The entertainment was over. Men moved off towards the baths; women went home with their purchases. Ignored for a merciful moment, I tried to stand again, but I found I was too dizzy. If my stomach had not been empty, I would have vomited. The midday sun beat down and rose up from the stones, glared off the buildings. Nothing in my life had prepared me for this moment. Nothing. Not incest, not childbirth, not exile or shipwreck. Not even watching my beloved disappear in the mists on the other side of the Menai Straits. Esus. Esus. Would I ever see him again? I had never doubted until this moment.

"Red, a word to the wise. Unless you're sailing on a ship or seasoning a broth, salt water is of no use whatsoever. Dry up. If there's one thing men can't stand, it's a whore with leaky eyes. They get enough of that at home."

I didn't know the word whore, not in any of the five languages I spoke. Didn't even have the concept. I was named for an infamous warrior queen who had thirty men a day, if she chose. If she *chose*.

"Stand up." She put a strong hand under my arm and pulled me to my feet. Pug Face undid my shackles, then lifted the plaque from my neck. "And don't you dare faint on me," she added. "If there's anything I hate more than weepers, it's fainters."

She put her arm around me as I stepped down from the block. Her touch was kinder than her face or voice. It confused me.

"Can you walk?" she demanded. "I'm open for business in three hours. You've got a lot to learn. Fast. Bone," she called, and an enormous eunuch hove into view. "Take her other arm. Let's go."

"Good riddance to bad rubbish," Pug Face muttered behind us. I heard him spit, and a blob landed next to my foot. Before I could even think of retaliating the woman grabbed my chin and locked my face into forward position.

"You're going to have to get used to scum, Red," my new captor told me.

"My name," I began, but I couldn't get it past the lump in my throat.

"Is whatever the clientele decide to call you," she finished for me.

With that she and the giant eunuch led me out of the relatively open spaces of the Forum through the crowded squalor of the notorious Subura and then up hill to Mons Esquilinus.

CHAPTER TWO

CAT HOUSE

Maybe you are relieved to know that I was forced into prostitution. Sold. No choice. Some people insist there is no evidence that I was a whore at all; they are eager to save my reputation—which implies that they think there is something wrong with being a whore. It is true that his official chroniclers never called me a whore, just a crazy bitch, or in polite language "a woman infested by seven demons." (We'll get to that part later.) Everyone seems to agree that I was saved, cleansed by his healing (asexual) touch and that I went on to become an important, if unacknowledged, disciple.

There is more to the story or I wouldn't be telling it. And I hope you will discover, if you don't already know, the difference between a stereotype and an archetype. Stereotypes are flat, one-dimensional, like the donkey you blindly pin the tail on. Archetypes are rich, lush, juicy. Sometimes they go underground, submerge in mist and myth, like the Loch Ness Monster. But I am here to tell you:

You can't keep a good archetype down.

I didn't know any of that yet. As I said, I didn't even know what a whore was, but I must have had a premonition. I knew I was fucked.

"Don't think you'll get much out of this one today," the hulk said, as we turned from a street into an alley where it was a squeeze to walk three abreast. At least here there was some respite from the garishly painted statues and frescoes that assaulted my eyes. You may be accustomed to thinking of the ancient world as full of white columns and torsos missing arms and busts with chipped noses. That's only because the paint doesn't last. Think Las Vegas and you'll be closer to the Rome of my day. "If I was you, I'd clean her up—she stinks of fish—feed her up, and let her sleep for a day."

"Well, you're not me, and I don't pay you to think."

"You don't pay me at all, O my mistress and O the delight—"

"Cut the crap, Bone," she waved away his words with her free hand. "You know I offered you and Bonia manumission years ago, and you wouldn't take it."

"Mistress, you have my balls. I can never leave you."

"*I* didn't whip you into that sacrificial frenzy. You know how I feel about those hysterical eastern cults. And manumission or no manumission, with your tips and your side rackets, you're wealthier than I am."

"Nevertheless, you are my goddess, my Cybele."

"Then don't question my ways, Attis boy. The girl is strong, healthy. It's never too soon to start getting a return on an investment."

"But my sweetness." *My sweetness?* That hard-faced predatory woman? "You don't want to put a horse in a chariot race before it's broken to the harness. Sure way to lose the race and disappoint the bettors."

"You may have a point, Bone. In any case, I'm turning her over to Bonia. I'm off to the Palatine today. You know where. I'm taking Helen."

"Yes, I remember. And I beg permission to accompany you, if you will allow me. I believe a certain *cubicularius* is ready to be indiscreet."

Apparently one of the eunuch's many functions was to get the goods on as many highly placed officials as possible in case his mistress ever needed a favor. Espionage and blackmail were a way of life in Rome.

"No, Bone, I need you here today. This one is going to bear watching."

"But I've been softening him up since—"

"The goddess speaks."

"Oh, all right. Have it your way. You always do," her devotee sulked.

"Here we are, Red," the woman addressed me for the first time since we left the Forum.

The alley gave onto a street. Across from us was a portico, the entire wall around it brightly painted. A grape vine and a fig tree framed the doorway, illustrating the name of the establishment. Yes, that's right: the Vine and Fig Tree, straight out of Hebrew scripture. Both the figs and the grapes had enticing suggestive shapes—visual double entrendre. If you missed the point, scantily clad nymphs frisked to the right and the left for almost half a block. The most striking feature of the fresco was the cats, more cats than women, of every stripe and color in every conceivable pose.

The eunuch opened the thick wooden door, and I heard the sound of running water. Among my people, wells and springs were considered sacred, a source of vision and healing, an entry way to the Otherworld. The sound made me homesick, but I couldn't afford to let down my guard now, so I blinked hard and swallowed my tears. When my eyes focused I saw that I was in a courtyard or atrium. A fruit tree of some kind (not a fig) gave a tiny bit of shade, and the sound of the water came from a fountain—something I had never seen before, because the Celts did not share the Roman obsession with plumbing. All around the rim of the fountain sat cats, sleek, elegant cats—black, striped, calico, orange, grey—watching goldfish dart around the pool. I stared at the small beasts in fascination. Celts had domesticated dogs and of course cattle, but cats—wild cats—I'd only glimpsed at a distance.

"It's the *novica*."

The voice came from above my head. I looked up and got my first glimpse of the women I would come to know more intimately than I knew my mothers. Their barely covered breasts spilled over the balcony railing. They had only just woken up; they looked tumbled, tired, blowsy, their eyes a little smudged or puffy. They were as varied as the cats, a full range of hair and skin color, shape and size. They all stared at me, sizing me up, their new comrade and competition.

"Would you get a load of that hair!"

"She won't need a lamp in *her* room."

"I wonder what kind of dye she uses to get that color?"

"By the tits of Isis, look at her bush. It's the same color."

"Oo, I don't think I'd want to use dye down there."

"No, *stulta*, I mean she must have been born that way."

"That's enough, ladies," said the eunuch. His boss had disappeared into the deeper recesses of the house. "Be nice. Sooner she settles in, the better it'll be for everyone."

"She can't understand us, Bone. She's a barbarian," said a big blonde woman.

"Oh, really, Berta. Like you're not," said a small dark one.

"She speaks Latin like a sailor," put in Bone, but they ignored him.

"I did not mean it as an insult, Succula. I am proud to be a barbarian. You hear me, proud. Who would want to be Roman?"

My sentiments exactly. I looked at the woman more closely, wondering if she were a Celt. Her accent didn't seem quite right. But maybe she would be an ally. Maybe she wanted to escape.

The *domina*, who clearly owned everything and everyone in sight, re-entered the atrium followed by a female version of the hulk and two little girls. At the sight of her, all the women turned tail and scurried back to their rooms.

"Here she is, Bonia," my captor said. "I leave her to you. Bone doesn't think she should work today, but we're going to be one short, so you decide. Don't give her to anyone who doesn't like some lip. With training, I think she might learn to crack the whip. Until she's broken in, you're going to have to keep her on a short leash.

"Helen!" she barked. "I told you to be ready at the sixth hour sharp. Go get Helen," she instructed the little girls.

Before the little girls had finished mounting the stairs, Helen appeared followed by a woman who seemed to be her hairdresser and make-up designer.

"You like, *domina*?" the attendant inquired.

"Very nice," the *domina* understated.

Helen gave a whole new meaning to the word golden; blonde had nothing to do with it. Her minimal attire was just a shade lighter gold than her skin and hair. She drifted down the stairs as if a slow breeze carried her.

"Yeah, a thousand ships, give or take a few," commented Bone.

"Go see if the litter is ready," the *domina* ordered the girls. "Step on it, Helen. Save the undulating grace for the senator."

"There's a girl could go far," remarked Bonia as the two women left. "If she had any brains, that is. Fortunately for Domitia Tertia she doesn't."

That was the first time I had heard my captor's name. It seemed possible that Bonia might be the sort of person who keeps up a running commentary. I decided to pay close attention.

"Come along, dearie," Bonia turned to me, giving me a quick once-over. "Not the Helen of Troy type, but I expect you'll do. I don't always follow her reasoning, but Domitia knows how to pick 'em."

After following Bonia through a confusing series of corridors and rooms, I found myself in a back courtyard off the kitchen that had a high wall and no exit that I could see. Bonia gestured for me to recline on a bench and sent the little girls to fetch wine and food. I ate ravenously—bread with a black paste made of olives, as well as cheese, figs, and grapes. I'd had barely enough food to keep me alive since I'd run away from the mountains in Iberia where I had been the revered, even worshipped, prisoner of a Celtic tribe whose youth, male and female, had been killed or taken captive by—who else—the Romans. One of their remnant had found me washed up and near dead on the shore and the surviving old women had, it is true, saved my life. In return I was supposed to single-handedly—or wombedly—repopulate their village. But I had had other plans. I still had other plans.

After my long fast, the wine hit my veins like a spring flood, weakening my guard. I struggled against the feelings of comfort and familiarity Bonia roused in me. She was big-boned, plain, older than me and completely sure of her place and her purpose. Until I was fourteen I had lived on an island with women only, all of whom had considered themselves my mother and alternately bossed me and spoiled me. When I went away to druid school, the black-robed priestesses of Holy Isle took firm charge of the female students. Now here I was again, being taken in hand by yet another woman, an extremely competent woman. But that did not mean she had my best interests at heart. As little as I understood of my present predicament, one thing was clear to me: the only interests that mattered at the Vine and Fig Tree were Domitia Tertia's.

"Run along," Bonia said to the little girls. "Go help old Nona with the washing."

"We want to watch the one with fire in her hair."

"Not now. I have to instruct her."

"We want 'structions."

"Don't be in such a hurry, silly things. Shoo!"

She cuffed them, not too roughly but not too gently either. I stared after the girls. I had been my mothers' only child, and even after I'd left the island I'd seen few young children. I craved some image of what my daughter, no longer a baby, might look like.

"How old are they?" I asked.

"The little one about four and the other, six, I believe," said Bonia as she fetched a stool and sat down beside me. "Some of the older ones are being trained to be *ornatrices*. A good skill for the ugly ones, and the pretty ones will begin to learn the profession from the girls. Domitia Tertia doesn't hold with auctioning a girl's virginity till she's fourteen. In most brothels, they're doing a full night's work by age ten. She won't budge on that rule no matter who's bidding, and some gentlemen like 'em barely out of the cradle."

I still didn't know—or, more precisely, didn't want to know—what she was talking about. My stomach lurched, and I took a deep breath, determined to hold onto my lunch.

"You mean she—"

"The *domina*," Bonia instructed me. "That is how you should refer to her."

"She buys little girls...as slaves?" I ignored her directive.

"*Mater Matuta*! You really are a barbarian. Why would she have to buy little girls? She picks them up off the street, off the refuse heaps."

"What do you mean?"

"Exposed, dear. Don't you know? People don't want the expense of raising a daughter, not more than one or two anyway. The only people with the sense to see the value of female children are the brothel keepers. Moreover, Domitia Tertia has a bit of a bee in her bonnet about infant exposure. No one knows for certain—she doesn't talk much about herself, not even to me—but the story goes that her father tried to expose her. She was the third daughter, as you can tell from her name."

"From her name?" I repeated. "Oh, you mean the Tertia part?"

I didn't yet know of the common Roman practice of naming daughters after the father, distinguishing them only by number.

"Dear me," Bonia clucked. "For all you appear to understand Latin, I swear you're more of a barbarian than Berta was when she arrived without a word of any tongue but what they speak in those savage northern places. Always sounds to me like pigs rooting in mud. I better get some idea of what you do and don't know. First things first. You do understand what the *domina* bought you for."

I felt such shame at the idea of being bought at all. I stared down at the remnants of the food. I'd lost my appetite.

"Answer me, girl." Her voice was sharp as the slap that would doubtless follow. Not that I was afraid of a smack in the face, but there was no point in antagonizing the woman who had immediate charge over me, the first obstacle in my path to escape.

"She bought me to be her slave." But I am no one's slave, and I never will be, I added to myself.

"Well, obviously, dear. We're all her slaves, from the old women to the little girls. It takes a lot of slaves to run a house like this one. Only a few of the slaves are whores. Surely I don't need to explain to you what a whore does."

I hated to admit ignorance to this woman who believed she had power over me.

"I am the daughter of warrior witches, who are the daughters of a goddess. I was educated by the Cailleach of Tir na mBan and the druids of Mona mam Cymru. I speak the languages of my people as well as Latin, Greek, and Aramaic. I know that all Romans are greedy, cruel, rapacious, and without honor or honesty. If there's anything else I need to know, you'll have to tell me."

By this time Bonia was whooping with laughter. I would have preferred just about any other response. But she kept right on laughing until she finally sighed and dabbed her eyes with her sleeve.

"What's so funny?" I demanded. "I just insulted your people."

"Not my people, dearie. Bone and I are Greek. You'll find that a lot of slaves come from somewhere else."

"Then why did you laugh?" I lowered my voice. "Do you hate the Romans, too?"

That started her off again. "No, dear. I don't bother my head with politics. The Romans rule the world, and that's that. No, it's just the *domina* said you'd be one for cracking the whip. I believe she's right. She ought to train you herself."

"To do what?"

"Some gentlemen like to be humiliated, dear. Some gentlemen like a woman who will give them a fight. And some gentlemen like an educated woman. Yes, I think Domitia may have made a good investment. Always a risk, though. The stupid ones are easier to handle. Like our Helen."

"So," I said, "a whore is someone who insults people?"

"You really don't understand, do you?" she sighed. "All right then. Now I know you're not a virgin. Domitia said you've borne a child; I can see that, too. You know what men and women do together, call it what you like. That's what a brothel sells, dear. Same as a tavern sells drink or a bakery, bread. Men pay for that, and they pay all the more if a brothel is clean and well run, as this one is, and the fare is dished up in exotic and entertaining ways. Now, tell me you understand. I can't make it much plainer."

I gaped at Bonia, a surge of adrenaline clearing away the drowsy haze of the wine like a sudden storm. You may have wondered how I could have failed to figure it out before, what with Domitia demanding to know if I was clean, the suggestive frescoes, the semi-clad women. You would have picked up the cues immediately, but I had no context for them. Slavery was bad enough. It had never occurred to me that my body could be sold again and again—to profit someone else. Specifically the hard-faced woman who thought she owned me.

"I will not do that." The calmness of my voice struck me as bizarre.

Bonia gave me a sharp look, alert for trouble. Until that moment she hadn't taken me seriously.

"Oh, but you will," she said. "And if you have a brain in your head, you'll count yourself lucky. You'll thank the gods for your good fortune. Wherever you come from, you're in Rome now. There are brothels here no better than rat holes. And there are whore masters here who will work you till you're dead. And why not? It's easy enough to replace a whore, and don't you forget it. Rome's crawling with 'em, and more coming every day. Slave and free. Now Domitia Tertia can be hard. She expects a good night's work and no nonsense. But she's fair. More than fair. She lets the girls keep their tips. More than one talented whore has bought her manumission and set herself up with her own business. Most brothel owners wouldn't tolerate that. They'd be afraid of losing clients, but Domitia Tertia has never stood in the way of an enterprising whore. She's always held that there's no shortage of high-class clients. Quality knows quality."

"You mean there are women who buy their freedom?" I wanted to get this part straight. "And then go on being whores or buying their own whores?"

"Why on earth wouldn't they? It's what they know. It's a good, steady, profitable business. Look at Domitia Tertia."

"Domitia Tertia, the *domina*," I corrected myself when Bonia frowned. "She was—or is—a whore?"

"Domitia Tertia was born the daughter of a senator," began Bonia, shifting her weight from one buttock to the other, settling herself to tell a favorite story. I recognized the signs. "Her father married her to a close friend of his who was always off trying to advance his career in unsuccessful military campaigns. Now everyone knows men can have mistresses, concubines, and whores by the score. Well-bred young ladies have to keep their legs shut or else sneak around all the while bribing slaves to keep their mouths shut. That didn't suit our Domitia Tertia. Back in the good old days of Emperor Augustus, when the *domina* was young, a woman could register as a prostitute to get around the adultery laws. So that's what she did, and just in time. When that old pervert Tiberius came to power, he closed the loophole. Ever notice how the more depraved a man is, the more he tries to ruin other people's fun? Of course, even when it was legal under Augustus, a woman had to give up all rights to any inheritance. Being young and headstrong, Domitia cared more about her freedom.

"After a few years of being a high-priced mistress, she found herself out on the street one day. The fancy *domus* she thought she ruled and all the slaves she thought she commanded belonged to him—and so had she, until he found someone younger to take her place. That was twenty years ago. She learned her lesson. Never be dependent on a man, whether it's father, husband, or lover. Don't just own yourself, own everything. That's her motto. If that makes her greedy and rapacious and whatever else you said about Romans, so be it. But she is not without honesty and honor, and you'd do well to respect her for it."

"I thought you said she doesn't talk about herself. How do you know all this?"

"Domitia Tertia doesn't have to talk about herself. Everyone knows who she is. Even the Emperor. She may have been disinherited, but she's got the bloodlines, and she's gotten rich by her own wits. What's more she knows everything about everyone. People are careful not to cross her. A word to the wise, dearie, Domitia Tertia knows how to cut her losses. She doesn't give people second chances. If she decides you're a bad investment, she won't hesitate to send you straight back to the slave block. Believe me, you won't have an opportunity like this one again.

"All right then." She stood up and snapped her fingers for someone to come and clear away the tray of food. "There's just time for you to have a little cat nap before the baths. Just sleep where you are. I'll send one of the girls to fetch you when it's time."

I closed my eyes and rested my head on my arms. Beside me I heard a soft thud; then something tickled my face. Through half-opened eyes I met a green-gold stare. Then the cat curled against my breasts, purring, and we both went to sleep in the sun.

CHAPTER THREE

A NIGHT IN THE LIFE

"**H**ere is the way how to think of it, *liebling*," said Berta. We were all soaking together in the *caldarium*. I had grown up with springs and surf, but I had never been in hot water before (at least not literally). I was distressed to find myself enjoying the sensation; I was becoming Roman already. The big blonde, my fellow barbarian, had taken me under her wing; that is, she had a plump arm draped over my shoulder. The other whores sat across the pool, whispering and tittering as they eyed me and listened to Berta hold forth. Well, they could hardly help it. She had a voice as big as she was—the voice of someone who'd once lived in the open.

"You have been raped, yes? Who has not? I myself have been raped by a whole legion."

"Oh, not the legion again," said the little dark one. She caught my eye and winked at me.

"You know it's true, Succula," Berta scolded. "So. The Roman legion comes to my village. They burn the huts; they put the men to the sword, and they rape all the women. It is the same story everywhere. I was a virgin...."

"It is the eve of her wedding day," added a woman, who was blacker than anyone I'd ever seen, with coil upon coil of snaky hair.

"She hears the thundering of many hooves," another woman continued.

I was shocked that they would mock such a terrible story. It took me awhile to understand. We all had terrible stories. Mockery kept the terror at bay.

"All right, all right," said Berta crossly. "I wasn't going to tell the whole story. I have a point to make."

"So make it already," the black woman said.

"If you would all shut up maybe I could."

The others pantomimed sealed lips and made strangled noises.

"The point is," Berta ignored them, "we have all had it stolen from us. Now we make them pay. It's good. Yes?"

The lips came unsealed with general laughter and agreement.

I felt myself frowning. I was still tired and disoriented, but I knew something was faulty in their thinking.

"No," I said, "Domitia Tertia makes them pay."

They regarded me coldly, and I realized my mistake. I needed the good will of these women to survive.

"Well, at least she's a woman," I amended.

"And a whore," Succula added.

"And a hardnosed, tight-assed bitch," said the black woman.

"You got that right, Dido." Everyone chimed in; this description was apparently a compliment to the *domina*.

"As you say, Red," Dido added, addressing me directly for the first time. "She makes them pay. Does she ever. Nobody fools with her, and you won't either, Hot Twat, if you know what's good for you."

Apparently these women identified with Domitia Tertia. I found their admiration perplexing.

"So," said Dido, who shared a name with the fabled Queen of Carthage. "Are you really a *novica*? Never been a slave? Never done it for money?"

"I did it for passage on a ship."

Applause greeted this admission.

"But it didn't exactly work out," I understated.

In fact, that was when everything had gone wrong. Maybe I was being punished—an unfamiliar and disconcerting line of thought for me.

"Don't tell us." Dido held up her hand. "The bastard drugged your drink and you woke trussed up and on your way to market."

"And on the way he sticks you every time he feels like it," added Berta. "Don't feel bad, *liebling*. It's not your fault. There is nothing you could have done to stop it."

Yet that's where the shame was, that it had happened to me at all. How could I have allowed it? How could I have been so stupid?

"Hey, none of us know until it's too late: you gotta drug *their* drink first," Dido answered my thoughts.

"That's right, *liebling*," Berta patted me and made comforting clucking noises.

Suddenly I was undone. Their unexpected kindness loosed my tears. I covered my face, expecting my weakness to be met with contempt. Instead I found myself surrounded by female bodies. Breasts brushed against my cheeks, bellies against my breasts. I breathed in the sweet, salty scent of women, the scent of home and I cried even harder.

"I was born," I said when I could speak again, "on an island of women."

"Only women!"

"I had eight mothers."

"Sweet Isis!"

"And one old, old woman."

"My granny used to take care of me," someone sighed.

"And then the Romans came?" prompted Berta.

"No. No, Romans. The Romans will never find my mothers' island. It is not in the same world."

"Then why did you leave there? Why would you ever leave?" Dido sounded angry and wistful at once.

Why? I knew, but I could not begin to say.

"It's all right," soothed Berta. "You will tell us your story when you're ready, yes? Listen now, *liebling*. Let me tell you how we do things here. You stick by us, we stick by you."

"Don't try to act like you're better than everybody else," Dido explained.

"Don't steal anyone's regulars," added Succula.

"And then we teach you everything we know. All the little tricks."

"How to spit it out without him knowing."

"The sure fire hand job."

"How to keep your womb locked up tight."

I was a long way from druid school.

"Don't worry," said Succula. "Tonight everyone's gonna know you're new. Novelty will make up for lack of technique. You'll catch on."

"So, are you with us, Red?" Dido fixed me with a deep black gaze; she was gorgeous. "We're all foreigners here, except for Succula. She was raised in the house. What matters is we're all whores. You can be out for yourself or you can be one of us. How do you want to play it?"

I looked at the women surrounding me, their impulsive kindness now replaced with wariness. If I got close to them, would they hold me back or would they help me? Part of me wanted to say, I am not one of you; I will never be one of you. You are slaves to the Romans, and you accept it. Then I remembered my beloved, prophesying in a druid grove. "Rome is not a place," he had said. "Rome is cruelty." And here, among these women, I had, for a moment, been back home on Tir na mBan.

"I'm with you," I said.

"Good. Now let's show her how we seal a deal."

As one the women rose to their knees and dipped their forefingers into their vulvas. They waited until I did the same; then we all pressed our hands together, and each woman gave me a smacking kiss on the mouth.

"Now you're a whore, *liebling*!" exulted Berta.

I felt like nothing so much as a pig ready to be roasted for a banquet. I lacked only an apple crammed into my mouth. (Though I did have wool and honey stuffed up my twat in case *coitus interruptus* failed.) Celts like jewelry well enough, being excellent metal workers and lovers of gold, silver, and bronze. And, yes, they do lime their hair and paint their bodies with woad for battle. But decoration is not the same as artifice. I had always taken my attractions for granted and done little more than run a comb through my hair now and then to keep the birds from nesting there. I'd never worn anything more elaborate than a tunic, and had a tendency to toss my bracelets and torques into votive wells as I found them cumbersome.

Now I was wearing very little—a filmy hot pink whore's toga, a sexy imitation of what senator's wore—but all the simplicity was gone. My breasts were jammed together and thrust up towards my chin. My hair had been wound into a beehive on my head, and it's a wonder I wasn't followed by a swarm of bees, I was so heavily scented. My freckles had been painted over, my eyes outlined with kohl; my lips and cheeks were almost as bright a red as my hair. All this binding and dabbing and fluffing had been accomplished by the horde of *ornatrices* who descended on us after the bath.

By the ninth hour—that's three in the afternoon your time—we were all assembled in the receiving rooms, reclining on couches, striking poses as we leaned against erotic statuary, doing our best to look as languid yet alert, as soft yet potentially dangerous as the cats who rubbed against our legs or nestled against our breasts. As I gazed around the room I was struck again by the women's variety—a small united colonized peoples with Domitia Tertia representing Rome as an equal opportunity exploiter. The rainbow display must be good for business. Bored Romans could fuck ethnic, and nostalgic foreigners could get a taste of home.

Clients began to trickle in, mostly regulars, it seemed. Bone played the genial host, but stayed near the door. No one could go in or out without encountering him. Bonia directed the little girls who fetched and carried trays of food and drink and she kept a sharp eye on the whores who did the actual serving—a form of foreplay. Figs and olives nestled in cleavage; grapes were held suggestively between lips. Frequent signals passed between Bonia, and the cashier. I later learned that dalliance in the lobby was not on the house. There was a charge for everything.

According to Bonia's orders, I was to stay on the sidelines and observe as much as possible my first night on the job. If someone wanted a twosome, she would send me along to learn under another whore's tutelage. If anyone insisted on having me or if there was a shortage, I'd be on my own to sink or swim. (Sinking meant back to the slave block.) Meanwhile Bonia was constitutionally incapable of tolerating idleness.

"Here." She came around to my hideout behind a potted palm. "You might as well learn how to pit and peel. You've noticed how the men love to have little morsels popped into their mouths."

She gave me a brief demonstration, then left me to my task, which I found oddly soothing, though I didn't see how I was to accomplish it without becoming sticky. My fingers tips were soon black with olive pulp. The grapes were no less messy and much juicer. Also I could not resist sampling my wares, and my lipstick wore away, replaced with darker stains. I was so absorbed in my task as I sat in my dark little corner that I did not notice a man approaching me until he spoke.

"And who is this fresh, new delicacy?"

I looked up and saw a man bending over me. Instead of a purple fringe, his toga was trimmed in gold braid.

"General Fullanus!" (Yes, that really was his name.) "Always a pleasure to see you, *General*." Bonia's emphasis on his title was clearly for my benefit.

"And you, Bonia, and you." He addressed her with perfunctory respect. "I heard rumors that the house had acquired a *novica*. She seems in need of some assistance. Permit me."

He knelt and began to lick the olive and grape juice that had spilled onto my breasts. I saw Bonia make a hurried signal to the cashier; then she turned back to me and made silent gestures I didn't understand—or chose not to. Having my body tongued by a total stranger was apparently part of my job description, but I just wasn't used to it. Then—I couldn't help it—staring down at his shining crown while his Roman nose tunneled between my breasts, I yielded to temptation. As subtly as I could—no one could say I spat—I dropped a fleshy olive pit on his pate.

Before the general could figure out what had happened, Bonia swooped in and whisked away the evidence of my insolence.

"The flies," she explained. "They're dreadful at this time of year." She narrowed her eyes at me, her lips disappearing in a tight, grim line.

"Oh, yes," he said vaguely, surfacing for air. "I don't suppose there's any chance she's a virgin?" He spoke to Bonia but he kept his lusty little eyes on me.

"I'm afraid not, general. It's almost impossible to buy a virgin these days. You have to raise them."

"Ah, well," he sighed. "At least at the Vine and Fig Tree you know you get honest wares—no fakery, no stitches and chicken blood. I don't suppose any of the current crop are ripe yet?" he persisted.

"No," said Bonia. "Not presently. You know how strict Domitia Tertia is. But you can put your name on the list of bidders and we'll send you word when there's an auction."

"The last time you auctioned a virgin I was away on a campaign. Of course, to afford one of Domitia's virgins I'd need to conquer another territory." He turned his attention back to me. "Tell me about this one."

"I hardly know what to say, general. Fresh off the block, untried." Bonia sounded hesitant, reluctant. Then she leaned closer to him and whispered, "I'm afraid she's a bit of a savage, sir."

I felt sick: Bonia wasn't protecting me. She was pitching me.

"She'll need a firm hand then," said the general, as if he were buying a battle horse. "Do I understand correctly that I will be her first in what we all hope will be a lucrative career in this illustrious house?"

Bonia beamed and signaled the cashier. "There's an extra charge for that privilege as I'm sure you know, sir."

"Of course," he shrugged. "Though by rights you should pay me for breaking her to the saddle."

"No doubt we should, general," Bonia laughed. "But that's how it works."

"Well, I don't come to the Vine and Fig Tree unless I'm prepared to bleed gold."

All during this exchange I hadn't said a word. I was cornered. Outnumbered and outmaneuvered. If I fought, I would be raped again and sent back to the slave block for worse. I was running out of options. I prayed to the goddess Bride for inspiration.

"So where is this barbarian beauty from?" the general inquired.

"She's a Gaul, sir."

I opened my mouth to correct her, then stopped myself in time. It would be very stupid to let on that I came from the unconquered Celts and could have intimate knowledge of a druid stronghold. I might be an exile, but I would not be a traitor.

"Ah, the Gauls. An undisciplined and unruly people." He licked his lips. "Has she any Latin or Greek?"

"Very, *very* little." Bonia skewered me with her eyes. I got the message. Keep your mouth shut.

"Good. I rather like it when they can't talk. This one reminds me of a wild mare." He was very unoriginal. "Yes, Bonia, I believe I'll take a ride."

"Very good, general. Bone will have someone escort you to her chamber while I have a brief word with her."

"You speak the barbarous tongues, eh Bonia?" He was sharper than I'd thought.

"The language I speak, all the girls understand. I'll send her right up, sir."

As soon as he was gone, Bonia grabbed my arm, pulled me to my feet, lifted my toga and smacked my bottom—hard. "Now listen, you silly little twat, you try anything like that again and you'll be back on the slave block so fast this place will seem like a lost dream. The only good way out of here is to fuck your brains out, that is if you have any. And if you play your cards right, there'll be plenty of opportunity to spit on men—and to piss on them, too, but they have to ask for it, and they have to pay for it."

"All right, then, dearie," she softened slightly. "Don't be afraid. He won't rough you up. House rule, and all our gentlemen respect it. Just do whatever he wants; that's good enough for now. Your room is upstairs, third on the left where the blank plaque is hanging. When we find out what your talents are—if you have any—we'll write 'em up. Remember any woman can spread her legs—a classy whore knows how to put on a show. Speaking of that, wait a minute." She turned away, rummaged in a wooden chest, then returned to me with several lengths of rope. "You might need these. Do you know how to tie a knot? Good. Off you go then."

I walked across the atrium and up the stairs as slowly as I could, the sound of the fountain lost in the noise of general carousing. As I passed Succula and Berta on the stairs, they giggled at the sight of the rope.

"Oh, I bet she's got the general. Don't worry, Red. You'll be all right. Have fun."

Fucking a Roman pig? Fun? I fumed as I climbed the rest of the way and came to the door of the room Bonia called mine. It was veiled in gauzy material and strings of beads. Inside, the general belched. I closed my eyes for a moment.

It's not just before death that your whole life flashes before you—or maybe it is. Crossing that threshold would be a kind of death. All the life I had known before rushed in with one breath and sang in my blood. The woman-shaped isle of Tir na mBan, my mothers, the druid groves, my classmates, my kind foster-father King Bran, the black-robed priestesses of Holy Isle. Yet all that dear life was just a mist that swirled around a boy with eyes dark as the well where the salmon of wisdom leapt. When I breathed out, I let it all go.

Back. Down. Deep under the hard layers of Rome, to bedrock, molten rock, dark rivers.

I stepped though the veil, so to speak, into a tiny chamber. By the light of a lamp—whose base depicted a coupling so complicated that it could put your back out for life—I saw the general waiting for me. He no longer wore his gold-trimmed toga or anything else that would distinguish him from any other body. He lay spread out on the bed—a shelf built into the wall with a mattress and several layers of removable coverings—arms behind his head, legs splayed, all his vital organs exposed in what I found a confusing mix of arrogance and vulnerability.

I had seen naked men before but never one so utterly on display. So I inspected him, from his hard face with the softness of dissolution just under the surface, to the muscular arms and chest, just beginning to lose their tone with age, his still-trim waist and, of course, his appendage. Having grown up on an island where the only males were animals, I had always felt that penises were a sort of afterthought on humans. The general's was large, soft, flopped over on one side, and—I peered more closely—hooded. You understand, of course, that the only penis I knew well was circumcised. (You don't want to hear about that penis? Better stop reading.) Under my interested gaze the general's appendage began to stir and poke its purplish head out of the foreskin. The general's breathing quickened.

"Barbarian bitch!" His voice was hoarse. "You have captured me. I am utterly at your mercy. Now what are you going to do to me!"

Clearly this was my cue. Never mind that I could think of plenty of things I'd rather do to him than play with his appendage. If I didn't want to go back to the block, I'd better get on with the job.

"Roman dog," I said in Celtic, remembering that I supposedly didn't speak Latin. I advanced on him with the rope. "First I will smear you with honey and let the ants swarm over you like the armies of Rome," I continued as I took my time tying him up with fancy Celtic knots. "Then I will marinate you in excrement for three days and three nights. After that I will roast you slowly until you are almost dead. Then I will feed you alive to the swine."

Actually I was beginning to enjoy myself—just a little. I pulled the knots tight. It was true. He was at my mercy. At least for this nanosecond. Suddenly I was overcome with a sense of absurdity. My mothers had once captured a man and ravished him against his will. (The true story of my conception—a truth I found out too late.) Now here I was with a man who was paying to be ravished, and it was my job to do it.

"Bitch!" Romans certainly lacked the verbal prowess of the Celts. My poor, mad, dead father would have been eloquent at least. "Naked, savage, barbarian bitch," he prompted desperately, straining against the ropes, his appendage swollen to near bursting.

Oh, all right, I thought, struggling to get out of my silly garment. I felt much better naked, almost free. I had to stifle a war cry as I pounced on him. Then I played with him cruelly, dangling my body over him, not quite letting his appendage touch me.

"Bitch," he screamed. "Let me have it!"

He was so loud, I was afraid Bonia would come charging upstairs. When I finally lowered myself onto his weeping cock, I have to admit it filled me quite satisfactorily.

"Take any pleasure you can," I heard my namesake Queen Maeve of Connacht whisper in my ear. "If there's no Fergus around it might take thirty men to satisfy you." She paused a beat. "But it looks like you've got all night."

It was all over in a few strokes. He sighed and looked so relaxed I caught a glimpse of the child he might once have been.

"Untie me now," he commanded. The Roman general was back.

I considered not comprehending. I was a savage, after all. But what was the use. I was trapped here. One of the old women came in with washing water and towels.

"Mistress Bonia wants to know, will you be wanting another half hour."

"Yes, yes," he said. "I believe I will. My compliments to the house on a fine new acquisition."

When the serving maid had gone, he got out of bed and gestured for me to lie down.

"Now then my hot little barbarian. Your turn."

And so began my life as a professional. Before the night was over I understood what many people don't: whoring is hard work. I'm not going to give you a blow by blow description of all my engagements that night. I did not have thirty men in succession as Queen Maeve boasted she had, but I did service quite a few. When I came back downstairs after the general, my sister whores feted me, feeding me grapes and figs and pouring me a cup of unwatered wine. Then it was back to work up and down the stairs with men, old men and young, fat and thin, handsome and ugly.

Twice I went with another whore. As promised, Berta gave me instruction on the care and feeding of the male member. No doubt he paid extra for being the object lesson of a *novica's* education. When I went with Succula, we took over the bed while the man watched. I had never made love with a woman before, but as my first experience of orgasm had been with two snakes in a cavern deep in the earth, I was open to the unexpected and to the naturalness of what other people might consider unnatural. After the clumsiness of some of my customers, I felt nothing but admiration for Succula's skill and a desire to improve my own.

As I look back on that night, I see choices I didn't recognize then. I could have disavowed my body. That's not me straddling the general. That's just my body. Or I could become my body, its opening and resistance, its capacity for cruelty or compassion. But there is another possibility, and I think I sensed it even then: that I—this fraught ecstatic coupling of body and soul—could become the conduit of some wild force, the mediator of it, the priestess.

I don't remember how that first night ended. I suspect, after finishing with some man, I just didn't get back up again and Bonia, in her mercy, let me sleep. I do remember the dream I had near dawn.

I am standing by a river that swirls with mist. The reeds rustle with the wind. Then I see something floating on the water, parting the mists, a wooden box, wider at one end than at the other. A coffin. Suddenly I know he is in that box, my beloved, floating down the dark river. I rush towards the coffin but the waterweeds bind my legs. The current flows past me and I float helpless, my arms streaming towards him.

I woke disoriented in close, airless darkness. Maybe *I* was in the coffin. I could still hear the sound of the river and the wind rattling through the reeds. Then I saw grey light leaking through the gauzy curtain covering my doorway. I got up and stepped out onto the balcony. Below me the fountain played, and an old woman swept with a broom made of sticks. When she saw me she smiled toothlessly.

"Go back to bed, my sweet," she said. "Isis love you! It's much too early for a whore to be up."

A whore. By Bride's breasts, she meant me.

CHAPTER FOUR

LOSING MY STORY

Yes, me. Whoever *that* was. Red, the hot new whore at the Vine and Fig Tree? After a few weeks it became apparent to everyone that my popularity was not just due to novelty. The plaque hanging by my door was no longer blank but crowded with my praises. I had an aptitude for the work, unmarred by my bad attitude, which seemed, if anything, an asset. I fit the bill as Savage Barbarian better than Berta who had more appeal as the kindly, maternal, all-forgiving type despite her avowed hatred of Romans.

Every day was much like another. We slept through the morning; then we ate, bathed, submitted to the *ornatrices* before working non-stop from midafternoon till near dawn. I had little time to think. But whenever I had a moment to myself, I was plagued by the same sense of disjuncture I had felt that first morning. I could not connect my past and present. I had been born of herowomen and raised as one. I came from a world where everything—rocks, trees, wells, winds, the flight of birds—was a form of oracular speech, where the very earth under my feet was alive and holy. Confined as a slave within square walls (for I was on probation and not allowed outside) with tile floors between me and the dirt, I felt as you might if you suddenly had to operate without one of your senses. I, who had once shape-shifted into a bird, who could see across worlds in the waters of a sacred well, I had no magic anymore. After a while I gave up gazing into the artificial fountain. Among the milling carp, no salmon of wisdom would ever leap.

But there was something more troubling still: I feared I had lost my story. The story I had been so sure of that I'd told it to a festival crowd on the Druid Isle, the story birds' wings had once spread across the sky, the story that had been my offering to the dolphins who kept me alive when I was cast out to sea. The story of Maeve and Esus.

The more time passed, the more desperate I became. How was I to remember him? Did he remember me? If you've ever loved and lost someone when you were very young, then you know what it's like. You cling so tight to your memories—as if they are air and water—and then one day you open your hand and find nothing there. My dream troubled me. He whose gaze held the mystery of the heavens, whose very hair felt alive to my touch, how could a coffin contain him? He was not dead; he could not be. But if I lost hope of finding him again, I would die. I had to find some way to keep the story alive.

So one day I yielded to Berta's curiosity and began to tell the story to the other whores during our baths. It was far too grand a story for one sitting, so I told it in daily installments.

The response was gratifying.

"And so, Red," someone would prompt. "What happened next?"

"Where was I?" I would pretend not to remember.

"You got to the part about the three black-robed priestesses standing on the cliffs watching you in your little boat. That made my hair stand on end."

"And the birds in the sky," someone added. "They spelled your name— and his."

And I would resume the story, spinning it out fine, so that they could see, hear, and feel it all with me, so that I could live it again, believe that it was true. Though my mothers had told me everything but the truth about my own begetting—and I had come to great grief because of it—there was part of me that still accepted their axiom: A story is true if it is well told. So I gave it all I had.

And then, one day, my story was done.

"Ah, *liebling*," sighed Berta, wiping away her tears. "So romantic. Now you can be faithful to your Esus forever."

"Berta," said Dido, raising one perfectly shaped eyebrow. "She's a whore."

"That is what I mean. Wife to all men is wife to no man. A whore is like a virgin. In her heart she belongs only to her true love. Like me and my poor butchered betrothed."

No, I wanted to shout. I am not like you, and my beloved is not dead.

"I will find him" was all I said.

"Yah, *liebling*. Sure you will." Berta patted my arm.

I wanted to scream.

"Listen, Red—"

"Dido," Succula pleaded. "Be nice."

"I like you." I could feel Dido's gaze, but I wouldn't look at her. "We all like you. You're a good sport. You told a good story. Whether it's true or not is beside the point. I'm telling you this for your own good. Get over it. He's gone. You're here. That was then. This is now."

An aphorism not invented at the turn of *your* millennium. I looked down at my navel. Little flakes of faux woad floated in the water. Domitia Tertia had agreed to let me dress—or undress—the part of a barbarian. The past few nights, I'd dispensed with my toga and gone to work in blue paint. I felt ashamed now. I had betrayed my people—and my warrior queen namesake— by play-acting a stock character in a Roman fantasy.

"You do know," Dido continued, enough kindness in her voice that I couldn't just hate her, not hear her, "that if he survived the journey—and it must have been a long and dangerous one—and made it back to his own people, he's probably married by now. Maybe he'll always remember you; maybe he'll even love you, for what that's worth. But Red, honey, life goes on. Don't waste yours."

"I don't have to waste it." I could taste the bitterness of my words; I savored it. "Domitia Tertia is wasting it for me."

"*Diobolara!*" Succula, my sometime lover who had been nestling beside me, drew back and practically spat. In case you are wondering, she had just called me a two-bit whore. "You are spoiled, as spoiled as our baby Queen Helen of Troy here."

"Eat me," said Helen languidly, not ruffled at all.

"Maybe you like it here, because you've never known anything else," I shot back. "Though how you can defend a woman who raised you just so she could sell your virginity to the highest bidder is beyond me."

"You know nothing about it, Red, so shut up. We've all heard your story, daughter of the shining isles. Not one mother, no, she has to have eight. You want to hear my story? I wasn't exposed as a baby," Succula hurtled on, "though if my mother had been looking out for herself, she should have left me in a ditch. So I know about the streets. I lived on them till my mother died under a bridge, right where the sewer empties into the Tiber. There's no dole in Rome for women and children. Did you know that, Red? Only for men. My mother worked the streets till she got sick. Sometimes we rented a room, mostly not. I tried to take care of my mother. I begged. I stole food, but she died anyway, and I was all by myself, fair game for any and everyone.

"That's when Domitia Tertia found me. This great rich *domina* in a *stola*— she never did wear a toga; she likes breaking stupid laws. And you know what she did, hard-ass, kiss-my-ass Domitia Tertia? She paid for my mother to be buried properly in a catacomb with her name inscribed on a plaque. And she gave me a place at the Vine and Fig Tree. I had food every day and a warm place to sleep.

"When it came time for the auction, I wasn't ignorant. The other whores had been getting me ready, training me. Before the auction there was a party for days and days, and I was the queen of it all. It was like being a bride but better, because I wasn't going to have to leave home to be some man's property and see his ugly face day after day. I was going to have a nicer room and more clothes. I was going to be one of the whores.

"And it wasn't like just anyone was allowed to bid. Honey, it was invitation only. You had to be rich. You had to be a gentleman. You had to pass Domitia Tertia's personal—and I mean personal—inspection. On the day of the auction, while the men were bidding up front, I was in back with the whores. Remember, Berta?"

"Yes, I was there, still a *novica*. We had wine and the best cakes I'd ever tasted."

"And I stood in the middle of you all, and everyone oiled me and perfumed me and put flowers in my hair and made wishes for me. And sweet Isis, I didn't feel like a whore or a bride. I felt like a goddess."

"You were, *liebling*, you were."

"I was so high, I wasn't really scared. Or only a little. My cherry burst with a tiny ping, and I thought well, that's that. No big thing. While the senator thought he was on Mount Fucking Olympus with Aphrodite in her nightie."

Everyone laughed, and the tension was dispersed for a moment.

"That's a good story," I said to Succula.

"And it's true. Do you understand now, Red. Why I was so mad at you?"

"Yes, but—"

I didn't finish the sentence, and no one pressed me. Succula leaned against me again. I looked up and found Dido still watching me.

"What about you, Dido?" I asked. "What is your story?"

If eyes are the windows of the soul, she had just drawn the curtains.

"I don't tell my story, Red. It's the one thing I have that's all mine."

I don't think Dido meant to wound me, but her words went in deep, piercing me in all my vital parts. No, it wasn't the words; it was their truth, a truth I already knew. Now my story was outside of me, dispersed on the air; worse, given some fixed form, like those Roman statues, lifelike but not alive. So why am I telling you my story now? Did I learn nothing from that loss? Yes, I did. Only now I know more. Dido knew one secret: don't tell. In time, I discovered another. Tell, lose, tell again. Live, die, live again. Let the story change. Let the story change you.

Then, all I knew was the loss.

Losses that are invisible or unreal to others can be hard to bear. There are no ritual releases. No funeral rites, no mourning garb. Now I did not even have words. The words I thought would give me back my life had betrayed me. Hardest of all was the sense that my life had been diverted—the way the Romans took free flowing water and made it go where they wanted. And I was left behind, as I had been in that terrible dream, helplessly tangled in the weeds while the river kept going.

Then one night the river tossed me something tantalizing, brought it almost—but not quite—within my reach.

It was early evening, and business at the house was slow; people were still at their banqueting. I was learning a lot from the cats and tended to drowse when I could. I came to abruptly when someone smacked the back of my head.

"Lolling is one thing. Snoring and drooling are another." It was Bonia. "I don't know what's gotten into you or gone out of you. You've been off the mark lately, and after such a promising start. Remember the rules: only drink with a gentleman if he wants the company and no unwatered wine! There's no place in this house for sodden whores. Now look lively. Domitia Tertia is here tonight with an important guest. He likes to meet the new girls. You're still on probation, and his opinion counts a lot with the *domina*."

The idea that anyone could have influence on Domitia Tertia was mildly intriguing, but I found it difficult to feel much of anything—excitement or fear. Yet when Domitia Tertia strolled into the reception rooms with her visitor all my senses went on the alert before I quite knew why.

The man at her side appeared to be her contemporary, that is, not young, not old, greying, in good enough health, but a little stooped, his bearing neither military nor athletic, and he had a squint. He wore a simple but well-made tunic of good material. His face was clean-shaven, though the hair on his head was thick and somewhat longer than typical. Then he made some remark. I couldn't catch all the words, but I knew he was speaking Greek, not unusual among educated Romans, except suddenly I knew he wasn't Roman, nor was Greek his native tongue. I would bet my tiny stash of tips on it.

He caught me looking at him; cat-like, I looked away, pretending he hadn't been the object of my scrutiny. I knew that I was now the focus of his. In another moment I sensed his approach, but I was totally unprepared for his greeting.

"Rhuad," he said, and he continued to speak to me in Celtic. "You must find it strange to live in square walls in a walled city. Are you from Gaul or from Pretannia?"

At that moment, I looked as though I came from the goldfish pool.

I gawped like a carp. It wasn't only that he was the first person to address me in my own language. It was his accent.

"Who are you?" I demanded rather gracelessly. "How do you know my language? If you are a Jew, what are you doing in a Roman whorehouse?"

I hurled these questions at him in Aramaic.

Now it was his turn to look like a fish out of water.

"Can you speak Greek?" he finally managed.

"Yes, and Latin, too, though I'd rather not." I said in Greek.

"Finally," he said in Greek, "an educated girl. How many times have I told Domitia Tertia, she could have a house full of witty, lettered women, like the *heterae* who had their own schools in Athens. Do you mind if we converse in Greek? My mind always feels clearer when I do."

"We can speak whatever language you prefer as long as you answer my questions."

For a moment he frowned, his squint even more pronounced, then—as if he'd had to think about it first—he decided to laugh.

"You certainly are bold, but I'm not surprised, having done business with some of the women of your people. May I sit?"

I made a welcoming gesture. I liked his deference, his apparent desire to converse. There was a charge for talk, of course, though perhaps this friend of Domitia Tertia's had special privileges.

"Please," I said, "am I right that you are from …from Galilee?"

"Galilee! No. Do I look like a peasant to you? I am from Judea, from Arimathea, a town between the port of Joppa and the city of Jerusalem."

Jerusalem. I wrapped my arms around myself to keep my hands from shaking.

"I am in the tin trade and have traveled often to the Pretannic Isles. As a merchant, I must have a base in Rome—though it is a crass place, its arts and letters but a crude imitation of the Hellenic."

"But you live near Jerusalem," I persisted.

"When I must." He was abrupt. "Why are you so interested in Jerusalem? How do you come to speak Aramaic? I have never heard it spoken among the *Keltoi*. It is time for you to answer some questions, Rhuad."

"Maeve Rhuad," I said before I could think. "My name is Maeve Rhuad."

He bowed his head. "And my name is Joseph."

Joseph! "I am Yeshua ben Joseph ab Jacob ab Matthan…" my beloved had said to the druids, tracing his lineage much further than the required nine generations, keeping us up all night with the story of his people.

"Do you have a son?" I blurted out.

"Why do you ask me that?" He was wary and, I sensed, pained.

"Your name—"

"—is a very common one." He cut me off. "Now then, am I to presume that you know a young Galilean Jew whose father is named Joseph? How did that come about?"

Now I was wary. I did not want to tell my story again, to make polite conversation about the ripped out, broken heart of my life. I just looked at him, and then, for the first time since my capture, I had a flash of second sight—more than sight. I could smell the sea, and hear the sound of wind in a sail, feel the pitch of the boat. Joseph was there with someone else—someone I couldn't see, someone I sensed he was helping.

"Take me with you," I heard myself saying. "Take me to Judea. Buy me from Domitia Tertia. You have influence with her. She will sell me to please you. And I will do whatever you want. Anything. Just take me with you out of Rome."

He looked at me intently; when he did not squint, his eyes were appealing, their expression gentle. I looked away so he couldn't read my face. I regretted my outburst. Now he would tell Domitia Tertia I was desperate to escape.

"You give me no reason why I should do such a thing," he said at last. When I didn't answer he added, "and you greatly overestimate my powers. I am an old friend of Domitia Tertia's and an investor. I sometimes give her financial advice. But I don't tell her how to run her business. I never interfere between her and one of her girls."

Then I did something that, given my profession, you may be surprised to know I had never done before. I turned my face to him and looked up through my lashes. I drew on all my fire and concentrated it in my eyes. I called on the waters to well and make them shine. I held him with my eyes, for just the right space of time, and then I spoke softly, so softly he had to lean into me and breathe my scent.

"Never?"

He closed his eyes and took me in through his pores.

"Never," he sighed, and opened his eyes again. "But I will tell you what I will do. I will buy you a night of rest, and I will come and lend you scrolls from my library."

"I do not read," I said proudly. "Reading destroys the memory."

"Nonsense!" he growled. "I see you must have been in training with the druids. I didn't know they taught women. It is an unfortunate bias on their part. If your literature is only in your head, it can be destroyed with your people. Listen, I will teach you to read Greek and as much Latin as necessary. I will come every day when I am in Rome."

"How about Hebrew?"

He squinted at me again. "Greek first."

"You never did answer my questions," I reminded him. "Are you a Jew? And if you are, what are you doing here at the Vine and Fig Tree?"

"Don't tell me you're a proselyte," he groaned.

"Answer my questions, please."

"All right, all right. I am a Jew, yes, and of a prominent family. I hold an inherited seat on the Sanhedrin. But does that mean that I must be ignorant of the great ideas and literatures of the world? Because I have read Plato and Aristotle does that make me a gentile? Because I must do business in Rome, am I a collaborator?"

He was arguing with someone—but clearly not with me. Maybe with someone like my beloved, someone he'd like to dismiss as a Galilean peasant.

"And the rest of my question?"

"What am I doing in a Roman whorehouse? Come, show me to your room, and I will answer you."

Well, maybe it was a dumb question. What is any man doing in a whorehouse?

Despite my status as a probationer, I was pretty seasoned by now, a quick learner, everyone said. But that night my native shamelessness faltered. This man knew something of my people. He knew what a free Celt looked like—I was glad I had given up my imitation woad and resumed the whore's toga. More inhibiting still, this man might have stood beside my beloved in the Temple of Jerusalem. To my dismay, my hands began to shake again as I undressed; then my whole body trembled uncontrollably with a sudden chill.

Still fully clothed, Joseph came and put his arms around me. His touch was as gentle as his eyes. He murmured comforting words—in Hebrew, a language I had never heard except in my beloved's voice. I couldn't help it; I broke down and wept.

"There, there," he soothed, and he put me to bed. "You have known sorrow. I have known sorrow. We will not speak of it," he said in Aramaic. "Not tonight. Tonight you will rest. I will stay with you until you sleep. Rest now, Maeve Rhuad."

I closed my eyes and hoped he would think I was sleeping. His kindness was too much. I didn't want to trust anyone. I didn't want to love anyone. I didn't want anyone to love me. Not here. Not now. Not this way.

I must have fallen asleep; I did not hear him go. I woke much later when the house was finally dark and quiet, my favorite cat, a golden tabby named Olivia, purring next to my heart.

CHAPTER FIVE

THE GODDESS FINDS ME

Joseph, whom my fellow whores called Uncle Joseph, was as good as his word. He came every day for an hour before we went to the baths to give me lessons in written Greek. The letters amazed me; they were so tiny and precise, moving in lines from left to right, each word so small compared to the amount of space it would take to write the same thing in *ogham*. But then Celts modeled *ogham* after the flight of birds—the whole sky for a scroll. Greek looked more like the scratch of small bird feet.

At my insistence, Joseph began to teach me the Hebrew alphabet, too, which went in the opposite direction. "Backwards!" he muttered. "A stubborn and stiff-necked people, our God calls us. We always have to be different." The Hebrew letters were easier for me to remember, because they came from living things, like gimmel, or camel, shaped like the strange humped beasts my beloved had described for me. Though I was still wary of the written word, I looked forward to the distraction of my lessons with Joseph, the brusque impersonality with which he taught that covered, for the most part, the unnerving tenderness he had shown me on the first night we met. Nor did he ever go upstairs with me again. I knew he'd dined several times with Domitia Tertia, but he kept away from the whores' parlor. I didn't know what to make of his eschewing my bed, but I confess I was relieved. I did not want to ask myself why.

Then, one morning, Joseph didn't show up for lessons. I noticed that I was mildly disconsolate, but I didn't have much time to wonder about his absence. Just as I was heading back upstairs, Bonia came to summon me to Domitia Tertia's private chamber, a place I had never been before, the secret center of The Vine and Fig Tree.

The *domina* received me reclining on a couch, which was where wealthy Romans generally were when they were not walking around the Forum or soaking in the baths. Behind her a mosaic depicted a scene I did not recognize. I did not know Greek or Roman stories. (Uncle Joseph had insisted we begin by reading Plato, as he found me utterly lacking in any rational philosophical foundation. The poets and playwrights could wait.) The mosaic featured a severe yet also seductive woman, not unlike Domitia Tertia—or one of my mothers. She stood on an island; stylized waves lapped the shore. She was surrounded by animals—lions, wolves, and a whole herd of pigs. The mosaic evoked a sense of wildness, remoteness. In fact, it made me homesick.

"You like the mosaic," Domitia Tertia observed, not inviting me to sit. "Do you know who the woman is?"

"I think it might be you, *domina*."

"You're perceptive. I asked the artist to depict Circe on her island. An insolent but talented young man, he manages to hint that there is a likeness between us. Do you know the story of Circe?"

"No, *domina*."

"Sit." She indicated a low stool on the other side of the table from her couch. "Long, long ago, much longer ago than those philosophers Joseph wants you to read, in the time of the gods and heroes, Circe lived on Aeaea, an island off the coast of Italia. Some called her a goddess, some a sorceress. She was the daughter of Helio, the sun god, and Perse, an ocean nymph."

Just the opposite of me, the daughter of the sea god and my mother Grainne of the golden hair, the sun herself, I mused, lulled by the storytelling, forgetting for a moment that god my father was a lie my mothers told because it made a better story than the truth.

"When a lover displeased her or rejected her, she turned him into an animal. All except Odysseus," Domitia went on. "He cheated. Hermes gave him an herb called *moly* to protect him against Circe's magic. She had turned his advance guard into swine. But she let Odysseus go unharmed, though he had been her lover for a year. She did more than that; she helped him, gave him directions to Hades, so that he could consult with the spirits of the dead. That is how the story goes. People are always telling stories of heroes outwitting witches. But I personally don't think the *moly* affected Circe's actions at all."

I waited attentively. Whose story was she telling me?

"The name Circe means hawk. A predatory bird with keen sight. I think she saw it all. I think she knew exactly what she was doing."

"Now then," she shifted from story-telling mode to her more familiar business manner, "do you know why I called you here today, Red?"

Suddenly I had hope, wild desperate hope. Joseph had changed his mind; he was buying me from her. He was even now making preparations for departure. Like Circe, she would help him go home…with me, even though he had been her lover. Holy *Moly*!

"I would not presume to know your reasons, *domina*," was all I said.

She gave me a sharp look. My imitation of a good, submissive slave must have seemed just that—an imitation, a subtly mocking one.

"Listen, Red, Rhuad, whatever Joseph calls you. You be straight with me and I'll be straight with you. As you know, you've been on probation and under keener observation than you might imagine."

I had no doubt of that, though it seemed rather absurd—obsessive-compulsive to use one of your terms—to expend so much effort monitoring a slave, a disposable commodity as I had been repeatedly reminded. I made no comment as I studied a chipped fingernail that one of the *ornatrices* would have to fix today. I knew my display of indifference bordered on insolence.

"Look at me when I speak to you."

I raised my eyes and met hers. They were fierce and dark and distant, all at the same time. Hawk woman, sorceress, ruler of her own little walled island. Did she turn her discarded lovers into cats?

"You have a gift, Red. Like any gift, wealth, talent, beauty—you could squander yours."

"What is my gift?" I asked after a moment.

"You are a talented whore."

Fucking great, I thought. My eyes twitched, I wanted so badly to roll them.

"You don't want to be here. Why else do you think I've kept a potential gold mine under house arrest for so long? You despise being a slave. You're very bad at it. You despise me. You don't hide it well. Yet when you are a whore, you are a whore. You don't stint. It's like a craftsman doing some minor job with care and precision, though no one else will notice. You can't help yourself, can you?"

I didn't despise her—that word implied contempt. But I hated her very much.

"Why did you call me here? Where is Joseph?"

She looked ruffled, angry for the first time. "Joseph's whereabouts are no business of yours unless he requires you. Don't get ideas. And no, in case you're wondering, I didn't put a stop to the lessons. He is perfectly right; an educated whore could be an asset. In fact, he left you a scroll to keep reading while he's gone."

"Gone? When will he come back?"

"Did I or did I not just tell you Joseph's business is none of your business?"

"You did." I said. If I shed a tear in front of Domitia Tertia, I will find a way to cut out my own heart, I vowed to myself. A soothing thought. There.

"As for why I have called you here, I swear I have almost changed my mind. I told you to look at me."

I did with all the calm of renewed hopelessness.

"Flavius Anecius is giving a banquet for his son, who puts on the manly toga tomorrow. He is also hosting chariot races at Circus Maximus. He has reserved a block of seats for the Vine and Fig Tree, and he has asked that you be among the entertainers at the banquet. Such occasions can be lucrative. Joseph has told me about doing business with your people. I know you count wealth in cattle. I want to make sure you understand: if you save your coins and bank them with the House, you can buy your freedom within years. Mere years. Do you understand?"

I'm not stupid, bitch. I know what a coin is worth, but you have no idea what a year costs me. "Yes, *domina*."

"You do know what happens to runaway slaves?"

"They are killed." My shoulders wanted to shrug, but I caught them in time.

"Ha! If they had only death to fear, there would be far fewer slaves in Rome. Listen well, Red. Runaway slaves are publicly beaten; their flesh is branded, and they are sent to the salt mines to be worked to death."

No answer seemed to be required.

"Joseph says you're too smart to be stupid. I have my doubts about that. You decide who is right. Go now. Be dressed and ready to go with Bone to Circus Maximus at the third hour tomorrow morning."

I stood up, looking again from Domitia Tertia to her likeness Circe— what Domitia might have been if she'd lived on a shining isle like my mothers, if she were wild instead of hardened, if she were a goddess, instead of a Roman brothel keeper.

"Wait. Here is the scroll." She reached under the couch. "When you are not studying, Bonia will keep it locked in one of the chests. No," she cautioned, "this scroll is inferior work not worth much money. Don't even think about trying to sell it."

I hadn't in fact thought about it; I needed to learn to think like that.

"Thank you, *domina*."

"Thank Joseph," she sighed.

And for just a moment she looked merely human and very weary.

All right. I'll admit it to you. I was excited to be going beyond the confines of the Vine and Fig Tree. My mind knew perfectly well I would be no freer outside the walls than in, but my body shouted, yes! And my imagination, some fertile mating of the two, whispered, anything might happen. There's a chance now, there's a chance. You can imagine my disappointment when I discovered that we were being transported in curtained litters. I wanted to walk. I wanted to know the lay of the land with my feet. But Domitia Tertia conscientiously flouted any law enacted against whores. We had to ride in litters precisely because it was illegal for us to do so. Another reason oral law is better than written; if you have to hold a law library in your head you stick to the essentials.

Bone and his assistants, three male slaves on loan for the day from Flavius Anecius, escorted us on foot (well, it would have taken a dozen litter bearers to heft the eunuch). They kept an eye out for the *aedile*, and Bone repeatedly and futilely shouted at us to stop sticking our heads outside the curtains. He could hardly be heard over Succula and Berta's tour guide patter as they called to me from their litters, "And here is the best place to buy pigeon pie, and look over there. That entire block of *insulae* belongs to Claudius Appius, and he owns all the shops, too. They say he is richer than Croesus."

I didn't catch all their words, and I didn't pay much attention, because neither of them was saying things like, "and if you take that street there, it leads to the nearest gate out of the city." So I just took in the bustle. Everyone was out and about trying to finish errands early. Some vendors were already closing up or packing their wares to sell to the crowds at Circus Maximus where all Rome, rich and poor, would soon be.

Our route became increasingly hilly and circuitous, whether to keep us disoriented or to find the least crowded approach to the Circus Maximus I wasn't sure. We were winding down a hill on the other side of the Circus from Palatine Hill with its enormous temples, palaces, gardens, everything on a god-like scale. I was more interested in the sky; I had been starving for it after seeing only a small cut-out square of sky for months. Now here it was, a heaping bowl of blue, enough for everyone, with birds circling it—high up an eagle, lower down the flocking birds wheeling and turning, now invisible, now flashing as the light caught their wings at different angles. Then the sky narrowed as we wound down the hill towards the Murcia Valley.

"Red," called Succula, "we'll be coming to the Temple of Venus Obsequens soon."

The compliant Venus, I translated to myself, the accommodating Venus. I had barely become acquainted with Roman deities; they struck me as petty and cruel, like the Romans themselves. You had to wonder about a people who worshipped their emperors as gods. Civic religion has always struck me as both dismal and dangerous to the health of the general population.

"She's the protectress of whores and adulterers," Succula went on.

I was not impressed. In Rome there was a Venus for everything, including Venus Cloacina, the goddess of the sewer—she helped the Romans maintain the illusion that their shit didn't stink.

"What does she protect us from?" I quipped but not loud enough for Succula to hear. If Succula wanted to believe there was a goddess who cared about whores, let her. As for me—I stopped for a moment, not quite prepared for my next thought—I had no gods. I had left mine behind in the wells and groves of Tir na mBan and Mona. Or you could say they had abandoned me, cast me out. I was a slave and an exile in a place where I had no connection with the local gods and wanted none. As for my beloved's god—the invisible one, the jealous one, the portable one who was any and everywhere—I thought that Joseph was quite right to take refuge in Greek philosophy. I was through with gods, I decided.

"It's right down this alley," called Succula.

With no warning, the dream I'd had my first night at the Vine and Fig Tree came back to me—only now it wasn't a dream. I could hear the sound of the water moving through the reeds, the whispering rasp of snakes; I smelled the mud; then the drums started and the women's voices singing, keening, wild as wind, high as birds. Before I knew it, I was running in my silly Roman sandals on the hard stones, in the narrow alley, running straight into the dark mouth of the Temple, the dark waters of the river.

You may argue that what I saw was a trick of the eye caused by going from bright morning light to cavernous dusk of what turned out to be a hole-in-the-wall shrine. But in that suspended moment I felt as though I had stepped into the cosmos, stars and comets blazing by me, the waters rushing past me. And then I saw her, shining horns above a face black and luminous as a clear night, her head crowned with a many-petaled star. Her breasts flooded the sky with milk; her wide wings were made of fire, of fine mist, of colors I did not know how to name. I had known her all my life, and I had never known her before now. But she had called me. She had found me in this terrible place far from home, and she called me to her.

"Bride," I tried to whisper, for so she must be, "Bride."

"Welcome, daughter, in the name of Isis."

In a literal blink of an eye the goddess was gone. A plain middle-aged priestess in an unadorned white *stola* greeted me. A half-dozen other priestesses stood by, holding frame drums and sistrums. They made a semi-circle around a statue—a small unimpressive statue, garishly painted like all Roman statues and dressed in gold cloth. The figure held a sistrum in one hand and what I came to know as an *ankh* in the other. She had been garlanded with fresh flowers.

"Isis?" I repeated.

"Our goddess is called by many names: Demeter, Aphrodite, Dyktynna, Proserpina, Hekate, Bellona, a thousand other names. The Temple is known from the outside as The Temple of Venus. Within these walls we know the mother of all, mistress of the living and the dead, ruler of wind and water, builder of ships, guide of the planets, queen of the stars, star of the sea, giver of grain by her true name—Almighty Isis."

"Red!"

The door darkened with Bone's huge bulk. The priestess, who had been swaying as she chanted her goddess's attributes, looked past me towards the eunuch, her eyes mild as a cow's, utterly unperturbed. When I turned to face Bone, he hesitated in the doorway, not so much as a toe inside. There is something intimidating to a man about a phalanx of priestesses.

"Red?" He sounded confused, as if he wasn't sure who I was, though he was looking straight at me. Was the light that dim?

"I'm coming, Bone."

"If you are a fugitive, the goddess gives sanctuary," the priestess said.

"She is a slave," stated Bone, recovering himself.

"Our goddess makes no distinctions between slave and free."

"Your goddess may not distinguish between slave and free, *domina*, but Roman law does. There is no sanctuary for runaway slaves."

"Listen, Bone." I went to him. I had to assure him that I hadn't been trying to escape or I would never be allowed outside again. It was hard to persuade eunuchs of anything, because, in contrast to most men, their brains were actually between their ears. The usual methods didn't work. "I wasn't running away. I just got carried away. I heard the drums and the singing, and it reminded me of…of home." I didn't want to talk about my dream of the river. "I had to see what the music was. That's all. I'm sorry. Let's go."

"You will come back," the priestess called after me; it was neither a question nor a command; I recognized the tone: it was a prophecy. "You belong to her."

I looked back at the priestess; her face was impassive, masked in the maddening way of priestesses.

"I don't belong to…" anyone, I finished silently as Bone's huge hand closed easily around my upper arm.

But it wasn't Bone's unspoken assertion of Domitia Tertia's ownership that silenced me.

"No one belongs to himself or herself," my beloved had once insisted, angry with me for my arrogance. I knew what he meant: *he* belonged to *his* god, Yahweh. A god I resented and mistrusted, whom I had nonetheless invoked in the end to save Esus's life.

"Yeshua ben Miriam," I had said. *"In the name of the unnameable one, the god of your forefathers, the god of Abraham, Isaac, and Jacob, I command you to go."*

He didn't want to, but when I called his god's name, he had no choice. And so he left me on the shore with no god or goddess to protect me; or so it seemed then.

Now here I was, stepping out of some fusty little temple back into the streets of Rome not sure of what had just happened. Who was Isis? What did she want with me? And what did she have to do with my dream of the river and the floating coffin?

CHAPTER SIX

THE FIRE FINDS ME

The Circus Maximus took up the entire valley of Murcia between the Palatine and Aventine Hills. It could seat a crowd of fifty thousand. By the time Bone and I arrived on foot—he had sent the litters ahead—the huge stadium was almost full. The sound of the crowd was like nothing I had ever heard; the closest comparison is surf, storm surf in a high wind, but without the rhythmic ebb and flow. I had seen plenty of Romans up close; held them as they panted and heaved. They were just flesh, as vulnerable and absurd as anyone else. But to see so many all at once, more people than I had ever seen in my life, was overwhelming—and they were all Romans, of all classes. Slaves and freed slaves were not allowed to buy seats—another rule Domitia Tertia was flouting.

As Bone and I made our way to the top row, I found myself wondering, who are they all, how can there be so many, each one conceived in some heated moment, born of some woman's wracked body, each one with secrets and passions, each one with a story that might break your heart, if she knew how to tell it, if he knew. Looking into a star-crammed sky was no less awesome, though perhaps more aesthetic. And of course stars do not sweat or reek of garlic, so far as we know.

Only Dido was sitting in our row, looking bored and above it all. I glanced at Bone, but he did not appear concerned about the absence of the others. He gestured for me to sit down, while he stood at the end of the row. I was surprised that he hadn't berated me when we left the Temple, though I'd caught him casting uneasy glances at me. Something about what happened at the Temple had unnerved him.

"Where were you?" Dido demanded. "I know you're green, but I didn't think you were stupid—running down a dead end street your first day out of the house."

Before I could answer or decide if I wanted to, Berta returned, puffing and sweating, and plopped herself down next to me.

"Three is enough for me!" she mopped her brow with her sleeve. "Succula's already done five. Where were you, *liebling*? We were so worried about you. You have to stay with us. You don't know your way around the streets yet. Dido, did you tell her? Anything we make at the Circus, we keep."

"I think she better stay put for now," Dido cut her eyes in Bone's direction. "Besides, Berta, you know what I think about doing just anybody. It's not worth it."

"When I am free, Dido, and you're still on your back, we'll talk—or maybe not. I'll be far away eating roast pig and drinking beer. Oh, here come the mimes!" Berta clapped her hands and laughed at their antics.

Dido had her eyes on other things. "Look across the arena, Red. No down," Dido gestured. "That's the Emperor's box. The purple is arriving. There! I think that's the Emperor." Dido gripped my arm.

Her excitement surprised me. I would have thought she'd scorn imperial Rome on principle. As for me, I had grown up believing I was of divine descent; I was the foster daughter of Bran, a valiant, if fallen, king. A balding dissolute emperor, who had banished his first wife for orgies in the Forum, Tiberius did not impress me. My standard for husbands was King Ailill, a generous man who counted Queen Maeve's chief lover as his comrade.

"There's the Emperor's mother," Dido continued. I looked at the spare, elegant older woman with more interest. Livia was the first lady of Rome. Widow of the Divine Augustus (as he was called) as well as mother of his stepson now Emperor, whom the late Augustus had disliked, Livia had masterminded and micro-managed her son's ascendancy. "And here comes Anecius. He's sitting in the Imperial box. What a coup. Well, he is spending fortunes on this election."

"Election?"

"Get with it, Red. You didn't think this circus is really for his son's putting on the toga, did you? That's just the occasion. The man is running for *praetor*. By all the gods, Red, look, do you see? That's Domitia Tertia. Sitting in the second row, behind Livia with some of the Vestal Virgins. That whore has testicles any man would die for!"

"Why do people always think of testicles when they admire someone's nerve?" I complained. But I had to admit, if only to myself, that Domitia Tertia had a certain style. She'd thumbed her nose at the conventions of the ruling class; she ripped them off on a regular basis; she broke laws like fingernails, and they fawned on her for it.

"For the love of Isis!" Dido exclaimed.

Isis, Isis. People called on her an awful lot. Now the name meant something to me. But what?

"Red, see way up there?" She took my head between her hands and positioned it.

"Is that our Helen?" I marveled. "In the box with Aetius? Doesn't he have a wife who's some sort of relation to the Divine Augustus? Where is *she*?"

"Childbed," said Dido. "When did having a wife ever stop a man from having or flaunting a mistress? Hell, a box is nothing. He's setting her up in her own house. Maybe you didn't hear about it yet. He just bought Helen."

"Bought her! I thought Domitia Tertia never sold her whores."

"Oh, she does. If the price is right."

But Joseph hadn't bought me. He'd refused. Now he'd gone off somewhere. Where? Where I wanted to go. Where I would give anything to go.

"That's one way out of the Vine and Fig Tree, but not the one I want," said Dido.

"Why not?" I asked.

"When I leave there, honey, I am going to belong to no one but me."

No one belongs to himself, I remembered my beloved's words again, but I did not speak them to Dido. I just nodded. I knew exactly what she meant.

Succula finally clambered into the row, stepping over Berta and squeezing in next to me, "Red, sweetie, you're here. I was afraid Bone would send you home."

"How many bets did you make, Succula?" Berta asked. "The girl's a sibyl when it comes to the races," she said to me.

"Trouble is," said Dido, "she hardly ever gets to collect her winnings. Bunch of crooks out there. She never learns."

Succula shrugged. "It makes the races more exciting."

The mimes were now mock-fighting their way out of the arena; the crowd had already lost interest in them. I could feel the collective energy gathering, rising in anticipation of the chariots. Suddenly horns blared from every direction, filling the huge elliptical bowl with sound. There followed an extraordinary moment of hush. Then the thundering of hooves began and the horses and chariots blazed into the arena. The crowd found its deafening voice again, but I could still feel the vibration of the hooves through my seat. No stranger to chariot racing, I leaned forward, curious about the Roman style. From that distance it took me a moment of close scrutiny to realize what I was seeing. Then it hit me. Hard.

"Ow, Red!" protested Dido. "Stop digging your nails into me. The race hasn't started yet. They're just parading."

"Dido," I said. "The charioteers are Celts, at least two of them are. See that one?" I pointed to a big lion of a man, his bare arms swirling with woad, his chariot built in the graceful style I remembered. At home our warriors fought bare-headed, their hair limed and sculpted into fantastic spikes. Here they wore helmets. That was the only difference.

"Well, of course, Red. Didn't you know? They use Celts, Scythians, and Thracians for chariot races. Prisoners of war. It could be worse. My people they hunt and capture and use for bestiaries. Wait'll you see those shows. At least no one is slaughtered or eaten alive in a chariot race."

I don't know why it hadn't occurred to me that the Romans would import their athletes; they enslaved anything that moved. At druid college I had heard horror stories of war captives paraded in chains through the Forum. Most Celts killed themselves if they could to avoid that fate. I had never thought about what happened to prisoners after the parade. I'd assumed they were executed—or died of shame.

I looked away from the ring to my own hands clenched in my lap. I did not want to watch my *combrogos* (the companions, as we called each other) demonstrate their prowess for the entertainment of Romans. Their shame was my shame. It knotted my stomach; it pressed against my heart. And there was something else, hovering at the periphery of my memory, something deeply agitating. I was torn between wanting to push it away and needing to know what it was.

I closed my eyes, and everything around me receded, except for the sound of the horses' hooves and the cry of a bird. I was back on Mona, the druid isle, in the teaching grove. Warriors galloped towards us from the Menai Straits still covered with dirt and blood from battle.

"Do you come from my father?" cried Branwen, my friend, my foster-sister.

"Branwen, daughter of King Bran the Bold, your father and my king is still living."

"Anu!" Branwen let out her breath. *For an instant her muscles relaxed; then she braced herself.*

"King Bran has been taken captive. Unless—may the gods give him strength and cunning—unless he has escaped, he is on his way to Rome."

I forced myself to open my eyes again. I searched the field and found him, the charioteer with the broad chest and the arms like big oaks. Arms that could lift you as if you weighed nothing, a chest that smelled of the earth and its goodness, that rose and fell like a gentle sea.

"Red, what's the matter?" asked Succula. "You're crying."

I just shook my head. I couldn't speak yet.

"I…I don't…I can't believe," I stopped, as if saying it might make it so. "I think, I think one of those charioteers might be my foster-father," I finally managed, my hands shaking as I pointed. "That stupid Roman helmet makes it hard to see his face."

"The Gaul? He's the one I've got my money on. Did you say he's your father? I thought your father was dead."

"No. My *foster*-father." I said impatiently. Then I reminded myself: Succula had never had a father at all. I could not expect a Roman street child to understand the meaning of foster kinship to my people, how such ties were as strong as blood and wove a complex web of loyalties among the tribes. "And he's not a Gaul. He's from the Pretannic Isles. Succula, you placed bets on him. What's his name?"

"Sia, Sia something with a B. I'm sorry, Red. Those barbarian names are so hard to pronounce. Everyone just calls him the Big Gaul."

"Bran?" I pressed. "Could it have been Bran?"

"I don't think so, Red, but I'm not sure. Look, they're in place now."

The huge Celt was positioned second from the inside; there were seven chariots in all. If you have ever looked across a crowd, straining to see someone you thought you'd never see again in this life, you have some idea of how I felt. One minute you think, yes, it's got to be him, and the next, no, it can't be. For me it was even more fraught. I longed to run to the first man I had ever known, who had adopted me and treated me with as much tenderness as he did his own daughter. I also wanted desperately to be mistaken. I couldn't bear to think of King Bran as a captive and slave.

And what if it was my fault, whatever his fate, my fault?

Why my fault, you ask? The fate of a king? It was King Bran's capture that had prompted the druids to offer the Great Sacrifice, to send a messenger to the gods, on behalf of the *combrogos*. Could that sacrifice have brought Bran home unharmed? No one would ever know. Because of me. I meddled with the mysteries. I stopped the sacrifice. There. Now you know why I was exiled. I am sure you can also guess who was chosen to be the victim.

"Red, what are you doing?" Dido and Succula grabbed hold of me. "Sit down!"

"I've got to get a closer look," I struggled to shake them off. "Don't you understand?"

"Sweetie, of course we understand. You're the one who doesn't. You can't go wandering around the stadium in your whore's toga annoying people by blocking their view. Sit. We'll find a way to see him afterwards. Trust us."

Impulse control is not my forte, but that's what friends are for. And they were my friends; I could feel it in the fierceness of their grip. We sat together on the edge of the stone bleacher, like any people from any time watching a race. You know how it is. Your heart races, too, flying out of your chest to light on one particular contestant. Your vision telescopes. The tension in your limbs, the bearing down of your will merge with the one you have chosen. I became one with my Celt; the roar of the crowd receding, till I swear I could hear his breath and the steady pounding of his horses' hooves. After the first circuit, he was holding third place. The other Celt and a Thracian were neck and neck in the lead. By the end of the fourth round two chariots began to fall behind, and two began to gain on the leads. One of these was my Celt.

Now Succula and I were both on our feet, Succula shouting instructions in street Latin about what he should do with his *podex* (that's right, Latin for ass) while I loosed an authentic Celtic battle cry. So authentic and so Celtic that I swear you could hear it above the trumpets and all the bellowing citizens of Rome. My Celt looked up; I was afraid I had distracted him till I realized that he had seen—or sensed—something else: three crows wheeling over the Circus, the noon day sun sending their shadows racing over the ground. For Celts, crows were not just birds; they were the Morrigan, the triple goddess of battle, slaughter, and death. Before it happened, I knew it would.

"Look out!" I screamed. "Look out!"

The next moment, one of the Thracians hurled a spear into my Celt's wheel—a movement so swift that it could easily have been missed by most of the onlookers. The spear broke, but jammed the wheels long enough to upset the delicate balance of the speeding chariot. The Thracian had timed his move perfectly. The chariots were just rounding the sharp curve at end of the circus. The Celt's chariot tipped on its inside wheel. As if by pre-arranged signal, another Thracian chariot sideswiped the outer wheel, and the Celtic chariot went over, spilling its rider onto the track, the spooked horse going wild and thrashing and rearing as it dragged the wreck behind it. The Celt on the ground rolled nimbly in an acrobatic display and dodged the wheels of the oncoming chariot and somehow made it off the track to the median.

He had also managed to keep hold of his spear.

Several grooms scurried out from the stable under the circus and struggled to catch the driverless horse. Once off the racetrack, they swiftly parted him from the wreck and led him away. An eerie calm fell over the circus as the chariots raced towards the opposite end of the ellipse from where the big warrior stood, clearly waiting. I could feel him sinking his roots down into the Roman dirt, sending them across land, across water to gather strength from his own soil, his own gods.

Now the chariots rounded the far curve and began to move towards the warrior again. He remained motionless, but the three crows circled lower and lower till they were only a few feet above the his head. The chariots were nearly on him now, the Thracian just ahead of the second Celt. The crowd held its breath; all you could hear in the whole valley was the sound of hooves and wheels, the cry of the crows. I thought I saw the warrior tap his nose. An instant later the second Celt sprang from his chariot and cleared the track in an amazing series of aerial somersaults. Then the big Celt roared his war cry, a deep bellow that made every hair in the circus stand up, that would have raised the very hackles of the mother wolf of Rome. The seven hills shook with its power. If the Thracian charioteer could have turned back, I think he would have.

But it was too late. The Thracian's horse reared; the Celt didn't even need to cast a spear. The chariot careened out of control, and the Thracian hit the dirt. The charioteers still driving headed for the nearest exit. They knew what was coming. The crowd started pouring out of the bleachers, a human flood as dangerous as a burst dam—or a tidal bore.

"Bran!" I screamed. "Bran."

I started to struggle, clawing and biting the huge restraining force that thwarted my will until I was sobbing with desperation and rage. The arms that held me only tightened.

"Easy, girl, easy." I realized my captor was Bone. "That's a full scale Roman riot down there. We stay right up here. Does everyone understand? This is the only place we don't risk getting trampled to death. Look, the purple's already made it out. They have a private escape route. Soldiers will be here soon to clear out the rabble. We stay put till then. Red, if you'd stop bawling, you'd see that your man is holding his own. Trained fighter by the look of him. Matter of fact, I'd say he's enjoying himself. And as far as I can make out at least half the crowd is on his side; they're brawling with the other half. The rest of 'em don't know what they're doing. We've got the best view here."

I calmed down enough to see that Bone was right. My Celt, my *combrogo*—yes, I felt a surge of pride—was in great form. What is more, the crows were helping him, swooping down and going for the eyes of his assailants. When the soldiers marched into the circus, most of the crowd turned tail. The charioteers, with nowhere to go, stood quietly and futilely defiant. All except for the Thracian who lay, dead or unconscious, on the ground.

"Ladies, let's go." Bone still had both his arms around me. "Trust me, Red, you don't want to see this part."

"No, Bone, no. Please. I have to know what happens to him."

Bone swept me up in his arms and started carrying me down the steep steps as if I weighed nothing.

The Forum Boarium, where we emerged and joined the milling throngs, was the oldest part of the city and the most squalid. There were filthy children everywhere begging or stealing from market stalls. One small boy was aggressively soliciting for a whore—his mother?—who'd set up shop in a fornice. (Now you know the origin of the word fornicate—doing it standing up in an archway.) There wasn't an alley, recess, or shadow that didn't have some trade. Every tavern and eatery has its own whores. Bakeries sent whores into the street to sell pornographic cakes and lure customers into cells in back. Bone guided us to a relatively clean establishment off the main thoroughfare and bought us wine and meat pastries, which I felt too sick to eat. All of us were subdued.

"All right," Bone sighed when we had finished. "Who's up for a visit to the athletes' pens?"

I turned to look at him, startled. He avoided eye contact, clearly embarrassed by his kindness.

"Bone," I said before I could stop myself. "I love you."

With the dropping of coins along with Domitia Tertia's name, we gained entrance to the aptly named pens—horses, wild beasts, and men all quartered in the cellars of a huge imperial *insularium*. Our progress was greeted with whistles, catcalls, and innuendos in all the languages of the conquered. When we reached the charioteers' quarters I returned some of the insults eloquently and in three different dialects. The Celts were thrilled to have their lineages disparaged in their own tongue—or acknowledged at all, come to that. They promptly fell to their knees before me and begged to be of service.

"Siaborthe might as well die happy," said one of the men when we told them who we wanted to see.

"Siaborthe?" I repeated. "Die? But he was fighting so well when we left."

"Sure, he had the battle spirit on him. The rest surrendered, but he took on the whole century with his bare fists. Ah, if any of us here were bards, his fame would be sung and his story told to all the tribes for all time."

I'm a bard, I almost said. But I wasn't. I was a failed first year student turned whore and slave. If any bard knew my story, he would be silent for shame.

The men showed us to a cell. My charioteer lay on his side in the straw, his hands shackled, his face turned to the wall. His breathing was shallow and labored.

"Has no one tended him?" asked Bone. "Owners usually take better care of their investments."

"Not when the purple thinks they're dangerous," said one of the men.

I knelt beside the charioteer. As soon as I touched him, I could feel that he was in critical condition, bleeding on the inside.

"Is he, Red?" Succula whispered. "Is he your father?"

I shook my head, because I couldn't speak. It wasn't Bran, thank the gods, but it was one of my *combrogos*, one of my people, big and brave as Bran had been, but much younger. And he was dying, dying in pain in a Roman prison.

"Can you do anything for him?" asked one of the Gauls.

"She's a whore not a healer," said Bone. "I'm afraid he's past needing her services."

"I think you're wrong, man. She's one of ours. Look how she's feeling of him, like her hands have eyes. She's had training. She has the healer's touch. I'll swear it."

He was right. I called it the fire of the stars; it started in my crown like a swarm of honey bees, burning through my body like strong drink, only sweeter and hotter, burning me clean as it went, burning in my hands, burning unbearably until I had learned what it was for. I followed the fire into the man's body, found the places where the blood stopped and pooled instead of flowed. The fire poured from my hands—redirecting, mending, shoring up, restoring life and strength.

"What if she is, then?" someone spoke bitterly. "What's the use of his being saved just so someone can stick a blade between his ribs or hand him a cup of poison?"

"Ssh," said Berta. "Let her be. She must do what she can."

"So he's a marked man," said Bone. "What's he done?"

"It's not what he's done, it's what they think he'll do. Best not to speak of that, if you get my meaning."

No one did speak after that or if they did, I didn't hear them. I was far away inside the warrior's heart, which grew stronger and steadier. I breathed with him slower and deeper. At last I rose. He was out of pain; he would live. But I didn't feel eased or happy. He might have planned this chance to die in battle, and now I had ruined it.

Before we left, I described Bran to the other Gauls—for so they were; none of them came from Pretannia.

"He was before my time in the pens," said one man; he was older than I was, older than Siaborthe, more slightly built, with a curved scar on his face. "I remember hearing about him. One of the Silures, you say?"

"King of the Silures."

The man shrugged. "King doesn't mean much in the pens. It's how a man carries himself. I heard that Bran was a fierce fighter but fair. Men trusted him. Purple doesn't care for that."

"What does it matter to them?" I asked.

"Name Spartacus mean anything to you?"

There was an uneasy silence. All of us here were slaves, however well or badly off. All of us lived on that edge of rebellion and hopelessness.

"Was Bran killed?" Without meaning to, I lowered my voice.

"No one knows. At least I've never heard for certain. He just disappeared."

"He might be alive then?"

"I'm sorry I don't know more, lass. Your foster-father, was he?" he asked, gentleness overcoming the wariness by which he survived.

I nodded. If I spoke, I'd weep. The pity I saw in his eyes was unbearable. Worse, I knew he felt shame for me, the foster-daughter of a free King, now a Roman whore in a filmy red toga. He was ashamed, too. We were both ashamed for staying alive at all, for in some degree choosing life as a slave over an honorable death. When did the moment come and go when we could have killed ourselves but didn't? Or did it recur again and again? Poor Siaborthe. What had I done to him?

"Come along, Red," said Bone. "There's nothing more for you here."

"When he wakes up, give him bread softened in wine, if you can," I said over my shoulder to the Celt with the curved scar as we left the pens.

Would I ever see a free Celt again?

Berta and Succula walked with their arms around me. No one spoke as we made our way out of the pens, but the silence held a charge. It was Dido who finally confronted me, stopping our party just before we went out into the noise of the streets.

"Red, I'm sorry. I can't ignore what just happened in there. Something came into you or over you. I don't know what. I mean that man was *dying*, and you brought him back to life." She fixed me with her blackest gaze. "Who are you, Red? Why have you been hiding from us?"

I returned her look as steadily as I could. I didn't know how to answer her questions. Or maybe I didn't want to.

"I told you my story," I said shortly.

"Hmm," said Dido, narrowing her eyes. "Then I guess your story ain't over yet."

As we made our way through the streets, Dido's words resounded in me. I thought I had lost my story, as I had lost my mothers, my child, my people, my gods, my love. But today some goddess had found me in a tacky

Roman temple. The fire of the stars had come to me in a prison and healed a man through my hands. Lost. Found. Dido was right; the story wasn't over. Maybe I would find my way again. Maybe, just maybe, I was on it.

"Watch your step!" Dido called.

A moment too late. Not everyone in Rome had plumbing.

CHAPTER SEVEN

ENCOUNTER WITH THE ENEMY

"We can forget about getting a litter now." Bone held his nose. "I swear I can't take you anywhere, Red."

And so my wish for a long walk was granted. I got to see extremes of poverty and wealth as we left the slums, where the plebeians tossed slops and stood in long lines for public baths, and began to climb the Palatine with its terraced gardens and sprawling palaces. Anecius had a particularly classy address on the Forum side of the hill not far from the Via Sacra.

With her legendary skill for flouting the conventions and intimidating the members of her own class, Domitia Tertia had arranged for us to be received as guests at the front door. Without turning a hair at the sight of a bevy of bedraggled whores, the *ab admissione* (a slave title that translates roughly as the perfect butler) escorted us to a room furnished with couches. Here, he informed us, we could rest and dress for the evening's festivities after enjoying the house's private women's baths. At the mention of the latter, he could not resist a pointed sniff.

We were more than happy to take the hint and wasted no time in stripping off our whores' togas and slipping into the bath robes the house had thoughtfully provided us. But when we entered the *caldarium*, we were greeted by gasps and shrieks.

"Well, I never! What is the meaning of this intrusion?"

Through the steam we saw a dozen women clutching their bosoms. It seemed we had walked in on Anecius's wife and her distinguished guests.

"Pardon us, *dominae*," said Bone, who was still with us.

"By Diana, is that a *man*?"

The woman was not taking Diana's name in vain. The virgin goddess had once punished a peeping Tom (or Acteon in this case) by turning him into a stag and hunting him down with his own hounds. A popular theme for bathhouse décor. (Not that any of the assembled qualified as virgin or goddess.)

"No, dear, of course not. It's a eunuch."

"We are the guests of the Senator," Bone explained. "We do not mean to disturb you. We shall retire until you are done."

"Why, they're whores!" someone hissed. "Filthy, dirty whores." The woman sniffed. (Guess I should have lost the sandals.) "This is an outrage."

"An arrangement of my husband's, it would seem," said the hostess, a gaunt colorless woman, who spoke almost without moving her lips. "A failure on the part of his staff to communicate with mine. My apologies to all of you. I assure you, those responsible for the error shall be beaten."

"Come on, ladies, let's go," said Bone, under his breath.

"Calm yourself, Marcia dear." I looked back to see an older woman with a beautifully kept body rise from the bath. "Such misunderstandings can occur in the most efficiently run households." The woman's tone implied that they never occurred in her house. "Weren't we just remarking that it is time to dress?"

This woman clearly outranked all the others. Could she be Livia? We stood and waited while she snapped her fingers for her slaves, who helped her from the bath and robed her. The others had no choice but to follow her lead.

Their dismissal of Bone's offer to leave, I suspect, had to do with arrogance. If they had allowed us to withdraw, they would have acknowledged us as persons, however undesirable. By making a show of being finished with their bath, calling their attendants, and dressing in front of us, they made it plain that our existence was of no consequence. For our part, we struck poses of nonchalance and boredom.

It was all a sham. We wanted to stare at them—the female counterparts of the men we serviced—and they wanted to gawk at us. In fact, there wasn't much difference between us. Expensive whores and wealthy matrons both spent hours every day tending their flesh, maintaining appearances in order to please and control men. The main difference was in the face, the expression. The *dominae* looked peevish, as though nothing was quite what they expected. They looked disappointed. If we did not, it was because we didn't expect anything. Or if we did—(who am I kidding)—we didn't let it show.

Now they began to file past us out of the room, not turning their heads to acknowledge us—except for the last one. She was younger than the rest with masses of dark hair piled carelessly on her head. Her expression was even more petulant, but she didn't bother to hide her curiosity about us—or her rather sumptuous breasts. As she passed me, she contrived to brush her breasts against mine. I felt her nipples go erect.

"*Scorta!*" Succula spat the rudest Roman street term for whore as the woman's swaying hindquarters disappeared into the mists.

"Who is that?" I asked.

"Only the latest wife of Appius Claudius," said Bone, who knew these things. His tone was dismissive.

"The one who owns all those *insulae* near us?"

Bone nodded. "The man is rich, but he has no pedigree. Believe it or not, the bitch does. Old republican stock."

We all eased into the hot water; a collective sigh rose with the steam.

"Claudius is not exactly in his first youth," Bone became expansive with the heat. "Rumor has it he can no longer rise to the occasion. At least not for a woman."

"That is not just a rumor, *kinder*," Berta winked. "What I went through with that man the last time I had to do him. A few years ago it is now, thank the goddess. Never let anyone tell you whores just lie on their back and spread their legs. Before he can get it up, I have to stand the man on his head and fuck him upside down. I tell you it's no joke," she protested as we all started to howl. "Stop! I will piss the bath water!"

"Too bad we didn't get the bath *first*," said Dido.

"Those cunts are pissy enough as it is," said Succula. "Not that I'd mind giving any of them a golden shower, especially that horny, little—"

"Now, now, *liebling*, she can't help it if she's horny. Look what she married!"

"Why can't she take a lover?" I asked. "Would the husband care?"

"The husband, no," said Bone. "Probably not. He doesn't even much care about an heir. He's got a pretty good racket going. Lots of gorgeous young men hanging around him, flattering him, hoping to be adopted."

"But then why lumber himself with another wife?" I persisted. I did not understand Roman ways.

"Simple. Her *pater's* connections. Why Publius Paulus ever agreed to the match is more of a mystery. Some of the old families are cash poor, but I suspect there's more to it than that. Anyway, he kept the *manus*. That's not done much nowadays, even in the old families. But Paulus made a point of it."

"The *manus*?" I had not heard the term before. "What is that?"

"It comes down to who owns her. A daughter is a father's property unless he gives the *manus* to the husband. If he keeps it, the father has the right to protect or punish his daughter as he sees fit."

"To put it crudely, honey, if she gets caught with her *stola* up around her ears, it's daddy, not hubby, who gets to strangle her," said Succula. "I could almost feel sorry for her—almost." She nestled against me and cupped one of my breasts. "Bitch better keep away from these or I'll show her who's got *manus*."

"Her father could kill her without a trial?" I didn't know why my hands shook and my stomach churned. I certainly didn't care about some spoiled young Roman matron.

"Red," said Dido, "this is the real world. Fathers don't need trials to dispose of their daughters. When did they ever? I thought Uncle Joseph was trying to civilize you with those Greek lessons. Didn't he tell you about Agamemnon, sugar? Need a fair wind? Sacrifice a daughter." Her tone was angry, bitter. "Are you seriously trying to tell us it's different where you come from?"

"Tell them, *liebling*," Berta urged. "Tell them who is really the barbarians."

I wanted to tell them. Damn right, it's different. We have a law older than all other laws called mother right. Women of my people own their own herds; we can be queens; we can make poems and recite law. And we can fuck whomever we want to fuck. We have sovereignty, goddess bless us.

And yet hadn't my father raped me, and no one would believe me? Hadn't my father tried more than once to kill me? In the end, when he killed himself, hadn't the druids blamed me for his death? Even when they learned the truth, they sang his praises.

Me they put in a boat with only a knife and let the tide take me away.

So I didn't answer Dido. I leaned back in the bath. For a moment the steam thinned and I could just see the high ceiling. There were birds flying around in the upper reaches. Were they looking for the way out—or had they forgotten the sky?

"How in the three worlds" (I reverted to Celtic cosmology when I was in extremis) "am I supposed to dance after eating all that! No one told me there was going to be dancing."

I clutched my stomach. I could feel the bulkiness of sugar-glazed meats. The spicy sauces of stewed vegetables and fruit repeated on me. Then there were the cakes, at least twenty different kinds. I'd kept a loose count as I sampled them all. We ate well enough at the Vine and the Fig Tree, but I was used to scanter, simpler fare. And for Bride's sake, I'd been raised on oats and apples and the occasional roast pig.

"There's always dancing at banquets," said Succula. "Why do you think we've been practicing that routine?"

"I don't know these things," I groaned. "I didn't even know I was going to a banquet till yesterday."

"That's right," Berta said. "It's your first time out. You'll learn."

"Didn't I tell you to stop stuffing your face, Red?" said Helen, who had joined us for a swan song performance. "No, *stulta!*" she raged at the *ornatrix* who was arranging her hair. "Not like that. I told you. I want it exactly like the *domina* Livia's hair. Ouch!"

It seemed Anecius's slave—or his wife's—did not like being ordered around by another slave and a whore at that.

"Do you really think that's wise, Helen?" asked Dido. "Do you think the first lady of Rome wants to be imitated by a tart?"

"She'll be flattered," said Helen with unshakable confidence. "Besides, the style will look better on me than it does on her."

Bonia was right. Helen was stupid. Domitia Tertia was not. She was unloading a dumb whore at a premium price. In a few years, when Helen's looks were gone, she'd be a dead loss.

"Don't worry, *liebling*," Berta clucked over me. "So you eat a little too much at a banquet. There will be that much more of you to jiggle so prettily."

I groaned. "If I jiggle too much I'm going to be sick."

"Ew." Helen moved further away from me. "Then go to the *vomitorium*. Now."

"The *what*?"

"Red, don't tell me you don't know," said Dido. "All the best homes have a *vomitorium*. I'm sure Aetius is having one built specially for Helen. How else do the best people keep their figures? If they're going to gorge every damn day, they have to disgorge."

"They make themselves vomit?" I was horrified. "They waste food? On purpose?"

"It's not such a big deal," said Helen. "Everybody does it."

"I'm not going to do that."

"Honey." Succula came over and put her arm around me. "I think maybe you better, just this once. You don't look so good."

"If you vomit on the purple during the dance, you'll end up looking a whole lot worse," said Dido, "and Domitia will never let you out again."

"I'll go with you," said Succula.

"Thanks, honey, but there are some things I'd rather do alone."

"It's actually considered a social activity," Dido informed me.

One of the house slaves had to escort me or I would have been hopelessly lost. When we finally arrived, I found that Dido was right. The *vomitorium* was the place to be seen. Anyone who was anyone was there. I hung back for as long as I could, hoping not to be recognized by any of the aging nymphs from the baths. When the traffic thinned, I took my turn. Kneeling before the gutters that were being continuously sluiced by slaves, I imitated the best people, stuck my finger down my throat, and gave most of my dinner the old heave ho.

I had to admit I did feel better. I rose and stretched, began to take a deep breath, then thought better of it. It really didn't smell very good in here despite the unceasing efforts of the slaves. Ignoring the woman retching next to me (how did people manage polite chitchat when they were puking?) I headed out.

"You!"

How did I know so certainly that "you" meant me? And why didn't I keep walking anyway? One of those reversals of fortune, you could say. I turned. I did not immediately recognize the woman in the gold colored, purple-fringed *stola*. She had a jeweled filet over dark hair coiled and wound up and around so that it added inches to her height. On the swell of her pushed-up breasts flashed huge stones that I now know to be sapphires. In fact, it was her breasts that I recognized first.

I'd had one brush with them already.

"What's your name?" she demanded.

No way was I telling this woman my true name. For the first time I was sincerely glad that I had a *nom de twat*.

"They call me Red."

"What kind of dye do you use to get that color?"

"I don't."

"Come on now. All whores dye their hair."

"How do you know I'm a whore?"

The woman threw back her head and laughed. She had a very long white but somewhat thick neck. Her breasts bulged almost to her collarbone.

"What else could you possibly be?"

I decided not to answer that.

"All right." She smiled at me, a smile that could have been used to illustrate the word "seductive." I knew she had practiced it for hours in front of a mirror. "I want proof."

As she started swaying toward me, I realized she was drunk. I backed away, but not fast enough. She grabbed my toga and lifted it.

"Oo la la!" she giggled.

And before I knew it, she had her hand between my legs. I had been a whore for months now, but I still hadn't quite grasped the fundamental fact that to a member of the aristocracy, all slaves are up for grabs. Before I could stop myself, I slapped her face.

She withdrew her hand and put it on her cheek and stood there open-mouthed, too shocked for a moment to speak or even breathe.

"I may be a whore," I said. "But I'm not your whore."

"I could have you flayed alive for what you just did." Unfortunately she'd found her voice again.

I shrugged. "That's up to Domitia Tertia."

I turned and sauntered away with confidence, though my escort had fled.

"You haven't seen the last of me, you red-bushed slut."

I didn't answer, but suddenly I realized that I had given her all the information she needed to find me again. That was the problem with having a smart mouth. I had a tendency to shut it a moment too late. Oh well, she could have found out where I came from simply by shaking her tits at Anecius. So it didn't matter what I'd said. What mattered was that I had assaulted her, a senator's daughter.

In all honesty, I can't say I was very sorry.

All right. Let your imagination run to glitzy stereotype. We did look like a Las Vegas version of middle-eastern belly dancers minus the stage and the high-tech lighting. Oil lantern is flattering as lighting goes, and certainly would not make us sweat. The rooms that opened onto the atrium where the guests reclined in various groupings (the drinkers and gamers, the literary and the philosophical crowd, the randy young men, the matrons with their virgin daughters making a show of spinning wool) were heated with charcoal braziers, but the atrium, open to the stars, was downright chilly.

I was in a bad, bad mood as we huddled together in a corridor awaiting our cue. My first day and night out in the big Pomegranate had made one thing clear to me. Rome was nothing but one big brothel. I existed for the entertainment of the senatorial class, just as the charioteers did. That we were good at what we did only made it worse.

"Red," Succula pinched my cheek, "stop scowling. This is the fun part."

I loved Succula, but she just didn't understand.

"Take a swig." Succula passed me a wineskin. "They're so in their cups we'll never catch up."

I took a big, long, thirsty drink.

"That's enough." Succula snatched the skin away. "Only a dumb whore gets drunk. There's our cue. Get your *podex* in gear, girl."

I don't know if it was the sudden rush of unwatered wine into my bloodstream or the Middle Eastern rhythms—Romans liked ethnic entertainments—or the flickering lights, or the flash of stars overhead, but I let myself go. As we danced, swaying back and forth, circling each other, our hips switching, our arms moving as if we held live serpents, I heard the sistrum, its music a rasp that evoked the wind moving in the river reeds. I smelled the sweet smoke of the Temple of Isis or Venus, whoever she was.

Then I saw it: not the Temple of Venus Obsequens alone, but all the temples that had come before it, in all times and places, one after the other, each temple more ancient and vivid than the last, skin after shed skin revealing what pulsed beneath, the colors and patterns brighter and bolder each time. Then at last there were no more temples, only rock and earth and a chasm where stars spilled through.

When I came to myself again I found I was in a chamber with a frightened boy who wanted to fuck his first whore and instead found himself face to face with some wild divinity. For a moment, I almost felt sorry for him as he cowered on the couch, unable to summon the contempt for a slave that should have protected him and kept him in control.

But then I made myself remember: his people had enslaved and maybe murdered my foster-father. I looked at the soft, pimpled flesh of this over-indulged Roman youth and felt a rage and revulsion I had never known before. I wanted to be sick again. No, I wanted more than that: I wanted to kill him. The hairs on my neck rose as it dawned on me that I could. There he was, alone and vulnerable. Here I was, full of power and fury. I could tear him to pieces.

I closed my eyes and clenched and unclenched my hands. If this is meant to be, I spoke to something I did not name, if I am meant to be an instrument of revenge, use me.

I waited, and my crown ignited as the fire of the stars rained down.

No, I protested silently, not knowing fully what I meant. Not for him.

Open your eyes, a voice inside me said.

Reluctantly I obeyed. When the boy saw me staring at him, he began to whimper.

Find the god in him, the voice prompted.

No, I answered. I hate him. I hate what he will become.

Call forth the god.

The fire was burning in my hands and in my sex, but still I resisted.

Why bother? I challenged the voice. These people already think they're gods.

Look again. Look deeper. The voice was implacable.

The boy kept his gaze on me as if I were the goddess, death, fate, all in one. And I was. He saw the truth. So I looked at him again. I looked deeper, and I saw it: earth and grain, sun and rain in the form of this boy. In that instant I knew something I could never again forget: all flesh is innocent.

I let out a long breath I hadn't known I was holding, sat down at one end of the couch and took his feet in my hands, pampered feet, hardly calloused, bigger than the rest of him. I explored their shape, the tendons, the length of the toes. The fire flowed through my hands as I touched this humblest part of the body, the farthest from the head, the closest to the ground.

Then the boy started to cry.

"I don't know what I'm supposed to do," he said.

"You will." I released his feet and stretched out beside him.

"Don't tell anyone," he begged.

"I am the keeper of secrets. I am the temple of mysteries. Enter."

The voice that had spoken within me now spoke through me. All distinction was lost between myself and whatever power claimed me. I was the chasm and the stars. I was the riverbed; through me the source flowed relentlessly to the sea.

Afterwards the boy slept on my breast and drooled. I was alone again with my small self, the force that had filled me ebbing away.

"Who are you?" I whispered aloud. "What do you want from my life?"

I heard nothing but the boy's soft snores.

CHAPTER EIGHT

THE LOST THREAD

I did not speak to my friends about what had happened to me with Anecius's son—for so he was—my sense that some deity had taken me over for her own purposes. I say *her* purposes, because I had definite suspicions about Isis. I was wary of this roaming Egyptian goddess and even more alarmed by the priestess's insistence that I belonged to her. Being a descendant of the goddess Bride—so my mothers claimed—I had taken goddesses for granted, and never felt the need to become a devotee any more than you might worship your grandmother, however much you loved her. I didn't like the idea that a goddess could control my life. Deities ought to stay in their place, I told myself, in their own groves and wells and be thankful for the votive offerings that came their way. Though my ears pricked up whenever someone swore by Isis or prayed to her, I made no attempt to seek her temple again.

Bone had apparently decided not to report to Domitia Tertia my bolting from the litter and running off to a disreputable temple. As the whore chosen to initiate Anecius's scion, I was in especially good odor. I had passed muster; my probation was over. I was allowed to go to onsite jobs—private orgies, power baths, literary soirees. Bonia also set up an in-house schedule for me, so that my regulars could count on finding me at home, so to speak.

In short, I was a success, more of a success as a whore than I had ever been as a student. On the surface of my life everything glittered. Winds of excitement and bustle whipped my waters into saucy little whitecaps. If I were a lake or a sea, you would want to sail on me. I'd give you a good ride but (mostly) not capsize you. No one could see past the sparkle to the depths where strange life forms lurked and currents no one suspected crossed and pulled, where the full force of me waited to be raised by some storm.

No one, that is, but Isis, who had staked her claim, whether I acknowledged it or not, who had begun training me as her priestess even before I knew her story and how it would restore the lost thread of mine.

The man appeared to be what we call an easy one—not arrogant, not awkward, not old, not young, not demanding anything in particular—or so I thought. I lay on my back for this simple sunny side up sort and reached for his cock to ease him in. He was ready. Ten strokes, I bet myself as I sometimes did to add interest. Then suddenly he leapt off me. He must have had strong upper arms for it seemed as though in one motion he was in the opposite corner of the room (granted it was small) pressed against the wall, staring at me with terrified eyes.

Slowly I rolled to my side and raised myself on my arm. No sudden moves. I had seen eyes like these before that looked at me but saw something else. It was one of the few things that frightened me. I looked to see if my bell was within easy reach, the bell that would bring Bone running. It was by the lamp. I began to inch my hand towards it.

Wait. There's something here, a voice within me spoke. Yes, that voice again.

I didn't want to hear it, but after a moment I answered: Then tell me what to do.

He needs a priestess, the voice said.

He came to the wrong place then, I shot back.

Did he?

I looked at the man and noticed details I had missed before. He was beginning to grey; his face had some deep lines, but in this moment he looked young, terribly young.

"I won't hurt you," was all I could think of to say.

He shook his head; then he covered his eyes. When he uncovered them, I saw that he was back from wherever he had gone. He knew where he was—in a tiny room with a whore who meant nothing to him. But his face was so bleak, instead of feeling relieved I felt my own sorrow stirring.

"Forgive me," he said and turned to go.

"Is that what you need?" I asked.

The man stopped in the doorway; very slowly he turned around, and looked at me, really looked at me, as he had not before.

"What did you just say?"

"Do you need someone to forgive you?"

He didn't answer right away, but he remained in the doorway.

"I cannot be forgiven."

I sighed. If I had had a watch I might have looked at it. What did I care what this man had done? He'd had his time with me; let him pay and go.

He is a stranger, the voice inside said.

He's strange, all right.

The god-bearing stranger, but the god in him is wounded.

Not this god shit again.

Yes. Will you help him?

I have a choice?

The voice inside was silent. There would be no force here. I looked at the man, the stranger, and suddenly I remembered how everyone at druid school had called my beloved the Stranger; they feared him, too; they thought he was a god; they tried to make him one—on their own terms.

"Tell me," I heard myself speaking to the man. "Come and tell me."

"Are you a priestess?" he asked.

"Yes," I said, surprised by my certainty. "Come closer to me."

For I suddenly knew I needed to hear whatever he would tell me not only with my ears but also with my hands. Without instruction from me, he knelt before my low bed. As he spoke, I put my hands on his heart. He poured out what seemed at first an ordinary tale of youthful indiscretion—a love affair with a young married woman, no more than a girl, really, whose marriage had been arranged by her father. A typical story. They were caught, of course, and brought to trial. Guilt meant a fine for him, divorce for her, and separate exiles for both. Or so he thought, persuading himself that once outside of Rome they could meet again and begin a new life.

"The night before I left, I bribed my way into her husband's house in secret. She begged me not to leave. 'He's sending me back in the morning,' she kept sobbing, 'back to my father's house.' But I didn't understand what she was saying. I went over our plans of how and where we were to meet. She clung to me and wouldn't be comforted. I was afraid we'd be caught again, so I tore myself away and headed for the port to board my ship in time for the next tide. While I was sailing free into the rising sun...." He paused and seemed not able to breathe for a moment. I waited, silent, my hands burning on his heart. "...her father strangled her."

My throat closed, too. All my muscles tensed. I wanted to fling him away. He had left his beloved to be killed by her father. Killed by her father. I would not forgive him; I refused. He was right; he could not be forgiven—even if it was not his fault.

As I looked at the man kneeling before me, trying to control my rage, I saw Esus galloping across the Menai Straits, not looking back, leaving me alone to face the druids, to face my father who reviled me as his daughter and wanted me dead. My father would have killed Esus, too. Made him a holy sacrifice. I had forced Esus to go; I had commanded him to go. It was not Esus' fault, not his fault that he had left me.

I hadn't known until this moment that I blamed him.

Suddenly it dawned on me: What if Esus blamed himself?

Esus could not know that my father had killed himself. He could not be certain that I had survived. Why had I never thought of that? This man trembling between my hands was unable to forgive himself. Could my own beloved be suffering this way?

I closed my eyes and had the dizzying sense of being able to see everyone's story—this man sailing away while his beloved died; the girl staring into her father's face as his hands closed on her throat. Esus seeing the hard, exposed Cambrian rock rise up before him as a huge, black tidal bore swept the straits cutting off his pursuers. And I saw myself, calling the storm, howling as my water broke and my childbirth began.

Then all the images dissolved as I saw everything through the eyes of the one who weeps rivers, the one whose lover drifts away in a coffin.

"Since then," the man was saying. "I have not been with a woman. Whenever I have a woman in my arms, I see her face; I hear her begging me not to leave her."

He fell silent and stayed motionless with his head bowed, waiting for my judgment. I became aware that I was breathing evenly again, a great steady tidal river of breath. The fire flowed through my hands into the man's heart. But something more was wanting.

If you are willing, the inside voice said, I will open the way.

I am willing.

Again I saw through the eyes of the one who had known all sorrow.

"Beloved," I answered in her voice. "I am the mistress of the living and the dead. Speak to your love, and she will hear. Comfort her and be comforted."

I raised him from his knees, and held him in my arms while he called her by name and wept. When he entered me, she received him; I received him as the lover I had lost.

One morning not long after this encounter, I woke early feeling cold. Outside the wind stirred, wakeful like me. I could hear the dried, fallen leaves of the atrium's vines and trees scudding along the stone.

It was almost *Samhain* by my reckoning, my people's new year, the season of my birth, the time when boundaries between this world and the Other World shimmered and thinned. Soon the Pleiades would rise again in the night sky; wandering bards and bands of warriors would find a place to winter; the cattle would come down from the hills; the migrating flocks of birds would disappear. The thought of all this movement made my tiny, stale room unbearable. I took my mantle and coverlet and went down to the atrium where I sat in a corner and leaned my head back to see what I could of the sky. It was that dim indeterminate color that dawn watchers know goes on and on before the light quickens. I pulled my wraps around me and decided to wait for the sunrise. Olivia the cat found her way under my cloak and curled against my heart.

I must have gone into a light doze, halfway between sleeping and waking. I became aware of a low tuneless humming, a humming almost like human purring. Or maybe it was only Olivia. It went on and on, and a whispering rhythmic sound became part of it. The sound soothed me, like the sound of small waves on a pebble beach. Then I heard a song, or maybe I dreamed it.

> *I am the mother of the living*
> *I am the lover of the dead*
> *From the womb I knew my lover*
> *Now I seek him in the riverbed.*

The song rose and receded, rose and receded, the waters of a river, the river I had dreamed before, the dream of being tangled in the weeds. Now I drifted in a boat shaped like a crescent moon. In the shallows I would reach into the water and pull out a hand, a foot. I felt no horror at my finds. I was aware only of a diligent sorrow and the song going on and on until I knew the song was mine.

> *I am the mother of the living*
> *I am the lover of the dead*
> *From the womb I knew my lover*
> *Now I seek him in the riverbed.*

No! I wanted to speak. He is not dead. I saved him; I sent him away across the straits and raised the tide to protect him. But the song kept singing through me, and the boat kept drifting through the reeds, blown by a hot, malodorous wind....

I opened my eyes to find an old woman's face inches from my own. Her breath stank and whistled through the gaps in her teeth. She held a tiny glass vial, from which she pulled a stopper that proved to be a tiny blade. With it she delicately but firmly scraped my cheekbone, just below my eye. She held the blade poised for just a moment; it held a single, intact tear, which she carefully slid into the vial. Then, with the same precision, she harvested two more tears before she sealed the vial with the stopper.

I had been too astonished to speak, but now, as she drew back (and I could breathe again), I saw that old Nona the sweeper had accosted me. I had seen her only rarely; she swept while the whores slept, and went to bed around the time the house opened.

I managed a feeble, "What the fuck?"

"Whores' tears." She grinned, displaying all three teeth. "Cure anything. Couldn't waste 'em."

"I've never heard that claim before," I said with more resignation than indignation. My life had been riddled with crazy old crones. It was as much a relief as an irritation that one of them had caught up with me here.

"Old Nona's the onliest one who knows," she crooned, and then she cackled. "How do you think I live so long?"

She was speaking Latin but with an accent I couldn't place—or it could have been the effect of her near toothlessness.

"Those are *my* tears." I felt ornery.

"Not anymore."

Nona slipped the vial, which she wore around her neck suspended on a string, inside her tunic where it rested between whatever was left of her breasts. Then she picked up her broom and began sweeping the fallen leaves into a crescent shape. She hummed while she worked, and I recognized the tunelessness. It was her voice that had threaded through my dreams.

"Who are you?" I demanded. I had met old women before who turned out to be goddesses or close relations. You couldn't be too careful.

"Nona, Nona, Nona. No name Nona," she replied unhelpfully. "That's what everyone calls me. I don't remember my other names."

She started to sing.

> *I am the mother of the living*
> *I am the lover of the dead*
> *From the womb I knew my lover*
> *Now I seek him in the riverbed.*

"You sent me that dream," I accused.

"What dream would that be, dearie?"

"The river, the boat, searching for my lover. *You* know!" I insisted.

My tears welled again, and I knuckled them back into the ducts before she could come and steal them with her tiny scalpel. She paused in her sweeping and eyed me intently, her eyes black, her head cocked like a bird's. Then she laid her broom against the wall, crossed the atrium and prostrated herself before me. The next thing I knew, she was kissing my feet.

"Stop!" I protested. "Are you crazy?"

I hardly needed an answer, I thought. But she did stop, and when she got up again, she plucked my hand.

"Stand up, *domina,*" she urged. "Come."

Domina? I was too confused and, I confess, curious to resist. Besides, this tiny old woman's grip had the fierceness of a newborn's, and the authority of a mother's. Dislodging Olivia, I stood and followed where she led me. I was disappointed when we only went as far as the *Lararium,* a miniature temple, a sort of dollhouse for the gods. All Roman households had one on display, a locus for the care and feeding of the family's personal gods. The Vine and Fig Tree's *Lararium,* complete with miniature columns and a fresco depicting Mount Olympus, was tucked away in one of the smaller reception rooms. It was quite crowded both with such jolly well-known types as Venus and Bacchus as well as more obscure figures crudely fashioned by the whores and other house slaves to represent the gods they remembered from home. Bone's many breasted—or, as he insisted, testicled—goddess was displayed prominently, and there was a Priapus, whose enormous prick was garlanded with single earrings that had lost their mates. Even the cats had a deity, a stately obsidian cat Dido had introduced as Bast.

I'd never had more than a nodding acquaintance with any of these figures and had not added to the population. My gods, untamed, shape-shifting gods, did not belong here. I would never insult them by giving them a fixed form and cramming them into a little box, as if they, too, could be confined and controlled, as if they, too, were slaves.

Nona dropped my hand and beckoning me to look more closely, she pointed to a figure in the back that I hadn't noticed before. She stood a little taller than the rest or maybe it was just the horns she wore that cradled the star-like flower. She was robed in gold, just like the statue in the Temple of Venus Obsequens. In one hand she held a sistrum; in the other an ankh.

"Almighty Isis," said Nona.

"We've met."

Nona just nodded. Then she reached into her tunic, lifted the vial from around her neck and handed it to me. I looked at her uncertainly.

"Pour some for her."

"But I thought you said you lived on whores' tears," I argued for the sake of argument.

"These tears are her tears," said Nona. "Pour the tears over her."

I shrugged. There was no harm in humoring her. Taking care not to knock anyone over, I reached into the *Lararium* and poured a few drops of the salty water on the figure's head. It pooled in the petals of the flower, then overflowed and began to trickle down her terracotta face.

"Her tears," Nona repeated.

I closed my eyes, and the dream came back, the boat curved like the moon, the river, the mud, the severed limbs, the sorrow.

"When the moon is full again, it will be the *Isia*," Nona announced.

"The *Isia*?" I felt a prickling at the base of my skull. Whatever it was, this *Isia* happened at the same time as *Samhain*.

"The mysteries, the sorrows. We who belong to Isis mourn with her, search with her. The priestesses go in moon-shaped boats to seek the Beloved in the waters. When he is found, we rejoice. We embrace the stranger, and everyone eats."

I suddenly understood—no, that's wrong; I didn't understand anything—but I knew: I had been dreaming Isis's story. Why? Why was this goddess pursuing me?

"Little Bright One," she called me by my mother's name for me, and I could no longer see, but I felt her take the vial from my hand. How could a flood fit in that tiny container? "You belong to her."

Before I could argue, Old Nona was gone.

CHAPTER NINE

WHORES' DEAL

"All right," I said when my sister whores and I settled into the bath. "Tell me everything you know about Isis."

"Why do you want to know?" asked Succula.

"You started it, Succula." I accused. "The Temple of Venus Obsequens. Did you know it's really a Temple to Isis?"

"Well, sure. But you didn't expect me to shout it out in the street, did you?"

"Why not?"

"Red," said Dido, "don't you know? Isis is *dea non grata* in Rome. Temples to her are prohibited inside the city walls. It's been that way since good old Queen Cleopatra, her late representative on earth, led first Julius Caesar and then Marc Antony around by the dick. Cleo had the audacity to want to be more than a Roman puppet. She had some notion that her country existed for some other reason than to feed Rome. What *was* she thinking?"

"Well, she lose in the end, poor thing," sighed Berta. "But at least she was no captive. Do you know the story, Red? She puts poisonous snakes in her bosoms and when Roman soldiers break into her palace, they find her dead."

"Original." I was impressed.

"That's not the only thing the purple have against her," Succula said. "They're afraid of her, because she draws riff-raff, slaves, foreigners, whores."

Well, that description fit everyone within splashing range of me.

"That's not entirely accurate, Succula," said Dido. "If her followers were only from the dregs, the purple would pay no attention. She's also popular with some of their own wives and daughters. It's a trend—like wealthy matrons becoming Jewish proselytes and sending money to Jerusalem. The purple don't like that kind of mixing. Their silly wives might end up funding an insurrection."

Isis was sounding more and more appealing.

"So what is it about her?" I asked. "Rich, poor, slave, free, Roman, foreigner. Sounds like she takes all comers. She sounds like one of us."

Everyone laughed and we did our whores' high five (fingers in twat, then pressed together).

"You know, Red," said Succula thoughtfully. "You have a point. Do you know the story?"

"Oh, let me tell it," Berta pleaded. "So romantic. Just like your story, Red."

Something inside me that had been drifting and dreaming woke up all the way.

"Listen, *liebling*. Isis loved her brother Osiris—it's Egypt, *kinder*, that's the way they do things down there and besides she was a goddess—they are twins, and they are lovers, you know what I mean, lovers even in the womb."

Berta gave a gusty sigh and continued the story with lots of interruption and embellishment from the others. I closed my eyes and listened with my whole being. Berta didn't know how right she was; she was telling my story, the story of my beloved and me, eternal twins in the great starry womb.

"After the wicked brother Set kills Osiris and sends him floating down the Nile in a coffin..."

A coffin! If I had needed more confirmation of the connection between Isis and my dreams, there it was.

"...Isis searches the world for her beloved. She wanders for years and years. She never gives up..."

Neither would I. Then I shook myself. The story was wrong, all wrong. *My* beloved was not dead. Why was I dreaming Isis's story? What did she want from me?

"...she finally finds his coffin in a tamarisk tree, a column in Astarte's temple. She brings him back home. She fans the air with her great bright wings, she breathes the breath of life into him, and he lives again to make a child with her..."

"Then he dies again—but she's got the baby, so who needs him anymore?" said Dido.

"Dido! You are heartless! Heartless! You always ruin my stories. Now where was I?"

"The nasty brother cuts him into fourteen pieces, and Isis goes fishing."

"Dido, stop. *liebling*, don't listen to her. Isis is true to her love. She gives a sacred burial to each part of him—"

"Except his prick," Succula interrupted. "A crab ate it."

"Really?" I opened my eyes and appealed to Berta, who nodded sadly. "And that's what the, whatever it's called, the *Isia* is? Everyone searching for body parts?" After such a promising start, I confess I found the end of the story disappointing and disturbing. It was not how I wanted my story to go at all. "I don't get it."

"Ah, *liebling*, don't you see? Isis knows. She knows love; she knows sorrow. Just like us."

"That's not it for me," said Dido. "What I like is that she rules—not just one little piddling thing, like these Greek goddesses, and their cheap Roman imitations—but everything—life, death, stars, seas, wind, thunder, everything people make from ships to looms. And she's smart; she tricked the sun god Ra into revealing his secret name—"

"But that's not the best thing about her," said Succula impatiently. "Do you want to know the best thing? Berta left this part out. Almost no one knows, but it's true." She paused for effect. "Isis was a whore."

"I have never heard this part. How do you know it?" Berta demanded.

"And what's wrong with being a whore?" Dido countered.

"Shut up, both of you," I said. "Let Succula tell the story."

"Well, she's wandering around the world for years. How do you think she supported herself?"

"Succula, she is a goddess. She doesn't have to worry about such things."

"Berta, you said it yourself. She's just like us. When she was in Byblos, in Astarte's Temple, she was a whore. They were all whores. Only in those days, people didn't despise whores. *Whores* ruled. They were fucking priestesses. They were more important than kings. A king had no power at all unless the high priestess took him as a lover. When she did—if she did—she wasn't just a priestess, she was the goddess."

"Like Cleopatra," said Dido.

"Where do you hear these things about Isis?" Berta still resisted any interpretation that departed from strict romance.

"Domitia Tertia," Succula said solemnly.

There was a moment of silence. Succula had invoked her ultimate authority.

"Domitia Tertia!" I couldn't help it. "She doesn't worship any gods. I heard her making fun of Bone's devotion to Cybele. She believes only in herself."

"I didn't say she was a devotee." Succula was surprisingly calm. "I heard her arguing with Uncle Joseph. He was going on about the Greek *heterae* the way he does, and she went him one better. Also, Domitia admired Cleopatra—not many people know that either. She actually saw her once when she was a little girl. Her father was stationed in Egypt for a time. That's when she started keeping cats."

Circe and Cleopatra. Two women who ruled—or tried to. Too bad Cleopatra hadn't turned Julius Caesar into a pig. Then my people could have roasted him.

"Succula," I marveled, "you know more about Domitia than Bonia."

"Bonia told me the story about Cleopatra," Succula admitted. "Bonia's been with Domitia a lot longer than I have. But I've taken the trouble to know as much as I can. You can hate her if you want, but as far as I'm concerned Domitia Tertia rules."

We were all silent for a time, the bath water lapping at our separate shores. It was a comfortable, comforting silence, the silence of sisters who could insult and forgive each other as easily as we breathed. I was so at home with these women. But that was the trouble; I didn't want to be at home. I wasn't meant to be at home. When Osiris disappeared, did Isis sit telling stories in the bathhouse?

"Why have none of you ever told me about Isis before?" I finally asked.

"She is just there," said Succula. "We don't think about her. We know she loves us. We can't be real devotees, going to morning hymns, observing periods of celibacy. But Isis knows how it is with us. Isis understands."

"But can we go to the *Isia*?" I persisted. "Will the priestesses let us?"

"It's more a question of will Domitia Tertia let us," said Dido. "And the answer is no. Not if it interferes with business."

"But, *kinder*, listen. The third day, the procession to the river when the priestesses go in the boats, it happens at dawn. We come back in plenty of time to work."

"Dawn," shuddered Dido. "Ugh!"

"Just this once," said Berta. "We get up, all together, we go. Succula will ask Domitia Tertia."

"Will you, Succula?" I appealed to her.

She looked at me, her dark eyes strangely fearful. I knew that next to Domitia Tertia, Succula loved me more than she loved anyone. I knew that love sometimes gives people the sight. What did she see?

"You never answered my question, Red," she said. "Why are you so interested in Isis now? Why does the *Isia* matter so much to you?"

I had become so self-protective, so secretive. My first impulse was to evade her question. Succula loved me. I was asking her to do something for me out of that love, so I made myself answer.

"I had a dream, Succula. I dreamed about the *Isia* before I could possibly know what it was. I think it's a message. A message from Isis."

Succula continued to watch me, her eyes no less troubled. Dido and Berta for once held back, watching, the silent chorus to some drama none of us understood.

"All right, Red," she said. "I'll ask her. And I'll go with you. We'll all go." And she turned her fierce gaze on the other two. "Whores' deal."

And we sealed our agreement according to our custom.

Whatever her apprehensions, Succula kept her word and succeeded in securing permission from Domitia Tertia. An hour before dawn on the appointed day, we rose in the dark having barely slept. In the atrium we found old Nona waiting for us with her arms full of something that looked like moonlight. When we approached her she held up white linen robes just like the ones the priestesses at the temple wore. Wasting no time or breath and with a curious authority for someone at the bottom of the slave heap, she made it clear that she would dress us, and she did so with efficiency and care, making sure to tie the knot of the fringed mantle so that it fell in two pleats down the front. In the damp, chilly dregs of night, we were so glad to have some extra garments that none of us questioned her. Then Bonia came out with mulled wine and bread.

"Magna Mater!" She almost dropped the tray. "You look like a gaggle of virgin sacrifices. Where on earth did you get these garments? Please don't tell me you robbed a temple."

"I made them," old Nona said with that eerie command, and she stuck out her lower lip. "Long ago, long since for this very day."

"I'm afraid I'll have to check with the *domina* about this. You're breaking the law not wearing your whores' togas. Not to mention impersonating priestesses."

"We are not impersonating priestesses," I countered. "Obviously this is what a priestess looks like."

Bonia was already gone. She returned with Domitia Tertia more quickly than I would have thought possible. I had never seen her face naked, untended by her *ornatrix*. The moon, I thought looking at her, she is like the moon—stark, removed, beautiful, and, if possible, even less vulnerable than usual—which struck me as odd. She eyed us without expression.

"They look dignified," she pronounced at last. "At these festivals many devotees wear white, I believe. They will blend in. Remember," she addressed us now. "Even if no one recognizes you, you are from the Vine and Fig Tree. You have our reputation for quality to uphold. The *Isia* attracts the *vulgari*. You are not to mix with them. Nor must you allow yourselves to get carried away in unseemly emotional displays. Is that quite clear? Go then. Be back at the sixth hour. No later." And she turned and disappeared into the recesses of the house.

"Drink up," said Bonia. "Take the bread with you."

Old Nona made some kind of blessing or protecting sign over us.

"Where's Bone? Isn't Bone going with us?" Succula sounded panicked.

"He has important business to attend to for the *domina* today," said Bonia. "It's not his job description or mine to indulge your whims. I don't know why she's allowed you to go at all. I told her I didn't think it was wise. Gadding about Rome on your own when decent people are still asleep. Most mistresses are not so lenient. Don't make her regret it or you'll regret it. All right, I'm going back to bed. You're on your own."

CHAPTER TEN

THE CROSSROADS

O n your own, on your own, I repeated the words over and over to myself as we trudged through the quiet streets. It was the first time since
my capture that I'd had no one watching me, guarding me. I felt dizzy
with the illusion of freedom. I knew it was illusion, but I was having difficulty
remembering. The air tasted different; my body felt light and unfamiliar.

Gradually more and more people joined us, in little streams and
tributaries, until we all merged with the festival procession in the Via Sacra.
The priestesses and priests led the way, sustaining a hypnotic rhythm with
frame drum and sistrum as we danced through the heart of the Forum, past
Capitoline Hill and out through the Flumentana gate. There we walked along
the Tiber River with its thick dawn fog floating and swirling above it until we
came to Campus Martius—broad, flat fields where games were held and
military formations practiced.

During the *Isia* a festival city had mushroomed with the usual vendors
and side entertainments. The priests and priestesses went directly towards a
central pavilion—a large golden tent on a raised platform. The laity fell back as
the priesthood entered the makeshift temple. It is a very strange thing to stand
in a large, silent crowd. Even more so in the half-light before sunrise in a field
full of ground mist with the last stars faint but still there. Then the priestesses
emerged from the tent and began to sing a song full of piercing, sweet disso-
nance—the way stars might sound if we could hear them.

> *Look how the sky's doors open to your beauty*
> *Look how the goddess waits to receive you*
> *This is death. This is life beyond life.*

Look how the day is breaking in the east.
Look how the goddess awakens you.
Listen to us singing to you, there among the stars.

I closed my eyes, and I was somewhere else, somewhere I had never been, standing in a high place overlooking wide water, wide sky, full of those star voices—no it was my voice, my voice singing to my Beloved.

I opened my eyes again when the singing stopped. Two priestesses stepped forward, one robed in gold, wearing a horned headdress and a lotus crown. She sang the part of Isis, the other of her sister Nepthys. As they sang a call and response lamentation, they descended the steps. The crowd parted as the priestesses, followed by the rest of the priesthood, led the procession to the river, which was no longer the Tiber, but *the* River, the river of life, the river of sorrow, the river of re-membering.

"Come on," I urged my friends. "Let's fall in with the priestesses. We'll get a better view."

"I don't know, Red," Succula hung back, but I grabbed her hand and dragged her along, trusting that Berta and Dido were right behind us.

When we reached the water's edge the whole crowd began to sing while the priestesses boarded the waiting moon-shaped boats.

You are the mother of the living
You are the lover of the dead
From the womb you knew your lover
Now you seek him in the riverbed.

All at once I knew exactly why I'd had the dream, why old Nona had provided the priestess robes. There was a purpose here. Everything had been prepared. All I had to do was act. I dropped Succula's hand and made for the nearest empty boat. Before anyone could stop me, I was launched, the fog shrouding me, the black water sliding beneath the smooth curve of the boat. The sound of the singing came through the mist, clear, disembodied, but not loud enough to cover the sound of Succula crying my name.

"Row." I hardened my heart and turned to the oarsman. "By Isis, mistress of the living and the dead, ruler of wind and water, row for all you're worth to Ostia."

"Ostia?" He sounded confused, but he did not question my authority. "I thought we was only going to Tiber Island. I never heard nothing about no Ostia."

"It is the goddess's command."

Well, it was. Wasn't it?

"But *domina,* what about the rapids?"

The rapids?

"And with the rain we've had this autumn, the river is running swift."

"The goddess will protect us," I said with more assurance than I felt, and then I thought to add, "And you will be well-rewarded."

Through the mist I could just see the other boats; the priestesses singing a high, wordless lament as they trailed their arms and hair in the water searching for the scattered god. Around a bend in the river, Tiber Island hove into view, and the other boats veered toward it. My oarsman was looking frightened; I thought I saw him surreptitiously pulling us to the right out of the current.

"Don't even think about it," I said.

"But, *domina—*"

"You are more afraid of the rapids than the goddess's wrath?"

And then, in a flash, we passed the point of no return. The current became stronger as the river narrowed and divided. Just before we hit the rapids the sun shot up and turned the mist golden. I had just time to think, how beautiful, and then the river took the little boat into the foaming torrent as if it were no more than a stick a child had tossed into the water. The oarsman screamed as we hit a rock, and he lost his oar. He lunged after it, and the boat capsized, pitching us into the water right where the Venus of the Sewer, Cloacina Maxima, relieved herself of her tribute.

In other words, we were in deep shit.

The rapids swiftly took us to a deeper part of the river where the current was still strong. The water was frigid and foul, but I could swim; one glance at the oarsman told me he could not. He flailed and sank, flailed and sank, so I made for him as fast as I could. After a struggle that nearly finished us both, I managed to get him in a classic lifesaver's hold and pull him out of the current and then onto the bank of river where he promptly passed out.

Now what? I looked around me, dazed. It was a beautiful morning, too beautiful to make sense of what was happening. What had happened to the divine plan? How did I come to be standing here on the riverbank stinking of sewage in bedraggled priestess garb with a half drowned man at my feet? The small bag of coins that I'd worn under my clothes was gone, forever lost like Osiris's prick. I had no idea how far it was to Ostia or how to get back to Esquiline Hill from here.

My oarsman was lying awfully still. Since I did not know what else to do, I knelt beside him, checked his breathing and his pulse, then I searched his head to make sure he hadn't hit it on a rock. I found no injury, but the man groaned and then began to shiver convulsively. In a flash, the fire of the stars ignited in my crown and flowed into my hands. I followed its lead, touching the man's face, throat, lungs, legs, feet.

"Isis," he sighed. "Sweet Isis."

I looked up and saw that the man had raised himself on his elbows. He was gazing at me with awe and adoration, which made no sense considering I was soaking wet, stinking of sewage and had nearly cost him his life by forcing him over the rapids.

"So it's all true." His plain diffident face had been transformed. "You do save us. You welcome us in the Land of the Dead."

I held on to the man's feet, trying to bring him to earth. But I wasn't about to contradict him.

"My son," I spoke the words that came to me. "You are saved indeed, but you are still in the land of the living. Go home now. Get into dry clothes. Drink hot wine."

"I obey, my goddess and my queen."

He bowed before me; then obediently went his way, his step young and sprightly.

Then the fire that had filled me died away. I felt cold all over. I knew I had to do something, make a decision, but my mind felt numb as my feet. Get up, get moving was the best I could do, but when I tried to stand, my legs buckled under me. Where is Isis when *I* need her was my last conscious thought.

I can smell the river, the mud banks baking in the sun. I can hear the sound of water and wind moving through the reeds. And there is the black coffin carrying my beloved away from me. I rush towards the box but the water weeds bind my legs. The current flows past me and I float helpless, my arms streaming towards him.

"You must become the river," a voice says.

Yes. I begin to dissolve, turn into water, but someone is pulling at me, slapping me, forcing me back into solid form.

"I was right," a voice spoke, a different voice, voluptuous with satisfaction. "I do know this woman. She is a whore, not a priestess, a whore and a slave, a *runaway* slave."

I kept my eyes shut. I was dreaming, I decided. I'd had that dream of the river. Now I was simply having a nightmare. Nothing more.

Another blow; half my face exploded in pain. My ears rang, and my eyes opened against my will. Two large breasts blotted out the sky. Then the face above them leaned over me. A young, beautiful face, empty except for malice. I had seen it somewhere before. I didn't care to see it again.

"I am a priestess," I managed to say. "A priestess of Isis."

Then another blow fell, and I got my wish. Everything went black.

"She's burning up with fever."

I felt the touch of a woman's hand kindly and competent on my forehead. I made an effort to sit up. That's when I discovered my hands and feet were shackled to the floor. I had no idea where I was, except that I was inside, and it was damp and chill and stank of piss. I focused on the woman kneeling beside me. She was dressed in priestess's robes, and after a moment I recognized her as the priestess from the Temple Venus Obsequens.

"She's lying in her own urine," the woman went on. "And no one has given her dry clothes. This woman is a priestess. Do you not fear the gods, man?"

"If the woman is a priestess of yours, you can take her and welcome."

"Very well," said the woman. "Call for a litter at once."

"Not yet, *domina*," said the *aedile,* a bored looking low-level bureaucrat. "We have a witness who says she's a runaway slave from the Vine and Fig Tree. We can't settle anything till Domitia Tertia gets here."

"But I told you. I *know* who she is," another woman spoke. Oh shit. The bitch was here. "How dare you doubt my word, dog! She should be publicly flogged and branded at once. And when I tell my father about the disrespect you have shown me, you'll be next."

I turned my head and saw the black-haired beauty pushing the *aedile* aside. I had the urge to vomit but was too weak to roll on my side, not to mention I was chained.

"By your own account, *domina*, she belongs to Domitia Tertia who must claim ownership and make the accusation against her," the *aedile* said wearily.

"If we wait much longer, she'll die unpunished." My nemesis sulked.

Death, I mused. Not a bad idea. And I was seized with a chill so violent my chains rattled.

"Get her a blanket, fool!" snapped the priestess.

If I hadn't been debating the merits of dying in a puddle of my own piss or living to be flogged in the Forum, I might almost have felt sorry for the man caught between these two furious women. Then the third fury made her entrance.

"Ah, Domitia Tertia." The man sounded terribly relieved. "I am sorry to disturb you. Thank you for coming so promptly. *Domina* Paulina Claudii has identified this woman as your property. She believes her to be a runaway. We await your confirmation."

The three women stood over me. In my fevered state it looked to me as if they floated. Or maybe I floated, suspended, in suspense, as they deliberated over my fate. I could see it, held in their hands, a red thread, a crackle of green lightning. The malicious beauty tugged at it. The priestess held her end lightly and serenely. Domitia Tertia was in the middle. She held the thread taut.

"Paulina Claudii is mistaken." The thread snapped. "No woman of my house would make a public spectacle of herself."

She turned away, and I felt, to my horror, as if I had lost my last mother all over again, as if I were some exposed girl child Domitia had tossed back on the refuse heap. I tried to cry out, but no sound came. My persecutor was shrieking, but I couldn't follow the words. I closed my eyes as if I could block out the sound that made everything red and throbbing. Then someone was handling me, taking off the cold shackles, pulling me to my feet. Stars fell all around me like burning rain.

Somehow I have escaped them all. I don't know where I am; it is dusk or dawn, half-light. I am on some sort of an island; three rivers wind away into the hills. No, they are roads. Or strands of light cast by a lantern. A whispering begins; at first I think it's only the wind blowing dead leaves over the hard bare ground. Then I hear the words.

> *Tri-via, tri-via, tri-via*
> *Three roads, three rivers, three worlds.*
> *Leave a message on the post*
> *Tell us where you choose to go.*
> *Each way leads towards and away*
> *from the others.*
> *To the country of life*
> *you can go, you can go.*
> *To the country of death*
> *you can go, you can go.*
> *To the place between*
> *to the crack in time*
> *you can go, you can go.*
> *Tri-via, tri-via, tri-via.*

I look around for the singers of this strange song. All I see is a pillar.
Look look look
And I see that the pillar is a statue with three heads, each looking down one road. But I know these faces; it's not a statue. This one is old Nona. There is Anna of Jerusalem whom I met in a dream, and the other is the Cailleach, grey as the rocks of Tir na mBan, the island of women, my home. They are all here, and yet they are not. They are guiding me, and I am alone.

To the country of life
you can go, you can go
to the country of death
you can go, you can go
to the place between
to the crack in time
you can go, you can go.
each road leads toward and away
from the others.
Find what you seek
seek what you find
go go go.

"I want the one that leads to him."

My own voice startles me; the air shimmers with it.

"Come look, then," the voices answer so softly now; it's less than a whisper. It is my own breath. Now I am the three-headed one. I can see in all directions at once. At the same time, I can hone my vision. Each distinct road opens to me or I open to it. Each world has its own force, its own crosswind that propels me toward it.

The country of death is quiet. The light there does not come from the sky but from inside each thing—that huge boulder, that stand of copper beech, the stream winding, without sound, through the landscape. And the light comes from my father, too. He is there resting after his long, long time in the sea. I am curious. Now will he know me? Will he speak to me? His eyes are so bright in his fox face. He is looking at me. I try to take a step forward, but I can't seem to move.

I look down and see someone's brown, dusty, bare feet. Beautiful feet. When I look up, he is there, my beloved, standing before me. So this is the road! I guessed right the first time. He is holding his arms out straight from his sides, but not to reach for me and gather me into an embrace. He is blocking the way.

"Don't touch me," he says, his voice as gentle as the words are harsh.

The road to this world thins to a thread.

"Not yet," he whispers, though I can't see him anymore. "Not yet."

The Otherworld opens to me. My true home, my birthright. Here there is always sound, wind and waves, women's voices singing, loose lines of poetry flapping across the sky on cranes' or ravens' wings. Dwynwyn is here, the old witch from the druid isle, with whom I once changed shapes. She is putting something into her cooking pot. My mother is there combing light into hair or hair into light. And on the sandy shore, playing with pebbles, there is a small, fiery-headed child. Myself as a child? No. I suddenly know. She's my daughter, my daughter. I will go back to the Otherworld, to Tir na mBan, the Land of Women. I will never, ever leave again.

Someone is crying.

Not my daughter who plays happily, oblivious of me.

I will stay here.

The weeping goes on.

No.

"Maeve."

It's his voice. With huge sorrow I know I can't find him in the Otherworld.

"Come back."

The country of life makes me weep. The stones here are so hard. They cut my feet. It takes so much time to walk this road. Yet I know the other worlds are here, too, at the edges of my vision. There is the silent stream that will cool my feet. There is sea spray shimmering gold around the island. But I am tired, and I hurt. Someone keeps crying.

Then, for an instant I am in a garden; the dew is cold; the earth smells spicy, sweet. Where am I? The joy is unbearable. Which world is this one? I want this one, no matter what it costs. This one.

And then he is with me.

"Don't die, Red. Please don't die."

"Choose," he says, and he is gone.

I wake in the country of life with Succula's tears on my face.

THE HOUSE

OF

MY ENEMY

CHAPTER ELEVEN

SAVED?

Life is a hard choice. You say you have no choice? Life is all you know? I don't believe it. You remember the restfulness of not being, of no pain, no yearning. We may fear death, but we don't always know if we can make it through life. It's the suspense that keeps us hooked. We want to know what happens next. Of course, there's a reason we don't know. Because if we did, we might say forget it, just forget it. I'm not signing on for that.

If you want to find out what happens next in my story, I'll give you fair warning: the next part is tough. But if you persist, you may recognize your own story of times too hard to bear that seemed as though they would never end. You may find the hidden gifts of those times. You will know that I know all about it. And I won't give you any crap. I won't say things to you like god—or goddess—never gives us more than we can bear. I won't lie. Sometimes life *is* just too much. When you want to lie down and die, I won't judge you. I'll sit and howl with you. Just remember: I am still here, I am telling you this story. And it's not over.

"Yes, Isis loves you, yes, Isis loves you," crooned Old Nona. She had been my attendant since Succula left me. "Yes, Isis loves you, she tells you—"

"Spare me," I snapped, irritable as any convalescent.

"Oh, she has, dearie. She has."

If spared meant lying on a pallet somewhere in the back of the Vine and Fig Tree instead of drowned or dead of fever, then yes. How I had even come to be here I did not know. The last I remembered, Domitia Tertia had publicly denied any knowledge of me. Old Nona wouldn't or couldn't answer any of my questions, and Succula had not returned. Nor had I seen any of the other whores. No doubt I was being punished. Maybe Domitia Tertia intended to demote me to sweeper or latrine cleaner. I didn't know. And worse, I hardly cared. I rolled over, covered my ears and escaped into sleep again.

I woke to the touch of someone's lips on my cheek. A man's kiss. I kept my eyes shut for as long as I could, wanting it to be him, the one I searched for in all my dreams.

"Maeve," the man said softly; the name was right, but not the voice.

"Joseph?" I opened my eyes, and caught the look of tenderness that he quickly covered as he drew back from me. "Where have you been?"

"You're the one who needs to answer some questions. Why did you do it, Maeve? Why? *Why*! If only you had waited."

He was practically wringing his hands. What did it matter to him? I looked at this man, who had walked on the same ground as my beloved, this man who had the power to come and go, who traveled from Pretannia to Rome to Jerusalem whenever it suited his purposes. I wanted to rage at him, but I couldn't summon the strength. I felt powerless, as I did in the dream, my feet tangled in the weeds.

"You know why," was all I said.

He turned his face away as if I had struck him a blow; then, very deliberately, he looked at me again.

"I deserve your reproach."

"No, Joseph," I said wearily. "You don't owe me anything."

"Except the truth."

Now he had my full attention. "What do you mean? When have you lied to me?"

"I didn't lie, I just didn't tell you what I knew or rather what I suspected. Now it's too late."

"What do you mean, it's too late? What's too late? Tell me."

"Listen then." He sighed, and he sat down next to me on the floor; I could feel him wanting to touch me, but he wouldn't let himself. "Do you remember you asked me if I had a son? I did once, a son and a wife whom I caused great suffering; they are both dead now, but that is another story."

"I'm sorry, Joseph." I touched his arm lightly; he brushed it away without noticing as if a fly had lighted on him.

"When I met you my interest was aroused. A Celt in Rome is not unusual, but one who knows Aramaic is highly unusual. I couldn't help wondering…" He broke off; he was having difficulty with his narrative. "Let me start again. Some years ago on a trip to the Pretannic Isles, I met a young Jew in the company of three Hibernian women. I would have been curious anyway, but he reminded me of my son—"

Joseph stopped again or maybe he didn't. Maybe I just couldn't hear him over the roar of surf in my ears, the whole salt ocean pressing behind my eyes. I clutched Joseph to keep from being utterly lost.

"He's alive," I spoke without knowing I spoke. "He's alive."

"Yes, Maeve, he's alive, if we are talking about the same person. When I first saw him, he was distraught, beside himself. It was hard to make sense of what he was saying. A crazy story of being chosen as a human sacrifice, then being rescued by a woman he kept insisting was a prophetess in the Temple of Jerusalem. I was sure he had lost his mind."

He hadn't lost his mind; or anyway his account was true insofar as he understood what had happened. An old woman *had* rescued him—me in disguise. When he had mistaken me for Anna the Prophetess in his drug-induced delirium, I had not contradicted him. I had borrowed her authority. *"I sent you here, Yeshua,"* I had said in Anna's voice. *"Now I've come to send you home."*

"I felt responsible for him," Joseph went on, "a fellow Jew, and the Hibernian women were clearly anxious to be shed of him."

In my hag form, I had also rescued them, political prisoners in rebellion against the druids. They had paid their debt to me by taking him with them across the Straits, just before the tide turned, and I raised the tidal bore that forced their pursuers to retreat.

"They'd brought him to Glastonbury to dump him on the priestesses there, so, of course, I said I'd take him with me back to Palestine. But he didn't want to go. He kept saying over and over, 'I've got to go back. I should never have left her. How could I have left her?' He couldn't eat; he couldn't sleep. He was ill and feverish."

I felt sick, just as he must have felt sick, wracked with guilt to think that I had caused him such anguish when I only meant to set him free.

"The priestesses kept him under watch—under guard really. Finally, he begged them to use their arts to find out what had happened to the young woman he had left behind."

Joseph paused as if waiting for me to tell the other part of the story. I just nodded for him to go on. I couldn't yet speak.

"I don't know if you can understand, being a Celt and accustomed to divination, what it meant for him to ask that. We have a story of a king who went to a witch—"

"Saul," I put in.

"Ah, you know our stories. Yes, Saul. And so you know that after Saul went to the Witch of Endor, the Most High abandoned him."

My beloved had finally chosen me over his jealous god. When it was too late. When it could not help either of us. Oh, Esus, Esus.

"What did they tell him?" I spoke so softly Joseph had to lean closer, close enough so that I could smell the man smell of him, the sweat, the sorrow.

"They told him you had been found guilty of various crimes and exiled in a boat with no food or water. I told him it was a death sentence, but he refused to believe it. That's when he decided to go with me, to try to follow you, though I had agreed to no such plan. As it turned out, I didn't have to argue or make my case. Just before we were to embark, a terrible storm came—high winds, waves like mountains. No one believed you could have survived that storm. No one."

"But the priestesses," I was weeping now. "Surely the priestesses knew. They called the storm. I know they did—they blew me to safety."

Joseph said nothing for a moment; I could feel he didn't believe me.

"If they had any knowledge that you were alive, they did not say so; they said nothing more at all. When the swells calmed, we sailed for Palestine."

For a while neither of us spoke. I just sat with my head in my hands, hearing the slap of the waves on the boat, feeling his desolation as he went back—with what? Anna the Prophetess of Jerusalem had told him to step outside his world. She had promised him that when he came back he would see his people with new eyes, love them with a new love. And instead he had returned grief-stricken and sick with shame.

But it was not over yet. It could not be over. He was alive. I was alive.

"Joseph, where is he now?" I turned to look at him, and again he looked away.

"I don't know."

I waited. There had to be more. There had to. I took his face in my hands and made him look at me.

"Maeve, don't you understand? That's where I went when I left last summer. To find him. I didn't want to tell you, because I wasn't sure. But I thought I had to find him. I had to make sure of him, because, because—"

"Joseph, don't spare me anything."

"Well, you see, I had helped to arrange his marriage."

The words went in, went in so deep I couldn't comprehend them.

"I told you he reminded me of my son. Such a keen mind. That much was evident even when he was most desolate. I tried to help him by teaching him the rudiments of Greek philosophy—so spacious and spare compared to the Torah. He paid attention at first out of courtesy, but I like to think the mental exercise brought him some relief. I rejoiced whenever I could draw him into argument. You of all people can understand, I'm sure, that after spending so much time with him on the journey, I became attached to him. I even went back with him all the way to Nazareth where I met his family."

I was jealous, jealous even of Joseph.

"I made a point of checking up on him whenever I was in the country. Often as not when I went to Nazareth, he wasn't home. He picked up odd jobs in Sepphoris, carpentry, enough to keep him in drink. His older brother had thrown him out of the shop at home, and I'm sorry to have to tell you this, but he became wild and dissolute. His mother, she's a widow and very eccentric, never wavers in her belief that he has some great destiny. She goes on about it, and all her other children just roll their eyes. They resent him; it's understandable. He's the favorite, and what has he ever done but bring her grief and worry while they stay home and do her bidding?

"Last time I was there his mother told me: 'He needs to get married.' That's not the strange part. What mother wouldn't say that? She kept insisting that he's supposed to marry a woman named Mary. He must marry Mary."

"No!" I burst out.

"Do you want to hear the rest of the story?"

"Yes, but that's not how the story goes."

"Well, listen. When she said the name Mary I remembered a cousin of mine in Bethany. Her family had tried to arrange a marriage for years, but—"

"She's hideous." I was hopeful. "Foul-tempered. Mad."

"No. Just brilliant. She cares only about learning. She wants to be a rabbi."

"So?" I was worried now. Esus would love having someone with whom he could dispute the fine points of Mosaic Law.

"Among our people that is not considered normal. Men can be quite put off by a woman more learned in Scripture than they are, and one, moreover, who is almost completely ignorant of housewifely arts. But I thought, well, two misfits. And her passion for study might reawaken his, so I offered to broker the match."

"He *agreed*?"

"Maeve, he thought you were dead."

I was rocking myself now, back and forth, back and forth.

"I was going to go back for the wedding in any event. But when I realized who you were—or might be—I went sooner."

"You were going to tell him I'm alive?"

"I have to tell you the truth, Maeve. I hadn't decided. I wanted to see if he was still haunted or if, if he might want this new life with Mary. Maeve, you must know, even if he wanted to, he couldn't marry you. A gentile barbarian and you know—"

"A whore."

"Well, yes," he paused delicately. "But, in any case, when I got there—"

"Wait, Joseph, just give me a minute."

There was something I needed to know about myself. Would I, could I give him up—if I had a choice? Which of course I didn't. It was true; it had always been true, that he couldn't marry me. I knew less about marriage than most people. My mothers had not been married, nor had the druids. But I knew marriage was important to other people. Maybe to him. Could I give him up— to life, to ordinary life?

Tears were rolling down my face now. Giving him up meant giving up the story, too, the story of Maeve and Esus, the lovers, the lovers of the world. His mother and Anna the prophetess had all prophesied greatness. So had the druids, though they thought he had to be dead first. Maybe he was destined for greatness. Without me. Maybe I was just a short episode. And now he had to marry Mary.

"So," I spoke at last. "What did you find out? Has he forgotten me? Is he happy with her?"

"The thing is, I don't know, Maeve."

"What do you mean? I thought you went back to find out."

"I did, but he was gone. They were both gone. Three weeks before the wedding, they disappeared. No one knows where they are."

"Together? They ran off together?"

"They are both gone. That's all anyone knows."

"Gone," I repeated. "But not married. They ran out on their wedding?"

"So it seems."

I did not know what to make of this information. Or at least my mind didn't. My heart had already taken off, skipping, soaring. Not married. Not married to Mary. He's somewhere in the wide, wild world, and I can find him. I will find him.

"Joseph!" I turned to him and grabbed hold of him with both hands. "Now you understand. How I wish I had told you everything before. But now, now you must see why you must take me to Palestine. You must. And Domitia Tertia will be glad to be rid of me. I disgraced her; she's already denied me publicly. She'll be itching to sell me."

Joseph didn't answer, and his silence was dreadful.

"What is it, Joseph? What's wrong?"

"Maeve, she's already sold you."

"What?" I felt as though the hard floor gave way, I was falling. "How can that be? If she's sold me, why am I here?"

"You were sick, Maeve. Remember? That was her agreement. She'd keep you till you were strong enough to walk."

"But who? *Who*?"

"She wouldn't tell me. Maybe couldn't tell me. I don't know for certain, but I suspect she's being blackmailed. She saved you, you know."

"Saved me?"

"Runaway slaves are as good as dead. You must know that, Maeve. That's why she denied knowing you, don't you see? She told me she let the *aedile* think you were a priestess. Then she made some kind of a deal and had you smuggled back here. She won't tell me more than that. It was a generous act, and she's now furious with herself. It goes against her grain to risk herself for someone else. You owe her your life."

I looked at him blankly. My life? What life? I could see nothing but that empty sickening space that had no end; that held no air.

"Joseph, save me. Save me." My voice was flat in the void.

"Ah, Maeve, Maeve, if only I could. If only I could have taught you more. Listen to me. You must hold fast to philosophy now. Remember as much as you can."

I could hear his desperation. He couldn't bear to be helpless to help me. "Remember your Plato, Maeve. *'If a man, fixing his attention on these and the like difficulties, does away with the idea of things and will not admit that every individual thing has its own determinate idea which is always one and the same, he will have nothing on which his mind can rest; and so he will utterly destroy his reasoning…'*"

Joseph went on quoting, but all I could hear were fragments of a poem, my beloved's voice raised in lamentation when he told the story of his people's exile from Jerusalem. *'How deserted she sits…all night long she is weeping…she never thought to end like this.'*

"Ah, Maeve, dear Maeve, how I could have loved—" He stopped himself. "It's better I go now. If I find out where you are…. No. No promises. But I will do what I can. Meanwhile, remember what Aristotle said, 'Hope is a waking dream.'"

"A dream? Joseph, this is a nightmare."

"I'm sorry, Maeve."

And he was gone.

That night, my last night at the Vine and Fig Tree, I tossed and turned and woke again and again from restless sleep shouting: "I'm alive, Esus, I'm alive. Wait for me. Wait!" Lying awake between nightmares, I tried to console myself. He must know, deep inside he must know or how could he have come to me in my vision, blocking the way to the country of death, offering me the choice of life? I tried to send myself to him in my dreams as once long ago on Tir na mBan my dreams had taken me to him in the Temple of Jerusalem. But now, awake or asleep, all I could see of him were his feet, his beautiful feet, dusty and bleeding, as he walked over rocks and rubble of some dry, dead land.

Finally old Nona came and held me in her arms. Or maybe it was Anna the Prophetess of whom I had once dreamed so vividly, Anna whose words had come to me that rainy night on Mona when I loosed my beloved's chains.

"There, there, my little dove," she crooned, and I could sense my bird form, feel my swift bird's heart beating in her palm.

After that I must have slept deeply for a while. I woke to cold dawn light and the sound of voices in the corridor.

"I won't have it." I recognized Bonia's angry tones. "The *domina* said she is to go quietly before the rest of them are awake. We don't want a lot of wailing, red-eyed whores. We don't want the house in an uproar."

"Well, that's exactly what you'll get if you don't let them see her. Tears now or later. Take your pick."

"No, Bone. Domitia just wants her to disappear. The others will get the message; they'll be too frightened to make a fuss."

"Don't bet on it."

"Well, no matter what you think, those are her orders. How can you even question them?"

"Just because I worship Domitia doesn't mean I worship every decision she makes."

"Hmph! Some devotee you are. You're fickle, that's what. The girl has gotten to you. Admit it. How, I don't know. Magic, sorcery. You can't trust the *keltoi.*"

"She's gotten to you, too, Bonia. Why else are you so upset? She's gotten to everyone. She's changed the whole place. I told you what I saw that day at the temple, the day of the races." He lowered his voice. "Ever since then—"

"And I told you to stow that rubbish. The *domina* is right about those cults. Look what happened. How I wish they'd never gone to the *Isia.*"

"I'm going to wake the others," announced Bone.

"If the *domina* finds out, on your head be it."

Bonia came in to get me ready. There wasn't much to it. She'd brought me a clean plain tunic with my accumulated tips sown into a pouch.

"Find a good hiding place for that," she advised. "Most houses don't have a bank for slaves and they're always stealing from each other."

"Where am I going, Bonia?" I asked listlessly and hopelessly.

"No one knows. You're lucky to be alive. Remember that."

She had also brought me bread and wine.

"I'm not hungry," I said.

"Don't be stupid, girl. You can't be sure when you'll eat again. I told you!" She couldn't contain herself anymore. "I told you the first day you were here, it doesn't get any better than the Vine and Fig Tree. Now you're going to find out." She brushed a tear from her eye as if she was trying to punch herself out. "Come on, then. It's time."

The other whores were huddled in the courtyard, shivering and red-eyed.

"Red," wailed Berta. "We forgive you. We know you did it for love."

"That is such a crock," wept Dido.

"Red," Succula flung herself at me. "I hate you."

"I know," I said, trying not to cry, as old Nona elbowed her way into our whores' huddle with her tear scalpel. "I love you, too."

Olivia the cat rubbed against my legs. I picked her up and buried my face in her fur. The cat embodied the Vine and Fig Tree, soft, feline, female, warm—everything I was about to lose.

"Strip her." It was a man's voice from behind me.

"When a whore leaves this house, she keeps her clothes," protested Bone.

"Tell your mistress she'd better guard her reputation. Rumor will spread that she's soft. In the head."

I heard a thwack, and the man cried out. I guess Bone had socked him.

"I meant no offense," the man whined, suddenly obsequious. "I have my orders."

"Bone." Domitia Tertia appeared in the entryway. "That was the agreement. No clothes. No belongings. Bonia, strip her and put everything back in the safe."

I kept my eyes fixed on Domitia Tertia as Bonia lifted the tunic over my head. I wanted to communicate something, though I didn't know what—gratitude, defiance? But she would not meet my gaze. She was willing me out of existence.

"There was one more condition, *domina*," said the man, who was still behind me.

She made an impatient, dismissive gesture. I was no longer her concern. But she couldn't quite sustain her indifference. For just an instant, she caught my eye. What was she saying? *I know you. You will haunt me.* Then the blindfold blotted out everything.

I could hear the other whores sobbing, and I fancied I could also detect the faint brush of old Nona's scalpel. Then my hands were bound behind me, my feet shackled so that I could only just walk. A scratchy rope was fastened round my waist. With a vicious jerk that made me stumble to my knees, the man began to drag me away from the Vine and the Fig Tree, from my sisters, from a place, I realized too late, where I had belonged.

CHAPTER TWELVE

MY STRIPES

I have been publicly naked before. I am not particularly distressed by it. But being chained to a wall, blind-folded, with my bare ass exposed to a room full of people, gave nakedness a whole new dimension. To distract myself from my condition, I focused on sound and smell. Yes, smell. Food was being served, scents wafting past me as slaves carried meats and pastries. There was a cacophony of voices, male and female, becoming louder as wine flowed. Clearly I was on display—perhaps the centerpiece of some midday banquet? The dessert? The entertainment?

"Does Claudius always put new slaves on view to his guests?"

Some man had come closer, and I could smell his breath. He must have eaten a raw onion for breakfast. I wished he wouldn't breathe on my neck.

"Never seen him do it before," replied his companion, whose voice I recognized from the Vine and Fig Tree. A senator. What else. One of Berta's regulars. "Not a bad idea, what? Teach them their place right away. This one looks rather fat and sassy. Maybe she needs a lesson."

"I can think of other methods."

"So can I. And if there weren't ladies present, I'd demonstrate. Wouldn't I just love to spread those luscious cheeks and take a plunge."

They both sniggered like the overgrown schoolboys they were.

"Damn," said the first man. "You can't hide anything under these to-gas."

"I know. I've got one, too. Nothing to be ashamed of. Give the ladies something to talk about."

"I hear the lady of the house talks of little else."

They both laughed in absurd appreciation of each other's puerile wit as they moved away, presumably to recline at table. The feasting began in earnest and went on interminably. Still weak from my illness, I was also hungry. I'd had nothing to eat since the bread and wine I'd barely touched that morning. Added to all my other discomforts was a bladder near bursting. I gave my mind to a serious question. Would it be more humiliating to me or more insulting to the banqueters if I made a puddle on the floor? This dilemma distracted me from graver questions such as: where the hell was I and what was to become of me?

The answers came all too soon.

"May I have your attention please," commanded a male voice.

An excited hush fell. How did I know it was excited? My senses and extra senses were heightened. Let's say I could smell it.

"My very dear friends," the man continued, jovial and pompous in equal measure, "I'm pleased to inform you that we have arranged an entertainment for you today. Like all the best entertainments, it is also designed to be morally instructive and uplifting."

Morally instructive. Not a good sign. That meant I couldn't get by with tap-dancing—or lap-dancing, either.

"We are all only too aware of the dangers posed to decent society by rebellious slaves. If you let a slave get away with one transgression, it leads to another and another, until you find yourself one day with a blade between your ribs, a cup of poison at your lips, or a full scale insurrection in your kitchen and stables."

His listeners were getting worked up. Shouts of "Well said!" and "Hear! Hear!" punctuated his stagey pauses.

"Masters who do not chastise slaves endanger us all in our very homes, in our very beds. This insolent vixen insulted a lady, a very important lady: my wife. And this outrage went unpunished by the vicious slut's former mistress. As for me and my house, we now accept the full burden of responsibility for this depraved creature's moral rehabilitation. So great is my wife's concern for the safety of honest Roman citizens that she herself will administer the first lashes."

Cheers and applause greeted this announcement. A typical wanker's fantasy, I thought dismissively, forgetting for a moment that here—unlike at the Vine and Fig Tree—I had no control over how to play it out.

Then someone breathed damply in my ear.

"It's me."

Oh shit. Oh no. Oh yes. Of course. The bitch.

She pressed herself against my back, her breasts filling the hollows under my shoulder blades. Her nipples were hard enough to prick me.

"Do you know what I'm going to whip you with," she whispered throatily. "A bull's pizzle. A big, long, thick bull's pizzle."

How could Domitia Tertia do this to me? How *could* she? She called this saving me? When I could have died in a salt mine—a swift, simple end.

The crowd was getting restless. "Have at her, *domina*. Go on. Teach her a lesson she'll carry with her on her back."

"But take care not to scar that delectable rump," someone shouted.

All the men brayed like the asses they were.

I narrowed my focus. Bladder control. The question was now settled. "Never piss yourself in front of the enemy," Queen Maeve of Connacht had advised me long ago. I called upon her memory for strength. The first lash tore into my back to the cheers and applause of the crowd. I sucked in my breath and squeezed tight the muscles of my twat as skillful whores learn to do. Soon the crowd became silent, entranced no doubt by the sound of the whip singing in the air, cracking across my flesh. I made no sound, and after my first flinch, no movement. I had learned a thing or two at druid school and distracted myself from the pain by reciting in my head from *Invasions*, the beginning of the story cycles first year students learn by heart.

I barely noticed when the woman tired and turned the whip over to someone else. Soon I stopped waiting for the lashes to end. The rhythmic lines of poetry came to life, and I was on the battlefield with blood and pain all around and the death crows screaming overhead. At last someone carried me off the field, dead or alive, I didn't know or care.

When I woke up, lying on my stomach in a dark, cold place, still naked, except for a thin blanket someone had thrown over me, I knew I was alive. Being dead could not hurt this much. My back was inflamed and at the same time stiff and immobile. I pulled my thighs and knees up under my belly, and then I slowly sat up. The blanket stuck to the wounds on my back. Suddenly I felt so helpless and alone, I broke down and wept.

I was still weeping when a woman came in with a torch, which she set in a holder. I could see now that I was in a storage room full of oil jugs and grain sacks. The woman, a lower rank slave in a plain tunic, knelt next to me and handed me a flask of wine laced with something else, drugs for the pain, I hoped. She waited while I took a drink. Then lightly—so lightly—she touched my shoulder, rose and disappeared, returning with a basin of scalding water. With her hands and some kind of knife perhaps—I couldn't see—she removed the blanket and began to bathe my wounds—an excruciating relief. When she had thoroughly washed me; she rubbed a soothing salve all over my back. Last she pulled out from her tunic some fresh bread that she pressed into my hands. Only after she had left did it dawn on me that she had never spoken a word.

I must have slept again. When I woke there was a little light coming in through small barred upper windows. I could see and hear feet passing by outside. As I had guessed, I was in a basement storeroom. Just before I mounted the slave block, I had been stowed in the back of a fish shop. Perhaps the bitch was planning to sell me again, now that she'd had the satisfaction of beating me. With these wounds on my back—the mark of a recalcitrant slave—I'd be sold to the salt mines, anyway.

The slave who'd tended me last night had left me a slop bucket. As I got up to use it, I heard the sound of a door being unbolted, opened, then bolted again. In a moment the woman appeared, carrying a pitcher and a basin. She had straight black hair streaked with grey, pulled back tightly from a sallow face that had the shuttered look common among low-ranking slaves. She did not greet me, but kept her eyes averted till I was done with the bucket. Then with gestures she asked to see my back.

"That salve you rubbed on me helped," I said. "Thank you."

She didn't answer, just went on tending the wounds.

"I guess you must have been told not to speak to me."

Her hands halted their ministrations, and she clenched them.

"What is it?" I turned towards her.

She looked at me directly. Then she pointed to her mouth and shook her head.

"You can't speak?" I asked. "I'm sorry. I didn't know."

She shrugged; then she tried to turn my back to her again.

"Wait," I twisted around. "May I ask you some questions? Can you answer yes or no?"

She looked wary but nodded.

"Am I still in..." What was the bitch's name? "The house of Paulina Claudii?"

She nodded.

"Do you know what she intends to do with me?"

Just then we both heard the door open. The woman gestured for me to be quiet and almost roughly turned me around and began to rub in the salve.

"Boca!" At what was apparently her name (Mouth!) the mute woman's hands began to tremble. "I told you to fetch me as soon as she recovered consciousness."

Boca rose, and I turned around. There was Paulina dressed only in a shift and shawl (in other words in her undergarments). I was still naked, but I made no attempt to shield myself, nor did I stand. I just gazed at her with the insolent nonchalance I had learned from the cats at the Vine and Fig Tree.

"Has she been trying to get information out of you, Boca?"

Boca gestured incomprehensibly. Paulina slapped her.

"You're perfectly capable of answering yes or no."

Boca shook her head, keeping her eyes lowered.

"It's amazing how someone with her tongue cut out can still lie."

Boca flinched, anticipating another blow, but Paulina abruptly lost interest in her.

"Your duties here are done. Go back to the kitchens."

Boca practically ran for the door, and Paulina and I were alone together for the first time since our encounter in the *vomitorium.*

"Well, aren't you going to ask me anything?" she demanded.

I shrugged.

"You better find your tongue before you lose it."

"Is that why you cut Boca's out, because she wouldn't answer your questions?"

She looked confused for a moment; she had already forgotten who Boca was, since she had no need of her at the moment.

"Never mind about her. I can have *your* tongue cut out if I want. I can do anything I want with any part of your body. So you better show me proper respect."

It took all my self-control not to laugh. Instead I bit my lip and continued to stare at her. Suddenly she heaved a sigh and flopped down on a sack of grain, as if it were a reclining couch.

"I can see it's going to take more than one beating to teach you your place. Too bad it wasn't as much fun as I thought it would be."

She pouted and idly began to trace patterns in the dust on the floor. I found this shift of mood curious.

"What will I do with you now?" she wondered—a bit like a child who has begged for a puppy and now discovers it has to be fed, groomed, and housebroken.

"Oh," she said, looking up from her dust doodles, "you have one of those whore anklets."

I had forgotten I still had it, a gift from Succula. Paulina reached out, accustomed to taking what she wanted. I was about to slap her hand, when she withdrew it.

"There's no point. No one ever even sees a respectable matron's ankles. And besides you look rather luscious sitting there with nothing on but your slutty little bauble." She paused for a moment considering. "I think I'll let you keep it as a sign that you're still a whore, my own personal whore."

"Is that to be my official position in your household, *domina*?" I asked, my tone cool and professional.

"No, *stulta*! Your unofficial position. Let's see." She put one finger on her pouting lips and pondered the possibilities. "Officially you will be—"

"I can read and write." Well, I was learning. "I can speak five languages."

I had spoken too eagerly. I saw my mistake. To offer or ask anything gave her power.

"*Cara stulta*," (dear stupid one) "we have Greeks for that sort of thing. Scores of them. You, I think, will assist the *a cubiculo*. Empty slops, hold the mirror for the *ornatrix*, the things none of the other slaves want to do—they're so particular about their positions. But we must have a title for your position. Ah, I know just the thing. You will be my *pedisequa*."

"*Pedisequa*?" I repeated. I didn't know the term but figured it meant something like a female slave who sits at the mistress's feet, a human pet.

"Yes, you will attend me at all times; you will do whatever I ask. Is that clear?"

It was clear. Clear as a barren desert under a harsh noon sun.

"Yes."

"Yes, what?" she demanded.

"Yes, *domina*."

I finally lowered my eyes. Insolence took too much energy.

"Show me your back."

Lightly she traced the wounds, as if they were inscriptions she was trying to decipher.

"I don't think you will scar. Not much anyway," she said, whether with regret or as reassurance I couldn't tell. "Listen, Red." Abruptly her tone changed; she almost whispered. "I need someone. I need someone who belongs to me. Someone I can tell things to. Someone I can trust, who won't…who isn't a spy for someone else. Do you understand?"

I looked at her again. Her face was very close to mine, unguarded. I had known before that she was a young woman, but now it hit me—she was as young as I was, maybe younger, and far more frightened. She was also crazy. The woman had just had me publicly beaten and humiliated. And she wanted me to be her trusted confidante?

I didn't answer her. And just as suddenly her face closed again.

"I will have a tunic sent to you," she said as she rose to go. "You will report to my bed chamber at the second hour."

"How will I find it?"

"You'll have to figure that out for yourself." She smiled nastily. "It will be the first test of your obedience. I'll give you a tip, though. Don't even think about trying to escape. All the porters have your description, and they are all rather attached to their body parts—the ones that still have any. Bribing them with whorish tricks won't work."

With that she flounced away, trailing a ragged bit of her shift in the dust.

CHAPTER THIRTEEN

ANT HILL

T he Vine and Fig Tree had seemed a large and complex dwelling to me. I'd grown up in a round wattle and daub hut; accommodations at druid school were only variations on the same theme. *Domus* Claudius seemed more like an enclosed city than a house. It had four stories, not including the basement storerooms, and as Succula had pointed out to me, it took up an entire city block. Four long streets, all with shop fronts, enclosed its numerous atriums, each with a four-story cluster of rooms surrounding it. There were countless bedrooms, several banqueting halls with corresponding kitchens, as well as receiving rooms where the clients lined up every morning and of course the house had private baths—though everyone went to the lavish public ones anyway—as well as private stables.

Even more overwhelming than the size of the house was the sheer number of slaves and hangers on who inhabited it. You couldn't easily tell the difference between the two. Some of the slaves were richly dressed, and some of the ne'er-do-well relatives and friends looked like they should be plucking chickens or pushing a mop. There were almost one hundred titled slaves in *Domus* Claudius, and dozens more without titles. Like everything Roman, including the Latin language, the household was hierarchical and bureaucratic. The titled slaves jealously guarded their status. If your title was *a purpuris*—servant in charge of purple garments—then you were a cut above the *a vesta*, who had charge over ordinary clothes. Likewise the *ab ornamentis*—the servant in charge of hair and accessories for ceremonial occasions—held rank over the *ornatrix*. There were slaves whose only job was to dust busts and statues, and slaves who did nothing but keep track of unguents.

Of course, it took me months to learn all the overt and covert rules of slave society and protocol. On my first morning poor tongueless Boca brought me a plain tunic like hers and guided me for what seemed like miles of corridor and courtyard, as well as up and down staircases. None of the scurrying people we passed paid any attention to us, not even a curious glance. Everyone seemed as enclosed and lifeless as the *insularium* itself. I had lived in square walls at the Vine and Fig Tree, too, but at least from my room I could hear the sound of the fountain, and the cats gave relief from the relentlessly human scale and focus of city life. I did not know how I could survive in *Domus* Claudius. I did not.

At last we came to yet another courtyard, and Boca stopped, gesturing across it. I turned and looked at her; her eyes were so huge and empty I could see my reflection—a flash of brightness like a salmon leaping into an alien element. She shook her head as if I'd asked her something. Then she turned and fled.

"You botched abortion," a woman shrieked. "Your mother should have exposed you at birth!"

I did not need further guidance to find Paulina's *cubiculo*. The invective continued, but the words were lost in the sound of something shattering. A moment later two female slaves scurried out of the chamber and down the stairs to the courtyard.

"That's the third mirror she's broken this week," one muttered to the other.

"You know why she's been so touchy lately, don't you?"

"What do you mean? That spoiled brat is always like that."

"Well, if you don't know, perhaps I'd better not say. But there's them that ought to know, and when they do—"

At that point, they caught sight of me and abruptly ceased their innuendo.

"Who are you?" the one who had spoken first demanded.

I could not bring myself to say, I'm the *domina's* new slave, her *pedisequa*. Or maybe it was the effect of spending time with Boca, the only person in *domus* Claudius who had shown me any kindness. She had imprinted on me, as if I were some motherless duckling. I shrugged and gestured ambiguously.

Before I knew what was happening, my cheek was stinging with the woman's slap, and inadvertent tears blinded me.

"What the fuck—"

"Oh, so you do have a tongue. Then answer me civil like. Who are you?"

My eyes cleared. I looked at the graceless woman. She was thin and bony with a pinched face. I was a big, strapping barbarian. I could easily pick her up and hurl her into the far corner of the courtyard. I gave the idea serious consideration.

"Oh, I know who she is," said the other woman, a bit broader of beam; I didn't know that I could take on both of them. "She's the one the *domina* tied up bare-naked and flogged in the banquet room."

"What's going on out there!" Paulina roared from her *cubiculo*.

"Tell you what, you get the broom," said Bony. "I'll get the mirror. We'll take our time about it, too. After all, it is not our job to fetch and carry like untitled slaves, so why should we rush? You," the skinny one poked me in the ribs, "get in there and take what's coming to you—*and* to us."

"The gods are good," said Broad Beam as they sauntered away. "They've sent us a whipping girl."

An unidentified flying object hurtled into the courtyard just too late to hit the two laggard slaves. I managed to duck. When I looked up again, Paulina was in the doorway looking down at me.

"You!"

The sight of me momentarily diverted her from her rage. I could hear the slaves in the chamber behind her hurrying to set the rooms to right.

"Yes," I agreed.

"Yes, what?" she prompted.

"Yes, it is me, I mean I," I corrected the case.

Let her throw the curling tongues at me; let her throw the entire contents of the room. I wanted to stay outside as long as I could.

She frowned. "Yes, *domina*, delight of my eyes," she prompted.

"Just say it, toots," a male voice called from within the room.

"Shut up, Reginus," said Paulina. "She's my *pedisequa*. I'm training her."

I'd had lots of acting experience at the Vine and Fig Tree, I told myself. Playing Paulina's *pedisequa* was just another gig. Another trick to turn.

"Yes, *domina*, delight of my eyes."

"With feeling this time."

"It's true," I said thoughtfully. "You're not hard on the eyes. Glossy hair, smooth skin. Great tits. But you'd look a lot better if you stopped sticking out your lower lip."

Whatever doom was to befall me, I had the pleasure of seeing the blood drain from her face, then shoot back up in two big red blotches.

"You asked for a mirror," I said, taking advantage of her speechless shock.

"Very well, then," she said, recovering with surprising swiftness. "My mirror you shall be. Upstairs. *Now!*"

I found out what Paulina meant when the skinny one returned. At Paulina's order, the sullen slave handed the mirror to me and huffily resumed her proper duties as *sarnatrix*, (mender of clothes)—though Paulina, I noticed, still wore the torn shift. You might think holding a mirror would be a simple job requiring no great skill. In fact it was exacting and exhausting. Paulina sat in the center of the crowded room, while the *tontrix* and *ornatrix* hovered over her and three slaves, including me, circled her with mirrors. The only thing more tedious than her minute directions—a little higher, to the right, no, that's too much, lower, *stulta!*—was when she settled on an angle she wanted and we had to hold our arms absolutely still, the brass-backed mirrors growing heavier by the second.

Although it was late November now, and the air outside held a distinct chill, Paulina's chamber was stuffy with heat and smoke from the charcoal brazier and the torches. The *tontrix* sweated as she rolled Paulina's thick black hair—that needed no improvement—into long sausage curls, and then wound them one after the other in a rising beehive dome. The *ornatrix* plucked and shaped Paulina's eyebrows and outlined lips that were already vivid. Paulina had stopped raging for the moment, but the atmosphere was silent and tense. It was all so different from the same rite at the Vine and Fig Tree with the whores trading friendly insults, the old women cackling over lewd jokes, the little girls competing to help and getting in the way.

At last Paulina's face and hair were done. The *ornatrix* and the *tontrix* stepped back, and Paulina again examined herself from every possible angle. There was a collective holding of breath as everyone waited for the verdict.

"*Stola!*" She snapped her fingers.

A colorless little woman who'd been standing on the sidelines now stepped forward with a dull looking garment the color of an old bruise. To call it aubergine would have been a stretch. The woman's hands shook as she held it up.

"Not that one, *stulta!*"

The woman nimbly skipped just out of range of Paulina's raised hand.

"But, *domina*, I thought—"

"No one has my permission to think anything unless I say so. Put it back." She sighed as if she were a patient long-suffering adult surrounded by backward children. "I told you before. I will have the red."

"*Domina*, honey." I recognized the voice of the man who had called out to me before. He had been standing, almost leaning against the far wall, plainly bored. Now he took a step towards her. "May I remind you that your esteemed *pater*, the honorable senator Publius Paulus, is calling today and plans to dine."

"I know my father's name," she snapped. "And no, you may not remind me. I'll do the reminding. You are in charge of my chamber, not my life, Reginus. Just because you belong to my father, and I can't discipline you myself, doesn't mean he won't do worse than I could ever dream of doing if I tell him of your insolence."

The man made an obscene gesture with his hands, which were hidden behind his back even as he bowed to her, saying. "Yes, *domina*, delight of my eyes." He couldn't quite keep the sarcasm out of his voice.

"As for the rest of you—" Paulina stopped mid-sentence. If she had been a dog her ears and nose would have been quivering; she might have whined softly in anticipation as the voice she strained to hear came closer.

"Quick," she hissed to her attendants.

For someone who'd taken almost two hours with hair and make-up alone, Paulina jumped into the *stola* in record time. She could barely stand still as the *ornatrix* fastened it with a brooch at the shoulder and tried to drape the folds as modestly as possible, which was difficult as the fine, soft-spun wool had a tendency to cling to her curves.

"You," Paulina shoved the *ornatrix* aside and pointed to me, "fix my breasts!"

"What?" Her breasts needed no improvement as far as I could see.

"Tie the girdle under them. Push them up. You're a whore. You know!"

I decided it was useless to point out that when I was a whore I'd had my own *ornatrix* and *a veste*. I knew the effect she was after.

"You," she said to the *ornatrix*. "Get the garnets."

I arranged her breasts as if they were roasted twin birds on a platter while the *ornatrix* fastened the necklace of dark garnets that would draw every eye to the depths of her cleavage. Then she hurtled across the room to the door. As soon as she crossed the threshold, her entire bearing changed. She moved languorously to the balustrade, stretched as if she had just woken up, and then leaned over it, resting her chin in one hand. Those of us inside the chamber could hear the sound of one male voice below.

"Why Decius Mundus," she cooed, yes cooed. "My favorite equestrian. What a surprise. I didn't know you were back."

There were a few soft snorts from the chamber slaves and a great deal of eye rolling.

"Ah, my dear *domina*. What a vision you are. Like a goddess calling from on high to a mere mortal."

The slaves were now in an agony to keep from exploding with laughter. I might have bonded with them then, I suppose, but no one caught my eye, and I felt a new and unwelcome wariness. How could I know who was trustworthy? How could you trust anyone in a place as miserable as this one, where body parts could be lopped off on a whim?

"Are you in Rome for long this time?"

"I've been posted here for the winter, *domina*."

"Then I shall expect you to dine with us today, Decius."

"It will be my great pleasure, *domina*. Until then!"

Paulina turned from the balustrade, her enticing smile still in place for an instant. Then she discarded it—that's how it seemed—and the petulant expression was back.

"Get me the other *stola*," she said wearily.

Wisely no one questioned her. Everyone welcomed the brooding silence into which she had fallen. She was tractable as a doll as the *a veste* removed the red tunic and dressed her again in the somber one.

"You." She roused herself and focused on me again. "Can you spin and weave?"

"Not very well." My mothers had been so busy teaching me things like how to cast a spear from a moving chariot that they'd neglected the traditional female arts.

"Neither can I," she sighed. "But I have to pretend I can every damn morning while the clients line up to see Claudius."

"Why?" I asked sincerely puzzled. Wasn't that the point of having slaves? To do the work for you?

"Don't you know, honey?" the male slave jumped in. "The *virtuous* wife of Old Republican Stock, like our lovely *domina* here, is industrious." The man seemed incapable of getting his tongue out of his cheek. "She clothes her household. Why, the great Emperor Augustus himself only wore garments made by his womenfolk—"

"Shut up, Reginus!" snapped Paulina; clearly if it was up to her, he would have been as tongueless as Boca. "Nobody asked you, and nobody is to answer her questions anyway, which she has no right to ask.

"Now hear this, all chamber slaves: Red is *my* slave. *Mine*! I bought her. I beat her. I'm training her as my *pedisequa*. She is to attend me whenever I want her and to do whatever I tell her to do. Right now I'm taking her with me to the textile room. If anyone has any complaints about her or notices any disrespect or shirking in her, you are to come directly to *me*. Not my husband. Not my father. Is that understood?"

There was a hearty chorus of "Yes, *domina*!"

She could hardly have isolated me more, if she told everyone I was her personal leper.

"Come!" she snapped her fingers.

I had a momentary vision of simply lying down and forcing her to drag me—to my death no doubt, which would be the honorable course to choose. I glanced around the room to see if there was a shard of glass. Then I could cut her throat or mine. Where was a sword when you needed to fall on one? Or a vial of poison or a basket full of asps?

"Red!"

I shrugged and followed her out of the chamber with the eyes of other slaves lodged in my back like knives.

CHAPTER FOURTEEN

PEDISEQUA

The only thing that kept my first day from being as tedious as countless days to follow was the novelty. I might as well tell you about it, because then we can skip over days and weeks and months at a time. After the labor-intensive toilet, we enacted the fraudulent tableaux of the industrious matron in a room adjoining the antechamber where Appius Claudius spent the morning receiving his clients. He lolled in purple-trimmed splendor on a sumptuous couch cushioned not only by pillows but by his own rolls of fat. His crown of laurels—too small for his thick, bald head—was frequently rearranged by one of the pubescent boys who clustered around him, a phalanx of overgrown cupids. Although Berta claimed that she had serviced him standing on his head, I did not recognize him as a Vine and Fig Tree regular.

I did, however, know many of the men lining up to flatter, deal, or receive their private dole. Some of them stopped by to greet the lovely, virtuous young matron, but, to my initial surprise, none of them gave any indication that he remembered me. Considering that I'd given most of them blow jobs, you'd think the top of my fiery head alone would jog their memory. How could I be so forgettable? For a while I tried to tell myself that I was simply out of context for them, but there was no point in hiding from the truth. Unless they wanted something from me, I was just a brand x slave girl.

"Stop gaping at your betters," Paulina reprimanded me. "By Hestia, your thread is even more uneven than mine."

It wasn't true, but there was no point in arguing. Hestia help me, I might as well turn my attention to the spinning, get good enough at it so that I could lose myself in the rhythm of it, disappear into mindlessness.

As the clients thinned out, various slaves reported to Paulina. The social secretary, the courier, the chef, among others. They all pretended deference to her. And although Paulina was rude and capricious, she only played at giving orders. She wasn't really interested in the workings of her household, and her slaves had no intention of taking direction from her. Paulina, I realized, had no more power or responsibility than a child.

After some mid-morning refreshment, which she did not share with me, Paulina perked up. It was her favorite part of the day: shopping. She rode in a litter to the markets followed by six slaves, including me. When she alighted to bargain and haggle and pick over merchandise, we were there to carry her purchases: costly fabrics—so much for weaving her own cloth—make-up, exotic beauty treatments like asses' milk and Nile River mud packs, absurd hair ornaments, perfumes, and when we came to that part of the market, food delicacies such as pickled larks' tongues and jellied eels.

At the end of the morning, we headed for the women's baths where the leading matrons held the first century equivalent of a coffee klatch before resuming their duties as hostesses at the midday banquet. They all had half a dozen slaves with them, who waited in the foyer till they were needed to redo their mistress's hair and makeup. I hung back with the others, relieved to have a break from Paulina. But when she discovered I hadn't followed her, Paulina came back and yanked me by the hair (in the absence of a leash).

"You are to stay with me unless I dismiss you! Is that quite clear?"

None of the other matrons seemed to think it strange that Paulina wanted me in the bath with them. In fact, some of them had their own pets—eunuchs, little boys, and a couple of other women like me. You could tell us apart by our silence and our downcast eyes. Later I would understand that smart slaves, while appearing deaf, dumb, and blind, listen to every word. That first day the words just flapped over my head like so many birds. No, birds I might have paid attention to.

By the time we returned for the midday banquet, which was attended by at least half of the people who had fawned on Claudius that morning, I was exhausted, ravenous, and snappish as a wild beast. Paulina ordered me to sit by her feet while she reclined and sampled appetizers brought round by slaves—olives, cheeses, tiny meat pastries—that were not offered to me. Now and then Paulina tossed me a tidbit, which I stubbornly refused to touch. If I was to be an animal, I decided, I would not be a tame animal. I would not take something from her hand unless I took with it a part of her hand, a well-manicured finger or two. Almost as if she sensed my mood, Paulina dangled a pastry just under my nose as if daring me to lunge.

Then suddenly her whole body stiffened. She stuffed the morsel into her own mouth and rose from her couch.

"*Pater!*" she called out, hiding her hands behind her back like a guilty child caught sneaking a treat.

I peered around Paulina and saw a spare silver-haired man crossing the dining room. He did not smile upon seeing his daughter but held his face and body rigid—it was a wonder he could move at all; he looked as though nothing in him would bend.

I recognized him, I realized, not his face but his rigidity. I had held it in my arms. It had been like fucking a marble column. No, he had been lighter than that, for he had never trusted his weight to me. He had kept his body stiff and still, barely allowing himself to breathe, while I did all the work. Before he came (it had taken forever) he grunted as if he were trying to pass a hard stool, his face strained and purple, all the veins on his brow alarmingly engorged. "Don't worry," Succula said when I described him to her later. "He's not a regular; he only shows up once every couple of years."

Now in full command of himself, Publius Paulus greeted his daughter gravely, pecking her on both cheeks and sniffing as he did so. The original breath test. Overindulgence in wine was considered unseemly in women—another thing for which a husband or father could strangle a woman if he saw fit. Paulina, I noticed, was trembling.

"*Pater.*" The word came out almost as a whimper. "I'm so glad you could come."

"Thank you, *filia*," he answered formally. "I rejoice to find you in good health."

Then *Pater* got down to business. Without looking at me, he pointed in my direction. "What is *that*?"

Conversation had lulled. Only Appius Claudius was oblivious to the tension in the room as he brayed on and on recounting some tedious joke.

"She's my new slave, *Pater*. I'm training her to be my *pedisequa*. You said I could have her." Her flimsy attempt at defiance degenerated into wheedling almost instantly. "Remember? She's the one who insulted me at *domus* Anecius. I've disciplined her myself, and Appius Claudius made a speech about how important it was for the safety of all Roman citizens—"

"Be that as it may, *filia*," *Pater* firmly cut her off, "it is not seemly for a Roman Matron of an Old Republican Family to have a *pedisequa*. It is a modern degeneracy that encourages idleness and corruption among slaves. You must put her to work. Industry is what keeps a slave in order, what keeps a household in order, and what keeps a country in order. Send her to the kitchens at once. Let her scrub pots."

During this pompous speech I had kept my eyes lowered, modestly I thought, while I examined my nails. The paint from my last manicure at the Vine and Fig Tree was already chipping. Suddenly my hair was yanked, and my head snapped back.

"You stand when my father speaks."

I got to my feet and gave Publius Paulus a cool look. He did not return it, but Paulina caught it and slapped my face.

"*Filia*," said *Pater* sharply. "A public display of temper is no way to discipline a slave. You must be in command of yourself before you can command others."

"I'm sorry, *Pater*." To me she hissed, "Go to the kitchens, Red."

When I glanced back at her, she was almost crying.

"Sure thing, *domina*," I said, giddy with relief.

As I walked away I heard her gasp, but it had nothing to do with me or with *Pater*. A man had just entered the room. No doubt it was her favorite equestrian, the one for whom she had leapt into her red dress. He had a head of short black curls, the tanned, wind-toughened complexion of a man who's lived outdoors, an athlete's body. I had to pass him on the way out. The testosterone was wafting off his skin in long rolling waves. Paulina better recline again before one of those waves hit her right in the knees.

No one had told me where the kitchens were, so I just followed the first slave who left the dining room with an empty platter through a maze of twists and turns to the inferno of the kitchens. A couple of dozen slaves performed a multitude of tasks in assembly line fashion from raw ingredients to artfully arranged platters. Other slaves, Boca among them, turned meat roasting on a spit. She nodded when she saw me, but did not leave her task. In a small adjoining room, several slaves appeared to be having a meal of bread and olive paste. I recognized some of them from the *cubiculo* and asked if I could join them. No one greeted me or offered me food or even acknowledged my presence until, driven by hunger and anger, I sat down and helped myself to a hunk of bread. Suddenly all conversation ceased.

"Who is this?" a squat, unpleasant looking man demanded.

I was sick of people talking about me instead of to me, but my mouth was full of tough chewy bread, and I could not speak for myself.

"It's the *domina's* new *pedisequa*."

I recognized the speaker as the sarcastic chamber attendant—what was his name—Reginus? A strange name made of a word that did not exist—the masculine form for queen.

Everyone appraised me silently. The hostility was palpable.

"Hey," I said when I swallowed my bread. "It wasn't *my* idea."

"Oh," said one of the women, "was she the one who was—"

"—publicly beaten yesterday," I finished for her, hoping to make it abundantly clear that my association with Paulina had nothing to do with any allegiance to her.

No one asked me what I had done. Everyone knew that no reason was necessary for a punishment. Now that they had me pegged, no one spoke to me further; they seemed utterly lacking not only in kindness but curiosity. I made a couple more fruitless attempts to join in the talk; then I gave up and left without a word.

I found my way through a back door into a *cul de sac* with a drain where the water from washing was dumped. At least I was alone for a moment, and I could see a slab of chilly sky. As I looked up, a few small winter birds flew over, a flash of life and movement in this narrow, cheerless place. My prison. Who would save me as I had once saved the Hibernian women? Why couldn't I save myself? I sat down and closed my eyes, willing to shift into my bird shape, as I had once before when my life was in danger on the druid isle. But whatever power had come to me then, whatever grace, it could not find me here. I wrapped my arms around myself for warmth and slipped into a doze. The only release was sleep.

"Wake up, toots." A hand closed on my upper arm, not gently but without intent to hurt. "She wants you in the *cubiculo*. Pronto. I'll show you the way."

I rubbed my eyes, feeling groggy and disoriented. I started to get up, but my back, where I'd leaned against the wall, was still stiff and sore.

"Come on," said Reginus, and he helped me up, careful not to touch my back.

I followed a pace or two behind him, trying to memorize the turns and count the number of corridors and courtyards. If I was ever going to get out of here—or even survive here—I'd have to learn my way around, but high walls and right angles confounded my natural sense of direction that had been based on observation of light and water, the contours of land, the moss on rocks and trees.

When we reached a deserted atrium, Reginus dropped back beside me.

"Don't ask me why I'm doing this," he said in a low voice, looking around to make sure we weren't being watched. "I guess it's out of the goodness of my heartlessness. Trust me!" He held up his hand as if I'd protested, which I hadn't. "I don't have a heart. I cut it out myself a long time ago and ate it, because I was starving. I do have my balls, in case you were wondering about that. I just don't do it with women. The noble Publius Paulus, in whose house I served for many years, found my predilections disgusting—though I'm not quite sure why, considering the perpetual stick he has up his ass. He was going to sell me off to a bathhouse (dear gods, I wish he had; how have I offended you?) when it occurred to him I'd make the perfect *a cubiculo* for his would-be slut of a daughter. But forget my life story. Not that you asked. It's just that I hate to see those dumb, dazed animals in the beast shows that just wander into the arena and get slaughtered. A weakness of mine. But you get my drift."

His patter was a little hard to keep up with, but this image went home.

"You mean—"

"Enough said," he cut me off. "Now I'm going to explain some things to you this once. But don't look to me for help after this. I'm not your friend. I'm not anyone's friend. A few words to the wise, then you're on your own. Got it?"

"Got it."

"Everyone here, everyone you see is working for someone. The ones who like to play dirty and dangerous are working for more than one someone. The ones who are really good at the game have people reporting to them. They're information brokers."

That had been part of Bone's job description. I was not unfamiliar with the pettiness that was Rome.

"So?" I said. "What's that got to do with me?"

"Tell me you're not that stupid."

"I'm a stupid slut," I said with disinterest. "That's the general consensus."

"Play it that way if you want to." He shrugged. "It might work. Depending on who you're working for."

"What if I don't want to work for anyone?"

"Then you really are stupid. Listen, honey, in Rome everyone from emperor to the slave who empties the slops is out for himself. But no one belongs to himself."

There was that phrase again, that charged phrase. No one belongs to himself.

"The only power you have at all is how you play the game. You can be clever or you can be a fool. I'll give you a tip. Now that Decius Mundus is back, the stakes have gone up." Reginus was whispering now. "Appius Claudius still hasn't chosen an heir. The contenders are like buzzards around a wild beast show. You can be sure Claudius will play them for as long as he can, but it's a dangerous game—"

"Wait," I interrupted. "I don't get it. Isn't that the main reason he's married to Paulina—to get an heir? Why else would anyone marry a spoiled little harpy who—"

"Ssh!" Reginus put his hand over my mouth as we heard someone approach from the other direction. "You'll have to figure out the rest for yourself. Now drop behind me again, there's a good rookie slave."

When we got to the courtyard below Paulina's *cubiculo*, my guide stood aside and gestured for me to pass.

"You first," I said.

"I'm not going." He grinned, not a very nice grin, more like a leer. "Thanks to you, I get to have an afternoon with the boys at the bath."

"Thanks to me?"

"She's cleared everyone else out. Have a ball." He walked away, whistling so softly I could only hear him for a moment.

Here goes everything, I thought, and I mounted the stairs.

CHAPTER FIFTEEN

EQUALS

When I stepped into Paulina's *cubiculo*—for all its luxurious appointments still small and stinking of perfume and hair oil—I had a moment's false hope. She appeared to be asleep, sprawled on her couch, one arm under her head, the other under her breasts, her hand resting on the curve of her pubic bone. Her shift rode up her thighs stopping just short of where her hand lay, as if she had been lifting it and then thought better of it. Her bare legs were shapely, her feet slender with beautifully curved arches and well-tended toenails painted silver. Her elaborate hairdo had come undone, and her hair fanned out like the rays of a black sun. I studied her face, her lips moist and slightly parted, her eyelids twitching a little.

Then her breathing quickened, and I realized: no one sleeps that artfully. She knows I'm here. This is a test. The mistress spread out, seemingly vulnerable in her sleep; what will the slave do? I sat down, leaned against the wall, and narrowed my eyes to slits. If she was going to fake sleep, then I would, too. For quite a while we each regarded the other through a thicket of eyelashes.

"Red."

She gave up first. Score one for me. No, wait. I am not playing.

"Red." Her voice was plaintive when I didn't answer. "Don't make me cross. Look at me."

When I opened my eyes, she pulled up her shift the rest of the way, shifting her legs and parting her thighs to reveal her swollen, glistening sex.

"Now we're back where we started," Paulina said. "Only I'm not going to make a grab for you this time, and I don't think even you would be stupid enough to raise your hand to me again. Why should you? You're a whore. My whore. Mine. You know what to do. Do it."

I looked at Paulina spread out like an oversweet pastry on a baker's tray—one of those pornographic ones so common in the Subura. I wondered fleetingly how that dry, tight stick of a man could have spawned someone so round and lush. From an aesthetic point of view, she was lovely, near flawless. But nothing about her moved me. She was like a painted Roman statue, vibrant and vivid on the outside, cold stone underneath.

"And if I refuse," I said, "what then? More luncheon floggings? The salt mines? No, I know, you'll tell *Pater.*"

I saw a spasm of fury rip through her. If she'd been on her feet, she would have struck me, or plunged a knife into my heart. There was that much force in her for an instant. Then, just like that, it was gone. She crumpled, making herself small, pulling her knees up to her chest, hiding her face. Her shoulders shook, and I heard her sobbing—not loud theatrical sobs, but the kind you try to swallow. I stayed where I was, still wary. When the sobs subsided, she sat up, disheveled and puffy-eyed. I rummaged in a chest and found her a handkerchief.

"He won't let anyone," she said at last.

"Won't let anyone what?"

"Touch me."

"What do you mean? You're a married woman."

She shook her head. "Appius Claudius doesn't sleep with me."

"Ever?"

"Never. Not that I want that repulsive old satyr, but I can't have… I'm guarded all the time. I wasn't going to tell you, but…" She paused and looked away.

"Tell me what?"

"I'm a virgin."

Shit. I stared at this child-woman with her pouting lips, her sumptuous breasts, her little, wet twat now drying in the breeze.

"Please, Red."

She was almost meek. I couldn't take it. A virgin matron with a split personality.

"Can you do it…I mean, so no one will know? I mean…"

"So your hymen won't rupture?"

She nodded. Her eyes welled with tears again.

"Sure," I sighed, "I'm a pro."

Paulina was right about one thing. I did know what to do; I'd had plenty of experience at the Vine and Fig Tree with the other whores, though I'd never had a female client before. There wasn't much to it. Paulina just lay there with her eyes closed and received my ministrations. She did not touch me at all, except—typical of her—to yank my hair when she climaxed. One thing puzzled me, though. Not that I'd had experience of any woman's virginity but my own, but I couldn't see or feel her hymen. Had she been lying to me? I wouldn't put it past her, yet she had seemed genuinely concerned about preserving the evidence of her virginity, which was also odd, come to think if it.

Something smelled fishy, and it wasn't just Paulina's twat.

When it was over I sat back down on the floor while Paulina cooled, so to speak, re-congealed. If she were a man, and I was still a whore in the traditional sense, she would toss me a tip and leave. If she were my lover, we would lie in each other's arms and talk and drowse. But she was neither. I was stuck with her, and I had nowhere to go.

"Get me my *stola*," she said, sitting up. "Quickly, *stulta*."

Clearly she was giving me my cue. I was to act as if nothing had happened, as if she had not been a mass of quivering nerve-endings a few moments ago. I decided to see what would happen if I didn't get the hint.

"So, Paulina," I said handing her the *stola*, forgetting that she wouldn't have the slightest idea of what to do with it herself.

"What did you just call me!" She handed the *stola* back and stood up, gesturing for me to dress her.

"Oh, yeah, I forgot. *Domina*, delight of my eyes."

She bit her lip. To keep herself from laughing? It was hard to say. Clumsily I put the *stola* over her head. Neither of us knew what to do with her arms. The dresser was supposed to move them for her.

"So, *domina*," I said, fighting my own impulse to give in to hysterical laughter. "What in Hades is going on here?"

"I don't know what you mean."

We'd finally gotten her arms through. She sucked in her breath while I tied the ribbon under her breasts.

"I'll tell you what I mean."

"Fix my hair," she interrupted. "I suppose I'll have to hold the mirror myself."

She snapped her fingers as if she expected the mirror to jump into her hands. That's what slaves were for, to give their masters and mistresses the illusion that the world was at their command. I ignored her and began to brush her hair. After a moment she picked up the mirror herself. I didn't know a thing about dressing hair, but I enjoyed brushing Paulina's. It was thick as a horse's mane but softer; its texture made me think of water—smooth, almost cool. If I knew nothing about hair styling, I did know something about sex. I knew something Paulina didn't. That orgasm had blown her wide open; her petals hadn't folded back yet into a tight-fisted bud. She was relaxing into the sheer sensual pleasure of my hair brushing.

"All right," she said. "Tell me what you meant by your question while you still have a tongue."

"To begin with," I said not breaking the rhythm of my strokes, "why are you married to an old man who won't fuck you? I can understand why you wouldn't want to fuck him, but that doesn't usually cut any ice. Doesn't he want to get heirs by you? As repellent as you find him, don't you want children?" I fought to keep the wistfulness out of my voice. "I thought Roman matrons who produced three or more children got direct control of their property."

She pursed her lips, frowning at her reflection in the mirror.

"Why should I tell you any of that? You're just a slave."

"Yes, just a slave," I repeated. "Like all the other slaves who are watching and listening and whispering."

Her knuckles on the mirror's handle turned white. No doubt she would hurl it—what was another shattered mirror to her—but then she sighed, and all her muscles went slack.

"This mirror is too heavy. Just fix my hair, and I'll look afterwards."

"I don't know how to fix hair, *domina*. I'm not a *tontrix*."

"Just keep brushing it then. The other slaves will be back soon."

So I kept brushing; she leaned her head back, her face tired and childlike.

"My mother was very beautiful, they say." She spoke in a dreamy voice I'd never heard before. Suddenly I regretted asking anything. I didn't want her to trust me. I didn't want to be anything more to her than a mirror she could pick up, put down, or toss away. "My father caught her in bed with some equestrian. I think my father had him killed. My mother was sent into exile. I think," she lowered her voice, "My father would have killed her, too, but her family rescued her. They took her away. Far away."

"Did you ever see her again?"

"No. She died of a fever a few years later."

"How old were you when she went away?"

"Four. I can't remember her."

Her voice was a monotone.

"Then my sister," she went on in the same flat voice, unstoppable now, "my oldest sister, less than a year after she was married, she committed adultery with a senator's son. I thought that would be better than with a slave. I was still a child; I didn't understand. I was glad when I heard she was coming home, but then my father killed her. He strangled her."

My hands started to shake so I couldn't hold the brush. My stomach heaved into my throat. I got to the slop bucket just in time. My body knew before I did: The guilt-wracked man who had come to me at the Vine and Fig Tree had told me the same story; I had acted as confessor and priestess to her dead sister's lover. I had also serviced her hateful father. It was unbearable, I had to throw up, get it out of me, this knowledge, this contamination.

Paulina just sat there not moving, not speaking.

"Did I give you permission to stop brushing?" she demanded when I was done.

"Would you rather I had vomited into your hair?"

"You people have so little self control. It's disgusting. Now pick up the brush and get on with it. By Juno, it wasn't *your* sister."

My hands were still shaking as I went back to my task. I needed the soothing rhythm of the brush strokes more than she did now.

"My second sister—"

"I'm sorry I asked. Don't tell me any more."

"She died in childbirth," Paulina went on impervious. "She was a virtuous wife. My father adopted her son."

Someone should strangle Publius Paulus before he harmed another generation.

"He didn't want me to be married at all. There was an opening for a new vestal virgin. I was still young enough. Our family is ancient and distinguished. I had a good dowry. They should have taken me, but they chose someone else, someone from an upstart family. That was around the time my sister got caught with the senator's son. Those old virgin bitches probably sat around congratulating themselves on not choosing me. That's when the rumors started. The rumors of a family curse. Poor *Pater*. It wasn't his fault. All the bad blood comes from my mother's side."

I opened my mouth to loose a stream of invective against poor *Pater* the *filiacide*, but realized she could not and would not hear any criticism of her father. It was not the story she was wanted to tell herself.

"So even though I had a good dowry, I didn't get any marriage offers."

"What about Appius Claudius?"

"I'm not sure, but I think my father knows things about him that Claudius doesn't want anyone to know, things that could ruin him, maybe even get him thrown out of the Senate."

"So, let me get this straight." I couldn't hold back anymore. "Your noble *Pater,* of the ancient and distinguished family, is blackmailing that kinky sleaze ball into being your jailer."

I could not see her face but as I brushed her hair, I could feel the muscles of her face pulling her scalp forward as she frowned.

"You must not speak disrespectfully of *Pater,*" she stated, though I thought I detected just the slightest interrogative tilt in her tone. "I will not allow it."

"Fine," I said. "He's your father, not mine."

Thank the gods. Mine was at the bottom of the sea, at the back of my mind, at the treacherous shifting edges of memory. Not that Paulina had asked.

"*Pater* knows what is best for me," she droned on. "I may not love Claudius…"

Love? I'd never seen her so much as have a conversation with him.

"…but at least I have a place in society. I am a respectable Roman matron. I am restoring the honor of my family."

She was clearly speaking by rote, repeating what she had been taught, renewing her will to believe it. I said nothing; there was nothing I could say that would not be disrespectful of *Pater.* Then, without warning, Paulina's mood shifted again, and she buried her face in her hands.

I stood there, the brush suspended, my life suspended. How I longed for a sea wind, raw and bracing, how I longed for sky and the piercing cry of wild birds. Instead here I was in a place thick with human secrets and secretions.

"Red," she whispered, "I need someone to, someone—"

To love you, I finished silently. But I can't. I can't.

"—to be on my side. Someone who won't betray me. Someone I can trust."

There was that request again, the one she had made of me in the storeroom when I sat naked with my wounds exposed. I understood it better now, but I still didn't know how to answer her. Everyone is working for someone, Reginus had said. I could say, "Yes, trust me, Paulina," and get the goods on her easily. I could become an information broker. Who would buy her secrets? Some lackey of *Pater's*? Or Claudius's? Or that walking erection Decius Mundus? There would probably be plenty of takers.

"Red, I'm talking to you, Red. Can I trust you or not?"

"Trusting someone is always a risk," I said. "I don't know that I would trust a slave I'd bought through bullying and blackmail, one I had publicly beaten. I mean, think about it, Paulina. Why wouldn't I have every reason to spy on you and betray you?"

She was so nonplussed she didn't even notice that I called her Paulina.

"But you're mine," she almost whimpered. "I can kill you if I want to. I can make your life so miserable you'll wish you were dead."

"You can threaten me all you like. It makes no difference. I'm already miserable. I already wish I were dead. Listen, Paulina, I may be your *pedisequa*, but you can't buy or force loyalty. Why should anyone be on your side when you can order them beaten or killed or lop off a body part in a fit of pique? When you regularly throw tantrums and break mirrors, threaten to tattle to your precious *Pater*, and in every way behave like a petty tyrant and a spoiled brat? What do you expect? What are you *thinking*?"

Paulina making loud gasping noises, as if she couldn't get enough air in her pipes. I wondered if she were going to faint or have a fit. But instead she stood up, white-faced and blue-lipped, and turned to face me.

"How dare you, how dare you speak to me as if," she sputtered, "as if—"

"As if I were your equal? Because I am."

"What," she managed after a moment, "what on earth can you possibly mean?"

"Honey," I said, "we're both prisoners."

Before Paulina could figure out what to say or do next, we heard voices in the courtyard below, and then the sound of feet on the staircase.

The guard had returned.

CHAPTER SIXTEEN

THE LONGEST NIGHT

"Isis!"

I stand before the tawdry painted statue at the temple of Venus Obse-quens; only it's not the temple; it's Paulina's *cubiculo,* dark except for the coals in the brazier and filled with the breathing of wall-to-wall slaves.

"Isis, you have betrayed me."

"Then make your complaint, daughter, make it well, as the druids taught you."

She wants me to make a poem, this plaster and paint goddess who led me to the river and overturned my boat, who abandoned me to slavery.

Suddenly I have a sistrum in my hand; I am shaking a rhythm with it, the rhythm of birds' wings beating the sky, the rhythm of the river where it meets the tides of the sea. I hear my voice wailing. There are no words, but my voice dissolves the walls, and there is only light, bright, unbearable.

Then I am in a grove of trees, a dark grove, like the ones on Mona. I am drawn to one tree in particular—a massive tree it would take six men to ring, a tree with bark like the flow of water, the current of a river. Lodged in the hollow of the trunk with the tree growing all around it as if it were a wound, I see the coffin.

"How do I get him out?" I cry out. "How do I free him?"

As if in answer, my foster-father King Bran appears beside the tree. He gazes at me, and the leaves of the tree turn gold, not autumn gold, gold as the sun, as light itself.

"Ah, lass, we all want to be free."

He holds out his arms, but before I can reach him—

I woke up cold and cramped in Paulina's room. It was dark, but there was a particular quality to the cold and to my wakefulness that told me dawn was not far off. Wrapped in my cloak that doubled as a blanket, I went outside and sat down in a corner of the courtyard. It was colder away from the sleeping bodies, but I needed to be by myself. Those other bodies, however warm, were not my friends. There was no comfort in their nearness. The fierce, faraway stars seemed kindlier than my chamber mates, so I sat and looked up at them.

The dream left me aching with longing, but I welcomed it. It was the first dream I could remember since I had come to domus Claudii. If I only had my surface life as a slave, the same every day, flat and featureless, I might as well die. I would die. Underneath, even if I could only know it in sleep, there was a world of great dimension, of numinous trees, a loving king, and a story that was not over yet. Curiously, the dream had changed. In waking life, I felt more trapped than ever, but I had not dreamed of being bound by the riverweeds. I had dreamed of the tree—in Isis's story, she finds the coffin in a temple pillar. But for a Celt the grove is a temple.

"Hey," said a startled voice. My thoughts scattered and hid as someone entered the courtyard from the passageway. "What are you doing out here?"

"Who wants to know?" I was angry. My cold dawn sanctuary had been invaded.

"I do." I recognized Reginus's voice as he neared me.

"Leave me alone," I growled. "Or I'll tell Publius Paulus that you were absent without leave."

"'Atta, girl, Red," Reginus encouraged me, ignoring my threat. "Now you're catching on." He sat down next to me and huddled close for warmth. "I've been meaning to have a chat with you. This is too good a chance to pass up. And besides I've got a flask of wine, and some fresh baked bread, so be nice."

"Have a friend in the kitchen, do you?" I said, tearing off a hunk of bread. "Oh, I forgot. You don't have friends. You're screwing someone in the kitchen."

"That's right," he said amiably, and he passed me the flask.

"So what do you want with me, Reginus?"

"Idle curiosity. What have you done to the *domina*?"

"What do you mean?"

"She's different since you've been here."

"Different how?"

"She keeps looking to you, as if she wants your approval. I've never seen her do that with anyone but Publius Paulus."

"I don't know what you're talking about." I recoiled at the thought of having anything in common with that man. "She throws fits with me the same as she does with anyone else."

"But with you, she's watching for a reaction."

I shrugged. "What do you care, Reginus? Oh!" I suddenly got it. "Of course. You report on her to someone. Her father. You're his slave. Well, get this straight, I wouldn't pass on information to Publius Paulus about my worst enemy, which Paulina is. It may be your job description to tattle to him, but it's not mine. And if you want to keep those balls you're so proud of, don't try to weasel secrets out of me."

"My, my. Aren't we the savage Celt?"

I didn't even bother to say shut up.

"I'll tell you something, Red, in confidence—"

"Don't."

"You're wrong about me. I don't report to Publius Paulus. I—"

"Listen, Reginus," I stopped him, "if you're not trying to trick me, why are you telling me anything at all. What do you care about what I think of you?"

"The hell if I know!" He sounded genuinely perplexed. "Hey, if you want to work for the bitch, work for her. Just leave my balls alone, ok?"

There didn't seem to be much point in explaining to him that I wasn't working for anyone, that I wanted no part of this dismal place and its pecking order. It was all Reginus knew.

But I knew something else. At least in my dreams.

"Red!" It was Paulina, half-furious, half-panicked. "Where is Red?"

"Well," said Reginus, helping me to my feet. "I will say I don't envy you. Why I'm bothering with you, I don't know, but take it from me, Red, if you're working only for Paulina, you may be backing the wrong horse. If I were you, I'd hedge my bets."

I didn't ponder much over Reginus's hints, though I knew what he meant. Paulina was not a player. She had no power; she was just a pain. People with real power didn't have to beat up on their slaves; they had more interesting victims. Ambitious slaves did what they could to ally themselves with power. But I did not want to succeed as a slave—to succeed would be to concede that I was a slave, which, of course, outwardly I was. But in my heart, I still fiercely guarded my sovereignty, though I no longer knew if it existed.

The light waned toward the darkest time, and the cold grew bitter. Then Saturnalia began, days and days of nonstop partying. The festivities kept Paulina distracted and the chamber slaves frantically busy as she changed her clothes, hair, and makeup half a dozen times a day. Now and then Paulina took me with her to a banquet. More frequently she left me behind, specifically whenever she knew or feared that *pater* might also be attending.

Though a break from Paulina's demanding company was always a relief, those long nights were also lonely. I was homesick, more homesick than I had ever been in my years of exile. In the Holy Isles, winter was the time of storytelling and music. There was no storytelling at *domus* Claudius, only talebearing. The slaves who were not busy serving at banquets sat around the braziers in numb silence—too cold, wretched, or mistrustful to talk, at least when I was there, hopelessly tainted in everyone's eyes as the *domina's pedisequa*. Only Boca ever made me welcome in the kitchens, saving me scraps of food and making a place for me at the outskirts of the hearth where she hovered, barely sure of her own place. In return I defended her from cuffs and taunts. We were both at the bottom of the slave heap.

This time of year also stirred my sweetest memory. It was on the shortest day that Esus and I had become lovers. I was already five months gone with my father's child. But it hadn't mattered. When we made love on that grey, cold day under the yew trees, summer came in midwinter, and the air turned warm and golden all around us. But when the memory rose, as I went through my tedious day with Paulina, I pushed it down. I didn't want to expose it to the dead Roman air of the *insularium*, stale with perfume and the stinking breath of too many wretched people.

On the longest night, with Paulina away at the imperial festivities on the Palatine, I decided to go for a ramble through the *insularium*, despite Boca's hand wringing and head shaking. She considered it dangerous for a woman to walk the corridors and courtyards alone, but warrior witches had raised me, and I'd picked up a few more pointers from the whores at the Vine and Fig Tree.

The sky was extraordinarily clear, the stars so distinct that they appeared to dangle at different depths, this one nearer than that one, like fruit on a tree. I wanted to pluck one from the night, feel it burn on my hand, burst on my tongue. When I came to an atrium that appeared to be deserted, I lay down in the center of the courtyard, trying to see only sky, no walls, only the stars making their silent journey from east to west. Had he seen the same stars lying out on that hard, dry ground I had glimpsed in my vision? Did he ever think of me?

He thought I was dead. Joseph had said so. And no one knew where he was or if he was alive. Why had I dreamed of the coffin sealed in a tree? Don't let him be dead, I prayed to something. Or if he is dead, let me die, too.

The stars blurred, and I closed my eyes. It was so cold I could feel the tears stop and freeze on my cheeks. I knew I should get up, but it would be so easy not to. I could just slip away, out of this body that Paulina thought she owned. I could go, to the cold, to the stars, to the night. And not come back.

Sometimes temptation is like that, so distant and dreamy, you don't recognize it until it's too late.

I don't know what forces intervened, but just as the potentially deadly drowsiness overcame me, someone stumbled into the atrium, gave a loud belch followed by a long fart and the unmistakable sputtering hiss of piss on cold ground. I raised my head and saw the archetypal arc gleaming in the torchlight. Most people would not interpret a stream of urine as sign of divine intervention, but the sight recalled my first vision of my beloved. Before I ever shared the same ground with him, I beheld him across the worlds in the well of wisdom on Tir na mBan taking a leak in an alley. God has spoken. Selah.

The owner of this appendage gave it a shake and dropped his tunic. Only then did I look higher and recognize the handsome profile of Decius Mundus.

"Holy Isis!" I said out loud without meaning to.

He turned and saw me, a slave woman supine on the ground. Not a good position for self-defense, I realized. For a moment he scowled becomingly (he did pretty much everything becomingly). Who wants a witness when he's farting and pissing? Then he brightened. After all, I was only a slave. Unlike the male slave holding his torch for him, I presented certain possibilities.

"I think," he said, grinning, "that you would be more comfortable lying on my couch. Come along."

He snapped his fingers and began to walk away. Then he surprised me by turning back and helping me up. Pressing his hand on the small of my back, just above the swell of my buttocks, he guided me down a corridor in the direction of a raucous sounding party. I was still a bit dazed and had not determined what to do. Decius Mundus was a guest of Appius Claudius and a famous equestrian. I might have to think of a more subtle method of extrication than knee in the groin. Right now, frankly, welcoming the warmth of his body and cloak, I was putting up no resistance.

I could smell the fumes of wine, sweat, and musk before we even stepped into his room. Decius was giving a party for his buddies, all male, all drunkenly shooting craps. Though the game was clearly hot, my entrance caused a stir.

"Hey, Dec! I thought you were just taking a whiz? Where'd you find this?"

"She have any friends?"

"You gonna share, right? I haven't had any since—"

I sighed. I had entertained parties of drunken soldiers before but not without a lot of help from my sister whores. I glanced at the door. Decius's torchbearer or bodyguard, a hulk I didn't recognize, blocked the way effectively. Shit. Seven to one. Seven guys too drunk to come in a hurry. This would not be pretty.

"In your dreams, " Decius laughed. "This one is mine. I found her."

"Hey, what happened to that oath we swore? Remember, share and share alike."

"Yeah," said Decius. "What's yours is mine, and what's mine is mine."

I was practically drunk on the fumes. I could imagine how muzzy-headed the men must be. Decius, playing host, handed me a glass of wine.

"That's right!" someone shouted. "What's mine is mine and—"

"Naw, naw, that ain't it."

"I know, I know!" Another drunk lurched unsteadily to his feet. "Let's shoot for her."

"Yeah. Fair's fair." A chorus of assent.

"All right, boys." Decius threw up his hands. "Have it your way."

Then he caught my eye and winked, a gesture I interpreted to mean: Don't worry, whoever wins, I'm still in control. Was I reassured? Not hardly.

"Wait just a minute," I interrupted. The wine had hit my bloodstream like a spring flood when the snows melt. I could feel myself growing larger, bolder. "If y'all are gonna roll," (Don't ask me where the y'all comes from; in Latin, of course, I said vos.) "I'm gonna play, too."

This concept was apparently too complex for the soldiers to wrap their tiny sodden minds around. In a collective stupor they sat and scratched their heads, that is, the ones who weren't already scratching their balls.

"But I don't get it," one of them finally blurted out. "If you won, what would you win?"

"Myself," I said quietly; then louder, "myself, myself!"

There was a silence; I sensed they were all a little uneasy.

"Never heard of no woman playing craps," someone grumbled.

At the Vine and Fig Tree, the whores rolled the die whenever business was slow. But I did not think now was the time to mention my erstwhile profession.

"Well, fair's fair," Decius Mundus settled it.

So in Decius Mundus's small but elegant guest apartment, we crouched on the floor in a circle as if we were in an army barracks or camp and took turns casting the die. We each had three rolls, and a one in eight chance of winning. Better odds than I'd had in a while. Better odds than the soldiers knew. While I waited my turn, I could feel my hands growing hot. I held the smile that wanted to spread across my face inside.

When the die came to me, I acted cool, unconcerned, ignoring the breath of the men hovering too close and the laughter of the man who was winning—

so far. I rolled once. Surprised grunts. I rolled twice. Shock followed by held breaths. I rolled a third time.

"Shit!" exploded the man who had just lost to me. "That's fucking unbelievable."

"Believe it!" laughed Decius Mundus. "All right, everybody. Party's over. Clear out and you'll still have time to hit the brothels on the way home— those of you who have any money left."

It took awhile, but the room finally emptied of soldiers like the last glug, glug, glug of a flask of cheap wine. I waited, not wanting to leave in their company. When his guests had all gone, Decius draped himself alluringly on his couch. If my luck held, he would be out for the count in a minute. I glanced at the doorkeeper, a perfect slave, feigning indifference. Thanks to Reginus's tutelage, I knew better. My presence in Decius Mundus's apartment and everything that happened would be reported to the highest bidder in the information market.

I checked on Decius again; his eyes were mere slits. I would just go now, a stray slave woman waylaid by a drunken party. Nothing more. I headed for the door.

"What's your hurry? Where're you going?"

Decius roused himself, and the slave, who had been standing aside, moved again so that he completely blocked my way.

"I won, remember?"

"You won," he agreed. "So you can do what you want. Don't you want to stay awhile?"

Did I?

"Take a break, Fido." He sent his man away. "The woman will do as she pleases."

A man who respected a woman's sovereignty; that was more seductive to me than the way he lay back, shifting his leg to best display his pelvis, his arms open and resting on the couch, his whole posture inviting. A slow smile spread over his face as he took me in, starting at my feet and moving up, lingering on my thighs, belly, breasts, with a heat I could feel across the room, before he finally connected with my eyes. A hot look, a wind blowing from southern places. Yet as he held me in his gaze, something in me knew: he is no different from Paulina. He's looking at himself. I'm just a mirror. I'm supposed to reflect how irresistible he is, how unnecessary force is for a man like him.

I closed my eyes to shut him out. Inside I found a desert and a dreadful thirst. What did it matter? I could take a plunge with Decius Mundus, let him plunge in, bring down my juices, awaken my secret springs. Why should I wish for cold, distant stars when I could have hot stars exploding in my belly, my breasts, my head.

For a moment I saw the green gold light under the yews, felt the heat of my sudden summer with Esus. But he had left me. Long ago now. I'd been a whore. I'd had hundreds of men. What would one more matter?

"Come here," Decius groaned.

I opened my eyes. He was holding out his arms, his cock rising, making a comical tent out of his tunic. All I had to do was ease myself onto him. It would be easy, so easy.

Too easy, a tart voice inside me said. Way too damn easy. For him. To have a slave woman, send her off with dripping thighs back to her servitude. At the Vine and Fig Tree, men had at least paid for the privilege, and I had the means there to keep my womb plugged up tight. If I went to Decius now, we might both have pleasure. But only one of us would pay.

"Sorry, Dec," I said lightly. "Thanks for the offer. But not tonight."

The blood abandoned his cock and rushed to his face. That's it, I thought. Now he'll jump me. But he recovered quickly, too lazy, too tired, too generally pleased with himself to press me.

"Your loss," he shrugged.

Loss, yes, but not of Decius, though he might have provided a brief distraction.

"Wait," he said, as I turned to go. "I'll escort you. You shouldn't be wandering around alone at night, especially not during Saturnalia. If someone else had found you, it would have been a different story. Where are you quartered?"

"The *domina* Paulina's *cubiculo*."

"Ah." He sounded interested, though I couldn't see his face as we walked single file through a corridor. "That's why you look familiar."

He hadn't said so before.

"My title is *pedisequa*," I sighed.

"What were you doing on the other side of the *insularium*," he asked a trifle sharply; no doubt he brokered information like everyone else. "Her quarters are almost half a mile away."

"The *domina* was out," I said shortly. It was none of his business what I did or why.

"Ah, yes, on the Palatine."

"Were you there earlier?" I steered the conversation away from myself.

"I wasn't invited." He answered candidly, but for the first time his tone was serious, almost grim. "My rank's not high enough—yet."

"Yeah, mine isn't either."

"But you're a slave." He didn't catch my irony. His sense of humor evaporated when it came it himself.

"Listen, Dec." I turned around.

He collided with me and caught me against his chest. For all the wine fumes and the smoke from the brazier, he smelled like the outdoors to me, like the world beyond the walls. However vain he was, there was something so uncomplicated about him, simple. Refreshing in Rome. Maybe he was just stupid, but in that moment, I wanted the comfort of that simplicity so badly I almost wept.

"You can always change your mind," he murmured into my hair.

"I can find my own way from here." I gently pushed him away. "You know and I know, the walls have eyes and ears. It would not be cool if anyone saw me with you."

"Why not?" He was diverted from his lust. "Would it jeopardize my standing with Claudius in some way?"

Yes, it was all about him.

"It would jeopardize my standing."

"You have influence with Claudius?" he asked eagerly.

"I meant my standing with Paulina. If she found out I'd had you when she can't."

As soon as I spoke, I regretted it. Damn! I needed to work on my slave mentality. Never give away information. Never.

"Oh, ho!" Decius grasped the implications immediately; what mental acuity he had was entirely focused on advancing himself. "So that's the way the wind blows. And do you think the *domina* has much influence with her husband?"

"It all depends." I shrugged; ambiguity is all. "But if I were you I wouldn't breathe a word to Paulina about tonight."

"Right," he said.

I left him pondering insofar as he was capable of it. As I crossed the courtyard to Paulina's *cubiculo*, a gust of wind lifted my cloak. I felt my ass flapping in the breeze.

CHAPTER SEVENTEEN

TAKE ME THERE

You don't need to know much about the rest of the winter. It was cold and cramped, damp and wretched. Rain and sleet frequently confined us all to the *insularium*. Decius Mundus carried on a cautious flirtation with Paulina that kept her in a constant state of arousal that I was obliged to relieve. I did not see much of Decius as *Pater* dined at *domus* Claudius more often than not, and whenever *Pater* was there, I was banished to the kitchens. I would have thanked the gods for that respite, but I still wasn't speaking to them, specifically not to Isis, except in my dreams with their tantalizing snippets of her story—or mine.

The only other part of the day that gave me any relief was our late morning trip to the baths. The palatial buildings were the largest indoor space in Rome, cavernous, with ceilings so high birds nested on the ledges of pillars. Doves mostly. Their sound brought back my dream—if it was a dream—of the Temple of Jerusalem and Anna the prophetess sitting below the walls in the terraced garden surrounded by birds. Sometimes, weightless in the warm water, I could feel my dove form hovering over me just out of reach. If Isis was all sovereign, one of her titles, why couldn't she just pick me up in her hands and toss me lightly into the sky as Anna had in my dream?

As it turned out, it was in the baths that Isis reentered my life by way of idle gossip. The gods are like that; they will stoop to any means.

"Do you know what I heard?" said Agrippina Lucilla, as she did almost every day. A well-preserved older woman, with skillfully dyed hair, she knew everything and everyone, and her life centered on imparting her knowledge.

"I am sure you are going to tell us," said Faustina Gnaea, who liked to pretend indifference and even disapproval of rumor spreading, but subtly encouraged people to be indiscreet.

"Well, ladies, it's about Libo."

"Which Libo?" someone asked. "Scipius Libo Bassanius?"

Roman nomenclature was complex and burdensome, I found, worse than declaiming nine generations of lineage, and getting worse all the time as the Romans became more self-important.

"No, *cara*, Marcus Scribonius Libo Drusus."

"Well, what about him? He's always struck me as a bit of a nonentity."

"You can't call the great grandson of Pompey a nonentity," objected Agrippina.

"And isn't he related somehow to Scribonia, you know, the first wife of Augustus, when he was still called Octavian?"

"Grand nephew, I believe. But, my dear, that's not a connection to be mentioned in polite circles."

"That poor woman was maligned. Accused of moral perversity just because she objected to her husband's mistress. I ask you," said Maxima Fabia, a handsome woman who had managed to keep control of her own considerable wealth as well as her docile husband's.

"Well, it is perverse," pronounced Faustina. "A wife's duty is plain."

"Oh, yes," ventured Paulina. "She has to put up with her husband's adultery, but risk exile or death if she gets up to anything on her own."

There was an awkward silence. One or two women coughed discreetly. Everyone knew Paulina's appalling family history, and everyone speculated, behind her back of course, about the condition of her marriage and morals. But it didn't do to be too outspoken about your discontent.

"Yes, well, as I was saying," Agrippina resumed once everyone had registered Paulina's gaffe and stored it up to use against her, "I have it on good authority—and of course I am not at liberty of reveal my sources—that Libo is about to be appointed *Princeps Senatus*."

There were various gasps and exclamations. I was indifferent. What did I care who headed the Roman Senate. It would make no difference to the condition of the slaves who carried the senatorial class on their backs.

"Oh, now I know the one you mean," Paulina caught on. "I sat next to him at a Lupercalia banquet. He's cute."

There is no exact Latin equivalent for the word cute, but that was the sense. I was embarrassed for Paulina. I was *pedisequa* to a ditz. Then I was further horrified that I identified with her enough to wish she wouldn't be such an idiot. I didn't want to care.

"Are you quite sure, Agrippina?" said Faustina. "Apart from his ancestry, I don't see what he has to recommend him. The position requires age, experience, and of course, superior morals."

"There's something more here than meets the eye," quavered Drusilla Livilla, an old woman who seemed to be everyone's mother-in-law but no one's mother. She liked everyone to admire her perspicuity, though she didn't usually follow up her clichés with any actual observations.

"Well, I'll tell you one person who won't like it," said Fulvia, whose other names I couldn't remember. She was one of the younger wives, like Paulina.

"Whatever can you mean, Fulvia? Don't just hint about it," demanded Agrippina.

"Well, it's no secret. The Emperor."

"Why, what could he possibly have against Libo?"

"Don't you know?" said Maxima. "Libo is always running off to astrologers and dream interpreters. Too un-Roman, darling," she laughed. "Dear Tiberius," she paused so that everyone could catch the note of intimacy. "He does rather have a bee in his bonnet about foreign cults."

"But everyone consults astrologers," pointed out Agrippina. "Tiberius has his own astrologers on staff."

"But I have heard that Libo goes to extremes."

"We don't want extremists heading the Senate," croaked Drusilla. "Moderation in all things, as what's his name said."

"Libo doesn't just go to astrologers," said Maxima. "He has a scribe by his bed in case he wakes up and remembers a dream. I have heard he goes to a dream interpreter in Jew Town."

I remembered my beloved's story of Joseph sold by his brothers into Egypt who worked his way into the Egyptian elite with his astonishing ability to wrest messages from dreams. I began to pay more attention.

"I will admit that I have heard rumors—and I am sure they are just rumors." Faustina pretended reluctance. "I heard that he's involved with that *other* Egyptian cult."

"Honey," drawled Maxima. Only she would have the nerve to contradict Faustina. "Jews aren't Egyptians."

"I didn't say they were," snapped Faustina. "All I said was, I believe Libo has been seen in attendance at one of those primitive Egyptian rites in one of those illegal temples. I'm sure it can't be true. And you didn't hear it from me."

"Jews, Egyptians. They're all foreigners," Drusilla condemned them roundly. "They should all be shipped to Sardinia."

"You can't lump all foreigners together. It is really too ignorant of you," said Fulvia with some heat. "And speaking of primitive rites, what about our own Roman practices? What about the cult of Bona Dea?"

Here several *dominae* turned pinker than they already were from the heat of the *caldarium*. I had heard about Bona Dea from Succula. Twice a year the vestal virgins and society ladies honored their goddess in a drunken, ecstatic rite that culminated in the slaughtering of a sow. Men were strictly forbidden to attend, and when one snuck in, disguised as a female harpist, with the intention of debauching Caesar's wife, there was a great scandal. Caesar—at the time *Pontifex Maximus*—divorced the woman pronto and made his famous mealy-mouthed statement, "The wife of the high priest must be above reproach." Gag me.

"Jews, on the other hand," Fulvia went on earnestly, "are a very upright people. They don't get divorced at the drop of a hat. They buy each other out of slavery. They are loyal to their religion. They send money to their Temple in Jerusalem no matter where they are. They have a very sophisticated system of moral law—"

"Why, Fulvia!" Agrippina was shocked. "I declare you sound like a proselyte."

"If I am, I wouldn't be the only one." Fulvia was defiant. "You don't have to be a proselyte to admire the Jews. Lots of the better class of Romans keep the Jewish Sabbath and some of the dietary laws. I haven't eaten pork in a year. Pigs are dirty animals, if you think about it, scavengers. They eat anything. Ugh. That's one reason I can't abide the Bona Dea rites. The Jews have such a clean religion."

"Well, I never." Drusilla filled the awkward silence with another meaningless expression.

"You know," mused Maxima, "if I was going to convert to an oriental religion I would go with the Egyptians. Worship of Isis offers a woman a great many advantages. If you don't want to sleep with your husband, you can always say you're doing one of the purification rites. On the other hand, if you want to step out on your husband, you can say you're attending an all night ceremony."

"Maxima Fabia, that is a dreadful thing to say," said Faustina, "and for your sake, I am going to pretend I did not hear it."

Paulina, on the other hand, had taken in every word. Sitting next to her in the bath, I could feel her coming to attention like a dog about to fetch a dead duck.

"Faustina, dear, don't distress yourself. I am not speaking from experience—yet," Maxima added provocatively. "That's the reputation those temples have. They're like religious brothels."

"That is exactly why Tiberius is right to keep these temples out of the city. They corrupt the morals of decent Roman citizens."

It was hard sometimes to pretend not to hear. I wanted to snort.

"So, um, where do you find these temples?" asked Paulina. Goddess, she was transparent.

"There's a new temple being built outside the city walls near Campus Martius. My sister-in-law's cousin Cynthia is a patroness. I am sure she would not be involved in anything loose or immoral," said Fulvia the just. "Those are just nasty rumors."

"I suppose rumors are inevitable," said Maxima, "Whenever women have any power or influence, men say they are having orgies. I say, why fight it?"

"Bite your tongue, Maxima," said Agrippina. "That's not true at all. No one says that about the Vestal Virgins."

"Except at Bona Dea," Fulvia harped. "Well, so far as I know the morals of the Isaic priestesses are impeccable."

"Oh," sighed Paulina.

"That may be true of the new temples, but I have heard that the older ones," Maxima lowered her voice, "the illegal ones are a little more racy. The problem, as I see it, is that they attract members of the lower classes. I think it might be high time women of rank had their own temple of Isis. I may just look up your cousin-in-law, Fulvia."

"Sister-in-law's cousin," corrected Fulvia. "Do. I'm sure she'd be delighted."

"But where are they, the old temples?" Paulina persisted.

"Why, Paulina," cried Drusilla. "What would your poor long-suffering *Pater* say if he knew you were asking directions to a whores' haunt?"

As usual, the invocation of *Pater* shut her up. Temporarily.

"Take me there!" Paulina panted.

Her nails dug into my back, coils of my hair caught in her fingers. Ouch! Paulina's orgasms could be quite painful for me.

"Take me there!" she cried again.

"I just did," I said crossly, disentangling myself. "Three times in a row is enough."

Paulina was even more hot to trot than usual today, and I knew why. The damn moon was full again. She was ovulating—so was I, for that matter. And

Decius Mundus had attended the midday feast, while *Pater* had graced us with his rare absence. Lucky me, I had gotten to sit at Paulina's feet while Decius fawned on her and flirted with me behind her back (or attempted to). The air was so thick with hormones and pheromones, I swear, every now and then I had to put my head to the floor in order to be able to breathe.

"How about *you* taking *me* there?" I challenged her.

Of course it had never occurred to Paulina to reciprocate any more than it would to turn around and do her *tontrix's* hair. Which generally suited me fine. I could take care of myself with much less muss and fuss, but I wanted to bring her up short.

"How could I take you there, *stulta*! I have no idea where it is."

"Roughly the same place yours is."

I put one foot on the couch where she reclined and lifted my tunic to demonstrate.

She gawped at me for a moment. Of course she had seen me undressed before, living as intimately as we did, but a burning bush on full display is a wonder to behold, as even my beloved's god knew. That's how he got Moses's attention.

"Don't be silly, Red," she waved me away. "I don't have time for that, even if I had the inclination. I'm not a follower of that lewd woman who wrote in Greek."

"Sappho," I supplied, suddenly weary. "So what are you talking about?"

"The Temple of Isis, of course." She sat up full of post-orgasmic vigor. "The old one that Maxima was talking about. Where women meet their lovers. I want you to take me there."

"How would I know where it is?" And why would I take you? I added to myself. Instinctively I knew it would be a bad idea, a very bad idea.

"Red." Her voice had an edge, a reminder of the whip, not that I cared. "I know you know about it. That priestess, the one who lied for you that day you tried to escape, she obviously knew who you were or she wouldn't have taken a risk like that."

"Maybe she was just a kindly woman who tried and failed to save me from a fate worse than death."

Paulina narrowed her eyes, not quite sure of what I had just said, but suspecting the worst.

"Red, I am not asking you, I am telling you to take me to the Temple."

"I was only there once." The truth would suffice, I decided. "I don't know where it is. I haven't exactly had the run of the city."

"Think, Red, think. You must remember something."

"*Domina*, even if I knew exactly where it was, you know we would be followed. Someone would report to *Pater* within the hour. So why are we even having this conversation?"

The word *Pater* had its usual effect. Paulina looked like a frightened rabbit. I sat down on couch and relaxed, ready for the nap we supposedly took every afternoon. Then Paulina surprised me.

"Red," she said, gripping my shoulders and turning me towards her. "Listen to me. I will not be thwarted in everything. The men are away at the baths, and anyone left here is probably asleep. No one is expecting to see me for another two hours. Let's go now, Red. Please."

Please? Did that word change my mind? Or was it her unprecedented urge to assert her will against *Pater's* that persuaded me? For whatever reason, I relented.

"It's called the Temple of Venus Obsequens—otherwise known as the Venus of Whores and Adulterers. It's somewhere on the other side of Circus Maxiumus. That's all I know."

"Let's go!" She sprang from the couch naked, and held out her arms for her *stola*.

"Wait, if we're going, let's not be stupid about it. Why don't you wear my spare tunic and cover your head. Then you might be able to pass unrecognized."

"I? Dressed as a slave?" She seemed more incredulous than angry. "All right. I'll do it. Red, you better cover your head, too. Your hair is very conspicuous."

Half an hour later, two lower rank female slaves left *domus* Claudius by the west portico near the kitchens. Paulina had written a pass for us, just in case. But we didn't need it. The porter was snoozing. It was a mild day in late February, the first flies of the season awake and buzzing in and out of his open mouth.

Somnolent porter at west exit. I filed this information for future reference.

CHAPTER EIGHTEEN

WHORES AND ADULTERERS

P aulina, shed of her jewels, rich clothes, and ridiculous hairdo, all the trappings of her petty authority, was undergoing a transformation. She was positively giddy and could not stop laughing. The trouble was, I couldn't join her. Though I was younger than she was (by a year or so, anyway) and a slave, I felt weighted with responsibility for a reckless child. I resented her more with each step. Being impetuous was *my* prerogative. And damn it, now she'd taken that, too. Or that's how it felt.

"Shut up, Paulina!" I hissed at her as we turned into a more crowded street. "You'll draw attention to us. Slaves don't giggle."

"Why not?" Paulina gasped, still out of control.

"Because it's not funny to be a slave," I snapped. "Not funny at all."

"I think it is," she hiccuped. "I think it's hysterical."

"No, *you're* hysterical. And I'm going to smack you if you don't get a grip."

"You wouldn't dare!"

"Try me."

"I would have you flayed alive!" She followed up the threat with another burst of laughter.

"How you do harp on that," I said, and I pulled her into an alley.

"What are you doing, Red?"

"I want to make sure no one's following us."

I peered around the corner but could not detect anyone looking around to see where we'd gone.

"Oo, Red, this is so much fun."

"Come on."

But Paulina was leaning against the wall with her legs twisted together.

"Red." She was laughing so hard, she could barely breathe. "I'm about to piss myself."

"Not in my spare tunic you don't. Squat," I commanded.

"Oh, Red, I can't!"

"Over there." I pointed to the back of the alley. "Now. I'll stand guard."

Paulina was a little more sedate with her bladder empty, which was just as well, as we had to ask directions a couple of times before we finally found the temple, tucked away on its obscure side street.

"But this can't be it," Paulina protested as we stood before the entrance, the walls around it decorated with faded, lewd frescoes. "It's so small and unimpressive. And where are all the, you know—"

"The whores and adulterers? Well, *we're* here," I pointed out, but she didn't get the innuendo. "Let's go in. Maybe we'll find one of the priestesses."

"But it's dark in there and smelly."

Paulina was right. It startled me that she had noticed it before I had, the river smell—baked mud, river weeds, fish, a faint hint of the sea, of blood, a woman smell, moist and fecund.

"Come on." I took Paulina's hand and pulled her in after me, as, of course, she wanted me to.

I wasn't about to admit it to Paulina, but I was inclined to agree with her; the Temple of Isis, a.k.a. Venus of Whores and Adulterers, was a disappointment. If Paulina had anticipated orgiastic rites, I had wanted something more elusive: to hear the river singing in the dark, to see the flash of crescent horns, to receive some sign that I hadn't lost my way. Except for the hiss of the tapers, the temple was as silent as the statue of Isis. She was just a bit of plaster like so many other deities in Rome, dressed for the day in her worn and faded finery that matched the rest of her temple. Suddenly I couldn't bear it—that there was no more magic here or anywhere else in my life.

"That's it," I said to Paulina, not bothering to keep my voice to a reverent whisper. "Let's go."

As I turned away, I saw a motion at the edge of my vision. We must have disturbed some worshipper I hadn't noticed before in the dim light.

"Red? Red!"

The woman came forward.

"Succula!"

In two steps we were sobbing in each other's arms while Paulina looked on appalled.

"Oh, Red," said Succula when she could speak. "I thought I'd never see you again. Domitia Tertia wouldn't tell us where you went. She won't even tell Joseph. And now here you are. My sweet, sweet Isis has sent you back to me."

"She has done nothing of the kind!" broke in Paulina. "Now take your hands off my property this instant!"

"Who the hell are you?"

Succula turned on Paulina, who, you will remember, was dressed exactly as I was, devoid of emblems of rank. Before Paulina could answer, Succula recognized her.

"*Diobolare!*" Translation: two-bit whore.

Then Succula lunged for Paulina. If I hadn't caught her arms, Succula's long nails would have added some interest to Paulina's too perfect beauty.

"Succula, don't," I cautioned.

"Are you protecting this society bitch, Red?" Paulina had shrunk back against a temple column, no match for a feisty, street-wise whore. "Come on, Red. There're two of us. We can take her out."

"Yes, and we can be executed together or, if we're lucky, live happily ever after in the salt mines. Very romantic, I'm sure. And we can count on Berta to make us an immortal legend in the whores' baths. No, Succula. No, sweetheart."

Succula was weeping again. I held her against me.

"How could she, Red? How could Domitia Tertia have sold you to *her*?" Succula was suffering two losses, I realized.

"She had her reasons, Succula. It could have been worse," I said without much conviction.

"You're damn right it could have been worse." Paulina left the shelter of the pillar but took care to stay out of striking distance. "And don't you forget it. Now listen here you little *quadrantaria*—"

I had to restrain Succula again. Paulina had just gone her one better than *diabolare*. A *quandrantaria* did it for a crust of bread. Where had *Pater's* daughter learned such language?

"—your girlfriend here was a runaway slave. I know it. Domitia Tertia knows it. And if I choose, the *aedile* can know it, too. And he can also know that Domitia Tertia lied to protect her. I can ruin her anytime I want. Is that clear?"

Paulina didn't know it, but she had just done Succula a huge favor. She had absolved Domitia Tertia of any guilt for what had happened to me.

"Perfectly clear, *domina*," I answered. "I couldn't have said it better myself."

Paulina eyed me suspiciously as well she might.

"Come along then, Red. As for you," she said to Succula, "I hope you know that I could have you arrested, tried, convicted, and crucified for assault."

"She could," I added. "But she won't."

"How can you be so sure I won't?"

"Because," I took a step toward Paulina, "if you even think about doing anything that would harm anyone at the Vine and Fig Tree, I will see to it that *Pater* knows everything about you that I know. Is that clear?"

Paulina opened her mouth, then closed it several times, looking like one of the carp in the fountain at the Vine and Fig Tree.

"You bitch," she finally said. "That's blackmail."

"Yes," I agreed. "Now go relax against a pillar or go play in the court-yard till I finish visiting with my friend."

Paulina stared at me; her eyes welled with tears.

"But you're *my* friend." She sounded all of five years old. "Mine!"

"Paulina," I sighed. "We'll go in a minute."

Paulina went to pout by a pillar. I turned back to Succula.

"By Isis, Red, you have to put up with that every day?"

"And every night. I'm her *pedisequa*."

Succula scowled. "Is that some fancy word for lady's whore?"

"That's about it."

"Oh, Red, I can't stand it. I can't stand to think of you—"

"Then don't," I cut her off. "Tell me about everyone at the cat house."

So we talked for a time as if we were any two friends, catching up with each other, as if I would not be dragged back to my pen on a short leash.

"Red," whined Paulina from her pillar.

"I guess I've got to go. Please give my love to Berta and Dido, and Bone and Bonia and everyone and Olivia and—" A thought suddenly occurred to me and filled me with so much hope for a moment I started to tremble. "And if you see Joseph, tell him, tell him where I am."

Succula was silent for a moment. "Red, if Domitia Tertia wouldn't tell him, maybe I shouldn't. Maybe I should keep her secret."

I couldn't trust myself to speak.

"Oh, Red, why couldn't you have just stayed with us?"

"You heard Paulina. She blackmailed—"

"I don't mean that." I could hear the anger in Succula's voice. "You tried to run away. That wasn't Domitia Tertia's fault. It wasn't even the bitch's fault. It was yours."

"I had to go." I have to go, I added silently, I have to. Isis, hear me.

"Yeah and you really got somewhere. You're a whole lot closer to finding him than you were. *Him*. Always him," she said bitterly. "And now you're stuck with her. I hate that I love you."

But she put her arms around me anyway.

"Red!" Paulina cried in a panicked whisper.

I turned and saw why. Three women had just entered the temple. One was the priestess who had lied for me, as Paulina put it. She was flanked by women well known to Paulina: Maxima Fabia, who had expressed her admiration for Isis worship at the baths; the other I guessed to be Fulvia's relation Cynthia from the suburban temple. They seemed to be conferring about the *Navigium Isidis*, the goddess's spring festival—for among other things, Isis ruled the stars and the sea, and had invented navigation.

Paulina had flattened herself against the pillar and was frantically gesturing to me.

"I've got to get her out of here before those women see her," I said to Succula. "If word gets back to her father that she visited a disreputable place like this, she could be in big trouble. Publius Paulus," I added. "Remember him?"

"So? What do you care, Red? Why should you protect her?"

"Succula, do you want to ruin my career as a budding blackmailer? It's the only thing I've got going for me."

"Oh, all right, if you put it that way. Once those three are clear of the door, we'll flank her and hustle her out."

Paulina allowed herself to be peeled off the pillar and even accepted Succula as a shield. We were all three so intent on obscuring Paulina from view that we had forgotten about me. One of the blessings and curses of my life is that I stand out. I'm of a good height and robust frame—noticeable especially in the Mediterranean world where people tended to be smaller than the average Celt. I have breasts no one can ignore, and then there's the red hair. Though my head was covered, odd tendrils had escaped their confinement and flared out catching whatever light there was. The priestess must have seen me out of the corner of her eye. She excused herself, and then she stood before me.

"Welcome, *domina*, in the name of our goddess." There was no question that she was addressing me. "I rejoice to see you well again. We have been waiting for you."

Who was "we," I wondered. The priestess and Isis? Well, this was not the time for a theological question and answer session.

"Yes, well, thank you very much. For everything," I said, remembering I owed the woman my life. "I'd love to stay longer, but—"

"May we have the honor of an introduction?" Cynthia asked.

She and Maxima Fabia, perhaps noting the deference in the priestess's tone, had wandered over and now stood directly in front of us, blocking our way.

"Alas, *dominae*," I thought fast. "I have made a sacred vow to reveal my name to no one." Unless I want to, I added silently, hoping that would count with the gods.

"Why, how solemn and mysterious," said Maxima Fabia. "But there is something familiar about you. I will stay awake all night trying to remember where I've seen you."

Paulina started to shake all over.

"Perhaps she has come here seeking healing for her friend," said Cynthia kindly.

"Have you a fever, daughter?" The priestess placed her hand on Paulina's forehead and her mantle slipped back.

"Why Publia Paulina Claudii, what a surprise," said Maxima. "And, my dear, what *are* you wearing?"

Paulina was too flustered to answer. I considered explaining that her slaves had gotten together and decided to cut out her tongue, but I didn't think anyone would get it.

"She also has a secret vow," I improvised. "No one must know she was here."

"Especially not my father," Paulina blurted out.

She would definitely be better off as a mute.

"I see," said Maxima, and clearly she did. "Cynthia, you and Paulina know each other, I'm sure."

Pleasantries were exchanged.

"The priesthood at Venus Obsequens have graciously invited us to join in their procession to Ostia for the *Navigium*, since our temple isn't finished yet," Cynthia excused her own presence here. "Has Maxima told you about our new temple? Perhaps you would like to come and see the building one day next week."

I glanced at the priestess, who looked on with detached amusement as a potential benefactress was siphoned off under her nose.

"Excuse us for a moment," Maxima said to the priestess, and the three society bitches, as Succula would have called them, went into a huddle.

"I have to go, Red," Succula said. "I'm late. Will you be all right?" she asked as if there was anything either of us could do about it.

"Sure," I said, and she was gone, leaving me alone with the priestess.

She turned to look at me, and I looked back. Neither of us spoke, but there was no awkwardness in the wordlessness and no sense of heightened intimacy either. It was a strangely impersonal exchange. Restful, like sitting and gazing at water. Or having a cool drink when you're thirsty. I wasn't even surprised when I heard the sound of the river again. I closed my eyes. It was carrying me along. I could feel the movement.

"We need a healer at this temple."

I opened my eyes. Why did she have to call me back? What did she want? Why did everyone in Rome want something?

"Are you asking if I am a healer?"

"I know you are a healer."

"*Domina*, whether or not I am a healer, I am a slave."

"Slave or free, it makes no difference to Isis."

"Well, it makes a difference to me," I snapped. "You can tell your goddess I said so."

I knew I was being rude. To my surprise the priestess appeared to take no offense. She even smiled.

"Red!" Paulina called to me. "Come."

Instead of speaking, the priestess bowed her head to me. As I turned away, I thought I saw her making some sort of sign of blessing and protection.

Paulina said nothing until we were safely out of range of the Temple and the two matrons, who had likely blackmailed her into making a donation to their cause. She was in a pickle. If she didn't cough up, they'd make sure *Pater* heard about the escapade, and if she did, she would be hard pressed to hide the transaction, since her accountant was doubtless a spy. It was enough to put anyone in a bad mood. It was predictable that she'd take it out on me. Still, I wasn't prepared when she yanked my hair and twisted my neck. Before I could react, she smacked me across the face.

"What the fuck is wrong with you, Paulina!" I did not exactly turn the other cheek, but I believe I showed great restraint in not punching her out.

"Don't you dare call me Paulina ever, ever, ever again. I'm the *domina* here and don't you forget it."

"Get over it," was all I said.

But Paulina wouldn't. She grabbed my hair again.

"You disrespected me in front of that little whore bitch girlfriend of yours."

Enough was enough. I grabbed Paulina's hair with one hand, and held my fist to her face. But before I could do any damage, someone grabbed my arms from behind and pulled me away, and I had to be content with watching Paulina gape and turn bright red.

"Why Decius Mundus, I do declare," she gasped.

That's not an exact translation. We weren't in the ante-bellum South, after all. But Paulina was doing a fair imitation of Scarlett O'Hara. She even managed to flutter her eyelashes.

"*Domina!*" He breathed the word over the top of my head.

He really didn't need to be holding me quite as close as he was, but the joke was on him. He had created a little (actually a fairly big) problem for himself: his cock was standing firmly against my buttocks. As long as they were there, it wanted to be there. If he loosed me, Paulina might see his predicament before the blood retreated to more discreet locations.

"Are you unharmed, *domina*? Perhaps I misinterpreted the situation—"

"Oh, no, you didn't. And I thank you for saving me. I have been far too lax with her. But I think it's safe to let her go now."

"Er, if you're quite sure."

He didn't have much choice. I stepped aside and left him unshielded, his cock pointing straight at Paulina. If she noticed, she no doubt took it as homage to herself. She was also still extremely flustered to have Decius see her at such a disadvantage.

"Oh my, Decius, you must be wondering what on earth I'm doing in this part of town dressed this way."

A glance at the equestrian's face told me he hardly knew what she was talking about. Like many men, he didn't much notice clothes; he was too busy mentally stripping them away.

"You see, my *pedisequa* here had a vow to Isis, and I couldn't let her go alone, so I thought I would just disguise myself and…" Paulina trailed off vaguely aware that she wasn't making much sense.

"And pass unnoticed through the streets?" the gallant Decius came to her rescue, giving Paulina credit for my brilliant but obviously unsuccessful plan. "Very ingenious, *domina*. As it happens, I was just on the way to the temple of Isis myself."

"You, Decius?" Paulina was surprised. "Aren't you a follower of Mithras?"

"Naturally, as a man of battle, I am," agreed Decius. "But sailors tell me Isis rules the ships and the seas."

"Oh, I thought Neptune did that." Paulina looked confused. She didn't know anything about Isis except her alleged sympathies with unhappy wives.

"Who knows how the gods and goddesses sort things out?" Decius shrugged. "I would rather appeal to a goddess."

A slow, deliberate smile spread over his face. He bathed Paulina in his gaze as if she were the goddess to whom he made his appeal. Paulina was melting, her hard edges getting all soft and blurry.

"But what do you have to do with the sea?"

"Ah, *domina*, I am making a journey."

"No!" breathed Paulina.

"I was hoping to find an opportunity to speak alone with you." He took a step closer to her. "Already the goddess hears my prayers."

I backed further into the shadow of the wall. They had both forgotten me—or my presence didn't matter. I was a non-person.

"But where are you going, Decius? Why are you going?"

"There's trouble on the Parthian border. General Fullanus is taking a legion, and he is giving me a high-ranking post. I sail the length of the Mare Internum, and then go over land to the Euphrates. With my share of the spoils, I could make my fortune!"

Paulina looked completely blank, but I was reviewing my geography lessons. Decius would be going into the ancient land of my beloved's stories, to the fourth of the rivers that flowed from Eden. He might pass through Galilee, though more likely they would land further north in Antioch. Perhaps I could persuade Paulina to be a camp follower, since she had such a fascination with whores.

"Oh, but Decius!" Her voice quavered as it registered that he was leaving Rome.

"*Domina* dearest, don't you see? I can't keep hanging around Rome and its old men who sit on all the power and all the wealth that other people fight and sweat for." Here he clenched his teeth and his fists. "I'm a man and a soldier."

Oh, please, I thought. But Paulina was goggle-eyed.

"But Decius, everyone here admires you so. Why you're like a son to Claudius."

Could Paulina be smarter than I thought?

"Like a son," Decius repeated. "Like a son."

"And I believe that soon he's going to choose an heir."

"*Cara.*"

Paulina took a ragged breath. You could see her heart go pitter pat, making her breasts heave like unquiet seas.

"Claudius has been saying that for years. I can't wait anymore. He will respect me more if I make my own way. Surely it has occurred to him, and to you, that you may bear your own sons. You're young yet." He caressed her cheek.

Paulina shook her head; her eyes welled with tears, magnifying their luminous darkness. (Is this starting to read like a romance novel, or what? Sorry.

But what else is a narrator to do with Paulina?) Against my will, I started getting caught up in the story.

"Oh, Decius, Decius." Paulina flung her arms around him. "I can't stand it. Take me with you. Take me away with you."

Decius Mundus was one of those men possessed of a very smart body. He knew just how to hold Paulina, murmur to her without promising anything. He also had the instincts of the genuinely self-interested. When Paulina had quieted, he pressed his case.

"Claudius is an old man, and we are young. We have only to wait, and we can have… everything. Put in a good word for me when you can."

"Oh, Decius, I would do anything for you. Anything."

Oh, Isis, spare me.

"Then, dearest *domina*, wait for my return. Meanwhile, no one must know." He placed his finger on her lush, pouting lips. "About us."

And then he bent and grazed her lips with the barest kiss. Suddenly I was furious. I wanted to kick him in the balls, then knock him down, straddle him, and pummel his face. I knew full well his next stop after the temple would be a whorehouse. Then he'd be off on his goddamned adventures, fucking his brains out in every port along the way. Meanwhile, I'd be stuck with Paulina, who was practically swooning in his arms, scratching her itch and getting slapped for my pains. I could kill him—or her. Or myself. Or all three. It didn't much matter at the moment.

"*Domina*, I must leave you now. Will you find your way home safely?"

I suddenly came conveniently back into existence.

"Can I trust you with this…?" He looked confused, remembering that he knew me from somewhere. "I mean is everything all right?"

"Peachy," I said. Unless, of course, I succumbed to the urge to commit *dominacide* in some alley.

Paulina turned and looked at me in a daze. She might as well have had a frontal lobotomy. She had utterly forgotten my one-woman slave revolt. Her attention returned irresistibly to her hero.

"But will I see you again before you go, Decius?"

"I sail at dawn."

"I will pray to Isis for you every day."

I could almost pity Isis. Almost. There were a few more passionate embraces. Then Decius, looking rather desperate, thrust Paulina at me.

"Take care of my *domina* for me," he said to me.

He hurried away while I dragged Paulina, weeping and blowing kisses over her shoulder, in the opposite direction.

How could you do this to me, Isis, I demanded silently. How could you?

CHAPTER NINETEEN

TEMPUS FUGIT

I could not know it then, would not know it for a long time yet, but the seeds for my liberation were sown that day at the Temple of Isis a.k.a. Venus of Whores and Adulterers. There have always been people willing to plant trees whose fruit they will never taste, bless them, but I am not one of them by temperament. I sometimes wonder if the cause of strife between mortals and the gods doesn't have to do with timing—or with time itself. The gods don't get what time is, unless they are incarnate, and then three years—or three hours—can seem pretty long. This preamble is all to let you know we're going to skip over a couple of years now. Or fly over them, or fast forward. Pick your metaphor.

What essentials do you need to know about this flying time? (Note: This *tempus* did not *fugit* very fast when I was actually living through it.) Paulina became surreptitiously involved with the new temple of Isis. She contrived to make donations through Claudius's accounts. The society temple had a veneer of respectability, in any case—or at least it was fashionable. Seasons and celebrations came and went. Now and then I had brief encounters with my friends from the Vine and Fig Tree or with the priestess from the old temple, who seemed so sure of me as a healer-priestess that she was content to wait for my approach. I gradually became guarded friends with Reginus. Though he generally eschewed women, we would sometimes sleep together out of boredom or loneliness—not love making, just sexual release. Boca was my only other friend at *domus* Claudius. Paulina pined relentlessly after Decius. Being witness to their romance made me lock away my own longing. I did not want my loss to be in the same room with Paulina's. I shut down more and more in order to survive.

I heard nothing from Joseph. Either he was no longer in Rome or no one had told him where I was. Of course there was a third possibility. That he had thought better of further involvement with me. That he had found his renegade protégé happy somewhere, with or without the studious Mary, and had decided to leave well enough alone.

I still dreamed of my beloved from time to time. Sometimes I dreamed of the past. We were back under the yew trees, lost in each other, but never safe. My father was always there, lurking, as he had been in real life. Once I dreamed that Esus was with me in the falling-down cairn where I had given birth. When he held my daughter in his arms, she shone, living flame. I knew we'd have a girl, he said. We. It took me days to recover from that dream.

Other times I dreamed of him in a place I had never seen. A dry, stark, empty place of mountains pock-marked by caves. Sometimes I saw other men with him, all of them intent on prayers, chores, reading scrolls, or writing on parchment. His face looked closed. I could not see inside. I could not make him see me or hear me. I was simply not there.

More than once I dreamed of the tree, the tree in the dark grove, the tree with Osiris's coffin in its heart. In one dream, I opened the coffin to find no body inside, only sky, dawn sky full of fading stars.

In only one dream did we speak.

It starts with his feet, walking on dusty ground. Then there is another pair of feet walking beside him.

"I'm not dead," I point out. "See? Those are my feet."

"I never said you were," he answers crossly.

"Yes, you did. You said so to Joseph."

"No, Joseph said it."

"But you believed him," I accuse. "You were going to marry Mary."

"Do you want to argue or do you want to eat?"

Before I can speak, he feeds me something sweet. A ripe fig. I could still taste it when I woke up.

At first, I tried to persuade myself that the dreams must mean I would find him again. But the energy it took to maintain belief wore me out. In the end I just let the dreams come and go, let whatever bliss or pain they brought roll through me. I stopped plotting how to escape from Rome—its reach was just too far.

Time wears away hope, like water wears away rock. As for faith, I remained in a standoff with Isis. But love, as Paul of Tarsus was to say, is greater than hope and faith; it can survive without either. Love was all I had. And it would not go away; it would not die, even though sometimes I wished it would.

So the days and then years passed, and insidious fear began to make its incursions. That nothing would change, that I would grow old with Paulina, who was already a case of arrested development: not a wife, except legally, not a virgin, except technically, not mistress of her household, except in name. Not a mother, though I don't think she minded that except for the status sons might have given her. In short, she remained a child but without a child's innocence or appeal. Sometimes I could pity her, but I couldn't love her.

Paulina wasn't happy either, but we didn't know how to ease each other's grief. It seemed we were doomed. Both of us were too young to know: Nothing—and no one—lasts forever.

Pater died. Suddenly, or so it seemed. Actually he must have been concealing pain and illness for months. Prostate cancer would have been the diagnosis today.

Are you surprised by this development? Did you believe that I had set you up for some further drama with *Pater* and the one daughter who hadn't died or been killed off? Did you speculate that I might save her life or cause his downfall? That she would free me in gratitude? Don't worry. A person doesn't have to be alive to have a part in a story. You'll see.

Dear old, horrible old *Pater* died, and Paulina was undone. She was hysterical for days, shrieking, tearing her skin with her nails, refusing to eat or be dressed. At first people praised her for what they assumed was her devotion to her father and her extreme grief, but then they began to murmur that her display of emotion was excessive, which is to say, un-Roman. Claudius, who had now become her legal guardian as well as her husband—until her nephew came of age—called in a physician and had her heavily sedated so that she would be able to attend the funeral orations.

I knew her better than anyone else by this time. I had been with her since she received the news, and I suspected something no one else did. Paulina wasn't as much grief-stricken as terrified. If *Pater* had confined her, he had also defined her. She did not know where she was now or who. If you've lived all your life in a cage, and suddenly someone opens the door, chances are you'll cower in a corner.

It was *Pater's* will that finally propelled her. Or rather it wasn't *Pater's* will, but something *Pater's* will had not been able to circumvent. It seemed that Paulina's exiled and long dead mother, Sylvia, had accomplished a feat virtually impossible according to Roman law: she had kept a villa and considerable lands, given to her outright by her father, out of her husband's hands. As Paulina's legal guardian and keeper of the *manus*, Publius Paulus had administered the estate, but he had no power to dispose of it. According to standard Roman law, it should have gone to Paulina's nephew. But the Sylvani—a powerful, if suspiciously un-Roman family (too much old Etruscan blood)—had found some loophole or more likely bribed some official.

Pater had also left Paulina an ample income payable directly to Claudius as her guardian, enough to insure that Claudius would lose by divorcing her. But the villa, and any wealth generated by the surrounding lands, was under Paulina's direct control.

Paulina, who had never thought about where money came from or questioned anything that *Pater* did, was bewildered by the will. Many Romans went on summer retreats to the mountains or sea; some lived permanently at their villas, and only came to Rome on official business. Paulina had visited a number of her father's properties—but this one she had never known about, much less that it belonged to her. At first she didn't even want to think about it; she assumed Claudius would manage everything for her. But the Romans being Romans, with everything having to be written and documented, she could not dispose of it so easily.

Which gave me time to maneuver. I decided on a dramatic approach. During one of our siestas I began to pack.

"What are you doing, Red?" Paulina whined from her couch.

"Getting ready for our journey."

"What journey?"

"To your villa at Nemi."

"Who said anything about going to Nemi?"

"It's obvious. You have to go. Would you anger the gods by disrespecting the will of both your parents?"

She looked uncertain.

"But *Pater*— "

"Is dead," I reminded her. "Look. *Pater* kept the revenues from the estate in trust for you." He might have been a psychopath, I wanted to add, but as far as we know, he wasn't a crook. "He must have looked after it to some extent. And your mother gave you this villa. Now it's your job tend to it."

"My mother," she repeated without comprehension. "My mother."

"And Decius…" That got her attention. "When Decius comes back, do you want him to find you lying around with nothing to show for the time you've been apart? Or do you want to greet him as a woman of independent wealth and property?"

"Like a whore," she said dreamily. "Like Domitia Tertia."

"If you want to put it that way," I replied as I continued to pack.

And *tempus*, after sitting perched on *domus* Claudius for so long, spread its great dark wings and flew on ahead, settling in the branches of an ancient oak by a mountain lake where it waited for us to catch up.

REX NEMORENSIS

CHAPTER TWENTY

DIANA'S COUNTRY

I could breathe again. That's what it felt like to me. I know everyone breathes all the time without thinking about it. The reptilian brain takes care of it. We all eat, too, if we can. And if there's only stale bread and stagnant water, we'll swallow it willingly to stay alive. That's the way I had been breathing in Rome. Now, as the Appian Way took us further and further from Rome, my breathing became like feasting. The air had texture, scent, color—a blue that shimmered in my throat, the taste of things growing in dark dirt. And sound. I breathed in birdsong; I breathed in the whisper of the wind in trees. Even the sounds of our ridiculous over-burdened caravan—wagons creaking, slaves shouting—gave me pleasure. The human world seemed in the right scale: small.

I could breathe again. But breath brings more than bliss. Pain that I had numbed came alive again, too. Buried longing thrust toward light, as fiercely as green shoots in spring. Tears that had gone underground gathered and rose. Out of long habit, I found myself holding my breath again—or trying to. But it didn't want to be held back anymore. So, I let it out, a huge storm. If tears came with it, so be it.

"What is wrong with you, Red?" demanded Paulina, who had grown increasingly peevish as we jolted along in the carriage. "You can't be having your courses again so soon."

"*Domina,* I'm going to get out and walk for a while."

I had learned that if I made announcements rather than requests, she would sometimes forget her absolute authority. It was worth a try anyway.

"Don't be silly, Red! You can't get out of a moving carriage."

"Sure I can."

A fifty cart cavalcade, laden with clothes, jewels, even furniture, not to mention food, wine, oil, a full complement of slaves, did not move as fast as I could walk. I jumped out, landed neatly on my feet and was walking beside the carriage before Paulina could make any further objections. After a while, I stopped and untied my sandals; then I ran a few strides to catch up with Paulina and tossed the sandals into the carriage.

"Ow, Red! What are you doing?"

"Sorry, *domina*."

"Is this your way of assuring me that you're not going to run away?"

"Whatever," I said noncommittally.

Let Paulina think what she liked. She would anyway.

"You stay where I can see you, Red," said Paulina, sounding more like a frightened child than a demanding mistress.

Then for a blessed moment, I forgot about Paulina.

In a very different voice, the earth spoke to my feet, and my whole being was bent on listening. Beloved, the earth said, we were made for each other. I gazed down at my pale feet on the brown earth, brown like my beloved's feet. Then my eyes flooded and the world turned to water and fire. But I didn't need to see where I was going. The earth and my feet met like long lost lovers who could never get enough of each other.

The journey to the villa took two days. On the second day we left behind the planted fields and began to climb into the Alban Hills where the trees grew thicker, evergreen and oak. In early June, the mountain streams were running almost full spate, and the sound and scent of water were everywhere. It was all very fresh and pristine. God's country, you might have called it, but you would have been wrong. These wooded mountains with their clear, secluded pools, belonged to the goddess, Diana, to be specific. Paulina's modest little hundred-room villa perched on cliffs overlooking a crater lake carved into the side of the mountain. The lake was known as Diana's mirror.

I first saw the lake from the colonnade that ran the considerable length of the villa. I had wandered away while the other slaves scurried around attempting to give the appearance of obeying Paulina's erratic, sometimes contradictory, commands. The resident slaves were in fact taking direction from the steward while the Roman slaves looked to Reginus. I had no authority and was glad of it. So I stood, for as long as I could, watching the lake change color as the sun set.

"Red?" Paulina shrieked as she discovered my absence. "Red!"

I went inside the cavernous villa where dusk had already come. Instead of reproaching me, she just clutched my hand when she saw me.

"If I may be permitted, I will show the *domina* to her suite," said the steward.

We hadn't gone very far when Paulina stopped.

"Where are we going?" she asked the steward. "Aren't my rooms in the other wing?"

"Ah, the *domina* must be remembering the nursery." He coughed nervously.

I looked at her sharply. She had told me she'd never been here before.

"Begging your pardon, I hope I have done the right thing. We assumed you would prefer to occupy the master suite, the one the late Publius Paulus used when he visited. It is larger and nearer to the baths and the library. And the eastern wing isn't...that is, I hope you will find the master suite satisfactory."

I could sense Paulina wavering, debating whether or not to throw a hissy fit and refuse the arrangements that had been made. Then her hand began to tremble. There was something else going on here, more than bad temper.

"When were you here, *domina*?" I asked suddenly.

"I was never here," she snapped.

"I expect you would have been too young to remember, *domina*, you were—"

"I was never here."

That was an order, and both the steward and I knew it. Paulina did not have to make sense. She was the *domina*, and if she wanted to say day was night, it was no part of anyone's job description to contradict her.

"I will inspect the entire villa tomorrow," Paulina decided. "Show me to the rooms you have prepared. I hope you have not neglected to heat the baths."

"Do you think it's all right?" Paulina whispered to me.

We stood together on the threshold of a large, torchlit room, watching the slaves arrange the furniture and put clothes, jewels, makeup and unguents into various cabinets and chests. It would be a dark room even during the day; there were no windows, and an antechamber separated the master suite from the colonnade.

"It looks tidy and in good repair," I answered.

It was also surprisingly warm. I later learned that a duct from the nearby baths funneled heat into the bedroom—a luxury that had no doubt offended *Pater's* sense of Old Republican Virtue.

"I don't mean that," she said. "I mean is it all right to stay in *Pater's* room?"

Was she afraid of ghosts? Romans had a tendency to be fearful of the dead in a way quite alien to Celts. Our dead went off to the Summerland in the Isles of the Blest; they were too busy enjoying themselves to bother anyone.

"You are the *domina* here," I reminded her. "Everything you see is yours."

While we prepared for the bath, I tried to decode the story painted on the walls. In one panel, a half-naked man looked back in terror as he ran through a stylized forest. In another, a beautiful nymph sat at the foot of a waterfall, but despite her perfection, her expression was haunted, hunted. She reminded me of someone, but I couldn't place the resemblance. In a third scene a man with a bloody sword stood over another who lay crumpled at his feet. There was a tree in the background, an oak, massive and dark and yet somehow each leaf emanated light. *Like the tree in my dream.*

Maybe Paulina was right to wonder about sleeping in this room.

But sleep she did, or it might be more accurate to say that she passed out.

After the baths, which she complained about loudly—the caldarium wasn't hot enough, the dressing room was drafty, there were chipped or broken tiles here and there—Reginus gave her a rather savage massage, taking out on her his frustration at being exiled from Rome and the men's baths. Finally Paulina slapped him. I saw the villa slaves exchanging looks of dismay. The good old *domina*-less days were gone, and moreover they had to put up with the contempt of the Roman slaves, who looked down on them as crude rustics.

When she was fully dressed and made-up again, Paulina attended her own banquet for one, complete with Roman and rustic slaves pelting back and forth and getting in each other's way. Reginus elected himself wine steward, and saw to it that Paulina drank far more than she should. As he poured her a fifth unwatered cup, I tried to catch his eye

"Don't you think that's enough?" I suggested.

Reginus ignored me. What did he care? He wasn't the one she'd be sick all over.

"Shut up, Red," she slurred. "Sh'none of your business. Sh'none of anybody's bishness what I do. No one can tell on me. Theresh no one to tell."

Then she started laughing—it was not a pretty sound, one drunken *domina* laughing with indifferent slaves looking on until she got a violent case of the hiccups. I had to half-carry her to the toilet; then I wrestled her out of her clothes, with the help of two other slaves, and shoveled her into bed. As I looked down at her pretty, empty face, I suddenly felt her vulnerability in the pit of my stomach. Here she was in a remote mountain villa with some hundred assorted slaves, many of whom hated her, none of whom loved her. What was she thinking? What were any of us thinking in consenting to this bizarre, arbitrary order of master and slave?

I was too tired to figure it out. I left one taper burning, as Paulina preferred, and, like a good *pedisequa*, made a pallet for myself at the foot of her bed. No sooner was I settled than I found myself looking straight into the eyes of the nymph in the fresco. It was an unnerving encounter. In the almost darkness, her eyes seemed desperate, furtive. She was hiding something that she also wanted to reveal. She was pleading for help.

"Don't ask me," I heard myself speaking aloud. "I want nothing to do with it."

I shut my eyes, determined to go to sleep. Maybe I did for a while. When I woke up, the other slaves had returned from feasting on Paulina's leavings, and the chamber was full of their snores. I decided to get up and look out at the night, the wild, naked night uninterrupted by city walls and lights.

It was a dark night—the gibbous moon wouldn't rise till late—but very clear. I sat at the edge of the colonnade; there were gardens below and a wall around the whole villa, but not one that obscured my view. Stars outlined the mountains, and as I became oriented, I realized that there was some kind of light on the edge of the lake, a fire or maybe just a torch. Its reflection shimmered and shifted with the wind. On the way to the villa, we had passed a village populated by slaves who worked the terraced vineyards, and freemen who leased the land for raising swine or hunting. But the village nestled into the south-facing mountainside above the lake. This light on the shore shone all alone.

I was curious about this singular light surrounded by such unrelieved darkness. I wondered how long it would take to wind down the cliff path (if there was one) to the lake—not that it would be a wise thing to do on such a dark night. It would be too easy to find a fatal short cut.

And yet the impulse was hard to resist. Here I was with a huge, dark wilderness before me, and Paulina dead drunk inside the villa. I could just start walking, find a way over the wall, and never look back. And if I broke my neck or got devoured by wild beasts, who was there to care? It would be a way out, an honorable end. But I am not being entirely honest here; it wasn't a death wish that made the forest so compelling—it was a hope that I could not bear to acknowledge: that in the wood, among the great, breathing trees, my magic would come back to me.

When someone tapped my shoulder, I jumped and whirled around.

"It's only me," said Reginus.

"What do you mean by sneaking up on me like that? You startled me."

"I was testing your instincts," he said. "You flunked. You must have been a million miles away."

"Yeah. In my dreams."

"Me, too," Reginus sighed. "In my dreams I'm still in Rome. I've had a great afternoon at the baths, attended a raucous all-boys banquet. That old pervert Claudius has sated himself with someone else. And I'm free to end my day—or I should say my night—sleeping spoon style with Dmitri." His latest flame. "How 'bout you, Hot Twat?"

"Reginus, did you ever…" I hesitated; he was a Claudian spy, among other things, but he was also my only friend here. "Did you ever think about running? I mean just look." I gestured towards the mountains.

"Into *that*! That unbounded horror out there? Honey, no way. The very thought of it makes me want to shit myself. Don't you know how dangerous these trackless wastes are? Savage beasts. Uncouth ruffians. That is, if you saw anyone at all. But never mind that. You wouldn't get very far. Alive. Our lady of the unsated lust would have the dogs after you. So I'm gonna pretend I didn't hear what you just said, and I certainly didn't understand the implications."

"Of course you didn't," I agreed. "Your head is way too far up your ass to hear anything but your own digestion."

"Indigestion, you mean. I wouldn't call that old goat we were obliged to gnaw on digestible. If it was a goat—and I shudder to think what it was if it wasn't."

"So what are you doing out here, since you're clearly not contemplating escape?"

"Oh, your basic insomnia, aggravated by homesickness and lovesickness. Hey, you wanna do each other? It might help."

"Maybe," I said without much interest. I was more than homesick. I was heartsick. I was soulsick. I had been for years. Breathing the scent of the trees, of water, of the earth rich with season after season of leaf fall, I couldn't ignore my condition anymore. "Reginus, do you know what that light is down there?"

"That? Way down there?" He looked obligingly. "I think that's one of those whatchamacallits, eternal flame thingies, you know, tended by so-called virgins, like the eternal flame in the Temple of Vesta."

Reginus could be superstitious in the old Etruscan way—avoiding black cats, broken mirrors (hard to do around Paulina), always throwing spilled salt over his shoulder—but he wasn't much interested in religion

"So that's just another temple to Vesta?" I was disappointed. Vesta, Roman goddess of the hearth, had little to offer as far as I was concerned. I didn't care if Rome was sacked again. Too bad my people hadn't done a better job of it three hundred years ago.

"No, not Vesta. Diana, bloodthirsty bitch."

Diana. I remembered her from the fresco at Anecius's baths.

"Ssh, Reginus! If that's so, then we're in her woods. Show some respect."

"Well, it's true," he insisted, but he lowered his voice, as if that made a difference to the goddess. "Personally, I don't see how such things can be allowed to go on in any part of the Empire. We're supposed to be a civilized state." Reginus, slave though he was, identified himself as Roman. Like Succula, he'd never known any other place. "The divine Augustus—may he frolic among the immortals—outlawed it in the conquered territories."

"Outlawed what?" I pressed, though I was beginning to get an inkling.

"Human sacrifice, honey. You being a barbarian and all, maybe the idea doesn't shock you the way it does a nice Roman boy like me."

I may be a barbarian, I wanted to say, but I stopped a human sacrifice once. I hadn't had time to be shocked. I'd had to do something—melt shackles with my bare hands, steal horses. But I didn't want to reveal that part of my life to Reginus, even though—or perhaps because—that world of mystery, danger and fantastic power seemed closer tonight than it had in years.

"Are you telling me that they sacrifice people to Diana? Down there, by the lake?"

"Well, maybe it doesn't qualify as human sacrifice exactly, but as far as I'm concerned, it's the next thing to it."

"What do you mean?"

"There's a guy down there, the steward was telling me. Now maybe he's just trying to spook me, but I've heard the story from other people, too, back in Rome. This guy is down there, not where the light is tended by the pretty little virgins, but in the darkest, deepest part of that nasty wood. He's prowling around night and day with a sword. They call him *Rex Nemorensis.*"

The King of the Wood, I translated for myself, feeling the hairs rise on my arms and the back of the neck.

"Really he's just a runaway slave. But as long as he's got the title, and is guarding this big old mother tree, no one can take him back into slavery."

Guarding a tree, a huge tree. My dream rose in the dark, the tree with Osiris's coffin, the coffin that held the starry dawn.

"But there's a catch. He's king until some other fugitive breaks off a branch of his friggin' tree. Then they fight to the death. And as far as I can make it out, Diana gets off on it. She demands blood. Ugh. You won't catch me running around in those woods challenging any mangy, flea-bitten kings."

I almost laughed out loud at the image of Reginus as a contender for the title.

"But Reginus, bloody or not, I wouldn't call it human sacrifice—unless someone is chosen by sacred lot to be the challenger."

Of course, as I knew, sacred lots could be rigged, too.

"You're the expert." He shrugged. "What would you call it?"

"Single combat, a do or die battle for kingship."

"Well, I call it nuts. If you win, you lose. If you lose, you lose."

I wasn't so sure.

"Has there ever been a female *Rex Nemorensis*?" I asked.

"Listen, honey, don't get any ideas or I'll have the *domina* put you under house arrest. Promise me you won't do anything dumb."

"Well, it's a long time since I did any sword fighting," I said lightly. "I'm all out of practice."

I might not be qualified as a contender for the title, but I knew somehow I was going to have to find that tree.

"Come on, sweetie." Reginus put his arm around me. "You're dreaming on your feet. Let's curl up together and go to sleep."

And for the moment my longing for the wild and the wood, for risk and magic, seeped back under my skin. I leaned against Reginus, appreciating the sheer animal comfort of a friendly fellow mammal, someone close and familiar in the dark unbounded night.

And then we heard the scream.

CHAPTER TWENTY-ONE

OPEN-EYED DREAMS

The empty rooms amplified the sound. Another scream followed and another and another. When Reginus and I got to the master chamber, we found Paulina standing in the middle of the room still screeching. The other slaves were flattened against the wall; two were hiding under the couch. No one would go near Paulina, who continued a high-pitched wailing, her eyes wide but unfocused.

"She won't let us near her," one of the slaves said.

"I *won't* go near her," said another. "She's got an evil spirit in her."

"Come on, Reginus," I said, "help me."

When we tried to touch her, she began clawing and flailing without appearing to recognize us.

"All right, then, all right," I said more to myself than to Paulina.

She wasn't falling down or crashing into things or in any immediate danger of hurting herself. So I stood out of range of attack and waited for a clue.

"All of you," I said to the other chamber slaves, "go to the kitchens and fetch some food, warmed goats' milk and honey, bread. And bring a basin of hot water."

Ordinarily they might have resented taking orders from a *pedisequa*, but now they were only too happy to comply. They all fled, except for Reginus. I motioned for him to stand behind her, in case she needed restraining. Then I moved directly in front of her, placing myself between her and the fresco of the nymph.

"Paulina, Paulina."

I didn't shout to make myself heard over her screams but just kept speaking her name in a low, rhythmic voice, the way my mothers had taught me to do when we approached wild horses on Tir na mBan. In time, she began to quiet. If she were a horse, her ears would have shifted towards me. Since she was human, it was her eyes that found me. I don't think she knew me yet, but she saw me. I lifted my hand and held it out to her. She took in the gesture but appeared not to comprehend it. I kept my hand still. My arm began to ache, but at last she gave a deep sigh and moved towards me, her eyes closing. I thought she might collapse and signaled Reginus to be ready to catch her.

"Paulina," I said again.

She opened her eyes as if it took an immense effort, as if their lids were made of stone instead of skin.

"Red?"

"You're all right, Paulina. Let's get you back to bed."

She allowed me to put my arm around her and guide her. Once she was settled, she began to shake with more than cold.

"You, Red. Where were you?" She was awake enough to reproach me.

"I'm here now," I said.

When the other attendants came back, Reginus made a show of sniffing the milk and honey, cautiously testing it by dipping a finger and licking a drop before he nodded and handed it to me to hold to her lips. Reginus was savvier than I was; I hadn't thought to take this precaution, though poisonings were common in Rome, and many of the wealthy employed tasters. Of course, Reginus hadn't ingested enough to put him at risk. He merely wanted to signal to the other slaves, especially the rustics, that someone was paying attention. It wouldn't do anything for his brilliant career if the *domina* died on his watch.

After Paulina ate and drank a little, I bathed her feet in the basin of hot water, which seemed to dispel her chill. During all these ministrations, she was uncharacteristically quiet and docile.

"Sleep with me, Red," Paulina said, when the midnight snack was cleared away and all the attendants had settled down again. "Sleep in my bed. Don't get up again."

I got in next to her.

"Hold me, Red."

No one who hasn't been a slave or a servant can imagine what we had to do and be for our masters. To them we had no separate existence. We were appendages, arms, legs—brains, hearts. They asked of us what you should only ask of dogs or gods, unconditional love, no limits.

I put my arms around her.

"Stay with me, Red."

She sounded so young. What had she seen in that open-eyed dream? Where had she gone? And to what time?

"I'm here, Paulina."

She slept in my arms, soft and heavy as a child.

Paulina's usual morning temper was not improved by a hangover from too much unwatered wine followed by nightmares she could not remember. Or so she insisted when I asked her what she had dreamed. She flatly denied that she had stood in the middle of the room screaming.

"And what's more, I'm not getting up today," she announced to her chamber attendants. "No more pretending to spin while Claudius's clients come and peer down my *stola*. Now go away, everyone, and leave me alone."

She scrunched down in her bed and pulled the covers over her head to everyone's silent jubilation—especially mine. Beyond this dim chamber with its dismal frescos, the real world waited—sunlight, water, trees, rocks, birds, bees. Alive, alive. I was practically skipping out of the room.

"Except you, Red." A puffy eye peeked out of the covers. "You have to stay here in case I need anything."

"What you need," I snapped, "is a life."

I saw her hand groping around for something to throw, but she was too lazy to sit up and look for it. Then unexpectedly life, Paulina's to be exact, intervened. A nervous little villa slave stood and knocked at the entrance to the chamber.

"Go away!" Paulina snarled. "I expressly gave orders that no one is to disturb me. Anyone who bothers me again will be flayed alive."

The only thing that kept the slave from bolting was her buckling knees.

"Don't mind her," I gestured to the querulous lump in the bed. "She always says that. You can give me the message."

"It's just that I thought the *domina* would want to know. The clients are waiting. Many of them have been here since sun-up. Please, what am I to tell them?"

"What clients?" Paulina's head emerged from under the covers. "Claudius isn't here, and *Pater*...." Her voice wobbled to a stop.

"They're *your* clients, Paulina," I said

"From the village, *domina*, and the temple," added the villa slave uncertainly.

More of Paulina appeared, and she propped herself up on her elbow.

"But I'm not—"

"You are now," I pointed out.

For a moment, Paulina looked thoroughly disoriented. But she found her direction—and started giving directions—with impressive swiftness.

"Tell them to wait," she told the messenger. "I will come presently. And serve them some wine—water it well—and some bread and cheese, figs and olives. And send the chamber slaves to me. I will dress at once."

"Yes, *domina*." The slave bowed and scampered away.

"You." She still had her annoying habit of speaking to me as if I were a nameless minion. "Don't just stand there. Fetch me a *stola*—the dark blue with gold trim."

Seeing her receive her clients that morning, no one could have guessed that she had never done more than spin and shop, bathe and banquet, that she had administered nothing but cuffs and slaps, never so much as decided on a menu, didn't know how to read a household account. Reginus and I exchanged glances, reluctantly impressed. Paulina received everyone graciously, appeared appreciative of condolences, and listened gravely to concerns without promising anything. She invited several people to dine with her and discreetly opened her purse now and then. She seemed perfectly at her ease until, near the end of the audience, a lone woman came forward.

I don't know what it is about priestesses. You can always tell. Or at least I can. I suppose it's like people who have gone to Catholic school always being able to spot a nun, in or out of a habit. Having been schooled and scolded by priestesses, I knew a woman in authority when I saw one. Most women, now and then, concern themselves to some degree with pleasing men or people in general. Priestesses don't. They have bigger game. Their eyes show it, watchful, weathered eyes that scan the skies for storms or auguries, eyes that can narrow and focus on human foibles, the way an eagle can see from a mile above when a fish leaps or a mouse twitches its whisker. The priestess was looking at Paulina that way, keenly, from some remote place.

"Egeria, high priestess of Diana from the Temple at Nemi," the steward announced.

Robed in a short tunic, with a ceremonial bow and quiver of arrows strapped to her left shoulder, the priestess bowed her head, and I saw the strands of grey in her hair. Otherwise the woman showed no age. That's another thing I've noticed about priestesses—unless they are very young or ancient, you can never tell how old they are.

"Welcome to Nemi, Paulina, daughter of Valeria Sylvia of the Sylvani."

I glanced at Paulina. Her jaw tightened, and a nervous twitch seized the muscles around her left eye.

"How dare you." Paulina barely breathed the words.

The priestess gazed at her without expression—or human expression. Again she was birdlike, an owl, perhaps, unblinking. She had Paulina in her sights. Don't move, I almost wanted to warn her.

"I said, how dare you! Answer me at once."

"Pardon, *domina*. I do not know how I have offended."

"You have greeted me as the daughter of one whose name was banished with her person by my late and beloved father, Publius Paulus."

Paulina seemed to have forgotten for the moment that she was reclining in the villa the banished one had bequeathed to her.

"I offer you condolences on the death of Publius Paulus, but you are Sylvia's daughter whether you will name her or not. You have the look of her. I knew her well."

"Well, I didn't!" The composure Paulina had displayed was wearing out; her lower lip stuck out in her habitual pout. "Anyway, I don't suppose you have come to prate of my ancestry. What do you want?"

"Very well. I will not waste your time or mine with meaningless pleasantries. I have come for the bequest your mother left to the Temple. It has never been paid."

"I know nothing about it. My father never mentioned it to me."

"How would he, if he never spoke your mother's name?" The priestess shot back. "Nevertheless the bequest exists. In his otherwise faultless administration of your mother's estate, Publius Paulus failed to honor this bequest."

"You are mistaken. My father honored his duty in all things."

Her words were confident, but her tone wavered. The priestess could hear it, too.

"Publius Paulus was a man." The priestess spoke carefully with a surprising gentleness.

"Your point?" Paulina said when the priestess did not continue.

And sometimes men fail, I answered silently. Sometimes they don't forgive. Sometimes what you see is only the bright surface of something cold and deep.

"What is done is done. What is undone is still undone. For whatever reason." The priestess sidestepped the question of Publius Paulus's honor. Priestesses could be very practical, especially when it came to money. Whatever she thought of the man, Paulina was the one who mattered now. "If the *domina* will be so kind as to come to the Temple record rooms at her convenience, we can show her the written record of the bequest made by her mother, Valeria Sylvia, for the sustenance in perpetuity of the *Rex Nemorensis*."

The King of the Wood. The fine hairs at the base of my scalp rose. I looked at Paulina to see if the words had any effect on her. Her face was closed, as if someone had fastened all the shutters; you couldn't know if anyone was inside peering out.

"You will leave now," she informed the priestess.

I had never heard her voice so quiet and contained, deadly—just like *Pater's*.

This round was over; the priestess knew it, and she knew that it would be better for her cause in the long run to acknowledge that Paulina had won this time. She let the silence lengthen for a few dangerous heartbeats, and then she bowed.

"As the *domina* wishes. Until we meet again, the blessings of Diana, the peace of her grove."

Peace. I wondered about that.

There was certainly no peace in the villa that day. Now that she was up, Paulina was running. She planned an elaborate mid-day menu and dispatched slaves to find the impossibly rare ingredients. Then she conducted her threatened inspection of the villa, which took the rest of the morning. Of course, I had to go with her. She didn't slow down or stop giving orders to the dwindling army of slaves that trailed her until we came to the last series of rooms at the easternmost end of the villa.

Unlike the rest of the property, which was moderately well-kept, this part had been allowed to fall into a disrepair that was close to ruin—fallen or rotten doors and shutters, weeds cracking the paving stone. The rooms, ranged on three sides around an atrium that opened onto the colonnade, had plenty of windows. In the early morning the place would have been bright and cheerful. Now, with the sun near its height, the interiors were shadowed, and the atrium—which no longer had any living trees—was hot and exposed. A fountain slept dry with dead leaves obscuring the mosaics. There were statues draped in heavy cloth to protect them from the weather, and the frescos of Diana and nymphs cavorting with their animal friends were chipped and faded.

Paulina wandered slowly and silently in and out of the rooms. She did not walk with her usual arrogant saunter, but almost tiptoed. The remaining slaves hovered uncertainly in the atrium waiting for the other sandal to drop, so to speak. In one of the smaller chambers, Paulina stood still for a long time. When I went to see what held her attention, I found her in front of a fresco: the same nymph and the same waterfall as the one in the master bedroom. The expression on her face here was different, laughing, almost mocking—but not cruelly. The fond, teasing look you might give a lover or a beloved child.

"What is the story of this nymph?" I asked Paulina. "Do you know?"

"No," she said abruptly, and as Paulina turned away, I glimpsed the other face of the nymph, the haunted, furtive face.

"Oh!" I said out loud, but Paulina had already gone ahead of me out of the room.

"Who is responsible for this negligence?" she demanded.

No one answered.

"Don't think to spare him or yourselves. I will find out."

"Begging your pardon, *domina*, but it was your late lamented father, Publius Paulus—"

"Enough!" She advanced on the slave. "Do not sully my father's name with your worthless tongue again, or I will rip it out. Listen, all of you. In one month's time, I will be entertaining a large party from Rome. I want this wing repaired and restored at once. The fountain must be flowing. There must be a lush garden flourishing. The frescos must be refurbished—except for the one in that room. Leave that one alone. Is that clear?"

We walked back along the colonnade, because it was the quickest route from one end of the villa to the other. Paulina walked so briskly I could barely keep up with her. She was clearly in no mood for the questions I wanted to ask, so I paused now and then to look at the lake. Today I noticed that it was shaped like an eye, or like a vulva—they are the same shape, really, those openings to the body's mysteries. The water was dark and bright at once—also like an eye. Or maybe it depended on our own eyes, whether we saw light and sky or the darkness of the grove in Diana's mirror. The wild goddess who both hunted and protected animals, who helped women in childbirth and killed men who trespassed without a qualm. The fierce goddess who soaked up the blood of the vanquished *Rex Nemorensis*.

"Quit dawdling, Red," Paulina shouted at me over her shoulder.

She kept walking, angrily, like a grownup with no time for children or childish things. She walked as fast as she could without breaking into a run.

The banquet went well enough. Fortunately Paulina was too flushed with wine and with her success as a hostess to notice the discrepancy between the food that was actually served and the fanciful menu she had ordered. I sat at her feet, as usual, eating freely of food that was simple and tasty (despite Reginus's complaints) and adding water to her wine whenever she wasn't looking. Perhaps, I thought, letting down my guard as I drank my own wine, we were in for a jolly holiday, after all. No *Pater* to cast a pall over everything, Paulina with new interests to keep her occupied, and me with gardens and woods waiting to be explored.

But when we retired to the perpetual gloom of the master chamber, Paulina lurched around the room, drunker than I had thought. She should have been exhausted after the restless night and busy morning, yet she seemed agitated, unable to settle.

"Come on, Paulina. Let me help you out of your *stola*." As usual during the post- banquet rest hour, I was her only attendant.

"No." She was belligerent. "You take off your clothes. Take off your clothes and lie down. Now."

I sighed. I supposed the wine and the fawning attentions of her male guests had made her randy. Maybe she'd take a lover while we were here, and I'd be off the hook.

"I said, lie down, slut." She stumbled into a chest and barely kept herself upright.

Suddenly I was wary. Even when she was tipsy and amorous, she didn't much care whether my clothes were on or off as long as I serviced her.

"Lie down and spread your legs."

"Why do you want me to?" I played for time; something was not right here.

"Want to see what men see. Want to do what men do."

I considered my options. I could refuse and risk a drunken rage. No big deal. Or I could comply and hope that as soon as she lay down she'd be out for the count. She didn't look well. Her eyes were glazed and her temples were beaded with sweat.

"Do as I say. You have to obey me."

I didn't have to obey her, I told myself. Yet I felt afraid, not of Paulina, but of something else, something I couldn't name as I found myself slipping out of my tunic and lying down naked before her. Of all the times I had taken this pose, I had never before felt so exposed. She stared at me, at my secret blind eye, with what felt like hatred.

"Slut, little slut." She came closer until she stood swaying over me. "Wider!" She grabbed my knees and pulled them apart. "Wider! Lie still!" I hadn't moved. "I said lie still, you little bitch."

She lifted her hand as if to slap me, but instead of hitting my face, she brought it down between my legs. With her other hand, and both her knees, she pinned me down. Ordinarily her strength would have been no match for mine, but there was a fury in her that I felt helpless to counter.

"You are a whore and the daughter of a whore." She spread the lips of my vulva and rammed her hand in. "You will take this now, and she will see what she has done, what she has made with her stinking, filthy whoring ways."

The part of me that could reason went away, leaving behind a terrified child shadowed by a huge beast who tore her open, its terrible claw reaching for her insides, in and out, in and out. Hurting. A monster who'd stolen her father's face. She squeezed her eyes shut, but the darkness was bad, throbbing with the wet, swollen heat of shame. Then a hand came over her nose and mouth. She couldn't breathe.

Thrashing and gasping, I fought free, the last throes of a painful orgasm shuddering through me.

"Red?" a voice said. "Red?"

There was Paulina looking disheveled and panicked, as if she had just woken up and could not remember where she was.

"Red, you're crying." She put her hand on my cheek. "Who hurt you? Why are you crying?"

Until she'd asked, I hadn't known that I was. Then a big sob tore loose—from her or me, I couldn't tell, for suddenly she was crying, too. Then she flung herself into my arms, and we both cried, without comprehension, until we slept.

CHAPTER TWENTY-TWO

SLEUTH

But not long afterwards, as soon as I recovered from the initial shock of her assault on me, I did comprehend—or I began to. I understood, as you must, what *Pater* had done to Paulina. I had *been* Paulina, the terrified child she refused to acknowledge. I knew in my own body the memories locked in hers. That much was clear to me. But why? That part was harder to grasp, and it made me uneasy. Some mystery of my own was playing itself out, sounding and resounding its theme. Have you ever noticed that the deepest wounds of your life resurface, taking subtly different forms? Or maybe it's not the wound that changes but our relation to it. I had been a helpless girl when my father had raped me. I suspected that I could now have a different role. If I chose. If I *chose*?

On this point I was confused—and angry. Not with Paulina, not even with her horrible father or mine—deranged, murderous wretches, both of them. Like a priestess (did I just say that?) I was after bigger game. Life itself, the gods, the way they use us, take our lives and stories and turn them to their own ends. Did I really have a choice? If so, when did I make it? I wanted my father to love me, not to rape me, get me with a child I couldn't keep, and try to kill me. I wanted to be in Galilee feasting with my lover, not enslaved to Paulina. And that fearful moment, when I became the child Paulina, knew what she knew, felt what she felt—had I chosen that? Did I have any choice in the exercise of this gift for taking on another's pain? If it was a gift.

I didn't know the answers, but I entertained the questions, like frequent dinner guests. Hell, they moved in and set up housekeeping. Questions do that sometimes, and then your only choice is whether or not to be a good host. Of course, the villa was huge, and there was plenty of room for all the questions—especially in the east wing.

Without quite realizing it at first, I hit upon a role for myself: sleuth.

I soon gave up my attempts to confront or question Paulina about what had happened between us. The most she would allow was that maybe (*maybe?*) she'd had a little too much wine. I should get over it. Subject closed. I decided it would be more fruitful, in any case, to do a little private investigating. Here Paulina became my unwitting accomplice. Though she still woke screaming most nights and clung to me like the desperate child she was, she put increasing distance between us during the day.

It was partly that she was busier than she had ever been and did not need me for company or diversion. She received clients, planned menus and entertainments for her daily and nightly guests, went over accounts, directed renovations, and planned endlessly for an elaborate house party in August when she intended to fill all the rooms by welcoming half of Roman society. In all these matters, especially the party, Reginus was her right hand, even more, her chum. The pair of them gossiped and argued over the guest list—who should be included, who subtly or ostentatiously snubbed. When there was nothing else to do, they went over her wardrobe incessantly. I was free to wander but not too far. The question "Where's Red?" still had to have a prompt and specific answer. The biggest change was nap time. Whether she was protecting herself or me, I don't know, but she now demanded the presence of all her attendants, not just me. Exhausted by broken nights and industrious days and always a little tipsy, she slept heavily (and snored horrendously).

I could hear her all the way across the atrium in the library where I went to snoop in the late Publius Paulus's library for personal documents. I'd had enough tutelage from Joseph to recognize that *Pater* had a standard literary collection, as if he had ordered some slave, a Greek no doubt, to stock it as befitted his rank. Nothing appeared to reflect his personal taste in poetry, plays, or philosophy. The largest and most used-looking section had to do with law, accounts of the senatorial debates and decrees. But then, of course, Publius Paulus had been a senator. Since I was following *Pater's* scent, I ignored my own preference for poetry—if you could call written poetry real, harrumph!—and began to look among the law scrolls, choosing the most worn. In one of these I found myself perusing a history of cases pertaining to paternity—the perennial patriarchal obsession, because, in the days before DNA tests, you could never really know. And therein lies many a tale of woe.

The Romans had their own way of dealing with this uncertainty. Paternity was entirely up to the *pater*. It did not happen at conception (although Romans believed that women were just breeding containers for the almighty seed). It did not even happen at birth. In fact, the child was not considered officially alive until the ceremonial occasion when it was presented to the prospective father. He could refuse to acknowledge it, order it exposed or sold as a slave, or he could claim it as his. If he did accept the child, he picked it up and raised it to his knee (*gens*, the root of genus, generation). Only then did the child become his, legitimate, fully human. If I was reading the case studies in this document correctly, there was a catch. Though more than one man had apparently tried, once he raised a child to his knee, he could no longer deny paternity, no matter what evidence surfaced subsequently. This legal form of paternity was irreversible.

I read the cases over again, pondering their possible significance to Publius Paulus. Reading was a new, painstaking skill for me, and I lost track of time and no longer kept an ear cocked for Paulina's snores or paid attention to my surroundings at all.

"Rule number one!"

I dropped the document. Thank the gods, it was only Reginus, but my hands were shaking as I bent to pick it up.

"If you're going to snoop, don't stand with your back to the door, you silly twat!"

"Quit sneaking up on me. You do it on purpose," I complained. "And I am not snooping. I am merely improving my mind. You ought to try it sometime."

"Rule number two: if you are caught snooping, have a better line ready than the one you just handed me. Slaves don't have minds, unless their masters happen to need the use of one at the moment."

"You may be right about how they think, but you and I both know it isn't true. Did you know that at one time I was studying to be a druid? They're the lawgivers among my people, oral law, of course. I was curious about Roman law, how the written word affects it. Not for the better, I can tell you that much."

"Honey, the only thing you need to know about Roman law is that you don't exist as a separate human entity. Now what are you really doing?"

I looked at him speculatively. He was probably Paulina's spy now, since she was the only game going, but maybe I could get him to work for me, too.

"Aren't you the least bit curious about what's going on here?"

"I'm not curious unless someone pays me to be. Curious about what?" he added in spite of himself.

"Just little things, like Sylvia's bequest, why Publius Paulus wouldn't pay it, what it all has to do with the *Rex Nemorensis*."

"Are you still on about that, Red? Oh, I know. I bet that butch priestess with the bow and arrow is paying you!"

"I wish," I said, knowing outright denial would only confirm false suspicions he might then report to Paulina, which would not be helpful. "Maybe I'm just bored. You seem to have taken my place as *pedisequa*."

"Low blow, Red!" he protested, thrown off the scent as I hoped he might be. "Wait, I know, you're jealous."

"Give me a break, Reginus." In fact, what I needed was a longer break than the ones he had given me. Enough time to get down to the lake and back.

"Come on," said Reginus. "Let's get out of this musty old tomb. Our lady of sodden somnolence is still out for the count. Come sit with me in the sun and tell me why you want to stick your nose in this sorry old mess. I mean, they're all dead. Who cares about a bequest to some runaway lunatic slave?"

"Because it's not over," I said, reaching for Reginus's arm as my eyes adjusted to the sudden light. "Don't you wonder about the nightmares?"

We went to sit at the edge of the colonnade. In daylight you couldn't see the reflection of the perpetual flame on the water, and the temple complex—if there was one—was obscured by the heavy cover of trees.

"I only wonder when I'm going to get a decent night's sleep."

"My guess is you're not. Not until she can remember those nightmares. Reginus, listen." Forget discretion, I needed to talk to someone. "Something happened here. Something terrible. In this villa."

Reginus was silent for a moment.

"Do you think there might be unquiet shades around?" His attempt at a mocking tone failed. "They say the entrance to the Underworld is not far from here."

He shuddered. I could feel the goose bumps on his arms.

"Yes," I said. Wherever *Pater's* shade might lurk, the evil he had done lived after him. I wanted him gone, I suddenly realized—out of Paulina's nightmares, out of her blood and bones, out of this place, out of this time, out of her life—and mine.

"And you, being a barbarian witch and all, can see them?" he asked nervously.

"Yes," I said solemnly. I had found suave, cynical Reginus's Achille's heel.

"What do they look like?"

"Trust me, you don't want to know. Not to worry. They are no match for a barbarian witch like me. I'm going to hunt them down. But I need your help."

"You've got the wrong boy, Red. I'm not going to creep around at night gathering hellebore or mandrake or mashing up spiders or gutting toads or whatever you witchy types do."

I was having a hard time not laughing.

"Besides, I'm really busy. The house party is only two weeks away now. Did I tell you Dmitri's coming?" he said brightly, doing his best to change the subject.

"I'm happy for you. Reginus, listen, I don't need help making potions or communing with the dead, ok? I'm just investigating. What do you know about the man Paulina's mother got caught with?"

"Only what I've heard. Equestrian class. Well-connected. After the shit hit, he went off to some godforsaken outpost for the duration. The usual story."

"You weren't around?"

"Honey, please. That's ancient history. How old do you think I *am*?"

"Older than Paulina," I said severely. "She was around four years old."

"Well, my golden childhood, so to speak, still hadn't come to an end. My father didn't sell me till me I was ten."

"Oh, Reginus, you never told me that."

"Debt, you know how it is." He shrugged away whatever he felt, as I sensed he had for years. "Why do you want to know, about the equestrian, I mean? Is his shade hanging around?"

"Just a hunch. You know how you could really help me? Think of an errand for me and talk Paulina into letting me go to the village."

"Why do you want to go to the village?"

"I don't." I decided to tell him the truth; that way he'd be more likely to lie for me. It would be more pleasurable for him. "I want to go to the temple. I need time."

"The temple? With those vigilante virgin priestesses? You couldn't pay me to go there. I suppose you want to go nosing around about that bequest. I wouldn't put too much stock in it, if I were you. Priests and priestesses are notorious money-grubbers. She could have made the whole thing up."

I thought of the priestess, her steady, far-sighted gaze. I doubted it.

"Still, I want to find out what I can. Will you help me?"

Reginus considered silently for a moment.

"All right, if I can, though I don't see what's in it for me, but then it's no skin off my nose. Here's what bothers me more, what's in it for you? What do you care about that sorry little bitch who makes a petty misery of all our lives?"

"You've been getting along with her well enough lately," I said lightly. "Besides I thought you wanted a decent night's sleep."

"There's more to it than that," Reginus accused.

He was right, but I didn't know how to explain what that more was, even to myself. The detective story—What happened when Paulina was four? Were the lovers caught here? Why did Publius Paulus take revenge on his daughter? What did the unpaid bequest to the *Rex Nemorensis* have to do with it all—gave me a focus, relief from the deeper mystery, the wellspring of the questions I still could not answer.

"Do we have a deal or not?"

"Deal," he sighed. "I'll try to get you sprung tomorrow."

CHAPTER TWENTY-THREE

PRIESTESS TO PRIESTESS

Reginus was as good as his word, and I had to admire his inventiveness in contriving a suitable errand for me. I had gone shopping with Paulina almost daily in Rome, so she knew I didn't have much aptitude for the sport, wouldn't know a bargain if it bit me, had no idea how to ferret out hard-to-find luxury items. Reginus persuaded her, however, that being a savage from remote isles (beyond the empire, even!) where people ate nothing but oatmeal and pigs, I would know everything about how to choose the best suckling piglets to roast outdoors at the festival of Diana in August when all the Roman house guests would be arriving. I was, in short, sent out to interview pig farmers. I had the entire afternoon.

My first step beyond the walls of the villa was ecstatic. I could hardly remember what I was doing. It was enough to take one step after another, unimpeded, unaccompanied. It was a hot day, clear day, the sort where you can hear your own breath and the sound of your footsteps emphasizes your solitude. After some preliminary exploration, I concluded that there was no direct path to the temple from the villa. The drop was too sheer. So I headed towards the village, where I was supposed to go anyway, figuring I could ask the way to the temple there.

The village was quiet, the market stalls beginning to close for the midday break. In response to my questions, most people just shook their heads, then tried to sell me the wilting remains of their morning wares. I had forgotten, after my insular life as Paulina's slave, that people from small remote villages are suspicious of strangers.

"No one is allowed to go to the temple or the grove," one old woman finally explained to me. "Except at Diana's feast. Or the goddess will be angry. And the king, too. Very angry."

"I see. Well then," I changed the subject, not wanting to lodge in her memory as someone intent on trespassing in sacred precincts. "Can you tell me who raises the best pigs around here? The most tender and sweet?"

The answer was long and detailed and involved the intimate history of several families. I listened attentively, making mental notes. Pig raising and eating was an important subject, whatever my beloved's people felt about scavengers with cloven hooves. Perhaps they had never tasted pigs that had fed entirely upon acorns. Fortunately the old woman dozed off mid-sentence, the village square emptied, and I set off eagerly to find the path on my own. It couldn't be that hard. There was up and there was down.

And down and down. If there was a wider path used by villagers at festival time, I hadn't found it. Goats must have made the one I traversed, back and forth, back and forth in long zigzags. It was so steep and the path so narrow, I soon abandoned my sandals; they didn't give me enough purchase. To gaze fathoms down at the tops of huge oaks was dizzying, so I tried not to look. At last, the path became gentler and greener. I could smell and hear rushing water. Around a bend there it was, a waterfall hollowing out a deep, clear pool. Maybe it was just an unexpected breeze, shifting the leafy canopy to admit a flash of light, but for a moment I thought I saw her, the nymph from the frescoes, naked by the pool, smiling and beckoning to someone. An instant later, she was gone. Hot and tired from my harrowing descent, I knelt by the pool and bent to drink and splash my face. When I looked up, someone was there again.

It was not the nymph. And no amount of blinking could turn the priestess, bow drawn, arrow aimed at my heart, into a vanishing apparition.

I considered my predicament for a moment and decided that if I were going to be shot, I would rather be standing. So I rose and faced the priestess across the pool. She kept me in her sights, but when she realized I wasn't backing or running away—the intended effect—she lowered her bow and with an exasperated gesture indicated that I should meet her further downstream away from the roar of the falls. When the stream narrowed and quieted, she addressed me, bow not drawn but clearly at the ready.

"You are in Diana's Sacred Grove and the jurisdiction of her temple. You are forbidden to enter unless invited and escorted by her priestesses."

"Naturally," I agreed.

The priestess frowned; she was clearly accustomed to commanding awe and fear and found my response perplexing.

"What are you doing here? State your name and business."

Maybe it was the rich, loamy smell of the wood, or being in the presence of a fierce priestess; I took a deep breath, and began to intone in ceremonial Q-Celtic:

"I am Maeve Rhuad, daughter of the warrior witches of Tir na mBan, daughters of the Cailleach, daughter of the goddess Bride, daughter of Dugall the Brown—"

"I didn't ask your lineage," the priestess interrupted me. "You are a Gaul, I observe."

"No," I decided not to let the mistake pass; Gaul was a Roman word for the Celtic tribes they had conquered. It meant something like dumb cluck, an insulting word for a chicken, Succula had told me. "I am of the free Celts. Do you speak the language?"

"No," said the priestess. "I recognized the rhythm. So, Maeve Rhuad of the free Celts, what are you doing in Diana's sacred grove?"

Good question. For a moment I couldn't remember the answer. Remembering my real name had disoriented me.

"Speak," the priestess raised her bow by way of nudging me.

"Um, I am here on an errand for the *Domina* Publia Paulina." That was more or less true. "I am to examine the record of the bequest you claim her mother made."

I chose my words carefully, but I felt a little uneasy, obfuscating the truth, if not outright lying, in a sacred grove.

"The *domina* has sent me no word of your coming. I have been to the villa every day, and she has had me turned away at the gate."

I wish someone had told me that. But then, why would they?

"And if she has changed her mind, why has she not come herself, as I requested?"

"What? Down the goat path?" I laughed. "You've got to be kidding."

The priestess was having a hard time restraining a smile.

"That is not the way people usually come to the grove, as you would know if any official arrangements had been made between the villa and the temple for your visit. Tell me, Maeve Rhuad of the free Celts, do you always choose the hard and dangerous path?"

"More often than not," I admitted.

We continued to regard each from other across the stream.

"If the *domina* did not send you, then why are you here?"

"Whether or not she sent me, priestess of Diana, I am here on her behalf."

Now that was the truth. It gave me some ground to stand on. And so I stood. The priestess waited for me to continue. I let her wait. She could shoot me; she could call the temple guards and have me hauled away, but if she asked me another question, I would win this round. She knew it was a contest, too. She sighed and conceded.

"Explain."

"Not here."

She gave me a long considering look. I looked right back.

"Too bad you are a slave. You might have had the makings of a priestess."

I suppose she meant that as a compliment, but it really got up my nose.

"How do you know that I am a slave and not a priestess?" I demanded.

"Why else would someone who boasts of being a free Celt run errands for a Roman mistress? Also I can't believe that a Roman matron of distinguished family would follow the gods of a such a, well, remote place as the land of your people."

Remote was no doubt a polite word for primitive, uncivilized.

"What if I told you I was a priestess of Isis?"

The priestess face betrayed a flicker of interest.

"So the rumors are true then."

"What rumors might those be?"

"That Publia Paulina is flirting with that faddish Egyptian cult."

She was a snob, I realized. Here she was running around in the woods in a short tunic, hunting down a bequest for a king who would one day be slaughtered in ritual combat, and yet she felt free to condescend to worshippers of Isis, queen of stars, ruler of the seas, mistress of the living and the dead, and so on and so forth. I didn't know whether to laugh or splash across the stream and slap her silly.

"You know," I said, shifting my weight to one leg, putting a hand on my hip, and tapping my foot for good measure, "if I was so hot to get my hands on a bequest that I hiked up a damn precipice every day—or however you get up there—I might show a little respect to my prospective patroness's goddess." Here I launched into a hymn praising Isis's numberless attributes. "I would humbly acknowledge that my little grove goddess wore but one of Her many faces. And I wouldn't keep the priestess of said goddess standing on the other side of the stream, hungry and tired and getting chewed up by the midges breeding in that puddle you call Diana's mirror."

The priestess tried to keep her face impassive, but her mouth twitched, and she kept blinking and swallowing.

"In the name of Diana, welcome to the Temple Grove," she said at length. "Come with me."

I jumped across the stream and followed the priestess through thick woods that gave way to stately avenues of trees, evenly spaced like temple columns, and then to actual columns as we arrived at the temple complex beside the lake. I noticed that there was a dock where boats could be moored. I surmised that the easier route must be by water from a more accessible part of the shore. A little further on, the perpetual flame burned right beside the lake, as I had seen from so far above. It was sheltered from the wind in an obsidian shrine shaped like an eye—or a vulva. The rest of the temple spread out behind the flame, the porticoes and antechambers leading to the caves in the cliffs.

"The oldest part of the temple is from the time of Aeneus," said the priestess. "The records are kept there, but first you will have some wine and something to eat."

She had taken my rebuke about hospitality to heart. We sat on low stools—no couches here—while young not-quite-adolescent girls served me bread and fruit on a plate made of some kind of leaf. The wine was dark and spicy and came from the local vineyards. A lake breeze stirred to life, bringing relief from the afternoon heat. I was beginning to relax and enjoy myself as a visiting priestess. This was more like the life I was supposed to be leading.

"Great spot for a sacred grove," I remarked. "Always pleasant to have a body of water near by. Sorry I called it a puddle before."

But the priestess was not about to let an audience she had so reluctantly granted degenerate into a genial chat.

"You will now explain what you meant when you said you were here on the *domina's* behalf, though you acknowledge that she did not send you, and, I assume, does not know that you are here."

"All right," I sighed, my brief fantasy holiday over. "I sleep in the *domina's* chamber. Almost every night she has nightmares that she can't remember. I think there's a connection."

The priestess looked expectant, but I did not want to be the one to make things explicit. Let her do some work.

"A connection between?" she prodded.

I nodded encouragingly, but she folded her arms, signaling her willingness to outwait me.

"Between the bequest to the *Rex Nemorensis* and whatever is causing the *domina's* nightmares. I heard the *domina* tell you that she knew nothing about the bequest. I'll tell you something more. She didn't know this villa existed, much less belonged to her, until Publius Paulus's death. I wonder why. Awake, the *domina* insists she has never been here before this summer. Dreaming, I think she remembers things she wants to forget. Everyone in Rome knows that Valeria Sylvia was exiled for adultery with an equestrian. So the story goes. I believe that there is more to the story, and, whatever that more is, it happened at Nemi. I have a hunch that someone at the Temple—you, for example— knows whatever secrets there are to know."

There, that was enough. More than enough, Isis knows. I shut my mouth and folded my arms in a perfect imitation of her pose. We sat like that and sat, the cool, water-scented breeze, washing over us.

"Supposing," she said at last, "supposing there are such secrets. We should divulge them to you because?"

"Because," I said, not knowing what to say, irritated by this form of interrogation, beginning a sentence I was supposed to complete. "Because. Because I am a healer."

As soon as I spoke, I wanted to take the words back. I'm just nosy, I wanted to say. I'm a rich woman's toy, and I have nothing better to do. Pay no attention to me. But it was too late. The truth had been spoken, and the priestess and I both knew it.

"And so, you want to find out what is tormenting the daughter of Valeria Sylvia and free her from her terror."

"I don't want to, exactly," I suddenly felt cranky. "The truth is, I don't even like her much. But, whatever god or power wants to heal her seems to be using me."

The priestess nodded. She understood.

"I cannot tell you secrets of this grove that have been entrusted to my silence. You will find them out—or not—as the goddess wills. But I will gladly show you the documentation concerning the bequest. Come with me, priestess of Isis."

No one had ever called me that before. The words went through me like an icy bolt of lightning.

"You can read?" she inquired as she led the way into the caves.

"Of course," I said, managing not to add: though reading is for stupid literate Romans with not enough room in their tiny brains for a decent memory.

Two of the young girls held torches as the priestess found the relevant scrolls. It may come as no surprise to you—living in an age when legal documents fell whole forests, and a lawyer is required to complicate the simplest of transactions—that the terms of the bequest did not give me much information. But I was disappointed. The priestess also showed me copies of appeals made to Publius Paulus as administrator of the estate. When those were ignored, the temple wrote to various courts in Rome. From time to time, dates had been set for a hearing of the case, but they were always canceled or postponed.

Finally there was nothing more to see; the priestess led the way out of the caves.

"I have arranged an escort to take you back to the villa," the priestess announced, making it clear that my visit was at an end.

"That's kind of you. But I can find my way back up the path. I left my sandals."

And I wanted to poke around the grove a little more. The priestess knew that.

"I insist. It is too dangerous to make that climb with the late sun in your eyes. Someone will find your sandals and return them to you tomorrow. I have already sent for a bargeman. He will be here presently. I will wait with you till he comes."

Translation: And keep an eye on you until you are safely out of the grove. It is very difficult to argue with a priestess, especially when she's on her own sacred turf.

"Thank you very much for your hospitality. I will do what I can, when I can, to persuade the *domina* to pay the bequest."

"On behalf of the Temple and the Grove, I thank you."

"By the way, how is old *Rex* getting on? Without his bequest, I mean?"

She gave me one of her eagle looks, distant and deadly.

"He is the *Rex Nemorensis*. The goddess provides."

The temple priestesses take care of him, I translated for myself.

"Does the *Rex Nemorensis* make an appearance at Diana's feast?"

"This is not Rome," the priestess's voice was cold as the lake. "This is Diana's Sacred Grove. We have no spectacles or spectators here."

"I understand. Believe me, priestess of Diana, I am no lover of Roman spectacles. And I am no stranger to the sacred groves."

And I knew all about trespassing in them and how dangerous that could be. I knew also that somehow I was going to find this king.

"I believe you, Maeve Rhuad of the free Celts, priestess of Isis."

She put together my true name with the title she had bestowed. I had an impulse to throw my arms around her, but her reserve, not to mention her bow and arrow, did not encourage displays of affection.

"I think I remember that your name is Egeria?" I said instead.

"It is now. The high priestess of Diana's Temple always takes the name of the nymph of the waterfall."

The nymph in the frescoes, the nymph I had glimpsed by the pool.

"Was Valeria Sylvia a priestess?"

Egeria was startled by the question.

"Of course not. Why would you think so? She was married to Publius Paulus."

I hesitated. All along we had been playing the game of who could say the least and find out the most. But it could be carried too far. I decided to show my hand.

"There are frescoes of the nymph of the waterfall at the villa. Perhaps you have seen them? It is my belief that they are the likeness of the *domina's* mother."

"Surely you have been in Rome long enough to know that artists will often use their patroness as a subject. It is a common form of flattery."

"You told the *domina* you knew her mother well." I tried a different tack.

"Yes." She did not elaborate; she was better at withholding than I was.

"Did you know her lover?" It was worth a try.

The priestess just looked at me, her eyes dark as the lake in shadow.

"The barge is here," was all she said. "Perhaps we will meet at Diana's feast. The *domina* and her household are, of course, invited to the Temple then."

"Perhaps, we will. Just one more question," I said as I stepped into the barge.

"I do not think that is wise." Translation: don't push your luck.

"Who raises the best pigs?"

I had the pleasure of seeing the priestess look utterly perplexed.

"Is that a sacred riddle, priestess of Isis?"

I burst out laughing as the barge floated out onto the bright water.

"I'll tell you the answer next time I see you, priestess of Diana."

And—I couldn't help it—I blew her a kiss.

CHAPTER TWENTY-FOUR

CURVE

I will confess to you now, though sin has always been a hard concept for me to grasp and I've run a shame deficit most of my life, I was almost happy at Nemi. You see how I cling to the "almost," as if covering myself with a verbal fig leaf? For how could I be happy when I had lost him whom my soul loved and had no idea if I would ever find him? How could I be happy when my daughter was growing up far away without me? Happiness can be heartless, can make us feel that we have broken faith with pain, with the past. Life is both merciful and merciless that way. It makes us go on. It can heal us without our consent—sometimes only to tear us apart again.

My lightened mood persisted over the next two weeks as preparations for the house party intensified, and the first guests began to arrive from Rome. I decided to wait for Diana's feast to pursue my quest to find the *Rex Nemorensis*. I didn't want to risk encountering Egeria again and rousing her suspicion or ire. I made the most I could of my new role as pig inspector and went on a number of additional outings with the chief cook, Rufus, whose nose, I realized, had been a bit out of joint when he was not consulted. I also made friends with Alisa, the old woman who tended the kitchen gardens and gathered wild plants for medicine. I'd had some instruction in plant lore from the priestesses on Mona, but my chief gift was in my hands, where the fire of the stars had begun to flow again for the first time in years. Many mornings I helped Alisa in an impromptu clinic attended by slaves and freemen alike.

When the rustic slaves discovered that I was a country girl and did not look down on them, I gained acceptance and enjoyed more camaraderie than I had known for years. It was not that there weren't dramas and feuds among them as there are among people everywhere, but the rustic slaves lived largely in their own society. The intricate web of spying and counter-spying, intrigue and double-crossing that so prevailed in Rome was irrelevant. There were crops to get in, animals to tend, weather to watch for and outwit, and gods to be propitiated to insure survival.

Pater, it seemed, had only come once a year. No one liked him; he dealt out severe punishments, including flogging or being sold away from the estate, but they grudgingly admitted his management had been competent, his appointment of overseers, judicious. They were wary of Paulina, but inclined to be tolerant, because they regarded her as a Sylvani—the time when the Sylvani spent summers at the villa had taken on a perhaps unrealistic luster as a golden age by the older slaves. As they came to trust me, I learned more about Paulina's mother.

"She was a wild thing," Alisa told me when we were out foraging for soapwort, "always outdoors. We called her the wood nymph; she didn't seem quite human. When she was ten or eleven, she begged to be allowed to serve at the Temple with the other young girls, and she did for a summer or two. She would have lived at the villa year round if her family had allowed her to; she hated going back to Rome. Sometimes used to hold everyone up for days by disappearing into the woods. Her father didn't know how to say no to her, laughed and pinched her cheek, when most others would have beaten her and locked her in her room. That was his mistake, you see, to indulge her like that all her life, and then take it all away."

"What do you mean take it away?" I pressed.

"Well, it never occurred to her that she would have no say about marrying. And it never occurred to him that breaking a wild thing like her to harness was bound to cause trouble. The Sylvani were kind masters, didn't interfere with us unnecessarily, but I sometimes find that city people are not very shrewd, don't you? No mother wit. I put it down to plumbing, drinking water out of pipes. Not healthy."

And, as you know, history proved her right. Encouraged by her confiding tone and our solidarity as people who knew it was better to drink from springs, I asked the burning question.

"I know Sylvia was caught with her lover here at Nemi," I stated; I had no doubt of that much. "Do you remember him?"

Alisa was quiet for a moment, as if digging up the roots of the soapwort required all her attention. When she had the roots dangling in the air, she looked behind her and up and all around. As if she thought someone might be hidden and listening.

"We don't talk about it. She wouldn't like it."

"Who wouldn't? Sylvia's shade?"

Alisa shook her head. "Her. Her of the Grove. It's her secret, isn't it, dearie? We better get back then. Old Lena will be there already waiting. I promised her a tonic."

I didn't ask any more questions of Alisa. Her answer was almost like Egeria's. Her secret, the secrets of the grove, something even the loquacious Alisa dared not expose. You will find them out—or not—as the goddess wills, Egeria had said.

Diana, I spoke to the goddess silently. I am Maeve Rhuad, daughter of the Shining Isles, priestess of Isis, seeker of secrets, healer of old wounds. If you find me worthy, guide me to the heart of your grove.

Then in the midst of my busy life as a sort of sacred busybody—spying on and for the gods, so to speak—life threw me a curve.

Though Paulina no longer required my constant presence, I still sat at the foot of her couch at twice-daily banquets. I was used to it. Unlike the early days when Paulina teased me with tidbits and I refused to eat, I now helped myself freely, and listened to the conversation or pursued my own thoughts if the company was dull. There was a degree of rustic informality to our villa meals. Neighbors dropped by unexpectedly, and guests from Rome arrived at all hours. The evening feast especially tended to go on and on. Paulina encouraged anyone with talent (or without) to entertain with songs or stories. Sometimes the villa slaves danced. I would have liked to join them. I even considered telling some of the tales I had learned at druid school or from my mothers, but something held me back. The more myself I felt, the more I realized how little Paulina knew me—except as her all-purpose slave and sometime whore. Her self-involved indifference gave me a sense of having a secret reserve of power. I wasn't sure I wanted her to know me.

I was pondering this question between courses while some old geezer wheezed on about the Catiline conspiracy, for Catiline had hidden out in mountain caves and passes not far from here. I was on the side of Catiline or anyone who wanted to subvert the Roman state, but the narrator wasn't, and the bulk of his story was badly mangled renditions of that prig Cicero's condemnatory speeches to the senate. We were all in something of a stupor when the *ab admissione* announced the arrival of more guests.

"The distinguished *domina* Maxima Fabia and her entourage."

We all rose, and I looked on with mild interest as Paulina rushed to air kiss one of the three women who had suckered her into funding the new Temple of Isis at Campus Martius. A society bitch, as Succula called her, Maxima had a ruthlessness that reminded me of Domitia Tertia, but she lacked

Domitia's directness. I supposed it was more amusing to manipulate and deceive. I glanced at her claque to see if there was anyone else I knew from the baths.

Then, thank Isis, Paulina gave the signal to resume our seats. If she hadn't, I would have collapsed. Standing quietly at the periphery of the new arrivals was Joseph of Arimathea.

He had seen me before I saw him. His eyes had been beseeching, calling me to turn to him. And I understood, with no need for words, that this meeting was not an accident. He had come here looking for me. After almost three years. He had not forgotten me. I turned my face away to hide my tears, but then I forced myself to recover. I did not want him to think that I reproached him.

But when I looked back, he was caught up in introductions. I could tell he was on his best urbane, Hellenic behavior, allowing only just a trace of his more exotic origins to show. This mix no doubt entranced Maxima, who liked to think of herself as bold and unconventional. Joseph's charm was working on Paulina, too. She had called for more couches and wedged his in next to hers, which meant that I would have to lean forward and peer past the whole length of her to get a glimpse of him, which did not seem wise. So I just strained my ears to catch snatches of conversation, not easy to do as the new arrivals had notched up the noise level. But I heard enough to figure out that Joseph had involved himself as a supplier of metals for the Temple of Isis. Not something a good Jew ought to do, perhaps, outfit a heathen temple full of graven images and idols, but Joseph had never pretended to be good. Business was business.

Joseph waited a decent interval, partaking of a few courses, and then excused himself, pleading fatigue from the journey. As he walked out towards the colonnade, he caught my eye. I nodded, but cast my eyes toward Paulina. Again, without words, we agreed that he would wait for me until I could slip away unobtrusively. Maxima Fabia, who would spend her visit subtly (or not so subtly) outdoing Paulina, had brought her own mime troupe with her. When the performance began, I crawled out of the room, careful not to block anyone's view.

Out on the colonnade I moved away from the doors to the banquet hall and into the shadows. Before I could even look for him, I was enfolded in Joseph's arms. For a long time I just wept and Joseph murmured incoherently.

"How did you find me?" I finally asked, stepping back to look at him.

"Come, let's talk," he said.

We walked further along the colonnade, away from the banquet hall, and settled near where I'd sat with Reginus the first night, the dark mountains defined by stars and the light of the perpetual flame shimmering on the lake below. I tried to pay attention as Joseph told me of his travels the last few years, back and forth to Pretannia, to Alexandria, to Greece, but his account washed over me without sinking in. I knew I was waiting for one thing, one word, one name. It did not come.

"Ah, Maeve, I have done my best to forget you. I told myself you were a whore, a slave, and a barbarian, not someone to be taken seriously. But I have failed. Domitia has steadfastly refused to tell me who bought you. I think now she wanted to protect me from myself, from my own folly. But no one can do that for another. Finally Succula told me that she had seen you at a Temple of Isis. She is too loyal to Domitia to say who owned you, though I am sure she knows, but she did admit that you were in the company of some prominent Roman matrons. So I took pains to discover what fashionable women had taken up with the Egyptian cult. I was soon led to Maxima Fabia, and through what I pride myself was a most subtle and discreet inquiry, I found out where you were at last. And here I am."

"Yes, here you are," I agreed, and to my astonishment I had no more words. What was there to say of the intervening years? How could I recount the crushing sameness of my time with Paulina, holding her mirror, holding her body, holding my tongue. I did not know how to bridge the gap between past and present, or between this man beside me and the one I longed for.

"And so," he said uncertainly, waiting for something from me.

"And so," I repeated helplessly.

"And so, Maeve, I have come for you, don't you see? I will buy you from this vain, uneducated woman who squanders your gifts. We can live anywhere. You will be my Aspasia, and I will be your Pericles—well, perhaps not Pericles; I am no politician. Did you know that Socrates himself sought Aspasia's society?"

I did not know. And I did not know how to tell Joseph that I had forgotten who Aspasia was, if I ever knew. I had forgotten Plato and Aristotle. I had not forgotten Joseph, but there was some terrible discrepancy between our memories.

"Joseph," I finally plunged in; there was no easy way to ask. "Joseph, have you been back to Judea or Galilee?" Say it, I told myself. "Do you know what has become of Esus, I mean Yeshua? Please, Joseph, you must understand, I have to know."

There was a long silence. I was grateful for the darkness that hid our faces at least. But nothing can hide the voice; it is always naked.

"I was afraid you would ask that, but I dared to hope you might have given up on him. I should know better. Didn't I love him, too? I have let my own foolish dreams deceive me. I wanted to protect you; I still want to protect you."

"From my own folly? Ah, Joseph, as you have said yourself, no one can do that for another."

I'm sorry, I wanted to add, but I wasn't sure for what.

"I will tell you what I know," he sighed. "And perhaps you will see for yourself how impossible it is. How impossible he is. He's disappeared. Again."

"Again? When did he come back? Where had he gone? Did you see him?"

"I arrived just too late, in the wake of the scandal. Our family is a prominent priestly one, you know. My cousins are disgraced. I heard about it as far away as Alexandria. I went to Judea to find out what had happened first hand."

I wished he would get to the point; with effort I curbed my impatience.

"When Yeshua and my cousin Mary ran away together, that was bad enough. Rumors abounded. After a while, the family decided to mourn Mary as one dead, though privately they had received word that she was alive and well. Not even her sister Martha knew where she was until she was found out."

"Found out?" Could my rival have become a prostitute or an idol worshipper?

"Mary and Yeshua joined an Essene community in the Judean desert. It is hard to say which is more shocking, that she disguised herself as a man or that she allied herself with a cult of extremists who defy the authority of the Temple of Jerusalem."

"She disguised herself as a man?" I marveled at something that had never been an option for me. Did that mean she had meager breasts? A masculine face or demeanor? I have to admit; these were my thoughts. "But why?"

"The Essenes practice celibacy. Some communities allow women in separate compounds, but women do not do the work of scholars. Learning is what Mary wanted."

"Celibacy," I repeated. "No sex? As in no sex between Mary and Esus?"

"Maeve, I am surprised at you, with your brilliant mind, your worldly experience that you would concern yourself with such details when so much more is at stake."

But I am a woman, I wanted to shout at him, a human being. Don't you get it? Fuck learning. I want to know if they were lovers.

"Go on." I managed to control myself.

"When Mary was discovered, Yeshua turned himself in as her co-conspirator. Well, no one ever said he was not honorable. Just headstrong, misguided, and a source of grief to anyone who loves him. He went back to Bethany with Mary and offered to make restitution to the family with seven years of labor. Strangely enough, her brother Lazarus accepted. He is the head of the family, their father being dead, and just as well or the shame would have killed him. Why Lazaus didn't have Yeshua stoned to death is a mystery to everyone, but there is some sort of friendship between the two men, and even Martha clucks over the miscreant. But, I hardly need say, he was more trouble than he was worth. The errant pair attracted both censure and curiosity. Mary was forced to become a recluse. And Yeshua, Yeshua is gone again. No one knows where. Out of the country, it seems."

For a moment I let myself believe: he is looking for me; he will not rest till he finds me.

"He has gone to Rome...?" I wavered between a statement and a question.

"Ah, Maeve. I think I know what you want me to tell you, and I can't. He didn't know. He still doesn't know that you're alive. He doesn't know where you are."

"But, Joseph, didn't you tell Mary's family? When you went back for the wedding that never happened?"

"Martha and Lazarus were beside themselves when Mary and Yeshua disappeared. It was hardly the time to discuss his previous misadventures."

"Misadventures? *Misadventures*! But Joseph, don't you see? Do you still not see? That's *why* he didn't marry her. He's never forgiven himself for leaving *me*. He blames himself for my death. Oh, Joseph, Joseph. If you had told them, if they had told him..."

I tried to swallow the sobs that wanted to tear me open and wept silently, bitterly. Though he hadn't moved, I could feel Joseph drawing away. He couldn't bear it either.

"I'm sorry, Joseph," I finally said. "It's not your fault. Of course you didn't tell them then. But they must know about me now, that I'm alive. So if he ever, if they ever..."

I couldn't finish. Ever was such a desolate word, as dead as that desert I had seen in my dreams, as a long life unlived, as thirst unquenched.

"Maeve, this is why we need philosophy; the sweet rule of reason. Passion brings us all to ruin. But what am I saying? My words are meaningless, worse than meaningless. They are lies."

"Joseph, what do you mean?"

"Maeve, I didn't tell them about you. Not this time either."

"I don't understand." My mind didn't, but my body already knew. I felt as though I might be sick.

"I didn't tell them, because...because I wanted you for myself."

His shame was palpable; it filled the night air and clung to my skin like moisture.

"You must believe…I have to believe that if I had seen him, Yeshua, I would have told him everything. I would have told him you were alive and loved him still. But, he wasn't there, and I didn't tell anyone, I said nothing. Ah, Maeve, Maeve, can you ever forgive me?"

Ever. Ever forgive. How could I forgive him? Yet how could I not? You're a man, I could have comforted him, a human being.

Before I could speak, we heard footsteps approaching. Someone held a torch. We got quickly to our feet, and then there was Paulina, flanked by two villa slaves, swaying drunkenly before us in her bright red *stola*.

CHAPTER TWENTY-FIVE

NOT FOR SALE

"I t's one of my distinguished gueshts," slurred Paulina. "What's his name? I can't remember."

"Joseph of Arimathea, *domina*, at your service." He bowed stiffly.

"Josheph." It was a hard name to pronounce when drunk. "You want to service me, Josheph? I don't do that kind of thing with distinguished gueshts. *Pater* wouldn't like it. I'm not a whore, you know, but Red is. Red!" She registered my presence. "What are you doing here? Did I say you could turn trish with my distinguished gueshts?"

I glanced at Joseph, who, even by torchlight, I could see was turning purple.

"Joseph is an old friend of mine." I tried to keep my tone neutral.

"No, Red, no. You don't have friendsh. You're mine. You're my pedish-ishkabob," she giggled. "And before that you were a whore. Domitia Tertia's whore, but I showed that bitch. Now you're mine." She turned and frowned at Joseph. "If you want to borrow her, you have to be nishe. You have to ashk. Because she'sh mine."

"*Domina*," said Joseph; I could hear his barely checked rage. "I will pardon your unspeakable rudeness and indecency to me, because I can see that you are drunk and not in command of yourself. But I refuse to pardon your disrespect of Maeve Rhuad."

"Maeve *who*?" Paulina looked genuinely confused. Her eyes crossed, and she was no doubt seeing double.

"My point precisely. You don't even know her name. You say she is yours, and it may be that you purchased her from Domitia Tertia, but she will not be yours for long, because I am here to buy her from you."

Paulina's eyes snapped into focus. She was still drunk, but she'd just gotten a shot of adrenaline.

"She is not for sale."

I shook my head at Joseph, trying to signal him to stop, but he ignored me.

"I will pay any price."

I should have warned Joseph right away: Paulina would never agree to sell me. She didn't need money. Unless Joseph was willing to steal me and smuggle me out of the country, which would now be next to impossible, there was no escape.

"She's not for sale," Paulina shouted. "She's mine. If you want a whore, go out and get your own whore. Red is mine."

I quietly went to the edge of the colonnade and threw up into the shrubbery below. Neither Joseph nor Paulina noticed.

"She is no one's whore, *domina*," Joseph answered heatedly. "I will not allow you to speak of her so."

But I am a whore; I acknowledged silently. I am a whore and a slave, and Joseph can want me as his *hetaera*, his mistress, his Aspasia, but it's all the same thing. Even if he gives me my freedom, I will not be free.

"Shut up!" I said out loud. "Shut up, both of you. I'm sorry, Joseph. Don't think I'm not grateful, you coming all this way to find me, but can't you see it's no use?"

"You tell 'im, Red."

"I said, shut up, Paulina." I turned on her. "You're disgustingly drunk. I'm putting you to bed."

"Maeve," Joseph called after me. "Oh, Maeve, I'm sorry. I'm so sorry."

Get over it, I wanted to say, but I didn't.

"It'll be all right, Joseph," I said instead, but I didn't believe it.

If Paulina hadn't passed out, I think I would have knocked her over the head, but she fell asleep (at least temporarily) as soon as I got her horizontal. I thought of going to find where Joseph was quartered. I knew he would be sick with self-reproach. It wouldn't take him long to figure out that he had ruined any chance of rescuing me—unless we made a mad dash tonight. I knew in my heart Joseph would never take a risk like that, and I didn't want to throw it in his face. So how could I comfort him? How could I comfort myself?

I just sat next to Paulina without moving, dry-eyed, as if I could keep the pain at bay by sitting perfectly still, the way people keep predators away by sitting near a fire. The other chamber slaves slipped in and took their sleeping places, but no one spoke to me. Reginus was the only one who might have, and I knew he was spending the night with the new arrival, Dmitri. Just as well. I wanted to be alone, and the closest I could come to solitude was being the only one awake in a room full of sleepers.

Without really intending it, I had fastened my gaze on the fresco of the nymph, the nymph who laughed and beckoned in the fresco at the other end of the villa, but here seemed to pause, for an instant, like a wild animal that knows this time it cannot outrun the hunter. I still don't know whether I crossed over into dream or waking vision.

The change was seamless.

I am inside the fresco; I can hear the waterfall, and smell the damp night earth. I can even hear the panicked breathing of the nymph. I cannot see inside her mind, but I know she has just witnessed something terrible, terrible and final. She is gathering the strength to go on. When she gets up, I follow her, though it is not clear to me whether I have an actual physical form in this world, for I am able to climb without feeling out of breath. Yes, climb, for in a moment I recognize the goat path. The dust and the cliffs are bright with moonlight. We walk on and on, back and forth, but before we reach the village, she takes a turn I didn't see before. It's hardly a path. It's a precarious scramble from handhold to foothold up sheer rock face, and then we are at the bottom of the villa wall. She moves towards a portion of the wall covered with thick wild grape vine, and she pulls herself up and over.

Sylvia, the wild thing, the wood nymph.

Once inside the wall, she stops still and listens. I can hear it, too: a child screaming, screaming in terror for her mother. Sylvia moves so fast, it is more like flying than running. She gains the colonnade, and her bare feet touch it like rain as she races towards the east wing, towards the child. She crosses the atrium. The air is dense and sweet with night blooming moonflowers. She doesn't see the man hiding in the shadows. I have no way to warn her. Just before she crosses the threshold to the child's room, he seizes her and locks her in a stranglehold.

All at once I am the woman. I see what the man wants me to see: the child, my daughter, flattened against the wall, naked and screaming. I see the blood between her legs. The man is speaking, spewing his hatred, but I can't hear him. I am crying—though I can barely breathe—crying out to my daughter, trying to tell her everything, everything, because I know I will never see her again.

Then I am myself again, waiting in the moonlight. The man is dragging the woman away across the atrium. She looks directly into my eyes. She sees me. She is beseeching me.

"I will," I promise her.

And then she is gone.

"Ma, ma, ma." The little girl runs into the atrium.

"Ma, ma, ma," screamed Paulina, her eyes wide, unseeing as she stood in the middle of the room, as she had so many nights.

"She's here," I answered. "I'm here."

And I got up and gathered Paulina in my arms, leading her back to bed. She made herself small and rested her head against my breasts.

"She never wanted to leave you," I whispered to Sylvia's daughter and to my own daughter far away. "Your mother never wanted to leave you."

And long after Paulina had fallen back asleep, I wept into her hair.

My dream or vision had been so vivid, I hoped somehow Paulina had seen it, too. When I tried to tell her about it, she adamantly refused to hear a word. If she did not remember her dreams, she was amazingly cognizant, considering how drunk she'd been, of her encounter with Joseph. She alternately berated and clung to me, bombarding me with questions without stopping for answers, which was just as well, since I had none.

"I will see Joseph of Arimathea at once. Privately." she decided. "Before I receive my clients. If he wishes to remain a guest under my roof, we must come to an understanding. And you, you, Red, I don't want you gadding about the countryside anymore. You stay with me the way you are supposed to."

Petrus, the villa slave sent to fetch Joseph, returned to announce that the gentleman had been called away suddenly on business and begged his hostess's pardon, thanking her for her gracious hospitality and so on.

"And he left this for you."

Petrus swiftly handed me a wax tablet he had been holding behind his back, knowing full well that Paulina would try to snatch it from me.

"I order you to give that to me," she said. "I won't have secret communications between you and that, that duplicitous Jew."

"No," I said flatly.

"You dare to defy me?"

"Yes. Besides, Paulina, you can't read Greek. Leave me alone. I'll come find you when I'm done." I bent my head over the tablet. "Go on. Your guests and clients will be waiting."

She wanted to say something. She wanted do something, but all she managed was huffing noises. I ignored her, and when I looked up again, she was gone. I resumed the arduous task of reading, which was made easier because I could guess the gist of what Joseph would say:

> *My dearest Maeve, forgive me. Perhaps you will condemn me as a coward for leaving without seeing you again. I thought it best, for I have nothing now to give, and I fear I might only cause you more grief and trouble.*
>
> *I have failed you and failed you. No philosophy can ease this knowledge. Nor should it. You know that I am not pious. I hardly know how to pray, and I am not worthy to address the Most High, whom I have always thought of as the Idea. If I could pray, my prayer would be to have another chance to serve you, this time without thought for myself.*
>
> *I do not know if the Nameless One or Fate—whichever one governs our lives— will be so kind to me, but if it is true, as Heraclitus says, that a man's character is his fate, then I have hope—for you.*
>
> *Maeve dearest, if you are ever in trouble, danger or distress and have need of anything I can give you, send word to Domitia Tertia. She will know how to find me.*
>
> *Ever your Servant,*
> *Joseph*

After I finished reading, I sat for a long time, running my fingers over the soft wax of the tablet. I stared at the letters till they turned back into abstract shapes devoid of meaning and finally disappeared altogether as I slowly erased them.

Only one thing remained clear to me. I didn't know why it was my task or why I should care at all, but it was only the comfort I could find this morning—I would go to the sacred tree. I would find the king of the wood.

CHAPTER TWENTY-SIX

KING

O
n Diana's feast day, August 13th, her mirror showed her most benign aspect. Heat drew moisture into the air, softening all reflections: the sky's blue, the edges of rock face and mountains. The dappled light under the trees had a honeyed quality. The heavy, fruit-scented air might have been oppressive except that it kept moving, lightly skimming over the water, then turning back on itself as lake breezes often do when surrounded by mountains.

Except for Reginus, who eagerly volunteered to stay behind with a skeleton staff, our entire household made a procession in the cool of the morning through the village and down a long, gently-sloping path (the one I had not taken) wide enough for carts and litters. Paulina did not for a moment consider walking the mile or two to the docks where barges waited to ferry merry-makers to the Temple. When we arrived at the lake, everyone from all the surrounding villas and villages had gathered there as well in a huge milling holiday crowd that included hunting dogs, Diana's favorites, sporting garlands of flowers on their heads and necks—whether they appreciated the honor or not.

The Temple traditionally provided roast kid for Diana's feast and vats of wine, but most parties had picnic baskets laden with breads, olives, fruits, cheeses, and many carried their own wine skins, and were already feeling quite jolly by mid-morning. (And, yes, we did have a pig roast for our fifty-some guests at the villa the night before, with Rufus and me comparing notes on recipes. Our picnic basket included smoked spareribs.) The women were also laden with ritual paraphernalia—votive lanterns, terracotta figurines of the goddess, huge bunches of wild and cultivated flowers. All along the lakeshore people would build their own shrines to Diana, lady of the beasts, fierce guardian of virgins, and compassionate midwife.

Paulina was never at her best in the mornings. She always managed to receive her clients in the cool, shuttered halls of the villa, but coming out into bright morning sunlight was a stretch for her. If she'd lived in your time, she would have worn designer sunglasses to conceal the effects of her hangover. As it was, she kept the curtains drawn in the litter, and then took care to sit under the striped canopy on the barge, fortifying herself now and then with the hair of the dog. She did not entrust her wineskin—the contents well-watered by me—to anyone else, but had it strapped to her side. I knew Paulina was nervous about venturing onto the Temple's turf with the matter of the bequest still unresolved. Last night she'd tried to beg off, but Maxima wouldn't hear of it.

"But darling, it sounds so quaint and picturesque, how can you resist? Imagine, eating from plates made of leaves, and all the lovely little lanterns reflected in the lake at nightfall. Besides, you own a great deal of land here." Maxima's tone was close to reverent. "Own it in your own right, you lucky thing. It would look very odd if you did not patronize the Feast, don't you agree?"

Disagreeing with Maxima would have taken far too much effort. Now as we made our slow, dreamy progress in the barge along several miles of shore, Paulina's eyes glazed over while Maxima kept our party entertained with running commentary.

"And of course," Maxima was saying, "what else is the ritual slaying of the famous *Rex Nemorensis*, but a re-enactment of the death of Osiris, just as Diana is clearly an aspect of Isis. When you trace it back, everything comes from Egypt. Isn't it marvelous, darling?"

"Oh, piffle," said her husband. "You're as bad as that Jew you took under your wing—what was his name—with his Greeks. Greeks, Jews, Egyptians. Why do so many Romans fawn on 'em? We've got the Empire, by Jupiter. Bigger than anyone else's ever was. What do we need with other people's gods? Diana is Diana, I say. Likes to hunt, likes to bathe. Wholesome. No funny business like all those Greeks or Egyptians, always getting up to something with their sisters, brothers, or mothers."

"Pay no attention to him," Maxima advised. "He's hopeless. Oh, look. There are the temple columns, running right down to the water's edge. How charming."

I did not turn toward the Temple. I kept my eyes trained on the wooded shore, straining for some clue, a broken branch, a disturbance in the understory that might point the direction to the tree with the golden bough where the *Rex Nemorensis* endured his hidden reign.

"What are you looking at, Red?" Paulina demanded.

Lately she had seemed jealous of my very thoughts and had tried to cur-
tail not only my movements but my mind. I turned to reassure her. Her eyes
were as shadowed as the deepest part of the wood. That's when I saw it, reflected in her pupils—a sudden flash of gold, and a dark figure pacing under the
canopy. When I turned back to the shore, it was gone.

"Nothing," I answered. "Nothing."

For the first part of the day, I stayed with Paulina and confined myself to
assessing Temple security. I confess I enjoyed seeing the cool, watchful priestesses transformed into harried hostesses dancing attendance on their patrician
guests. The temple guards had their work cut out keeping the plebs in their
place. As at festivals anywhere, there were speeches and games, dancing,
songs, and parades, and constant eating and drinking. When the midday feasting began in earnest, I hit upon a strategy. Every time Paulina held out her wine
cup for a refill, I told her how many she'd already had. When she began to flirt
with a married senator, I hissed in her ear that his wife was watching and she
mustn't be so obvious.

"Isis, Red!" she finally snapped. "You're acting like some old biddy. Stop
spoiling my fun."

"It's my job," I insisted. "It's my job to see that you maintain proper
decorum befitting your station, *domina*."

"No, Red. It's your job to do as I say. Now go away and leave me alone."

She went back to her rather outrageous flirtation, giggling as she deliberately spilled a little wine on her massively exposed bosom. After checking to
see that his wife wasn't looking, the senator obligingly lapped it up with his
tongue. I pictured Bonia signaling to the cashier. Paulina had definitely missed
her calling.

My timing was good. Everyone was feasting or serving those who feasted; in a little while, slaves and masters alike would sleep until dusk when the
festivities would begin all over again. The temple guards, I noticed, were not
exactly sober, either, it being a day of general laxity. Egeria was the only one
who might have guessed my intentions, and Maxima had appropriated her. I
wandered, with apparent aimlessness, down the neat avenues of trees until I
slipped unseen into the perpetual dusk of the wild oak wood.

If I had not imagined that reflection in Paulina's eyes—and I could not
be certain at all that I hadn't—the sacred tree would be somewhere on the shore
we had passed in the barge. I looked around for some sign of a footpath. Unless
the king had to hunt and gather all his food in addition to guarding the tree, the

priestesses must come and go with offerings. But there was not much undergrowth in the thick of the wood, so it was hard to be sure. And perhaps they varied their routes to the tree for this very reason.

As I stood considering my direction, a breeze stirred, and a blade of light sliced down through the trees, hovering for an instant before it disappeared again.

"Sylvia," I suddenly sensed her. "Show me the way."

So I followed flickering light, subtle rustlings among the fallen leaves, the call of a bird, on and on, for much longer than I had expected. The air was thick with moisture, and my tunic clung to me; now and then, in boggy places, biting insects whined. The wood grew darker, the canopy so thick, it was hard to remember the sky. All the trees were old and huge, but none of them had a trace of gold, their leaves so dark a green, they were almost black.

Then suddenly, without warning, I stepped from the thick of the wood and saw it: the sacred tree, so huge, it parted the forest around it like waves turning the whole wood into ripples. It rose up and claimed the light, now burning in its crown. I did not see the king until his shadow leaped high, shielding the tree like a lover, his whole being staked between his beloved and any harm. I stepped back into the cover of the wood; I had no business here. I was an intruder in a lover's bower. But the man had sensed if not seen me. Hair and beard wild and knotted as tree roots, clothes in tatters, mad as he must be after years of sleepless solitude, there could be no doubt of his identity as the *Rex Nemorensis*. Sword at the ready, he paced beneath the holy tree and roared his challenge.

"I know you are there. Come at me then, come at me. Do not dare to hide and skulk like a slave if you would be king. Come, show me the stolen branch, if you would challenge me. I will fight you sword to sword. If you have no sword I will fight you hand to hand as a man fights a man, and a king a king."

There was something so familiar about the cadence and the rhythms of his speech. Then it dawned on me: the man was speaking Celtic. I began to tremble all over as I looked more keenly at the king, trying to see the face beneath a beard thick enough for birds to nest in.

"The Holy Tree will take no coward for her consort. Come out now and show yourself. I will fight you with joy. With joy I will claim your life or if you are the king that is to come, with joy I will meet my death at your hand."

But I didn't need to see his face. I could never forget this voice, the note of kindness it held even when he challenged an unseen enemy.

"Bran," I whispered, and then I shouted, "Bran!"

And I ran towards him with my arms open, heedless of his naked sword, which fortunately he dropped in his bewilderment a moment before I flung myself against his huge chest. I breathed the smell of him, sweat, smoke, leaves, musk that had so overwhelmed me when I first met him, the first man of my life, my foster-father. His thick arms encircled me—imagine being hugged by an oak tree. His heart beat and his chest rose and fell like the sea. He lifted one huge hand and held it over my head—not quite touching it—as if my hair were flame.

"Maeve?" he breathed my name. "Maeve Rhuad, are you really here? I've had so many visions...." His voice trailed off.

"I'm here," I mumbled into his chest. "Are you here?"

I was not coherent. I hadn't taken it in, couldn't put it together. At the same moment we both drew back to look at each other in the late light, almost dusk, the shape-shifting time of day when one world might open onto another.

"Have you come for me, dear heart?" said Bran. "Have you come to take me to the Isles of the Blest I've longed for all my life? I'm so glad it's you, Maeve, chit of a girl that you are, but your mothers' daughter, for all that. I always thought I would die by violence. Anu knows I've lived by it. But perhaps I'm dead already and have forgotten. It doesn't matter. You're here now, and I'll go quiet, quiet as a newborn lamb."

He smiled at me so sweetly; then he placed his hand in mine. Huge as it was, it made me think of my tiny daughter's blind trusting grip.

"There's just one thing I would ask of you, Maeve, daughter of the Shining Isles, if it is in your power to grant it, I'd like to see my Branwen again, a vision would do, just to know she's well."

Ah, if I had the powers he thought I had, what wouldn't I do for him?

"Bran."

I hardly knew how to begin. I didn't know if he'd gone mad with loneliness and grief or if my appearance was so startling he couldn't fathom it any other way. The truth of how I came to be here did not make a pretty story. My mothers would have discarded it. Bran's assumption that I had stepped into this grove from an enchanted Otherworld sounded so much more appealing to me.

"Bran," I tried again.

"But if you can't, no matter. I don't know how it works, you see. If you must shed my blood first, I'm ready. Just let me say goodbye to the Tree, then I will lie down in her lap and give her my death as I have given her my life."

He turned toward the great tree with his arms outstretched, and my dream came back to me. In waning light, the leaves still shone with their own fire. At the heart of the huge trunk, there was a scar or gash, big enough to shelter a man—or a coffin. But it was empty; there was no doorway to some mysterious dawn, no Osiris, no Esus. Just Bran, exiled and homesick.

"Come then, here's my sword."

He picked it up and handed it to me. Then he lay down, cradled by the enormous roots of the tree. Lifting his beard, he showed me where the blood coursed in his neck.

"Easy for you, painless for me. Don't fret, lass. I keep my sword sharp and clean. I would rather die at a stroke from you than from the finest warrior in the three worlds."

I stood dismayed as he closed his eyes and waited, the sword dangling from my hand like a dislocated limb. I wonder still if I should have killed him, let him die with his sweet illusions intact. Or maybe they weren't illusions. Maybe I was called by some power within me or beyond me to do just as he said: send him to the Isles of the Blest.

If that is so, judge me who will, I failed.

CHAPTER TWENTY-SEVEN

TO SING OR RETURN TO SILENCE

After a time, Bran opened first one eye and then the other.

"Here I am forgetting, old fool that I am, you're a druid in the making and cannot wield a weapon. Here I am presuming to know the ways of the Otherworld, mistaking them for my own. Pardon an old warrior, sweetheart, forgive your old foster-father."

He did look old and so weary. I laid down the sword and went to him, curling beside him among the roots.

"Bran," I said, my head resting against his shoulder, so I didn't have to look into his face. "I am not a student of the druids anymore. Being here with you and the Tree is the closest I have come to the Otherworld since I left the Holy Isles. As for Branwen, the last time I saw her on the shores on Mona when the druids sent me beyond the ninth wave, she was well, as well as she could be in her grief for you. I can tell you that she bore herself bravely, always, and she is and will be a great poet. Of that you can be sure. Your name will never be forgotten among the *combrogos*."

"What? What are you telling me, Maeve Rhuad?" He sat up and passed his hand over his eyes as if trying to clear them. "Well, if you have not come from the Otherworld just now, and if, as I fear, that means we're not going there just now, let me stir the fire to life, and we will tell each other stories."

He got up, and uncovered the banked embers, and added wood to campfire set in a ring of stones. Then he settled back against the tree. We sat silently for a time, both of us with our stories, stories no bard would ever sing.

"The ninth wave," he finally said. "You were always a bit headstrong, but the ninth wave?"

I shrugged—a stupid gesture—as if I had not lost everything in the world.

"I interfered with druid mysteries. Helped the quinquenniel sacrifice to escape, that sort of thing."

"Ah, Maeve, Maeve. And I was not there to help you, to intercede for you. My foster-daughter an exile."

"Dear Bran, I don't think even you could have lightened the sentence. And, as you see, the gods ruled in my favor. I survived."

"Ah, and you being the daughter of Manannan Mac Lir, son of the wave, how could you not? Surely, the druids must have reckoned on that."

"Yes, well," I hedged, reluctant to inflict further disillusionment.

"Tell me everything, Maeve. Who was this quinquennial sacrifice then?"

So I told him the story. How Esus was chosen as the sacrifice in a crooked lottery, how I exchanged shapes with the old witch Dwynwyn and rescued him with the help of the outlaw Hibernian women. How the fugitives thundered across the straits just before the druids were cut off by a tidal bore.

"But why didn't you go with him, lass? Ah, no, how can I ask. You are of the *combrogos,* and he is not. Though you defied injustice and corruption, you still felt bound by our holy law."

"Er, not exactly. It's just that, well, I was nine months gone with child. I bore my daughter hours later."

"You were carrying his child, and he left you! I thought better of the Stranger than that. Why, if I ever see that young scoundrel—"

"It wasn't his child, Bran." I put a restraining hand on his arm, as if he were about to thrash Esus here and now. "And I have since found out that he has suffered terribly on account of my forcing him to leave."

"*Your* forcing him?" Bran was skeptical. "How could you force him?"

"Word magic, Bran. Believe me, I did force him. I forced my will on everyone."

"Strong-willed you are, lass, but you take too much on yourself. You a wee girl against the druids of Mona."

"No, Bran, listen. That sacrifice, rigged lots or not, the druids decided to make it when you were taken captive. It was for *you,* Bran, and for the *combrog-os.* And I stopped it. I may have saved Esus's life, but he has never known peace anywhere in the world since. And here you are, all alone and far away from your daughter and your people, and I, well, never mind about me—but I've mucked it all up, Bran. Don't you see?"

"No, *cariad,* no." Bran held me against him; my tears soaked into his warrior's chest like rain into a broad new-planted field. "I don't see that. I'm no seer, mind, but I've a true enough eye. All I see is a brave young girl saving the life of a boy she loved."

"But if his death could have saved the *combrogos*, saved you....?"

He took me by the shoulders and held me so that I had to see his face.

"Look at me, Maeve Rhuad, and tell me honest and true, knowing what you know now, would you go back and undo what you did, see the young Stranger killed three times over by stabbing, hanging, and drowning?"

"No, I would not."

I hadn't known how heavy a weight I'd carried till Bran's blunt question lifted it from me.

"Well then, let be, *cariad*, let be. The ways of the gods are strange. Our only choice is to play our parts with honor or without. Your honor is not in question. Not for a moment, but there is someone else's whose is. Now then, if the young Stranger did not father your child, who did?"

Bran had admired my father, a great political strategist, and worked closely with him. Why inflict more pain?

"It doesn't matter now," I said.

"I see you don't wish to speak of him. No doubt you have your reasons. But the child, Maeve? Where is your child?"

"They took her from me. She is fostering among the Iceni." My voice was flat.

"A wealthy tribe, known for its warrior women," Bran approved. "But you have never ceased to grieve for her."

"No more than you have ceased grieving for your daughter. Though your grief must be greater still, since you raised Branwen and you know how much she loves you. That's what I still can't bear, Bran, that by stopping the sacrifice I might have been the cause of Branwen's loss of you."

"You had nothing to do with my capture, Maeve. Though I have no doubt your queen mothers—bless their lustrous, honeyed thighs—schooled you in battle and shape-shifting both, could you impersonate a treacherous Roman ambush? As for whether the triple-death of some Stranger could have saved me, I leave that question to subtler minds than mine. But personally I've always suspected the druids went in for bloody bullhide oracles and reading of entrails because they've never known the blood of battle. Once and for all, lass, let be."

He was right, I suddenly saw: I was still clinging to the belief that I had caused all our sufferings—Bran's, Esus's, my own. It had been a relief to have it lifted from me for a moment, yet where did that leave me? At the mercy of life's plotless indifference?

I shivered and drew closer to Bran.

I did not want to tell any more of my story. What meaning did it have now? I had forgotten all about my detective work. I could not connect the sordid mess of Paulina's life with the poignant sweetness of this time out of time. I was with Bran in the Otherworld. Nothing else mattered.

"Tell me how you came to be the King of the Wood," I begged.

Bran sighed a sigh that filled the night; sparks flew from the fire on his breath; the great tree groaned and swayed.

"I'm sorry," I said. "I don't need to know if it gives you pain."

"What does pain matter?" he said. "If I don't tell you, then who will I ever tell? I want to tell you the truth of it. Then it will be yours to sing or return to the silence. I am no bard, so bear with me. You know the part about the ambush. How I had agreed to fight the Roman's champion in single combat?"

"Yes," I said, "and you were betrayed. They surrounded you, and you fought bravely and made them pay dearly. And your men fought hard, too."

"They tell it that way on Mona, do they?"

"Of course."

"Well, that much is true. I fought and killed as many as I could till I lost my sword, then I fought with my fists and my feet, until someone knocked me out with a blow to my head. When I came to, I was bound hand and foot, gagged, loaded into a wagon like so much salted meat. The Romans know full well that any Celtic warrior will fall on his sword or kill himself any way he can to avoid the dishonor of captivity, so they guard him well, especially a king. The idea is to keep him alive to parade him before the crowds in Rome."

"Oh, Bran," I said.

"There's a worse shame than being forced to walk in chains through the Forum. It's that I lived to do it."

"But Bran," I objected. "You had no sword. You were shackled."

"True enough. Yet I ate their food, didn't I? I drank their water. Well, after I was jeered in the forum, I thought I'd die of shame. I almost did. I fell into a fever. For weeks after that I was lost to myself. I wandered between the worlds, searching and searching for the way to the Isles of the West, listening, listening to hear the road calling me home."

"The road to the country of life is hard," I said softly, remembering my own delirium. "It blisters your feet and breaks your heart."

"Ah, I speak to one who knows. Poor Maeve. Then you can imagine how I felt when I came to myself in the charioteer's pen. My *combrogos*—I call them that, though many were Gaul or from tribes I once called my enemies—had kept me alive. Not that I cared to live, but I had lost the will to die, too. Death would find me soon enough in the ring, I thought. Fatal accidents were commonplace. Yet somehow it stayed just out of my reach, as if I hadn't earned it yet, wasn't worthy.

"In time, so I hardly noticed it, the will to live—and to be a leader of men—took hold in me again. My *combrogos* and I, joining with the gladiators and bestiaries—Huns, Scythians, Africans, all of us captives together—began to plan an uprising. In Rome there are spies everywhere, even in the pens, and I became a marked man. Yet every attempt on my life failed—loose spokes in the wheels, poisoned food. I was becoming a legend. So in the dead of one night, soldiers came, clapped me in irons and marched me out of the city with a chain gang of other slaves. I knew we were bound for the salt mines. Certain death, to be sure, but not a death that sang my name, not a death that would open the way to the Isles of the Blest. I knew I had to escape or die in the attempt.

"Slaves can be bought and sold, but loyalty is something else again, and there is an unpredictable quality in even the poorest man that makes him willing to do a noble deed. One of the soldiers in charge of herding us to the mines was a great fan of the races, and he had won money betting on me. He considered me good luck. He found a rotten link in the chain and gave me the tools to sever it.

"By then we were well out of Rome. The smell of the earth, the sound of running water, the deep-rooted life of the great trees gave me strength. I knew I didn't have much chance, but I knew, too, it would be better to die in the wild wood than in the mines. So I ran for all I was worth, trailing the broken chain all the while, into the mountains above this lake. It wasn't long before the dogs were after me and their masters close behind. I didn't have time to think or hide. When I saw the water, I made for it, thinking only to throw the dogs off the scent.

"I was about to take the plunge when a woman stepped out from the trees, dressed in a short white tunic, with an arrow at the string aimed straight at my heart. Now here's a lovely death, I thought, at the hands of one of the *beansidhe*, for so I took her to be. But when she saw my desperate condition, she lowered the bow and spoke to me. 'You won't get far swimming in irons. If you have the courage—and I believe you do—there's a better way.'

"Then she told me of the Holy Tree and the golden bough and the *Rex Nemorensis* waiting to meet his challenger.

" 'But why should I kill another man who is as wretched as I am?' I asked her. 'He is no enemy of mine.'

"The woman looked me dead in the eye.

" 'To kill him,' she said, 'would be a kindness.'

"The woman drew a sword from the scabbard at her side, handed it to me, and led the way.

"I beheld the Holy Tree and loved her before I saw the man beneath her. And with one giant leap I broke off a piece of the great golden bough. But when I saw the gaunt, half-crazed king I was to battle, I thought, how can I challenge this man? It would be like fighting a cripple or a beggar. Then he rose and faced me, and I saw the fierce, glad fire of kingship in his eyes.

"After that everything happened quickly and at the same time so slowly, as if another lifetime had been given to us. I am told that we fought for a full day and night without ceasing, neither of us knowing that a crowd had gathered beyond the glade—priestesses and the slavers who had pursued me. They did not exist for us. We lived in a hot, vivid world of breath and blows, the battle forging us into something bright and molten.

"Those who have never fought a man to the death don't know, but it sometimes happens that you come to love each other. You become more familiar to each other than the closest kin. Your enemy's face is seared into your flesh. His eyes look out from your eyes, and you see with his. When I drove my sword home through his heart, he fell forward into my arms. I held him against my own heart as he died."

Bran fell silent and we sat for a time, listening to the fire burn, watching the sparks rise and die in the gathering darkness.

"And so I am a king again, Maeve. It is a strange fate, guarding a Holy Tree so far from the Holy Isles. Yet here in her embrace, I know I am not so far. When you see my Branwen again and my sons, tell them I am free and a king. Promise me, Maeve Rhuad."

"If I ever see the Holy Isles again—" My voice broke.

"But surely, Maeve Rhuad, surely, now that the gods have found in your favor, you can return. Surely the druids would not—"

"Bran," I stopped him. "Bran, I am not only an exile. I am a captive, too. I know what it is to lose the will to die and the will to live. I was sold into slavery. I am a slave."

"Maeve, how can that be? You, the daughter of the warrior witches of Tir na mBan. I don't understand. You a slave?"

It was the worst thing I could have told him. It was a deathblow to his dreams. I hated myself for it. Why hadn't I just promised what he asked and left him in peace?

"I'm sorry, Bran. I'm so sorry."

"It's no shame to you, Maeve Rhuad, no shame. The shame belongs to the people who think to enslave the whole world for the sake of their greed and vanity. But if you are a slave, how do you come to be here alone?"

Before I could think how to answer, where to take up my tale again, Bran jumped to his own conclusion.

"How can I of all people ask?" He struck his forehead. "You've escaped. I was right the first time; you *have* come to kill me, to send me home. Who else but Maeve Rhuad would dare to be the first *Regina Nemorensis*? And now you don't know what to do, because the King of the Wood is your foster-father. Ah,

Maeve, Maeve, don't let our kinship stand in the way. Trust me, to kill me would be a kindness."

"Oh, Bran." I wrung my hands.

Stepped out of the Otherworld, escaped slave come to challenge the *Rex Nemorenis,* how paltry and unpalatable the truth was in comparison: I'm a rich woman's human pet. I came here sniffing out the secrets of her past like some hound.

"Did I guess wrong again?"

I nodded.

"Are you going to tell me, lass?"

A sudden wind lifted the leaves. Looking up into the shifting branches, I glimpsed the stars, and I remembered that there was another reason I had searched for the tree.

"I had a dream, Bran, a dream of this Tree. I had forgotten. It was years ago now, and you were in the dream. But I wasn't looking for you. I was searching for him, for Esus. I found him buried in the tree, the way the Egyptian goddess Isis found Osiris in a temple pillar. Then you were there; I asked you how I could set him free."

"Ah, lass, we all want to be free."

"That's just what you said in the dream, Bran. Just exactly what you said. Now you're here, and I'm here, and the Tree is here, but he's not. It's hollow. Hollow. What can it mean?" I felt desperate to know.

"Maeve, I am no ovate to know the meaning of dreams, just an old warrior waiting for his last battle, a king whose kingdom ends at the edge of the glade. But you, brave heart....Wait." He stopped and stared, not at me, but at something I could sense, shimmering and dancing at the periphery of my own vision. "There is a tree, Maeve; two trees. One is dead, and the other, oh!" His breath caught in his throat. "And you Maeve, you and the Stranger. I can't keep you straight. You keep changing places...."

Then he shook his head, and looked at me helplessly. "There's no more, Maeve, I'm sorry."

But for an instant I had glimpsed it, too, the bare tree against the sky, the cracked lips, his, mine. And the other tree, the one I had seen in a vision long ago, the tree with golden leaves that shed their own light, the tree we were meant to stand beneath, my true love and I.

"It's enough," I whispered to Bran. "I see."

I did see. My sight, my second-sight, had been restored to me. For one suspended moment, I could see all the worlds and times held secure and balanced.

The moment passed, as moments do. And then the worlds collided.

CHAPTER TWENTY-EIGHT
WHO WE ARE

"T reachery!" a voice shrieked. "Trespass, treason, sacrilege. I knew it! I knew it! Arrest her now. Seize her!"

Paulina stepped into the firelight, flanked by priestesses and temple guards. She pointed her long beautifully shaped finger (for some reason I noticed this detail) straight at me.

Bran leapt to his feet so fast, the old dry leaves under the tree rose and whirled. He sailed over the fire, his sword flashing. No doubt he'd had a lot of time to practice, and his reflexes had to be on a hair trigger. Still, his grace and fleetness were impressive. By the time I scrambled to my feet, Bran's mouth was going full spate. Like all Celtic warriors, he was as agile with his tongue as with his sword.

"I am Bran, King of the Wood, sometime King of the Silures, ab Fendi-gaid, ab Llyr Lleidiaith, ab…"

His recital of his lineage went on and on, the effect both terrifying and hypnotic. My would-be assailants could not move; their eyes glazed over.

"And he—or she," Bran continued when he was finally done naming himself, "who seeks to lay hands on my foster-daughter, who would harm even one single hair on her shining head, who so much as looks at her with evil intent or without the honor due to this daughter of queens, his—or her—life I value less than the life of a flea on the hide of a dog, less than the life of a worm boring into fruit, less than the life of parasites hanging from a sheep's—"

I don't know how long he might have gone on—he was only just warming up—but suddenly I realized he was speaking Celtic.

"Bran," I hissed.

"—miserable, stinking ass. Don't interrupt, Maeve. And he—or she—"

I tugged at his arm.

"What, Maeve, what?"

"Bran, they don't understand a word you're saying."

"What makes you think that, lass? Can't you see they're shaking in their flimsy Roman sandals. Now then, where was I?"

"You're speaking Celtic, Bran. Can't you speak Latin at all?"

"Enough to get by and only when I must. It gives me the headache. Mangling language with cases and conjugations; whoever invented Latin ought to be pounded into the pit." (An ignominious death the Celts reserved for captives and slaves.)

While we conferred with each other, Paulina recovered.

"Seize her, I said! What are you waiting for? Seize her now!"

The temple guards took a tentative step forward, but retreated when Bran raised his sword.

"O *Rex Nemorensis*." Egeria assumed her mantle of authority as high priestess. "We look to you for honor and truth. What business have you with this woman, who calls herself a priestess of Isis, while Publia Paulina Claudii claims her as slave? Whoever she may be, she has entered these sacred precincts without the knowledge of the Vestals. You appear to stand ready to defend her. Illuminate us. Who and what is she?"

Bran followed the gist of the priestess's Latin well enough. Then he surprised us all. He threw back his head and laughed, a torrent of laughter, like cataracts of water tumbling down a cliff or a huge wind driving leaves, waves, birds, the smoke of old fires, the fog of old fears before it.

"Who is she, you ask, what is she? Listen well. This bright one you see before you, this radiant one, whom I am honored to call my foster-daughter, is no less than Maeve Rhuad, the daughter of the warrior queens of Tir na mBan who trace their lineage to the great goddess Bride. Her father is Manannan Mac Lir—what do you call him here?—Neptune. Yes. As for Bride, I suppose she would be your Ceres, your Cybele, your Juno, your Diana all in one. If Maeve Rhuad says she is the priestess of Isis, she is being humble. For Isis wears the horns of Bride, too, so I've heard. No doubt Bride and Isis are two names for the same goddess, which makes our Maeve no mere priestess but a daughter of the divine lineage. So here she stands, daughter of gods, daughter of queens, foster-daughter of a king—"

"Piffle," squeaked Paulina.

"But a slave? I don't think so." His voice now was soft and dangerous. "Not in my grove she's not. Now then," he spoke directly to Paulina, "if you have anything further to say about my foster-daughter, step forward and say it to—"

He suddenly stopped. He was staring at Paulina, and, to my astonishment, huge silent tears began to roll down his cheeks. Then he opened his arms wide and held them out to her.

"Come, maiden. Come, my child," he murmured to her in Celtic; then he remembered and shifted to Latin, his halting formal speech limpid with tenderness. "Come to me, daughter of my dearest foe. Come to me, and I will sing to you of your father's valor."

As amazing as Bran's sudden shift in tone was the change in Paulina's face. It began to wobble and blur, not the way it would if she were struggling against tears, but as if her face were being unmade, the hard, set lines erased, melting into something raw and unformed.

"Come," Bran said again softly.

The wood was so still now you could hear the leaves breathe. Paulina moved towards Bran as if she had no will of her own. She stopped before him, head lowered, her eyes on the ground until he took her face between his hands and lifted it.

"I am glad to see that the blood and bone of the great one who was *Rex Nemorensis* before me live on in you. I don't know if you knew your father, lass, but you can be proud to claim him. He may have come to this grove a slave, but he died a king, which makes you the daughter of a king. I would have been glad to die at the hands of so noble a foe. But fate ruled otherwise. I can only hope that the one who is King after me is as worthy as the one who was King before me."

I could not tell if Paulina understood what Bran was revealing—or saw revealed in her. But suddenly she crumpled to the ground. The priestess and guards rushed forward, but I reached her first. I thought she might have fainted, but when I sat beside her she crawled into my arms and buried her face in my breast. She was trembling all over. I held her and rocked her.

"The lass is in shock," said Bran, sinking to one knee. "Perhaps she didn't know her father had died. Perhaps she hoped to find him living still."

"I don't think that's it exactly," I said to Bran; then I spoke to Egeria who stood over us. "Did you know that Paulina is not the daughter of Publius Paulus?"

A tremor shook Paulina. Good, I thought, she's hearing. Now all the pieces of the puzzle were assembled. No matter how ugly a picture they made, it was time to put them together.

"We did not know, but we suspected. We knew that Sylvia and the slave Virbius, her childhood companion, were lovers long before they were discovered. But according to Roman law, Paulina *is* the daughter of Publius Paulus.

He acknowledged her and raised her to his knee. By the time he suspected that he might not have fathered her, there was nothing he could do."

"That's where you're wrong." I said to the priestess. "There was plenty he could do and did."

I paused. No one questioned me or tried to silence me. I decided to go on the way you might force yourself to dig out a thorn embedded in someone's infected flesh.

"It is my belief that when Publius Paulus discovered his wife's adultery and realized Paulina was not his daughter, he raped the child to punish the mother. When Sylvia heard her daughter screaming, she came running and found her child naked and bruised, her thighs bloodied, pressed against the wall in terror. But Sylvia could not comfort her. Publius Paulus dragged her away, and she never saw her daughter again."

My last words were lost in Paulina's screams. She screamed and screamed as she had each night since we'd come to the villa. Bran and Egeria took a step toward her and stopped as if her screams threw up an impassable barrier.

But I was inside the wall of sound, Paulina's screams tearing through my body as if they were my own. I did not decide what to do next; I just did it. I slapped her across the face. The screaming stopped abruptly, and Paulina stared at me with huge, pupil-less eyes, panting but quiet.

"Red, did I have another nightmare?" she asked as if we were alone.

And we were alone, the way Bran and his dearest foe had been, the spectators shadowy and distant.

"No, Paulina. You're awake now. Listen to me. The man you called *Pater* tried to destroy you. He raped you when you were four years old and took your mother away from you. Do you remember now?"

Paulina flinched, but she did not deny it.

"But he didn't stop there. He married you to a man who wouldn't touch you. He threatened you with death if you ever took a lover. He tried to take your life more subtly but as surely as if he had killed you outright.

"The man who gave you life lived and died in this grove. It was the only chance at life he had, once Publius Paulus discovered that he was your mother's lover. I'm pretty sure your mother insisted he take that chance. That's why she left a bequest to the *Rex Nemorensis*. And that's why Publius Paulus refused to pay it. Because the late *Rex Nemorensis* was your mother's lover and your father.

"Know this, Paulina, and you won't have to have nightmares when you sleep, and in the daytime you will become more than a spoiled, loveless child. You can learn to be a *domina* in truth, not just in title."

Paulina's face turned red with rage at this insolence from a slave. She raised a hand to strike me, but then the color drained from her cheeks, and she buried her face in her hands.

"Slave," she mumbled. "I am the daughter of a slave and an adulteress."

"Get over it, Paulina," I said with less sympathy than I felt.

She lowered her hands and for the first time really looked at me—not her fantasy of a prostitute, her substitute for a lover or mother, her all purpose slave—but me. Then she narrowed her eyes and thrust out her lower lip.

"That's easy for you to say. According to him," she gestured toward Bran, "you're some sort of barbarian princess, with a more divine lineage than Julius Caesar. Not that I believe all that. But how on earth did you end up a whore at the Vine and Fig Tree?"

"That's a long story. If you really want to know, maybe I'll tell it to you some day. Or maybe I won't. But, for now, I will tell you this much. I am King Bran's foster-daughter and proud and honored to say so. I am, also, the daughter of the warrior witches King Bran hails as queens."

"More than one?" Paulina interrupted.

"Yes, eight mothers, nine if you count the Cailleach. She was more like a grandmother, I suppose."

Paulina looked understandably confused.

"My father, the man who got me on my mother—"

"One mother?"

"Technically. Anyway, my father, whom I didn't know was my father, turned out to be a very important druid. A priest and a counselor," I explained to the priestesses, who were all ears. "Yes, my father was Lovernios," I said to Bran.

"Well, even if he wasn't a god, that's a lot better than having a slave for a father." Paulina was still put out about her paternity.

"You may think so, but you would be wrong. This man, who fathered me, also raped me, taking my maidenhead, and got a child on me. I didn't know he was my father then, but in the end, everyone knew, though he never acknowledged me."

By the time I had finished speaking, the priestesses, the temple guards, and Bran were sitting around us in a circle. Bran was holding his head and moaning softly, rocking back and forth. I reached out and touched his cheek.

"I'm sorry, Bran. I didn't want to tell you."

"Ah, Maeve, *cariad*. Don't soften your words for me. Warriors know better than bards that not all stories are pretty. They don't all end well."

He took my hand and held it in both of his. Paulina sat, gazing at her hands in her lap, as if some wisdom pooled there.

"I want to make sure I have this straight," she said at length. "You didn't know who your father was. I didn't know who my father was. You thought your father was a god, but he turned out to be some crazy priest who raped you. The man I thought was practically a god was not my father, but he raped me anyway. My real father was a slave who became the *Rex Nemorensis*. Then your foster-father, who was already a king, came along and killed my father. Is that right?"

"That's the gist of it." I was impressed.

"So, um," Paulina struggled for words. "I mean, well, what does that mean?"

"What do you mean, what does that mean?"

"May I be permitted a question?" Egeria broke in.

"Sure, why not?" I said, as if I were in charge.

"I have heard you called divine, royal, daughter of a barbarian priest, mother of a child of incestuous rape. You have been claimed by the *domina* as her slave, and, if I do not mistake the reference to the Vine and Fig Tree, you have also been a whore. Yet I remain curious on one point, are you or are you not a priestess of Isis as you claim to be? No one else has identified you so."

I looked at her. Who and what makes a priestess, I wanted to ask. I had never been initiated into a temple hierarchy and had no desire to be. Yet whenever I became still, I could always hear the river moving through the reed beds.

"Isis alone knows," I said at last.

(Have you noticed that people were already asking me: who are you, who are you? As they later kept asking my beloved.)

"Well-answered," King Bran laughed. "That's our Maeve. You won't catch her out that easily. She's like a clever, red fox—" Bran stopped abruptly, remembering that my father's name, Lovernios, meant fox.

Then a silence came over the whole glade, as if the air itself held its breath. Not a leaf stirred; even the fire burned soundlessly. Paulina looked at me; I thought I knew what she was asking, and I didn't want to answer. I turned to Bran, my own unspoken appeal in my eyes. Bran, after meeting my eyes briefly, looked to Egeria. It was she who finally spoke.

"Publia Paulina Claudi, for so you still are, your name and fortune in the world remaining unchanged, now that you know your mother's secret, will you carry out her bequest at last?"

"I remember him," Paulina said suddenly. "A tall man with black curly hair and huge bulgy arms. I remember I liked to feel his muscles. He brought me a puppy once. He used to make my mother laugh. Oh!" she cried. "I remember her. Red, I can remember her."

I took her hand and squeezed it. Then she let go, and rose to her feet, more sober and grown-up than I had ever seen her.

"I will honor my mother's wishes, though the man who was my father no longer lives. I shall make good the bequest to the *Rex Nemorensis*," she said to Egeria. "Come to the Villa tomorrow."

"It is well done, *domina*," said Egeria.

"You are your father's daughter," approved Bran. "And your mother, may she grow young on the Isles of Apples, must have been a great lady."

Then the moment I had been dreading arrived.

"It's time to go, Red. Come with me." She tried to make the words a command, but I could hear her fear of losing me.

Everyone was on their feet now, Egeria beside Paulina as they waited for me.

"Bran!" My voice and my heart broke. "Can't I just stay here with you?"

I was more a child in that moment than I had ever been in my whole life. And Bran was my father, my good father.

"No, *cariad*, this place is my fate, not yours, much as I would like to keep you close and safe. You will find your way. Never doubt it, lass."

"But I've lost my way, Bran."

"Ah, Maeve, it only looks that way now, because you don't know where you're going."

"I'm not going anywhere, I'm trapped," I said bitterly. I didn't care if Paulina heard; I wanted her to hear.

"Not for long, sweetheart, not for long. Anyone who could get herself sent beyond the ninth wave and survive won't be trapped for long in Rome."

Then his eyes unfocused and he stared just beyond me as he had before. A chill passed over me.

"Hear me, daughter of my heart," he cried. "Within the year, the great maw of Rome that has swallowed you will spew you forth."

It was a vivid and rather grotesque image. I waited for more. But Bran rubbed his eyes and became once more the brave, weary man waiting for an honorable death.

"Red," Paulina implored.

By Roman law, I was still her slave, as soon as I set foot outside my foster-father's kingdom. I couldn't bear it. I buried my face in Bran's chest. I put my ear next to his great heart where I could hear the waves breaking on the shores of the Shining Isles.

"Maeve?" Paulina called me by my name for the first time.

"Go now, Maeve Rhuad," Bran whispered. "Bride with you."

"I love you, Bran," I spoke into his heart.

I walked numbly, as if my feet were deaf to the earth. Paulina walked ahead with Egeria and the other priestesses; the temple guards walked behind me. We took a different route from the one I had found earlier, and soon came to the shore. In the distance I could see not only the perpetual flame but hundreds of lights in the makeshift festival shrines outlining the contour of the lake.

Then our whole party halted at the sound of something large crashing through the dark wood. It stopped panting next to the lake, a tall black man, darker than the dark water, trailing irons. When he saw us, he froze for an instant; then he made ready to fling himself into the water.

"Wait!" I pushed past Paulina and the priestesses till I stood before the man who stared at me fiercely. "If you have the courage—and I believe you do—there is a better way, a way to live or die with honor, to die a king or at a king's hands."

"Tell me," he said in accented Latin.

So I told him of the Holy Tree and the golden bough, and the *Rex Nemorensis* who waited there.

"Why should I kill this man? What harm has he done me?"

"To kill him," I said, "would be a kindness."

Tell him, I wanted to say, tell him Maeve sent you. Tell him the way is open to the Isles of the Blest. But I could not get the words out.

"Will you guide me there, priestess?" the man asked.

Then Egeria stepped forward.

"Priestess of Isis, this is not your task. You have done enough. The Temple of Diana is forever in your debt. Guide the *domina* and her priestess the rest of the way," she said to the others.

And she disappeared with the challenger into the wood.

When I tried to walk again, I could not find the ground until I fell on it. I had no will to get up. Then someone's arms went around me, surprisingly strong and comforting, like a mother's arms. One of the priestesses, I supposed.

"Come on, Red. Lean on me."

She helped me up. Keeping her arm around me, Paulina led me from the Grove.

PRIESTESS OF ISIS

CHAPTER TWENTY-NINE

BACK INTO THE MAW

I wish I could tell you that after this moment of revelation and reversal, everything was utterly changed between Paulina and me, that when she recognized my divine—or at least royal—descent, she could not countenance keeping me as a slave. It would make a prettier, tidier story.

What happens next is messy. There are things I did that I still regret. Innocent people got hurt. And those who were saved perhaps did not deserve it. I will leave it for you to judge. It is no coincidence that in the events to come I had my first brush with history—(as distinct from the shape-shifting, time eluding Otherworld where the mythic and the mundane move in and out of each other). No, I do not appear in the accounts of Josephus, Tacitus, or Suetonius, but Paulina and Decius Mundus do. And I happen to know better than all those famous Roman historians what really happened and why.

We did not stay long in Nemi after Diana's Festival. Without any of us needing to discuss it, we knew our time there was over. People talk about the dog days of August, when the air is hot and so still it hardly feels like air at all. Everyone lies around sweating and panting. But there is another kind of August weather when the wind picks up, driving the first dry, dead leaves before it. The mornings are cold. Get moving, this weather says, find your winter place.

By the end of the month, we were on our way back to Rome. I walked barefoot beside the cavalcade as I had before, my feet listening to the earth. The bones of your foster-father are cradled in the roots of the Holy Tree, the ground whispered, and he has gone on to the Summerland. Beloved, keep walking. I will lead you where you need to go. Nemi, Rome, trees, stone, living, dead. I am always there beneath you.

Reginus came along and interrupted the conversation.

"Aren't you cold with bare feet?"

"No," I said, not elaborating.

"I know. You're a rugged country girl. You're sad to be leaving, aren't you?"

"Not as much as I expected to be," I said. "I suppose you're glad."

"Not as much as I expected to be," he sighed.

"That's just because you had a fight with Dmitri before he left. Don't worry, Reginus. You'll make up with him. Or you'll find someone else."

"You think I'm shallow," he accused.

"I don't." Did I?

"You do, Red. Or you would have told me what happened that night at the festival. Because I know something did. The *domina* is behaving so strangely."

"Do you have a problem with sleeping through the night?" I asked.

"No, and I have to admit, she doesn't scream as much during the day either, and she hasn't broken a mirror in a while. And she's way too nice to you, Red. It's not natural."

"We'll see how long *that* lasts." I tried to shrug it off.

"It spooks me, Red. I had my life figured out. I didn't always like it. But I knew what to expect. Now I don't. It makes me nervous. And I know you're holding out on me. Not that I can blame you. I was the one who told you never give away information for free. But you're my friend, Red."

"Reginus, I'm touched. You told me you didn't have friends."

"Now you're being evasive."

I was, and I had to wonder why. I had no reason or obligation to keep secret what had happened in the sacred grove of the king. As Egeria had observed, Paulina's legal identity remained unchanged. Yet if word got out that she was the bastard child of her mother's adulterous liaison with a slave, there could be unpredictable consequences. Was I protecting her or could it be that I was instinctively hoarding my knowledge in order to make use of it later? I found both possibilities so repellent that I almost blurted out the whole story to Reginus, then and there. But something I could not name held me back.

Instead I told Reginus my part of the story, of finding my foster-father, then losing him again, sending his longed-for death to him.

"Aw, honey," was all Reginus said, and he put his arm around me.

And in that moment, walking with my friend on the road back to Rome, I understood what my feet already knew. Seeing Bran had brought back my past and at the same time cast me loose. Cast me into some future as seed flung by a sower, as a flock of small birds skittering into a huge, stormy sky.

On the second day of our journey, it rained, and Paulina coaxed me to ride in her wagon.

"I've been thinking, Red."

That sounded ominous.

"When we get back to Rome, I'm going to make an addendum to my will."

Many Roman women did not have wills, but at Claudius's urging, Paulina had made one, because of her independent wealth. Of course, he was an interested party. Until she had a male child, everything went to him. As far as I was concerned, this making written lists of possessions and property was more evidence of the inferiority of Roman culture. Celts did not own land; it was a living, sovereign entity. They counted wealth in cattle, and if there was a dispute over a herd or the use of grazing land, they could always have a cattle war, and the bards could compose another poem.

"I am going to leave you your manumission." Paulina looked at me expectantly. "Don't you understand, Red? When I'm dead, you'll be free!"

"Don't tempt me," I muttered.

"You know, you could be a little grateful, Red. To be left manumission in a will is a great honor."

She really didn't get it.

"Paulina," I sighed. "You're only a couple of years older than me."

"So?"

"You could live a long time. Maybe longer than me."

"Your point?"

"If you want to free me, free me now. Lots of people free a slave who has rendered special service."

"And what exactly have you done for me, Red? Remind me. Did you save my life when I wasn't looking?"

"Paulina, I helped you find out who you are."

"And I should be grateful to you for that?"

"Yes," I said without hesitation. "Now you don't have nightmares. You can remember your mother and your real father, and you have the satisfaction of knowing that you're not the spawn of that cold *filicidal* fish you used to call *Pater*."

"I loved him, Red. Maybe I shouldn't have, but I did."

"I know." I acknowledged this complicated truth. "But you were terrified of him, too. Now you're free, Paulina, don't you see? Free. I want to be free, too."

She was silent for a moment. I could hear the rain falling on the wagon roof and the wheels scattering fine drops from the wet stones of the road.

"But Red, if I freed you, you would leave me," she said with unnerving, childlike simplicity. "Don't leave me, Red. I need you. I love you."

I had never felt more trapped.

"Besides, I'm not stupid, Red. I know you think I am, but I'm not. You know things I don't want anyone else to know. I need to keep you near me."

Paulina was still herself, shifting from vulnerability to unabashed self-interest with no awareness of her effect. I shook my head. Of course she was stupid. I was, too. All I had to do was say to her: Paulina, give me my freedom or by tomorrow night everyone will know you're the daughter of an adulteress and a slave. Why didn't I? Why?

"Let me tell you something, Paulina, as long as you have a secret, anyone can blackmail you. If it's not me, it will be someone else. You've lived in Rome all your life. Don't you know that yet? So why keep your parentage a secret?"

"Why? How can you ask that? If Claudius knew, he'd use it as an excuse to try to steal my inheritance. And, well, I'd never be able to go to the baths again. Maxima would ostracize me at the new temple of Isis. You know how she feels about mingling with the lower classes. She is dedicating her life to bringing Isis to the senatorial class, making her a respected goddess."

I did know, and the new suburban temple of Isis, built to exclude the slaves, whores and plebeians, was a sore point between Paulina and me.

"You know what, Paulina? You're the slave here, way more of a slave than your father ever was, more than I ever will be. You're the one who needs to be freed, but no one can give you your freedom, if you won't take it."

"I have no idea what you're talking about, Red."

"No, you don't," I agreed.

We rolled on in silence for a time, both of us sulking.

"Red, don't you love me at all?"

"You don't have a right to ask me that."

"Yes, I do, you're still my slave. I can ask you anything. You have to answer."

"As long as you keep me a slave, I have no answer to that question. You can order me to give you one, but I won't."

"I don't see why. Lots of slaves love their masters and mistresses."

I didn't respond.

"You know, Red, sometimes you have a stick up your butt, just like *Pater*."

I wished she would be consistently stupid, but when she fought, she knew where to hit. I couldn't think of anything sufficiently insulting to say in response and me a Celt whose mothers raised insult to an art form. But then, they usually relied on disparaging each other's lineage. And *Pater* was now out of the line-up.

"Look out of the curtains, Red, and see where we are. We must be getting near."

Of course, I was the slave, so I was the one whose head should get wet. I didn't mind really. I stuck my head out and held the curtains to my neck, so at least part of me was alone. The suburbs were closing in around us. On the right, Caeline Hill rose up obscuring part of the Servillian wall. Vallis Camenarum opened up on the left. You could look across the valley to the aqueduct. Beyond the wall, Rome rode the swells of its hills.

"Well, where are we?"

"Via Latina just merged with Via Appia."

"Oh, good, we're almost there." She clapped her hands.

For a moment I tried to see Rome with the eyes of a native instead of a captive, a lover instead of a contemptuous stranger. There was a fevered energy here, human squalor and splendor pressed up against each other like illicit lovers. Someone was always awake, plotting or pursuing pleasure. The hills gave the city scope; the river linked it to the sea. Rome was the heart of a ravening, sprawling empire. People who wanted their fingers on the pulse or in the pie had to be here.

"Listen, Red. Maeve." Paulina's tone was almost timid. "There's something more I want to say. Pull in your head for a minute."

I complied. The curtained wagon felt suffocating after the cool, rainy air.

"I can't...I just can't let you go. Not yet. But, well, I could change your title. You don't have to be my *pedisequa* anymore. I know you hated that title. That's why I gave it to you. I...I'm sorry now. Could you, would you be my priestess, my resident priestess? You could spend as much time as you wanted at the temple."

I raised an eyebrow. "The temple?"

"You know. The old temple. Venus of Whores and Adulterers. I'm sorry, Red. You know how Maxima feels about the new temple."

"Paulina, I wouldn't go to the temple on Campus Martius if you ordered me to."

"Well, I'm not. Believe it or not, I'm not ordering you to do anything. I'm asking: Will you be my priestess?"

I looked at her. Without meaning to, Paulina had answered the question that had been plaguing me: Why didn't I use my knowledge to force her to free me? It wasn't to protect her social position or because I was a good slave. At Nemi I had acted as a priestess on Paulina's behalf. I had called myself a priestess of Isis, a goddess who shared with my beloved's god that annoying trait of being able to go everywhere. Damn.

"I already am your priestess," I sighed.

"You don't sound pleased about it," she complained.

"Being pleased is not a requirement of the priestesshood."

I poked my head out of the curtains again just as the Capena gate came into view, and very maw-like it looked in the rainy dusk. As Rome swallowed me again, I prayed that Bran's prophecy would be fulfilled.

CHAPTER THIRTY

PLAYING IN TRAFFIC

Back at *domus* Claudius everything was the same, but Paulina was different, as the resident slaves soon discovered and as Claudius noted with some alarm. At Nemi she had developed a taste and a flair for having her own clients and running her own household. She was not about to go back to pretending to spin while Claudius had all the fun and wielded all the power. I counseled getting a divorce and setting up an independent establishment, but Paulina was uneasy and evasive when I raised the subject. And I had to admit that what I did not know about Roman law could and did fill libraries. It was Reginus who explained the complications to me.

"Listen, honey," he said one morning, looking around to make sure we were alone. "Don't even use the "D" word around here. If Claudius thought she was considering divorce, he'd beat her to it and try to set her up on an adultery charge. That way he'd get to keep the loot, and she'd be packed off to an island like her dear old *mater*, and we'd all have to go with her, Cybele forefend."

I wondered did each adulteress get her own island? It didn't sound so bad to me. Were there enough to go around?

"Claudius can't afford to let *her* divorce *him*," Reginus continued. "He'd have to return most of her dowry, and a court might appoint her nephew guardian of her estate. He's coming of age next year. Besides, the *domina* has no grounds for divorce."

"What do you mean she has no grounds? What about Claudius's adultery?"

"Honey, he only does it with men, slaves, and whores. Unless he did it with another *domina* from the senatorial class, it doesn't count."

It counted when Paulina's mother did it with a slave, I almost said, but then I remembered that Reginus didn't know about that.

"What about the fact that the marriage has never even been consummated?" I asked instead.

"Could you prove that? Technically, I mean." Reginus cleared his throat. "You would know better than I would."

"No." I was blunt. "Don't look at me. I had nothing to do with it. But Reginus, she has no children. He doesn't sleep with her. Surely that's a reason for divorce."

"Claudius could use it, if he wanted to, but she can't. Barrenness is always the woman's fault. Didn't you know that?"

"I should have guessed," I grumbled. "Listen, Reginus, you know as well as I do this is not a stable situation. Paulina is not going to want to be celibate forever. I was a stopgap, because she thought she could keep me hidden from Publius Paulus. At some point she's going to want a man."

"And she can have one—or half a dozen for that matter. Discreetly. Unlike that twisted son of a bitch Publius Paulus, Claudius doesn't care who she fucks. He cares about the money, and he cares about his social standing."

"But you just said he'd get to keep the money if he divorced her for adultery."

"He'd get to keep the dowry," Reginus clarified. "But he'd only divorce her for adultery if he thought she was trying to do him out of money. He doesn't want a big scandal, if he can avoid it. Bad for business, and business is all that matters. You know I'm fond of you, Red, but let me handle this one. I have connections in both camps, and if anyone can smooth out the new balance of power in *domus* Claudius, it's me. Don't rock the boat, Red. You're a priestess now. Go do whatever it is priestesses do."

Go play in traffic, he might as well have said. In Rome there was plenty of it. And that's essentially what I did for a time. Because I had no clue what a personal priestess did on a day-to-day basis, and neither did Paulina. Despite her permission to go to the old Temple of Isis whenever I liked, I avoided it. I wasn't sure why. The priestess at the Venus Obsequens had been so certain that I would eventually join their ranks. I had no reason not to, except perversity, a desire to cling to the illusion that I had at least some free will. Or maybe I was afraid that if I embraced the role of priestess, my path would end at that temple. I would have my place and purpose in Rome, and that would be that.

So I spent a lot of time just walking through the city, not exploring exactly; that implies some intention. I mostly kept moving, just to keep moving, the
way some caged animals do, for I was still caged, however new and improved
my perimeter. A few times I ventured into the suburbs. As long as I was in
densely settled places, no one took any note of me. But a woman or any lone
person on the open road was cause for suspicion and a target for slave catchers,
who were always on the lookout for runaways—or fresh merchandise. I had
learned the hard way not to make an impulsive dash for freedom.

I quickly learned to steer clear of the Lavernalis Gate and any other that
led to Via Ostiensis. That heavily trafficked road to the seaport was the Roman
state's favorite site for crucifixion, the preferred punishment for everything
from stealing to inciting a riot. There were almost always half a dozen people
dying slowly, with bored soldiers in attendance supposedly for crowd control—except that they never did anything to stop the taunting and spitting.
Public humiliation was part of the punishment.

Paulina did not concern herself with my comings and goings as long as
I was there when she needed me in the lazy hours of the afternoon. The other
slaves noticed my changed status, but did not know what to make of it, so they
assumed I was going out to spy. I was followed a few times, which amused me,
especially as I was good at losing my trackers. Since I never led anyone anywhere, after a while the would-be counterspies lost interest. Only Boca seemed
concerned for my safety, so I usually stopped by the kitchens to reassure her
when I came back in. One day, when I returned, she was in such a state of high
agitation that she acted out a pantomime of violence, complete with a scene of
chase and capture.

"I'll be all right, Boca," I said. "I'm just a slave. When I have to, I cover
my hair and lower my eyes, and no one pays the slightest attention to me. I
know how to disappear when I want to."

But that did not satisfy Boca, who went and tugged at the sleeve of one
of the sub cooks, an older man, and kindlier to Boca than most of the others.
She acted out her pantomime again.

"I think she's trying to tell you about the pack," said the cook.

Boca nodded emphatically and stroked the cook's arms in thanks, encouraging him to go on.

"Senators' sons," he elaborated. "It happens from time to time. Too
many young men putting on their togas but with nothing to do till their fathers
die. Too much time, too much money. They can't all go off and be generals, I
suppose. Well, sometimes they run wild together, robbing people for kicks,
chasing down women. It's a bad business, but the *aedile* can't control them.
Their fathers are rich, see, and well-connected. If they get arrested, their fathers

bail them out. Say it's all just boyish fun. The packs come and go. There's been a new pack around lately, mostly in the Subura. Nothing to worry about, as long as you're not in the wrong place at the wrong time. We're safe here, and I only go to the markets early in the mornings when the carousers are passed out from drink."

"Thank you for warning me," I said to Boca and the cook. "I'll be careful." But I knew as soon as I spoke that I had no intention of altering my aimless routine.

I met the pack a few days later when it was neither late at night nor was I anywhere near the Subura. I had gone for a morning walk by the Tiber. Around midday I started back by way of the Forum Boarium near the Circus Maximus, the most direct route back to *domus* Claudius. Then I remembered that there had been a bestiary show in the Circus that morning, and the crowds would be pouring into the market place between rounds in search of food, drink, and the plentiful street whores, so I skirted the area, climbing the narrow, less frequented alleys of Aventine Hill.

I was the only one on the street when I heard shouts and laughter coming from somewhere close by. I might have ignored the commotion, assumed it was a dice game or a party, but a woman's scream broke through the male voices, only for an instant. Then it was cut off; that's what it sounded like to me— a hand coming down over a woman's mouth. I started to run.

I recognized the pack as soon as I saw them down a filthy cul de sac. There were about a dozen of them, and they wore the clothes of their rank, torn and dirtied by the chase. I couldn't see the woman they had cornered. But I knew exactly what was happening to her, as you must, too. Two of them held her down, a third raped her, while the others urged him on, shouting encouragement and insults.

"Hey," one of them tried to shout over the others. "Take your hand off her mouth. You're gonna suffocate her."

"Aw, what difference does it make," said another. "Dead or alive, we can still fuck her."

"I like a little fight in mine."

"Go on, take your hand away. Let her scream."

"What are you, crazy? Someone might hear her."

"No one's gonna hear, and if they do, they're not gonna care."

That's where they were wrong. I did not have to think. All I had to do was take breath, a deep breath that pulled in the power of the earth under the hard Roman stone, that drew down the fires of the heavens, and then I loosed the sound that was always there in the hollow of my bones, ready to rise—the cry of my mothers, the *beansidhe*. The sound went on and on; it shredded air, it tore into entrails and loosened bowels, it shriveled appendages. It poured through me, and I rode it like a wave or a torrent, without thought or fear.

And then it was done. Before I could fill my lungs with air again, the pack turned on me.

"Here's another one."

"I swear they're lining up for it these days."

They were nervous, even frightened, but all the more menacing for that as they advanced on me, leaving their other victim apparently unconscious on the ground. I had to think fast. I could not outrun them. I could not threaten them with the law. I might disable one or two with a knee to the groin or fingers in the eyes, but I couldn't fight them all.

"Stop where you are," I commanded. "Know this, all of you: the power to curse is mine. Do not call it forth or you will beg to unbreathe every breath you have ever taken, you will cry out to crawl back into your mother's wombs, and beseech your sires to undo your very begetting."

Why I didn't just say, you'll be fucking sorry you were born? By now you should know: I'm a Celt, for one. I was also doing my best to hypnotize them with the rhythms of my voice and the intensity of my stare. I was having some effect; they stood poised and uncertain. One or two had even taken a step back.

"Bollocks!" one of them shouted. "Have at her, boys!"

The pack surged forward again.

"Wait!" someone else called out, and elbowed his way to the front. "Stop. I know this woman."

I looked at the speaker, one of the older youths, with the scars on his face of a bad complexion. It took me a moment to place him. It was the awe and the hint of fear in his eyes that recalled him to me: Anecius's son, the one I had initiated some three years ago.

"So? Introduce us. Don't try to tell us she's your cousin or your aunt. Not with hair like that."

Oh, great, I thought. Boys, meet my first whore.

"She is a priestess," he said.

Was it that obvious? Should I be flattered?

"Oh yeah? What kind of priestess?"

"A very powerful one," he said.

Good answer. They looked skeptical but uneasy.

"If you leave," I seized the moment, "I will refrain (with difficulty) from speaking the words that will cause your pricks to fester and stink before they blacken and rot away altogether. As for your balls, I will spare them for now. But if you ever hurt or force a woman of any rank again, the curse that I hold in abeyance will hunt you down. Your balls will fall off and scatter to be eaten by feral pigs. Go! Before I change my mind."

"She can't do that. She's crazy. She's one crazy bitch."

I widened my eyes and began to roll them around as if I were about to have a fit. I bared my teeth and managed to work up enough spit to look as though I might foam at the mouth. Then I began to move towards them, pointing my finger and muttering. It wasn't long before one of them panicked and bolted past me out of the alley. That was all it took; the rest hurtled after him.

Once they had scattered, I hurried to the woman and knelt beside her, feeling her neck for a pulse. She was alive but unconscious. She was thin, with sallow skin and lank hair. It was hard to tell her age, because of the bruises on her face. Her clothing was badly torn and stained with mud and blood. Before I could do a more thorough examination, I heard footsteps approaching. I turned to look, and there he was again: Anecius's son.

"Nice bunch of friends you have," I snarled.

He looked a bit hurt; I suppose he was hoping I would thank him for saving my life, but I didn't feel particularly grateful.

"Since you're here, make yourself useful. We need to get her to some help."

"Wh-where shall we take her, *domina*?"

"How 'bout your little palace on the Palatine?" I suggested and had the pleasure of watching him blanch and squirm.

"Isn't that a bit far?" he hoped.

"I suppose." I looked around and suddenly I knew where we were.

"There's a temple to Venus. Venus Obsequens. It's not far from here. We can get help there, but I am telling you now, Anecius's son—yes, I remember you—I am holding you personally responsible for her convalescence and future support. Got that?"

"Yes, *domina*," he said meekly.

Domina again. I could get used to that title.

When I had determined that she had no broken bones beyond a few smashed ribs, we made a pallet of my cloak—it had been a brisk morning—and managed to carry her the few blocks to the Temple. Isis must have guided my steps, for I hadn't been there in some time. The door to the dingy little temple was open. Someone was singing and shaking a sistrum. As we entered, I called out.

"I have a wounded woman in need of help and refuge. Is there a healer in the house of Isis?"

The singing stopped, though the sistrum kept on or maybe it was the sound of the wind in the river reeds. Then someone called out an answer.

"There is now."

The priestess who had once saved my own life stepped forward out of the twilight at the back of the temple. In all my fleeting, noncommittal comings and goings, I had never learned her name. I had intentionally kept my distance. I didn't want to belong to a temple any more than I wanted to belong to anyone or anything else.

"All right," I surrendered. "I need water, wine, and clean cloths."

"We'll carry her to the back chamber," the priestess said.

She motioned and several others, male and female, came forward to help. Out of the corner of my eye, I saw Anecius's son begin to back away.

"You!" I snapped my fingers at him. "Stay. You are going to see this through."

I might as well have said, "Heel." He did instantly, and we all followed the priestess into a cheerful, homey room that opened onto an enclosed courtyard. An open door and window let in plenty of light. It looked as though some of the priestesses lived here. There were sleeping pallets rolled up against the wall, and an open hearth for cooking. We laid the woman on a pallet, and the priestess got a knife to cut away her clothes. She was covered with cuts and bruises, as I'd suspected she'd be. I closed my eyes the better to see with my hands as I moved them over her body. As soon I touched her, I could feel the fire of the stars begin to flow.

Then someone began to pour water. I knew that it was only water from a pitcher being emptied into a basin, that I was kneeling beside an injured woman in a temple in Rome. Part of me remained there, fully intent on what I was doing.

But part of me is somewhere else. Water gushes from a spring and runs over rock through a walled garden. A fresh wind is blowing, a wind that smells like water and fish and roses. I don't know where or who I am in this place, but my sight is directed to a tower in one corner of the wall. Two people stand in silhouette against a dawn sky full of dim, disappearing stars.

Then the sound of the water stopped, and the vision was gone, leaving behind, like an after-impression, a joy so poignant I still don't know how to describe it or explain it. You may have had dreams like that, dreams you don't understand and can hardly remember. You don't speak about it. You don't dare. It was like that. The joy lingers after you wake.

I opened my eyes and picked up a cloth soaked in water and wine. As I began to wash the woman's wounds, she moaned and stirred. It was a good sign. She would be all right.

CHAPTER THIRTY-ONE

MY LIFE

And so as simply and inevitably as that, I became a priestess-healer at Venus Obsequens, our lady of whores and adulterers, a.k.a. Almighty Isis. I ceased my aimless ramblings and spent much of my time at the temple. On a typical day I would arrive early in the morning for the hymns and the vesting of Isis. Then I'd hold a clinic until noon when I'd return to Paulina. More often than not, I'd go back to the temple in the late afternoon and stay for the evening hymns when the statue of Isis was divested of her robes and garlands until the next day.

I liked singing the hymns; they were poetry, and I had once been a bard in training. I began composing, adapting some of Bride's praise songs and adding elements of my own. Unlike the priests and priestesses at the suburban temple, Aemiliana, the resident priestess at Venus Obsequens, was not a stickler for tradition and did not insist that all hymns had to be ancient and authentically Egyptian. And so I introduced a wild, haunting Celtic note into the great tradition of Isaic aretalogy.

Word soon spread that there was a healer at Venus Obsequens. Most of what happened at the clinic was simple first aid, if you want to know the truth. The rest of the time, I just touched people. The fire flowed through my hands and gave my hands sight. Not X-ray vision; I did not see kidneys or gall bladders, but I saw images, some I didn't understand, some as simple as a clear pool or clouds dispersing, and I directed them with my hands to the site of the illness or injury. Sometimes I would hear a song and sing it, sending the sound through my hands. But I am not sure any of that matters.

I want to tell you: being a healer is no different from being a whore, a paradoxical mix of the intimate and impersonal, the receiving of another human being without judgment, the bone-deep knowing that you are not separate from this other. You recognize the river flowing under all skin, the tidal rhythms of breath, the darkness of earth giving rise to and claiming all flesh.

I was known as the Red One, and if you are wondering if I was enjoying my fame or being seduced by its power, the answer is no. Perhaps you are disappointed. Perhaps you were hoping that I would be faced with the temptations of pride and succumb (later to be redeemed, of course). That's a classic plotline, but it's not the one I'm working with here. On the other hand, if you're concerned that I'm about to turn self-effacing and saintly, relax. That's just the reverse side of the pride story. I'm not interested.

One day my reputation brought me an entirely unexpected visitor. We had just finished the morning hymns to Isis. As people milled about, greeting each other or making their private petitions to the goddess, I noticed a tall woman near the entrance, her stance at once commanding and ill at ease. When she saw me looking at her, she nodded her head ever so slightly. It was the quality of the gesture—ironic, stiff, faintly mocking—that I recognized first.

"Domitia Tertia?" I took a step towards her.

"Red," she greeted me. "Or should I call you something else, now that your status is so elevated?"

"No more elevated than the slave block in the Forum where you first found me."

"Oh, come now, Red. They tell me you are a priestess. Half my household is running over here every chance they get. They've all converted," she said with marked distaste. "I was curious. I thought I'd come and have a look at you myself."

A delayed reaction caught up with me, and I was suddenly struck with the strangeness of her presence here. Domitia Tertia seldom left the Vine and Fig Tree, except on business. Like Circe's island, her house was the seat of her power. That she would set out to see a slave in the hole-in-the-wall temple of a goddess whose worship she considered a lot of overblown twaddle was unusual, possibly unprecedented. It behooved me to be gracious.

"Will you take some refreshment?"

I saw her hesitate. I sensed that she had come here impulsively without a clear purpose, and her own behavior disconcerted her.

"Thank you," she said at length.

I took her to the back room, and the other priestesses, perhaps at some cue from Aemiliana, nodded politely but gave us what privacy they could. I invited Domitia to recline on one of the only couches and fetched wine, bread, oil-cured olives and cheese. We ate and sipped in silence for a time. I found myself at a loss for words. How's business, didn't seem quite right. And, as she had noted, my friends from the Vine and Fig Tree visited the temple frequently, so I did not need to inquire for their health. I decided to say nothing. Maybe being a priestess was having some effect on my character. I never used to be able to keep my mouth shut.

"All right," said Domitia after taking what can only be described as a gulp of wine. "It's more than idle curiosity that brought me here. A lot of whores come and go at the Vine and Fig Tree. I take good care of them while they're with me, because that's the way I do business. But when they go, they're gone."

She paused, waiting for me to say something, waiting for me to help her say what she wanted to say. I merely nodded.

"But you," she sighed, "you have not disappeared satisfactorily. In fact, you are becoming notorious."

Odd, to be so notorious, yet to feel so unknown. Or maybe that is a common side effect of notoriety.

"I was very angry with you when you pulled that caper with the boat," she continued. "I believe I still am. You put us all at risk, and threw away everything you could have had with me. I didn't want to sell you to that little piece of baggage, but I had no choice. I'm angry with you for that, too. And I am angry most of all, because my dearest friend lost his head and his pride over you."

"Angry or jealous?"

"What a conventional assumption, Red. I am disappointed in you. Not that I owe you any explanation, but Joseph is a great deal more to me than a lover. We helped each other survive in times when either of us might have ended it all. That's a more enduring bond than the one people make in bed. Too bad you cut short your career as a whore or you might have learned that."

How can I know, I wanted to say. My beloved and I never even had a bed.

"For Joseph, you are a fantasy—"

"I know that," I cut her off, irritated by her condescension. "I was supposed to be his Aspasia. I'm not right for the part, any more than you were, but I suppose I showed more promise." I couldn't resist a dig. "Look, Domitia. I can't help what Joseph saw in me. I never set out to deceive him or use him."

"But you shamed him. He came back from seeing you at Nemi broken and humiliated. For that, I cannot forgive you."

"Don't then."

There was a charged silence between us. If we had been cats, you would have seen our tails lashing and our whiskers quivering. I broke down first.

"Did he tell you what happened?" I demanded.

"No. He said only that he failed you. Then he tried to extract a promise from me that if you were ever in trouble, I would send for him. I did not answer; I'm afraid he assumes my compliance. Tell me, Red, why should I honor such a request?"

"Because your dearest friend asked it of you?" I suggested.

"If I am his friend, perhaps I should do all I can to protect him from you."

"You already tried that," I pointed out, "and it didn't work. You're powerful, Domitia, and shrewd, but you're not all-knowing, for goddess sake. You're as mortal and foolish as the rest of us. If Joseph didn't tell you what passed between us, I won't either. You can believe me or not: I did nothing to shame him."

And that was the truth. It irked me that I felt compelled to defend myself. So I clamped my mouth shut and resolved to give her nothing more. We had another silence, and I felt a mild triumph when she spoke first.

"I find I do believe you."

I had an impulse to shrug—it was becoming a very bad habit—but I restrained myself, because it would have been a lie. Whether I liked it or not, Domitia Tertia's opinion did matter to me.

"Thank you," I said.

"That still doesn't mean I'll fetch Joseph for you, and I'll tell you why."

"No need," I said.

"Yes, there is a need. Rome is not a healthy place for Joseph to be. I have no intention of calling him here for any reason. In fact, I've urged him to stay away. Tiberius is not the friend to Jews that Augustus was. He's made it no secret that he resents the Jewish community's prosperity and independence and especially their loyalty to their temple in Jerusalem. Even scarcely observant Jews like Joseph faithfully pay the temple tithe. And there are an increasing number of proselytes from the senatorial class, especially among the women, who are sending money to Jerusalem, too. Not that Tiberius likes Isis worship any better. Slaves converting their mistresses, as you have done, he finds distasteful and potentially dangerous, upsetting to the natural order."

"I did not convert Paulina," I objected. "Besides, she spends most of her time at the new temple with Maxima Fabia where women of your class don't have to rub elbows with the riffraff."

Domitia Tertia did not rise to the bait. Instead she drained her wine and did not stop me when I poured her more. She seemed to be settling in for more than a brief visit.

"That's another thing," she went on. "If I were your Paulina—"

"She is not *my* Paulina."

"—I'd keep a distance from Maxima. She presumes too much on her connection with Livia. It's a risky strategy, trying to win Livia's approval and patronage of her new pet cause. But if there's trouble, Maxima won't take the fall. Someone else will. Paulina, for example, if she's as rash and luckless as her mother. That might be exactly why Maxima is cultivating her acquaintance."

"You knew Paulina's mother!"

"Oh, we all knew each other. Valeria was a few years older than me. Very beautiful and a bit wild. Then she married that pompous bully. I don't know why I'm telling you this—"

Because you have had a considerable amount to drink, I did not say.

"—it's all a long time ago, what happened to Valeria. But when I found out about it, I decided, that's it. That's never going to happen to me. That's when I registered as a prostitute. I gave up everything to do it."

Isis save us, she *was* drunk. She was getting maudlin and melodramatic.

"Do you regret it?" I asked.

"No," she said thoughtfully. "No, I don't." She frowned and peered into her wine cup as if it were an oracular well. "And what about you, Red? Do you regret what you gave up?"

"Do you mean the Vine and Fig Tree?"

She nodded.

"Oh, *domina*, it's not the same. I had already lost everything."

And I had only sipped *my* wine!

"That is how you would see it, I suppose."

"How would you see it? Have you ever stood naked in a slave market?"

"Just about." She did not elaborate. "Well, whatever you lost, here you are, a priestess, a healer with a growing following, a slave who virtually commands her mistress, and yet I sense you are not satisfied. What is it you want, Red?"

What did I want? What did I *want*? I closed my eyes for a moment and felt dizzy. Images swam up out of some dark place. I saw his bare feet on a rocky path and mine beside them. I heard the sound of water, could feel its coolness on our sore feet. Last I saw the tower and the two people standing there. I want *him*, but even as I thought it I knew that was not quite right. I wanted the stars, the water, the rocks. I wanted the joy, the danger, I wanted—

"My life," I said out loud.

She gave me an odd look.

"You are having it, Red," she said. "Hadn't you noticed?"

"I am not free," I said stubbornly.

"Freedom," she snorted derisively. "The whores who lean against the fornices in the Subura are free, Red. Is that the kind of freedom you want?"

"What about the kind you have, *domina*?" I turned the question on her.

"I pay for mine," she said.

No, I almost said, your whores do, but I was suddenly too tired to bait her. I didn't want her life or her freedom. I wanted mine. *Mine*. It seemed farther away than ever.

"Excuse me, Red," Aemiliana came in from the temple. "There are people waiting. Will you see anyone more today or shall I send them away?"

"Yes, I will. In a moment." This was my life.

"I have taken enough of your time." Domitia rose a little unsteadily to her feet.

I got up and offered a hand she would not take.

"The wine may have loosened my tongue, but I think I can manage to walk to my litter. It's just outside."

"Thank you for coming," I said politely.

"I didn't come for your benefit, I came for mine. Listen, Red, Rhuad—whatever Joseph calls you—if you get into trouble, I will not promise to call Joseph, but I will offer this much: get word to me, and I will help if I can."

I wanted to ask her why; instead I said something I knew would mortify her.

"You're a good woman, Domitia Tertia." I found that I meant it.

"Not at all." She meant it, too.

As I watched her walk out of the back chamber, I gave her the blessing of Isis. Very softly, so that she would not hear.

CHAPTER THIRTY-TWO

ECSTASY AND EXCREMENT

We were entering the season of sorrow when Isis and Nephys would search again for Osiris, picking bits of him out of the Nile. The word mourn derives from a root that means remember. When Isis mourned Osiris, she re-membered him, literally. Maybe all remembering has the same purpose, to restore what is lost, to make the unruly fragments of lived experience a coherent whole. Which is why memory is the mother of the muses. Memory is something we make, the primordial art form. But if a poem or a story or a memory is alive, it shapes us, too.

It was three years now since I'd tried to turn the Tiber into the Nile, myself into Isis, not Isis seeking the pieces of Osiris but Isis hightailing it off to find her lover in the wide world. Maybe that's why it hadn't worked. It was the wrong part of the story. Maybe it was the wrong story altogether. If I ever found Esus, I didn't want to find him entombed in a tamarind tree, and I didn't ever want to dredge a river for him. To hell with my dreams. What good had they done me?

For as long as I could, I'd held my capsized boat against Isis and kept her at a distance. Now here I was, installed in her temple, all my bottom-feeding memories rising to the surface, stirring up the sludge. This year I would be an official priestess with a sanctioned place in the boat, and yet as the holy day approached I found myself in a funk. I hated the whole idea of the ritual, of ritual itself, re-enacting the same story over and over with no power to change the plot. How could I bear to lament and troll the smelly old Tiber, year after year, everything lost, nothing gained.

"Child, you look so weary," said Aemiliana.

It was the eve of the *Isia*. All the priestesses had gathered for an all-night vigil in the temple. Hundreds of tapers burned, and the temple tonight looked more impressive, with the smoke of incense rising and shape-shifting. Instead of seeing dulled or chipped paint, I saw rock formations and lichen, as if we were in a cave. Outside rain lashed and wind moaned, most atmospherically. The statue of Isis was shrouded in black. Someone had draped a fish net over her arms, making it appear that she held it ready to cast.

"Come, speak with me a moment before we begin the silence."

She led me to a quiet nook behind a pillar and motioned for me to sit beside her. I wished I could be the child she had called me. I longed to lean against her. I was tired, but I held back from the comfort I wanted. I was not a child. My mothers were lost to me in another world.

"Your spirits have been low lately," Aemiliana observed. "I'm afraid we ask too much of you."

I shook my head. It was not the work, not the people I touched or whom the fire touched through me. I called it fire, yet river might be just as accurate. I rode the current; that was all.

"My spirits have been low for a long time, Aemiliana. It's nothing new."

"Will you tell me about it? What oppresses you?"

It seemed like such an effort to find words for something that had become pervasive, elemental. Yet Aemiliana meant to be kind. I did not want to rebuff her.

"Three years ago, I tried to escape, tried to find my way. Now here I am."

"Three years ago, I recognized you as a priestess. Now here you are."

We were silent for a time. The rain lulled, but the wind kept searching the streets, restless, not finding what it sought.

"I don't want to be ungrateful to you, Aemiliana, but being a priestess of Isis in Rome is not what I had in mind."

"Oh, I see, you thought you had a choice." Her tone bordered on teasing. I did not want to be jollied.

"Whether the gods choose or whether we choose, I don't know," I said. "But I thought I had been chosen for something else."

Aemiliana allowed a silence. I could hear her doing it. The silence became a well on a tiny tidal island, where eels swam up from some bottomless depth. It was *Samhain*, and a full moon would soon rise.

"Tell me," Aemiliana said at just the right moment.

And so I began.

"There was a seer, an old woman with wild, white hair, and a girdle of skulls. She told me: 'You will be a great lover.' Later she said to us both, my beloved and me: 'You are not just the lovers of each other, you are the lovers of the world.'

"But I lost him, Aemiliana. I let him go. I made him go, and it hurt him. Now, sometimes I can hardly remember him. I can't picture his face, just his feet. I don't know how to love the world. I don't want to love the world. I am so angry and lost. If this is my life, if this is my place, why can't I be at peace?"

"You cannot force peace," said Aemiliana.

"Doesn't the Roman sword force peace? Why not a *pax Romana* in my heart?"

"Is that what you want?" she asked.

"No," I admitted. "No."

"Let go of time, daughter. Stop holding it so tightly. Don't you know the river is always rising and always meeting the sea?"

I didn't know what she was talking about, but her voice seemed to come from some great distance, from Tir na mBan, from the stars beyond the wind and the rain. At the same time her voice was inside me.

"Our lady Isis knows all about loss, longing, searching, exile. Pray to her tonight. Pray for a dream. A dream to show you what is true."

For the vigil, we all found places near the statue of Isis. Some priestesses knelt; others lay prostrate. I sat with my spine straight, my legs before me with my knees forming an M on the tile floor. Now and then a priestess rose to cast incense or dried herbs on the charcoal brazier that provided the only warmth in the temple. I did not look at the figure of Isis mourning but stared straight ahead, focused on nothing. The glint of light on the mosaic walls became abstract and appeared to float on the smoky air

Pray, Aemiliana had said, but I wondered if I knew how to pray. Once I had believed I was the daughter of a god, the great granddaughter of a goddess. The gods had been my kin; they hallowed the wells and the hills. They inspired poems and songs, sacrifice and bravery. But had I ever prayed, the way my beloved had prayed to his god, his invisible god, always with him, talking and listening, commanding and quarreling? For all I called myself her priestess, had I ever prayed to Isis who troubled my dreams, who called me to love people I did not want to love in a place I did not want to be?

"Isis," I heard myself whispering; or maybe it was only the wind. "Isis, Isis, Isis."

The fire of the stars began pouring into me; my hands burned. There was no one sick or wounded to tend; the other priestesses were deep in their own devotions. The burning was becoming painful; I had to do something with these hands. Slowly I brought them to my heart and held them there, my fingers pressed together lightly, so that the palms and thumbs formed a chasm.

Isis, Isis. Esus, Esus. Yeshua, the name Anna called him, the name his mother must call him, Yeshua, Yeshua. His name was saying itself inside me, in the rhythm of my breath, in the rhythm of waves rushing in and out of a sea cave. Yeshua, Yeshua. I chanted his name till it was not a name anymore, but sound itself, longing itself, the sound of longing, the loneliness of the gods, a primal yearning that could call worlds into being, stars, galaxies.

Then he was with me—not a memory or a dream. Not past or future. He was present. I did not see him; I did not hear him. I just knew him. He entered me, filled every opening. I was an opening—vulva, heart, crown, all only ways to receive his total penetration. Insistent and gentle, dark and bright, sweet and salt all at once. I let him all the way in; but how could I let in the whole sky, the whole earth, the hard rock and the rolling seas, the huge leviathan? Wave on wave, breath after breath, his hardness and heat flowed through me until I burst, the way a seed splits open, the way ripe fruit spills seeds. Uncontained, dying, ecstatic. Then slowly, achingly his presence ebbed and emptiness gave me back my form.

I was awake, sitting in the same position, my hands still held at my heart when the other priestesses began to stir and make preparations for the procession to the river. I wanted to be alone for a moment before I got swept up in the festivities as any woman might after a blissful night with her lover. I rose to my feet, noticing that my limbs were remarkably warm and fluid for having sat so long on a cold floor.

Outside the pre-dawn air was chilly, but the clouds had blown away overnight. Venus had risen high enough that I could see her over the cityscape. She looked so clear and close that I had a child's impulse to stand on my tiptoes and reach. I paid no attention to the sound of approaching footsteps. Just someone coming to join the procession, I assumed. The stretch felt good, so I extended it, my cloak falling away, the cold air stiffening my nipples. I registered no discomfort in the cold; everything was sensual.

Then the footsteps stopped. I heard a gasp and a noisy clattering. When I looked down, there was a man prostrate before me in the street.

"Sovereign Isis," he began intoning into the paving stones, "inventor of navigation, mistressh of the winds, shtar of the sea—"

He was slurring his words. No doubt he was a sailor in Rome for the *Isia* whose sacred vigil involved drinking all night in a tavern. His voice sounded familiar, but then I'd known a lot of men.

"—um, queen of all sea going vesshels, and er—"

He seemed to be running aground. Clearly he was not a Celt or he could have kept singing my praises indefinitely. Though many sailors were foreigners, this man's Latin was not accented and seemed to be fairly upper crust.

"Keep going," I instructed.

My voice, in contrast to my appearance, must have given me away as merely human. I could not keep my amusement out of it. The man dared to look at me, first my feet, which may have been a little muddy after yesterday's rains, then the rest of me, his head bending further back as he raised himself on his elbows. Finally he got to his feet, accepting my hand to help steady him.

"Pardon me, priestess, you dazzled me so, I took you for the goddess herself."

"Never apologize for mistaking a woman for a goddess, Decius Mundus."

For so he was, standing before me, a little worse for wear and reeking of drink.

"Oh," he said, his focus narrowing. I went from goddess to priestess to "You're Paulina Claudii's slave woman, her *pedisequa*. I remember you."

"I preferred your first impression."

Was I flirting with him?

"Are you still of her household?"

"I am." I saw no need to elaborate.

"It's all coming back to me." The shock of recognition seemed to be sobering him up. "I saw you here with your mistress just before I sailed for the East. You were quite badly behaved, as I recall."

He looked at me speculatively; I knew the look: What a saucy little slut you are.

"What are you doing here?" I asked, turning his attention from me to his favorite subject.

"Oh, I just came to give thanks to Isis for my safe return."

And to find a cheap whore into the bargain, I bet.

"And how was the looting in Parthia?" I asked.

"Not too bad," he answered without shame. "We put the rebels in their place for the time being. A long time to be away from Rome, though."

"The city of old farts who sit on all the power and all the wealth that other people fight and sweat for?"

I quoted him to himself, and then I felt mildly embarrassed that I apparently remembered that conversation so well.

"True enough, but still the old mother wolf for all that. By the way, I heard that Publius Paulus died. Is it true?"

Speaking of old farts, he might have said. It was a logical leap.

"Yes. A malignant growth in his asshole," I added unnecessarily.

He winced squeamishly. "How is your mistress bearing up? Surely by now she has children to comfort her? She is still the wife of Claudius?"

And you are still a fortune hunter, I did not say aloud.

"Ask her yourself," I said, instantly regretting my words. I had as good as invited him back into her life.

"Thank you, I will. I'll wait for her here until she finishes her devotions."

"You'll wait a long time, then," I said.

I turned to go back inside, when he put his hand on my arm and pulled me toward him. If I were a goddess, I would smite him for such familiarity. But unfortunately I was a woman. His hand was warm, strong and compellingly male.

"Don't play with me," he said with just the right degree of hoarse sincerity.

Why not? What else are you good for, I felt like saying. But I resisted. I could hear the other priestesses bustling. Lay devotees were beginning to arrive. I had other fish to fry that day—or Nile crabs, as it were.

"Look, Decius, Paulina's not here," I said.

"But how can you be here without her?" His muzzy little brain was puzzled.

"I'm her priestess now, and I go where I please, not that it's any of your business. And if you're a devotee of Isis, you'll know that today is the *Isia*. So if you'll excuse me." I removed his hand. "I'm very busy."

"I meant no offense, priestess," he grabbed hold of my hand and held it for just a moment, looking at me with his black thick-lashed eyes, his expression somewhere between mocking and caressing.

Suddenly I burst out laughing, "Get out of here."

With the hand he'd just released, I patted his cheek, shaven in the Roman style but bristly with morning stubble. In another moment that cheek was against mine, and he kissed me before I could stop him. Then he turned and sauntered away like the naughty boy he was, forgetting all about his prayers of gratitude to Isis.

(Aside: Are you wondering how I can move from a rapturous, mystical union with the divine lover—who in his own mortal form was wandering around with mud on his feet, too—to flirting with and, I'll admit it, being mildly aroused by, a self-involved twerp like Decius Mundus? It is part of the mystery that largesse and pettiness, beauty and absurdity can coexist, must coexist. Whoever thought it up—if you want to call it a who—willed it so, ecstasy and excrement all mixed up together. If you can't laugh or weep, or preferably both, you're in big trouble. It's called being human.)

I joined the procession, and I spent a long day by and on the river, singing and drumming into the evening. Despite my earlier resistance to it, the ritual served its purpose. My own particular sorrow, so narrow and familiar, expanded, deepened, became one with all sorrow. I felt emptied and cleansed, and, by the time I got back to *domus* Claudius, I was exhausted.

I found the other chamber slaves dozing where they sat, for Paulina wasn't back yet. After waiting for a while, I gave up, presumed on my privileges, and crawled into the wide couch I so often shared with Paulina. I fell asleep instantly and deeply.

I did not wake up when Paulina came in, and she did not demand that I attend her as she undressed and undid her complicated hairdo, but neither could she wait till morning to talk to me. When she got into bed, she shook me awake, which took some persistence on her part.

"I'm here," I finally mumbled. "Didn't steal a boat this time. Let me sleep."

"Red." She put her mouth right by my ear, jangling all the delicate bones in there. "Red, wake up. It's important. He's back. Do you hear me, Red? He's back!"

"Mmm." I put my hand over my ear, and tried vainly to slip back into sleep.

"Decius Mundus, Red." She pulled my hand from my ear. "I saw him at the festival. He was in the crowd when I was standing on the pavilion steps with Maxima. Our eyes just locked!"

I groaned as I came all the way awake.

"It was like he sent a bolt of lightning straight into my heart."

Her heart. Right. But it was her crotch she was pressing against me, wrapping her legs around my thigh.

"Then the procession to the river started, and I lost sight of him in the crowd. I was wild to find him again. I sent Reginus out looking for him, and then," she gave a big ragged sigh, "someone—I just knew it was him—put his hands on my shoulders and turned me towards him. I practically swooned. No, I did swoon. He had to catch me and carry me to one of the pavilions."

If you were a respectable matron or a well-guarded young virgin, swooning was an effective way to get yourself into a man's arms.

"He brought me wine and food and stayed until I was quite recovered. He says he will call on Claudius soon—but of course we must be discreet. But oh, Red, when he touched me, I just melted like hot wax in the sun."

(Note: that was her over-worn simile. I take no responsibility for it.)

"Oh, Red, Red, what am I to do?" She murmured into my neck, her breath sour with wine. "He loves me. Do you think he loves me? He must love me."

I wasn't surprised when she reached for my hand and placed it right at ground zero of her meltdown. Do you think I should have answered her question then and there? Gotten up and fetched cold water to throw on her fantasies? No, Paulina, he doesn't love you. He's in love with himself, and he's out for what he can get, in this case Claudius's money and/or yours. If I had, could I have changed the course of history? Who knows? I didn't answer her. I took the path of least resistance. I did what she wanted me to do, thinking that was the best way to get us both some sleep.

Paulina was so hot, and my hands were so skilled, it didn't take long. Her climax was violent; her whole body convulsed. I was shaken, too, not by ecstasy but the images that rose unbidden in my mind: a screaming crowd, people being rounded up in the streets, nails pounded through flesh. The images flashed by so quickly and with so little context, that I did not recognize them as a warning—until it was too late.

CHAPTER THIRTY-THREE

BEDROOM FARCE

ecius Mundus began to come to *domus* Claudius almost every day, paying homage as a client in the morning, often remaining to dine and go to the baths or the games. From what I observed at the rare banquets I attended, Decius was charming and entertaining, full of tales of his exploits in Parthia with General Fullanus (of whom he did a sly, unflattering imitation). Claudius was amused and made Decius a favorite, to the distress of other hangers on and heirs hopeful. He did not, however, offer him a room as he had the last time Decius wintered in Rome.

To her dismay, Paulina had little private access to Decius. He was always outwardly correct, honoring her as his patron's wife, but he sent her just enough lingering glances, augmented by the odd discreet touch or murmur, to keep her in a state of perpetual anticipation and arousal. After a while this exquisite frustration began to tell on her. She slept fitfully and was too distracted to eat properly (though she never forgot to refill her wine glass, I noticed).

Now that Claudius had adjusted to Paulina's relative independence— i.e., having her own clients instead of spinning demurely—he ignored her as he had before. Paulina's infatuation with his pet equestrian appeared to trouble him not at all—if he even knew about it. I wondered if double-agent Reginus was keeping him informed. I hadn't seen much of Reginus since I'd been spending so much time at the temple. But one day we encountered each other on the way back to the *insularium* and decided to stop at a tavern for a tête-à-tête. Reginus often picked up tips at the baths, so he had enough to buy a full wineskin.

"What do you think the chances are that Claudius will ever choose Decius as an heir?" I asked after we'd caught up on other news.

Reginus, seasoned spy that he was, carefully surveyed the room before he answered. He stretched, and then casually brought his elbow down closer to me, so as not to look as though he were leaning in for a confidence.

"The real question isn't will he choose Decius but whether he'll choose an heir at all," said Reginus. "You see, to Claudius, death is hypothetical. He has no intention of actually having one. Naming an heir can be bad for your health. Adoptive fathers have been known to meet mysterious and untimely ends. Besides, if Claudius named an heir, the fun and games would be over. He'd be just another boring old pervert, and buff young equestrians would stop spreading their luscious little cheeks for him."

"Have you ever told Paulina what goes on in the men's baths?"

"Come on! Do you seriously think she wants to know? She'd probably have my tongue cut out. Let her have her own little fantasies. They're harmless."

"I'm not so sure about that," I said.

"Why? What's the worst that could happen?" He was both curious and dismissive.

"You know, Reginus, I'm not sure I should talk to you about Paulina. You're working for Claudius, after all."

"Oh right, and you're such a loyal slave." He rolled his eyes. "Well, never mind. These days I probably know more about what goes on with the *domina* than you do."

"True," I agreed. "So what's your take? What do you tell the other camp?"

"I'm not sure I should talk to you about what I tell and don't tell Claudius," he came back at me. "But seriously. What's to tell? So she's got the hots for Decius. Who doesn't?"

"Are you speaking for yourself, Reginus?"

"Should I be speaking for anyone else?" He gave me an intent look.

"He's sexy," I admitted. "He might be fun in bed. But he's not my type."

"What *is* your type, Red?" He was serious. "You haven't been with anyone but the *domina* or me since I've known you. Frankly, that strikes me as unnatural. Do you have some deep, dark secret?"

I thought of my night in the Temple, and a wave of heat broke over me. A smile spread from my lips over my whole body.

"Damn! Who is he?" said Reginus.

I just shook my head. My secret. Dark, bright, deep. Untellable.

"Not Decius. I'll tell you that much. If I got up to anything with him, Paulina would definitely kill me or at least pull out all my hair. Not worth it. Maybe you see another side of him when he's with the men, but I'm getting sick of the way he's playing her, giving her just enough to keep her panting. What's his game plan?"

"You may be giving him more credit than he's due. Most of what that boy's got going for him is packed between his legs."

"He has a smoldering gaze, too, don't forget." I interjected. "Women like that."

"His eyes may be in his head, but that doesn't mean he has brains behind them. I doubt his plan is much more complex than 'hedge your bets, play both sides.' If Claudius dies intestate, everything goes to Paulina. Did you know that? So then there's this lusty young widow dying to marry him. That is, if Decius ever gets *his* divorce."

"He's married!" I was taken by surprise.

"Oh, yeah. Some putative heiress in some godforsaken outpost, I forget where. He tries to keep it quiet in Rome. It was a case of double hoodwinking, I gather. Each party thought the other had a fortune. It's tied up in lawsuits. Meanwhile, our boy is trying another route to riches."

"Does Paulina know?" I wondered.

"I haven't told her, and I'll lay odds our hero hasn't either. I wouldn't be the one to break it to her if, I were you."

"Maybe it would bring her to her senses."

"What senses? Any senses she's got are completely under his control."

"That's for sure," I sighed. "But still, she's got a right to know. I'm going to tell her, if you won't. I can at least do that much. After that, I can't help it if she runs to him, and he hands her a line about how his marriage was all a mistake, and he's trying to get a divorce, and his heart is only hers, and if only—"

I stopped. If Decius ever did get a divorce, the pair would have a compelling motive for murder.

"That's right." Reginus confirmed my unspoken thought. "But don't worry, honey. It would take a lot of effort and planning to carry it off. I'm not sure either of them is up to it."

"Reginus." A chilling thought occurred to me. "You wouldn't—"

He took some time to answer; he was seriously considering. What if Paulina offered him manumission with enough money to set him up for life?

"Naw," he finally said. "I don't have the stomach for it. Would you?"

I thought about it and questioned my initial horror. What difference would it make to me, a savage Celt? What objections could I have to killing a

Roman? Still I found that the idea of helping Decius and Paulina become successful assassins held no appeal.

"Naw, me neither."

"I think we need another drink," said my friend. He poured one. "Here's to us."

The last dry leaves of autumn blew away. Saturnalia came and went with its frenzy of licentious festivity. Decius took advantage of the season's laxness to push the limits with Paulina, but he never went beyond them. Unlike Paulina, he had plenty of opportunity for orgiastic release. When he had money in his pockets, he went to the Vine and Fig Tree, where he was popular for his charm and good looks. So many men were sheer hard work to fuck, I understood how my sister-whores might welcome him.

Too bad there was no comparable place I could take Paulina. Since the *Isia*, I wasn't who or what she wanted. I did not have the appendage in question, an item she had fixated upon with a volatile mix of longing and fear. Remember, as a woman, she'd had no intimate experience of men. Her early encounter had given her nightmares she was only just shaking off. One dreary afternoon in early February, after months of fleeting kisses and vague promises, Paulina flung herself on my breast and wept in sheer frustration.

"Paulina," I said when she'd worn herself out, and I was weary of stroking and soothing. "Just have the man. Or tell him to leave you alone."

"We can't, Red. You know we can't. We have to be careful. It's only a matter of time till Claudius names Decius. It could be any day now."

"Oh, Cybele's balls, Paulina."

I had been over this ground with her before. I had made Reginus's arguments, and I had told her about Decius's marriage. Just as I'd predicted, when she confronted him, he'd snowed her.

"You don't like him," she accused. "You're always so unsympathetic."

I made no comment. I had nothing new to say. After a few more attempts, she gave up trying to draw me into argument or agreement and just lay against me, worn out.

"Red," she said, just as I'd begun to hope she was falling asleep, "if we decided, well, if we couldn't, didn't want to wait anymore, would you help us?"

"Paulina, you're a big girl now. Trust me, you'll know what to do. The two of you don't need any help from me, much as Decius might enjoy two at once."

"Don't say things like that about him!"

Honey, I *know* things like that about him, I could have said. Berta and Dido had once given me a blow by blow(job) description of a threesome they'd had with him. But it wasn't worth the breath.

"Anyway," she continued. "That's not what I mean."

"Then what kind of help are you talking about?"

"Help, you know, arranging it. A place, a time."

"Paulina, you could do it anywhere. Do you really think Claudius would care?"

"I have no idea. But we couldn't possibly risk it. Not now. I don't see how you can take, well, adultery so lightly." She was whispering now, even though we were alone. "You know what happened to my mother and my sister."

"Honey," I stroked her cheek. "He's dead now. Publius Paulus is dead. He can't hurt you anymore. You're safe now."

But no one ever is, really.

"You didn't answer my question, Maeve." She never called me Maeve unless she was serious, dead serious—or desperate. "Would you help us?"

"Well, I still don't see the point, but yes, of course, I would help you. But I want to make one thing clear. Adultery, yes. Murder, no. Do you understand me?"

"I understand," she said, sounding like a little girl promising to be good.

I couldn't help but notice that the mention of murder did not seem to surprise her.

I confess I did not take Paulina's plea for help very seriously. The mention of murder notwithstanding, I still assumed we were in the realm of bedroom farce, a genre Roman playwrights and theatergoers relished. I apparently had a bit part as the devoted female slave who lived to further her mistress's love interests. I found this petty role demoralizing, so I dismissed the matter from my mind, figuring it was only a question of time till lust overcame the pair and they had at each other in some deserted passageway without the need of my services.

Meanwhile, I wanted to get on with my own story. That night in the temple on the eve of the *Isia*, I had conceived something I will call hope, for lack of a better word. I can't even say hope of what, exactly. Hope that I would find my way again. Like a woman in early pregnancy, I hardly dared admit my hope for fear of losing it. But as winter wore away, and the first signs of spring appeared—a balmy day here, a hint of green there—I felt it quickening. I didn't know what would happen next, but I felt a new confidence that something would. Change was coming.

I was right. But I could never have predicted the form it would take. Nor did I recognize its harbinger.

"Oh, it's you!"

I looked up from emptying a basin in which I'd just bathed a man's infected toe to discover Decius Mundus standing in the doorway.

"So you're the one they talk about," he continued. "The Red One. I should have guessed. That's why I hardly ever see you at *domus* Claudius anymore." He sounded tremendously pleased with his limited powers of deduction. "What is your name again?"

"There is no need for you to know it," I said shortly.

"Oh, come now. Why so severe? You're not some solemn vestal virgin. You're a priestess of Isis. You can afford to bend a little, be gracious like our merciful goddess."

How would he know what I could afford?

"Was there a reason you came here? Apart from idle curiosity. Because I'm very busy with the clinic. People are waiting."

"And I am one of them, *domina*. I'm your next patient." He smiled hugely, as though he had just bestowed a costly gift on me and anticipated my surprise and pleasure.

"Oh?" was my minimal response.

"I fell from a rigging," he explained, a bit dampened. "I thought it was just a sprain. The foot's better, but all my joints on that side still ache when it's damp."

"That is to be expected," I said without sympathy.

He looked abashed, and even hurt, like a little boy whose mother is being inexplicably withholding.

"You'll be able to predict the weather," I offered. "A useful skill."

He looked at me incredulously. Charm was his currency; he wasn't used to having it refused. I was beginning to enjoy myself in a not very nice way. Perhaps I *was* cruel.

"But I don't want to predict the weather. I want to be *healed*," he said dramatically, as if he were a cripple. "They say you can heal with your touch alone. They say you work miracles."

"People exaggerate. I would have thought a sophisticated, well-traveled man like you would know that."

"I'm just a simple equestrian, ma'am."

If he had been wearing a cowboy hat, he would have tipped it. As it was, he smiled so beguilingly that my resistance was put at risk. It was hard to ignore those dark eyes, long lashes any woman would kill for. His face was still hardened by his recent outdoor life with just a trace of boyishness lingering. No wonder Paulina was a wreck.

"Lie down, then." I kept my tone curt and gestured towards the couch.

He complied at once and immediately took advantage of the position, gazing up at me with a look of calculated vulnerability: Here I am, all laid out before you, all my vital organs exposed. What more could any woman want?

I ignored him.

"Show me where the worst pain is."

He rolled towards me. Hip joint, he indicated, and his coccyx. Of course. Keeping my face carefully blank, I placed one hand on his hip and one on his tailbone. I closed my eyes as I often did when seeing with my hands. In this case, I also wanted to shut out the distraction of Decius himself. I began to settle as I opened myself to the fire and saw beyond the man's insistent personality to his pain. The joint was indeed inflamed and the muscles around it under strain.

"I don't know why you dislike me."

He sounded sincerely puzzled. For if I did not respond to him as he expected, his little, tiny belief system received an unwelcome jolt. Chaos threatened.

"Be quiet," I told him.

"No, really," he persisted. "I want to understand. You know, your mistress is devoted to you. I find that quite touching."

Isis help us, he was sentimental as well as conceited.

"I'm sure it distresses her that you feel such antagonism towards me."

I tried to keep my focus strictly on his hip and back. The fire flowed though my hands in a cool, silver stream, dissolving the red, loosening the knotted muscles.

"What are you doing?" he asked.

"If you were in the middle of a battle, would you want me to ask you that question?"

"Point taken," he said with surprising good nature, and he managed to keep his mouth shut until I was done.

"You can go now," I said.

He rolled onto his back again, but made no move to get up.

"I am not going anywhere till you answer my question."

I put my hands on my hips and looked at him with exasperation. "Idiot child, don't you know I can call the temple guards and have you thrown out on your *podex*? The only reason I hesitate is respect for the work I just did on that part of your anatomy. Now rise up and get your miraculously healed butt out of here before I change my mind."

Slowly and insolently he moved to a sitting position.

"Your antagonism only makes you more challenging and alluring, you know. I wonder if you are doing it on purpose." He looked at me speculatively.

"If I am, which I don't concede, it is not for the purpose you suppose."

As soon as I spoke, I knew I shouldn't have.

"What purpose then? Because, you know what? I think you want me. You're fighting it, but you want me."

Oh, Decius, you have guessed my secret, I could have said, but out of loyalty to my mistress, I must resist you, alas. And he would have sauntered away, his belief system restored, and left me alone. Maybe he would have left Paulina alone, too. But mouthing off is an addiction, and once you start it's hard to stop.

"You want an answer, Decius Mundus? Brace yourself. I keep you at arm's length, because you are bad news. You are a loser. You have neither guts nor fortune, but you think glory and wealth should come to you without any risk or effort. Charm and looks are your only claims to fame, and you squander both. Apparently you are not smart enough to see that Claudius is playing you—and a half a dozen like you—for a fool. Meanwhile, you are playing Paulina for a fool. Yes, a fool. But she, at least, is sincere, if deluded, in her passions. I don't like what you are doing to her. And I don't like you.

"As to my wanting you. Yes, I believe it would probably be fun to fuck your brains out, that is, supposing you have any. But even a whore and a holy whore, priestess of an all-gracious, overly-accommodating goddess, has her standards. If you inherited a double fortune, you would not be able to afford my services. And if you ever tried to force me, the way equestrians do to slaves all the time, you'd have to look for your balls in the far reaches of the empire—"

I was speaking Latin, but my Irish was up, as the saying goes. I was in love with the sound of my voice, and the roll of the words on my tongue. It didn't matter anymore what I was saying. I was about to start in on his lineage, when Decius threw me a curve.

"Awesome!" he said gazing up at me. "You are truly awesome. You are like a towering flame. You are like...a goddess!"

Isis save us, the man was serious. With all my experience, how could I have failed to guess that he might be one of those men, so common among military types, who enjoys abuse? Did I really have a calling as a dominatrix? (Notice the Latin root.) Bonia and Domitia Tertia had thought so. Decius apparently agreed. Now what was I to do?

"It is time for you to go," I said in my flattest voice.

He got up, and then fell to his knees where he bent and kissed my feet, which were bare, each toe separately. It was hard, but I managed not to kick him in the face. It would only have encouraged him.

"What can I do to serve you, priestess of Isis?"

"Nothing. If you worship Isis, your service is due to her, not to me. And for Isis's sake stop tormenting Paulina."

He rose and gave me an adoring look. Where had all his cockiness gone?

"I hear and obey, *domina*."

He was making me very nervous, but before I could say anything more, he bowed and turned away.

CHAPTER THIRTY-FOUR

THE SHIT HITS

For the next couple of days, a sense of foreboding plagued me. I debated saying something to Paulina about the encounter with Decius Mundus, but I wasn't sure how to couch a warning. It wasn't Decius's attempts at seduction that bothered me. That behavior was in the realm of the ordinary, and Paulina would only deny it or blame it on me. How to tell her about his bizarre—and, I hoped, temporary—adulation of me? As February passed with no further visits to the temple from Decius, I began to hope that whatever had come over him that day was a fleeting aberration.

The exuberant spring festival of *Navigium Isidis* was now only days away. There would be a procession all the way to Ostia to bless the ships that would sail to the grain baskets of the empire to bring back wheat. I was busy helping to build and paint our temple's float when Aemiliana told me that someone wanted to speak with me privately.

"Male or female?" I asked with trepidation.

"A female, I believe, but incognito. So I suppose it could be male. Whoever it is, is waiting in the backroom. Call if you need help."

"Maeve!" hissed the shrouded figure as I entered the room, and I knew at once who it was.

"Paulina, what are you doing here in that ridiculous getup?"

"I've come to seek the counsel of a priestess."

"It's not like you never see me," I said crossly.

"I must say you are not being very hospitable," she complained. "In fact, I find your conduct unbecoming to a priestess of Isis. Doesn't our goddess say, come unto me all you who are heavy laden, and I will refresh you?"

(Note: Yes, Isis said it first.)

"Honey, you don't know from laden."

"Oh, shut up, Red. I didn't come here to be lectured about how over-privileged I am by my over-privileged slave. I came here for a reason. I can't talk to you at *domus* Claudius. I need to tell you something privately." She dropped her voice. "Secretly."

She gestured questioningly towards the doors.

"We're as safe here as anywhere," I sighed. "All right. Sit down."

Before I thought better of it, I poured us both some wine. She tore off her veil and gulped hers, and I took what can only be described as a slug of mine. The Celt in me anticipated the invention of one hundred proof whisky.

"He has asked me to become his lover." Paulina leaned close to me, her mouth at my ear. "He says he can't wait anymore."

I felt hot and claustrophobic. The wine hit my bloodstream. A moment later it flared in my cheeks.

"It's about time," I said lightly.

But my foreboding began to drift into the room in wisps like smoke from a sacrifice. Stop tormenting Paulina, I had said to Decius. Was this his answer? I didn't want it to have anything to do with me.

"I'm scared, Maeve." She looked at me, her eyes round and childlike.

"It will be all right, Paulina," I said, feeling more maternal towards her than perhaps was wise. "Do you know how to prevent conception?"

Despite the wine she'd already downed, her face paled.

"I haven't even thought about it."

"Listen then. I'll tell you what to do."

I gave her an introductory course in contraception while her eyes glazed over.

"Maeve." She clutched my hand, and I wondered if she'd taken in a word I'd said. "Maeve, you have to help us. Decius says we must do it in the temple of Isis."

"In the temple of Isis! But why?" I asked, afraid of the answer.

Did he hope to make me jealous? Did he want to impress me with some kind of twisted piety? Add mental unbalance to amoral opportunism and what did you get? Nothing I wanted any part of.

"I don't know!" Paulina wrung her hands. "So that the goddess will protect us and Claudius won't find out, and he'll name Decius his heir, and then maybe he'll die, and Decius will get his divorce, and we'll get married, and I'll have sons, only sons. I don't want any daughters, Maeve."

"Sweet Isis, Paulina! Has Decius said all that? Do you really believe life works that way?"

"Why do you ask so many questions?" She was on the verge of tears. "Just make it all right. If we do it here, it will be safe and holy. I know it. The goddess will be honored. I mean this *is* the temple of whores and adulterers, isn't it? Trust me, I will make it worth the temple's while."

"What exactly are you asking me to do?"

"Open the temple for us. Let us in. At night. If anyone asks where I am, you could explain that I have been chosen for a special rite. It could even be true. Don't the gods take lovers? I mean, maybe not Osiris, I wouldn't presume. But what about what's-his-name, Anubis?"

"Paulina, let me get this straight. You want to use this temple as a trysting place for adultery. And if anyone asks, I am supposed to tell them that Anubis, a jackal-headed god most Romans consider an abomination, has requested the sexual services of a respectable Roman matron? Mother of Isis, wouldn't it be simpler—and less risky—to rent a room somewhere? Or how about a little spring vacation on your estate?"

As soon as I said it, I knew I had made a fatal mistake. That was where her mother had been caught.

"Maeve." Her voice wobbled with tears. "You know I can't go there. Not just because of…you know, what happened. But think about it. There are hundreds of slaves at the villa. Someone would tell. You have to help me. You promised. This is the most important thing that has ever happened to me, Maeve. Decius loves me. No one has ever loved me before."

I love you, I almost said. What stopped me? My stubborn insistence that I couldn't love her if I wasn't free? My refusal to say it when she'd asked? If I had told her then: I love you and know you far better than Decius ever will, would it have changed the course of events? I'll never know.

"Listen, Paulina, if you want a safe discreet place, I can arrange one, a nice one, a classy one."

"Where? How?"

"Domitia Tertia told me that if I ever needed her help, she would—"

"Domitia Tertia!" If Paulina had been a cat, she would have been hissing and puffing her tail. "You've been seeing her?"

Why hadn't it occurred to me that Paulina would resent Domitia Tertia just as she resented anyone who'd had any claim on me?

"She visited me here once. She knew your mother, by the way—"

I stopped, but it was too late. What was wrong with me today? My instincts were dangerously dull.

"Don't talk about my mother in the same breath as that hard-nosed flesh monger," she snapped. "And how dare you! How dare you even suggest that I meet Decius in a brothel? As if I was a whore instead of a sacred bride meeting her sacred bridegroom. That's what Decius says. Our marriages don't count; they are just crude, legal arrangements. Our love is sanctified, holy—"

"If your love is as holy as all that, it'll be holy in a brothel, and you'll be safer and more comfortable there than here."

It was getting on my nerves, this distinction between holy lovers and lowly whores, sacred temples and profane brothels. I had seen the inside of both, and there wasn't as much difference as people supposed.

"But if word ever got out—"

"Paulina, that's the point. Domitia Tertia is rich and well-connected. She can protect you. The priestesses here are neither. They've been kind to me; I don't want to put them in danger. This temple isn't even legal. If Decius Mundus thinks this is a safe place, he's even stupider than I thought."

"And you," she said, eyes narrowing, lip protruding, "are cowardly, disloyal, and a liar!"

"Oh?" I sighed and downed the rest of my wine. "How do you figure that?"

"You promised to help me."

"I will on my own terms."

"*Stulta*! Slaves don't have terms."

"Well, priestesses do. This priestess does. If you and Decius are so determined to consummate your love in the temple of Isis, why don't you go to your own temple? You practically own it. Don't the priests at All-Sovereign take bribes?"

She stared at me for a moment, white-faced with rage. Then, with exaggerated care, she got to her feet. Despite all the wine she had swilled, she managed not to weave as she walked to the door where she turned to confront me.

"You don't love me. You don't care about me. It's all a lie and a pretense. You're not my friend. You're not my priestess. You're just a slave, a worthless slave. You've betrayed me, and I…I don't love you anymore."

With that she burst into tears, yanked down her veil, and ran from the temple.

I should have run after her, wrestled her down, slapped her silly, and loved her back into her right mind. But I didn't. I let her go. I persuaded myself to shrug it off. Another tantrum. So what else was new?

Plenty. Paulina was serious this time. Dead serious.

Paulina did not come home that night. Or the next or the next. When I saw her after the midday meal, she just smiled, stretched, and went to sleep. If she was angry still, she didn't show it, except by refusing to speak to me. I, of course, was too proud to ask her anything. Everyone assumed that I knew where she was. I covered for her, pretty much as she had asked me to, without going into what I considered unnecessary specifics, like she says she's fucking a god. I merely indicated that she had important business at the temple, a vow to fulfill, a vigil to keep. I didn't say which temple, and nobody asked. They all made their own assumptions.

Then a couple of things happened in close, fateful succession. The *Navigium Isidis*, always a high-spirited festival, got out a little out of hand. The procession from Rome to Ostia (where I'd been captured) consisted not only of the priesthood and a handful of lay devotees but attracted the worst elements from the Subura and all the idlers and vagrants in every hamlet on the way to port where sailors of all stripes, who'd been drinking since dawn, greeted the Roman throng with riotous joy. Before too long, between hymns to Isis, people were making incendiary speeches. One wealthy citizen's ship had its cargo of purple dye tossed overboard.

To top it off, by some quirk of fate or the lunar calendar, this year the *Navigium* coincided with Purim. As Isis worshippers made their riotous way to Ostia (think of Carnival in Rio) the Jews of Rome celebrated Queen Esther's deliverance of her people by getting stinking drunk. Jews rarely made public displays of themselves, but on Purim excessive imbibing was undertaken as a pious duty. All things considered, there were relatively few disturbances in the Jewish quarter, a brawl here and there and lots of noise that unfortunately carried across the Tiber to the Palatine where Tiberius had his palace.

From their own point of view, Jews and Isis worshippers had had nothing in common since Moses led the people out of Egypt thousands of years ago and then came raging down Mount Sinai to burn the golden calf his people had backslid into worshipping. (The first two of the Ten Commandments made it clear there was to be no more of that.) But to Tiberius, and other Romans of rank, it must have appeared that the city was being overrun with oriental cults and their raucous, disorderly rites. And so the two disparate groups became yoked in the imperial mind. At least that is what I think, and it may help to explain what happened later.

After the melee, all the priestesses from Venus Obsequens made it back from Ostia safely. When days passed, and no officials came sniffing around the temple, we began to relax and return to our old routines. Those directly involved had been arrested, but no general purge had been ordered. The incident might have been forgotten, dismissed as the excess of a festival day, if another scandal hadn't followed so closely on its heels.

One day I returned to *domus* Claudius at noon and found the house sibilant with the whispers of hundreds of slaves. It sounded like a hive about to swarm. A survey of the dining room told me Paulina was not at the midday meal, which was more sparsely attended than usual. Claudius was carrying on as always, holding forth and telling jokes, as if he had a large audience, but I noticed he had taken the precaution of having not one but two tasters present. Even with them, he seemed disinclined to eat.

I hurried to the *cubiculo*, where I found Paulina under heavy sedation.

"What's going on?" I asked Reginus who was in attendance; without realizing it, I was whispering, too.

"Decius Mundus got thrown out this morning. He has been declared *persona non grata*. The *domina*, as you can imagine, was hysterical. I thought it was best to knock her out before she said anything stupid."

"You mean Claudius accused her of adultery?"

"No. That's why she needs to keep her mouth shut."

"But surely he knows. Why else would he give Decius the boot?"

"Of course he knows," said Reginus. "But he didn't care until yesterday."

"Come on, Reginus. Don't keep me in suspense."

"Decius's divorce came through. The idiot told everybody the good news."

"Oh." It took a moment to sink in. "Oh, you mean..."

"Yeah, what you and I were talking about. The irony is, I don't think either Decius or our *domina* dodo bird here has figured out the implications of his divorce. The greedy little innocents hadn't gotten around to thinking of murder—yet. But Claudius put two and two together pretty quick and figured out it might mean one less—of him. So Decius is out on his ass."

"But isn't Claudius going to accuse them of adultery? He could get rid of both of them that way."

"Who can know for sure, but I don't think so. He doesn't want the scandal. He knows Decius will run away with his tail between his legs. I guess he figures he can handle the *domina*. All he has to do is hint to her that he knows about Decius. That's how I see it anyway. We just have to keep her quiet for a few days, and it'll all blow over."

I wished I could share Reginus's optimism. I wanted to feel relieved that Decius was banned from the house, and effectively from Paulina's life, but my gut wasn't buying it. I felt more frightened than I could remember being since my father had tried to kill me. I stayed with Paulina for the rest of the day and night, holding her while she raved incoherently.

In the morning when she was somewhat more rational, I was able to get her to understand that Claudius had not accused her of adultery and she must try to behave as normally as possible, receive clients, go about her business as usual. I offered to stay with her instead of going to the temple, but she had other plans for me.

"Red, you've got to find out what's happened to him," she whispered. "You can go to both temples. Ask Maxima. Maybe he'll even come to Venus Obsequens to take refuge. Red, if you see him, tell him, I love him. I'll run away with him, I'll…"

"Ssh," I cautioned. "Don't say any more. I'll see what I can find out."

I did not have to go far. Succula was waiting for me at Venus Obsequens. She took my arm, and hustled me to the back room before she spoke.

"Listen, Red," she began as soon as we were out of public view. "You know I can't stand that bitch who thinks she owns you, but I figure if anything happens to her, it'll happen to you, too, so I've got to warn you."

She waved away my offer of wine and would not even sit down.

"Decius Mundus was at the Vine and Fig Tree last night. He was already three sheets to the wind when he arrived, so probably Bone and Bonia shouldn't have let him in, but he's been a good customer in the past. He doesn't just fuck and run, he adds to the atmosphere, you know."

"Yeah, I know." If the warning was so urgent I wished she'd get to it.

"Well, first Bonia tried to get him to go with Berta—she's his favorite—but he didn't want to go upstairs. He wanted an audience. Then his old pal General Fullanus came in with a party of senators. Decius was all over him, and then he started ranting.

" 'Gentlemen,' he said. 'Dishtinguished shenators.'" Succula imitated his drunken slur. " 'Welcome to the Vine and Fig Tree. There are some truly fine whores here. Honest whores. But you wanna know where the best whores are? Right at home. Yesh. Your wives and your daughters. It's a shecret. But you ask 'em what they do when they go to the temple of Ishish. Ask 'em. Ask old Claudiush.

" 'Ya know, I was like a son to him, took care of him like he was my own father. Then out in the shtreet. Well, screw him. I don't need to screw him. I already screwed him, and his wife, too. That'sh right. The lovely Paulina. He never screwed her. Couldn't get his dick out of his slaves' asses long enough. Well, I took care of her. I was a god to her. Fucking Anubish, that's what she told everybody. So listen to me: when you're here or when you're fucking some slave that pours your wine or shaves your fat chins for you, your wivesh are going to the temple of Isish. She provides.'"

"And he started laughing hysterically while Bone was dragging him out the door."

"What did the senators say?" I asked with dread.

"Oh, while it was happening; they just stood around looking as if some-body had made a bad fart, pretending to be above it all. They let Bone take care of it. That's what he's there for. But after Decius was gone and Bone had apol-ogized for the disturbance, they started to say things like. 'Things have gone a bit too far. Can't have chaps going around saying things like that about the *dom-inae*, what?'

"I mean no one takes Decius Mundus very seriously. But he came right out and said that their women are whoring around at the temple of Isis. Maybe they'll dismiss it as the ravings of a drunken fortune hunter who's just lost his shot at an inheritance or—"

"Maybe they won't," I finished her sentence.

We just stood for a moment staring at each other, silently taking in the implications.

"I'm scared, Red," whispered Succula. "Old Nona has always been odd, but lately she's been even more peculiar. She spends a lot of time staring into the goldfish pool. Sometimes she laughs; sometimes she weeps. She talks to the cats. She could just be a crazy old lady, but—"

"What does she say, Succula?"

I felt a sudden, urgent need to know. Old women and oracular wells—even if it was an artificial goldfish pool in a Roman brothel—were ignored at one's own peril.

"It's not very coherent, but I think she's talking about you. 'It'll be a great day for whores,' she keeps saying. 'If the Red One lives. Come down off that cross, you silly twat. There's springs to be tended, wounds to be washed. That's the place to build your tower. Where water rises and the morning stars sing. It'll be a great day for whores, when she finds that spring.' Things like that. Over and over."

I didn't understand the words any more than Succula did, but all the hairs on my body stood up, and a wind seemed to blow through the hollows of my bones.

"Get out of town, Red. Now. Promise me."

And she gave me a fierce embrace, as if she feared she would never see me again.

I needed no further persuasion, and I didn't think Paulina would either, once she realized that she could be facing the charge of adultery. I fully intend-ed to go back to the *domus*, grab Paulina, take Reginus for protection (goddess help us) and hit the road. But first I had to warn Aemiliana. Decius's ravings, if taken seriously by anyone, could mean trouble for the temple. So I sought out

Aemiliana and told her the whole story. She listened gravely but without alarm.

"Every day we are here, we risk arrest," she said when I urged her to leave Rome. "We've always known that as long as times are quiet, we will be tolerated, and when they are not, we will be targeted. Until I am forcibly removed, I will stay at the temple."

She spoke so matter-of-factly, calmly accepting whatever her fate might be. I envied her the certainty that she was exactly where she was meant to be, doing what she was born to do. I didn't want to believe that I had come into this world to save Paulina's ass, but it was plain to me that I had to try. As Aemiliana and I gave each other a farewell embrace, one of the priestesses burst into the room.

"There's a man here to see Red. He says it's urgent."

For one absurdly hopeful moment, I thought: Joseph. Thank goddess. Joseph. Just in time. Then Decius Mundus staggered into the room, dropped to all fours, and began to crawl towards me across the floor.

"You son of a braying ass! You spawn of a sea slug, you—" Being a Celt, I was obliged to think of a third epithet, but I was distracted by the unpleasant sensation of tears and snot on my feet. "You sniveling facsimile (a Latin word, note) of a semblance of a man, get the fuck off the floor, look me in the eye."

He stayed cowering and cringing at my feet until I kicked him.

"I did it all for you!" He gazed at me like a dog who knows its master is angry but doesn't understand why, one of those dogs with soulful eyes like a basset hound.

"Why are you here?" I had no time to rehash his motives with him, and I didn't want to think about what part I might have played in his disastrous stupidity.

"I'm leaving Rome?" he sounded as though he were trying to guess the right answer. "I wanted, oh, hell, everything's ruined. I thought—"

He was clearly incapable of thought.

"Decius Mundus, have you forgotten that you told half the senate last night that you fucked Paulina in the temple of Isis?"

"I was afraid I might have said something like that." He hung his head. "And oh, shit, oh, gods, that would explain why…" he trailed off.

"Explain what?" I demanded.

"Why I saw Paulina being escorted from the house by the emperor's guards. I was waiting outside *domus* Claudius this morning to see Paulina—I'm not such a dog as you think—but I didn't know anything was wrong. I thought maybe Livia had invited her…"

I had stopped listening to him. All I could think of was getting to Paulina, poor, foolish, lovesick Paulina whose worst fear was coming to pass.

"Where are you going?" he asked, as I pushed past him. "Let me go with you. I…I'll protect you."

If I hadn't been so furious, I would have laughed.

"Fuck off," I snapped. "No, wait. On second thought, yes. Come with me. You are going to tell the emperor, and anyone else who wants to know, that you were drunk last night and lying through your teeth, up to your eyeballs, and out your ass to get back at Claudius for throwing you out of his house."

"You know, I think maybe we should think this through," he reconsidered. "They might kill me or sue me. They might—"

Adrenaline gave me a surge of superhuman strength. I grabbed hold of Decius's wrist. He had no choice but to come with me or have his arm wrenched from the socket. I had every intention of dragging the whimpering equestrian all the way to the Palatine, but as it turned out I didn't have to go that far. Just as we turned onto Via Triumphalis, I saw Paulina herself.

"Paulina," I cried, letting go of Decius's wrist and running towards her.

She did not run to meet me. Looking pale and strained, she walked toward me stiffly and kissed my cheek.

The next thing I knew, I was surrounded by soldiers; my hands were bound behind my back, and my ankles shackled.

As for Decius, he disappeared, like so much smoke or vapor, as if he had never existed at all.

CHAPTER THIRTY-FIVE

BEARING MY CROSS

I couldn't tell where I was going; my guard formed a wall around me. But I wasn't surprised when I ended up in a dark, smelly holding tank below street level. It was damp, and I could hear sewer water running nearby. No one told me why I was being locked up. No one recited my Miranda rights. I didn't have rights. The only person who could have intervened on my behalf was Paulina, and she appeared to be in trouble herself. In fact, if I had allowed myself to think about it, I could have figured out easily enough that Paulina had panicked and betrayed me. But I wasn't ready to consider the full implications of what had happened.

I concentrated on my surroundings. A sliver of light came through a high barred window; I watched it move across the small cell, minute-by-minute, hour-by-hour. I could hear the scrabbling of rats' feet, and a roaring that rose and fell, which I finally identified as human. I speculated that my prison might be in the maze of underground passages and rooms that led to Circus Maximus, but the sound betrayed too much rage and terror to be the cheering of a sports event. Finally, in what must have been the late afternoon, I slept.

I woke to the sound of voices as soldiers returned with a dozen more inmates. When my eyes adjusted to the lantern light, I recognized Aemiliana and the other priestesses from Venus Obsequens as well as some priestesses from Isis All-Sovereign, the suburban temple. Clearly there had been a roundup. Aemiliana greeted me affectionately as if we had run into each other by chance on the street or at a party. The priestesses from All-Sovereign glared at me, as if our predicament were all my fault.

Finally each woman was chained to the wall, and the soldiers left, taking their lanterns with them. In the anonymity of the dark, people did not feel so constrained to be brave. Some wept, others prayed. Some even muttered curses.

"Aemiliana," I said softly; I knew she was somewhere near me.

"Yes, daughter."

"I have to know. It's because of Paulina that we've been arrested, isn't it?"

Suddenly the sound of the sewer water running was audible again. Everyone was listening.

"I believe that is so," said Aemiliana.

"No, it is because of *you!*" came another voice, not one I knew, and so it must have belonged to one of the priestesses from All-Sovereign.

"You do not know that, Caspia," Aemiliana defended me.

"I will hear what you have to say," I spoke to my unseen accuser.

"Our high priest was brought before Tiberius this morning. Paulina Claudii was there and also Maxima Fabia and the *domina* Livia. The emperor himself accused Paulina of adultery. This case is being taken very seriously. Paulina Claudii declared that she was innocent. That she had been deceived. She swore that a priestess of Isis had ordered her to come to the temple to do service to the god Anubis. Tiberius demanded to know the identity of the priestess, and she named you, the Red One."

"But I didn't!" I protested. "I told her it was not safe to meet at Venus Obsequens."

"So you admit you told her to go to All-Sovereign."

"That is not how it happened."

"We all know about you," Caspia went on relentlessly. "You were a whore once. Paulina bought you from Domitia Tertia. She made you a priestess, but you are still practicing your old trade—only now you're a procurer."

"This is going too far," objected Aemiliana. "Maeve is a priestess in good standing in my temple—"

"A procurer!" I was getting riled. "What are you talking about?"

"For your lover, Decius Mundus."

"Decius Mundus is not my lover! And even if he was, what possible motivation would I have for luring Paulina to spend a night with him?"

"Oh, come now." I could hear the priestess's sneer. "Don't play the innocent. Don't insult us by assuming we're as stupid as your mistress. Your motives are obvious. Blackmail."

"Blackmail?" I sounded dumb even to myself.

"Admit it. You and your boyfriend were planning to bleed her white. Only lover boy can't keep a secret, can he? Poor choice of an accomplice."

"But he isn't, and I didn't. I mean I wasn't…"

I wanted to defend myself, but I was distracted by her story, as perhaps only one raised on stories can be. Hers sounded so much more plausible and interesting than mine. *A story is true if it's well told.*

"We will stop this at once." Aemiliana's voice cut into the darkness. "To repeat malicious, unsubstantiated rumors as if we were idle matrons in the baths is conduct unbecoming to priestesses of Isis."

"Who says they are unsubstantiated?" my accuser shot back.

"Maeve does. As her high priestess, I have experience of her character. I believe her, and I vouch for her."

"Very well then," said Caspia. "I suppose I have no choice but to bow to your superior knowledge and let the matter drop. It is immaterial in any case what you think or what I think. It is what Tiberius thinks that counts, and he thinks the worst. He can substantiate any rumor he likes. We all know he's been waiting for an excuse to move against the priesthood of Isis. Now he's got it." She paused for a beat. "Now we're all going to pay."

We sat in silence for a time, a horrible silence that roiled like my stomach. I waited until I knew what to say or knew, anyway, that I must speak.

"Will the priestesses of Isis hear me?"

There was a slight pause, and then they all said, "We will," even my adversary, for she spoke last and alone.

"I wish to confess my faults."

"Maeve, dear," Aemiliana began to protest.

"Don't stop me, Aemiliana. I want to tell the truth. I was never Decius Mundus's lover. As for Paulina, she did ask me to arrange a tryst at Venus Obsequens, and I refused. I offered to arrange a meeting in a brothel. Paulina was offended. That's when I told her to go to her own temple, All-Sovereign. I confess that I told both Decius and Paulina to get on with their affair and stop making such a fuss about it. I am not guilty of attempting blackmail, but I am guilty of impatience, arrogance, and carelessness."

"You judge yourself too harshly," said Aemiliana. "You did what you could to protect the temple. Paulina and Decius acted on their own accord and shifted the blame to you as the wealthy and powerful often do to those who cannot defend themselves."

Other priestesses murmured agreement, but I did not want to be exonerated.

"No," I said. "I know Paulina better than anyone does. Maybe some of you remember her mother's exile and her sister's death, both on charges of adultery. But you don't know the rest of her story, and it's not mine to tell. But trust me, she must have been terrified before Tiberius. I can't bring myself to blame her. As for Decius, I knew him for what he was. I should have told her to have nothing to do with him."

"Do you really believe she would have listened?" asked Aemiliana gently. "You take too much on yourself, daughter."

"Well, it doesn't matter now, does it?" said Caspia. "It's too late."

"It's not!" I insisted. "At the trial I will confess. I will make it clear that I acted alone, and the rest of you had nothing to do with it."

"Oh, spare us the heroics," snapped Caspia. "The trial is over. Paulina Claudii's trial—you don't get one. She's already saved her skin by sacrificing yours. Because you are a priestess of Isis, the rest of us are guilty by association. We will all die."

"Die?" I repeated.

"I know you're a foreigner and a barbarian, but surely you've been here long enough to know what happens to enemies of the state?"

The air thickened with mortal terror. I knew; we all knew. In our collective minds' eye, we were all seeing the crosses that lined the road to Ostia. And ourselves hanging there, dying publicly and painfully for days.

"Forgive me," I said.

No one answered directly, but the silence deepened and settled. After a time, Aemiliana spoke again.

"Let us put to good purpose the time that remains to us. We who love Isis know we have nothing to fear from life or from death. If we are to be cut down, let us pray that our deaths be fertile: the sowing of seeds on the flood plain, the rich darkness of her womb. Let us rise as stars in her great night to guide those who come after us."

As she spoke her voice shifted to the rhythm of chant. Someone began to rattle her chain as if it were a sistrum. Aemiliana sang a line and we all sang back; then someone else sang another, and we answered, and the song grew as it flew from one to another of us, the same wind moving from tree to tree.

> *Isis dawn-bringer*
> *mother of light*
> *deliver us from fear.*
> *Isis the swift*
> *raise the winds of justice*
> *with your sky-wide wings.*
> *Isis navigator*
> *star of the sea*
> *guide our boat to your shore.*
> *Isis whose breasts*

are heavy and sweet
as clusters of dates
comfort your children.
Isis of the sorrows
Isis of the rivers
Isis who endures
we are yours
we are yours.
Isis who brings life from death
receive us.
Into your hands we commend
our lives.
Into your hands we commend
our death.
Isis who endures
we are yours, we are yours.

And so we passed most of the night until by some unspoken agreement, silence fell again or we fell into silence, a deep black well of it, and each one of us went where she had to go alone.

I am in the Valley between Bride's breasts where the light is thick and golden. The nine hazel trees ring the well of wisdom. As I near the pool, I see an old, old woman and a young girl, hardly more than a child. I want to believe the old woman is the Cailleach, the guardian of the place. Then I will not be alone; then there will be someone to tell me what to do. But I know different: the old woman and the young girl are both me. As soon as I acknowledge this truth, they disappear.

I kneel by the pool as I did when I was that young girl and the fire of the stars first came to me, and my hands, stretched out over the pool, turned the water to an eye, a mirror, a way between his world and mine. Let me see him again, I find myself praying, let me see him again before I die. And the dark water shines and shifts shape until I see that I am seeing his eyes with something bright leaping in them, the salmon of wisdom, the reflection of flame.

The vision becomes more detailed. He is standing in a shrine, lit by torches, gazing at an image. I can sense his discomfort; as a Jew he is not supposed to be in this place. But he is drawn to the image of a woman, a dark woman with a wild, ecstatic face, and many arms. Her breasts are bare and her skirts whirl. All around her wild creatures circle: birds, bees, snakes. As my beloved gazes at the image, the woman begins to move, dancing to some sweet, insistent music. Her hair turns the color of fire. And all at once I understand, he is seeing me. I am not outside the vision anymore. I am the woman in the shrine. I hear the sistrum and the drums; I am dancing.

You are alive, he speaks to me silently, though you are dead, you are alive.

Love is stronger than death, I answer him. Come dance with me. Dance.

I see a shiver run though him, as if the sound of the sistrum rose in his spine.

I reach out for him; our hands almost meet, and then I am alone again kneeling by the dark pool in the valley between Bride's breasts. My hands are an old woman's hands. Sleep now, I whisper to myself, as if I were old and wise. And I do.

At dawn the guards brought us watered wine and bread.

"Eat and drink hearty," said one guard. "Be a long time before your next meal."

"Shut up," said his companion. "Show some respect."

"Our last meal, is it?" asked Caspia pleasantly.

She looked pale, but calm, as did all the other priestesses. I was overcome with love for them.

"Could be," said the first guard. "How about a little last something else? Hey, you, redhead, I swear I've seen you in a whore's toga."

"Stop it!" growled his companion. "It's impious. You'll anger the gods."

"Well, the gods obviously want to be rid of this lot. And their goddess doesn't seem to helping them much—Egyptian cow."

"There's no time for your foolishness," growled our defender. "We have to have them at the Lavernalis Gate by the second hour. Drink up, ladies."

"Yeah, hasn't anyone ever told you it's rude to be late for your own crucifixion?"

We all had the momentary satisfaction of seeing the man get punched in the mouth. After that he was too busy fussing over his broken teeth to bait us anymore.

Our champion unshackled us from the wall and allowed us to use the latrine. Then we were chained together and herded outside.

I had never seen such a beautiful morning. Or maybe until then I had not understood the meaning of morning, the miracle of it. The sky was a delicate color, fragile as an eggshell, and curved like one. The birds flew into that roundness, the beat of their wings the lightest brushstroke. The sight of ordinary life moved me: a woman scrubbing her doorstep, a child running up the street with a loaf of bread. With every shackled step, even through the paving stone, I felt the insistent, pulsing life of the earth.

Our progress was not peaceful for long. Crowds began to gather; word spreads quickly when there's a mass crucifixion. Soon the streets were lined with bystanders who relished spitting, jeering, and pelting us with garbage. More than one chamber pot was emptied on our heads. If anyone felt sympathy for us, no one dared show it. Rumor had it that lay devotees of Isis were being shipped to Sardinia. People were eager to demonstrate their loyalty to the emperor.

When we reached Vicus Armilustri, the main route to the Lavernalis gate, we were ceremoniously presented with the cross beam, a six foot piece of solid, heavy wood. The soldiers loaded these on our backs, and, for the last hilly mile or so, we had to carry the instruments of our torture. The spring sun was growing hotter. We staggered under the weight of the beams, our eyes blinded with sweat. If we lost our balance and fell, a soldier would come and whip us until we managed to get on our feet again. The only mercy in this ordeal was that it kept our minds off the ordeal to come. No time to think of torn sinews and slow suffocation by your own weight. Even the roar of the crowd receded from my consciousness. There was just one excruciating step and then another. Nothing else was real.

Maybe that's why I didn't notice the eerie silence when it fell. I lost my balance again and stumbled forward onto the ground. I made no attempt to get up this time, just waited for the lash; they could beat me to death for all I cared, but I was going to rest for a minute. I waited. A breeze touched my hair; the cooling sweat felt so good, I was almost happy for a moment. That's when I noticed the hush. I lifted my head from the ground and saw the most elegant feet I had ever seen, slender and perfectly shaped, delicate blue veins like rivers seen from a great distance. The feet wore sandals of fine leather inlaid with jewels. I wondered if I had fallen in front of the statue of a goddess.

"Release them!" A woman's voice rang out with pure and absolute authority.

I used the last of my strength to stand up unaided. The woman towering in righteousness over those exquisite feet was no less than the Senior Vestal from the College of Vestal Virgins.

"It is the law, the sacred law of Rome. I, high priestess of Vesta, keeper of the eternal flame, invoke my ancient right and duty to stay the sentence of all those who cross my path on their way to execution. Remove the cross beams, unchain them." Then she looked directly at me. "You are free to go, Priestess of Isis. You are free."

That's the last thing I remember before I passed out.

CHAPTER THIRTY-SIX

A GREAT DAY

I am hearing the sound of water, and I do not want to wake up. I want to stay in this dream of the tower and the dawn sky, the mysterious joy that wells in me like the spring in the courtyard. Then someone lays a hand on my head, and I open my eyes.

Old Nona was gazing down at me.

"A great day for whores and priestesses," she whispered to me, and then she cried out. "She's awake!"

In a moment I was surrounded by my sister whores, as well as Bone and Bonia. Everyone was talking and laughing and crying at once. I did not try to make sense of what had happened, how I had gotten to the Vine and Fig Tree. I was too happy. A little while later, all the whores and the reprieved priestesses went to the baths together. No one understood exactly how it had come about or why, but apparently Domitia Tertia had taken it on herself to give us sanctuary.

"Domitia Tertia does not explain things," Berta told the priestesses. "When she wants you to know more, she will tell you."

At the ninth hour, the house opened for business as usual, and the priestesses retired to the back rooms to eat and rest. I fell asleep again with Olivia curled in my arms. It was dusk when Bonia woke me. Domitia Tertia wanted to see me. Privately.

My former mistress rose from her couch when I entered the room, but did not embrace me. Without a spoken greeting, she reclined again and gestured for me to do the same. One of the little girls brought us wine, cheese, and fruit.

"We must discuss your future," she announced after waving away my thanks for shelter and hospitality.

"My future?" I repeated. I found it was a concept I could not grasp. It was so abstract, compared to being alive, right now, eating a fig, instead of being dead.

"I've already spoken at some length with your high priestess, Aemiliana. I have offered her and her priestesses sanctuary here for as long as necessary. It is not clear whether the senior vestal's stay of sentence applies to exile as well as execution. I will do my best to inquire discreetly."

"You are generous, *domina*," I said. "But you must be aware of the risk. Why would you choose to harbor a cult that has been condemned and exiled? I thought you found Isis worship distasteful."

"I find many things distasteful. It is distasteful to me when different standards apply to women than to men in regard to marriage, divorce, and adultery. I also find it distasteful when an entire group is punished for the transgressions—or as the case may be, alleged transgressions—of individuals. Did you know that the Jews of Rome are also being rounded up and exiled to a penal colony in Sardinia?"

"No! Why?"

"Tiberius decided to do a clean sweep, get rid of all the exotic, trouble-making cults at once. He found a case to serve his purpose. A Roman matron, a proselyte, claimed that funds she sent to the temple of Jerusalem had been, shall we say, diverted."

"Is Joseph safe? Do you know where he is?"

"As it happens, I do know." She smiled mysteriously. "He is safe. Now."

I knew she wasn't going to say any more until she was ready. But I suddenly felt confused and overwhelmed.

"Pardon, *domina*, I don't understand what's happening. You said we had to discuss my future, and then you make it sound as though you've arranged everything with Aemiliana. What about Paulina? Is she all right? Has she been exonerated?"

Domitia Tertia poured us more wine before she answered.

"You are a mystery to me, Red. I suppose that is why I concern myself with you. Am I to understand that you are concerned for the welfare of a woman who handed you over to death to save her own skin? Her foolish actions have also cost many people their lives. I might as well tell you, not everyone was reprieved. And many more are being herded onto ships bound for the penal colonies of Sardinia."

I felt sick with shame. Why should I have been spared?

"I share the guilt," I said.

She regarded me for a long moment, as if waiting for me to say more, to explain what I meant. But I did not want to tell the story again, what I had done, what I hadn't done. How much of it was my fault, how much wasn't. People had died because of how this disastrous love affair had unfolded. I was going to have to live with that knowledge.

"The charge of adultery has been dismissed against Paulina," Domitia said at length. "She is anxious to see you, if you will receive her."

"*If* I will receive her? I don't understand."

Domitia Tertia rose and went to her desk. She returned with a piece of parchment and handed it to me. My hands shook as I untied the clasp and un-rolled the document, which was written in Latin and full of legal terms. I stared and stared at the words, trying to comprehend their power.

"Is it…it is. It's my…my manumission papers?"

"I thought Joseph taught you to read."

In the next moment, I couldn't see anything at all. The letters were swim-ming, flying, dancing.

"Bona Dea, Red, don't drip on the parchment. The ink might run. Here, you better give it to me."

But when she reached for it I clutched it to me.

"By whatever gods you disbelieve in, Domitia Tertia, tell me everything."

And she did, unfolding a tale that with all my knowledge of classic plot-lines, I would never have imagined. Instead of retiring to her couch with a wineskin after her ordeal with the emperor, Paulina had dressed herself in ser-vants' clothes, snuck out of the *insularium*, and gone straight to the Vine and Fig Tree to see Domitia Tertia.

"She got right to the point, which surprised me," said Domitia. "I didn't think she had it in her not to posture.

" 'I have done a terrible thing,' she said. 'I turned Red, Maeve—you know who I mean—over to the authorities.'

"And she told me the whole incoherent story she had blithered to the emperor. It sounded like utter nonsense to me, and I can't imagine anyone be-lieved it, but clearly her accusation didn't have to be credible to serve as a pre-text for a crackdown on the temples.

" 'And so,' I said to her rather severely, 'a lot of people are going to suffer for your squalid little affair. What do you expect me to do about it?'

" 'I don't know!' She wrung her hands. 'What about that friend of yours, that wealthy Jew? He tried to buy her from me. Couldn't he help her?'

"I was beginning to believe that however contemptible she was, she might be sincere. I decided to test her.

"'If he could help her, would you let her go with him? Leave Rome? Leave you?'

"'Yes, I would. I would do anything.'

"'And yet not more than an hour ago, you betrayed her to save yourself.'

"That's when she broke down and wept. Believe me, Red, I have seen my share of tears. Whores' tears and the tears of men that only whores see. I am not easily moved. Only a few times in my life have I seen someone so abandoned to grief, and those were children." She paused for a moment. "Against my will, I found myself remembering Paulina's mother. I thought back to those days when we all knew each other, all the daughters of senators—and I remembered someone else I knew well.

"'You may be unaware, *domina*, that the Jews of Rome are being persecuted, too,' I said when she had quieted. 'My friend is in no position to help her.'

"She was quiet for a moment; then she spoke so softly I had to lean close to her to hear her.

"'If no one can help her, then I must go to the emperor myself.'

"'And do what, exactly?'

"'Tell him the truth. Tell him I lied, because I was afraid.'

"'You would do that?'

"She was pale and shaking so badly I was surprised she could even get to her feet, but she did. Then she thanked me and headed for the door.

"'Wait,' I said to her, and she practically collapsed. 'As much as you might deserve whatever punishment would come your way if you confess, there is no point in fruitless sacrifice. Tiberius is not going to pardon Red or the others. Your scandal is just an excuse to purge the city of oriental cults. Surely you understand that. I have thought of something that might work. But there is something you must do before I agree to act.'

"'I will do anything,' she said again.

"'Go at once and have Maeve's manumission papers drawn up. When they are done and signed, bring them to me here.'

"And so she did," Domitia Tertia concluded her tale abruptly, suddenly embarrassed, I suspected, by her part in the drama.

"And you," I said, "went to see your old friend at the College of Vestal Virgins."

The old girls' network to the rescue. The most famous whore and the most famous virgin in all of Rome putting one over on the emperor. There needed to be a poem about it, a praise song.

"If you ever breathe a word of it outside this room, Red, I will personally see to it that your tongue is cut out and sold in the market place as a delicacy. What we did was strictly illegal. I will assume that you are grateful."

"Grateful?"

I couldn't help it. I laid my precious papers on the table, got up and knelt beside her couch, throwing my arms around her and burying my face in her breasts.

"That's enough now, Red," she protested, but she held me another heartbeat or two before she pushed me away. "Now, about your future. Have you given it any thought?"

My future. This time it was not abstract, it rose up like a sea swell and carried me forward. I could see rocky hills, green valleys, and deserts. I could see feet, his and mine. And I could hear the sound of water flowing and smell roses and fish. Stars outlined a tower, and I swear I could hear them, the voices of the stars singing.

"If you cry or faint, Red, I will slap you," warned Domitia.

"I'm all right," I laughed instead.

"Excuse me for interrupting." Bonia came into the room. "Now that Red is here, I was thinking we'd better untie our guest. He's getting rope burns."

"By all means, untie him and send him in," said Domitia. "I suppose Joseph may want to contribute to the discussion of your future."

After I had nearly knocked Joseph down by flinging myself into his arms, he gave me an abbreviated version of how he came to be there.

"When I heard trouble was brewing for the Jews of Rome, I decided to come and tie up a few loose ends of my business here. Instead I got tied up. For my own good—that's what a dominatrix always says, isn't it? Dido and Berta took turns feeding me grapes. No one even told me about your arrest until you were safe. When I found out they'd kept me in the dark, I was fit to be tied. And I still am, but I've had enough of the ropes."He rubbed his wrists. "You have unmanned me," he accused Domitia.

"But you're still alive," she observed. "And now you may actually have a chance to be of some use."

"Pardon me again," said Bonia, a bit breathless and harried. "Paulina Claudii is here with a manservant. She wants to know if Red will see her."

"Send her in," I said. "Send everyone in. Whoever wants to talk about my future."

"I think," said Domitia Tertia, "you are about to find out how complicated freedom can be."

Domitia's private chamber, that looked bigger than it was because of the seascape surrounding Circe's island, was soon crowded. Aemiliana had joined us, and so had Succula, Berta, and Dido. Old Nona wandered in, too, and took up a place in the corner where she murmured her singsong refrain, "A great day, a great day for whores and priestesses."

Then Paulina stood in the doorway, clutching Reginus's arm to keep herself on her feet; she was shaking so badly. At first she just looked at the floor, and the room hushed as everyone watched and waited. At last she lifted her eyes and gave me a look I had never seen before: a look of complete submission. This woman who had bullied me, enslaved me, loved me selfishly, and finally betrayed me, now waited for my judgment. It was too much. She had given me my freedom; when would I be free of her?

I closed my eyes for a moment. Give judgment over to me, a voice inside me spoke. Give judgment over to mystery.

When I opened my eyes, I felt light, relieved of a burden I had been carrying for much longer than these last few minutes. I looked at Paulina and shook my head: I'm not the one to judge. But Paulina mistook the gesture and, stifling a cry, ran away.

"Paulina, you idiot, come here!" I called after her. "Reginus, go get her."

When she returned, I opened my arms to her. There were no words; just a terrible knowledge of all we had shared.

"All right," said Domitia. "Sit down, everyone. It is time to make plans. Red, speak."

I looked around the circle at each person. For better or worse, I had shared part of my life with all of them.

"I think you all know where I want to go."

"Don't make assumptions, Red," said Domitia.

"I want to go to Judea and Galilee. I want to look for him."

"Ah, *liebling*!" Berta sighed gustily and clasped her hands to her heart.

"Him who?" Paulina began to recover herself; I had never told her about Esus.

"Him whom my soul loves."

"You've been holding out on us, honey," Reginus reproached me.

I turned to Joseph. He was the one who knew the whole story, even better than my sister whores. For he knew Esus.

"Maeve, dear, remember I told you he may have left the country. No one has seen or heard from him for some time." Joseph paused and passed his hand over his face, then resolved to go on. " He has made a mess of his life."

I said nothing. I did not want to defend Esus or to remind Joseph that he might have had the power to relieve my beloved's anguish.

"My point is, he could be anywhere, and you could go anywhere. Alexandria. Greece. On the Island of Delos there is a temple to Isis, I believe."

"I have heard of it," said Aemiliana.

"You could even go back home to your people, to Pretannia."

I shook my head. "I have been excommunicated and exiled."

"But surely your survival at sea proves your innocence?"

"Is that what survival does?" I asked.

The air in the room became heavy and charged. I let it be for a moment; then I went on. "There is nothing for me in Pretannia, except—" My voice caught in my throat, and I found I could not speak.

"Your child," said Joseph softly. He knew.

"Red, you had a baby!" said Paulina. "Why have you never told me anything?"

I closed my eyes and rocked myself for a moment. My daughter, not a baby anymore, a little girl in a tunic, part of the *combrogos*, part of a tribe. The Iceni, known for their strong and beautiful women, the priestess had told me. Did my daughter need a mother returning from exile, a mother who had been a slave in Rome? She would never be able to go to druid school or marry a king if she had to bear that taint.

"I cannot go back," I said. "I may not find Esus, but I must look for him."

"And if you don't find him—you need to face that possibility, Red," said Domitia more gently than I had ever heard her speak.

"I will have my life."

As I spoke I heard the sound of the water, felt the wind wash over my face. It was dawn, and two people stood together on a tower.

"But how will you live, Red?" Domitia Tertia was insistent. "It may take time to find this man. Even if you find him, from what Joseph says, he may be a vagrant. It is all very well to have idle dreams of freedom when you are a slave, but when you are free, you must look after yourself."

"Thanks to you, Domitia, I have skills. And to you, Aemiliana."

"A great day," Nona sang. "A great day for whores and priestesses."

"What about thanks to me?" blurted out Paulina.

"The less said about that the better," growled Succula.

"I am not going to use those skills anymore, Paulina. Besides, you told me yourself, I was an impossible slave."

"But what are you going to do, Red?" persisted Paulina.

"We all want a handle on that, honey," said Reginus.

"Old Nona has been trying to tell you," observed Aemiliana. "Maeve is going to open a temple of sacred prostitution. A house for holy whores."

"I am?" I turned to the priestess. "I have no idea what you are talking about."

But that wasn't true. I heard the water again; the wind smelled of fish and roses.

"Don't you remember, Red?" Dido said. "Don't you remember the temple of holy whores where Isis found Osiris in the tamarisk tree? In the time when whores ruled. Don't you remember?"

I had never heard Dido speak that way, with no hint of sarcasm or bitterness, her voice musical and rhythmic, as if she were a bard. And her words did evoke memories, memories I could not possibly possess.

"Those temples don't exist anymore." I spoke with effort as if breaking a trance. "Maybe they never did. Maybe it's…just a story." A heretical statement for someone raised on stories.

"Let go of time, daughter," said Aemiliana, just as she had on the eve of the *Isia*. "Don't you know the river is always rising and always meeting the sea?"

"I don't understand," I said helplessly.

"You will," Aemiliana assured me. "If Isis is calling you to found a temple of holy whores, she will show you the way."

"I want *you* to show me, Aemiliana," I said. "Come with me. "

"My place is in Rome at Venus Obsequens whenever I can return," she gently refused me. "You don't need me. You'll have plenty of help."

"I for one am going with you," announced Berta. "Close your mouth, *liebling*. You look like a carp. I have earned my manumission. That is why I am here tonight."

"Oh, Berta. I would love to have you with me. But don't you want to go home?"

"Home? To my village that is rubble? To my man who is dead? No, I go with you, Red. If you'll have me."

"The same goes for me, Red," said Dido. "I am also free. Free!"

I opened my arms to them, and Succula came into the whores' huddle with us.

"Red," Succula began, "I wish…but I can't, even if I'm free. Oh, Red."

"I know, Succula," I spoke softly. "Your place is here. With Domitia.

"That much is settled." Domitia brought us back to order. "Who is going to pay for their passage to Palestine? Or invest in their business?"

I am afraid everyone looked to Joseph, who sighed. If he had lived in your time, he might have complained to his therapist: Why is it whenever I fall in love with a woman, I end up investing in her brothel? All I ever wanted was a nice Platonic relationship.

"Am I to understand that I am to take a boatload of whores to the land of my forefathers where I am a member of a prominent priestly family with an inherited seat on the Sanhedrin?"

"Red," said Paulina timidly. "I wouldn't blame you if you didn't...I mean I can understand how you might not...but the thing is, I can't imagine..."

"Spit it out, Paulina," I sighed.

"Take me with you, Red! Please take me with you!"

"And an adulteress into the bargain!" Joseph threw up his hands.

"She's been cleared of the charge," Domitia reminded him.

Domitia was right: freedom was getting complicated. In all my imaginings, dreams, and visions, I had never seen myself with an entourage.

"But why, Paulina?" I demanded. "Your life is in Rome. Everyone and everything you know is here."

"But *you* won't be here!" Paulina burst out. "What do I care about everyone? Who's everyone? Maxima? Claudius?"

She had a point.

"I love you, Maeve." Then she leaned closer and whispered, "I think I'm going to have a baby; my courses haven't come. It would be best if I get out of town for a while. A provincial backwater might be just the thing. *Please*, Maeve."

"A pregnant adulteress!" Joseph had overheard. "It is enough to make me repent!"

"Besides," said Paulina. "Now that I've been cleared of all charges, well, people, let's put it this way: I have money. And *I* would invest in your whorehouse."

I regarded Paulina. I didn't have to take her with me; I didn't have to take her into consideration at all. I owed her nothing. On the other hand, I considered, she owed me quite a lot.

"I would have some conditions," I said.

"Name them."

"Free Reginus and Boca. Make sure they have enough money to take care of themselves for life."

"Oh, honey," said Reginus.

"Boca?" Paulina looked vague.

"The slave whose tongue you cut out."

Paulina had the grace to look ashamed. "I will free both of them at once. And do anything else you ask, Red."

"Reginus," I turned to him. "I can't imagine you'd want to leave Rome, but—"

"Hey, what has Rome ever done for me?" He cut me off. "Wherever you're going, sister, I'm going."

"And a flaming—" began Joseph. "Er, Greek."

"Joseph dearest," said Domitia, "a great deal is being asked of you. You've always managed to keep your life abroad separate from your priestly duties at home. Think hard before you do something that might damage your good name."

There was a silence as everyone gave Joseph a moment to reflect.

"My dear." Joseph came and knelt before me, taking both my hands in his. "My name, good or bad, would not mean much to me if I failed you again. I have a ship, anchored under a Roman friend's name, so I think we can leave in a few days without fear of pursuit. But I want you to think. Your chances of finding your Esus are small. And his chances of finding you, if you pursue this crazy, antiquated idea of temple prostitution, even smaller. What you are proposing is an abomination to a Jew. You may get your Greeks, your Romans, your Egyptians, your Syrians, your garden variety gentile, but you won't find a Jew in a whorehouse!"

Everyone waited a beat before we simultaneously burst into laughter. Joseph finally got the joke on himself.

"But I never said I was a *good* Jew. As you can see, I am being punished for my transgressions. Still, I would rather have this punishment than any reward I can imagine."

At that moment Old Nona came forward, gesturing for Joseph to move aside. She reached inside her tunic and lifted out the tiny vial of tears that she wore around her neck suspended from a braided cord. She placed the cord around my neck, and the vial nestled between my breasts.

INTERMISSION

MARE INTERNUM

We will have a brief pause now. If this novel were a theatre, you could go out into the lobby, wait in line for a drink or for the bathroom. Give people a chance to admire your clothes, hair, or jewels. Step outside for some air or a smoke. Backstage, the crew would be busy transforming the scenery. Actors would change their costumes and redo their makeup. Some would be done until final curtain, others awaiting their first entrance.

But we are not in the theatre, and I am not letting you go outside of the story, not really. Where we are is more like a pause between breaths. Whether you're inhaling or exhaling, there's a pause, just before, like the pause you can feel more than hear before the tide reverses. Where we are is the point of intersection in the figure eight. Turned on its side, the eight becomes the symbol of infinity. You can make this figure with your hips when you dance. Over and over, you will return to that point of balance before your weight shifts from one hip to the other.

The balance of this story is about to shift; the scenery is changing as we make our slow way across *Mare Internum*, a journey I am not going to describe. When the story begins again, some of the people you have come to know and love (or not)—Dido, Berta, Paulina, Reginus, and Joseph will appear less frequently. Domitia Tertia, Succula, Bone, Bonia, Old Nona, Aemiliana and Boca (who stayed in Rome and opened a tavern called The Nightingale's Tongue) you will see hardly at all. I don't like it when characters fade from a story, so I am apologizing in advance. But life is like that; we leave people and places and times behind. We encounter new ones. Sometimes we can't see the patterns or connections. But they are there, between one breath and the next, in the ebb and flow of tides, in the rhythm of the dance.

TEMPLE MAGDALEN

CHAPTER THIRTY-SEVEN

JERUSALEM THE GOLDEN

I confess that I begin this part of the story with trepidation. You may like to think of me as brazen and fearless. (I would like to think of myself that way, too, but his adherence to truth has rubbed off on me.) The truth is, it takes a hell of a nerve to tell another version of the gospel story. Until now I assume I've had your willing suspension of disbelief. A Celtic girl encounters the young Jesus at druid school? Unlikely, perhaps, but fun. After all, his lost years are up for grabs, and there is a certain literary tradition there. (See Blake's famous poem, "And did those feet?") My adventures in Rome as a whore and a priestess are strictly mine. You have no reason to question my authority.

But now I am venturing into tricky terrain. My story and his are coming together again. Only, his belongs to everyone in the world, believers and unbelievers, orthodox and heretic alike, as well as scholars and theologians, not to mention novelists and filmmakers. Everybody has theories, interpretations, angles, axes to grind. And why not? It's part of the tradition. Why do you think there are four canonical gospels in the first place, one of which presents an entirely different chronology than the others?

For more than two millennia, people have not been able to leave his story alone. Do we really need yet another version? I don't know. I only know I need to tell the story. So, if you're willing, suspend your disbelief some more. (A lovely word, suspend. It makes me think of bungee jumping, and of course, it is from the same root as the word suspense.) And I will do my best to deliver this passion story, to see it all the way through to the promised dawn.

"So we're here," sighed Reginus. "Now what?"

We had arrived last night at Joseph's well-appointed house in Arimathea after months of traveling, seeing the great sights of the Mediterranean world, and getting on each other's last nerve. Now we sat in the courtyard, surrounded by thick, whitewashed mud walls, eating a breakfast of fruits and goat cheese.

"We go shopping in Jerusalem, of course," answered Paulina.

Paulina's purchases in Alexandria were still catching up with us by camel. After three months of being sea, land, and morning sick, Paulina had perked up in her second trimester. She was feeling particularly well this morning, as the announcement that Claudius had died intestate had greeted her here. She no longer had to worry about whether or not Claudius would raise the child to his knee to make him legitimate. Claudius had died in embarrassing circumstances, the communication indicated, but there was no suspicion of foul play. Since he had named no other, Paulina was his sole heir.

(If this sounds too easy and convenient, just remember that inheritances have been the stock in trade of novelists since the form began. I'm not going to inherit any money. But I hope you won't begrudge me a wealthy benefactress.)

"But isn't Jerusalem another day's journey from here?" objected Berta. "I for one would prefer to lie around all day eating figs and taking baths. It is very hot here."

We had arrived at the end of summer, a few weeks before the Sukkoth, the feast of the Tabernacles.

"The baths here are not exactly like the baths in Rome," said Joseph nervously. "They are for cleansing before prayer."

"A very good idea to have a bath before prayer," agreed Berta. "Isis will like it."

"And water must be used sparingly, especially in this season," Joseph added. "I don't know if you noticed the cisterns. There's not much groundwater in these hills; we are dependent on rainfall."

"Surely the Romans have built aqueducts!" Reginus was alarmed.

Though he had impulsively chosen adventures with me over staying in Rome, he clearly had reservations about being stuck in a waterless backwater.

"For Roman use, yes. They don't feel obliged to supply every village."

"I want to hear what Red plans to do." Dido cut short the discussion on plumbing. "We came to Judea because of her."

I wasn't sure if Dido meant her remark as support or accusation or mere statement of fact. I knew she had never put much credence in the idea of reunion with my long lost love. How long could I expect any of them to stay with me on this quest?

"I want to—what's the village called where your cousins live?"

"Bethany," Joseph sighed.

"Well, I want to go there to see her. Her and her brother and sister."

"Her who?" demanded Paulina.

"Mary. The one he was supposed to marry."

"Are you sure that's wise, Red?" said Dido.

"Well, I want to see her, too!" declared Paulina.

"And I, too!" added Berta.

"No," said Joseph. "These are very private people who have had enough trouble and scandal in their lives. We can all go to Jerusalem; it is on the way to Bethany. But I insist that we rest today. There are preparations to make, and I need to send word ahead to my friend in the city and to my cousins. We'll stay tomorrow night in the city, then Maeve and I will go to Bethany alone."

Joseph looked harried. We were an unruly and motley crew. He was a brave man to take us to Jerusalem.

We set out at dawn the next morning, and made good time on some sturdy donkeys. Paulina wasn't up to a twenty-mile walk up increasingly steep hills. In the heat of the day we rested in a well-placed grove of oaks and terebinths, and so it was late afternoon when we crested a ridge and found ourselves gazing down at Jerusalem, the whole city golden in the western light, and the gold of the Temple roofs beyond golden, flashing like living fire. In contrast to this brightness, black smoke billowed from the Temple's sacrificial altars.

"It's not Rome," Paulina had to say, "but—"

"Or Alexandria, Athens, or Carthage or Damascus, but—" Dido parodied her.

"But, hey, it's impressive," Reginus concluded.

"The most famous view is from the East," Joseph felt obliged to point out; he had spent most of his life avoiding the holy city, but he wanted us to admire it. "From there you look straight at the walls of the Temple from the Kedron Valley."

"Is it very ancient?" Berta, a barbarian raised, like me, in wattle and daub huts, was clearly awed, even after all her years in Rome.

"The site is," said Joseph. "See where the city sits, crowning the mountains, the coast to one side, the desert to the other. Jerusalem has been the crossroads of the world for thousands of years. She's been torn to pieces more than once, people fighting over her like dogs for a prize bone. You see, whoever controls Jerusalem has his finger on the pulse of east-west trade. As for the Temple, it's mostly new. The late great Herod set out to make it one of the wonders of the world, and he has largely succeeded. All that gold, that huge expanse surrounding the Temple buildings, is his work, and it's still going on. He was very much influenced by the Greeks, of course. Wait till you see the porticoes."

We all gazed in silence for a moment. Confronted by this city that my beloved loved, I felt excited and daunted. Walled and watching from the heights, Jerusalem was a fortress, and whether or not Esus was actually inside those walls at this moment, the city held some part him. His invisible god, who could go anywhere, who could crop up as a burning bush, who could speak in dreams, who led his people out of Egypt into a long bloody tramp through the wilderness, this god lived here. It was his permanent address. I was an old hand at trespassing on sacred ground, but I felt the presence of a power that would not let me slip in under the invisible fencing, so to speak.

"Shall we go on?" prompted Joseph.

Disconcertingly, the vast Temple complex disappeared as we began our descent down the last ravine. On the other side of the valley, roads from the coastal cities—Joppa, Ceasaria, Acco—merged, and traffic thickened as we wound through the suburbs to the Fish Gate. At Joseph's insistence, we stabled the donkeys and hired a couple of boys to help carry our baggage.

I soon understood Joseph's reasoning. Jerusalem's streets made Rome's meanest alley seem spacious. Two laden donkeys passing in opposite directions created an instant traffic jam. The almost standstill pace of the throngs made it all the easier for vendors to hawk their wares, which they did loudly and competitively. In a couple of places, we had to make detours to avoid streets clogged with flocks of sheep and goats, who made their own contribution to the cacophony. Every now and then, the wind would shift and a cloud of smoke from the Temple would waft over us, the scents of charcoal, incense, burnt flesh, and offal in one dizzying mix.

"I have heard that Jerusalem is the best place to buy scent," shouted Paulina over the din. "We must find the perfume markets first thing tomorrow."

I thought she was being a pretty good sport. The old Paulina would have been threatening to faint, but perhaps she could see that if she did not go with the press of the crowd, she would surely be trampled.

At last we turned away from the commercial thoroughfares into a somewhat quieter area where, it seemed, the city's potters lived and worked. Now that I was not just looking at the backs or tops of people's heads, I noticed something—or rather the absence of something—which I hadn't registered before: No garish statues of gods or goddesses, no frescoes of their petty, immortal dramas, just rough, unfinished looking walls. We were in the city of the one god to whom idols and graven images were anathema.

Joseph stopped by one of the workshops and turned to us. "It's not the upper city, I'm afraid," he apologized, forgetting that none of us knew then about the elegant homes on the hill that housed the wealthier members of the priestly classes, Joseph's own class, in fact. "But Nicodemus is a good friend. I can trust him.

"Tell your master that Joseph of Arimathea is here," he said to a young man who must have been an apprentice.

"I know Nicodemus from the Sanhedrin," Joseph explained to us. "I inherited my seat, but he earned his. He is a renowned Doctor of the Law."

"Oh?" said Paulina. "I thought he was a potter."

Her confusion was understandable. There was no counterpart in Roman society for a Doctor of Law who gained distinction by virtue of long and diligent study, not birth into a class.

"For a Jew, it is possible to be both," said Joseph a little testily.

Just then a merry looking man with white unruly hair, and a mischievous glint in his eye, came from the house in back and enveloped Joseph in an embrace.

"Joseph, you old sinner! I can't tell you how glad I am to see you. We've heard terrible news from Rome, but you seem to lead a charmed life." He winked in our direction. And I could suddenly see how we must have appeared: four voluptuous women, one decidedly pretty man. We looked like a harem with a keeper. "Job's complaints are justified. The wicked prosper."

"I don't admit to wickedness, just waywardness, you pious old curmudgeon."

Their exchange had a ritual quality; I sensed they traded the same affectionate insults every time they met.

"As the friends of my friend, you are welcome in my house for as long as you wish to stay," he said to us. "Whoever you may be?"

"Perhaps we needn't go into that too closely." Joseph answered the note of interrogation in Nicodemus's voice. "Suffice it to say that they have all run afoul of Emperor Tiberius."

"Then you are doubly welcome," said Nicodemus gravely as he bowed to us. "Come in. Come in or my wife will be scolding me for keeping you standing in the street."

After raising one eyebrow and giving him a look that he ignored, Nicodemus's wife Hannah took in stride this superfluity of gentile guests and bustled about making us comfortable, washing our feet herself. I guessed that Nicodemus was often generous at her expense, but I also sensed she took an exasperated pride in his eccentricities. The house was already overflowing with children, grandchildren and apprentices. I don't think I ever saw Hannah, or any daughters or daughters-in-law, sit down, but when Berta and I offered to help we were firmly rebuffed. I didn't know then that anything we touched would have had to be ritually purified.

Nor did I appreciate how questionable it was for Nicodemus, as a Pharisee, an expert on the laws of purity, to eat with us at all: gentiles and women, not to mention once and future whores. If anyone had challenged him, he might have shot back: "Be kind to the stranger, for you were once strangers in Egypt." Many of his fellow Doctors of Law would have considered his interpretation of that text as too liberal and too literal. That's why Joseph trusted him; however pious and observant, Nicodemus was a maverick and a free thinker, too. They formed an odd alliance on the Sanhedrin.

"Nicodemus, do you remember that young man I introduced you to a few years ago?" Joseph finally asked the question he had strictly forbidden me to pose myself. "Yeshua from Nazareth?"

"The one you tried to marry to your poor cousin Mary? What was the Eternal One thinking putting that mind in a woman's body? Not that your protégé didn't have a promising mind, too. I remember him as a young boy. He used to come to the Temple and drive the doctors crazy, getting into debates as if he had a degree. I admired his spirit. But he needed discipline. Is it true that the pair of them ran off and joined the Essenes?"

"I'm afraid it's all true," said Joseph. "Mary's back in Bethany now. I was wondering if you had heard anything of the young man. Has he been seen around the Temple?"

Nicodemus shook his head. "Not that I know of, and I would have noticed him. He could never keep his mouth shut."

The night was warm, and the whole household slept on pallets close together in the small courtyard. I woke at dawn, and for the first time the city was quiet except for the soft cooing of mourning doves. Then I heard an extraordinary sound, a huge groan, as if some immense primordial beast lifted its voice in lament.

"What's that?" I asked aloud, sitting up.

"It is the Nicanor Gate that opens onto the Court of the Israelites," explained Nicodemus, getting to his feet. "Solid bronze. Twenty men it takes to open it. Jerusalem, awake!" He lifted his voice and opened his arms to the sky. "The day begins!"

There was a lot more groaning then on a purely human scale, but Nicodemus paid no attention as he turned in the direction of the Temple and chanted *"Shema Yisrael: Adonai Elohenu, Adonai Echod."* Hear O Israel: the Lord thy

God, the Lord is One. Hundreds of voices joined him all over Jerusalem. Then the trumpets sounded announcing the first sacrifices of the day.

All right. I was here in *his* city. There was no avoiding this god who claimed to be one god. I resolved to ask Joseph if we could visit the Temple on our way to Bethany.

"Maeve, pay attention," said Joseph. "Tell me what the sign says."

We were standing in the Court of the Gentiles near the entrance to the outermost court of the sanctuary, the Court of Women.

"I know how to read, Joseph," I said crossly. "You taught me yourself."

"I want to hear you read it aloud."

"Do you want me to read from the Latin or the Greek?"

"Don't get smart, Maeve. They both say the same thing. Read the Greek."

"No pagan may proceed beyond this point," I intoned. "Anyone who is taken shall be killed, and he alone shall be answerable for his death."

"That means you, Maeve. You're a pagan, do you understand?"

The Temple, it seemed, was arranged like a hierarchical onion (with steps leading upwards between each layer). Everyone in the world could be in the outer layer, for the one god was the god of all people, even if we did not acknowledge him and had not been chosen by him. One peel further in, Jewish women could go, beyond that, only Jewish men; further in, only the priests. At the mysterious empty core where the one god lived, the high priest alone was allowed to enter once a year on the Day of Atonement.

"Can I trust you on your own? I won't be long, but I need to meet with a couple of people. You can stroll about, listen to the debates, look at the view. We'll meet by the Southeastern gate when the trumpets blow for the midmorning sacrifices."

"I'll be fine, Joseph," I assured him. "I'll just wander around and see if I can find Anna the Prophetess."

"Anna the prophetess!" He looked at me warily. "What do you know about her?"

I decided now was not the time to tell Joseph about the dream I'd had when I was thirteen years old, how I had seen this Temple before. From atop one of those elegant Greek porticoes Joseph so admired, I had listened to a presumptuous boy from Galilee disconcert the Doctors of Law, just as Nicodemus remembered. I had fluttered down and perched on his head, where, alas, I lost control of my bowels—as doves are apt to do. When I flapped away in confusion, it was Anna who had called me to her and comforted me. She had also waylaid my beloved as he fled from the Temple humiliated by the incident with the incontinent dove (me). If anyone would know how to find Esus, it would be Anna.

"Well, she's very famous, isn't she?"

"Was, perhaps. She was an ancient-of-days when I was a youth. I haven't seen her here in years. Maeve, promise, you won't even think of going into the Court of Women to look for her. She can't still be living."

Once Joseph left me alone, I began to realize how disoriented I felt. Emerging from the narrow streets to the mountain of steps leading to the Temple platform had been overwhelming. The Temple utterly skewed my sense of scale; people, who took up so much space as they jostled through their crowded city, suddenly appeared antlike, if less organized, as they swarmed the steps and thronged the vast Court of Gentiles. The south end, especially, where people changed money and bought and sold animals for sacrifice was as noisy and chaotic as any marketplace. Yet somehow I had the impression of everything human being swallowed up or crushed by the immense weight and silence of the one god.

I preferred the Temple from a dove's eye view.

Here now, in my waking, walking, human form, I suddenly felt desolate. How could I have known so much when I was so young, had the power of prophetic dreaming and shape-shifting and now have to plod along in the heat of the day with a blister starting on my heel from the hard paving stones. 'He has been here, he has walked on these stones,' I kept telling myself, trying to stir some emotion, some sense of connection to him. But it wasn't working. I might as well have been in Rome.

I decided to wander past the porticoes where the rabbis were teaching or debating. If my beloved was anywhere in Jerusalem, he would be there. Though some of the debates were heated, there was no sense of the freshness, outrage and excitement my beloved had generated. I didn't peer into every face; I did not worry that I might miss him. I knew he wasn't here.

"Isis," I found myself praying out loud. "Oh, Isis."

I missed my goddess, I realized. I needed her here. If my beloved's god wanted to smite me for failing to appreciate his singularity, let him.

"Isis, I'm here in his holy place, and I'm still lost. Help me."

She can be subtle, my goddess; nothing much happened, but I immediately felt a little lighter, a little clearer. The air stirred, and a fresh breeze, spicy and sweet, washed over me. I followed it and found myself on a flight of steps that led to the gardens outside the temple walls. I recognized this place. I had been here in my dream, flown away from the laughter and jeering, from the heat of my beloved's shame, flown to Anna the Prophetess who had held my dove's breast in the palm of her hands. I closed my eyes and breathed the scent of the garden. I could hear the soft, liquid sounds of the doves.

"Come, my dove, my dearest, come to Anna."

Was I only remembering my dream? I didn't want to look and find that she wasn't there.

"Little dove," she called again, and I knew she was calling me.

I turned toward the sound of the voice. And there she was, impossibly old, smaller than I remembered.

"Here I am, Anna," I answered.

She did not turn towards me, just stared her blind stare, her eyes like pools with mists drifting over them.

"And here I am, no, not dead yet, though why *he* keeps me waiting so long, I don't know. The Eternal One has very little sense of time." She cackled softly at her joke.

I went and knelt beside her, and took her hands, placing them over my heart.

"My little dove?" she said again, more tentatively this time.

"Yes?" I answered, and I found myself tongue-tied. Suddenly it seemed presumptuous of me to believe that Anna knew who I was or shared the memory of my dream.

"You have grown," she pronounced, and she let one hand fall into her lap; with the other she explored my face with a light feathery touch.

"Well, I'm not a bird anymore," I blithered.

Maybe I was crazy; maybe she was, too, sitting outside the Temple day after day talking to escaped sacrificial doves. Maybe it didn't matter. Her touch and her voice were as much a comfort to me now as they had been in my dream.

"That is not what I meant." Her tone sharpened; and the mists seemed to clear from her eyes. "I know who you are, even if you don't. Yes, my dear, you seem a little confused today. So was he when he came to me, full of anger, bitterness, and reproach. As if it was my fault—well, people do sometimes mistake the medium for the message—though I will say I expected him to be more discerning."

"Who?" I knew whom she meant, but I longed for her to speak his name.

"Miriam's son. Who else?"

"Yeshua," I spoke the name his people called him; the syllables were like water on a thirsty tongue. "Yeshua."

"Oh, my little dove." She put her hand on my heart again. "Yes, bigger, broken, open. His, too, but he hadn't learned to appreciate it yet. He thought it was all a mistake."

"What was?" I whispered, afraid the answer was me.

"Going, loving, leaving, returning. All. He thought he had done it all wrong. He thought he had lost his way. And so he had. Being lost *is* the way, I tried to tell him, how else can you be found? How else can you find again what you have lost—sheep, coins, love? But it's no good telling people things. And so, my dove, I will give you my blessing, much better than prophecy any day of the week. Prophecy you can't understand until it's too late, but a blessing, now, a blessing comes in handy—like a pocket hanky. Best not to go on a journey without one. Now then."

But I did not want to be blessed and sent on my way. Not yet. I longed for the vaguest, most obscure prophecy.

"Anna, please. Do you know where he is?"

"That I can't tell you, dearie."

"Cannot or will not."

"Cannot," she paused to consider, "and will not."

All at once, I felt angry with her, and anguished. I knew she was withholding. I could feel it in my bones. I took a breath to keep myself from shaking her.

"Hear me, Anna the Prophetess." I felt myself expanding like a bird fluffing its feathers to make itself appear larger. Not that such a strategy could possibly impress Anna, who knew all about the ways of birds. "You spoke the words that sent Yeshua Ben Miriam to the Holy Isles. I spoke the words that sent him away, but he heard them in your voice. That is why he listened. If you will not or cannot tell me where he is, then tell me what to do. Tell me how to look for him. And if…if I am meant to give him up forever, then…then turn me into a bird and let me fly away."

I started to weep, but I didn't get out my vial of tears. It was already nearly full, and I damn well didn't feel like it. Anna reached up, touched my tears, then put her fingers in her mouth and tasted them. I wanted to be appalled by this strange, intimate act, but somehow I wasn't.

"Ah," she said. "Ah, there. I will die easy now, little dove. The Eternal One will give me wings." She paused for a beat. "It's the least *he* can do."

The breeze sprang up again, and I felt my tears drying. I felt light again, though I didn't know why.

"Little dove, come now, bow down your head. Receive my blessing."

This time I did not resist. She put her old woman's hands, light as a bird claw, on my crown. Her hands were burning, and I felt her pouring the fire into me. In the next moment it felt like water, cool dark water, flowing underground, then rising into light. I could hear it and smell it, the waters of the spring. I could see the dawn stars reflected there. For just an instant I glimpsed the face I loved best.

"Go then, my little dove."

She slid her hands from my head, and I turned them over, kissing each palm.

"Thank you, Anna. The wings of Isis enfold you."

"Yes," she said simply, turning not one hair at my implicit denial of the one god.

As I walked away, she called after me.

"When you see Miriam of Nazareth, tell her Anna said, 'I told you so.'"

When I turned to look back it her, she had a smile on her face that was both enigmatic and smug.

CHAPTER THIRTY-EIGHT

MARY B

At last I was on my way to meet Mary of Bethany, whom I shall henceforth call Mary B for short. The nickname may not sound very respectful, given the connotation that the letter B carries for designating secondary importance. I don't mean it that way, although there is such a plethora of Marys in the New Testament, you could probably get to E or F, if you wanted to sort us by letters. Given this excess, it is perhaps understandable that many people have assumed Mary of Magdala and Mary of Bethany, sister to Martha and Lazarus, are one and the same. In this version of the story, you will have no trouble telling us apart.

During our five-mile walk to Bethany (which I enjoyed; it was a fine day, and figs and olives were coming into season) Joseph told me more about his cousins. None of them, it seemed, had been lucky in marriage. Martha, the oldest, was a childless widow whose strong maternal drive had found an outlet in raising her baby sister, and then her brother's children from two wives, both of whom had died in childbirth. She was a fair, if demanding, mistress to the servants and laborers (none of them slaves) that worked the family's olive groves and vineyards, and she had a soft spot for strays and bad boys.

"If anyone looks lost or hungry, she'll take him in hand, clean him up, give him some work. She couldn't resist Yeshua."

The family was comfortably fixed. Not only did they own a farm, Lazarus was also a member of the same priestly class as Joseph. The priestly classes (there were twenty-four in all) served at the Temple on a rotating basis. And priests were paid amply for their tours of duty, in contrast to the Doctors of

Law, like Nicodemus, who taught for the sake of love or righteousness. Though Lazarus performed his priestly service faithfully, he was happiest out in the fields pruning vines and trees.

"Modest and retiring," Joseph described him. "That's why they don't have a house in the upper city like the other priests. He's no good at the social aspect of the priestly life."

Mary was the youngest by a dozen years. As a child, she had first amused and then horrified her family with her insistence that she would serve as a priest, too, just like her brother and her late father. When it was finally borne in upon her that she would never get beyond the Court of Women, let alone into the Court of Priests, she nursed an ambition to be a Doctor of Law and attended the public teachings in the porticoes. For a time, Nicodemus even gave her some private instruction, which ended abruptly at the family's insistence, when Mary became of marriageable age (about fourteen years old). Mary's only path of resistance was to refuse all suitors.

Then along came Yeshua.

"She fell in love with him!" I interrupted Joseph's narrative flow. "She must have. He would have been the first person, the only person, to understand her."

I was torn between the grudging sympathy and even admiration I felt for this stubborn woman and my growing fear that she might have been worthy of him. Maybe they fled their wedding only because *she* scorned the convention of marriage.

"It may well be," said Joseph unhelpfully. "At least she did not refuse him, and no one knows which of them came up with that insane scheme to run off to those desert fanatics."

Joseph shook his head; for all his urbanity and love of philosophy, he shared at least some of the prejudices of his class.

"Well, I intend to find out," I said with grim resolve.

Joseph stopped in his tracks and turned to me, taking me by the shoulders.

"Maeve, wait now. I should have thought of this before. We need to talk. We need to decide how we're going to present ourselves, I mean, um, you."

"What do you mean, Joseph? I thought you regretted not telling them about me before."

"Well, yes, that is to say, but Maeve, there is such a thing as delicacy. I know you're a strapping, forthright, uh, Celt." He managed not to call me a barbarian. "But we, you can't just go in there and interrogate them—"

"Joseph, give me some credit. I am a sophisticated former whore from the Vine and Fig Tree. I have served as a healer at the Temple of Isis."

Joseph took his hands from my shoulders and held them to his head and began to rock back and forth. If he had been a more pious Jew I would have said he was davening.

"I mean it's not as if I'm naked and painted with woad with my hair all spiked with lime. Come on, Joseph, how much more respectable and discreet can I be?"

My head was covered; though my tunic was sleeveless in this warm weather, I wore a shawl of soft blue-green wool. My jewelry and scent were minimal, despite Paulina's desire to tart me up.

"I'm sorry, Maeve, I didn't mean to imply...but you can see the problem, can't you. Who are we going to say that you are?"

I looked at him blankly. "Couldn't we just say that I'm me?"

"I know!" he said. "You're my ward. Everyone knows that I have traveled in Pretannia. So, let's see, your father was an associate of mine. He died, and I—"

"Is all this really necessary?"

"Hush, I'm thinking. And I promised to provide for you."

"But Joseph, I'm only here to find out about Yeshua and to tell them—"

"I'm getting to that part. So I promised to provide for you, and then it turned out that you were a childhood friend of—"

"Childhood?"

"Oh, I don't know. But don't you see? Domitia is right. I *have* kept my other life separate. I can't go to my cousins and say, here's a Celt I picked up in a Roman brothel. She might be the reason no good ever came of that marriage I tried to arrange for Mary."

I took a deep breath and let it out slowly.

"I've complicated your life," I said.

"It's not your fault, Maeve, but, well, now you can see why I've spent so much time away. Here there are rules about everything. Whom you can eat with, whom you can't—Nicodemus will be purifying himself for days—whom you can marry, whom you can't. What foods you can eat with other foods, what you can't. It's not as if Jews don't associate with gentiles, do business with them, even have friends among them. But the Law does keep us separate in many ways. And the Law is a whole cloth, seamless. You can't choose bits and pieces of it or the whole thing unravels. I forget when I'm away, but here... I don't know what to do with you here, Maeve. You don't fit; you don't make sense. You're like an unpredicted comet or a rare bird blown in by a storm."

I reached out, and touched his arm. I didn't know what to say.

"Well, are we going to go on?" I asked at length.

"They are expecting us," he allowed.

"Then let's go. I *am* getting hungry, and we could make a good case that I'm lost. Martha will love me."

"You don't *look* hungry," Joseph eyed my ample curves dubiously, "not the way Yeshua did. You don't have the build."

And people who fuss over bad boys don't necessarily have any sympathy for bad girls, I considered, but I didn't say so to Joseph.

If Martha was taken aback or put off by my appearance in any way, she didn't show it. It was a good half hour before she even glanced at me at all. It was the beginning of the olive harvest, and she had hired extra laborers, who had to have food and water carried out to them at the midday break (not every landowner provided such amenities) and therefore extra orders and instructions had to be given to the domestic servants. Lazarus's assorted children were underfoot. I couldn't help feeling that we might have come at a bad time.

"No, no," said Joseph. "She's always like this."

"Which one is Mary?" I whispered to him. Martha had greeted us, but she had made no introductions.

Joseph looked around the bustling courtyard.

"I don't see her. Lazarus isn't here either. He'll be out in the fields with the workers."

Martha gave an order, and servants scurried forward with hot water and towels to wash our dusty feet. Then more water was brought for our hands. When we were cleaned up, Martha led us into the courtyard where she had laid out refreshments for us in the shade of a fig tree. Wine, goat cheese, olives, grape leaves stuffed with some kind of fish paste, garlic, and spice. At Martha's insistence, Joseph and I reclined on cushions while she sat on—or rather hovered over— a low stool, ready to leap into action. Her conversation consisted mostly of urging us to eat and shooing away compliments like flies. She had the ageless look of a vigorous woman who has no time for self-reflection. I sensed that in her own way she was as uncomfortable with social occasions as her brother might be. Martha would have no problem preparing or serving a banquet, but she wouldn't want to sit through one.

When the topics of food, weather, and crops had been exhausted, Martha and Joseph moved on to Temple duty. Apparently Lazarus and Joseph's class was due to serve next week.

"I suppose someone has to serve during harvest," said Martha grudgingly, "but it is very inconvenient for us."

"The Eternal One should have put you in charge of scheduling," Joseph teased.

"Yes, he should have, blessed be his name now and forever," Martha agreed without a trace of irony. "Will you be staying with us, Joseph? Lazarus would like that."

Joseph did some nervous throat clearing. "Well, I don't quite know yet. I, um, have some friends with me from Rome, staying with Nicodemus at the moment, you remember him."

Martha gave a sniff, which I took to mean: I remember him all too well.

"I hadn't realized," Joseph continued cautiously, "when I came to Jerusalem that our class was on the roster so soon. We might take some rooms in the upper city."

"Joseph, you know your friends are welcome here."

Poor Martha. She was torn between being affronted that Joseph had not asked for hospitality and fear that he might accept her offer and bring the Roman Circus to her doorstep. So far, apart from urging me to eat, she had neither spoken to me nor looked at me. It wasn't unfriendliness, exactly. She just didn't know how to cope with my existence. She probably thought Joseph had gone round the bend and got himself a barbarian concubine—which is all very well if you were one of the old patriarchs, like Abraham, or a king, like Solomon, but hardly the thing for a respectable priestly widower.

"Oh, Martha, I couldn't impose."

I could feel the tension between them, the way you can see a rope quiver in a tug of war. Martha and Joseph were in a bind. I wondered if I could help them out.

"You are very kind, Mistress Martha," I said.

She was so startled it occurred to me that she must have assumed I couldn't speak any Aramaic, beyond "thank you" and "delicious."

"I am afraid my companion Paulina Claudii will not leave the bazaars of Jerusalem unless she is removed by force. She has only just begun to shop."

Martha looked both alarmed—how many foreign women had Joseph brought with him?—and relieved that we were not about to descend en masse.

"Um, yes, that is true, so perhaps it would be best if we...um, you see, Maeve, here, is my ward. It was her father's dying wish that I take care of her, and I brought along some of her little friends, so that she wouldn't be lonely. Thought they all might like to see a bit of the world."

Joseph launched into his absurd explanations that Martha had not asked to hear. If she had been dubious about me before, she was now downright suspicious.

"Joseph," I stopped him. "Let's just tell the truth."

"Oh, dear," said Martha and Joseph in unison.

"Martha," I turned to her, and against her will she looked me in the eye. The rest of her face was without expression. She made me think of clothing neatly pressed and folded and put away in a cedar chest. Every particle of her being was tidy, and I was about to remind her of a big mess. "It's about Yeshua. I think I might have ruined his life, by accident—I was trying to save it. And from what Joseph tells me, he may have ruined yours or your sister's. I'm trying to find out where he is. You see, he thought I was dead, but I'm not. "

From the look on Martha's face, I began to think Joseph was right. I might as well have been wearing nothing but woad. But mingled with the horror and fear, I saw something else—an unassuaged grief. Impulsively, I reached out to her. A mistake.

"You will excuse me for me a moment." She bolted.

"Now see what you've done!" Joseph hissed angrily.

"Well, at least she knows I'm not your mistress," I shot back.

"I wish to God you were," he said. "It would be much simpler. I could install you in some back alley and forget about you."

"Look, I'm sorry, Joseph," I began not very apologetically, "but I don't see the point of pretending—"

Then Martha returned, all smoothed out again, except for a lingering blotchiness in her cheeks.

"Martha, dear," Joseph stood. "Please forgive this intrusion. We're just going now. Thank you for your gracious—"

"Joseph of Arimathea," she cut him off with great authority, "you will not even think of leaving tonight. You must stay and see Lazarus. He will be hurt if you don't. Now if you will excuse me again, I have to oversee the getting of the evening meal. You will both take your ease."

It was an order.

Joseph and I actually did manage to nap, since we were not entirely on speaking terms. I would have liked to wander around the farm, but Martha had succeeded in putting the fear of something into me, and I didn't dare intrude.

Supper was simple, hearty, and tasty, a lentil stew, roasted vegetables, more cheese, olive paste, bread, and figs. The servants and the family ate together. Though Joseph's cousins were well-to-do and of priestly lineage, their household was not at all like any wealthy Roman one I had ever seen. I felt almost as though I was among the *combrogos* (except the food was better) with everyone sitting outside while the sun set and the stars came out. I felt wistful to think that I had no place here. Though I had found the Temple overwhelming—who wouldn't—and Jerusalem crowded, the land itself, the very air, seemed welcoming—not like my home, but somehow homelike in a way Rome had never been.

Lazarus was close to tongue-tied with shyness, but he had an air of kindliness and did not seem to find my presence as necessary to ignore as Martha had. From time to time he smiled at me, then ducked his head.

All of you know, as I did not, that Lazarus was the man over whom Jesus was to weep, whom he raised from the dead. I had none of my prescient flashes then, but I understood at once why my beloved might love this man who wouldn't know how to hold a grudge if someone put one in his hands and told him to squeeze. He had a large, loose frame, strong but with nothing of the warrior about him. He was as rumpled as Martha was tidy. If button shirts with tails had existed then, his tails would have constantly come untucked and buttons would have been forever flying off, giving Martha more to fret over. There was something restful and generous about Lazarus, like the shade of a big tree at noon. You could shelter with him, no questions asked, no explanations needed. His children clearly adored him, and he seldom had fewer than two or three in his lap or leaning against his shoulders. Much later, when I heard my beloved tell the story of the prodigal son, I recognized Lazarus immediately as the father running, opened-armed, to embrace his son.

As for the prodigal sister, no one introduced me to her. By the end of the meal, though Lazarus and I had barely exchanged two words, I felt sufficiently at ease with him to risk another gaffe.

"Please, may I be presented to your sister Mary?" I asked Lazarus. "Joseph has told me so much about her."

Joseph was not reclining near enough to me to kick me or he would have. As for Lazarus, it was fortunate there was no meat at the meal, and he only had to choke on lentils. Martha bustled to the rescue. She could have said Mary was ill or that she was visiting relatives, but instead she gave me a fierce, level look, and answered in front of everyone.

"My sister does not receive visitors."

And that was that.

It was another warm night, and everyone took bedrolls to the roof, women to one side, men to another, a few married couples and children in their own section. Full of good food and rich, dark wine from Lazarus's vineyard, I fell asleep right away, but woke to the light of the waning gibbous moon. All around me was the soft surf sound of sleepers' breathing. I got up as quietly as I could, locating Martha's shape as my eyes adjusted to the dark. Reassured to hear her snoring, I went to look out over the olive grove. Dull in the daytime, at night the leaves caught the moonlight, giving it back in tiny gleams. Patterns of light and shadow played tricks with my depth perception, the light seeming solid and three-dimensional. Then a figure moved into the grove, a human shadow breaking up the play of branch and leaf.

The blood pounding in my ears was louder than my bare feet as I stepped over the sleepers and then ran down the outer stairs into the grove.

"Mary," I called in a low voice. "Mary."

She stopped and turned slowly towards me. I had guessed right. We stood wordless for a time. I could not tell in that light if she was beautiful or plain or what color her eyes were. My primary sense of her was kinesthetic; I could feel her intensity the way you can feel heat or cold emanating. I could feel the sharpness of her mind, precise, probing, ruthless.

"I ...know...who...you...are." That is how she said it, each word separated from the next as if by a chasm.

"Then you must know why I'm here," I answered, and I waited. For a long time. I sighed. Was she going to be one of those people who let your words fall clunk, like a dead ball, until you became unnerved by the silence and tried again...and again?

"Mary," I said, "how the hell did you think you were going to be a Doctor of Law if you can't keep up your end of the conversation?"

"You and I are not debating the Law." Her response was quicker this time.

"Point taken," I said. "So what are we doing?"

She considered for a moment. "We're going for a walk."

She turned and began taking long confident strides. I hurried to catch up, determined to walk beside, not trail behind, her.

"Martha says you don't receive visitors. Is that her idea or yours?"

"Both," she answered curtly, and then, to my surprise, she elaborated. "Martha is afraid the villagers might want to stone me. I just want to be left alone."

We walked in silence for a time, leaving behind the orchards and following what seemed to be a goat path up a steep stony hill. I could see her a little better now. She was tall, even taller than me, and gangly. A surreptitious glance at her profile told me that she did not, as I'd suspected, have much in the way of breasts, so disguise as a man or boy would not have been difficult. Her hair was bushy and loose—rather sheep-like in its texture. In profile, I couldn't see much of her face, but I had an impression of angularity.

"So," I said, remembering that it was my turn to speak, "if you know who I am, then you know what I want to ask. Shall I just get on with it or would you rather I be veiled and indirect?"

I scanned what I could see of her face for a smile, a scowl, any sort of a reaction, a shift in pace, a catch in her breath. Nothing.

"Get on with it," she finally said.

I suddenly realized that I didn't quite know how to proceed. What happened between you and Yeshua? Were you lovers? I wanted answers, but I when I opened my mouth, the questions wouldn't come out.

"How do you know who I am?" I asked instead. "Yeshua..." There finally his name was out hovering in the air we both breathed. "...if he told you anything about me, he must have told you I was dead. That's what he believed."

"I was always afraid you weren't," she said.

So the male impersonator had at least a particle of women's intuition. That answered one question: she had been or was in love with him.

"When I saw you in the courtyard and heard you ask about him," she went on, "it wasn't hard to figure out. How many red-headed, Aramaic-speaking Celts with over-sized breasts can there be?"

"So he described me to you?" I decided to let the slur on my breasts pass for the moment.

"Of course he did. I know everything about him."

She was a woman all right.

"Things you will never know about him. Things you can't possibly understand."

She was pushing it.

"Such as?" I kept my tone cool, well, let's say icy. The kind of cold that burns.

She stopped in her tracks and slowly turned towards me. The moonlight was now full on her face. She was not pretty; her skin, though I couldn't be sure it was sallow, was at least pockmarked. But her complexion didn't matter nor did the bird-like sharpness of her features. Anyone who looked at her would forget everything but her eyes, fierce, black, challenging and, yes, beautiful.

"*I* know who he is," she said. "I know what he was born to be."

I waited for a moment.

"So...do....I." I left my own chasms between words. Through mine, cataracts of raging water roared. I could barely hear her through the din of the flood.

"You can't possibly."

I was beginning to feel sympathetic to the villagers; I was tempted to throw something at her myself. There were plenty of rocks handy in these hills.

"Why do you say so?" I restrained myself admirably.

She shook her head, as if I was hopelessly dense, and began to walk again.

"You are not of Israel. You do not know the Lord our God."

"I wouldn't be too sure of that," I interrupted. "Just because I don't worship him doesn't mean I don't know him."

"There is no knowledge without love."

That shut me up for a moment.

"Well then, in that case I know Yeshua better than anyone knows him, for I have loved him since before time began and will love him still when time ceases to exist."

I staked my claim without being sure of what I meant.

"Words only." She dismissed me. "You cannot love him if you do not love his God. If you do not live by our Law that is so much a part of him it is inscribed in his heart; it is in every breath he takes."

"You have a narrow view of love." I sounded patronizing, even to myself.

She sniffed and kicked viciously at a stone. I wondered for a moment if we were going to end up brawling, scratching each other's faces and tearing each other's hair out in clumps. I almost wished we would. It would be preferable to arguing over Eternally Annoying One.

"If my view is narrow," she said, "it is also deep."

"So why didn't you marry him when you had the chance?"

"You wouldn't understand," she said with fine disdain.

"Try me."

"Marriage was irrelevant to the bond we had. Have."

That could be true, I considered, but it wasn't the whole truth.

"And he was still in love with me." There. I'd finally said it. "And you knew it, and you couldn't stand it."

"I would not call it love." Her tone made me cold all over. "Torment. He was tormented by his memories of you."

We had arrived at the top of the hill, and there below us lay Jerusalem, the Temple outlined by torches along the walls. Though dawn could not be far off, the stars still shone in the deep sky. Mary stood for a moment, then she sat down on the ground, gesturing for me to sit beside her.

"Why have we come here?" I asked.

A wild hope rose in me: This was their trysting place. He had not left the country but was merely in hiding. For an instant, I didn't care what was between them, whether or not they were lovers, I just wanted to see him. Then everything would come clear.

"You will see," she said. "While we wait, I will tell you something that I have told no one else."

While we *wait*? My hope leapt out of bounds.

"He did not leave me," she went on.

I was right; he was here, somewhere close by, coming with the dawn.

"It was I who sent him away. I made him go."

"What?" My crazy hope plummeted like a bird wounded in flight. "What are you saying?"

"I told him to go away and rid himself of his ghost. I told him not to come back until he was free, pure, with nothing between him and the will of the Most High."

"Where is he?" I whispered.

She just sat not looking at me.

"Mary, listen to me! If he knows I'm not dead, he won't be tormented anymore. Don't you see? He'll be free for whatever his destiny may be. Mary, you have to tell me where he is."

"I cannot."

"Cannot or will not?"

"Cannot and will not," she answered, just as Anna had. "Hush. It's almost time."

I did not bother to ask her what she meant. I turned my face away from her and wept as soundlessly as I could. Birds started to sing, and I could hear the whir of wings as flocks hurled themselves into the sky.

"Now," said Mary, touching my hand. "Look."

My eyes still blurry with tears, I looked out across the Kedron Valley, just as the rising sun touched the Temple Wall and turned the east-facing gates to gold.

"The Beautiful Gates," she said in a strange, exultant voice. "The Messiah will enter Jerusalem through them one day. Look! Look and tell me what you see."

I didn't know what she wanted me to say. Yes, the gates were beautiful, the view from the east, impressive, just as Joseph had said. So? Then, in a literal blink of an eye, everything changed. It wasn't dawn anymore; it was impossible to tell what time of day it was. The temple was on fire; people were screaming, fighting all along the walls; the Valley of the Kings, with its ancient tombs, swarmed with soldiers. It was worse than that. I had a sense of time collapsing in on itself, as if caught in a whirlpool. The Temple fell and rose again, fell and rose again and again. I put my hands over my face to stop it, to shut out the smoke and rage and grief.

When I looked again; the valley was flooded with light; trumpets sounded from the temple as the gates swung open. Someone climbed towards the gate, and my vision carried me to the other side of the valley, so that I was near enough to see him. I knew the set of his back, the rhythm of his gait. I knew the way the earth felt when those feet touched it. He was walking, walking uphill to the gates, but inside the gates there was no Temple, there was nothing—

"Oh," I cried out aloud. "Oh!"

And then I was back on the ridge with Mary; there was no one in the valley but a flock of sheep.

"What did you see?" She turned to me. "What did you see?"

I just shook my head.

"Tell me." She held my arm, and turned those hot coal eyes on me. "You must tell me. I know the scriptures; I know the prophecies, but I can't *see*." Now she was pleading. "You! You are a sorceress. He said so. He told me that all your people see things that other people can't. Tell me. I need to know. I need to know if I am right. Or if it's all—"

She broke off abruptly and turned away as if ashamed of her loss of control.

"Mary," I said slowly, aware that I was on tricky ground. "I know enough of your Law to know that you're not supposed to ask a witch to give you foreknowledge. So let's agree that you never did. I'm not sure what good prophecies do anyone. You usually can't understand them until it's too late. That's what Anna the Prophetess says."

"You spoke with Anna the Prophetess! Did she say anything…about him?"

"Nothing that made any sense to me at all. She just gave me a blessing." And then a not very bright idea occurred to me. "I could give *you* a blessing."

She recoiled from me. I didn't take offense; I knew she couldn't help it.

"You have no power to bless me. All blessings come from the Most High, and me he has seen fit to curse, and there is no one who can change that."

"What curse?"

"I was born a woman."

With that, she got to her feet and started back to Bethany at a fast clip. I had all I could do to keep her in sight. When we reached the olive groves she disappeared altogether, and I went back to the house alone.

CHAPTER THIRTY-NINE

MA

"Next stop Nazareth," I announced to my friends.

We were all sitting on the roof garden of our palatial suite of rooms in the upper city enjoying a prime view of the Temple's southern steps. The speed with which Paulina had made friends and influenced people in the Roman ex-pat community was a little frightening. It was clear to us all that she was enjoying her cachet as a lovely, filthy rich young widow with a slightly racy reputation.

"But we only just got here," objected Paulina, "and I've accepted invitations to dinner into next week!"

"We don't all have to go," I pointed out. "In fact, it would probably be better if I went alone with Joseph again."

"You still haven't told us what has happened with this Mary he didn't marry," Berta reproached me. "We want to know everything!"

"My cousin Mary was indisposed," Joseph said abruptly. "We did not see her."

Dido raised one of her eloquent black eyebrows, and I shook my head and cast a glance at Joseph. Presenting me to his cousins had been difficult for him. I sensed that he had his suspicions about my encounter with Mary, but he did not want them confirmed.

"Did you find out anything about where lover boy might be?" asked Reginus.

"No one seems to know," I said, "but Lazarus promised to tell Yeshua that I'm alive if he ever comes back. I told him that Joseph would always know where I am."

"When did you talk to Lazarus?" Joseph was dismayed. "Couldn't you see from Martha's reaction that no one in Bethany wants to hear his name?"

"I spoke to Lazarus privately before he went out to the fields," I confessed. "I'm sorry I upset Martha, but Joseph, listen, I've traveled at least halfway to the ends of the earth to find him. How can I not ask?"

Joseph didn't answer. I was feeling more and more uncomfortable about how much I had demanded of him. I will admit to you, I would have been Joseph's mistress as a way of giving something in return if he had asked me, but I knew I couldn't offer without insulting his pride. Any scruples were his, not mine. And here was another coil: though none of us were slaves, Dido, Berta, Reginus and I were all dependent on Paulina's wealth. Our journey across the Mare Internum had had its own logic and momentum. Now that we had arrived at our destination, the oddness of our assortment and our lack of any purpose but mine was becoming more and more apparent.

"Only Nazareth and then—" I began to answer my own unspoken thoughts.

"And then what?" said Dido, giving me one of those cool, level, no bullshit looks.

And then…I didn't have a clue. All those plans we had made in Domitia Tertia's chamber seemed so vague and far-fetched.

"I must warn you, Maeve, I am not on good terms with Yeshua's brothers." Joseph rescued me from having to answer Dido. "However disastrous this botched marriage was for my cousins, I am still their family. They know I meant well. To Yeshua's brothers, I am a meddlesome fool. They resented his marriage into a priestly family in the first place. Then he had to go and throw away what they saw as undeserved good fortune and get mixed up with the lunatic fringe in the desert. Frankly, I don't think they want to be reminded of his existence, let alone his, um, previous misadventures." Joseph cleared his throat. "In any case, I can't take you next week, because I'm serving at the Temple, and soon after that it's the High Holy Days, and then Sukkoth, and then I really must make a quick trip to Alexandria, and then…"

"I'll go without you," I interrupted.

"You'll do nothing of the sort."

"I think it would be best," I said firmly. "I want to go right away before the Day of Atonement and Sukkoth to be sure of finding Miriam at home. Don't worry, Joseph, I won't bother with the brothers. I'll avoid them altogether, if I can. But I have to see her. I have a message for her from Anna the Prophetess."

"Harumph," is my best translation of Joseph's response. I took it to express overt disapproval at my willfulness and covert relief to be let off the hook.

"But is it safe for a woman to travel alone?" asked Paulina; she was, oddly enough, turning out to be the most practical of all of us, except perhaps for Dido.

"I go with her," volunteered Berta.

"Two women or three would be no better," said Joseph gloomily.

"All right, all right," said Reginus. "I can see where this conversation is heading. I'll go. Off into the wilderness, I suppose, to some rinky-dink one-camel town?"

"Nazareth is quite small and provincial," Joseph acknowledged. "Not at all Greek, though a lot of Greeks live in Sepphoris nearby. The two of you could be a married couple from Greece traveling to Sepphoris to visit relatives. It would be the same turn off the main route north."

"But why do we need to pose?" I asked.

"Because." I could hear the exasperation in his voice. "You won't be traveling by yourselves. I am going to a find a caravan for you to join. The hills are dangerous, full of robbers and rebels, and people are naturally fearful. The more ordinary you seem to others, the better. If you must go, and I see that you are determined, promise me that on the way back you'll join a group of pilgrims going to Jerusalem for Sukkoth. There should be plenty of traffic headed south then."

"We'll be careful, Joseph, and—" I stopped, wishing I knew just the right words to relieve the sadness I sensed in him as if he had come to the end of some long, fruitless journey of his own. "Thank you. Thank you all for coming so far with me when I don't even know…"

I let my sentence hang unfinished, and no one tried to complete it for me. We were silent for a time, watching the late light climb the Temple heights before it disappeared into the deep, sudden night of this country. Here there were no long twilights like the ones in the Holy Isles, that magical, dangerous hour when things had a tendency to shape-shift and one world opened onto another. I wondered if it was because my beloved's god would tolerate no half-light, no ambiguity, that there was such a sharp distinction between day and night.

So Reginus and I joined a caravan of jolly and not particularly inquisitive merchants, their cargo of oil and spice carried by camels. I soon fell in love with these cantankerous beasts who spat and belly-ached and occasionally bit, and had a generally bad attitude. I sneaked them dates and figs when I could. I enjoyed the journey out of dry Jerusalem-dominated Judea along the spine of the land, towards the greener north. The mornings were fresh and cool; and we always rested during the heat of the day. Along the way, the landscape was pleasingly varied, sometimes heavily cultivated with vineyards, orchards, and plains of wheat, other times forested with a variety of oak, the sacred tree of my people.

Best of all was the flowering, aromatic brush. One of our companions, knowledgeable in plant lore, took pleasure in reciting the names and making distinct the wild profusion around us: hyssop, aneth, chamomile, mint, bitter rue, and marjoram. And the mustard was in flower, turning whole hillsides golden. With such an abundance of shelter and food, there were birds everywhere, filling the air with sound, as they rose and dipped over the sea of brush as if they were stitching together earth and sky.

Though Reginus was a city boy, I think he took pleasure in the journey, too. We shared a sense that these might be our last days of holiday, when anything could happen, and decisions were suspended. There was only the changing scenery and the temporary, unbinding camaraderie with our fellow travelers. The future stayed in its place and the present was sweet and poignant. Some kind of reckoning was coming—but not yet.

In the afternoon of the third day, we parted from the caravan and took the road towards Sepphoris. It was only a mile or so till the turnoff for Nazareth, a dusty track hardly wide enough for two donkey carts to pass each other. Reginus and I approached on foot, and we met no one as we climbed towards the village that looked ready to slide down the hill it crowned.

"How much you wanna bet, we've already been spotted, and they're crouching behind the walls getting ready to pelt us with stones," predicted Reginus.

"Oh come on. We don't look that scary," I said dismissively.

"Well, we don't look Jewish, either. Joseph told me the Greeks and the Jews don't mix in these hills. A town is one or the other. So what's our story now? We were looking for Sepphoris and got lost and gee it's getting late, could we spend the night here?"

"Just leave the talking to me, Reginus. I speak Aramaic, remember?"

"Yeah, but I'm the husband. Aren't you supposed to defer to me or something?"

"Ok, so speak to me in Greek, and I'll translate. Don't worry. We'll be fine."

Still, our entrance into my beloved's hometown was a little unsettling. The population was small enough that it could hush itself by unspoken agreement. The children had been called in from the streets, and they peered out from behind their parents' legs as everyone stared at us, some openly, others surreptitiously.

"Wife," said Reginus a bit more imperiously than necessary. "Ask the local inhabitants where we might find an inn."

An old man, who appeared awestruck to hear his native tongue on the lips of a strapping barbarian (for I hardly looked Greek), managed to point out the local tavern. There were no rooms to let in Nazareth, the tavern keeper told us, but we might bed down in the courtyard, if we liked. Pleased to be paid in coin for food and drink, our host became friendlier, and I took the opportunity to ask where I might find Miriam of Nazareth.

"Miriam, you say." He scratched his head, and I sensed he was stalling. "That's a very common name in these parts. Whose cousin did you say you were?"

I hadn't. I didn't see how I could pass for anyone's cousin, looking as I did, but my almost perfect Galilean-accented Aramaic must be confusing. Clearly I was being asked for references.

"I have a message for her from an old friend of hers, Anna the prophetess at the Temple of Jerusalem."

The tavern keeper gave me a sharp look. Nazareth might be a small hill town, but it was a Jewish town. Everyone there had made numerous pilgrimages to Jerusalem.

"Are you a proselyte then?" He cast a dubious glance at Reginus. "Your husband is not a Jew, I think."

I didn't want to go too deeply into my marital or religious status.

"I have had some instruction. And I have known Anna of Jerusalem for a long time."

Both statements were true as far as they went, which was not quite far enough to satisfy the barkeeper of my credentials or intentions.

"Can you describe this Miriam you seek? As I've said, it's a common name."

"She is the widow of a carpenter named Joseph. She has several sons. Anna mentioned one of them by name. Yeshua, I believe."

I was not prepared for the effect of his name. The barkeeper scowled, and muttered something I could not catch. For a moment he seemed to forget we were there.

"You will want to rest after your journey," he said when he recovered himself. "I will have a bed prepared for you under the fig tree in the courtyard."

"You are kind," I said, "but I'm not tired. Can you just direct me to the widow's house?"

"I will make inquiries for you," he said. "You must rest now."

And so I did, just long enough for Reginus to fall asleep under the tree and for word of my presence to spread through the town. Then I got up and found an empty water skin among our things. Covering my head, for all the good that would do, I slipped out into the street. As I'd suspected they would be, women from all over town were walking with their water jugs balanced on their heads, heading for the village well, the source of all information.

My attempts to stand quietly in line without drawing attention to myself were in vain. The women fell silent at once and I stood uncertainly. It occurred to me that as a gentile I might defile their well if I helped myself. I was deciding how to ask politely when a thin woman with sharp features darted at me and took the water skin. When she had filled it, she handed it back, and leaned close enough to hiss in my ear.

"She will see you. Follow me."

I had to scramble to keep up as she led me up several narrow flights of steps, then down and down to the other side of town and then along a rocky path to the outskirts where a few ancient olive trees dwarfed a small square house with a woodworking shop attached. My beloved's childhood home.

Let me pause for a moment here to catch my breath and to prepare myself—and you—for this meeting with his mother, The Mother, you might say, a.k.a. The Blessed Virgin Mary to whom the old myths and titles still cling, bright gossamer threads woven into her mantle. Mother of God, Queen of Heaven, Star of the Sea. Virgin Mother, immaculately conceived, exempt from death, ascending bodily into heaven, with the power to appear on earth throughout the centuries to the simple and faithful.

"Ma!" called my guide. "She's here."

The woman disappeared into the house, leaving me to absorb the knowledge that she was his sister, his flesh and blood sister. Suddenly it was all too much. What was I doing here, vainly seeking him in a place and a past that excluded me? How could I sustain my faith—or illusion—that I was sister to his soul, lover to him from the womb? Who was I kidding? There was his sister, a woman with a pinched, bitter face, who had lived her whole life in this little village, who fetched and carried water from the well and shouted impatiently for their mother. Maybe I should just go, not even stay the night in Nazareth.

Then I heard a rustling sound and in the waning light turned and saw some flowering vines growing on a steep incline move as if of their own accord. A door in the hillside creaked open, and a woman emerged from what must be a root cellar, her arms full of onions. (Root cellar or grotto, woman or goddess: take your pick. If you go to Nazareth today to visit her church, mass is said at the subterranean level right next to the cave where I first saw her.)

Short and a little stout, she wore widow's weeds, her head was bent, her face in shadow under her mantle. She looked like any old peasant woman from any time. Part of me wanted to turn and run before she spoke, before I had to know that she was missing teeth and her breath reeked of garlic. Then she lifted her head and looked at me, and a fragrant breeze sprang from nowhere, and the last of the sun's light sought her.

Have you ever seen a lone tree in a field hollowed out and half-destroyed by lightning? That is the nearest I can come to describing her face. She looked as if some force had torn through her. She was god blasted or blessed. I had a strong impression that she was partly here in her yard holding the onions and partly somewhere else altogether where eternity pulled at her like a strong river current.

And she was his mother. There could be no doubt of that. She had his night sky eyes, but they lacked his intensity and focus. Even as she looked at me, her gaze seemed to wander and dream. Wherever she had gone, whatever strange realms she had inhabited, she was not all the way back.

As I gazed at her I felt myself coming under her sway. I couldn't speak or move. So we just stood there until slowly the onions slipped through her fingers, drifting down the folds of her dress and arranging themselves around her feet. At last she reached out a hand towards me. I could see earth in the creases, as if she spent so much time in the garden she could never scrub it all out. Yet when I took her hand it felt smooth and cool as water. She led me to a low, wooden bench under one of the olive trees, and we sat side by side while the twilight deepened, her hand still resting in mine. After a time, I gave her hand a squeeze as if my grip could moor her, pull her back from drifting on some timeless sea.

Then all at once, she was there. She turned to me, and I was grateful now to find myself facing a plain middle-aged woman with grown children, accustomed, like any other, to work and worry.

"What did Anna say?" she asked abruptly. Her breath did smell of garlic, garlic and roses all at once.

I felt embarrassed now. It wasn't much of a message after all. Cryptic and possibly antagonistic, but I had no other to deliver.

"She said, Tell Miriam of Nazareth, 'I told you so.' I'm sorry," I added. "She didn't explain what she meant."

The Blessed Virgin Mary, or Ma, if you will, made a rude noise in her throat, the kind that camels make when they are about to spit.

"She means to have the last word, that's what she means," she muttered, more to herself than to me. "Did she say nothing of my son?"

The way she said 'my son' there could be no doubt which one she meant. She might have given birth to half a dozen sons, but for her there was still only one. It was easy to understand his brothers' resentment. It was a wonder they hadn't sold him into slavery in Egypt—or Rome, as it would be today.

"She said—" I paused straining to remember the windings of Anna's speech, "that he thought he was lost. And then she said, being lost is the way, how else can you be found?"

"She is always saying things like that." Miriam waved the words away as if they were a cloud of gnats. "It is much easier to be his prophetess than to be his mother. I don't really need Anna, you know. The angels talk to me," she confided, her voice both dreamy and matter-of-fact. "They told me about you."

My hands began to tremble. All at once I felt afraid of this fey woman's knowledge as I never had been of anyone else's.

"Not that they needed to. I saw you. I saw you in his eyes when he came back from the far, terrible places where gods lurk who ought not to be, who have been forbidden by the Most High. Why did Anna send him there? May the Eternal One forgive her, for I will not. He came back hollowed out and haunted. You took away his life."

I felt that I could not breathe; as if a huge weight crushed my heart and lungs. I felt that I could not live. Then a furious storm rose in me and gave me the strength to throw off the weight.

"If that is true, then by your god and by my goddess, Miriam of Nazareth, mother of Yeshua, I and no other will be the one to give him back his life!"

The gale force of my words seemed to extinguish the last of the fleeting twilight. When Miriam spoke again her voice was disembodied, floating and swirling around me in the dark on currents of cooling air.

"It may be so, Mary of Magdala. May it be so."

It took me a moment to register that she had called me by a name—and it wasn't mine! Sweet Isis, how many Marys were there littering his past? How many women had ruined his life? I thought that distinction was mine.

"My name is not Mary," I said through clenched teeth. "And I don't come from Magdala. I don't even know where Magdala is."

She didn't answer right away, but I swear I could hear her shrugging her shoulders.

"That's what the angels call you," she said at length.

A shiver went through me, hot and cold at once. The breeze stirred again; it smelled of fish and roses.

"Don't ask me why," she warned, a hint of sharpness in her voice. "The angels never tell why."

We continued to sit, darkness a mantle that both concealed and connected us. Questions formed—did you want him to marry Mary of Bethany? When did you last see him? Did he tell you where he was going?—and dispersed unasked. It would have been easier to get answers from a tree or a stone.

"Ma!" The woman called into the night. "Ma!" I could hear her exasperation. "James is back. It's time to eat."

Miriam rose, and I did, too. She faced me for a moment, but she did not speak. Then she turned and went to the door. I got a glimpse of a crowded, lamp-lit room before the door closed firmly, leaving me outside. I wasn't sure of the way back, but it was a small village, and the new moon was drifting down the west, the new moon, jewel of the night that had guided me over the billows. As my mothers had taught me, I bent my knee and bowed to the new moon, singing her a song as I walked back over the hill.

CHAPTER FORTY

MAGDALA

Reginus was not best pleased when I informed him I wanted to leave for Magdala at the crack of dawn the next morning.

"Is it on the way back to Jerusalem?" he asked warily, as we got ready to bed down for the night.

"Not exactly," I admitted. "But the tavern keeper told me we could get there in a day, if we keep up a steady pace. Once we're out of these hills, there's a Roman road through the Valley of the Doves." An auspicious name, I thought, given that I had once been a dove. "It leads straight to Magdala."

"Yeah, don't tell me. You can't miss it, right? And we're going there why?"

Because a crazy woman thinks I come from Magdala, I did not say to Reginus. She also thinks my name is Mary, which irritates the hell out of me.

"I have had a sign," I answered. I might as well have said: just because.

"You think our boy might be there?"

"I didn't say that."

"Then why are we going?"

"Humor me," I said.

"What else have I been doing for the last six months?" he grumbled.

But I knew he wasn't really mad at me, and I wasn't mad at him.

"Shut up, and go to sleep," I said.

He was such a comfortable friend, I thought, as we pressed our backs together as we so often did. And unlike some of the men in my life, he was there.

"I love you, Reginus," I added.

"Love you, too, toots," he mumbled half asleep.

On our way to Magdala, Reginus regaled me with gossip he'd picked up at the tavern.

"Your sweetie has a bad reputation, Red."

"Tell me something I don't know," I shrugged, as we picked our way down hills that were practically cliffs to get to the valley. "He told me that much himself. Got thrown out of shul after shul for always having a smart remark. He also used to play at striking people dead by casting them into a trance. Supposedly he turned some children into goats because they wouldn't play with him. He was a terror."

"Did you know about the drinking, gambling, and loose women in Sepphoris?"

"Joseph has spared me nothing," I said a trifle grimly.

"Did you know that there's a rumor that the carpenter wasn't his father?"

"Who do they say his father was?" I hadn't known, but after meeting Miriam I somehow wasn't surprised. And, come to think of it, Anna always called him Miriam's son, not Joseph's.

"No one knows for sure. But everyone says she was definitely knocked up before she married the carpenter. No one believes those two were sneaking off to the vineyards. Old Joe was a widower with too many children to keep track of. Her family flat out wanted to unload her. People say she was touched, always wandering off by herself."

Talking to angels, no doubt, I thought to myself.

"Some say she might have met a shepherd or someone from Sepphoris, ye gads, maybe even a gentile. But the nastiest version is that she did it with a Roman soldier who was out in the hills on maneuvers. The wonder is that the carpenter went through with the marriage at all."

"Esus never told me any of that!" I felt stricken, that he had kept such a secret, something that must have caused him pain. For surely he knew the rumors, had suffered other children's taunts. No wonder he had turned them into goats—or threatened to.

"That's why our friend Joseph had to go south to find him a bride. No family in Upper Galilee would take the risk. Strange mother, unknown paternity."

We walked on in silence for a while; the slope growing gentler, the vegetation more lush and green. Soon we came to pastures threaded through with a bright stream. Fat sheep grazed happily. Galilee was a beautiful country, much less stark and forbidding than Judea, and yet everywhere, it seemed, people could be harsh and full of judgment.

"Honey, I've been thinking about something," said Reginus. "I don't want to offend you, but I feel like I ought to, well, just warn you."

"What is it?" I sighed.

"Let's look at our boy's record."

"Could you please refer to him as Esus or Yeshua?"

"How 'bout we call him Jesus then; the name is easier to pronounce in Greek. Saying Yeshua makes me feel like I'm sneezing. Anyway, first Jesus leaves you—"

"He did not leave me," I objected. "I made him go. He was running for his life."

"All right, all right. And I know you two had a sweet time together—"

"Maybe you better stop now," I suggested.

"Then there are the loose women. But when he finally meets a nice girl—"

"I would not use the word nice to describe Mary of Bethany."

"—does he marry her? No, he cross dresses her and goes off to live with a bunch of supposedly celibate guys. I hate to say it, but I know the type. A youthful fling, then hanging out with prostitutes, but when it comes down to it, he just can't do it."

"What are you trying to say, Reginus?"

"The way I see it, your Jesus likes men, but he can't admit it. Jews are notoriously intolerant of Greek-style love. So no wonder he tried to hide it, even from himself. You can't blame him."

I didn't answer; I was trying to control my expression.

"Oh, honey, I'm sorry. I didn't mean to upset you."

I gave up. I couldn't help it. I burst out laughing.

"I don't see what's so funny." Reginus was huffy. "I would think you'd have a little compassion for the man. It can't be easy. It's probably why he left the country."

"You may be right," I said, and I took his hand and swung it as we walked.

But I knew he was wrong, and for some reason, being presented with a worry I didn't have to worry about made me cheerful. Nobody knows, I said to myself, walking in time to the words. Nobody knows where he is or who. Not Anna, not Mary, not his Ma, not me. And, for the first time, instead of feeling lost and bereft, I felt light and free.

For Reginus, Magdala was love at first sight. It wasn't as big a city as Jerusalem, but it was just as lively and infinitely more profane. In Jerusalem life revolved around the Temple; people lived and breathed by the sacred rhythms of its daily rites and yearly festivals. The heart of Magdala was the waterfront, the biggest port on the Sea of Galilee, with the largest fishing fleet. There were taverns on every corner, and people of all kinds coming and going—Syrians, Greeks, Jews, Samaritans, Romans, Phoenicians, Egyptians, Gerasenes. In the streets, we heard dozens of languages, and saw the gamut of complexions and styles of dress. One of the main south-north roads in the region went right through the center of the city, which meant that not just fishermen but merchants and traders of all kinds frequented the place.

Magdala was a beautiful city, too, it couldn't help but be, with the dramatic red cliffs of Mount Arbel behind it and the lake before it with all its varying moods and mists, its constantly changing light and color. Even the meanest building was bright with mosaics depicting not gods but the life of the place, the waves of the sea and fishing boats riding them, fish leaping from the water and swarming the nets. If Magdala had a god, it was life itself, its abundance, its goodness.

We found an inn easily enough, and though we were tired, we got a second wind and stayed up late, drinking and playing dice. I had to quit the game after awhile, because, as you may recall, I have an uncanny ability to roll exactly what I want, and people tend to get upset when a person—especially a woman—wins too much. I sat back for a while and watched Reginus flirting with a Greek, who was apparently also a Greek in the other sense. I took note of the whores, who appeared and disappeared into a back room that seemed to exist for their use.

Was that why Miriam's angels identified me as a Magdalene, I wondered, because Magdala was a city where whores had plenty of work? How touching—if odd—to think that they might have concerned themselves with my livelihood. But why had the angels found it necessary to locate me at all? It puzzled me greatly, but then I didn't know much about angels or what made them tick. I supposed them to be some kind of otherworldly beings. But a worldlier place than Magdala was hard to imagine.

Seeing where things were headed with Reginus and the Greek, I eventually went upstairs to sleep alone. I woke a few hours later, scratching bedbug bites that made me disinclined to try to go back to sleep in the infested bedroll. The bar was finally quiet, but when I looked out the open window of the upper room, I saw that on the docks and in the boats torches burned as the fishermen got ready to go out on the lake. I decided to go down to the shore and watch.

The pre-dawn was chilly; my wrap served almost as a cloak of invisibility as I walked by the docks and the warehouses where fish were dried and salted and packed for shipment to landlocked cities like Jerusalem. No one heckled or cat-called; it wasn't the time of day for that. The men were busy, intent on hoisting the sails and arranging the nets in their sturdy, wide-bottomed boats. There wasn't much wind in the sheltered port, so the crew— about eight to a boat—rowed out to the open water where the sails could catch the breeze. Lakes make for tricky sailing; there's no prevailing wind, and the conditions on the Sea of Galilee were notoriously fickle with squalls that seemed to come out of nowhere. All this lore I learned later. Then, I just enjoyed the sight of the torch-lit boats, moving out on the dark water. Darkness made all the sounds more keen, the rhythmic groan of the oars, men chanting rowing songs in Aramaic and Greek.

I walked along the shore as the fleet fanned out further and further on the lake; the stars outlined the Golan Heights on the other side of this inland sea. Venus was rising, holding her own in the sky that was beginning to brighten. As I left the docks and warehouses behind, I came to a marshy shoreline, thick with water reeds. Though the sky above was clear, the water's surface swirled with little mists. I began to sing a song to Isis, made up on the spot, which caught the rhythm of the oars. A breeze sprang up and the reeds sang with me. Then as the first rays of sun dimmed the stars, birds everywhere lifted their voices and rose in line after line into the sky.

On the outskirts of the city, I came to what looked like it might have been an abandoned villa or farmstead. I decided to sit down and watch the lake changing colors with the light. That's when I heard it, not the soft lapping of the water against the shore but the sound of flowing water. I looked and in the growing light, I saw a small stream, really just a trickle, washing down a pebbly incline towards the lake. Something prompted me to follow the stream inland. I made my way through brambly thickets of wild roses. The way seemed to open for me, the thorns all but retracting so as not to catch my cloak or scratch my arms and legs. At the source, I knelt down and parted the thicket, and there it was, the spring at the base of a hill so steep it was almost a cliff. The water bubbled up from the darkness of earth, giving back the brightness of sky, like all springs, a way between worlds.

I was no stranger to sacred springs and magic wells; I was raised to revere them. I had first glimpsed my beloved in the well of wisdom on Tir na mBan. But this spring… I closed my eyes to listen to its sound, and I knew I had heard it before. The wind picked up, washing over me, scented with fish and roses. When it quieted again, I opened my eyes and gazed at the clear surface of the pool and for an instant I saw the tower and the dawn sky and the two people standing there. Then the image vanished, but I had seen all I needed to see.

"All right," I said aloud, to myself, my goddess, to Miriam's know-it-all angels. "Magdala it is. And by the way," I added. "My name is Maeve."

CHAPTER FORTY-ONE

HOME

Being born in a place is only one way to belong. Nor do you have to die there. I did neither in Magdala, and yet I came to be so closely associated with that place that it became one of my names. Mary Magdalen, people still call me. Or just the Magdalen, as if it were a title, as if Magdala was not just a place but an identity, as if it were a religion and I its priestess—which is not so far from what came to be the truth.

I knew at once that Magdala was home, because I felt sighted there again, second-sighted. It was not only the spring: in time everything spoke. When birds rose into the air, I could read the pattern of their wings, and the paths the wind made on the water carried messages. The very ground said: make a path here; plant herbs there. These vines are not dead, tend them, and they'll bear fruit again. Ancient trees offered shelter and wisdom as well as olives. And there were certain rocks that could absorb fatigue or agitation, leaving me refreshed and calm.

It did not escape my notice that my second home was the inverse of my first. I had grown up on an island surrounded by sea. Here the water was the island surrounded by land. The Jordan River flowed silently through the lake, connecting the snow-peaked mountains of the north with the deserts of the south. The whole of this inland sea, with its waves of surrounding hills, was a magical, between-the-worlds place. Surely Nile-borne Isis would be happy here. So we set about making a home for her and ourselves around the spring. The Temple of Isis at Magdala was its formal name. We called it Temple Magdalen for short.

Yes, time is passing, and so much is happening that if I described everything in detail, you might despair of his ever making his entrance. And yet I must give you some sense of how a pile of rubble at the outskirts of town became a notorious holy whorehouse. Although most of our story—his and mine—takes place on the road and in Jerusalem, the spirit of Temple Magdalen traveled with us. So you need to know something of how it came into being— miraculous in itself. And how we lived—outcasts and exiles, whores and sinners—in paradise.

The first miracle greeted Reginus and me as soon as we got back to Jerusalem. When Isis wants a temple built, she does not fool around.

"*Liebling*!" Berta welcomed us breathlessly. "You will not believe what has been happening here."

Only Dido and Berta were at home in our rented rooms; the spacious apartment seemed strangely silent and empty in contrast to the riotous celebration of Sukkoth in the streets below. Following Joseph's advice, we had made the return trip with a large pilgrim band. It took us more than an hour to make our way through the holiday throngs to the Upper City. Every possible cranny in Jerusalem was crammed with the colorful makeshift tabernacles, bedecked with autumn flowers and fruit. Wine flowed so freely it practically ran in the gutters and singing never ceased day or night.

"Where's Paulina?" I asked. "Who's with her? Isn't she a little too pregnant to be out carousing in these crowds?"

"Don't worry," said Dido. "She's with her boyfriend. He's built like a bodyguard."

"Her boyfriend?" Reginus and I said at once.

"No, her betrothed," corrected Berta.

"She hasn't said yes yet," Dido cautioned.

"Who?" we both demanded.

"*Kinder*, that is what I am trying to tell you. Our little Roman princess is being courted by the sewer king of Judea."

"Caesar Cloacus, if we want to be more Latin about it," suggested Dido. "He is a Roman, after all."

"Yes." Berta dropped her voice to a whisper. "But he is a, what do you call them when they are not rich?"

"He *is* rich; he's made a fortune," corrected Dido.

"Do you mean he's a plebeian?" asked Reginus.

"Yes, that's it. No lineage."

"But why do you call him the sewer king?"

"Red, you know how these Romans are about their plumbing," said Dido. "Well, he's the one who harnessed the tides to clean the sewers in

Caesaria. That's where the Roman procurator has his chief palace. Well, now he thinks Paulina's beau is a god. And maybe he is. He started out as a ditch digger, and now he's going to be the head engineer for the new spa city being built in Galilee."

"Galilee? Where in Galilee?"

"Some big lake. Tiberias, I think the city's called. Such an original name," Dido rolled her eyes. "So, of course, the emperor is funding it. A vacation hot spot for the legions."

"Reginus," I turned to him, "isn't Tiberias just a few miles from Magdala?"

He nodded, and we exchanged a long look.

"I think we're missing something here," said Dido. "Is there something you two haven't told us?"

"Well, in point of fact, we haven't told you anything yet."

"Oh, *liebling*." Berta was stricken. "Here you are just back from your journey, and we don't even ask how you are or give you anything to eat or drink. Let me get food and wine, and you will tell us everything."

And we began to tell them the whole story of our journey. Joseph came in just as I was getting to the part about Miriam and the angels.

"Joseph, sit," said Berta not wanting the narrative flow interrupted.

"So that's why we went to Magdala," I explained, "because the angels seem to think I come from there."

"Angels," muttered Joseph. "What are angels? Are they thought forms? Are they ideas? Do they serve a purpose? Maeve, I told you no good would come of visiting Nazareth. Can't you see? The poor woman has gone mad. Not that I blame her—"

"Ssh!" hissed Berta fiercely. "Tell about Magdala."

And so I did, just as I have described it to you. Joseph fidgeted and even got up at one point and paced, but I could tell he softened when I talked about the spring. He had spent time among my people. He could be open-minded about *foreign* customs and beliefs. The Greeks were the best, of course, but he could tolerate the Celts. It was only the religious quirks of his own people that got up his nose.

"So that's where we're going to build it," I concluded.

"Build what?" said Joseph warily.

"The holy whorehouse. Remember, Joseph? We talked about it with Domitia and Aemiliana."

"Do you have to use that word holy?" Joseph almost whined. "It makes me nervous, and frankly I do not see the point."

"Well, it is going to be a temple to Isis," said Dido, gently for her.

"Must it?" Joseph tried to appeal to Reginus as a possible fellow rational being.

Reginus gestured toward us, the three whore-priestesses.

We just eyed him in a baleful, bovine manner.

"It couldn't just be a house full of learned women like the Greek *heterae*?"

"To serve the goddess and to be educated aren't mutually exclusive," argued Dido. "Unless I'm very much mistaken, your friend Nicodemus is both a scholar and a man of god, and you yourself—"

Here she was interrupted by a loud groan from Joseph.

"It is true!" Berta took up the theme. "Look at our Red. It was you who taught her to read, Joseph. If you like, you can teach all our whores to read Greek—except for me. I am too much barbarian. Forget about it."

"This is my destiny? My fate?" Joseph appeared to be addressing the ceiling. "Teaching Greek to whores who worship a holy cow?"

"She has other forms beside the cow, Joseph," Dido pointed out. "Sometimes she has wings, but most statues depict her simply as a woman holding an ankh."

"Graven images," Joseph covered his eyes. "Idols."

"Well, it's not like Greeks don't have graven images," I said. "You told me yourself all Roman art is just a cheap imitation of the Greek. So who started with all the statuary?"

"And these angels, Joseph," Berta jumped back in. "The ones who have picked Magdala, well, they are Jewish, yes? So we should listen to them. This is their country. And now they have found this husband for Paulina—"

"She hasn't married him yet," Dido interjected.

"Ah, but she will. The angels and Isis have arranged it all. Why else would this new city her betrothed is building be so nearby to our temple?"

"Well, then they can't be Jewish angels!" Joseph threw up his hands. "Or they'd know that Tiberias is an abomination. Decadent Roman pleasure palaces built on an ancient Jewish gravesite. The Pharisees are in an uproar about it. Typical Roman arrogance. Not that I myself believe the dead would care. According to Plato, the soul—"

We were saved from a philosophical treatise by the entrance—and it was quite an entrance—of Paulina. At seven months, Paulina's pregnancy preceded her, a rounding moon, almost full, an entity in itself. Her face was rosier than usual, and her hair would not stay put and had half come undone. She looked the way anything living does, whether tree or animal, when it has come to fruition, to perfection, when it is exactly what it is meant to be. In short, she looked like a goddess. I'm afraid I gaped a bit, all the more so, because in her wake followed her suitor. As Dido had said, he *was* built like a bodyguard or like the ditch digger he had once been. His face was homely, lumpy as clay someone hasn't finished working. Yet there was something precise and delicate about him. Large as he was, he seemed to skim the air around Paulina like a hummingbird waiting to drink.

When she saw me, she shrieked and hurled herself into my arms. I just managed to keep my balance—and hers, as she wasn't capable of keeping it herself. I could smell the wine on her breath. (If you're worried about fetal alcohol syndrome, you should be, but Isis be praised, the baby was fine.)

"Red, darling, thank the goddess you're back. Now you can help me make up my mind. This is Lucius. He builds sewers, and he wants to marry me. In his favor, he does everything I tell him to do, and he is most attentive. Oh, he also says he'll adopt the baby. On the other hand, he is ugly and a little bit old, and he wants to take me to some city that isn't all built yet. Shall I marry him or shall I be a whore like you?"

Still holding Paulina, I looked over her shoulder at Lucius. He was either sunburned or deeply embarrassed, but he managed to meet my eyes. His gaze was steady, slightly apologetic—as if he was already assuming responsibility for Paulina's bad behavior—and utterly determined. For all his success with the bigwigs, the man had not a shred of self-importance. Comes of working with shit, perhaps. I liked him at once.

"Paulina," I said, still looking at Lucius, "I don't know if he should marry you, but you should marry Lucius. Immediately."

And so it came to pass that we did not lose a benefactress, but we gained a celebrity engineer, a sewer king, as Berta had called him. As soon as we could make ready, we all moved north to the shores of Lake Gennesaret, the newlyweds taking up residence in Tiberias and the rest of us renting temporary quarters in Magdala. Joseph, ever honorable if also cranky, kept his agreement to be our financial backer and sought out the landholder, which took some doing. For the man was an absentee owner who made his living foreclosing on people who couldn't pay their taxes. It troubled me to think that some peasant family had been driven off the land, but Joseph said it couldn't be helped, and he reminded me, rather sarcastically, about Miriam's busybody angels. Joseph's land purchase included a small olive orchard, complete with an ancient oil press, and the neglected vineyard that we later restored.

"Every whore needs to plan for retirement," Joseph explained, "and have a respectable source of income."

Paulina was Joseph's co-investor, and I was surprised and pleased to see how well they got on as business partners.

"She's got a good head for figures," remarked Joseph the night before he left Magdala for his postponed trip to Alexandria. "And I've never met her equal at haggling. She'll set up accounts for the temple and work out a payment plan, if you insist on it."

"I do, Joseph. Your money is an investment, not a gift. I want Temple Magdalen to belong to itself."

Paulina's financial investment was the construction of the Temple complex, materials and labor. She also volunteered her new husband as an architect. For Lucius, chief engineer at Tiberius by order of the Roman procurator, Temple Magdalen was moonlighting, sometimes literally, but he was the sort of man for whom leisure and work are meaningless distinctions. After the exacting work of building sewers, baths, and drains for a Roman resort city, designing a small temple was child's play to him, like making mud pies or sandcastles—or, as it turned out, caverns and tunnels. It was Lucius who discovered the honeycomb of passages and chambers in the hill behind the spring.

"*Dominae!*" he called us from our inspection of the vineyard. "I've found your temple! It is already here!"

And so all of us, including the now enormous Paulina, went spelunking, and Lucius's genius became immediately evident. Just as he had worked with the sea in Caesaria, he now proposed to work with the earth, not disturbing or moving it, but understanding its design and will. He found natural chimneys and skylights, hot springs and thermal stones. We followed in his wake, pointing out to each other niches for altars and chambers for couches.

"And, of course," said Paulina, "we will import marble to smooth out these rough walls, and—"

"Oh no, my love!" Lucius opposed her, perhaps for the first time in their marriage. "We don't want to lose the contour of the rock. Mosaic or painting right on the rock's surface; that's what's wanted here."

And he touched the walls of the passage so tenderly and knowingly that my own body responded. He must be an amazing lover. I hoped Paulina appreciated her luck.

"Hey, caves are all very well for exotic, erotic rites and whatnot," Reginus spoke up, "but we can't live in here. Or at least I can't. I can feel the fungus starting to grow under my fingernails already."

"Actually these caves are quite well-drained," said Lucius. "It's my belief they've been used before as storehouses. But my idea is to use the hill as one wall and to build three more walls to make a courtyard around the spring. That's where the kitchens and sleeping rooms would be—in the other three walls."

"And can there be a tower?" I asked. "In the corner nearest the lake. Not a big one, just tall enough for a view, with room for two people to stand together or sleep out under the stars."

Dido, Berta, and Reginus all gave me keen looks. Though I had told no one of my vision of the two people on the tower, they could hear the sound of dreaming in my voice. It was Lucius who answered me.

"*Domina*, a tower you shall have."

Galilean winters are mild, so work on the temple complex began right away. Most days Dido, Berta, Reginus and I were on the site, and all of us learned something of the building trade. Over everyone's objections, the due-any-day Paulina continued to visit us whenever she was bored. (She had elected herself city planner and eventually succeeded in turning Tiberias into a first-century super mall, but in the early days her scope was limited.) So, of course, Paulina went into labor at the temple site. Not only that, but just as her water broke, one of the lake's famous storms blew up out of nowhere and began to pelt us with cold, slashing rain. Reginus was dispatched to fetch a midwife from town and then to run on to Tiberias for Lucius. Meanwhile, the three whore-priestesses hauled the bellowing Paulina into the temple caves.

"I am not going to give birth in a hole," howled Paulina, "like some animal. I don't like it. Make it stop. I am not going to do it. Damn Decius to Hades. I hate him."

Those of you who have given birth will probably know at once that Paulina's labor was progressing very fast. She was already in transition.

"Do any of us here know anything about delivering babies?" Dido asked in a loud whisper that Paulina could have heard if she wasn't making so much noise.

"My *oma* was a midwife," said Berta, "and I saw my mother give birth."

"So what do we do?"

"We need water?" said Berta uncertainly.

"The hot spring," I said. "All the water here has healing properties. I know it. There's a pitcher down there at the outdoor spring. I'll go and get it."

"Red, stay!" screamed Paulina.

"I'll go," said Dido. "You know more than the rest of us, Red. You had a baby."

Yes, I had, inside a cavern of earth, while a storm raged outside, just as it did now. I closed my eyes and remembered. I could feel the priestesses holding me, supporting me while I squatted. Berta was big and strong, so I asked her to get behind Paulina, and Dido joined her when she came back. Someone had massaged my vulva, I remembered, to help me stretch and ease the baby's passage. So I knelt before Paulina, and as I worked, I sang to her and to the baby, whatever words came into my head. I heard the lapping of the dark sea waves, and then I felt the head crowning, a dark sun rimmed with fire. In another moment I caught Paulina's baby in my hands.

The tiny girl had a pair of lungs to rival her mother's as she indignantly but competently took her first breaths of this strange new element, air.

Dido stripped off her tunic and washed the baby with the hot spring water. I took off my own tunic, swaddled her, placed her in Paulina's arms, and helped the baby find her mother's breast. Then I delivered the afterbirth, the blood soaking into the earthen floor of the cave. Paulina was quiet now, still resting against Berta as she gazed at the tiny dark head of her suckling child.

"She will have two names," said Paulina. "One for you, Red, one for Lucius. Maria Lucia." She said the name like a caress. "Maria Lucia."

"Paulina," I said lightly, pushing away the potent mix of grief and joy that threatened to overwhelm me, "my name is Maeve."

"*Cara stulta*," she said. "Listen to the angels."

And Paulina drifted off to sleep holding her baby, just as I had after I had given birth. But Paulina and her baby were safe and beloved. No one would come while she slept and take her baby away.

"Red." Dido reached for me. She knew. And she drew my head down into the soft, warm night of her breast.

By late spring, we were ready to move to Temple Magdalen. If Paulina had had her way, Temple Magdalen might have taken centuries to construct, like a cathedral. But our needs were simple, and Lucius quietly ignored the wife to whom he absolutely deferred in all matters outside his expertise. Paulina had to be content with hiring artists for the ongoing mosaic work inside the caves. In time Temple Magdalen housed as many as twenty or thirty people. But we began with five. Dido, Berta, and I wanted to find out what we meant by being whore-priestesses before we trained others. So there were the three of us. The other two were Reginus and his lover, Timothy, whom he'd met the first time we came to Magdala.

Yes, I am introducing you to a lot of people you may not see much. Think of it as being at a large, chaotic party. Have fun and don't worry if you don't remember everyone's name. Timothy, born to a local fishing family, had grown up in Magdala and had worked and failed in every aspect of the fishing industry. He was tall and gangly and had a tendency to fall out of boats. When he worked at gutting, he narrowly missed severing limbs and fingers. Because people had known him since he was a tot, his clumsiness and sexual preference were simply accepted. No one wanted him as a son-in-law. But he was so good-natured, everyone liked him, and so inept, no one was threatened by him, and many felt a protective fondness for him. An insider and an outsider at once, Timothy was instrumental in helping us win over people who might have been hostile to a holy whorehouse dedicated to an Egyptian goddess. He also finally found his calling tending the temple's orchards and vineyards. The main thing you need to know about Timothy is that our suave, sophisticated, cynical Reginus was smitten with him. And all those who said it couldn't last were proved wrong.

So here we are, just before sundown on our first night at Temple Magdalen. We're having a fish fry to celebrate, and we have invited the whole town. The wine is flowing; the music is jumping. I can't hear the sound of the spring, but I know it's there. At dusk I slip away and climb the tower by myself. The first stars are sneaking out while the wisps of cloud still hold the fleeting afterglow. The wind picks up and washes over me, carrying the sound of the fisherman's songs as they make for port, the lanterns in their prow waterborne stars. The wind smells of fish and roses.

In the vision that brought me to this place, it was dawn, and two people stood in the tower. Now I am alone as night falls. For how long? How long?

I turn back to the courtyard. I hear Berta's raucous laughter and Joseph, who's back for the party, holding forth. And it comes to me: I have made a home here. I have stopped searching the earth for my beloved. Isis kept on till she found the coffin. Well, I don't want to find a coffin. I am changing the story. I have become someone else. I am Maeve of Magdala.

Now *he* has to find *me*.

CHAPTER FORTY-TWO

HOLY WHORES, HOLY LAND

When I think of those early days at Temple Magdalen, I see images of feet. Our feet, painted with henna, anklets jingling rhythmically as we dance ourselves into ecstatic trance. Our feet planted in the soft, new-turned earth of the gardens we made or cooling in the spring after a long day. Our feet climbing trees when we pruned the upper branches and our feet purple with crushing the grapes of our first harvest for wine.

I see the feet of the men, too, the suppliants who began to come, only a few at first, but as word spread more and more each evening. The pampered feet of Roman magistrates, the callused feet of soldiers and rebel hill fighters, the feet of peasants, the soil worked so deeply into their soles that the distinction between earth and feet is almost lost. And of course the feet of fishermen who stood among the fish guts and never seemed to be quite free of scales.

Picture all of these feet finding their way to our temple gate. No one is refused. Gold coins, a basket of fish, a loaf of bread, a morning's labor in the vineyard, all offerings are acceptable. Maybe it is because we are veiled, as we guide men through the honeycomb of passages in the temple, that I am so aware of the suppliant's feet. I hold the lantern low, so he can only see enough to take one step and the next. At every turning we pause, and he must shed something, his cloak, his insignias of rank, tokens of piety, or good luck talisman, and finally, his tunic, his undergarments, and sandals.

Some rich and powerful men turn back. This is not their idea of a whorehouse where they are accustomed to paying for (the illusion of) control. To become the god-bearing stranger, the suppliant must surrender, forget who he is in the world, be naked as he was at birth. When he leaves everything behind but himself, the whore-priestess leads him to a hot spring. She bathes him from head to toe. She anoints him with warm, fragrant oils. And here is our mystery, our surrender: to know that each stranger is the beloved of Isis. Through us she will know him, love him, heal him. Always it is when I touch the stranger's feet that she becomes fully present in me; there is no more distinction between goddess and priestess.

And I know something more. For it is my own beloved's feet that I picture most clearly when I think of him. It is his feet that walk beside me in my dreams, his feet, brown as earth, beautiful as the flight of birds. In the feet of every god-bearing stranger I remember him whom my soul loves. When I open myself to the goddess, he is restored to me again in the stranger's embrace.

That is all I am going to tell you about the mysteries of sacred prostitution. Because in some deep part of yourself, whether from this life or another, I know you remember. The light flickering on the curved, mosaic walls, the sound of water, the scent of spices, oil and honey. The way age and beauty and rank are consumed like so much candle wax by living flame. If you don't remember yet, someday you will.

In the ancient times when whores ruled, as Dido always put it, the sacred marriage of the god and goddess insured the fertility of the land. You can imagine that with all the holy goings-on in the temple, the adjacent lands were prospering wildly; in fact, the vineyards and orchards looked more like a jungle that first summer, and our small band could hardly keep up with the work. At the time none of us, including fresh-from-the-waterfront Timothy, had any agricultural experience. Moreover, we were in a standoff with our benefactress. She wanted to supply Temple Magdalen with slaves, and we, being former slaves, absolutely refused. Though she had freed Reginus and me as a personal favor, Paulina did not believe in paying wages to free laborers. She considered it a bad investment, like renting instead of buying a house. She refused to lend us the money she would have spent on slaves. Everyone was being extremely stubborn, and harvest time was fast approaching.

The way I see it, Isis intervened.

We were lying around in the shade of the trees one hot day—(the heat of Galilean summer is like a fifth element, made up of the other four intensified)—watching the olives ripen, when Paulina descended upon us, dragging a bedraggled and sullen woman by the wrist. Three equally ragged children followed her, crying and pelting Paulina with clumps of dirt and grass. At a safer distance, the baby nurse followed with Maria Lucia.

"I found this woman in the Temple courtyard stealing figs. This is the third time I've arrived to find the temple unguarded with the gate open. I swear Maria Lucia has more sense. I've left my driver there for the moment. Good goddess, you might as well send out an invitation to all the thieves in Galilee. Stop that!" She turned on the children. "Don't you know you can be flayed alive for attacking a Roman citizen?"

The mother spat at Paulina and would have scratched her face, if Reginus hadn't caught her other wrist.

"Paulina, Reginus," I said in Greek, figuring everyone would understand that language. "Let her go."

The woman looked at me, fierce, mistrusting. But she did not try to attack Paulina again. Her children flung themselves at her, and she held onto them tightly.

"You and your children are welcome to the figs and more," I said to her in Aramaic. "Stay and eat with us."

"I'll get some wine and bread," announced Dido. "Berta, come with me."

"Red, are you crazy!" demanded Paulina. "This woman snuck into the temple courtyard. She was stealing. Aren't you going to do something about it?"

"Yes," I said in Latin, hoping the woman would not understand. "I'm going to feed her and her children. Can't you see they're hungry?"

"You mustn't encourage indigence," began Paulina.

"I am not a thief." The woman spoke for the first time in Greek, though I could hear her Aramaic accent. "How can I steal what is mine? This fruit, these trees, this ground."

Timothy's mouth fell open; I guessed he knew the woman, but hadn't recognized her before.

"Please, sit down," I invited the woman. "Tell me who you are."

"Why should I tell you anything!" She remained standing, defiant, but her legs were shaking. "Thief! Foreigner! Whore!"

"Red, are you going to let her talk to you that way?"

"Paulina, if you're going to stay here, shut up! I *am* a foreigner and a whore. It's the thief part I want to understand."

"I think I can explain," said Timothy in a low voice.

But just then, the woman's legs gave out under her. Timothy and I caught her before she fainted. Her children all began to wail.

"Oh, my goddess, she's sick into the bargain!" shrieked Paulina, and she snatched Maria Lucia from the nurse and promptly carried her away from possible contagion.

Dido and Berta arrived shortly with wine, cheese, and bread as well as a jug of spring water and clean clothes. Berta dipped the bread in wine to soften it for the children. They were soon quiet as we examined the mother, who appeared to be suffering from malnutrition more than anything else. We bathed her face with the spring water and put a cloth soaked with wine to her lips. In a little while, she revived and sat up, her eyes now dull rather than defiant.

"You once lived here, didn't you?" I said.

"Yes," was all she said.

"I went to your wedding," Timothy ventured. "You might not remember me. I was just a kid."

She focused on him, and she almost smiled.

"You're the boy who fell into the wine vat and almost drowned."

Timothy nodded, blushing.

"Sweetie," said Reginus. "You never told me that one."

"Honey, if I recounted every near death experience I've had, it would take me the rest of our lives."

"I've got time," Reginus assured him.

"Will you tell me your name and what happened to you?" I asked, focusing our attention again on the newcomer.

"My name is Judith," she said after a time. "What is there to tell? The land belongs to my husband's family. We had some bad years, failed harvests, so we couldn't pay the tax. We were driven off the land. My husband's parents died the first winter."

"And your husband?" I dreaded her answer, but I had to know.

"As good as dead." Her tone was flat; I knew about that flatness. It was a lid on everything too painful to feel, everything you were powerless to change. "He sold himself when we were in Judea—we'd gone there to find work—and he gave me the money. Told me to come back here and wait, find a place for myself and the children. Sew, do laundry. Live." She paused for a moment. "I was robbed, of course. And…"

She stopped herself and looked at her children, still sucking on their bread. She didn't need to say it. I knew the rest of the story. Unthinking, I reached out and touched her hand. She snatched it away from me.

"You are a gentile, a gentile and a whore. Unclean."

"I wash myself everyday," I said lightly. "I'm not as unclean as all that."

She stared at me, as if I were not speaking Aramaic, and with a Galilean accent almost as thick as hers.

"But you are a foreigner," she said again. "And a thief."

"I come from a place where people do not believe land can be owned. But it is true that my friend Joseph bought this land from the man who stole it from you."

"And that Roman whore who acts like she owns everything?"

"She's not actually one of the whores here." Thank Isis, I added to myself. "She's only visiting. She built the temple."

"You are leasing the land?"

"We are paying my friends back, but the land belongs to Isis."

"Isis?" the woman looked confused. "Who's Isis? The fat blonde?"

Yes, I could have answered. She is the fat blonde and the tall black woman. She is me. She is you. Not to mention queen of the stars, ruler of the wind and water, mother of grain. I could have gone on and on. But the woman, whose teeth were so loose that she took care to soften her bread, didn't need theology.

"The blonde is called Berta," I clarified. "Isis is a great goddess known by many names in many places. The Egyptians call her Isis."

"An Egyptian goddess?" The woman made the sign for warding against evil. "How can an Egyptian goddess hold land in Galilee? Moses led our people out of bondage in Egypt and away from those wicked idol-worshippers. There is only one god, the god of Abraham, Isaac, and Jacob."

"I have heard of him." I tried to be respectful.

"Well, this is *his* land." The woman was belligerent. "All of us are his tenants. Everything belongs to God!"

"Exactly," I agreed.

"But you just said it belonged to Isis!"

"The Most High and Our Lady no doubt have an understanding."

She looked at me as if I were not only unclean but also insane. (The two states are related. For demons are after all unclean spirits that cause people to go stark raving mad.)

"The point is, the land the tax collector stole, that your family tended for your god, well, it belongs again to the divine. It is sacred ground, holy land. Dido, Berta, and I are here, but—"

"Whores!?" It was both a declaration and a question.

"Yes." I looked at her and held her eyes. "But what I am saying is that you are welcome. You and your children."

"I am no whore!"

Many are called, I might have said, but few are chosen.

"Some of us here are whores. Some are healers, too. There is also an orchard and a vineyard that need to be tended."

"The vines need pruning badly. And my herb gardens have been overrun."

"Do you know the plants around here? The healing plants?"

She nodded, wary.

"You could live here again," I stated.

She stared at me, her eyes full of anger and longing.

"I will not be a slave and a whore where I was once a wife, the one who made the challah bread, who said the Sabbath prayers over it. This was our place, my husband's and mine. We brought the best we had to the Temple, the finest oil and wine, the unblemished kid—"

"Goats? You kept goats? You know how to make cheese?"

She sat quietly for a moment before she answered. "How can I live here with you?" she wondered. "I don't understand."

I waited, too, before I spoke, waited for the words to be given to me. The warm afternoon air was still. I could hear bees buzzing, and even at this distance I could hear the sound of the spring water finding its way to the lake. Dido and Berta, Timothy and Reginus were quiet, too. Even Paulina, who had come back, too curious to stay away, miraculously kept her mouth shut as she suckled Maria Lucia. I put it down to the tranquilizing effect of nursing. Judith's three children leaned against her and drowsed.

"I don't understand either," I finally spoke, and I felt Judith's listening deepen. "Where I come from, the islands to the north of Gaul, where the Romans reach but have not yet grasped, we call ourselves the *combrogos*, the companions. We live in tribes, some bigger and stronger than others, some warring with others. Still, we are the companions. The children of Israel are all related, too, though you may disagree among yourselves. It's the same with Berta and Dido's peoples, I'm sure. What else do any of us have in common except that the Romans want us all to be their slaves and make their bread for them?

"Here at Temple Magdalen we are all exiles. I was exiled by my own people; Berta and Dido were captured and taken far from their homes. Even Paulina, a Roman, well, let's just say she had to leave town in a hurry. You were driven off your land. Our Isis was a wanderer, too, for a long time, looking for the body of her murdered lover."

Judith's eyes never left my face; they were huge, dark, and hungry.

"We don't come from the same places; we don't have husbands or families, just each other and this place to be for now. I want the people who come here to be able to eat if they're hungry, heal if they're sick, rest if they're tired. I want us to be able to dance together and sing. Can that be? I don't know. I only know you are welcome here—not as a slave but as a companion. Rest for now, stay the night and decide in the morning."

I began to pick up the wine flask and the cheese that remained, thinking to give Judith some time alone in what had been her family's olive grove.

"What is your name?" the woman said, as if it were an urgent matter for her to know, as if she knew what a difficult question it was for me.

"Mary?" I tried the name for the first time. "Mary of Magdala. At least that's what your god's angels call me." It still didn't sound right. "But you can call me Maeve."

CHAPTER FORTY-THREE

THE ROCK

But Judith never did call me Maeve. On the side of the angels, she always referred to me as Mary when she spoke to me or of me. She is greatly to blame for why I am remembered as Mary in the Gospels. Except that I can't really blame her for anything, for I don't know how Temple Magdalen would have managed without her. How she reconciled herself to living with a bunch of idol-worshipping whores remains a mystery to me, but once she made up her mind, she never second-guessed herself.

Judith's arrival marked the beginning of what I like to call our unintentional community. Isis knows we did not set out to found a prototype kibbutz (though there is a kibbutz on the site of Temple Magdalen today). We did not have strict rules or exacting requirements for membership. We were whores; we took all comers, whether they were suppliants seeking the embrace of the goddess or homeless laborers seeking work and shelter or sick people seeking healing. People came and went. There were seldom more than we could handle; for there was a built-in self-selection process: the censorious, the self-important and the humorless tended to leave in a hurry.

Our rules were simple if eccentric. "Worship whomever the hell you please" was one. Some of us sang hymns to Isis morning and evening, vesting and garlanding her graven image. All of us shared in a Shabbat feast with Judith presiding and reciting prayers in Hebrew. "Don't say it: Sing it" was another Temple Magdalen tradition. When conflicts arose, as they must when two or three are gathered together, they were aired in song. Try singing the next time you have a beef with someone. (Recitative: I'm sick of washing the dishes you leave in the si-ink!) You and your adversary will probably end up laughing till you cry and fall into each other's arms to keep from falling down. That's what happened at Temple Magdalen more often than not.

And of course we discovered the magic of the axiom "from each according to his ability, to each according to his need" millennia before Marx. Somehow there was always enough—enough help with the harvest, enough food to go around, enough people to mind the children or tend the sick. Maybe it was all the dancing we did on Friday nights after the Shabbat meal. Those who couldn't dance clapped and drummed and sang wild, wailing Middle Eastern melodies. We were all in the rhythm, trusting to the ebb and flow, the waxing and waning of moon, sun, and seasons.

Over the years, Temple Magdalen's reputation spread. We were known for many things besides holy whoredom: our rich red wine and aromatic oil, our healing springs and our healing skills. Among the many who sought us were wives who had not been able to conceive—a terrible plight, as a barren woman could be divorced and left destitute. If a husband was kind enough to keep her, she was still pitied or despised by her neighbors and in-laws. We offered herbal remedies and advice on diet. If I sensed the problem was in the woman's womb, I let the fire flow through my hands to try to clear any infection or blockage. But if the woman was healthy and apparently fertile, we had another remedy for the daring—or the desperate. I think you can guess what it was.

With god—and goddess—all things are possible.

And that is how I came to meet Simon called Peter, the apostle, the saint, the rock, goddess help us, on which the church was built, a.k.a. Rocks-for-Brains.

He showed up one evening at the temple gates with a cart full of fish. I watched as Reginus greeted him. He was a burly man, a bit awkward and surly, but honest-looking. I took him for a suppliant and liked what I saw of him from my tower perch.

"I'm here to see the healer," the man said.

"Which one?" asked Reginus.

The man furrowed his brow and shifted his weight from one foot to the other, as if wanting to be sure to get it right.

"The one with red hair. The one they call Mary. The fish are for her."

"Well, I'm sure she'll be thrilled," said Reginus. "That's a whole lotta fish."

"She can salt the ones she doesn't eat fresh," said the man.

"Lovely!"

The man scowled at Reginus. It wasn't hard to read his mind: What kind of establishment is this, with a Roman queer for a gatekeeper? I'm sure he wanted to bolt, but he had his mission. Give the fish to Mary. I started down when I saw Judith coming to investigate. Nothing to do with food could happen at Temple Magdalen without her overseeing it. (In case you're wondering, yes, we did keep kosher.) She startled when she saw Peter, for apparently they knew each other. I wondered if she was embarrassed about her present address. The man also looked nonplussed. Judith told me later that the pious Jews of Capernaum had refused to help her when she returned to Galilee, because she had been raped. She covered the awkwardness of the moment by fussing over the fish and calling some of the children to help unload the cart.

"The healer, is she here?" the man repeated. "I am supposed to give *her* the fish."

He started to scuff the dirt again. It was time for me to put him out of his misery, so I hurried down to the gate.

"I am called Mary," I greeted the man. "You are welcome here. Come have something to eat and drink while Judith unloads the cart."

The man blushed, which took some doing. He was wonderfully swarthy, having spent so much time on the water getting his skin leathered, accumulating those little lines around the eyes from squinting that make sailors look wiser than they may be. For this visit, he had put on a clean tunic, but he still smelled of water and sun and fish. A healthy man smell that I always enjoyed. As for me I had just bathed and oiled myself before soaking in the late sun on the tower. My hair was loose and wild the way I liked it. I was in glowing health, not worn out by childbearing as some women were at my age. If I were a fruit, I would have been at the point of perfect ripeness, bursting with juice and sweetness. In short, I was hot.

"N-n-no." The poor man began to stutter. "That won't be n-n-necessary."

"I thought you wanted to see me."

"Just to say thank you."

"I can't imagine I would have forgotten a man like you." I looked him up and down—I admit it—suggestively. "If I did you a good turn, I'm glad, but refresh my memory. Please."

"Not me. My wife."

Ah, a married man. Not that we never saw them here, but he looked like the faithful type.

"Was she ill? Tell me her name."

"Priscilla. No, she wasn't ill. We…she…she's just given birth to our son."

At the word son, the sun burst through all the clouds of awkwardness in the form of a huge, irrepressible smile. His big body expanded but there still wasn't room enough to contain his pride. "Seven years she was barren, but we never lost faith, and now the Eternal One has answered our prayers."

"Oh, yes. Of course. Priscilla from Capernaum. I'm so glad!"

I remembered her, a tiny woman—this huge man could have easily lifted her in one hand—fierce in her determination to have a child. The goddess, in her mercy, had sent us a lithe, small-boned man from Damascus to tend to Priscilla.

"Did the birth go easily?" I asked. "Is she up from childbed?"

"She's a wonder." He was at ease now. "Up and about the very next day. Thriving, mother and babe both. We'll be going to the Temple soon for the purification and the thank offering."

"Fish?" I asked, feeling a slight competitive edge on behalf of my goddess.

"Of course not!" The man looked shocked. "We will offer snow white doves and a kid without blemish."

He obviously made no connection between Temple Magdalen and the Temple of Jerusalem, between the fish and the prescribed offerings to the Most High.

"I'd better be going," said the man. "My wife thanks you for the tonic. She believes it strengthened her for the birth."

The tonic. I bent my head to hide my smile. My feet were hennaed. I wore a toe ring. I looked like what I was. I appreciated Priscilla's gesture, but it hardly seemed wise. She clearly had great confidence in the thickness of her husband's skull to send him here.

"I thank you and Priscilla for the fish," I said, leaving Isis out of it, though I was tempted to receive the offering in her name. "We never know how many people we'll have to feed at Temple Magdalen." The word temple slipped out. "We are grateful."

Just then Dido and Berta and some of the others began to sing the evening hymn to Isis. They sang in Greek, which most fishermen understood at least a little. The man looked confused and uncertain.

"Please give my greetings to your wife," I encouraged him to leave.

He bowed his head uncertainly and began to turn away, and all might have been well if a group of three fishermen had not been passing by the gate on their way to town.

"Hey, is that Simple Simon?"

"Yeah, it's Pete." That was his nickname, which does indeed translate as something like "the Rock" or "Rocky."

"Pete! I thought I saw you dragging that load of fish here, but I couldn't believe it. What are you doing here, man?"

"What do you *think* he's doing here, Andy?"

There was guffawing and giving each other the first century equivalent of the high-five.

Poor Peter looked like a stalled ox. Full of power and fury with no idea where to go with it.

I stepped past him to confront the men crowding around the gate. Probably not the wisest move on my part. I have always been what they call too smart by half, which is as bad or worse than being plain stupid. Predictably the men whistled and cat-called.

"Is there a problem here, gentlemen?"

"Hey, no problem. Don't let us interrupt anything, Pete. We won't tell Priscilla. We all know how it is, brother. Nothing for thirty days. You're lucky it's not a girl, man, twice as long to wait. Hey, don't worry, Pete. We're just giving you a hard time."

That no doubt was true. Peter was the sort of man everyone likes but can't resist teasing. It was so easy to get a rise out of him. I could feel the heat and humiliation emanating from him. I didn't even have to turn around to know how red his face must be. I decided I had done enough damage and stepped aside intending to return to the courtyard. But Peter decided to compound his predicament.

"Shame on you!" He shook his finger at his buddies. "Treating this woman this way. Don't you know she's a healer?"

"Sure, Pete, right, a healer," said the one called Andy. A tall gawky fellow with an irresistible grin, he caught my eye and winked.

Then I did something that had repercussions I could not have foreseen; for this moment marks the beginning of my long difficult relationship with the Rock. Hey, it was a beautiful evening, a healthy child had been born; I was high on the proximity of the men, their good-natured banter.

So, I winked back.

Peter saw me, and his denial cracked. A little earthquake on his face. He turned and began to run towards the docks with a strange stiff-legged gait, his knees hardly bending, his arms held straight and rigid.

"You forgot your cart!" I called after him.

Peter did not turn or slow his pace.

"I'll take it for him," said Andrew, a little shame-faced for having pushed the fun so far. "I'm his kid brother."

CHAPTER FORTY-FOUR

A VOICE CRYING IN THE WILDERNESS

Yes, I've just met Peter and Andrew, two of those who became known as The Twelve. Actually I've met four. The other two clowns with Andrew were James and John the sons of Zebedee, whom my beloved nicknamed the Thunderers for obvious reasons. They were *loud*—at both ends. If I don't seem very reverent or respectful towards the disciples, well, I wasn't. And if you read the Gospels, you will find that I am not alone. People complained constantly about the company Jesus kept.

So, yes, I am setting the scene in Galilee. You can picture the docks, the fishing boats. You've heard of Capernaum, and I hope you feel welcome at Temple Magdalen. Various characters are making their entrances. You wise virgins can start getting excited and trimming your lamps. The bridegroom, as he often refers to himself, is getting closer. Though as a wise-ass whore, I had no premonition until Joseph told me about the Dipper.

"Mmm," murmured Joseph appreciatively. "This wine is wise beyond its years."

Joseph was making one of his semi-annual visits, and we were sitting on the tower roof, enjoying some time apart from Temple Magdalen hubbub below. It was autumn—Joseph had just come from the high holidays in Jerusalem—but the day was hot and still. I could almost smell the sweat of men in the boats as they rowed, sails limp. I whistled softly three times, and the wind answered. We watched it making a path across the water, filling the fishermen's sails on its way to touch our faces.

"Do you really think you ought to do that?" asked Joseph.

"Do what?"

"It seems a bit frivolous. Commanding the winds on a whim. I mean shouldn't you save your weather witching for dire circumstances only?"

"Practice makes perfect," I said, enjoying both the breeze and Joseph's discomfort.

"I don't recall your practicing weather magic when you were in Rome. You have reverted to your savage Celtic ways since coming to Magdala."

"Joseph dear, in Rome I was an exile and a slave, and there was always stone or tile between me and the dirt. Now I'm free, and Magdala is my home place, my sovereign place, as much as Tir na mBan was. I've told you about my mothers; the weather was their plaything. They set a very bad example for me, I'm afraid. But I'll send the breeze back where it came from if it would make you feel better."

"That's all right," he said hastily. "I think the fishermen appreciate it."

We sipped our wine in silence for a time, and let the soft wind wash over us as the cooling shadow of Mount Arbel lengthened. The air was now just about the perfect temperature.

"You've made a good life here, Maeve, I'll admit that," allowed Joseph, mellowing in direct proportion to the wine in his bloodstream. "Not what I'd envisioned or hoped, but a good thing."

"Thank you, Joseph." I was touched.

"But still," he had to go on and ruin his simple compliment. "I worry about you, Maeve, living here with no protection."

"What do you mean by protection, Joseph? More men?" I bristled a bit. "Weapons? What?"

"Well, you would be wise to have an armed guard. Who do you think is going to look out for you if there's trouble? All of you at the Temple are outsiders, foreigners, except for Timothy and Judith, who have ruined their reputations by associating with you. You're not Roman citizens or Jews. You have no ties with any of the local gentiles. Yet you behave as if you had the freedom of that island—what's it called—where you were born. But you're not living on some misty, mythic island. You're in the midst of a cantankerous, divided country."

"This is not exactly news, Joseph," I yawned and stretched; I often had a nap in the late afternoon before the suppliants began to arrive. "Besides, that's probably our best protection, that we don't belong to any group; no one has any ancient feuds with us."

"It may be true that no one has a grudge against Temple Magdalen— yet," he conceded. "I just hope you don't get caught in the crossfire. I'm not sure you understand how bad it can get here. We're not talking about tribes skirmishing over cattle. Galilee has a reputation for spawning rebels, and Herod Antipas is a weak, corrupt ruler. Everyone knows he's just a Roman puppet. I know it's not a popular view around here, but Galilee probably would have been better off under direct Roman rule, like Judea."

I had learned something from my friends the camels; I began to expectorate, but the wind I had called up was blowing the wrong way, so I thought better of it.

"There's a new prophet preaching by the Jordan River who could be trouble."

"Joseph, this country breeds prophets like fleas."

"And when a dog has fleas, it scratches. If it has them badly enough, it runs mad."

"So what's so special about this one? And what's it got to do with Galilee? If he's preaching by the Jordan River, isn't he in Judea?"

"That's what I mean, Maeve. You don't understand how volatile things are here. This John—they call him the Dipper because he plunges his followers into the river—is upsetting a very delicate balance. There were meetings about him among Temple officials, and several delegations of scribes and Pharisees have been sent to investigate him. He seems to think he has a direct line to the Most High, that people don't need the priests or the rites of the Temple to make atonement. They can go to John and take a dip."

"You're right, Joseph. I don't get what's so dangerous about taking a dip. We do it at Temple Magdalen all the time. All our suppliants undergo full immersion before we receive them."

Joseph sighed so deeply, I swear the breeze reversed and headed back across the lake to the Golan Heights.

"Maeve, don't take this the wrong way, but Temple Magdalen is an eccentric reconstruction of an antiquated cult. You have no relationship to the Temple of Jerusalem or any other authoritative body. The Dipper comes from an important priestly family. As I understand it, he'd already turned his back on his lineage and joined the Essenes. But the Essenes keep to themselves. Now John has left the order, and he's preaching to the masses, the hoi polloi—"

"Wait, Joseph. Stop. Did you say the Dipper was an Essene? Could he have been in the same order as Yeshua? Do you think he might know him?"

Joseph turned and looked at me sadly. Then very tenderly he touched my cheek.

"How long, Maeve? How long?"

I knew what he was asking. It had been years now, more than a decade since I had watched Esus disappear across the Menai Straits. I had made a life for myself. Days, weeks, even months passed when I did not think of him or the thought was too far below the surface of life to be called thought. Bedrock rather, underground river, deep-buried vein of fire.

"You answer my question first."

"Well, yes." He was clearly reluctant. "They may have been in the same community. They may have overlapped. I believe they may even be related through their mothers, but Maeve—"

Joseph knew me very well; he would see that I was already packing camel bags for a trip down the Jordan River Valley.

"I suppose it's no use, but I'll say it anyway. Don't go, Maeve. This man is trouble. The Romans don't like rabble-rousers who won't even acknowledge the Temple's authority. The Dipper has also taken to castigating Herod Antipas for marrying his brother's wife—a messy situation, but why get involved, I say."

"Yeah, wife stealing," I agreed. "Big deal. It's not like he stole the brown bull of Culaigne." But Joseph missed my reference to Maeve of Connacht's famous cattle war.

"The worst thing is that people are flocking to the man, crossing that abysmal desert in huge numbers to hear him rant about repentance and the end of the world," Joseph continued his own rant. "My people have a long tradition of that, I'm afraid. Comes of scorning logic and philosophy. Prophesies of doom always get the people riled up, no matter how many times the world fails to come to an end. Please, Maeve, stay away from that nonsense. You've got a sweet deal here. Keep a low profile. Don't go looking for trouble."

I bent my head and bit my lip to keep from laughing in Joseph's face.

"All right, all right. Forget I spoke."

He threw up his hands, and suddenly we were both laughing. We laughed and laughed until we couldn't anymore. Then Joseph reached for me and surprised me with a kiss, a full-blown passionate kiss.

"I wish I could make you forget him, Maeve."

I couldn't answer; the air wavered in the last light.

"I know," he said. "I know."

His sorrow went straight to my heart.

"Be my priestess tonight," he said after a time.

"Full immersion then," I warned him. "The whole eccentric reconstructed antiquated cultic rite."

"Right."

Much later when I went to bed alone—I did not spend the night with suppliants, not even old friends like Joseph—it took awhile to fall asleep; I was too poised on the knife edge of something. A precipice, not just any precipice but the cliffs of Mount Arbel. I began to see the rock face as clearly as if I was the air itself. That's when I fell asleep.

Except I'm not falling but flying right off the top of the cliff, over the lake, into a clear cold dawn. From high above the water, I feel myself pulled by the invisible current of the river, the holy river that begins in the snowy peaks of Mount Hermon, runs silently through the Gennesaret, then carries its living waters south into the desert places, to its dead end in the Dead Sea. From high above, my floating sight follows the river from lush Galilee into the stark, wild desert where the river becomes a narrow ribbon of dusty green, a slow snake forever unwinding its sinuous length.

I come to a place where there is some dense, dark growth, spreading out from the riverbanks. Or maybe it's ants or locusts. But as my vision focuses I see it's a small tent city, and the milling life is human. I begin to smell cooking fires, hear the commotion of people waking for the day. There's one voice that rises above all the others, so harsh I think it's a raven's, piercing enough to be a hawk's. It could be the voice of the desert itself, dry, hard, and unforgiving.

I wish I could understand the words, but other senses remain stronger, and I find the Dipper by the stink of his rough camel hair cloak and leather loin-cloth that never dry out, despite the desert heat—for if he is not dipping, he is sweating. His hair is wild and matted and small birds dart at him from time to time, looking for lice or perhaps for a place to nest. He pays them no attention. He is in a trance. I can't see his eyes, but I know they burn. The air stirs around him; the crowds begin to gather on the banks to hear him, though at times their own shouts and moans drown him out. Then people line up and the dipping begins. They come by ones, twos or in families to be plunged into the cold water by the Dipper's strong hands. He holds them down till they begin to panic and thrash, then he lets them up gasping and sputtering. And of course cleansed of sin.

Then someone cuts line.

He cuts it with such authority that the shouts of indignation die away, and no one tries to stop him. The desert reclaims its silence. Water running over rock, wind moving through scrub brush, loose scree falling down a steep bank. The two men face each other; or rather they face off. Testosterone rises off their skins and mixes with the stink of sweat and camel hair. They don't use words; their words are all used up.

Finally the Dipper points to the hills, jerks his head.

The other man doesn't move. And doesn't move.

The Dipper finally throws up his hands and brings them down on the other man's head; the man sinks to the water like a star falling, like a salmon leaping, swift, bright, without weight. There is no struggle; the water loves him, the air waits to rush back in. When he rises, he looks up.

In a flash of white I am flying down, and he is laughing, lifting his hands toward my heart.

My beloved. The whole sky is singing. My beloved in whom I am well pleased.

CHAPTER FORTY-FIVE

JORDAN RIVER

S o, am I staking a claim to being the dove that descended from the heavens at his baptism? Well, yes I am. Wasn't that dove supposed to be the Holy Spirit? Didn't the voice say something about "this is my beloved *son* in whom I am well-pleased?" You can take my version or leave it. I will just add that the Hebrew goddess, Asherah, is often depicted as a dove, as is Aphrodite. Some people even believe that the Holy Spirit is feminine, despite the use of the masculine pronoun in the Nicene Creed (written centuries later). I have taken a dove form before, though my first appearance was embarrassing for both of us. I controlled my bowels better this time. According to all accounts, the heavens were rent (I reckon that would be the thinning of the veil between the dream world and the waking) and I descended, an unmistakable sign of favor and grace, and then I vanished—or anyway I woke up.

Don't worry. If you are skeptical, you're not the only one.

"All right," said Dido, "so you had a dream. Does it follow that you have to go charging off down the Jordan River Valley?"

I was having a conference with Dido, Berta, and Judith in the kitchen yard, and we were far from consensus.

"It most certainly does not." Judith was emphatic. "Dreams must be interpreted the way Joseph interpreted the Pharaoh's dreams. I mean, that dream about the seven lean cows coming out of the river eating the seven fat cows wasn't about cows."

"But it was about food," I pointed out. "Fat years and lean years."

"But the cows weren't cows, they were years."

"And the point is?" Dido tried to get us back on track.

"The point is," Judith pressed on, "Mary is not a dove."

"I wouldn't be too sure of that," said Berta, my fellow barbarian.

"Whatever," said Dido. "So you dreamed you had a dove's eye view of your long-lost love getting dunked. Judith is right. That doesn't mean it literally happened. That doesn't mean he's there. It just means you wish he was."

"It means I have to find out," I insisted.

"*Liebling*," said Berta. "When two people are lost—"

"I'm not lost—"

"Shush, let me finish. When two people lose each other, one of them has to stay still or they only go in circles and never find each other."

I didn't answer. That was the best argument anyone had made so far. I had to think about it.

"You told us that you were done searching," said Dido. "You told us that *he* had to find *you*. Remember?"

I frowned. "Did I promise never to search again? Did I swear an oath?"

"No, I suppose you didn't promise," Dido sighed. "You merely stated. But you led us to believe you had come to your senses."

My senses, the trouble was I had six of them. Life at Temple Magdalen satisfied five. There was comfort and camaraderie here, a good life, as Joseph said. Even a useful one. But my sixth sense was sure my beloved was near, and would not rest till I had searched the Dipper's camp.

In the end, after more meetings that included Timothy and Reginus, the companions, as we called ourselves, agreed to let me go, although it was not clear that I had asked permission. Still their blessing mattered. After more deliberation, we decided that Reginus should accompany me as stand-in husband and protector for old time's sake and as a guarantee that we'd be back as soon as possible. He did not like roughing it or being apart from Timothy for long. And so early one morning, we set out with some fisherman to Philoteria where we bought supplies and hired a camel to carry them down the river valley.

It was strange to travel on the ground through the landscape I'd covered so effortlessly in my dream, but I found I enjoyed the journey, the sometimes subtle, sometimes dramatic shifts in landscape and light. By the second day, we were surrounded by desert far starker than the dusty hills around Jerusalem. There was a loneliness, an otherness that I hadn't experienced since I rambled alone as a girl on Tir na mBan. We occasionally met other travelers or saw shepherds following flocks that somehow managed to find the few tufts of edible vegetation. But the desert is like the sea: anything human is small and easily swallowed.

As the air became dryer, the temperatures became more extreme. We found what scruffy shade we could and slept during the heat of the day, traveling by night almost as bright as day during the moon's full phase, the brightness intensified by the empty desert's answering shine. At dawn after the third night of our journey, we arrived at the Dipper's camp.

No one paid us much attention; pilgrims were constantly arriving and leaving the makeshift city on the riverbanks. I was more than usually covered to protect myself from the harsh climate, so my hair did not throw up an immediate red flag, so to speak. As we wandered uncertainly through the camp, a friendly peasant family invited us to join them at their breakfast fire. In case you are wondering, they were not eating honey and wild locusts. They were treating themselves to fresh-fried river eels. We shared our olives, cheeses and figs from Temple Magdalen.

"So you have not heard our John preach yet?" asked the patriarch of the family. "No? Oh, he's a powerful preacher; no doubt about it, the spirit of the Lord is upon him. He preaches it plain and to the point, not like those hair-splitting Pharisees, and the Dipper doesn't despise a man if he never had the chance to study."

I knew from Joseph that many Pharisees had a horror of the *Am-ha-arez*, the people of the land, who were illiterate and unobservant of the finer points of the law. The kind of people we saw a lot of at Temple Magdalen.

"Some say he's Elijah returned," the man went on. "Some say he is the Messiah."

"But *he* says there's a worse one coming," said the grandmother; the wife was silent, dark-eyed and kept a veiled watch on us, as she busied herself with feeding the children. "That one will burn the wicked like chaff; he'll whack them down at the root with his axe," she cackled. "Oh, there will be wailing. Wailing and gnashing of teeth!"

"But you haven't got any teeth, Granny," said one of the children.

"Hush, child," the father reproved. "Your grandmother won't need to gnash her teeth; she has repented her sins. Haven't you, Mother," he hinted loudly.

"Oh, yes, oh yes. I am clean as new-washed linens beaten on the rocks. But the wicked priests, the clever Doctors of Law, the greedy tax collectors, and the Roman scum, they will burn," the old woman exulted. "Their fat will crackle like the fat of fatted calves the thieving priests force the people to buy for a fortune. And the Most High will breathe the smoke like perfume."

"And will they gnash their teeth, Granny?"

" 'Course they will. Teeth is the last thing to go in a fire. Dear me, yes. They'll gnash a good long time."

"Mother," the wife finally spoke through clenched (if not gnashing) teeth in a tone that made it clear that 'mother' meant 'mother-in-law.' "You're frightening the children!"

But the children did not look frightened; they clearly wanted their grandmother to go on detailing horrors, the way children love to hear stories of people being eaten.

"We do not know if he is the Messiah or the Prophet of the Messiah," the patriarch took control of the conversation again. "When he talks about the One to Come he could mean the Most High himself. All we know is that the End is near and the Day of the Lord is at hand."

"Would anyone care for more figs?" Reginus endeavored to change the subject in his bad, heavily accented Aramaic. Excess religious zeal made him nervous.

"Where did you say you were from?" asked the patriarch, suddenly suspicious. John was being watched by the authorities. We could be spies.

"Galilee," I answered, before I remembered that Reginus, as the so-called husband, should be the one to speak. But my Aramaic was fluent, so I went on. "My husband and I are proselytes."

"Is that so?" the patriarch sounded skeptical. "And how did you hear of our John?"

"Oh, well, he's famous, isn't he?" Reginus prattled. "Delicious eels, by the way. We had to come hear him ourselves. I mean, when the End comes there goes Galilee, too. Poof! We thought we might as well repent while we have the chance."

As unobtrusively as I could I jammed my elbow into Reginus's rib. I should have coached him better. He was extremely unconvincing as a proselyte.

"Husband," I said to Reginus, "weren't you going to ask about our friend Yeshua from Nazareth."

"Oh, yes, good old Yeshua. We think he might be a disciple. We're hoping to run into him."

There began the usual exchange about families and relations designed to close the six degrees of separation, but it got us nowhere. Yeshua was a common name, and I could not give a clear description of him. I had barely glimpsed him in my dream, and my memories were all of a young man not yet grown into his full stature.

"When he was dipped, a dove descended from the heavens," I finally blurted out.

There followed a silence. The patriarch's brows drew together into an almost unbroken line. An eerie silence came over the camp as if everyone had suddenly stopped to listen. A wind rose out of nowhere and a dark cloud covered the rising sun. It felt like it might rain.

"That one," the man finally spoke. "He had his own ideas, that one. He was a disciple, but he will never more wear the hair of the camel or know the sweet crunch of honeyed locust." He paused. "He is gone."

"Gone?" I repeated. Again? Not gone again. Didn't he know how to do anything else? "Where?"

The Patriarch shook his head. "Only the Most High knows and maybe John, his chosen, his prophet."

"Where can I find John?" I began to get to my feet, abandoning all pretense of being a proselyte and a docile wife.

"But you can't speak to *him*!" cried the wife startled into speech by my breach of decorum. "Only his disciples go near him."

"You may come to the preaching like everyone else," said the patriarch sternly. "If you repent, you too can be made clean and behold the Coming of the Lord in his might and wrath."

"I can hardly wait," muttered Reginus.

So Reginus and I joined the crowd on the riverbanks as John preached, undaunted by a sudden pelting storm. He was hot as ever, and I swear steam rose from his skin as he ranted. The people, too, moaned and swayed and sizzled, and I can't say I heard a word of the sermon, but I had, by this time, gotten the gist of his message. Then people began to line up for the dipping.

"What are you doing?" Reginus grabbed my arm.

"What do you think I'm doing? It's the only way I'm going to get near him."

"Aw, hell no, honey. That water is muddy and freezing. You'll catch your death of cold or something worse. What is it about the gods, they all seem to want their devotees to be as uncomfortable as possible."

"I'll be fine," I insisted. "Wait for me here. Have the camel ready to go."

"Go where?" he called after me, but there was no point in answering.

It seemed that dipping wasn't a once and for all affair as baptism is in your time. It was more like Mass, and while they were in camp, people underwent immersion daily. By the time I reached the front of a long line, the brief storm had passed, and the heat of the sun was intensifying by the second. I was beginning to feel that dipping was a very sensible rite, apart from the wait. I think lots of people would have just plunged in and started frolicking, except for the camel-haired disciples whose main function seemed to be crowd control. Finally my turn came. I waded eagerly into the stream and bent down to splash water on my face.

"What are you doing, woman!" snapped John. "Come forward and repent of your sins."

Now that I had come face to face with him, I suddenly realized that I hadn't given any thought to what I was going to say.

"I hardly know where to begin," I stalled.

John sighed. "I keep explaining to people—perhaps I should have my disciples brief them—it is not necessary to go into detail. The Lord is not interested in your petty, personal sins. It is his people Israel who must be made clean, Israel who must return to his ways."

"Oh, well, then why bother with half-drowning everyone in turn?"

He snapped to attention then and regarded me fiercely. His eyeballs became as hairy as the nasty, scratchy tunic he was wearing.

"Who are you?"

I decided to drop the proselyte pose and let him have it.

"I am Maeve of Tir na mBan, daughter of eight warrior witches, daughters of the Cailleach, daughters of the goddess Bride, daughter of Manannan, well, of a great druid. I have been called Red the Whore and I am now also known as Mary of Magdala, priestess of the All-Sovereign Isis, who is the Queen of Heaven, mistress of—"

"Woman!" John cut me off, his eyes and his voice equally penetrating.

I was suddenly arrested by the resemblance between John and my beloved: a similar bone structure, perhaps, but more the intensity of focus, a gaze that took in everything but was distracted by none of it. But John had no trace of Yeshua's humor and sweetness.

"Woman, your antecedents and your idolatries are of no interest to me. I repeat: Who are you?"

"Have it your way, then. I am who I am."

John blanched at this blasphemy but stood firm.

"I am looking for Yeshua of Nazareth."

I lifted my chin defiantly. Unmoved, John continued to consider me, his eyes unfocused as he looked just to the side of me. All at once, I knew what he was doing.

"So how's my aura?" I asked.

"A…little…too…fiery," he spoke slowly and hypnotically, recapturing my gaze with his. "One, two, three, four, five, six, seven!"

Then he struck.

Before I had a chance to take a breath, he plunged me under. I came up fighting and took a breath, which I then promptly wasted.

"You febrile son of a desert toad, you flea-bitten git of a mangy camel, you sickly whelp of a rabid dog, what the fuck do you think you're—"

"I'm baptizing you, bitch!"

Down I went again and back up.

"I'm not even Jewish, you maniac. I told you I'm a priestess of Isis, and I call on Isis to—"

And he forced me under again into the waters that had flowed by Temple Magdalen on the way here. Didn't he know that all waters are sacred to one goddess or another? Well, he was about to find out. When I surfaced again, I was ready. Taking a deep breath, I hurled myself at John, knocking him off his feet, and we both went down, but I was on top. He flailed and struggled, then got a strangle hold on my neck. We might have drowned each other, but his disciples splashed to his rescue and hauled me off him. It took about ten of them, I might add.

"Careful," warned John, back on his feet again. "This woman is possessed of seven unclean spirits."

Now you know how that rumor got started.

His terrified disciples dropped me like a hot potato, and exhausted and half-drowned as I was, I fell into the water again. It was John who pulled me up, grabbing my arms and twisting them behind my back as he held me in a lock against his chest.

"Unhand her at once, you…you rustic boor!" Reginus waded gingerly into the water. Very brave of him, as he could not swim and had never immersed himself in anything deeper or wilder than a bathing pool.

"I haven't finished baptizing her yet," said John.

"What do you mean? You dipped me three times!"

"There are at least four more unclean spirits in you, woman."

"How do you know?"

"I counted them. "

So *that's* what he had been doing. I thought he was trying to put me in a trance.

"Demonic spirits can't stand water. I was driving them out."

If you are a little confused here about the difference between baptism and exorcism, so was I. But there may be a connection between the rites. Satan and all his works are still renounced at baptisms in your time. Or maybe John just got carried away.

"Who asked you?" I demanded. "You have a hell of a nerve dipping me without my permission. And if I am possessed of any spirits, I'm sure they can swim just fine. I'm the priestess of a river goddess, for Isis sake."

"If you didn't want to be baptized, why were you in line?" He sounded unsure of himself for the first time.

"I told you, I am trying to find Yeshua. If anyone's going to cast any unclean spirits out of me, he's the one. So just tell me where he is, and no one will get hurt."

"You heard the lady," said Reginus nervously.

John still had me in a lock, but his grip had loosened a little, now that his exorcizing frenzy had passed. I sensed he was feeling awkward and even foolish holding a dripping, voluptuous and obviously gentile woman in his arms. And he had another, growing difficulty. I could feel it pressing against my backside. He was caught on the horns, so to speak, of a dilemma. If he thrust me away from him, his loincloth would look like a soggy tent collapsing around a pole. And if he held onto me, his condition would only be aggravated. Cold, wet, outraged as I was, I burst out laughing, more evidence of demonic possession, as far as the onlookers were concerned.

"Leave us, everyone," John commanded.

"But Master," fretted his disciples, "what about the demons?"

"I shall rebuke them. Go," he said.

The disciples backed away, but Reginus stood fast and shivering in the shallows.

"Go ahead, Reginus," I said. "I have to finish this."

"All right," John hissed in my ear when the others had gone. "Turn around slowly and don't make any sudden moves or you'll be sorry."

"Oh, yeah?" I hissed back. "I bet I can make you sorrier."

I entertained an image of ripping off his nasty leather loincloth and exposing him to the multitudes. But when I turned around and met his gaze again, my antagonism seemed childish. This man was full of urgency. He had no time to waste. He was like a flame, flaring and leaping just before it goes out.

"Tell me," he commanded, his voice harsh with desperation. "Is he the One?"

I was taken aback. Someone else had demanded prophecy of me in the same harsh tone; I felt distracted trying to remember who it was.

"Is he the One who is foretold?"

"I don't know what you mean." And I don't want to know, I added silently.

"The One to deliver my people Israel, to restore them to the Covenant. I thought…I thought I might be the One."

His face was anguished, and I sensed I was hearing his confession, things he had never admitted to anyone else.

"I have never hesitated to do the will of the Most High. I have never wavered; I have done all the Lord has asked of me, no matter how hard…while he, he turned his back on his people, he…"

As John's voice trailed off, I stared at him, and the air around him roiled with bright red confusion. Some threat of violence hung over him. And things worse than violence—bitterness, despair. I surprised myself by reaching out and touching his neck, as if he were some spooked horse. He shied away at first, and then he seemed to soften.

"Tell me who he is, you, who saved him from his first death."

His first death. He knew who I was. Of course he knew; he had the sight. Still, his words chilled me, and I noticed for the first time how cold the water was.

"I don't know how to answer you," I said. "I only know I need to find him. Please, please tell me where he is."

At first, John didn't respond. Then slowly he raised his arms, spreading them as wide as they would go. As if he had invoked it, the Judean wilderness rose up all around me, desolate and vast.

"You will never find him," John said gently, almost kindly.

I couldn't bear it. Before I knew what I was doing, I smacked him across the face, and then I fell into his arms sobbing. The ascetic, fire-breathing prophet had the decency to hold me. We wept together, our tears mingling with the River Jordan on its way to the Dead Sea.

.

THE BRIDEGROOM

CHAPTER FORTY-SIX

BACK TO LIFE

A nd so I went back to my life at Temple Magdalen. Berta, Dido, and Judith plied me with questions, but I found I did not want to talk about what had passed between the Dipper and me at the River Jordan. I did not want their comfort or their exasperation when they found I could not be comforted. I did not want to be exhorted to count my many blessings—friends who loved me, enough to eat, a roof over my head, work that I did well. I did not want to be told to forget him or told not to give up hope. I did not want to justify my stubborn longing or my bitterness.

Increasingly, I kept my own counsel as I struggled to come to terms with John's pronouncement. I did not even talk to Isis, who I could not help feeling had set me up, led me on. Almighty goddess that she was, she was also all too human for me at that time. I found respite only in the non-human—water and wind, the rich earth, the constantly changing sky, birds, their song, their flight. And the cats; for a suppliant had brought us kittens, and we now had a thriving feline population.

And to you who know the secret shame of having everything but the one thing you want, let me tell you: I know the courage it takes to go on living, to keep coming back and back again to life, every day when you have lost your faith. Am I telling you that I lost my faith?

Yes.

Here is my good news: This is not a story about faith or faithlessness, reward and punishment, about those who deserve and those who don't. This is a passion story, passion that breaks time open wide, so you that can taste the mystery inside.

One wild night, rain on the way, the last suppliant gone, the gates closed, I went to the tower to breathe the wind, sense the moving darkness of the lake below. I didn't hear the knock on the door when it came, but Reginus did. He came up the tower stairs to tell me someone was at the door, claiming to have a sick man with him, a man near death. But it might be a trick, Reginus cautioned. They might be robbers.

The son of man comes like a thief in the night. You do not know the hour. Stay awake. Be ready.

Well, I was awake; I was ready for anything, a dying man or a thief. Isis only knew. I opened the door in her name. Though I had waited nearly half my life for this moment, I was not prepared for what I saw when I knelt by the dying man and looked at his face by the light of my lamp.

My heart knows before my eyes; my eyes know before my mind. All I know is I am lost. There are lines here that go on for miles, for years. I am looking at his face, and what I see are his feet, brown as earth, beautiful, lost. I see the sun wheeling out of control, and the stars trying to find him.

"Red, honey," said Reginus. "Why are you crying? What's wrong?"

"Whore's tears," I said. "Cure anything."

I soaked them up with the hem of my garment, and began to wash his wounds.

"The storm is going to break any minute," said Reginus. "We better get him to shelter. Where do you want him, whoever he is?"

Did I dare say it? Not quite, not yet, not aloud.

"You *know* who he is" was all I could manage.

"Holy shit!" said Reginus with proper reverence.

"I want to take him to the innermost chamber in the Temple. It's the warmest and quietest place. Can you help me carry him?"

"Let me get Timothy. We'll make a stretcher."

I wanted to lift him and cradle him against my heart, but I feared to injure him further by moving him without help. I kept washing his wounds, now and then stopping to trace the lines in his face with my fingers, as if they were sacred, secret inscriptions.

"You know this man?" asked the Samaritan, kneeling beside me.

I nodded but did not take my eyes from my beloved's face. How could someone so dark look so pale? But hadn't I been in the desert at night? Didn't I know the moon's cold touch? You will not die, I breathed on him. Fire, sun, life. Do not dare to die.

"He is a gentile, then. I was afraid he might be a Jew, and yet I couldn't have left him there to die if he had been my worst enemy, may the Most High forgive me."

"He *is* a Jew," I told the Samaritan.

There was a silence as the man registered the fact that he *had* helped the enemy.

"No matter," said the man. "You will care for him? That is all I need to know. I will leave you money for his keep, and look in on him when I come back this way."

"No need, no need," I said. "You have brought him to me. You don't know…."

And I began to weep again.

"It must be the will of the Eternal One," said the man gruffly. "Still, I will pay for his keep until he is well again. I took him under my protection, and I am a man of honor."

Something compelled me to turn and look at this ordinary, middle-aged man, a traveling merchant, no doubt with a wife and family to care for.

"You," I said, hearing my voice shift into oracular speech. "You are a man of righteousness, a man of mercy. Your deed will be told and retold age upon age. Do not doubt me."

The man looked shaken. Then Esus groaned, and I forgot all prophecy.

Reginus returned with Timothy and the wise whores, their lamps trimmed, their voices hushed, their faces full of awe and tenderness. Just before the heavens opened, we got him inside, carrying him through the winding passages to the chamber where Judith had made a fire in the brazier and set forth hot spiced wine and honey.

Once Yeshua was settled, Judith took charge of our Samaritan guest and led him away to be properly fed and accommodated. With tears in their eyes, Reginus and Timothy both kissed me and left the chamber. Only Dido and Berta remained with me while I finished tending his wounds. I was relieved to find no broken bones, nor did I sense any internal bleeding, though his breathing worried me; I feared he had an infection in his lungs. And his connection to life seemed so tenuous, as though part of him longed to let go.

"No. Not yet," I whispered to him. "Berta, Dido, will one of you get the vial?"

They knew what I meant, Old Nona's vial of whores' tears that we kept on the central altar to be used and replenished at need.

While Dido was gone, I looked at my beloved's lips, parched, cracked. I had seen them before in visions, terrible visions. But he didn't need to suffer anymore. He was here now. With me. Safe. Saved. Isis hear me, he is not dead. He will not die. I am going to give him back his life just as I swore to his mother I would.

When Dido returned I took a drop from the vial of tears, and some of the hot wine and mixed it with the honey. Coating the tips of my fingers, I touched his lips and the soft membrane just inside his mouth. His tongue stirred and reached for the sweetness, touched the tips of my fingers. O Esus, Yeshua. O my beloved.

"He will live," I exulted. "He will live."

At the sound of my voice, his eyes flickered open. I couldn't tell if he recognized me or registered what he was seeing at all. The muscles of his face barely moved, but his pupils widened, as if to drink me in. I held my breath, afraid to move or speak, as if he were a butterfly whose wings must be allowed to dry and open in the sun without interference.

Practical Dido handed me the cup of wine. She and Berta lifted and supported him while I held it to his lips. He managed to drink a little before his eyes closed again. With the help of my friends, I eased myself behind him, so that he could rest against me. Leaving the lamp burning, Dido and Berta tiptoed out of the room.

He slept with his head pillowed by my breasts (no matter what he said later about the son of man having nowhere to lay his head) and my arms around him, my hands over his heart, the fire of the heavens flowing through me into him at full flood spate. I could feel his heartbeat growing stronger, his lungs clearing, his breathing deepening. It even seemed that his hair, matted with dust and sweat (he'd have to have a thorough bath!) took on the fresh, springy smell of wild brush. Taking him in with all my other senses, I gazed at the walls of the chamber, the mosaic glittering in the soft light of the oil lamp.

The scene on the walls told the story of Isis finding her beloved in the tamarisk tree in the temple where she served Astarte, a temple made of trees with shining golden leaves, a sacred grove. There was Osiris, his coffin a dark wound in the tree. That same coffin I had seen in my dreams drifting past me on the river, always out of reach as I floated helpless in the riverweeds. Now the waters of the world had carried me here to my own temple, and he was in my arms alive, his heart beating under my hands.

I meant to stay awake all night, riding the waves of our breath, the fire of the stars melting in the fire of his heart. But the trees drew me into dreams of trees. I saw Bran under the great oak fighting his last battle, and the boy Esus lashed to a tree on a rainy spring night. I saw, too, the awful tree, the nightmare tree, stripped and stark against a parched sky. I could not have borne that sight but for the other tree, the one with leaves made of light that smelled of dawn and spice.

When I woke again, my beloved was still sleeping soundly, his body warm and relaxed, neither fevered nor chilled. I did not want to move but my left leg had gone numb under his weight, and my bladder, pressed against his back, was ready to burst. You usually don't hear those details in romantic stories, but cramped muscles and the need to eliminate are all part of the glorious mystery of incarnation. I managed to get up without waking him, and before I went out I stood and feasted on the sight of him. His color was restored, and his wounds had stopped bleeding. Though he was still terribly thin, death had clearly decamped.

It was full daylight outside, but no one had disturbed us. On my way back to the inner chamber, I saw that someone had set a basket of fresh soft bread, olives, cheese, figs, and grapes just outside the entrance as well as a vase of early spring flowers. In that moment I loved everyone and everything so much I could hardly bear it.

When I went back in with the offerings, I found my beloved awake. He did not look in the least dazed or disoriented as you might expect. Just glad to see me.

"Maeve." He spoke my name with such tenderness, I felt years of bitter longing turn to sweetness on his tongue.

"Esus," I answered. "Yeshua." I amended, a softer sound and his name in this place.

"Maeve," he said again.

"Yeshua."

I don't know how long we might have gone on with this call and response, but I couldn't wait to find out. I set down the basket and the flowers and went to his arms and covered his mouth with kisses.

"Maeve," he said, surfacing for air. "It's…it's all so pagan."

I kissed him again; eventually I'd have to break it to him that he had spent the night in a pagan temple (where I served as a whore-priestess), but not yet, not yet.

"Not that I'm complaining," he added between kisses. "I just didn't expect it. I don't know exactly what I did think it would be like. Jews are rather vague on the subject. What is *Sheol* after all but a way of saying 'Ssh! Let's not talk about it.'"

"Let's not," I agreed, and I kissed him some more, delighted and exasperated at how little he had changed since our days under the yew trees, days when he would go on and on debating theology with himself while I tried to seduce him.

"But really I thought I might meet Moses or Abraham, a few of my ancestors, that sort of thing."

I was gazing at him now, not really trying to follow what he was saying, just reveling in this sweet meeting of past and present. He still chewed his cheek when he was thinking.

"Not that I'm not glad to see you, Maeve. I am. But I'm wondering, did your people have it right all along? Or did I somehow take a different turn?"

"I really don't know what you're talking about," I finally admitted.

"The Isles of the Blest, the Summerland, being here with you. Not," he kissed me, "that I mind. I'm just surprised. It's all so bodily. Food, touch. I'm very hungry, by the way. Could it be that the Egyptians were right about taking along supplies? Hand me some of those grapes, would you?"

"Shall I peel one for you?" was all I could think of to say.

He shook his head, and started popping grapes in his mouth at a great rate while he continued to talk.

"I'm sorry you died the way you did, Maeve, all alone at sea. I blamed myself. I never got over it, you know. But now everything's balanced again, another one of those parallels you used to like to point out. One dies at sea, one in the desert. But what was it all for, Maeve? Do you remember how grandiose we used to be? How we were so sure we had some great destiny? And now here we are eating grapes in the afterlife." He popped another grape in his mouth. "Not that I'm complaining. It could be a lot worse, and I'm so glad to see you again." Another kiss, more passionate and lingering this time. "I didn't know you could do this in the afterlife, either."

"Honey, you don't know the half of it." I rolled over so that I was fully on top of him. "Shut up and I'll show you."

And after that there was no more talk of the afterlife, just moans of pleasure and occasional outbursts, "Oh, Maeve, your breasts with the blue veins like the rivers flowing from Eden. I remember. I remember."

He did remember. I remembered. We remembered each other, all the lost pieces of ourselves, restored, re-membered. And remember the word remember means mourn, and so we mourned, too, wept over each other, bathed each other in tears. Watered that dry desert, turned it into a garden, rode the waves of that sea, this time together. Oh, we remembered. We remembered those rhythms, knew them deeper this time, harder, stronger. Pleasure so intense it felt like wounding.

O Maeve O Yeshua O goddess O god O.

"Heaven," he said, holding me afterwards. "Heaven."

We stayed in the inner chamber of the temple all day. And my dear friends somehow contrived to keep everyone away. I took the role of the experienced one, wise in the ways of the afterlife, and only allowed my beloved to venture as far as the hot spring where I gave him a much-needed bath. And so we ate and drank and made love—sometimes all at once, my navel serving as a chalice for wine, various parts of both our bodies anointed from time to time with honey. This is all in the fine Jewish tradition of lovemaking. Read the Song of Songs, which my beloved chanted from time to time: "Your belly is a heap of wheat" or "I come into my garden, my sister, my promised bride, I eat my honey and my honeycomb. I drink my wine and my milk."

So, yes, I put off telling him what you would call the truth. But what is truth? Was his first guess so far off? We were in the Otherworld, the Summerland, Heaven. No less real because it couldn't last.

"Beloved," I finally whispered in his ear as we drowsed together, "there's something I ought to tell you."

"Go on," I felt him tense.

"I'm not dead," I said at length. "I never was. Neither are you."

There was a longish silence.

"I was afraid of that," he said.

And we held each other tight.

You might think I had a lot of explaining to do. He had some explaining to do, too, come to that, but you would be wrong if you imagined that we disentangled ourselves and started to talk. Both of us could be verbose, but in that moment we had the sense to keep silent, not dissipate the power between us. "My love is a garden enclosed," we silently sang to each other, "my sister, my brother, my promised one, a garden enclosed, a sealed fountain." And we let ourselves have that night without words; we extinguished the lamp and knew each other in the dark, the sound of the temple's springs flowing through us.

CHAPTER FORTY-SEVEN

SHABBAT SHALOM

When I woke I was alone. It was a terrible waking, with reason nowhere in sight. I can hardly explain the starkness of my grief except to say that all my losses, past and to come, gathered together in one huge blow. For a moment I couldn't move; I couldn't breathe.

Then I heard the morning hymns to Isis beginning, and reason caught up with me. He was just here; he couldn't have gone far, and I got up to go look for him.

As soon as I stepped out into the cacophony of morning at Temple Magdalen, I knew that he *had* gone far, far beyond my power to control the story. After that time out of time in the inner temple, the ordinary light of day smote me. There were Dido and Berta bringing out the statue of Isis and assorted children waiting to dress and garland her amidst a flock of raucous chickens. One of the old men sat in a corner playing a complicated game that involved loudly clicking stones together. In the far end of the courtyard Timothy sang fishing songs off-key as he got ready to go tend the vineyard. Reginus was arguing with someone at the gate.

In the midst of it, looking properly bewildered, stood my beloved with a distraught Judith apparently urging him to sit down and have something to eat. Several children danced around them in circles.

"Maeve?" he said when he saw me. "What is this place?"

I looked at him, and then at Judith.

"You explain it. I can't." She threw up her hands. "I'm going to wring one of those chickens' necks for Shabbat dinner."

Just when I thought it couldn't get any harder to explain, it did.

"Reginus!" A woman's voice became shrill. "You can't keep me out. I'm an investor for goddess sake. I just want to look at him."

And Paulina flounced through the gate with her entourage, including her newest baby and its nurse as well as the now six-year-old Maria Lucia.

"Is that *him*!" Paulina whispered loudly to Reginus as they walked towards us.

"Actually, he hardly looks like the same guy we hauled in from the storm."

"Isn't he handsome?" she tittered.

"Definitely," Reginus agreed. "If you like the type."

Because of the hill behind the courtyard, the acoustics were way too good. I could hear every word, even with blood roaring in my ears, and I'm sure Yeshua could, too. Neither of us made a move. You might think I should have taken charge of the situation; it was my home, after all. But with my past and present, my dreams and daily realities finally colliding, I had lost all my suave urbanity, such as it was, as well as my barbarian confidence and ease. I was clueless.

"*Liebling*!" called Berta, turning to us now that the vesting of Isis was complete. "Your patient looks so much better."

She and Dido came to greet us as Paulina and Reginus closed in on the other side. We were surrounded. I turned to my beloved.

"Welcome to Temple Magdalen."

In my visions of the two people standing on the tower, it had always been dawn—or so I thought. My beloved and I went there for the first time in the late afternoon when Mount Arbel cast its cooling shadow over the Temple complex while the Golan Heights still looked golden in full light across the lake. My vision had been so mysterious; it did not include a film of sweat that held the heat and tension of the day close to our skin; or the exhaustion of introductions, tours of the orchard and vineyard, all of us on our best behavior. When I closed my eyes for a moment, the wind picked up, and the salty, sweet smell of fish and roses reassured me and freshened my joy.

"Capernaum is near here," remarked Yeshua. He had figured out where he was, at least geographically. "I know some people there. I've been thinking I might visit them this evening for the Sabbath meal."

Have you ever seen a bird shot out of the sky, falling so quickly, too quickly to earth? That's what I felt like.

"You've only just recovered," I said. (You've only just come back to me, I did not say.) "Besides it's too far to walk to Capernaum before sundown."

"Not so far by boat."

"Well, we don't have a boat of our own," I told him. "You'd have to go to town to hire one." (Don't leave me. How could you leave me so soon?) "Besides, Yeshua, I told you, we celebrate Shabbat here, with Hebrew prayers and everything. You'll see."

There was a silence; every moment it grew heavier.

"But you see, I don't see." He turned his gaze from the lake to me, but I would not look at him. "Maeve," his voice softened. "Maeve, I love you. In some way I know you, I've always known you. And you know me."

I didn't answer; I knew there was more coming. I wasn't going to argue with him—yet.

"I also *don't* know you. That Roman woman calls you Red. The one who feeds everyone—Judith?—calls you Mary. The large blonde woman tells me you are a priestess of Isis and goes on about your skills as a healer, which I can attest to myself. The black woman won't say more than two words at a time, but watches me as though I might steal something. Those two men call you sweetie—but they call each other that, too. Just before we came up to the roof, a stranger knocked at the gate, and you told him there were no priestesses on duty tonight but he was welcome to stay and eat. I need a little more orientation. This...this temple of yours is way more confusing than druid school."

I finally turned to him and took his face in my hands. (You do know me, beyond any name, you know me, and I know you.)

"Your people," I began, "were once strangers in Egypt. That is how your story goes, if I remember, the story I translated into Celtic for the druids. They were slaves, and they wanted to be free. They escaped as a people and wandered in the wilderness trying to find home as a people. Here at Temple Magdalen, we were all lost from our people and exiled in one way or another. But we have found each other. We call ourselves the companions, and we welcome the stranger. We turn no one away from the feast. Is there anything more you need to know?"

He stared at me, his face changed. As if his body were mine, I could feel hairs standing up on the back of his neck and his skin raised with what we call gooseflesh—a strange word for what happens when some forgotten truth rises from the deep and feathers our skin like wind skimming over water.

"Tell me the story," he said.

So I told him the story I have told you, though not at such length and with lots of interruptions and exclamations as the various pieces fell into place.

"You mean the Roman woman—your enemy, your oppressor—has become your benefactress and...and friend?"

"I know she's overbearing." I felt a little embarrassed. "But somewhere beneath that sumptuous bosom beats a human heart. Her husband is a lovely man, far too good for her. You'll meet him tonight."

"Romans at Shabbat?"

He shook his head in wonder and chewed his cheek ragged, as I went on with the story. For the most part, he took in stride my account of my search for him, my meeting with Anna, my visit to Bethany. His affection for the Bethany family and his sorrow at having caused them pain were evident. When I pressed him for details about his relationship with Mary, he waved my questions away.

"We're hearing your story now. Not mine."

So I went on until the next outburst.

"My mother! You went to see my *mother*!"

"Well, of course, I did. What did you expect? She's the one who started this wretched Mary business, by the way."

And I told him about the angels' name for me and how I came to Magdala. He usually only chewed his left cheek, but now he started in on the right. But he listened without comment until Judith's entrance into the narrative.

"That's what I can't understand. I can see how this...this community might work for pagans who freely borrow each other's gods, but for a Jew, how is it possible?"

I guessed 'a Jew' might mean himself, not Judith, but I confined myself to answering his spoken question.

"I expect it might have something to do with her having been a starving woman with three children. The good Jews of Capernaum did nothing for her, by the way. She was unclean, you see. She'd been raped."

That shut him up for awhile, and I realized how parched I was from talking for so long. I thought I'd go get us some wine and fruit, but before I roused myself, he began to ask another question.

"So all of you at Temple Magdalen just live together and...farm? Make wine and olive oil? Take care of the halt and the lame? Heal the sick? Sing songs to assorted gods and goddesses, celebrate any holy day that involves eating and drinking?"

"Well, more or less."

"Did I leave anything out?" He paused a beat. "Did you?"

Why was I having such a hard time telling him? I who was named for Queen Maeve of Connacht who had a husband, a lover, and thirty men a day, if she chose? Who was never without one man in the shadow of another?

"Let me think," I stalled. "I did mention that I was sold into prostitution in Rome? That I was a whore called Red at the Vine and Fig Tree? Where I met

Dido and Berta?"

"Yes, you told me that part. I thank the Most High that you are all free now."

Your god had nothing to do with it, I wanted to say, but didn't.

"Free, yes, well. Actually, we do expect the suppliants to make an offering. I suppose that's not quite the same as payment, so in a manner of speaking..."

I was making a mess of my admission. What had become of my shamelessness and grace? In a word, my freedom?

"The suppliants?"

"Yes, the god-bearing strangers we receive in the name of Isis, for goddess sake," I said crossly. "Now do you understand?"

I could feel his eyes on me; he waited until I met his gaze.

"Yes, I understand. You receive them. The same way you received me."

I didn't flinch. I felt my courage rising again. My fierceness. My truth.

"Yeshua ben Miriam, I receive them *all* as you. Every one of them as *you*." He wanted to look away, but I wouldn't let him. "How do you think I survived all these years? How do you think I *lived*!"

All of a sudden it was there between us, my pain, his, huge roaring walls of pain, like the waters of the Red Sea rearing up and only a narrow passage between them. Could we walk it? Could we make it to the other side before the waters closed over us?

Then came the first call of the shofar, the one that summons the laborers from the fields to prepare for the Sabbath. It drifted across the water all the way from the synagogue in Capernaum, softened by miles of wind, suffused with the last light, its sound a poignant mix of longing and joy.

"Do you remember, Esus?" I reverted to his Celtic name. "Do you remember what the old witch Dwynwyn said to us just before we parted?"

"Just before I left you," he accused himself.

"Ssh!" I put my fingers to his lips. "That part is over now."

"And the rest?" He looked at me, as if I knew, as if it were true what I used to say when I teased him: I had the jump on him, because I hung around with crazy old women who had the Sight.

"Do you remember what she said?" I repeated my question.

"You are not just the lovers of each other." He knew it by heart. "You are the lovers of the world."

The second call of the shofar sounded. In the courtyard below, Judith would be taking the loaves of challah bread from the oven and wrapping them in cloth to keep them warm.

"But, is this," he made a gesture towards the Temple, "is this what it means? Isn't your interpretation a little, well, literal?"

"I don't know." I refused to argue with him, to justify myself. "It's what I've made of my life."

He nodded slowly, thoughtfully.

"And what have I made of mine?" I sensed he wasn't asking me. "What will I make?"

"Tell me," I urged him. "Tell me."

"I have a lot to think about, Mary."

"Don't call me that," I snapped. "You'll confuse me with that Mary of Bethany."

"Not a chance." And then he grinned hugely. "You're jealous!"

I looked away from him and wished I were a cat with a long tail to lash silently.

"Maybe we need new names," he considered. "Maybe we aren't Maeve and Esus anymore."

"Reginus says you should be called Jesus. He says Yeshua sounds like a sneeze."

"You know, he could have a point," he said. "Well, if we're going to have Shabbat dinner here, we better go and wash quickly."

The third call of the shofar came, the one that summoned the beautiful Sabbath Queen in all her bridal finery.

"Jesus," I tried out the name, "Shabbat Shalom."

"Shabbat shalom, Mary."

I waited for a moment, letting the name be. And I had one of those flashes of vision—almost too swift to register—of all that would become attached to the name: salvation from sin or insanity, penitence, piety, gratitude, a perpetual dogged following after the master.

"Nah," I said. "My name is Maeve."

Shabbat at Temple Magdalen resembled nothing so much as the feast my beloved described in the parable of the rich man: his invitation snubbed by the best citizens, he invites the beggars, the cripples, the wanderers. Everyone ate together, male and female, pagan and Jew. There was no distinction between servants and served. Unless it was rainy or cold, we ate outside in the courtyard, reclining on mats and pillows with food set forth on low tables or cloths on the ground. Wonderful food, the fresh Challah bread, fish of all descriptions, fresh and smoked, in a variety of sauces, stuffed grape leaves, oil-cured olives, chickpea pastes, lentil stews, roasted onion and garlic—and of course cheeses, grapes, figs, dates, whatever was in season—and tonight in my beloved's honor, a roast chicken as well. We drank wines from Temple Magdalen's vineyards and dipped bread and vegetables into our own herbed olive oil.

By the time the sixth and final call of the Shofar sounded, all the food was laid out; the Sabbath lamps had been lit, and everyone was assembled, freshly bathed and in clean clothes. Judith, her voice husky with barking orders all day, sang blessings in Hebrew over the lamps and the feast, swaying to the rhythms of the melody, her hands dancing over the flames. While she sang there were no sounds but her voice and the waters of the spring flowing to the lake. It always seemed to me that the stars came out just at that moment to hear her.

When Judith finished, she looked across the circle at Jesus, as I will now call him.

"Please, sir, you will recite for us the *Ma'ariv*." It was a command, not a request.

I found myself torn between pride that Judith recognized in my beloved some authority and jealousy that, like Mary B, she shared with him traditions that excluded me. Except that here at Temple Magdalen, I reminded myself, no one was excluded. I turned to look at Jesus, wondering if he would accept the challenge to say the evening prayers on behalf of this motley crew of Greeks, Romans, and Jews, many from the despised *Am-ha-arez*, Jewish by birth, but ignorant of the Law, not to mention assorted pagan whores. How must we appear to him? Certainly we did not qualify as a proper minyan.

Like anyone put on the spot, Jesus looked taken aback but also thoughtful. He did not hem and haw; he would not be rushed. He is changing, I heard the words in my mind without being sure of what I meant; he is growing bigger. There was something about his very silence that was big, the way stars make vivid the night's vastness. But not everyone was rapt in contemplation of our newest companion. An old man, the one who sat in the corner all day banging stones, started to grumble and grouse.

"Good god, let's eat. That's my prayer. I'm hungry. Get on with it, young man."

Then Jesus laughed. He had a wonderful laugh, like rain after a drought or sun after a storm. Everyone joined in—even the old man—and Jesus opened his arms, embracing us all. The Hebrew welled up and flowed from his lips like the waters of the spring, flowed over the feast and the feasters. Then we all began to eat.

I swear food never tasted better to me than it did that night. I had an intense awareness that I ate not only the bread, vegetables, olives, and grapes, but also the sun, the rain, the soil, the very mystery that called them forth from the earth. I took into my body the underwater life of the fish in the warm shallows, the cold currents and springs, the filtered light of sun and moon.

I reclined next to my beloved, sharing food with him and drinking from the same cup as we had in the temple chamber. Now instead of gazing at each other, we turned our faces to our companions, aware always of the heat shimmering between us. Most lovers want to be known for what they are, to see their bond reflected in other people's eyes. I had never fully known this sweetness before. On the druid isle we hid under the yew trees, and when our bond was noted it was regarded as portentous and dangerous. We were never simply sweethearts, surrounded by friends, safe and accepted.

I savored every moment of it; I did not ask myself if it could last.

CHAPTER FORTY-EIGHT

THE GREAT DIVIDE

With your hindsight, even crusted over as it is with centuries of church history—councils, heresies, schisms, reformations, counter-reformations, papal bulls in a china shop—you know that the story, his and mine, did not end at Temple Magdalen. In fact, you say, you've never heard of Temple Magdalen. You've never heard this part of the story at all. If it's true (and not just some wishful fantasy of mine) then why didn't it? End at Temple Magdalen, that is. Why didn't we slip into that peaceful, plotless obscurity storytellers have in mind when they conclude: "And they lived happily ever after."

That was my question exactly—or unspoken question, to be more precise.

What more could any man want than what was on offer at Temple Magdalen? Plentiful food and wine, days of honest labor leavened by nights of feasting, song, and lovemaking?

–Come on, Maeve, a voice inside me nags. He may be the son of god or the son of man or the son of Joseph (or not) but he's a guy.

–A guy? What's that supposed to mean?

–You know. He's a *guy*. He doesn't want to live in a matriarchal paradise. He feels like a drone.

–A drone! There's plenty of work to do here.

–Mary, Red, Maeve, Temple Magdalen is your place.

–Not just my place. Dido's. Berta's, Judith's, Reginus's, Timothy's....

–Your place.

–His place, too.

–No.

–If not here, then where?

–Birds in their trees have their nests, foxes have their dens, but the son of man has nowhere to lay his head.

–But he does! He does. We've been over that. Look at my breasts! They are the hills of Galilee. They are clusters of grapes, my belly is a mound of ripe wheat. I am the promised land, flowing with milk and honey. Take, eat, drink. I am the lady of sovereignty who bestows on him sacred kingship.

–You're getting carried away. There are other names for you that are not so pretty.

–I don't care what you call me. Whoever has ears to hear, listen. I swear to you, ye daughters and sons of this sweet earth, it may not end here, but it begins here, at Temple Magdalen, his ministry, his gospel, his passion.

Jesus stayed with us for almost four weeks, the end of the month of Sebet and the beginning of Adar—what you would call late February, early March— one of the most beautiful times of year in Galilee when the hills are bright with wild flowers and the fig trees turn a soft green; the vines flower, filling the air with such an intoxicating scent that you can get drunk just breathing it in. Jesus helped Timothy with the spring plowing, though it was clear that he didn't have much experience. He did, however, know which prayer to say, as he did for almost every occasion: "Lord, my task is red, the green is thine: we plough but it is thou dost give the crop."

"A rabbi," said Judith. "The man is a rabbi. He should be teaching."

Nevertheless, she happily exploited his carpentry skills, and many long-needed repairs were made around the place. He liked to eat, drink, and tell stories (though he revealed almost nothing of himself or his life to anyone, not even to me). He was not averse to playing craps, and he even mastered the old man's mysterious game of stones. I did notice that he made himself scarce during the hours when I saw people who came for healing. I wondered about that, but did not question him. I think now that he must have sensed what was coming, and some part of him still resisted.

Every night we fell into each other's arms and made love as if we were the spring sun and the rich, red, new-turned earth evoked in the prayer. By un-spoken agreement we fasted from speech and took all our nourishment from touch, instinctively storing each other in our cells. For those few weeks, I saw no other suppliants.

Then came the great divide.

In Rome, as you may recall, the Isis worshippers organized a festival pa-rade to Ostia to bless the ships—or they did till most of us got shipped out. In

Magdala we had introduced our own spring celebration of *Navigium Isidis*. We paraded along the shore from the Temple Magdalen to the port where we blessed the fleets, never mind that they were fresh-water fishing boats instead of sea-going vessels for carrying grain. We were quite sure Isis didn't mind, and the fishermen loved it. So did the local merchants. People came from towns all over the lake to drink and dance and garland everything and everyone with flowers.

That year, as in our last fateful year in Rome, the Jewish festival of Purim again coincided with the *Navigium.* We had planned to include the story of Esther's deliverance of her people in the festivities. Esther, Isis, Astarte, to us, all celebration was good. We assumed Jesus would join our procession, but when we left the gates of Temple Magdalen, Jesus turned in the opposite direction, towards Capernaum.

"I want to celebrate with my own people," he said to me. "Can't you understand that, Maeve?"

"No." I saw no reason to make it easy for him.

"I'll be back tonight," he said. "We'll talk then."

It sounded more like a threat than a promise.

"If you're a good Jew, you'll be too drunk!" I called after him.

I don't know if he heard me or not; he kept on walking.

When we came back to the temple in the late afternoon (a little the worse for wear) Jesus had not yet returned. The *Navigium Isidis* was one of our busiest nights of the year, the mood reminiscent of Beltane in the Pretannic Isles, everyone decked with flowers (and little else) slipping into the hedgerows to make love. Though we had taken a number of women into training as whore-priestesses, it would be a challenge to receive all the suppliants that would seek our gates tonight.

While we all bathed, usually our most relaxed time of day, I could feel Dido and Berta watching me, wondering what I would do but not asking. The tension in the air was palpable. I felt badly for ruining the party atmosphere of the whores' bath, and so I left abruptly, stealing away to my tower, training my eyes on the road to Capernaum. Just before sunset I thought I saw him, weaving a bit, walking in our direction. But then, there were a lot of other people heading our way, too.

"All right, Red." Dido with her cat-like tread took me by surprise. "This is it."

I felt strangely relieved at being confronted at last.

"There's a suppliant at the gate. He's asking for you. A farmer. He says he comes every year. He's drunk and spouting poetry, says you are his red earth, and he's the plow. You know the rest."

The way to a whore's heart. What priestess of the mother-of-grain could resist?

"Is it that pig farmer from the country of the Gerasenes?" He was a spring regular, and his offering meant a week of barbecue, though Reginus had to take over as chef, and we moved the party to the far reaches of the vineyard to avoid offending Judith.

"Smells like it," said Dido; she waited a beat. "So?"

"So?" I repeated, stalling for time.

"I need to know, Red. For myself: Are you still with us? Are you still with Isis?"

Or are you with him, she did not say, but I could hear it. Whose side are you on? Did it always come down to that?

My beloved is mine and I am his; he feeds his flocks among the lilies.

I am with him, and I am with my goddess, I wanted to say to Dido. I am with you, and I am with myself. I am that I am. Can you understand that, Dido? Can you understand that, Jesus?

Such is my love, O ye Daughters of Jerusalem.

"Tell the pig farmer I'll be right down."

Dido gave me a long searching look; then she turned to go.

It was very late at night when the last suppliant was gone and the temple quiet and dark, except for the lamp that always burned before the statue of Isis with her ankh and sistrum. I stopped at the spring to wash away the musk and sweat of more men than I could count; then I climbed to the tower where Jesus and I usually slept, though the spring nights could still be cold. I hoped he'd be there sound asleep. I just wanted to crawl under the covers and press against his warmth in a sweet animal way without any human complications. After standing and staring fruitlessly into the darkness all around me, straining my ears for the sound of his approach, I gave up and cried myself to sleep.

When I woke again, the darkness under the covers was close and hot; he was there with me, not asleep, a hard, insistent presence. As soon as I turned and reached for him, he was inside me. Our coupling (lovemaking seems the wrong term here) was ferocious and angry. Yes, angry, both of us consumed by a completely consensual rage. Orgasm like an act of god—flood, fire, earthquake.

We fell asleep, still fused. Then, at dawn, when darkness pulls away from light and day and night divide, we woke and drew apart to face each other at last.

"It won't work, Maeve." He spoke first.

"What won't." I knew, of course, but he was going to have to say it.

"You, me. Me living here at your temple."

He stopped abruptly as if afraid to trip over his tongue.

"Why not?" Let him stumble and fall.

He let out a long sigh that was more like a wind than a breath. I pictured it filling the sails of the boats. The fishermen were setting out from port, their rowing songs floating across the water. I relented a little; Magdala *was* my place, chosen for me by the angels. I was not the stranger here; he was.

"It's because I'm a whore, isn't it?" I did not say whore-priestess, whore-healer. It didn't matter in this moment. I didn't need to dress it up, the way we vested Isis, as if the robes or garlands made her any less or more a goddess. "You knew that, but last night, you saw it, felt it."

He got up and stood looking out over the lake; I went and stood beside him. Two people on the tower at dawn. The stars beginning to fade, the lanterns of the boats bobbing up and down on the waves. The wind with its scent of fish and roses. Was this the fulfillment of my vision? Was this *it*?

"That's not the reason."

"Jesus, son of Miriam, you lie."

I knew as soon as I spoke, the Celt in me was up; I was challenging him to fight, I wanted him to fight. I thought of Bran under the oak, talking of how intensely he came to love and know his foe. I wanted to be that close to Jesus, even if it killed us both.

"No!" he said; I felt him spring into action, sword in hand. "Well." He laid the sword down, and I felt let down; he wouldn't fight; he didn't love me enough or he loved something else more. "It's true. I hate…hate to think of you with another man. But that's not the reason I have to go."

"Go. Where." The words came out, one at a time, as if they had been waiting their turn but when the moment came, they had to be pushed into the air, into sound, into form.

"I wish I could tell you."

I turned to him, took him by the shoulders and made him face me.

"Haven't you wandered long enough, Esus? All these years, all these years. Ever since you rode across the Menai Straits. You nearly *died* wandering in the desert. Can't you come home?" Home to me, I bit the words back.

In the silence I could hear him chewing his cheek.

"About the desert," he said at length. "I haven't told you what happened there. I haven't told anyone."

"You haven't told me about the desert or joining the Essenes with Mary, where you ran away to after that or why you came back. Or why you left the Dipper's camp."

"You know about John?" He gave me a sharp look.

My own narrative had stopped with the founding of the temple. I hadn't wanted to go into further detail, as you may recall. I hadn't told him about my dream of being a dove at his baptism or about my encounter with John. And I wasn't about to; I wasn't going to tell him one thing more.

"You're leaving," I said flatly. "So, go already. Do it quickly. Leave."

He pondered me without moving.

"Do you mean that, Maeve?"

"What does it matter what I mean?" I shot back at him. "I have no choice in whether you go or stay. You're not asking me. You're telling me."

He didn't answer. What could he say? But he also didn't move. And I wouldn't move, because if I did, I would cling to him or hit him, and I didn't want to do either. Besides, the next move was his.

"Maeve, if I told you what happened to me in the desert, would you listen?"

The stars were disappearing one after another. Soon the birds would start to sing.

"Talk to me," I said. Talk to me forever. Never go.

Some of what he told me that morning, I already knew—his self-destructive aimlessness in Nazareth and Sepphoris, the marriage Joseph tried to arrange for him that turned into another sort of venture altogether. And yes, I did come out and ask the question I'd been waiting to ask for almost a decade.

"No," he answered. "Mary and I were never lovers, but if you want to know the truth, that's because of her. Not because of me."

"So," the next dreaded question. "Were you in love with her?"

"No." He was definite. "But I liked her; I liked Martha. I liked Lazarus most of all. I thought I could rest there in Bethany. Work the farm with Lazarus, have a lot of children, be ordinary. Forget the past, forget the future, too, all the prophecies everyone pronounced over me ever since I was six weeks old."

"But Mary said she would rather die," I guessed.

He nodded. "She didn't want to be ordinary, and she didn't want me to be ordinary. She joined in the prophetic chorus about my destiny. She has a passion for study, a single-minded passion. Finally, I thought, well, why shouldn't she, at least, find fulfillment? So I helped her run away. She was happy with the Essenes. I wasn't; I was bored and restless. My studies seemed dry as desert dust. But I didn't think I would be happy anywhere, so I stayed. I have to admit, I was relieved when we got kicked out. I pleaded with Mary again to marry me. I said I owed it to her family. That's when she sent me away."

"To lay the ghost," I said. "The ghost of me. That's what she told me. I thought she was jealous."

"She was," he agreed. "But not in the usual way. She was jealous on behalf of the Most High. She believed that my shame and grief over you came between me and the Most High's purpose for my life."

Shame and grief maybe, I wanted to say. But not me! Not *me*! Don't you get it? The Eternal One delivered you to my doorstep, for goddess sake. But I kept quiet.

"So I joined a caravan headed east, and ended up in Kerala. Jews have lived there since the Babylonian exile, but they are surrounded by people who worship all sorts of gods—and goddesses. Not like the Greek ones, who seem petty and predictable to me. That was the trouble. Their goddesses are fierce and wild—one of them dances girdled with skulls. They reminded me of your people's gods. They reminded me of you."

I wasn't sure he meant that as a compliment, but I decided to take it as one.

"One night I got drunk and went to one of the heathen temples and talked to, well, a goddess—may the Most High forgive me; I did not mean to be an idolater; I wasn't worshipping her, I swear. It was like a dream. And as I stared at her, for just an instant, she turned into you. She told me to go back to my own place, and she would send a sign. And when I saw the sign, I would know peace about you...and how I left you.

"When I got back to Palestine, everyone was talking about John. He's a cousin of mine. I knew him when we were both at Qumran, and he was a troublemaker, too, but in a different way. I asked too many irreverent questions and broke purity rules right and left, but for John the community wasn't stringent enough. Still, I admired him; he was fiery and outspoken. He held nothing back. He went on a rant once and called the community a bunch of self-satisfied wankers, who wouldn't know the kingdom of god from a hole in the ground. You're all living in holes, he said, like a bunch of desert rats.

"So when I heard he was on his own, preaching and baptizing, I became one of his disciples. I liked living outside, and a diet of honey and locusts is better than it sounds. I relished the idea that anyone could repent and be cleansed in a river, nothing between them and the Most High, no need for a whole hierarchy of priests, no need to be a monk either, cut off from the world. But I started to question him, too. About the Kingdom of Heaven, what it was, what it meant, how we live in it. People started to listen to me and follow me around, and John didn't like it. He never liked me all that much. Saw me as lazy and undisciplined.

"One day, he told me to get the hell out. Go wander in the desert—like all the other would-be prophets—shut up and give the Most High a chance to talk. And if I survived, maybe I'd be worth something, and if I didn't, good riddance. So I had to leave, but I didn't want to go without John's blessing or anyway one last dip. He tried to refuse, but I was determined. It was after he plunged me for the last time that the sign came."

"The dove." I had to say it.

He stared at me.

"So, it really was you."

"What's so surprising? It's not like it's the first time I've been a dove. I thought I did a pretty good job this time."

He looked at me, his mouth slowly spreading into a smile that transformed his face. He reached out and touched my cheek lightly.

"It was perfect. You were perfect. And Maeve, I don't know how to explain it, I wish you could feel it, the lightness that came over me, the joy. I finally felt free, forgiven, for the first time since I left you. More than that, I felt that you were blessing me, blessing my life, blessing whatever vision would come in the desert."

He had me now. I knew it. He knew it.

"So," I sighed, trying to loosen the tension in my neck, the tightness in my face. "The desert. Tell me."

You have all heard of my beloved's temptation in the Judean wilderness, so stark, so harsh as to seem almost another planet from lush, edible Galilee. But it is also beautiful, beautiful and bare, soul-baring. Nights full of stars so sharp it seemed that if you could walk across the sky your feet would bleed as his did walking over sharp stones into the vast remoteness. Days spent tracking the shadow of a pebble in the dust. After awhile, you welcome any company to remind you that you exist—vipers, scorpions, even Satan.

So the Adversary came to be with him, his god, as usual, being invisible. I'm sure his god was eavesdropping, though. To me the encounter sounded like a setup, the same as when Yahweh killed off Job's family and afflicted him with boils and made a wager that Job wouldn't curse him. I bet there's plenty of back room deals between those two that we don't know about: a naked light bulb overhead, the air thick with cigar smoke and whisky fumes, the sound of cards being shuffled and dealt.

–Ok, so I want you to offer him everything Rome's got. Bread? Hell, the Romans had to conquer Egypt for it. (Yahweh downs a shot.) Tell him, you can give him the power to turn stones to bread. As for circuses, let's see. (A puff on his cigar.) Try this: if he jumps off a cliff, the angels will come flapping to his rescue. That's always a crowd pleaser. If he doesn't fall for that, well, offer him the world at his feet. Here's the catch, he'll have to agree to worship you. And if he does that—(Yahweh cuts the deck and shuffles; a perfect arc of cards falls)—who needs him. He's all yours.

I could have told Yahweh and Satan that my beloved wouldn't take the bait. I know him better than they do. I could picture my beloved lying there, eyeing Satan with an amused detachment, too polite to interrupt the Adversary's earnest pitch. I imagined him cool and languid while Satan sweated it like a rookie insurance salesman.

It was after Satan gave up (oh, let's have him vanish in a puff of sulfurous smoke, why not) that the trial began in earnest. A doubt plagued Jesus. What if he had made it all up? God, Satan, everything. Who was he fooling? How absurd, clinging to the notion that the Most High had an exalted purpose for him, just because a bunch of women, mostly, wanted to believe it. Well, they must have been wrong. It was all so tedious, so pointless, his life. Nothing was real but sensation, heat, cold, hunger, thirst, and then even that didn't matter after awhile.

So why not just let go?

He could sense buzzards circling, feel the shadows of their wings wheeling over him. Why not will himself to turn into earth? It was already happening. The sun burned in him; the sky had fallen into his eyes. The wind called to him. He could just leave his bones, bits of charred flesh and gristle and go.

That's when it happened.

"I don't know how to describe it, Maeve, except to say that everything softened. The earth, the air, the light. And I heard the sound of water. Heard isn't the right word; it's more that I saw it, water so clear I could count the pebbles at the bottom—except there was no bottom. Do you understand?"

I nodded. I knew that water. I had gazed into it on Tir na mBan and seen him for the first time; I had plunged in my hands. The secret, sacred water of the world. I could hear it now rising and flowing in the courtyard below.

"Then I heard *his* voice, the Eternal One. I know it was his voice, but it was also a sensation, like a breast, soft and full. The voice said: paradise is here; my table is set, my feast is laid. Go gather the guests, go gather my people. And weak as I was, I got up, found my cloak and sack and started walking toward Jerusalem. I vaguely remember a sharp blow to the back of my head. The next thing I knew I was here. I'm still not clear how that happened."

I wanted to tell him that his god had lifted him up and dropped him in my lap or that the voice he heard was not his god's at all but the voice of my goddess.

"A Samaritan merchant found you," I said instead.

"A Samaritan! Are you sure?"

"Quite sure. He said a priest and a Levite had already passed you by and left you for dead. He brought you here; no one else wanted to take a risk on a dying man of unknown origin. He even insisted on paying for your keep. I tried to refuse, but he would not take no for an answer. In the end, I accepted it as an offering to the goddess. A thank offering," I added pointedly. "For her miracle."

He looked dazed, as if someone had just hit him again.

"Don't you see?" I demanded.

He shook his head slowly.

"Your god, my goddess, they arranged it. They brought you here. So I don't understand why...why you have to go."

I think he knew what it cost me to admit my bewilderment and longing. He took my hands and kissed both my palms.

"It's my feet," he finally said. "I need to let them guide me. You...Temple Magdalen, you've healed me, but now my life must be to some purpose. The voice told me to gather the guests for the feast, the feast of the Most High for his people: my people, Maeve, Israel. I just have to trust that I'll know where to go, what to do. That's what came to me as I was pacing in circles in the dark last night."

Here is another part of the story that the Gospels don't tell you: that he didn't know everything ahead of time, any more than any of us. Despite all the prophecies and prophetic scripture, the favorite plot device of his chroniclers, he still had to walk, one beautiful foot after another, into the unknown, the unknowable.

"I will go with you," I said.

"No," he said. "Your place is here at your temple."

"It is not my temple. It is the Temple of Isis."

"You are her priestess. Your work is here."

Some call me the disciple to the disciples, but I tell you, daughters of Jerusalem, if there was ever a chance of my becoming a disciple, he blew it. To others he said, put down your nets and follow me. To me, he said: stay where you are, you have work to do.

"How would you presume to know what my goddess asks of me!"

He had the grace to look shame-faced.

"You're right. It is not for me to know, but Maeve, if I am to go gathering the people, my people..."

"You can't have a red-headed, gentile whore on your tail."

"The words are yours."

"What if I repented?"

"Would you know how?" He kept his expression deadpan but I could feel his urge to laugh out loud.

"For your information, I have been baptized."

"Baptized? What are you talking about?"

"Dipped by the Dipper himself."

"How? When?"

"After my dove dream, I went to look for you. I got in line for dipping, because it was the only way I could get close enough to John to question him. He dipped me three times. Then I knocked him down and dipped him back. We had quite a brawl until his bodyguards hauled me off him. He told them I had seven unclean spirits in me. Three of them drowned, apparently. I don't know what happened to the rest. We ended up talking about you, and we both wept."

Jesus was speechless for a moment—no doubt picturing this bizarre scene—then he gathered me in his arms.

"Maeve, Maeve, my dove. How can I bear to leave you again?"

"You don't have to!" I tried one more time.

"But I do. We can't love unless we part. You said it yourself, remember?"

"That was then," I said. "This is now. Paradise is here. The feast is laid."

"Maeve, my beloved." He held me close. "You've given me back my life twice now. The first time I wasted the gift; I squandered all those years. Now I have another chance, and the Most High has spoken to me at last. I don't know what it means yet; I don't know where it will take me. But I have to go. Can you understand, Maeve?"

All at once I more than understood. I was a Celt, and I knew: Things happen in threes. I had given him back his life twice. Whatever fate awaited him, sublime or dreadful, I would be part of it. We would be together in the end.

"Will you let me go freely, Maeve, will you give me a blessing?"

A blessing comes in handy, I could hear old Anna saying. Like a pocket hanky. Best not to go on a journey without one. I waited for a moment, stilling myself, the clamoring grief and hurt. I waited till I was clear as that living water he'd heard and seen in the desert.

> *The blessing of Isis go with you*
> *queen of stars, mother of grain*
> *she whose tears are the rain*
> *she whose embrace is the sky*
> *her wings of protection enfold you*
> *her breast be your place of rest*
> *her river with you wherever you wander*
> *her river to guide you home.*

I sang the blessing as it came to me, one palm open to the sky, the other over his heart.

Then I kissed him and let him go.

CHAPTER FORTY-NINE

FOR THIS I WAS BORN

I could have watched him from the tower as he walked away along the shore of the Gennesaret in his new sandals, the only gift he would accept apart from a loaf of bread and some dried fish. But I didn't think I could bear it.

Besides, there was a better way to see.

In the silence of noon, when everyone found a shady place to doze, I sat by the spring and gazed into the water. At first I saw nothing more than the glare of light transposed over darkness, the play between the two when the breeze stirred. A vision cannot be commanded, but something told me to watch and wait that day.

I see only his feet; he is standing close to the water. I can hear the slap of the wavelets on the shore; I can feel the breeze. As if I am seeing with his eyes, I focus on a boat, not far from shore, where the men are making a cast with their nets. Then I am feeling what he feels; his heart is light, as if it might fly from his chest at any moment and skim across the water. All his life he'd been poised on the brink of something. Now he's making the leap. For this I was born, he is thinking, singing. For this I was born.

He shifts his whole attention to the men in the boat, hauling in their nets full of fish that flail and resist the alien element of air. I hear his voice carrying across the water.

"Come with me." Strong as beating wings, his words fly, skim the waves, find their mark. "I will make you fishers of men."

Now I see the men's faces; they look as stunned as the fish, as he calls them from the water, from the boats, from the catch, the scales and guts that have been their ground, to some unknown life. Why does he call these two?

I know who they are; I've met them before: Peter with his awkward, blundering ways and Andrew his mocking, lightweight brother. What does Jesus want with them? Why do they answer, put down their swarming nets and make for shore? Just like that.

I close my eyes, I am not seeing anymore; I am knowing: what the seed knows when it splits open. When something dormant suddenly stirs and wakes. For this I was born, the men answer wordlessly, helplessly, for this I was born.

When I opened my eyes again, the vision was gone, and I felt curiously empty—not bereft, just empty, emptied like a sky after a storm, or a pot that's been scoured, or a honeycomb from which every last drop of sweetness has been extracted. As if in accord, my womb contracted and my blood began to flow.

No child. No child.

Empty.

My friends were very good to me, kind, solicitous, tactful. After awhile I couldn't stand it.

"Listen, everybody," I announced as we rested together in the olive grove after the noon meal. "I'm all right, all right? Stop treating me as if I'm about to shatter."

Dido, Berta, Reginus, Timothy and Judith all exchanged looks as if deciding which one of them should speak.

"But *liebling*," said Berta, "we thought...I mean, *aren't* you shattered? Isn't your heart broken?"

"Mine is," said Judith boldly. "I wanted him to stay. I wanted him to teach the children. *I* would have married him in a minute." She almost accused me.

"So marry him already," I snapped at her. "You of all people, Judith, should know that he can't marry me. I'm as unclean as they come according to Jewish law."

"True, but we have our own rules here," she said stoutly.

You had to love Judith.

"But, honey, why did he go?" said Reginus, holding tightly to Timothy's hand, as if my parting from Jesus put all lovers at risk. "If you're not heartbroken, we're heartbroken for you. All these years you've searched for him. We can see that you're crazy for each other, and then he just takes off. We haven't wanted to ask, but it isn't really over, not for good, is it? It's just a lover's spat, right?"

"Not exactly."

"I know why he went," said Dido, looking the closest to remorseful that I had ever seen her. "I want to say I'm sorry, Red, but I'm not sure I am. Not sorry that you chose us, chose Temple Magdalen. But sorry that I forced your hand. So soon. Maybe if you'd had more time…"

I shook my head. "No one forced my hand, Dido. That's not why he left. We didn't quarrel, Reginus, or if we did, we made it up. He went with my blessing."

"I don't understand," sighed Berta.

No one spoke for a time. After awhile, I found I wanted to say something to my friends, my companions. Out of friendship, three of them had come with me across the Mare Internum; the other two had been a mainstay and support to us all for years. They had accepted my passion for this man they'd never seen, comforted me when I grieved, and then welcomed him into their midst. Now he had come and gone, blazing through their lives like a comet. Now they had their own sense of loss.

"My *combrogos*," I used the Celtic word. "I don't understand it myself, but it's not the same as before. Now he knows I'm alive; I know he's alive. I might miss him, but he's not missing anymore. He knows where to find me; he knows where to find *us*. We won't lose him. He's not lost anymore. Am I making any sense?"

My companions nodded.

"And you, all of you, you're the ones who have always been with me. Not him. And I love you, too, all of you. How could I not be all right?"

With that we all drew closer, and Dido ran to fetch the vial to harvest a fresh batch of tears.

I did not seek any further visions in the spring. I don't know if they would have come or not, but I felt a curious inhibition against it. I knew as much as I needed to know. If he wanted to go out alone, then I must leave him alone. I did not want to abuse the power I might have had to be inside his mind. Or it could be that my restraint had nothing to do with my own virtue, but that he had closed his thoughts to me. Since the day I had first seen him in the Well of Wisdom on Tir na mBan, I had claimed him as my twin, my other self. Not separate from me. I had spent most of my life waiting to find him again, after that first loss. To love him and let him go was a new, curious state.

Soon I had no need for second sight to have news of him. Stories of his healing and preaching spread throughout the lake country and beyond. The purpose that had eluded him—or that he had eluded—caught up with him, a river bursting its dam, a smoldering fire igniting. He was perfectly aligned with this purpose and whatever power had called him to it. It poured through him: poetry, stories, healings. All he had to do was open his mouth, open his hands. And he never made the mistake of supposing he was the source; he knew he was the catalyst, the conduit. Your faith has healed you, he said to people over and over. He also begged them, "Tell no one about this."

Of course they never listened.

Joseph came to visit, not long after Jesus left Temple Magdalen, and he was not happy about the wild stories and the rumors that had already reached Jerusalem.

"He only stayed at Temple Magdalen a month!" Joseph ranted. "What is wrong with him? What is wrong with you? After all those years of searching for him, waiting for him, you couldn't find a way to hold him here? Do you want him to be arrested like his cousin? That's what's bound to happen."

"John was arrested?" I ignored the rest of what Joseph said. My hands flew to my throat, as if something or someone threatened me.

"You hadn't heard? Yes, Herod Antipas has him imprisoned at his palace in Machaerus. Why he hasn't executed him yet I don't know. People say the king has a sick fascination with the locust-eater, who goes on ranting about the king's adultery and the ruin of the land from the dungeon. All the power John had—and for what? And now your Jesus seems determined to take his place. Where can it lead but to the same end?"

"No," I said, "he hasn't taken John's place. He's making his own."

"How do you know?" Joseph demanded. "Have you ever heard him preach?"

"I had to let him go, Joseph," I said, so softly that Joseph leaned closer to me to hear. "He has to find his own way."

"You asked to go with him, and he said no," Joseph guessed. "Prophets don't have mistresses, I suppose."

"Is that what you think he is? A prophet?" I asked.

"That's the polite word for it," said Joseph. "Such a waste of a mind that could have been trained to philosophy."

"Maybe we should go hear him, Joseph, the two of us."

And so Joseph and I set out to find him, to hear him, like so many others. That's how you knew where Jesus was, these days, wherever a crowd gathered he was likely to be at the heart of it, and I use the word heart deliberately; for his words had a rhythm, a vitality that was like a heartbeat, so strong that it reached every extremity—of poverty, sorrow, madness, desperation.

Joseph and I stood, anonymous, at the edge of the crowd, barely able to see him on the day he uttered the poem that is the Beatitudes. *Ashrei*, each line began with that caress of word, soft as air. *Ashrei*, blessed. Blessed are the poor in spirit...blessed are they who mourn...*Ashrei. Ashrei.*

That is all I will say, for it is not right to comment on what is perfect and complete. I can tell you this much; even at a distance, I could hear him as if he spoke inside me. And so could everyone else. That's when I knew: he's discovered what it means to be the lover of the world. That is what I thought, and here is what I will always see when I remember that moment: two birds, flying very high in a clear, empty sky.

"He's turning everything upside down," Joseph murmured to me. "He's turning everything inside out. I don't know how he's doing it. But he is."

When I turned to look at Joseph, he had tears coursing down his cheeks.

Jesus, and his growing band of disciples, traveled all over the lake country and surrounding hills, moving from town to town. I often heard news of him in the port and at the markets. And, of course, I knew Peter's wife, Priscilla, who kept much closer tabs than I did. Taking advantage of her husband's absence, she visited me now and then with her son Gabriel, a lively boy who loved to run wild in the olive grove with the Temple Magdalen children, while we swapped stories and rumors. I have to tell you she wasn't altogether pleased about the abandoned nets. Souls don't weigh or pay as much as sole (or the freshwater equivalent), if you'll forgive the terrible pun. Yet she did not resent Jesus for the utter disruption of her life and livelihood.

"It is the strangest thing, Mary." (Like most Jews, she called me Mary, Maeve being such an outlandish name.) "When he looks at me, I feel he knows all about me, all my secrets, and yet he doesn't judge me. You never told him anything, did you, about...you know, the way I conceived my son. No matter how it happened, I think of him as Peter's son."

"Of course, I didn't tell Jesus. I wouldn't. But I know what you mean," I said slowly, thinking it out, "by how he looks at you and knows you, how he sees you."

Was I jealous? I probed my feelings, the way a tongue probes for a sore tooth; except for a slight ache here and there, I found no pain, no inflammation.

"Are you in love with Jesus?" I asked suddenly.

"No! Well," she added after a moment, "yes, but, no, of course not. I mean, I love Jesus, but the strangest thing happens when he's around, I love Peter more than I did before. I see Jesus looking at Peter and suddenly I see Peter through his eyes and all the things that irritate me about Peter become endearing. Of course, Peter is a good man. Most men would have divorced me, or worse, for what I did. Peter just...decided not to understand. I owe him more than a wife's loyalty for that. How can I begrudge him anything, even if he bankrupts us by following Jesus all over creation? But it's hard having him gone, and when the men come back, how they eat! It's like Shabbat feast every day. And the crowds that gather! It's frightening."

"Send them over here," I said lightly, so that she wouldn't hear my longing.

"Oh, Mary. Send a Jewish teacher of righteousness and his disciples to a pagan, well, temple?"

"You don't have to mince words with me, Priscilla. We both know what Temple Magdalen is."

"May the Eternal One bless you and all within your house forever," she added fervently, as she watched her strong, handsome son swing down from a tree branch. "I do not repent the sin I committed here or the fruit it bore. May Jesus forgive me."

I was taken aback by her invocation of my beloved's name, but she remained tranquil, untroubled by blasphemy (ascribing Jesus a godlike power to forgive sins) or illogic (for how can you be forgiven if you don't repent). Priscilla was a practical woman, and the first of the many women to support Jesus and the disciples "from her own resources," as Luke, alone, has the grace to admit that women did.

I became the second, sending Priscilla home with a cart laden with Temple Magdalen cheeses, wines, and olive oil, things that could be stored to feed the men when they returned to Capernaum. Priscilla promised to send me word when they did.

Jesus and his posse came back in the summer, in the lull before harvest and all the fall festivals, when there was nothing to do but fish early and late (which many of the disciples still did whenever they could), and seek shade in the heat of the day. When I received Priscilla's message, I decided to go to Capernaum and take my chances on seeing him. It had been months since I'd stood in the crowd with Joseph. For all my conviction that I knew my beloved from before and beyond time, I wanted to know him *in* time, too. I wanted to know what had become of him, who he was becoming.

"Sure, I'll go with you," said Reginus, my faithful non-husband. "I've never missed one of your misadventures yet."

"My cousin could take you in his boat," offered Timothy. "It's too hot to walk."

To my surprise, Dido asked to come, too. She was the one who had kept most distance and reserve with Jesus. I sensed she still felt responsible for what she still saw as a rift, despite my reassurance.

When we stepped on shore and into the well-kept, upright town of Capernaum, the waterfront was almost deserted, and so was the synagogue in the town's center.

"Where is everybody?" Reginus wondered.

"Listen," said Dido.

We could hear it, maybe a couple of streets away, the sounds of a crowd, sometimes murmuring, sometimes ululating, now and then silent. We headed in that direction and soon found ourselves at the edge of a throng that filled a whole long street.

When there was a hush, I could just make out the sound of Jesus's voice, though not the words. He was on a roll; I recognized the rhythms of Hebrew poetry, the call and response repetitions. Then someone must have challenged him, and the rhythm shifted to the syncopated fits and starts of debate.

"Why isn't he teaching in the synagogue?" Reginus wondered. "Wouldn't there have been more room?"

"He was," said an old woman standing near us. "He went back to Simon's house for his meal, poor lamb, and the crowd followed him."

"Why?" asked Dido. "What do they want with him? Why do you stand here?"

"Why? We want to hear him or just be near the man, don't you? Never been a prophet like him before, eating and drinking and talking to unlearned people, even women. I never in my life dared go to the teachings—but him, I could listen to him forever, the lovely, shocking things he says! The other day one of them Pharisees says to him, How come you and your followers don't fast like we do? Even the Dipper's disciples keep the fasts. And you know what he says, bold as you please: The wedding guests can't fast when the bridegroom is with them. Whoever heard of a prophet calling himself the bridegroom, inviting everyone to the feast? Hush now, that's him again."

"I can't catch any of the words," complained Reginus.

"Ssh," said the old woman. "Just listen, the sound of it."

And so we did, the way you listen to birdsong, or wind in the reeds, while one word resounded in me. Bridegroom, bridegroom. And who was the bride? Did anyone ever wonder?

"We'll never get near him, Red," said Dido after awhile. "It's hopeless."

"And it's getting hot as Hades," added Reginus. "It's a good thing we didn't bring Berta. We would have had to carry her home." Berta suffered terribly from the heat and spent midday inside the caves with her feet in a cold spring. "How long do you want to wait, Red?"

Forever, I wanted to say, and not one minute longer. Both were true. How had I come to stand at the edge of his life next to an old woman who called him poor lamb? Lover of the world, he was as much her lover as mine. Where did that leave me? I closed my eyes against the glare of the day, and the stink of close-pressed flesh became that much sharper. The debate had begun again, the male voices rising, falling, attacking, retreating, in an intricate verbal rite that meant nothing to me. Maybe Mary B was right. I had been a mere obstacle, a distraction from the purpose he had found at last.

"Let's go home," I said.

Just as we turned away there was a commotion from a side street.

"Make way," someone shouted. "We must see the healer."

"Yeah, you and a few hundred other people!" someone shouted angrily. "Stand back and wait your turn. The healer is teaching."

"He can't stand, asshole, can't you see!" the man yelled back. "We've carried him all the way from Achbera. Let us through!"

No one budged. Dido, Reginus, and I had all lived in Rome and knew that crowds and belligerence were a bad combination.

"All right," said Reginus. "We're out of here."

"No," I said on impulse. "Let's go have a look at the man first. There might be something we can do."

"What? Like take him back to Temple Magdalen?" grumbled Reginus. "Cats, dogs, crazy people, always room for one more."

But he and Dido followed me as I skirted the crowd and came upon the man, carried on a stretcher by four weary-looking peasants.

"If we're going to have a fight, we better set him down," one said to the others. "I'm sweating like a gentile pig-eater in this heat. Hey, lady," he said to me, "stand back, this could get ugly."

"Will you let me look at him? I'm a healer."

They snorted derisively, but made no objection, glad for a moment's respite before they took on the crowd. I needed only a glance to see that the man was paralyzed, from the neck down, I suspected.

"How long has he been like this?" I asked the stretcher-bearers.

"Had a fall a few years back. His mother took care of him, but she died, see? No one in our village has enough to feed a mouth that can't work. So what's going to happen to the poor devil? This miracle healer here is his last chance, best we can do for him."

Though the men had made some effort to clean him up, the paralyzed man's garment was worn and filthy. I guessed since his mother died, he had been left to lie in his own shit more than once. I knelt beside him, and he stared up at me, as petrified as his limbs to see a gentile woman with fiery hair bending over him. Holding my hands an inch or so above his body, I ran them down the length of him.

"Here! What are you doing to him!" demanded one of the men.

His face—the only mobile part of him—relaxed a little.

"Just easing him a little." But I could heal him, I thought, if he would let me.

"I want to see the healer." The paralyzed man spoke for the first time. "The one they call Jesus. Will you take me to him?"

He spoke so trustingly, and I saw how young he was, young and motherless. Yet he wanted Jesus. Only Jesus. Not a priestess with the fire of the stars in her hands.

"Please take me to Jesus."

"Do you know the healer?" asked another of the men. "Have you got some kind of pull with him?"

I was once the lover of the lover of the world. But he left me, and you do not see that I, too, am a lover, a lover of the world.

"I have an idea," I said out loud. "Follow me."

"Red?" Reginus was alarmed. "What are you thinking?"

"This man wants to see Jesus, and I'm going to make sure he does. We'll go around the block to the back of the house. There's bound to be stairs or a ladder to the roof. We can get in that way."

"Red!" protested Dido. "You can't just go ripping up people's roofs."

"Sure I can," I said. "See? It's only palm branches and marl. Priscilla will thank me. She's been trying to get Peter to replace the roof for months."

"Did you know that John the Dipper says this woman is possessed of seven demons?" Reginus made small talk as the men picked up the stretcher. "Myself, I think his estimate is low."

"Oh, shut up, Reginus," I said, and everyone followed me around the block and down the narrow—and deserted—lane behind Peter's house where there was indeed a ladder leading to the slapped-together, leaky roof.

There is an account in Mark's Gospel of the paralytic man being lowered through the roof, but it doesn't give much detail. Picture the scene if you can. Jesus, disciples, and assorted scribes and Pharisees reclining or sitting cross-legged in the front room of Peter's house that opens onto the street where the crowd presses as close as it can. They are carrying on some earnest debate while bits of plaster and palm begin to fall on their heads; then a gaping hole appears, letting in the glaring sky. Next—and this is the part no one ever tells you—a strapping redheaded barbarian woman jumps down into the room, followed gingerly by a roman queer, and a regal-looking black woman

"What the fuck!" (Yes, the Rock on which the church is founded really did use an obscene expletive.) "This…this unclean, demon-ridden woman just destroyed my roof! She's defiling my house. Do something, Master!"

"He's right!" one of the Pharisees said. "The red-haired woman is de-mon-possessed and dangerous. I saw her myself at the Jordan River when the righteous John wrestled with her and nearly drowned."

All the other guests and disciples started in, and the crowd began to growl like the unpredictable beast it was. Jesus ignored everyone and just looked at me.

"What's he doing?" people asked each other.

"Watch. He's casting them out, the unclean spirits. See how she's quieted."

Little did anyone know: how hard we were both trying not to burst out laughing.

"Look alive!" shouted the men on the roof. "We're sending him down."

"Quick," I said to Jesus. "We need a few strong men to lower a stretcher."

At a nod from Jesus, Peter, still purple with rage, stepped forward with his brother Andrew and James and John. They received the paralytic man and laid him before Jesus. In the silence that followed we heard the other men scrambling off the roof and running down the alley. I guessed they didn't want to be around if the healing failed.

As Jesus turned his gaze on the paralyzed man, the hush deepened in the room. Priscilla bravely came to stand next to me to show I was not an intruder. Peter glowered a bit, but soon all the petty dramas subsided. The calm even spread to the crowd outside. Somehow, just by being still himself, Jesus had stilled everyone around him. All the agitation, that had darted and crackled in the air, now flowed steadily towards him. It was his to do with what he would. And he did nothing, or appeared to do nothing but look at the man lying before him.

When I shifted my attention from Jesus to the man lying on the stretcher, I saw that the miracle was happening. The terror and desperation had vanished from the man's face like shadows in a noon blaze. He was at peace. Whether he walked again or not, whether he lived or died, he was, in some mysterious way, whole, complete.

"My child," Jesus spoke at last with such tenderness; a collective sigh washed over the room. "Your sins are forgiven."

At that some people openly wept. But others, I noticed, were angry. His voice stirred them, touched them in places they did not want to be touched. I watched them struggle to regain control of themselves and of the world, as they believed it to be ordered. Jesus, by his very presence, seemed to draw chaos: Gentiles ripping off the roof, plopping a cripple at his feet. People sobbing un-controllably, falling to their knees.

"Only God can forgive sins!" the Pharisees thought to themselves. "This is blasphemous. What does he think he's doing? Who does he think he is?"

In Mark's Gospel, Jesus reads their minds. Not so hard, really. Disapproval, outrage, fear, they change the texture of the air. Now Jesus made one of his lightning shifts that so disconcerted people. One moment, only the man on the stretcher existed in all the worlds. Next he unfurled his focus like huge wings, an eagle ready to dive and attack. No one—no thought—could hide from him. I have to admit, he was scary.

"Why do you have these thoughts in your hearts? Which of these is easier: to say to the paralytic, 'your sins are forgiven' or to say 'get up, pick up your stretcher and walk?' But to prove to you that the Son of Man has the authority to forgive sins on earth—" He turned to the paralytic, "I tell you: get up, pick up your stretcher, go off home."

The room was silent and tense; you could hear the sweat falling, the walls expanding in the heat, a baby crying at the far edge of the crowd. The man pulled up his knees, rolled to his side, and slowly stood up, as if he were grain called forth from the earth that could not resist the sun. He stood up straight and astonished, and almost fell over again as everyone let out the breath they'd been holding. When his legs stopped trembling, he bent and picked up his stretcher, but instead of turning away, he turned back to Jesus, his mouth opening and closing as he struggled to speak.

"Go on. Go home now." Jesus's voice was kind but dismissive.

I shot a glance at my beloved and suddenly saw how tired he was; there were deep shadows under his eyes and a strange sadness in them.

"I...I don't have a home, not...not really," the healed man managed at last.

And here is another part of the story the Gospels don't tell. The lame walk, the blind see, the deaf hear, a moment of glory and wonder, and then complete disorientation. It was the flight from Egypt over and over again. Miracles right and left and then...the wilderness.

I did not think about what I did next. I just did it.

"You are welcome in our house," I said, putting my arm around the man but looking straight at Jesus. "The table is set, the feast is laid."

Jesus returned my gaze and nodded almost imperceptibly, acknowledging that something had just happened between us. Or beyond us.

For this we were born. I thought. Do you hear me, Jesus? Do you hear my thoughts? For this we were born.

Whatever *this* might be. Wherever *this* might lead.

CHAPTER FIFTY

CALMING THE STORM

W ho knows? Maybe Jesus did cast out my remaining demons that day at Peter's house. Lovers of numerology like to speculate on the significance of the number seven. Seven sacraments. Seven chakras. Seven Pleiades. Seven gates through which the goddess Inanna passed on her descent to the underworld. Seven is the sum of the magical three and the sturdy four. There are seven cardinal virtues (I can never remember them) and the corresponding seven deadly sins, which come to mind more easily: pride, anger, lust, envy, gluttony, sloth, avarice. Some of those sins have never been mine; others I have no intention of giving up until they die a natural death.

But that day, envy went out of me. I was not envious anymore of those he had called to follow him. In some sense, I was with him, whether we were in the same room or not. Nor did I mind that crowds flocked to him, while at Temple Magdalen we just went on as we always had, with people coming and going at need. I did not want to be a disciple or to have disciples. I had companions—people with whom I broke bread. That was enough. In the end, I believe, that was all Jesus wanted, too.

Jesus did not come to see us after the encounter at Peter's house, but he did get the idea that he could send us people who needed further care or feeding. Some stayed indefinitely; others only a day or two. The newly whole carried such a strong sense of his presence that we all felt it. It was like a party about to begin—not a dull, social party with people trying to impress each other, but a riotous party, a fiesta like—why not say it?— like nothing so much as Shabbat at Temple Magdalen.

But not everyone who had seen him arrived love-struck and transformed.

Late one afternoon, Judith came to fetch me from the whores' bath where we were just finishing tarting each other up for the evening: henna tattoos, kohl-lined eyes, perfumed breasts and thighs, flowers threaded into our hair (above and below). You get the picture.

"There's a whole group of people waiting outside the gate, asking for you, Mary."

"You didn't let them in?" I wondered. "You haven't *fed* them yet?"

"Well, of course I invited them in!" Judith was indignant. "And when have I ever refused to feed anyone. *Anyone!*" She emphasized the disreputable nature of some of our guests. "They insisted they'd wait outside for you. They're Jews, and if you ask me, they seem a bit hostile, as well they might," she added grimly. "I hope we're not in for trouble what with you destroying property in Capernaum. Honestly, Mary."

I confess I was intrigued rather than concerned, thinking perhaps I had merited a delegation of Pharisees or scribes, as John and Jesus had. (Ok, the sin of pride was still in residence.) I quite looked forward to a debate on my own turf. With a certain brazen eagerness, I stepped out the gate and stopped short. There, surrounded by four surly-looking men, one sour-faced woman, and a rather sweet-natured donkey (by comparison) was none other than my beloved's mother, her own peculiar scent of garlic and roses mixing with the Magdalen scent of roses and fish.

"I told you she'd be here," she said to her aggrieved brood.

"Mo-*ther!*" they responded in chorus.

And I heard all that was not said: You are impossible. What can you mean making us stand outside a whorehouse to see this painted creature with her half-naked bosom. We have put up with quite enough from you. This is the limit!

"Miriam of Nazareth." I went forward to greet her.

She met my outstretched hands briefly, barely. It was like touching the wind or blossoms on a bough.

"Mary of Magdala," she said calmly; she did not say: See? Didn't I tell you the angels call you that? But I could hear her all the same.

"My name is Maeve," I asserted, just to ruffle her feathers, but she remained maddeningly serene. My heart went out to her children. "Welcome, all of you. Please, come in and have something to eat and drink."

"Ma," warned her daughter. "We've got to get going. You said you just wanted to see if she lives here."

Of all Jesus's siblings, his sister was most like him in features, but only in the way a prune is like a plum. All the juice, all the sweetness gone. I wanted to take her hand, take her under my wing, feed her up, get her drunk, tell her bawdy jokes in the whores' bath, find her a lover, but I confined myself to a friendly smile.

"We don't know why she wants to see you," said one of the sons, half accusingly, half-apologetically. "Now that she has, we need to be on our way. Thanks all the same."

"She knows my son," stated Miriam, looking as if she had taken root.

There it was again: "my son," the others reduced to so much chopped liver.

"I'll just bet she does," one of them muttered, without adding: and this wouldn't be the first time he's taken up with a whore, but his mother heard it, anyway.

"That's enough, Jude."

"Jesus, I mean Yeshua, isn't here," I thought I'd better explain. "Not since Adar. He might be in Capernaum at Simon's house. It's about six miles from here."

At the mention of their brother's name, the siblings' faces darkened. I swear I could hear thunderclaps, catch a sulfurous whiff of lightning. Their frowns deepened like gullies cut by a flash flood.

No doubt you've guessed what had happened; both Matthew and Mark give an account of Jesus's refusal to see his family. (So much for Christian family values, an oxymoron if there ever was one.) Of course, he had his reasons, like not wanting to be carted off in the first century equivalent of a straitjacket. Mark puts it bluntly: his relations had set out to "take charge of him" because, they said, "He is out of his mind."

"We've already seen him," said a brother.

"You mean *not* seen him," corrected the sister.

"Whatever. We're on our way home. Come, Mother. Mother, *come*."

The donkey appeared to comprehend plain Aramaic much better than Miriam did, lifting his ears and shifting his weight from hoof to hoof. Miriam remained unmoved. The afternoon was hot and breathless; everyone else was sweating. A breeze sprang up that touched only Miriam, swirling her garments, blowing back her mantle. Her still-black hair came loose and floated around her. Then the breeze vanished as suddenly as it came.

"I am going to rest for one hour by Mary of Magdala's spring," she announced. "The rest of you," she paused and shrugged, "do as you please."

Without waiting for me to show her the way, she walked through the gates. The siblings and I looked at each other helplessly. Perhaps they felt my sympathy for them; we had a moment of bonding.

"Please come in and take some refreshment," I said.

Not knowing what else to do, they followed me. Judith immediately swooped down on them, bore them off to a shady corner where she had already set forth a small feast for the reluctant guests, including some sweet hay for the donkey. I fetched wine, bread, and cheese for Miriam, who had shed her sandals and sat soaking her feet in the spring. When I'd set the food before her, which she ignored, I sat down and waited for her to acknowledge me, which she seemed in no hurry to do.

"That's much better," she said at length. "They told me your spring would ease the blisters."

I did not need to ask who *they* were.

"It's a long way from Nazareth to the Gennesaret, if you're not used to going anywhere," she made conversation, as if she were a normal person. "Of course, I rode part of the way, but I got saddle sores and pains in my thighs and lower back."

I wondered if she would hoist her tunic and lower her hindquarters into the healing waters. I thought of suggesting it, but decided to leave helpful hints to the angels.

"He wouldn't see me." She spoke without affect, as if she were merely going on with her list of aches and pains.

"There are so many people around him," I suggested. "It's hard to get near him."

"Wouldn't even come himself to tell me to go away," she went on as if I hadn't spoken. "But I heard him. 'Who is my mother?' he said. 'Here are my mother and sister and brothers. Anyone who does the will of my Father in heaven is my brother and sister and mother.'"

Her tone of voice had not changed; her face was as still as the statue of Isis in the courtyard behind her. Then, without any alteration in her expression, tears welled in her eyes and ran down her face like rain. It was no doubt some consolation prize from the angels that she could weep like that, without noise, without reddening her eyes or nose.

"You didn't tell me," she accused. At last her tone had shifted; it was harsh and soft at the same time, and made me think of hissing snakes. "You didn't tell me it would be like this. Didn't *I* do your will? Didn't I?"

The hairs rose on the back of my neck—that's a true saying. It happens to all animals in the presence of a haunting. For I knew Miriam was not speaking to me or even to her angels.

"Who has known your will as I have known it? Who! Who has been torn open by it, taken it inside like fire? Who has lain under the cold, blue shadow of your wing? Who knows you as I have known you? Ah, you have named me well. For my name means bitterness, salt brine, deep and terrible as the sea. And you have dealt bitterly with me."

I wanted to reach out to her, touch her, comfort her in some way, but I would have had to reach across the worlds. Also, I admit, I was a little afraid of her, afraid of her terrible god. I wished he would go away. As if she heard my thoughts, Miriam turned from the Almighty, and focused her wrath on me.

"You said you would give him back his life, Mary of Magdala. Is this the life you have given him? A life of homelessness and poverty, scandal and scorn. A life lived for the *Father*—what does he know of his father!—a life in which he denies the womb that bore him, the breasts that gave him suck. Where can such a life lead? How will it end?"

Anguish tore through her voice, as if she were rending her soul like a garment, scratching her breasts, putting on sackcloth and sitting in ashes. Her eyes had unfocused, and I was losing her again. Suddenly I felt frightened and lonely. I wanted my own mother, Grainne. (Oh, if she could find me again, I would never turn her away.)

"Miriam," I called to her from my grief. "Miriam."

Slowly she came back, as if I tugged at some invisible tether, as if I were gravity and she some airborne seed that takes its time coming to earth.

"I am sorry, I am so sorry," I fumbled. "I wish I could answer you, but I don't know anything. I…I had to let him go, too."

Under her gaze, I felt the falsity of what I had just said. It was too easy, too slippery, the bond with her I'd tried to claim, the rope I'd tried to throw her. It could not save her, and we both knew it.

"He will come back to you," she stated, her voice again matter-of-fact. "But it won't be in the way you expect. No, not at all." She laughed out loud, a most disconcerting sound, as eerie as her silent tears.

"Did the angels just tell you that?" I asked.

"They tell me everything—except what I ask. When to plant onions, how to heal blisters. They gossip sometimes, but they won't tell me how it will end, what it will mean. I am an empty thing, a broken husk. The wind blows through me. Listen."

She started to sing softly, a wordless song with a wandering tune, and for a moment I could see the wild, desert places where she drifted when she disappeared, formless as wind.

"Why have you never borne another child, Mary of Magdala?"

She startled me; her song had laid me open, taken me to my own empty places.

"You know what I am." I shrugged, warding off the pain. "The life I lead."

"That is not the answer."

"No."

"Poor little child," she crooned. "You've lost your mother."

The hairs on my neck rose again, for I did not know if she spoke to me, to my daughter stolen from my arms, to herself, to her son—or to all of us.

"Come here, Mary of Magdala."

How did anyone—how did her precious Yeshua—dare to disobey her? I came and knelt beside her, not knowing what she would do, only that I would allow it. Very slowly, as if I was a wild animal she wanted to gentle, she placed one hand over my heart and one over my womb. Huge light flooded me; I was transparent, porous. The wind blew through me, and the sound of bells.

Then she withdrew her hands, and we became our apparent selves again, a gentile whore and a Galilean widow. She sighed and withdrew her feet from the pool. I dried them with my tunic and even kissed them before I helped her lace her sandals.

Miriam of Nazareth, blessed virgin (or not), difficult, demanding, and possibly daft, and a goddess, yes, a goddess.

In preparation for Jesus's prophesied return to me, I rehearsed a tongue-lashing concerning the respect due to "the womb that bore you and the breasts that gave you suck." But angels, like many Otherworldly beings, have no concept of time. Our doors remained undarkened by Jesus as he kept on with his wandering ministry.

Around this time, he began to speak in parables, a form that has become almost synonymous with his teaching. He was not the first rabbi or teacher of righteousness to make use of parable, but he turned the form to his own purpose—evoking the kingdom of heaven so potently that people would blink or turn their heads and suddenly see that they were in its midst. The tiny mustard seed growing branches big enough to shelter the birds of the air. Yeast leavening the bread. Lost coins and sheep found. A father forsaking his dignity and running to embrace his feckless son. For John the Dipper, the Day of the Lord was some catastrophic event that was on its way (like a tornado or tidal wave, I can't help thinking). For my beloved, the kingdom is here, happening, unfolding, blooming, proliferating, even in the midst of doom and disaster. Just turn (that is what repent really means), turn and look from a different angle. Paradise is here, even now.

Three out of four of my beloved's chroniclers recount parables, each narrator with a different emphasis. If I had to sum them up, I would say Matthew is fond of judgment, (separating wheat from chaff with a liberal dose of wailing and gnashing of teeth thrown in). Mark loves the mysterious (the seeds grow in the night, who knows how). Luke is famous for stories of mercy and forgiveness (the Good Samaritan, the Prodigal Son). Maverick John leaves out the parables altogether and reminds us that Jesus is a master of the Celtic Boast: I am the good shepherd; I am the vine, and you are the branches; I am the resurrection and the life. Only read *The Song of Amergin (I am a wave upon the sea; I am a stag of seven tines)* and you will see that my beloved paid attention at druid school.

Well, you can study the Gospels for yourself. I mention these storytellers now, because I have a bone to pick with them over the parables. The three who include them insist that Jesus spoke in parables to the crowd to fulfill some nasty bit of scripture (a device all of them overuse). Jesus allegedly says to his disciples, "To you is granted the secret of the kingdom of God, but to those who are outside everything comes in parables so that *'they may look and look, but never perceive; listen and listen, but never understand; to avoid changing their ways and being healed.'*" Bloody Isaiah 6:9-10. Then, in all their accounts, Jesus goes on to ruin the parable of sower by explaining it in painstaking detail. Why? Because they are the chosen ones? The inner circle? The initiates? Hell, no! Because they were too dumb to get it otherwise.

That's my interpretation. You may dismiss my criticisms as sour grapes; for it is true, I wasn't there. Yet I maintain that parables, like poems, are best left unexplained. Let them go to some deep place in you and germinate; someday you may be a shelter for birds. As for "those who are outside" listening and never understanding, I beg to differ. I was often one of them. Whenever Jesus was nearby, a contingent from Temple Magdalen went to hear him, standing at the far edge of the crowd with the other disreputable types.

"The Kingdom of Heaven is like yeast," we heard him say, "that a woman took and mixed with three measures of flour until all of it was leavened."

Judith put her hands to her mouth and actually giggled.

"What's so funny?" I wondered

"Don't you know, Mary? The rabbis consider yeast unclean. Only women handle it. Who but our Jesus would dare to compare it to the Kingdom of God!"

Many times I witnessed the gap-toothed grins of old women, and the clapping and dancing of younger ones as they recognized themselves and their lives in the stories: the persistent widow demanding justice, the woman throwing a party when she finds the lost coin. They needed no explanation.

They understood: the Bridegroom was here in their midst. They were invited to the feast.

And people were hungry. "A man does not live by bread alone," my beloved had answered the Adversary, "but by every word that proceeds from the mouth of God." According to John, he was that word made flesh. People could not get enough of him. And that wears on a person after awhile.

Despite my contention that the Twelve, far from being the spiritual elite, were in desperate need of remedial help in Parables 101, I will admit they did serve one useful purpose: the getaway. Peter's boat was kept handy for this purpose. Sometimes Jesus even preached from the boat. After a long day, he and the disciples would head way out into the middle of the lake where Jesus would spend hours watching the birds skim the swells, and the clouds drift over the mountains. Wind, sky, water, the land rising like still waves in the distance, the spaciousness, the silence of the elements replenished him, and soothed by them, he would fall asleep like a baby at the breast.

How do I know? How do I speak of his dreaming and drifting in that boat as if I were there? Because in some sense I *was* there; that is when I reconnected with him. I would stand on the tower, and let my mind soar over the water, light as a bird. As light. As a bird. So, of course, I was there for the famous storm.

It had been one of those hot, breathless days, the air thick and pressing down, as if it was the flat of some huge, heavy hand. Towards evening the sky turned a lurid yellow-green, and from the stillness a wind lifted, fat with rain. I climbed the tower as the sky began to spit. The laborers in the groves and vineyards picked up their hoes and pruning hooks and ran for home. Birds flew to shelter, and the fishing boats were making for port as fast as they could. The glassy stillness of moments before had given way to churning waves, their white caps foaming moons on the dark water. Then came the lightning and a clap of thunder loud enough to be heard over the wind. Children shrieked, dogs barked in the courtyard below. My tawny cat, Sekmet, came and rubbed against my legs, mewing in alarm. I picked her up and cradled her.

"Red!" Dido shouted from the stairs. "Are you trying to get struck by lightning? Get off that tower, for goddess sake."

"I'll be down in a minute," I said. "Take Sekmet. She's shivering."

"At least she has sense." Dido glowered as she reached for the cat.

"He's out there," I told her.

"And that means you should stand on the tower and offer yourself as a human lightning rod? Love! Isis save me from it."

"She didn't save herself," I retorted, but Dido was on her way down the steps.

I peered into the thickening darkness, watching the rain shift and billow on the wind like a curtain. Another flash of lightning lit the heaving water, and whether it was eyesight or sixth sense, I saw it: a frail boat hopelessly far from any shore, tossing like a child's abandoned toy. Before the thunder sounded, I was flying into the wind, weaving up and down, in and out, seeking the stream that would take me where I wanted to go. Wind is like water the way it moves, multi-layered. The trick is not to fight it, to ride it. Wind-borne, I was soon hovering above Peter's imperiled boat. Yes, as it is written, my beloved was asleep in the stern while the waves broke into the boat. Meanwhile, his terrified disciples bellowed orders at each other as they struggled to gain control of the sails—impossible with the constantly shifting lake wind.

"Master," sobbed poor Peter, "Master, wake up!"

"What does he know about boats!" A man I hadn't met snarled at Peter. "It's his fault we're out here in the first place. Didn't we all tell him it wasn't safe to cross!"

"Shut up and pull your weight, Judas!" snapped Andrew. "Matthew, either help or get down. Don't lean over the side."

"But I'm going to be sick," the erstwhile tax collector wailed. "I hate boats!"

"Master, please, wake up!" Peter pleaded. "Don't you care? We are lost!"

It was true; they needed help; or they were all going to be fish food, which might be a fitting end, considering that most of them were fishermen and all of them ate fish. But I wasn't interested in poetic justice as I fought my way through the updrafts, and landed on my favorite perch: my beloved's head.

"A dove!" someone cried. "In the storm! It's a sign!"

"Master, master, wake up. A dove!"

Jesus lifted his head and felt for me as a huge wave hit the side of the boat, nearly capsizing it. Yet his hand was calm, steady. He held his palm over my breast, and I knew he felt my heart beating. Satisfied that he recognized me, I fluttered into the air again, just above the boat. I knew what to do. I had called a storm once, called a tidal bore. My father had turned and walked into the wave, the door to his own realm, land under the wave. I was his daughter as well as the daughter of the eight greatest weather witches in the world. If I could call a storm, surely I could calm one.

As I set to work, I was in two places at once. I was the dove, riding the wind above the boat, and I was standing on the tower. I had called the tidal bore by unleashing the full force of my rage and grief, passions so elemental that they became the elements. Now I opened myself just as wide and sent my love out into the storm, strong and steady as the sun, my love not only for Jesus, but for the storm itself, its power and, yes, beauty. My love permeated the whirling fury of wind, rain and wave, and called it by its secret name. And the storm came to me. In my hands, the storm, a roaring, smashing thing, grew smaller. I not only shaped the storm but soothed it until it slept in my palm. Then I folded it into my heart where it dissolved altogether.

The wind now still, I flew high above the boat (yes, I was showing off a little) to catch the last light on my wings. It was a beautiful evening, fresh and clear and vivid. People spoke of it for years afterwards, the loveliness and calm that so suddenly and inexplicably spread over the lake and sky.

"Why are you so frightened?" my beloved said to the trembling, sodden twelve. "Have you still no faith?"

"Who can this be?" they murmured to each other. "Even the wind and the sea obey him?"

Jesus looked up at me, right into my bird's eye, and smiled. And then I was back in my own shape on the tower, wet to the bone, tired, but content.

CHAPTER FIFTY-ONE

HELP!

Maybe you are thinking that saving Jesus' life was becoming habitual with me, a bit obsessive-compulsive even. Those of you who are paying attention to the prophecies and keeping count of near-resurrection experiences may be wondering: "Does this episode mark the third time she's given him back his life?" Don't worry; it doesn't. First of all, Jesus was perfectly capable of calming the storm himself, and is on record as having done so. Believe whom you will. Second, I didn't save just his life but the lives of all those men who were to cause me (and the rest of the world, in my opinion) so much trouble later on. Really, it was no big deal. My mothers would have been pleased, but not unduly impressed.

No amount of love, weather-witchery, or psychic attunement on my part could keep my beloved out of trouble for long. And besides, I didn't sign on for that job. "You are the lovers of the world," Dwynwyn had prophesied. And what is love but a four-letter word for trouble?

A few nights later, I woke up suddenly, thinking it was raining, but the sky was starry, and the night was still. Then a spray of small pebbles and dirt came flying onto the roof. I got up and looked over the wall.

"Maeve!" the voice I loved best in the world called softly, barely above a whisper. "Maeve, please. Let me in quick before anyone sees me here!"

I didn't bother with my trimmed lamp for this bridegroom; I ran down in the dark and opened the gate. I was very glad to see him—or rather sense him in the moonless night; I could feel the gladness spreading to all my extremities. For a moment I exulted. Then I decided to take umbrage, deliberately, almost luxuriantly, because I could.

"So. You don't want anyone to see you sneaking into a whorehouse, Rabbi? If you are ashamed of me, of this Temple, where you were welcomed naked and half-dead, then turn around right now."

"Maeve," was all he said, his voice full of pain and bewilderment.

I have to tell you the hardness of my heart isn't worth much—the thinnest of veneers over a hopelessly melted center, just enough crustiness to add interest. We stood for a time, the spring sounding unnaturally loud in contrast to our silence. We both sensed that we were on a new footing with each other, but neither of us knew how to take the first step.

"Are you hungry?" I asked at length, remembering that I was the priestess and he, once again, the god-bearing stranger.

"Famished."

"Come on then."

I pulled him inside and bolted the gate securely behind him. We tiptoed to the kitchen stores, not wanting to rouse the house, and carried off a small feast of wine, bread, olives and figs to the roof.

"Are you in trouble?" I asked when his hunger was appeased.

"No, yes, not really," he answered variously. "It's...it's just all getting out of hand. I had to get away from all of them, from everyone. I didn't know where else to go."

This was not the most romantic of confessions. No "I miss you." No "I had to see you." But I decided to let it pass. I knew this man. He was tired, more than tired. All other considerations were moot. His head was nodding over his cup of wine.

"Come, *cariad*." I reached for his hand. "You need to sleep. The tower is too exposed, and it will be dawn soon. I'm going to take you to the inner chamber of the Temple where no one will see you or disturb you."

I made a bed for my beloved in the same chamber where I had first received him, the walls depicting Osiris in Astarte's sacred grove, the air heavy with the evening's scents of incense and oils. I covered him with a fine, woven cloth, but I did not lie down next to him. He fell asleep, the way he had fallen onto the food, with a kind of sensual gratitude. I stayed awake, watching him, feasting on the sight of him. The lines in his face had deepened; my eyes wandered his face as it mapped a journey I could trace. His hair had grown wild, into what you'd call dreadlocks. The look suited him, earthy and otherworldly at the same time. At last I let my vision drift and blur, so that I could see his aura flickering around him. Despite his fatigue the colors were bright, fiery, almost too strong, as if they would consume him.

"Maeve," he cried without seeming to wake. "Maeve."

I turned the lamp low, but left it burning in case he woke up disoriented. Then I curled up next to him. He was trembling in his sleep. When I woke again, Jesus was sitting a few feet away, watching me as intently as I had watched him.

"I raised a child from the dead, Maeve," he said without preamble.

Maybe it was because I had just woken up and was still half in the dream world, but somehow I was not surprised.

"Tell me," I said.

"I hardly know where to begin."

He had always had this problem, I recalled. The druids asked about his ancestors and his answer included a couple of thousand years of Jewish history. That's why parables were good for him; they gave him a short, poetic form to work within. Not that I know anything about brevity myself.

"Start from after the storm," I suggested. "That's where I left off."

Most people can't smile and frown at the same time, but my beloved managed it.

"Nice bit of weather witchery, by the way," he acknowledged, his tone off-hand.

"It was nothing," I tossed back.

"But you don't need to keep doing that."

"Doing what?"

"Keeping tabs on me, saving my life. I can handle it."

I raised my right eyebrow in one perfectly skeptical arch. "Honey, even your dumbest disciple knew not to go out that far on the lake that day. Do you ever listen to anyone?" He started to answer, but I cut him off. "I mean besides your precious god."

"No," he admitted. "Anyway, do you want to hear the story or not?"

So I shut up and heard his account of his first foray among the gentiles. On the day of the storm, he had been headed towards the country of the Gerasenes across the lake. People from a village there had requested his services as an exorcist.

I haven't told you much about his encounters with demons—apart from the story that he exorcised seven of mine. (In Celtic cosmology, we have the Fomorians but instead of exorcising them, we just make sure they have enough to eat.) Demons, and the demoniacs they possessed, seemed to be rampant in Palestine. The scribes put forth the argument that Jesus had the power to command the little devils, because he worked for their ruler Beelzebul. The demons, however, disagreed; they're on record as recognizing his divine nature before anyone else did, as in: "Oh, shit, here comes the Son of the Most High God. Now we're fucked." (My translation.)

Help!

The Gerasene demoniac was a terrible worry to the village. He was so violently possessed that he snapped any chains and fetters anyone managed to slap on him. No one could control or confine him (though why they felt they had to when he was living out among the tombs doing no harm to anyone else, I don't know). Maybe their intentions were kindly; the distraught man passed his time gashing himself with stones. Or maybe they were tired simply of the incessant howling. Demons are notoriously noisy. This particular set of demons (for it turned out to be a large infestation) was very clever.

"What do you want with me Jesus, son of the Most High," they hailed him. "In the name of God, don't torture me!"

"What is your name?" Jesus asked, sensibly enough; it's always good to know whom you're up against, and the demons had the jump on him in that respect.

"My name is legion; for we are many."

Then the poor, bruised demoniac started pleading on his demons' behalf. "Don't send them out of the country, Jesus, please." Perhaps he had grown fond of them. Who knows? The demons took full advantage of the man's pity and Jesus's dilemma. For demons, upon exorcism, don't simply vanish in a puff of smoke.

"Look, there's a whole herd of pigs over there. Send us into the swine," they begged. "Let us enter them."

"You did what they *said*?" I interrupted the story. "Didn't it occur to you that they might be trying to trick you?"

Jesus looked a little sheepish, if you can conceive of the Good Shepherd that way.

"Well, unclean spirits have to go somewhere. Otherwise they're just wandering around loose. Cast out one demon, and he might come back with seven of his friends. It's a problem. Besides, they had asked me in God's name not to torture them."

"You're a prince," I said. "So what happened next?"

"They went mad."

"The pigs?"

"Of course the pigs," he said irritably. "They started to snort and scream and then they stampeded over a cliff and into the sea where they…drowned."

"The pigs drowned! How many?"

There was an uncomfortable pause. "They said about two thousand."

That puts *my* alleged case of demonic possession into perspective.

"They?" I queried.

"The Gerasenes."

"Frankly, I'm surprised they didn't throw you off the cliff after the pigs!" My sympathies were all with the Gerasenes at this point. "Do you know how much food and wealth those pigs represent? If the Gerasenes were Celts, they would have spitted and roasted you. I'm surprised you got out of there alive."

"I am, too," he admitted. "And for a while, I thought I wouldn't. There was a whole mob gathered, but they appeared to be even more afraid than they were angry."

"So what did they do to you?"

"They kept spitting and making signs with their hands, I suppose to ward off evil and bad luck. Then the headman came forward and said, 'Leave, Jesus, whoever and whatever you are. Just please leave and never come back.' And so I got out of there."

"What happened to the man you healed?"

"He is now fully clothed in his right mind. He wanted to come with me, but I told him to go home to the Decapolis—apparently he'd been exiled—and tell his friends how much God has done for him, the great mercy God has shown him."

"God?"

"Yes, God. It's not me that casts out unclean spirits and heals the sick; it's the power of the Most High within me. Surely, you, of all people, understand that."

"I suppose that would explain the pigs then."

"What *about* the pigs? Why do you keep harping on them?"

"Your god has a thing about pig-eating. But he shouldn't go imposing his rules on people who don't worship him. I mean, one people's unclean animal is another people's barbecue. You ought to send the Gerasenes a shipment of salt fish by way of apology."

"Well, maybe you're right, but you're missing the point. The man was *healed*!"

"I didn't miss that point; I'm just making one of my own. But let's not argue about it now. Didn't you say you raised someone from the dead?"

"Oh, that." He seemed almost embarrassed.

"Get on with the story."

That evening Jesus and the Twelve went back to Capernaum. He'd barely set foot on the ground when a crowd began to gather. Not unusual, but Jesus had hoped they'd be able to press through it to Peter's house where Priscilla would feed them and hold the crowd at bay while they snatched a few hours of sleep. But Jairus, the president of the synagogue, who had till now disdained this wild and woolly teacher from the hill country, burst through the crowd and flung himself at Jesus's feet.

"My little daughter is dying," he wailed. "Please, I beg you, come and lay your hands on her."

"How could I say no, Maeve? So I went with him, and the crowd followed, like some huge, panting beast. That's the part that's hard. When I am face to face with someone, I know what to do. It is *given* to me what to do. But that crowd, always pressing at me, always hungry, always needing…like a rising tide I can't escape.

"I was walking as fast as I could, trying to ignore the crowd, when something happened. You know how it feels when the fire flows through your hands into someone. Only I hadn't touched anyone, someone had just taken it from me, stolen it. I whirled around and confronted the crowd; they stopped still and stared, the way cattle do.

"'Who touched me!' I demanded.

"I was angry, Maeve, maybe I shouldn't have been, but I'd had it. Peter tried to reason with me; with such a large crowd, who could know who'd touched me. And meanwhile poor Jairus was wringing his hands. I don't know what made me persist, but I asked again, I'm afraid I shouted: 'Who touched me!'

"Finally, a woman came forward and fell at my feet—"

"There's an awful lot of falling at your feet in this story," I commented.

"Way too much," he agreed. "The poor woman was terrified, Maeve. I felt badly for yelling. She was afraid I'd strike her or the crowd would turn on her, because she was unclean, and yet she had touched the hem of my garment."

"Unclean how?"

"She confessed she had been bleeding from her womb for twelve years. When I felt the fire flow out of me, that's when she touched my robe."

For those of you who don't know, contact with a "menstruous" woman (the term used in Jewish oral law), not to mention a woman with chronic female ailments, would make a man unclean for seven days. He would have to do rituals for purification.

"A strange thing happened to me then. I looked at her and felt such sorrow, not only for her illness, but for the shame she'd suffered with it."

"So what did you say to her?"

"'Your faith has healed you. Go in peace.'"

"Did the crowd let her alone?"

"They parted like the waters of the Red Sea to let her pass. For a moment there was such silence, and then someone came running to Jairus shouting, 'Your daughter is dead; let the teacher go; there is no more he can do.'" You might wonder if I reproached myself for the delay, but there was no time for that. 'Do not fear, only believe,' I heard myself saying. I had no idea what I meant; or what the Most High intended, only that I had to go to the child."

I could picture Jesus walking through the cramped streets, lamplight pooling from doorways. I could feel his silence and stillness deepening in the midst of all the commotion, the sounds of the crowd becoming like distant surf. But when they reached the house, a wave of grief rushed at him, threatening to overwhelm him. The whole household was wailing and keening. He spoke more sharply than he meant to:

"Why all this commotion! The child is not dead but asleep. Out, all of you. Out!"

He took with him only the child's mother and father and Peter and Andrew and went into the room where the child was laid out, a lovely little girl of about six years old.

"And *was* she only asleep?" I prompted; for he had paused in his narrative and seemed to go far away or deep inside himself. I sensed it was hard for him to tell the next part, and yet clearly he needed to.

"She was very still," Jesus said at length. "She wasn't breathing. I didn't think about what to do. I just took her hand. That's all. It was cool but not stiff yet. That's how death feels in the first few minutes, like cooling earth as though the body is turning back to clay. The same clay the Most High took in his hands and breathed life into.

"As I held her hand, I could feel a current of life flowing from me into her, feeding into her, like a stream into a river. And I just knew: the way back was not blocked; it was open. Then I bent over her and sent that current of life into my breath. And my breath flowed over her and into her. I could see it; it looked like honey, like fire. Like both at once. I remembered how you put honey on my lips, Maeve, and brought me back to life. So I asked for honey, and I put it on her lips. Her tongue came alive and tasted it."

He stopped again, buried his face in his hands and wept. I wanted to go to him, comfort him, but I knew it wasn't time. So I just sat with him, witnessed him silently.

"Then I said to her," he resumed 'Talitha cum! Little girl, get up.'"

Even in telling the story, after the event, his tone carried an authority that no one dead or living could ignore. The chamber inside Temple Magdalen resounded with it.

"And she opened her eyes. They were so clear, so truthful. They reminded me of yours, Maeve. And she got up and stretched, as if she'd just had a nap, though she looked a little bewildered when her parents started crying and kissing her frantically. I told them to get the poor kid something to eat. I've noticed that people have a tendency to forget the simple, practical things."

"Miracles can be so distracting."

"But it wasn't a miracle, Maeve!" He didn't want to be teased.

"What do you call it then?"

"I don't know," he struggled. "It just seemed like what needed to happen. You know, rain falls down, sparks fly up. Day follows night. A mother feeds her baby. A lover longs for…" He broke off.

I waited but he left the sentence drifting, unraveling.

"*Cariad*, all these things you name, they are a kind of miracle. But death does not reverse itself. Water does not flow upstream."

"Oh, but it does, it can! How can you, of all people, not know that, daughter of the Shining Isles where the rivers reverse with the tides? I'm not saying death can always reverse itself, but when there's an opening…or when it is the will of…"

He was having trouble finishing his sentences, but I could not finish them for him.

"Maybe it doesn't matter." He opened his hands in a gesture of helplessness and surrender. "I can't explain it. The trouble is, people think I can work miracles, and it scares them. Even Peter and Andrew. They were shaking; I don't think they meant to, but they backed away from me—like I was a leper or something…something not human. So I used their fear. I ordered them not to tell anyone what had happened, to go and wait with the others at Peter's house. Then I asked Jairus if there was a back way out of his house. I covered myself with a cloak and he led me down an alley to the open fields, and I…I came here. I ran here. No one knows where I am, not even Peter."

I felt a twinge of the jealousy I thought I'd overcome. Jesus had fled to me for a moment's respite, but Peter was his now his closest companion. Peter's house was his official headquarters. No doubt Jesus would be gone in the morning.

"Maeve, my beloved," he said tenderly, as if he had read my mind, which he probably had. "Will you hold me in your arms for a little while?"

Remember what I told you about my heart?

So he lay down again, and I held him. The fire of the stars flowed from my hands, from my breasts, my womb, from my very toes into every part of him. Rivers of fire, sweet and golden as honey. The way back to me was open. Maybe I could have blocked it, but I didn't try.

CHAPTER FIFTY-TWO

WHAT?

I woke again in the dawn chill. The lamp had burned down, but there was enough light coming in through the natural chimney that I could see Jesus pacing back and forth. My eyes were at the level of his feet; beautiful as they were, they were in need of attention—a thorough soaking and oiling at least, though I supposed it would be best not to smooth away the calluses. He needed them. But what was the use in contemplating spa treatments. He was clearly chafing to go. At least he'd had the decency to wait until I was awake.

"So you're off, then," I said briskly, sitting up and pushing my hair out of my face. No lovemaking, no lingering embraces. Better that way. I had a life, after all; I had my sovereignty, for goddess' sake. It was not so bad. "You must have something to eat before you go, or Judith will have my head."

I stood up and stretched

"Maeve." He alarmed me by suddenly plummeting to the floor, nearly knocking me off balance.

"What is the matter with you, Jesus? Are you sick?"

"I was throwing myself at your feet."

"Well, please don't. You're not very good at it."

"Maeve." He got up. "I have something to say to you."

"You don't need to say anything. I already know—"

"Yes, I do need to, and no, you don't know."

His fierceness silenced me. I eyed him warily.

"Get on with it, then."

"We are to be married."

Now it may be obvious to you who he meant. But my first thought was: Mary of Bethany, that bitch! Not pretty, but there it is.

"Well, aren't you going to say something?" he prompted after a moment.

"What to you expect me to say?" I didn't want to lose my dignity, but since it was inevitable, I decided I might as well throw it away with both hands. "I search for you for nearly half my life; I bring you back from the dead, restore you to health, just so you can leave again, tromp around all over the place with a bunch of village idiots, come back to me when you need a place to hide and a quick fix, and now, now...*this*! I may be a priestess of Isis, but if you think I'm going to be the all-forgiving, all-comforting, all-nurturing, eternally-on-tap-holy-whore-with-the heart-of-mush, you can forget about it, just forget it. I don't care about visions and prophecies. That's it. It's over. Long life to you. Goodbye. Don't come back."

"I didn't think you'd take it like that." Jesus looked completely nonplussed.

"How I am supposed to take it? Look, if you want to get married, it's your business. It has nothing to do with me."

"What do you mean? It has everything to do with you. I can't do it without you."

"I told you!" I was livid now. "I may be a whore, but I am not your mother or your nursemaid. I don't intend to hold your hand while you marry her."

"Marry who?"

"Marry Mary."

"Mary who?"

This is starting to sound like some silly knock knock joke, I know.

"Mary of Bethany!" Then an even worse possibility occurred to me. "Or is there someone else?"

"There is." A sly grin spread over his face.

"Did I or did I not just tell you to leave?"

"Don't you want to know who it is before I go?"

"No."

"The curiosity will eat away at you. You'll want to forget, but you won't be able to. You're better off knowing. Trust me, Maeve."

Bastard. "Make it quick."

"You. Maeve. You. I'm to marry you."

I am afraid my mouth dropped open, clichéd as it sounds, and I gaped at him.

"Are you asking me to marry you?" I said when I'd recovered myself somewhat.

"Not precisely asking, though it occurs to me that I do need your consent. I was trying to tell you, but I've made a mess of it."

Full sunlight now reached the inner chamber, long fingers of it, touching our feet. It felt warm, reassuring. Normal. The temple cats would be taking sunbaths; the little girls would be gathering flowers for Isis. I had a life here, a real life, a good life.

"I don't understand," I said slowly. "I'm a gentile, a whore, a pagan priestess. You can't marry me. It's impossible."

"With God all things are possible."

"God?" Here I broke a sweat. "What's God got to do with it?"

"The Most High sent me a dream."

"Are you sure it was him?"

"We were at some well-appointed villa in the hills—"

"A well-appointed villa?"

"Stop interrupting, Maeve. It was in the hill country, but it wasn't Nazareth. There were lots of people there, and they were all happy and tipsy. The air was fresh and spicy; you could get drunk just breathing it. We were in a vineyard. People's feet were still stained purple from the grape harvest. And they were singing to us: Love is as strong as death."

As he spoke, I could not only see the dream, it was as if I remembered it, too. As if I had dreamed it again and again, all my life. It was all mixed up with another dream: of a tree, and a garden of spice, the dew still on the ground. I turned my gaze from the dream world back to Jesus, and I saw tears running down his cheeks. Like his mother, he wept soundlessly.

"Esus, Jesus, my beloved." I touched his cheek, and then tasted one of the tears; Sweet, sweet and salt all mixed up together. "That is a beautiful dream. But...but how do you know it means we are to marry?"

"Because, it's the marriage song, from the Song of Songs. It's always sung at weddings. I was dreaming of our wedding, Maeve."

"Ah!" Now my tears were flowing, and it was hard for me to speak. "But it was a dream, *cariad*, a dream of the Otherworld maybe. The world beyond and before time."

"No, *this* world, *in* time," he said a little sharply. "Just after harvest, and definitely some place in Galilee. The Eternal One often speaks in dreams, and this one is so clear."

"How do you know *your* god sent you that dream?" That was the part that bugged me most; that marrying me was his god's idea, not his. "Look where you are."

I gestured towards the walls, the mosaic sacred grove, Osiris in the tree, and Isis who had searched the world for him, finding him at last. For just a moment Jesus looked taken aback, and then he actually shrugged. And I started to tremble, as I realized the implication of my own words—for me. What if Isis had sent him that dream? What if she had made some deal with Yahweh behind my back. But if she had, why hadn't the dream come to me? Because you wouldn't get it, she whispered, like a wind in the river reeds.

"I'm not going to argue theology with you, Maeve."

"You're not?" I felt desperate. "Since when?"

"Since now. Does it matter where a dream comes from if it's true?"

"Now that's a question for theological debate, if I ever heard one. Try it out at the Temple porticoes, why don't you. Come back and tell me what the rabbis decide."

"Maeve, you're being evasive. You're raising questions to avoid the question."

"Which is?"

"Will you marry me?"

"So *now* you're asking me."

"Yes," he said simply. "I want you to be with me, Maeve."

I noted the phrasing; he wanted *me* to be with *him*. If he wanted to be with me, he could just stay here at Temple Magdalen. I had been willing to go with him before. He was the one who had insisted on going alone. Now I wondered: did I want to go with him? Could I endure the crowds, the disciples?

"*Cariad*, I am with you," I hedged. "I've never not been, even when we're apart. Why do we have to be married to be together? What do you mean by marriage?"

"That no one and nothing can come between us."

Not Peter? I did not say aloud. Not the sick and the demon-ridden? Not your god? Not your... I would not finish the thought, let alone voice it.

"What is your answer, Maeve?"

He would not ask again. I knew that. Some dreadful decisive moment was here. Perhaps you do not understand my hesitation. You're thinking: you love him; you want to stand beneath the Tree of Life with him. What is your problem?

"Jesus, understand, if you marry me, you marry *me*: healer, whore, priestess. I am who I am. Do you want to marry *me*? What is your answer, Jesus?"

We locked eyes and wills, two flames, *love no flood can quench, no torrent drown*. One not to be subsumed in the other. Our whole story flared between us, a lightning vision too swift to hold.

"Maeve, beloved." He took my hands. "I know you. You're wild and thorny and sweet as the roses that always seem to be in bloom at Temple

Magdalen. I want to marry you. And I am who I am—which may not be much of a bargain—homeless, hounded, disreputable, and called to preach and heal by a God you deny. It doesn't make any sense; no one's going to approve, but the dream is real, Maeve. It's about us. Who we are."

The lovers of the world.

The words sounded silently between us. We both heard them. We stared at each other, almost sickeningly aware that we still didn't know what the words meant, but if we went ahead with this crazy dream we would find out.

"All right," I said at last. "I will marry you. On one condition."

"No conditions."

"No marriage then."

"What?" he sighed.

"We invite your mother to the wedding."

"Oy vey!" he said (or the first century equivalent), and he dropped my hands as he threw his up. "All right. So be it."

Jesus left soon after to go find his disciples. I confess I cherished a small hope that when they heard that he intended to marry me, they would peel away, decide he was off his nut, in need of an exorcist himself. They would come to their senses and go back to their fishing nets or tax collecting or terrorizing the Roman settlements or whatever it was they did before Jesus came and utterly disrupted their lives—as he was now proposing to disrupt mine. It is a measure of their devotion or their insanity (take your pick) that they did not.

I had my own companions to face. As luck, or Isis, would have it, Paulina was there that morning to go over the quarterly accounts. After the hymns, I invited Berta, Dido, Reginus, Timothy, Judith, and Paulina to the inner chamber (it somehow seemed fitting) where I broke the news.

"What!" A unanimous chorus followed by a unanimous moment of silence.

"Ah, *liebling*!" Berta clutched her heart and began to sob—she definitely did not have the gift of silent tears. "So clearly I remember the little *novica* telling us her sad, sweet story in the baths at the Vine and Fig Tree. 'I will find him,' you said. Do you remember that? And awful Dido telling you to forget him. And even I thinking he could be no more than a precious memory. Now, now you will be his *wife*!"

I turned green at the gills and wished I had not eaten so many figs.

"Did you forget the wife part, Red?" asked Dido astutely.

I nodded.

"Aw, honey," said Reginus. "You survived being a slave, surely you can deal with being a wife."

"But I don't know anything about being a wife. I don't even know any wives."

"What do you mean?" Paulina was offended. "I'm a wife."

That was hardly comforting. Claudius had oppressed her, and Lucius was oppressed by her, although I had to admit he didn't seem to mind.

"I was a wife," said Judith wistfully. "What I wouldn't give to be a wife again."

"I'm sort of a wife," said Timothy, giving Reginus a fond look.

"Your Queen Maeve," said Berta, "she was a wife."

I wondered how Jesus would feel about my having a lover or thirty men a day, if I chose. And how I would feel about not having "one man in the shadow of another."

"It's, it's just not me somehow," I said lamely.

"Well, you should have thought of that before," Dido gave me the archest of her looks. "It's too late now."

"Is it?" I appealed.

"If our dearest Rabbi is crazy enough to marry you, Mary, jump at it," advised Judith. "I can teach you how to keep a proper Jewish house."

"A house? What house?" I was alarmed.

"Oh, don't fret, Red," said Paulina. "Worry about housekeeping later. The question now is where and when the wedding will be."

Fortifying myself with large gulps from the wineskin we'd started passing around, I told them about the well-appointed villa and the stained feet.

"I know just the place!" cried Paulina. "And we have just about two months to plan. Oh my dears, what a lot to do. I will arrange it all—no quiet, all of you. I won't take no. You all rushed me through my own wedding and spoiled all my fun. We're going to do this one my way. Didn't Jesus say there were a *lot* of guests? Well, who else can organize an event like that? You must think of me as your mother, Maeve. Every bride needs a mother. And I'll send a message to Joseph at once; he can be your father."

"What does that make Lucius?"

"Lucius? What about Lucius? He'll do as he's told. He always does. Now no more questions. Just leave everything to me."

"I must ask one question," said Dido. "Maeve." She never called me Maeve. "Where will you live after you marry?"

"Sweet Isis!" chimed in Paulina. "You're right, Dido. And what will you live on! He's very handsome, but he hasn't got a *denar*—or what do the Jews call their coins?"

"*Shekels*," supplied Judith.

"I must tell Joseph to have a talk with your betrothed. If he's going to be a husband, he must have some reliable way to keep you."

The inner chamber seemed close and stuffy. What was I doing within walls in the first place, looking at a mosaic sacred grove? I was bred for the real thing. I started to feel depressed.

"Red?" prompted Dido. "Are we losing you, Red?"

Her question was resonant, textured with layers and layers of meaning.

"Are you going to follow him?" Dido pressed.

"No," I was suddenly clear about one thing at least. "I am not going to follow him. I will go with him. As to where we will live…" There was the sky full of clouds or stars, sun or rain. There were the hills, lush or barren. There were our feet, walking and walking over the earth. "I don't know if we will live any one place. But I sure as hell won't be staying at Peter's house when we're here. So I have to ask all of you a question. Is Temple Magdalen still my home, even if I'm not, not a …" I couldn't bear to say it.

"Not a whore?" Dido finished.

"But of course, she is a whore!" Berta was scandalized. "Once a whore, always a whore. Is that what is worrying you, *liebling*? Of course, your home is here."

Berta came and enveloped me in her arms, as everyone murmured assent and reassurance, but it was Dido's pronouncement I waited to hear.

"At Temple Magdalen," Dido spoke with authority as the high priestess she was, "people come and go, at need or will. They are free. We are free. Red, Maeve, my sister. You found this place; you founded it with us. How could Temple Magdalen not be your home? But I want to tell you something: life here will go on with or without you. That's the highest compliment I can pay you."

"What do you mean?"

"You are free, Maeve."

CHAPTER FIFTY-THREE

WEDDING EVE

T he excruciating preparations, during which I have been measured and fitted, fussed over and bossed (till I took to hiding in the olive grove) are over at last. It is the day before the wedding. Well before dawn, my hand-maidens (so to speak) dress me in gold and veil my face and generally ready me to be abducted from my maiden home (i.e. a notorious whorehouse) by the Bridegroom and his pals (the Twelve who have somehow been strong-armed into playing the role of traditional groomsmen). It is all very silly, I know, but believe me I have had no say in anything.

Picture the procession, me enthroned as a queen on a litter beneath a canopy of golden cloth; the poor put-upon disciples spelling each other as they haul me thirteen uphill miles to the "well-appointed villa" we've borrowed from a friend of Lucius's. Well-appointed is an understatement. Paulina and Joseph (my parents!) have spared no expense and considered every detail. The accommodations are lavish, plush cushions and couches everywhere; rich hangings; fresh flowers and fruit; the extensive baths heated and ready. The food is exotic and abundant. As for the wine, there are rivers of it endlessly flowing.

Or rather the supply should have been endless. As you already know, the wine ran out at the Wedding at Cana. (Surely you've guessed where we are.) If you want to know why the wine ran out, well, let's go straight to the party—or rather parties. For on the wedding eve there are two: one for the men, one for the women.

Of course I was not at the men's party, but Reginus was our mole. Here's how it looked to him at the outset. There were the Twelve, huddled in one corner, resisting the efforts of Paulina's genial husband to get them to mingle, and telling off-color jokes about shepherds and sheep—never mind that Jesus's brothers were in the carpentry business; apparently lake dwellers think all hill people fuck sheep. Lucius had no better luck with Jesus's brothers hunkered down in another corner telling off-color jokes about fishermen and fish. The brothers wanted no truck with the disciples, those low-life, lake scum, who were encouraging Jesus in his delusions. As for Lucius, despite his origins as a humble laborer, the Jews couldn't forget that he was a Roman, a desecrator of graveyards, and a builder of decadent spa cities. Nor did any of the Galileans have any use for Joseph, a rich ex-pat who went around spouting Greek philosophy and came home only to exercise his inherited Temple privileges. Then of course there was Reginus—a Roman poof and proud of it, and Timothy (who used to be an honest if inept fisherman) holding his hand. Only shy unassuming Lazarus, whose feet were still purple from the harvest, drew no dirty looks from any quarter.

And what about our bridegroom? He was not fazed in the least. He knew exactly what to do: keep pouring the wine.

The women's party was just as ill assorted, not only various and sundry gentiles, Jewish lake and hill dwellers, but perhaps more important divisions: whores, a madam (Domitia Tertia and Succula had come from Rome!) widows, wives, virgins, and one extremely improbable bride. But I will say the women were doing better at mixing it up. Domitia Tertia was paying her respects to Miriam. Though they made an odd pair, the tall Roman courtesan and the short Galilean widow, I noticed a similarity between them—they belonged to a peculiar aristocracy that has nothing to do with class or country. They recognized each other. Perhaps, too, Domitia felt she was more fit for the role of my stand-in mother than Paulina.

Priscilla and the other disciples' wives had embraced Jesus's dour sister Leah (I finally learned her name). They appeared to be telling tales at Jesus's expense, and Leah was almost pink with the pleasure of complaining about him freely. Martha and Judith, both used to being in charge of the care and feeding of the multitudes, spent some time sizing each other up. Instead of competing for who could be most competent and helpful, they cooperated in a coup against Paulina, who had organized the party but was now losing her edge as she slid deeper and deeper into her cups.

As for the bride, I was having a hard time tearing myself away from the whores' huddle, so comforting and familiar. Succula, of course, wanted us to tell her every detail about Temple Magdalen, and we were just as eager to catch up with her. A free woman now, she had become a priestess, too, serving as a liaison between the Vine and the Fig Tree and its affiliate the Temple of Isis Obsequens. Domitia Tertia and Aemiliana had joined forces in rescuing and training abandoned Roman street girls. Succula had found her vocation as novice mistress.

"Aemiliana would have liked to come," Succula said, "but the temple is still illegal, you know, and it's not safe for her to travel. She sent you a gift. I tucked it away with your things. Be sure you find it: an alabaster jar of spikenard ointment. She said: Tell Maeve she must save it for the time of the anointing."

"What does that mean?" I asked, feeling an odd sense of foreboding.

"I don't know. I'm not sure she does either. But she said you will know when the time comes to break open the jar. Keep it safe till then. It must have cost the earth! Now, Red, as much as I want you to myself, you better go mingle, honey. Who is that fierce-looking woman standing by herself? Someone needs to pluck the poor thing's eyebrows."

I looked and there across the courtyard was Mary B; she seemed to draw all the shadows to her, as she stood defiantly in the gloom.

"That's her. The Mary he was supposed to marry."

"I think she's waiting for you, Red," Dido said.

"Ah, *liebling*, you must go comfort her," urged Berta.

"Comfort her? She could be married to him with a slew of kids right now. She's the one who refused him, remember?"

"That doesn't mean she wants you to have him. Go on," Succula gave me a push. "Go face her."

Mary B was too honest to pretend she did not see me coming toward her. Her eyebrows did bristle and they almost met, just they way Jesus's did when he was pensive. Really, they were two of kind. Perhaps, I thought wildly, it's not too late for them. There was a whole night still before the wedding.

"Hello, Mary," I said.

"Hello, Mary," she said back.

"Call me Maeve, please."

"Miriam of Nazareth told me you had changed your name to Mary of Magdala."

"She changed it, not me. Why would I take the same name as you? It's way too confusing."

She looked at me but didn't answer. Her lips twitched; I couldn't tell if she was fighting a smile or had developed a nervous tic.

"Do you mind?" I asked abruptly. "Do you mind that he is marrying me?"

"Not at all," she said stiffly, and she turned her face away.

This woman needed a drink, I decided. So did I.

"I'm going to get us some wine."

"Please don't trouble yourself on my account."

"Mary, I wasn't asking."

But it proved impossible to get to the wine without encountering Paulina, who latched onto me, partly because she was reaching the point where she needed some help standing.

"Now whose thish, Red?" Paulina squinted at Mary B, trying to get her into focus.

"This is Mary of Bethany," I said, though surely Paulina had met her before. "She and her sister, Martha, and brother, Lazarus, are close friends of Jesus."

"Oh, I know who you are," Paulina hiccupped. "You're Jesussesh old girlfriend."

It is hard for someone as sallow as Mary B to blush, but she managed it. If we hadn't been in a corner, I think she would have bolted. I took advantage of the moment and passed her the wineskin. She gave in and took a large swig.

"You know Red hash an old girlfriend here, too. What did you shay your name was, Jesusesh girlfriend?"

"Mary." She took another drink.

"Well, you should meet Red's girlfriend. Succula wheresh Succula? Funny your name ish Mary. Some people call Red, Mary, don't they, Red? So if Jesush calls out your name in bed, it won't matter, right?"

"Paulina!" I protested, and I looked around desperately for help.

"You know, I do that sometimesh when I've had a little too much to drink. But my hushband—he's a nice man—he doesn't notish. I don't know if he knowsh about Red. I still miss her. She was the besh in bed, I mean—much better than that asshole, what's his name, who got me pregnant. Red's a professional."

"Paulina, Mary is not interested in your past. Or mine."

"Shut up, Red, of course she is."

"Yes, it's fascinating," said Mary.

Bitch, I thought. She wanted to know the worst about me, which until that moment I had never thought of as bad. Just then Succula, who must have observed my plight, came over and put a protective arm around me.

"Oh, Mary, thish is who I was telling you about. Jesusesh old girlfriend meet Red's old girlfriend. I used to be so jealoush of you, Succula, and I know you were jealoush of me. But that was a long time ago. We're all friendsh now, right?"

"That's right," said Succula, catching on quickly. "Now come with me and we'll talk over old times." To me she mouthed, "I'll take her to the vomitorium."

Mary B passed me the wineskin. I took a long drink and passed it back.

"All right," she said, after taking another drink. "I do mind. I lied before. Sorry."

Suddenly I liked her much better.

"Is it because I'm a gentile whore with a slew of old lovers, male and female?" I asked with more curiosity than animosity; the wine was doing its work.

"No," she said simply.

I found I believed her. Conventional thinking was not one of her faults.

"What is it, then? You told me before that I was not of Israel, that I was a distraction that kept him from his purpose. But he's found his purpose now."

"Then do not interfere with it!" She grasped my shoulders and turned me towards her; our faces so close now that I could feel her breath. "He belongs only to God. He must be inviolate. Beyond male. Beyond female. Beyond flesh."

"I see," I said. "Like you."

After all, don't we all make him in our own image after our own likeness? And is it so wrong? Doesn't the lover of us all come to us in whatever way we can receive him? So I have thought since, but I confess my thoughts were not so charitable then. Mary closed her lips into a thin straight line, angry with herself for saying so much.

"You think if he marries me, he won't be yours," I goaded her.

"You are proving my point," she refused to be drawn into a defense of herself. "You are incapable of comprehending what is at stake. You make everything base, crude, personal. He is not mine. He is not yours. He is the Bridegroom of Israel. That is why you must not marry him. You wouldn't, if you honored our history, our laws, if you honored *him*. But all you care about is yourself, your own satisfaction. Your life is nothing but sensuality, fornication, idolatry. You! You are the very opposite of inviolate!"

"That is where you're wrong, Mary of Bethany," I leaned in closer, close enough to kiss her. "That is where you are wrong."

I could feel her wanting to recoil from me, but she held herself rigid. How this standoff would have ended, I'll never know. Just then, Jesus's sister, looking a little wasted, approached us.

"Mary, Ma wants you."

Mary B and I both turned. It dawned on me, that if I married Jesus (and Mary was making a better case against it than I liked to admit) this peremptory summons from Ma would be the first of many.

"Not you, Mary," she said to me. "You."

Mary of Bethany, former daughter-in-law-elect, bowed her head and followed, leaving me alone at my own party, which was, damn-it-all, mine, and I could cry if I wanted to. And suddenly I did want to. I looked around at the festooned courtyard, the couches where some people were still reclining, picking at the remains of a sumptuous feast. All these friends, lovers, and strangers. Did anyone really want me to marry Jesus? Did I? I thought with longing of the silent hills outside the villa where the almost moon rose unfettered into an open sky. Perhaps it was not too late to, well, do a bunk. Before I could pursue this line of thought, Paulina was back.

"All right, everybody, listen up."

Succula was trying to restrain her, but Paulina, now somewhat sobered up, threw her off. Paulina commanded a sort of transfixed, horrified silence that people were powerless to break, because secretly they were dying to find out what she would do next.

"Darling Succula tells me I've been dreadfully indiscreet. But we all know our beautiful bride was once a whore. Don't we? I mean, does anyone not know?"

No one answered.

"Well, never mind," Paulina went on. "The important thing to remember is that everyone, I mean all of us, even Red, can be a virgin again! Just like Venus—for those of you who don't know, she's the goddess of love, screws everybody." She might not be slurring, but that only made it worse; people didn't know how drunk she still was. "Venus turned into a virgin again every day by taking a bath. I'm telling you, it works. I should know." She winked. "So what we're going to do now is go to the spa and—"

"Have a mikvah," Judith jumped in with a gallant appeal to the Jewish guests. She loved me, in spite of everything, and she loved Jesus. She also loved celebrations and did not want to see our wedding party end in disaster when it had barely begun.

"That's right," agreed Paulina. "A mikspa. It's all ready. So let's all go have a nice dip, and then our bride will be as virgin as the day is long, I mean, as the day she was born. Come on, everybody. Let's go. Except you, Reginus!" She stopped and stared. "What are you doing here? Women only!"

"But the men's party is so boring," Reginus complained.

"Well, *liebling*," Berta threw her arm around him. "You'll just have to go liven it up. Come. We'll help you. What they need is a dancing girl, yes?"

"Oh, no!" said Reginus.

"Yes, yes!" we all chorused, even those who couldn't have guessed what Berta was proposing.

Then one of those magical, unpredictable moments happened. Someone started clapping a rhythm; others picked it up. First one then another started to ululate. Then everyone was singing, weaving wild melodies and harmonies in and out of each other. Dido and Berta tore off Reginus's tunic, and the women pulled at the gauzy hangings and began to veil him. Someone whipped out some kohl and lifted his veil to paint his eyes; another got out a pot of rouge. And in case you're wondering, it was not just the pagans and whores who got into the act. Reginus graciously succumbed, shaking his imaginary tits and wiggling his hips, holding still only when (could it possibly be?) Martha and Judith fastened a girdle of coins around him, while even Mary B joined in the clapping.

Then—you had to have been there—Ma, a.k.a. the Blessed Virgin Mary—started dancing with him, while her poor daughter lost it, shrieking with laughter and loudly threatening to lose control of her bladder. At last, with Reginus and Ma leading the way, we all danced in procession to the men's wing, our lively rhythms contrasting with, well, if you want to know the truth, drunken sailor songs. The kind of singing where everyone is standing and swaying, and holding on to the man next to him to keep from falling on his face. We peeped, then shoved Reginus into their midst, which did indeed liven up the party as the men, too, began to dance and make lewd gestures, the ones, that is, who did not keel over. I caught a glimpse of the bridegroom dancing, his head thrown back, hair wild, and as I was borne away to the mikspa to be made virgin, I heard the unmistakable sound of my beloved's laughter.

The acoustics in the mikspa were great. Yes, the villa had Roman-style baths complete with mosaics of cavorting half-naked seas-nymphs and Venus herself rising from the foam. The Jewish women averted their eyes even as they sang (rather lustily) their own erotic songs. We all got into the bath, and an impromptu ritual began, which consisted chiefly of everyone pouring something over my head while chanting largely incoherent invocations. I had become the center of everyone's attention, and for one intoxicating moment, I sensed that everyone adored not me (some of them didn't even like me) but the goddess in me. Venus, Isis, Asherah. Some old memory wakened in their flesh and they saw in my eyes their own radiance. Then, as one, they reached their hands under me and lifted me up. I was flying, floating weightless—like a child in my mothers' arms. The next instant they lowered me gently into the water, all the way under, to the source, the warm formless dark where we all began.

When we finally went to bed, we all passed out, sprawled companionably together on pillows and couches. I slept dreamlessly for a time; then I woke abruptly and completely, my heart pounding. I listened for a while, soothed by the sounds of breathing, snoring, sighs, wheezing, all rhythmic dark sea swells with sleeping birds floating on them. I could sink back down into sleep, but then I would be lost. I would wake to my wedding day, and the chaos and clamor would carry me through it willy-nilly. My sovereignty would sink beneath the waves forever. Mary of Bethany was right: this marriage was all wrong for both of us. Never mind what Jesus thought he dreamed that night, overwrought as he'd been and under the influence of a pagan goddess. Dreams could not be taken literally. They had to be interpreted, for goddess sake. I needed to interpret myself the hell out of this mess before it was too late.

I would just go. I could walk back on my own to Temple Magdalen. If Jesus wanted me, he could seek me like any other suppliant, that is, if Israel (his true bride) ever gave him the night off. I got to my feet and stepped over the sleeping bodies, limbs flung and tangled luxuriantly in drunken abandon. I left the chamber with its sour-sweat smell and stepped out into the cool night air. It had a tonic edge that cleared my head. I decided not to try the gates yet, in case a watchman saw me and raised the alarm. So I walked along the outside walls, feeling for a possible purchase, and I came to a place where a stone had come loose and left a small gap, probably because of the vine growing there. Perfect. I grasped the vine and wedged my foot in the crack and tried to pull myself up, but my foot slipped. I tried again and again. The third time, the vine tore loose, and I fell backwards—into a strong pair of arms.

"Need a boost?"

His mouth was close to my ear, his breath warm and as sour with wine as mine was. I regained my balance and turned to face him whom my soul loves.

"Were you going to leave without saying goodbye?"

He sounded merely curious, and that made me furious. Just once I wanted to be the one to leave. Here he was in my way—well, perhaps not exactly in my way, he'd offered to help me over the wall. But still, in my way. The very fact of him.

"Yes!" I said crossing my arms over the breasts that had cradled his head, the nipples that stood up at a glance from him, let alone a touch. Mary B was right. I was hopelessly crude and fleshy.

"So was I."

"You!" I said, part exclamation, part accusation. "What do you mean you were leaving! This whole ridiculous performance was your idea. How dare you! How dare you even think of leaving me here, flapping in the breeze, in front of all your precious disciples and your sanctimonious Mary of Bethany!"

I wanted to hurl myself at him, pummel him, scratch his face. But before I could, something held me back. A deep stillness had come over him, as if he had grown roots, as if the setting moon had come to rest in his branches. There was something terrible in his face, not sadness, not anger, something akin to dread. I stood watching him, tremor after tremor shaking me.

"Maeve."

There was such anguish in his voice; I couldn't help it, my arms reached out to him, moonlight spilling helplessly over the sea. He did not move to meet them. Slowly I lowered them again and waited, my own roots now, sinking into the soil.

"Do you remember when I was buried inside the Mound of the Dark Grove on Mona all alone for three days and nights? Do you remember the vision that came to me then?"

"Yes." I had been there, too, at his druid initiation, inside his dream, inside my vision of the cracked sky and lips, the terrible pain.

"The vision came again tonight. Clearer, more terrible, more true. Listen to me, Maeve. I am going to die."

"No!" My hands flew out again, as if to catch him as he stumbled or to pull him back from some dizzying edge.

"Both of us know it, Maeve. I think we knew it even then. The druids knew it. The sacrifice I escaped on Mona was just a shadow of what is to come."

"The god-making death." Almost against my will, I spoke the words.

He hesitated. "I don't know. But whatever it is, whatever it means, it can't be stopped this time. I have to go through it."

The cracked lips, the cracked sky.

"I have to go through it alone."

"No," I said, suddenly certain. "Not alone. Remember the vision in the mound? You told me yourself: I was there. I took your place. I took the pain. I was there."

"Maeve, Maeve." He reached up both his hands as if he could grab the sky and pull it down. "Haven't you suffered enough for me already? Exile. Slavery. Finally, you've found your own place, your home. I can't ask you to come with me. I won't. I don't want you to go where I have to go."

That was it! That was all it was, him wanting to spare me. I was so giddy with relief, I almost laughed. Except how can you laugh when someone has just told you he's going to die and die horribly?

"So, you were going to leave me again. Like that was supposed to make me feel better? You know, sometimes you're such an idiot."

"You were going to leave *me*," he said, just a tad peevishly. I had ruffled his feathers. Good.

"That's different," I said. "And besides, you know what? I was wrong."

He looked at me skeptically. We had been arguing since we met, about everything, and I doubt I had ever made such an admission before.

"Yes, wrong," I repeated, enjoying the shock value. "Mary of Bethany said I shouldn't marry you, because you're the Bridegroom of Israel. I was afraid if I married you, I would lose my sovereignty. Well, get this!"

Here I slipped off my tunic and stepped into the last of the moonlight—my breasts and belly shining. Then I lay down on the ground. No, I was not abasing myself, unless you think the earth is base. Well, it is our base, our basis. If I was humbling myself, it was at the root of the word, humus, soil. I lay down, and opened to him the lush landscape, the sacred geography of my body.

"I *am* Israel. I *am* sovereignty."

"Ah, Maeve, *cariad*." He deliberately used the Celtic endearment. "You are a beautiful witch from the Isle of Women. And I am no king, just a Jew who worships the One God. And beloved, even if you were born and bred here, a queen, I could not mate with you the way pagan kings mate with the goddess of the land!"

I didn't see why not, but I decided not to argue the point. I was too in awe of my own splendor, too serene in it.

"You asked me to marry you," I said. My voice sounded rich and loamy, irresistible. "And I said yes. I am saying yes."

"I want to marry you, Maeve, a woman, my heart's beloved, not a goddess of sovereignty," said he, who had foreseen for himself the god-making death.

Suddenly none of it mattered to me: my terms, his, why he had wanted to run away or why I had. I could feel his legs trembling, barely holding him up. I looked at his feet, his beautiful travel-worn feet. I rolled over on my side and kissed them, kissed each toe and the tender place in the arch. He moaned. Oh, he was going down fast. I was a wicked, wicked seductress. Let me tell you: earthmen are easy, even the Son of Man. I had gravity on my side. He sank, like something beautiful and wounded, a bird from the sky, the last star. His body covered mine; he took my face in his hands and kissed me.

"Will you marry me, Maeve, just me, a man who is going to die?"

"Yes," I whispered. "Yes."

And the sky began to pale at the dawning of our wedding day.

CHAPTER FIFTY-FOUR

MIRACLE

I f there was bonding between the drunken wedding guests the night before, it was strengthened the morning after as everyone exchanged their recipes for hangovers. We had to recover ourselves enough for the men to engage in games of skill, and for women to dance enticingly in the vineyards, as time-worn tradition required.

The wedding rite took place as the sun set and the full moon rose. Though weddings were never held on Sabbath, the time of day called to mind the beauty of the Sabbath Queen. Descended from the goddess Bride, named for a warrior queen, priestess of Isis, I have never felt more queenly than I did at that moment, enthroned in the vineyard under the chuppa, in the mingled sun and moon light, the sky alive with flocks of birds winging from day into night. There I sat surrounded by women I loved: whores, wives, mothers, virgins—wise or foolish, who knows?—their lamps trimmed and burning but pale beside the splendor of the approaching bridegroom. We sang to him:

> *I hear my love,*
> *See how he comes*
> *leaping on the mountains,*
> *bounding over the hills.*
> *My love is like a gazelle*
> *like a young stag.*

And the bridegroom and his friends (wise and foolish) answered, singing to the bride:

You ravish my heart,
my sister, my promised bride,
with a single one of your glances,
with a single link of your necklace.
What spells lie in your love,
my sister, my promised bride!
How delicious your love, more delicious than wine.

He was almost here; the women's voices rose wilder, sweeter:

Awake, north wind,
come, wind of the south!
Breathe over my garden
to spread its sweet smell around.
Let my love come into his garden,
let him taste its most exquisite fruits.

The men advanced, their voices strong and tender as the winds invoked:

I come into my garden,
my sister, my promised bride,
I pick my myrrh and balsam,
I eat my honey and my honeycomb,
I drink my wine and my milk.

I rose to meet my Bridegroom as he came to stand with me under the chuppa, our own tent, visible now, that we would carry with us into the wilderness of our marriage. And we sang to each other:

How beautiful you are, my love
How you delight me!
Our bed is the greensward,
The beams of our house are cedar trees.

At what moment precisely we were married, I cannot tell you. In those days, there were no officiates, no rabbi, no priest or priestess—except the bride and bridegroom; we were the celebrants; we married each other. Everyone felt free to offer prayers, blessings, and more than a few bawdy jokes. But one moment does stand out in my memory. Miriam came forward holding a ripe pomegranate in her hands. She put it down on the ground before us and crushed it with her bare foot. (How had I failed to notice before that her feet were beautiful and smooth as if she were a young girl?) She stepped back and we saw the seeds spilling out on the ground, thick and numerous as stars, the dark juice soaking into the earth. Then she began to sing, not in the wandering, tuneless way I had heard her sing before but in a voice that made me think of ravens, throaty and harsh:

> *Who is this coming up from the desert*
> *leaning on her lover?*

> *I awakened you under the apple tree*
> *where your mother conceived you*
> *where she who bore you conceived you.*

Then everyone joined in:

> *Love is as strong as Death,*
> *passion as relentless as Sheol.*

The hairs stood up on the back of my neck as my beloved's dream of our wedding came true. Dream come true sounds so fatuous, so pretty. When it really happens, it is awesome, almost fearsome. And my beloved's description of his dream had not conveyed the somber note I heard beneath the joy.

> *The flash of it is a flash of fire*
> *a flame of Yahweh himself.*
> *Love no flood can quench,*
> *no torrents drown.*

I turned to my bridegroom and clung to him. Maybe it was only the wind in the vines, but I thought I heard the sound of the river flowing in the dark.

The feasting and dancing went on all night. The sounds of the drums, of pipes wailing, women ululating, men laughing, everyone clapping and singing followed us as we slipped away to our marriage bed in the vineyard. Our friends had brought cushions and coverings and left us dainties to eat and wine to drink. When they discovered our absence, they would seek us with puerile pranks and drunken serenades, but for a little while we were alone.

I am not going to describe our consummation, because I want you to imagine it for yourself. No, I want you to remember it. Because you do remember, if only in your most poignant dreams, the ones you weep for when you wake. God has been called our father. God has been called our mother. God has been born and reborn as a child. I am asking you now to know god as your lover, the one who fills you and surrounds you, who gives and demands everything. Yield yourself to him, to her. Lose yourself, find yourself. Remember.

In those days the couple did not take off with matching luggage and tickets for a cruise. They partied on with their friends and family for another six days. So what happened next is perhaps not surprising.

"There's no more wine!"

It was the afternoon of the last day of the wedding feast (aka the communal bender). I was half asleep in the shade, my head resting in Succula's lap. I did not need to open my eyes to recognize the sound of Paulina in an utter panic.

"What do you mean there's no more wine?" Reginus stirred himself; he tended to hang out with the women during the day, giving Jesus and the Twelve a wide berth. "There were vats and vats of it."

"I mean there's No More Wine!" Paulina snapped at him.

"Are you quite sure?" fretted Martha. "I was just in the storerooms yesterday."

"Of course, I'm sure," Paulina practically shrieked. "Don't you think I checked? There's only the wine that's just been stored, and it's not fermented yet. What are we going to do?"

"Do?" said Mary of Bethany. "Do without. There's been far too much drinking at this wedding already or the supplies would have lasted. 'Wine drunk in excess brings quarreling and calamities aplenty; it is the poison of a man's life.'"

I recognized from her shift in tone that Mary B was quoting scripture. I opened one eye and glanced at Paulina who was turning purple, her blood vessels standing out alarmingly. Clearly Mary of Bethany did not know from calamity.

"Surely," said Domitia Tertia from her couch under a shade tree, "we can send a servant to procure some."

"Domitia, this is not Rome!" said Paulina. "How I wish I'd never left! We're in a trackless waste, miles from the nearest town, and it's sundown in a couple of hours."

"We must speak to Joseph," said Judith. "I am sure he will think of something. He is the president of the feast, after all. He must be informed."

"I don't see what he can do about it," grumbled Leah. "I knew something would go wrong. With my brother around, it always does."

"There's still plenty of food," Berta tried to cheer us. "And maybe there's barley beer. Did you look for beer, Paulina?"

During this entire exchange my mother-in-law had been sitting and spinning with a drop spindle, apparently unconcerned. All at once, she set her work aside and stood up.

"I will go find my son."

Again, no need to ask which one.

"Oh, but you must not interrupt him!" cried Mary of Bethany. "He is with his disciples."

She sounded both wistful and protective. I thought she was being more than a bit presumptuous. Who appointed her to be his guard dog? Ma took no notice of Mary B or anyone else. She stalked from the kitchen gardens into the main courtyard where all the men, except Joseph who was resting inside, sat listening to Jesus. Paulina hurried after her, and the rest of us followed. We stood back a little as Miriam, without a trace of hesitation or diffidence, pushed past the disciples to confront her son.

"Yeshua!" Her voice was deep, almost a growl. "They have no wine!"

"Woman!" he answered back. "What do you want with me?"

She should smack him, I found myself thinking. But I saw I had no need to defend her. His faith in his god might be able to move a mountain, but his mother wasn't going anywhere. Neither were the rest of us. We had gone into suspended animation, like actors on a stage who freeze to become part of the background. There were only two principals in this scene. Jesus rose and faced his mother.

"My time is not yet come." He spoke softly, but the courtyard was so still, we could all hear.

Miriam did not answer him. Not out loud anyway. Who knew who else was in the conversation? The air suddenly stirred uneasily, the way it does before a storm, turning the leaves upside down, though the sky was still clear. Then Miriam spied some servants on their way back out to the fields. She called them to her.

"Do whatever he says." She nodded towards Jesus.

Her son sighed, a long sigh of exasperation and, I sensed, defeat. He looked away from his mother and caught sight of me. Suddenly he smiled with tenderness, amusement and memory, too. His look conveyed all his intimate knowledge of me. I thought everyone must be able to see it. I actually blushed, I trust becomingly. Still smiling, he turned to the servants, who stood by uncertainly. They reminded me of the slaves at Nemi, Paulina's country villa, used to being left to their own devices, doing things their own way—troubled by only occasional visits from the master.

"Fill the jars with water."

Jesus pointed to the large stone jars that the Jewish men had been using for ritual ablution, eschewing the Roman-style baths. (The women, even Mary B, continued to use the "mikspa.") Used to odd requests from this eccentric wedding party, the servants shrugged and went off to the household well. When they returned, we watched in silence as they filled the jars to the brim. Even Paulina was quiet, a miracle in itself.

"Now," said Jesus, "draw some out. Take it to Joseph of Arimathea, the president of the feast. You will find him resting inside the house."

With that, Jesus said nothing more, nor did he look at any of us. As if he were alone and slightly bored, he idly picked up a stick and squatted, using the stick to draw in the dust. We all watched him with a fascination that is hard to explain, unless you've felt it yourself: watching someone comb hair, or card wool, plant seeds or do any task in which he is unselfconsciously absorbed. Perhaps you know that peculiar state of sensual trance, as if it is your body that is being stroked and soothed. I could have watched him scratch that dust with a stick for hours. I was so lulled that I almost didn't notice: he was tracing and retracing the ogham for vine—one of the letters of the druid sacred alphabet.

"What's all this uproar about no more wine?" Joseph startled us out of our altered state. "This is the best wine I've ever tasted. Where did it come from? The best wine usually goes first."

"Wine?" breathed Paulina. She looked at Joseph. She looked at Jesus. Then her eyes fastened on the stone jars. "May I?"

Paulina took the cup from Joseph and dipped it into one of the jars for herself. Eyes closed, she lifted the cup to her nose and inhaled the bouquet. Then she took a sip, well, more like a gulp.

"My savior!" She opened her eyes and gazed at Jesus with pure adoration. Then she opened her arms as to embrace us all. "L'chaim, y'all! Party on!"

I don't know exactly what was in the wine. It tasted fiery and sweet. I suspect it was red mead: Maeve Rhuad. Mead mixed with red wine. An intimate joke, a pun made by the bridegroom that only the bride would understand. Its effect transcended any ingredient. It was like drinking life itself: new-turned earth, sun, wind scented with sea, blossoms opening at first light, the ripe perfection of fruit—the elements gathered on our tongues, lingering on our breath. It was like drinking love itself, the passion of the bride and bridegroom distilled, shared among the guests, flowing in all our veins, rivers from a single rise. If we were drunk, we were divinely drunk. We were in love. In Love. All of us. None of us could bear to part that night. The stars were so beautiful. We were so beautiful. In the end, we all slept together, no one alone, each one beloved.

BETWEEN

EARTH AND SKY

CHAPTER FIFTY-FIVE

IN HIS OWN COUNTRY

My beloved, (my Bridegroom and yours), is often thought of as a mediator, as if we need someone to make our case to his terrible god, to stand between divine wrath and human wickedness. Why not imagine instead a tree, mediating earth and sky? The roots know the mystery of the depths, the dark, the taste of earth and the leaves know the mystery of the heights, the light, the taste of sun. Both are good. In the heart of the tree, where Isis found Osiris, the mysteries meet. They meet in your heart, too.

We are all mediators of divine and human nature. As we drank and danced and embraced at the wedding, we glimpsed each other's radiance, saw our own reflected. The next day, remarkably rested and fit, considering, we saw our differences again, our annoying traits, our conflicting wills. But I am not here to condemn human nature or to exalt the divine. It's all good, the grit in the oyster, the stone in the shoe. Stop to shake out the stone. Take a moment to wonder at this place you find yourself: between earth and sky.

"But Master!" Peter was having—or trying to have—a private conference with Jesus; I was eavesdropping (accidentally) from inside the storerooms; Lucius had said we might take some cheeses. "She can't be coming with us! You never said anything about bringing her along. You know how we live, how you've taught us to live: wandering over the earth, sleeping under the sky." (How poetic!) "Trusting to the Most High to provide for our needs—you know, the lilies of the field thing. That's why none of us bring our wives. And this, this woman—"

"Maeve," said Jesus calmly, although I knew it wasn't customary for Jewish men to refer to their wives by name; they usually just said she, or the wife.

"Yes, well." Peter was all the more flustered. "Frankly, Master, excuse me for being frank, but frankly—"

"Peter, if you're going to be frank, get on with it."

"Well, she's used to living among the fleshpots, so to speak. She's used to luxuries. Why, she even has a Roman patroness." Peter lowered his voice in a vain attempt at discretion. "Judas is very troubled by her consorting with the oppressor, more than by her being, well, a gentile barbarian and a woman of loose morals. Frankly, Master, we none of us can understand why you felt it necessary to marry the woman. Not that we presume to question. No doubt it is a mystery beyond our understanding."

"No doubt." Jesus apparently felt no need to defend my honor, but then, how could he? Everything Peter said was true.

"So you are serious? You are taking her with us?"

"Maeve is a free woman," said Jesus.

"What?" Peter sounded utterly confused by this non-answer.

"I will not tell her what to do or where to go."

What happened to that urgent: "I want you with me." Was he having second thoughts? If he wasn't, I was. Give up my friends for his Twelve?

"But Master!" Peter was shocked as well as appalled. "She's your *wife!*"

"Good, Peter. I'm glad you noticed."

"Master, you are my master, but I've been married a lot longer, so take it from me: the wife obeys the husband. If you tell her what to do, she'll do it."

"Peter." Jesus's voice became conspiratorial. "I'm not going to push my luck."

I didn't know whether to laugh or cry; since I was eavesdropping I did neither.

"But Master—"

"No more buts. We'll all go to Nazareth for a few days. Then we'll see."

"See what?"

"What we see."

With that enigmatic response, Jesus and Peter moved away, and I finished packing the satchel. We would see, all right. Nazareth was only a day's walk from Magdala. If I didn't feel like wandering in the wilderness with the Chosen Ones, I could return to my fleshpots anytime I pleased. So I told myself. How else could I bear to part from my own companions? Hoping someone had thought to bring the vial of tears, I emerged from the storeroom to go in search of the Temple Magdalen and Roman contingents. Before I could find them, Mary B accosted me.

"May I have a word with you? Alone."

"We are alone," I pointed out.

"Where we can't be overheard."

Since I had just been eavesdropping, I realized she had a point. We walked out together into the vineyard where the chuppa had stood. I could still see the imprint of where my beloved and I had lain together. Why would Mary B want to confer near the site of a consummation she considered a disaster and an abomination? She seemed ill at ease, one of her hands pulling at the other.

"Well, what is it, Mary?" I was impatient. "My friends are almost ready to go. I need to say goodbye to them."

"I want to go with him, with Jesus. And the others."

I noticed she did not say: with you.

"You're a free woman." I borrowed Jesus's words. The tone was mine: unfriendly.

"You know it's not that simple."

"No, I don't know."

"I suppose for you everything is simple," she said. "You never question your will or whim."

I snorted. Look who's talking, I wanted to say. You're the one who ran away on a whim to join a celibate, all-male community with the man you could have married. How's that for willful? But I didn't say it. Mary was Jesus's friend, and he would not want me to be unkind to her. Such restraint was new to me. Marriage was complicating, if not ruining, my life already.

"Why are you telling me?" I said instead. "Or are you asking me?"

"I am not asking for your permission, if that's what you mean." She paused and twisted her hands some more. "I'm asking for your help."

"Help?" I repeated. "How can I help you?" At least I did not say: Why should I?

"By making it all right for me to go!" she burst out. "I've been wanting to ever since he started preaching and healing. I almost asked him last time he and the disciples stayed with us. He stays with us when he comes to Jerusalem. Did you know that?"

Well, if I didn't, I could have guessed. "So why didn't you ask him?"

"The disciples," she said; then, as if I were stupid, she added, "They're all men."

"But you lived with a bunch of men when you were with the Essenes. Why should that bother you?"

"Among the Essenes, I *was* a man! Don't you see? And the disciples, I knew they would resent me. They already do, because I spoke up during the teachings. I didn't want to cause trouble for Jesus," she concluded almost primly.

"So what's different now?" I sighed. "The disciples still don't want women to come with them. I just heard Peter pleading with Jesus to order me to stay behind."

"But you are going, aren't you." She had been avoiding my eyes. Now she looked at me directly, and I felt the full force of her intensity.

"Yes, I am." The sudden strength of my conviction surprised me.

"We're both women."

"Yes?" I said a bit doubtfully.

"That means women can be disciples."

"I am not a disciple!" I made an Egyptian hand sign for warding off evil.

"Whatever." She waved away my crucial distinction. "Just let me come."

"Mary of Bethany, I do believe you *are* asking my permission."

Whether from anger or shame or both, I don't know, but her sallow skin turned motley red, and then she flabbergasted me by bursting into tears. I couldn't help it, I went and put my arm around her, and she surprised me even more by allowing it.

"Come on, Mary," I said. "Let's go tell Jesus that you have chosen to join us."

With those words, whether she appreciated it or not, I restored her sovereignty. When we approached Jesus, my arm still around Mary B, we didn't have to say anything; he knew.

I am not going to describe in detail the parting with my friends, some going back to Magdala, some to Arimathea with Joseph before taking ship for Rome from Joppa. The vial of tears, as it turned out, had stayed on the altar at Temple Magdalen, but oddly enough, when the time came, there were few tears to harvest. Though I knew I would rarely, if ever, see Domitia and Succula again and though I would miss daily life with my *combrogos*, I felt curiously lighthearted, and I sensed the others did, too. Some grace from our last night together still touched us. I don't know how to express it, except to say that we knew, at least in that moment, that it was all a dance: meeting, parting, loving, leaving. Circle and turn, come together, take hands, let go, move on, meet again. And so we kissed goodbye, with some sadness, but with more merriment. We were in on the secret. We knew it was all right, knew we could not lose each other forever.

Nazareth was only ten miles or so from Cana, so we arrived well before evening. As you can imagine, our party caused quite a stir. The eccentric Miriam and her long-suffering brood, twelve strange (in more sense than one) men, and the prodigal son, so to speak, but with no wealthy father to greet him and kill the fatted calf. Everyone knew about the wedding—in a borrowed Roman villa no less. So. Nazareth wasn't good enough for him? And, of course, they were eaten up with curiosity about the bride. Was she really a gentile?

As soon as we had set up camp in Miriam's yard—for the house was too small to accommodate us all—Jesus upset his disciples further by taking Mary B and me on a private tour of his childhood haunts. Wherever we went, villagers came out to stare. Two women? A wife and a concubine? Who did he think he was, King David? A few people answered when he greeted them, but more pretended not to hear him.

"I don't think you're very popular here," I remarked.

"They just don't know him," Mary B said fiercely. "Who he really is."

If she kept defending him to me, she was really going to get on my nerves.

Jesus ignored us both and kept on walking up and up till we came to a cliff with a view of all the hills and valleys for miles around. Flocks of sheep grazed on slopes too steep to plough. We were high enough that hawks circled and floated below us. We all sat down and Jesus put an arm around each of us.

"This is where I used to come to get away from the shop, the village, everyone," he said at length. "No one would bother me here; people are afraid of this place."

"Why?" I wondered. "It's so peaceful."

"Not for the criminals who got driven or thrown over the cliff," he said. "Well, it's a quicker and more merciful end than stoning. Not a bad way to go."

For a time we sat lost in our own thoughts, in the vast space around us. A curious thing happened with the light. As the sun began to set, it found its way through a gap between two hills and flowed into the valley below like a river. With a prickling of my scalp, I had something like a premonition—only in reverse. The boy Jesus had come here over and over to watch that same trick of light. And I knew something more: so had his mother before him. Here in this place of terror and peace, she had met his father.

"I want to stay in Nazareth through the Sabbath," Jesus spoke from the silence. "I want to speak in the synagogue. There are things I need to say."

"Do you think that's wise?" asked Mary B.

"Probably not." He laughed, and the air, which had been still, almost ominous, stirred to life, carrying the scents of wild thyme and hyssop along with sheep dung. "Let's face it. I was a fuck-up. Arrogant, profligate, useless to my family. That's how I know, *know*," he repeated, "that the Eternal One does not love us because we are good. It troubles me when people think I'm good. Only God is good."

I thought of Yahweh's fondness for floods and plagues, his urge to destroy whole cities because of one or two sinners, his carping at his people because they spared a few women and sheep when he expressly said to leave nothing alive. If his god was good who needed evil?

"But Rabbi," Mary B had already jumped in. "Is it not written in the very first book of the Torah: 'God created man in the image of himself, in the image of God, male and female created he them.'" She quoted in Hebrew, but I got the gist. "Does it not then follow that we are good?"

Clever Mary B. I was beginning to see why Jesus admired her and would have married her. They could have spent their days arguing over scripture, while Martha chased after their children and cooked their meals. I could also understand why the disciples were threatened by her. She was erudite and outspoken. She wouldn't need a parable broken down into parts.

"Well, Mary," Jesus got to his feet and pulled us both up, "since we are also evil, or capable of evil, does it follow then that God is evil?"

Good question.

"Of course not," she replied without hesitation. "Evil came into the world because we listened to the serpent, the Father of Lies, and chose to believe him."

I had never been able to remember much about the Jewish Law, and frankly the prophets seemed scarcely distinguishable to me from your garden-variety demoniac, but I did have a good memory for the stories.

"Mary, as I recall there was no 'we' about it." I decided to get into the act. "Male and female created he them, maybe, but who takes the blame? Who takes the fall for the Fall? And what is it your people have against serpents? Isis had a cobra for a midwife."

"How bestial," Mary shuddered. "No wonder our people left Egypt."

But I could tell she was challenged; I think she had told herself my only hold over Jesus was physical. I might have his body, but she would have his mind.

"Think about it, Mary," I persisted. "That story is the beginning of all your problems. What does Adam say when God discovers them? Come on, I know you know it by heart."

" 'It was the woman you put with me; she gave me the fruit from the tree, and I ate it,'" she quoted.

"Now is that lame or what?"

Suddenly Mary B started to laugh, and I realized I had never heard her laugh before; it was a little squeaky at first—like a hinge that needs oil—but she didn't stop, and pretty soon the laugh took over her whole body.

"And did you notice," she went on speaking to me; Jesus who had been walking between us dropped behind a few paces. "Eve says 'the snake tempted me.' She acknowledges her choice, Adam doesn't. He only says, 'she gave me the fruit.'"

Mary B was off and running. She analyzed text with me all the way back to Miriam's house where a scrawny goat was roasting on a spit and the disciples sat glumly in the gloaming.

Three days later I found myself sitting in the women's gallery of the synagogue squeezed tight between Ma and Mary B. The place was jammed. Jesus was back, the bad boy, the scapegrace, who had set himself up as some kind of preacher and miracle worker, almost as notorious as the Dipper. He sat in the front of the men's section, waiting his turn to read.

"There are seven readers," Mary B whispered to me, the neophyte. For despite years of Shabbat feasts, I had never attended Sabbath teachings at a synagogue. "And after they read, each one gets to make commentary."

"You're kidding!"

"It can be interesting," she insisted. "Look where Jesus is sitting; he's going to be the *Maphtir*, the last of the seven. He'll read the portion from the prophets. It's an honor."

"Are you sure it's an honor?" I queried. "Maybe it's a setup."

"No, it's all right," Mary assured me. "His second cousin is the *hazzan*—see the man there who's reading over their shoulders to make sure they don't make mistakes? He's arranged it. We should pay attention now."

She appeared to hang on every word, though some of the readers droned and stumbled, and all of them commented at unbearable length. It seemed part of some sadistic tradition for the commentator to reach what sounded like a concluding sentence, then take a breath and plunge on to another conclusion—and another. After the second speaker, I passed my time in counting false endings. They averaged half a dozen each. The room grew hotter; children squirmed, and babies fussed.

I could not do this every week; I could not.

Then at last it was Jesus's turn to read. As he unrolled the scroll, the room quieted. It was so still that I could hear the sheep's bells ringing from the valley at the edge of town. Then I heard nothing but his voice.

The spirit of the Lord is on me,
for he has anointed me
to bring good news to the afflicted.
He has sent me to proclaim liberty to the captives,
sight to the blind, to let the oppressed go free,
to proclaim a year of favor from the Lord.

"The prophet Isaiah," Mary whispered to me, as Jesus rolled up the scroll and handed it to the *hazzan.*

Everyone remained silent and tense as Jesus sat down, facing the assembled.

"This text is being fulfilled today even while you are listening."

He paused, waiting, watching as hearing turned into comprehension, and the crowd came out of its torpor to agitated life. Like hornets, I couldn't help thinking. The buzzing began.

"Isn't this the carpenter's son?"

"Miriam's son. Look, his brothers are all here."

"What's he saying?"

"Who does he think he is?"

"Hey, carpenter's son!" someone called out to him. "We've all been hearing stories about miracle healings in Capernaum. What about us? Don't we have sick people here in Nazareth, too? Show us what you got!"

I looked at my beloved, sitting quietly, too quietly. Something was building in him, and it was going to blow any minute. Mary B sensed it, too; she clutched my arm, digging in her nails. I became aware of feeling trapped in the women's gallery. If anything happened, I couldn't get to him quickly. Of course, he had the Twelve to protect him, but somehow that didn't reassure me.

"In truth I tell you, no prophet is ever accepted in his own country." He spoke softly, but everyone heard him. His voice cut through the commotion and found the vulnerable place in each listener.

"There were many widows in Israel, I can assure you, in Elijah's day," he began to teach, "when heaven remained shut for three years and six months and a great famine raged throughout the land, but Elijah was not sent to anyone of these: he was sent to a widow in Zarephath, a town in Sidonia. And in the prophet Elisha's time there were many suffering from virulent skin diseases in Israel, but none of these was cured—only Namaan the Syrian."

I was having trouble following Jesus. My mother-in-law was humming loudly as if to drown out the angry comments erupting from the crowd. I also wasn't getting the scriptural references. I glanced at Mary B, who obviously did. The color had drained from her face, and she held herself rigid.

"What's he on about?" I whispered to her. "Why are people shouting at him?"

"The stories he's referring to, they're about prophets healing gentiles," she explained. "The widow took care of Elijah and gave him food. When her son died, Elijah asked the Most High to restore his life. Namaan was an army commander for the King of Aram. Don't you see now? They challenged him to work a miracle, and that's his answer. It's a terrible insult. Be quiet. We've got to listen."

But Jesus wasn't speaking anymore; or if he was I couldn't hear him or anyone clearly. Men were getting to their feet, ignoring the *hazzan* who called in vain for the final blessing. The whole congregation was massing on my beloved.

"Come on, Mary!"

I got to my feet, pulling her with me. Miriam grabbed hold of my other arm. I didn't want to be slowed down by her, but she wouldn't let go. The three of us managed to force our way through the panicking women's gallery to the riot outside, the air thick with curses and the thwack of fists connecting with flesh. The only way to avoid being trampled was to go with the press of the crowd through narrow streets. I had no idea where we were going until we came to the edge of the village, and I recognized the path Jesus, Mary B, and I had followed yesterday.

"The cliff!" I shouted. "Oh, Isis! Hurry."

"Calm down, Mary of Magdala," puffed Miriam, "this hill is steep. I'm out of breath. There's no need to worry. The angels are there."

And she held onto my arm like death. I couldn't shake her off and leave her to be trampled by the crowd. But before we got near the cliff, the crowd turned back, a wave receding, its fury spent to no purpose.

"Where could he have gone?" people asked each other.

"Did anyone see him disappear?"

"He must have slipped down some alley. Ran off like the thief he is."

By some unspoken accord, the three of us pressed on; encountering bruised confused disciples on the way, till finally we all gathered at the cliff's edge and gazed out over the valley where the sheep went on grazing. I fixed my eyes on a hawk, and sent out my vision, scanning the valley from a birds' eye view. At last I discerned movement as someone emerged from the shelter of an olive tree. Back on the cliff, I saw him waving to us from below. I waved back.

"I told you so," said my mother-in-law.

"*Cariad*," I said to Jesus as I lay in his arms that night in an open field. Oh, those are some of my favorite nights to remember, nights on the road under stars so clear and close, it felt as though you could pick them like wild berries. The hard ground and the chill air made our bodies seem even warmer and more yielding. "*Cariad*, must you start riots wherever you go?"

"You're asking me?" Answer a question with a question, a favorite device of his.

"I had nothing to do with the fuss you kicked up in Nazareth. And you know it. I could not have been more demure. I didn't even know what you were talking about. Mary had to explain it to me."

"I would think you would be proud of me." He nuzzled me and began to kiss the corner of my mouth.

"Why? Because you were citing scripture about the prophets showing favor to heathen gentiles like me? Really there's no need. I know you love me—you've caused enough scandal by marrying me. You don't have to preach about it."

"Apparently I do. The spirit of the Lord was upon me."

"Are you sure it was the Lord?

His only answer was more kisses.

"I'm afraid I'm only going to get you into more trouble," I sighed.

"Och, woman," he put on a Celtic accent. "Why do you think I married you?"

I guess it was a rhetorical question. There were no more words that night.

CHAPTER FIFTY-SIX
ARE YOU THE ONE?

Perhaps it is time for me to introduce you, briefly, to my fellow travelers now that I was getting to know one from the other and they were not merely the Twelve. They won't all figure prominently in the story—his four official chroniclers couldn't manage that either—but I'd like to give you some sense of the men who gave up home, comfort, and livelihood to traipse around with Jesus, if only so that you understand the sheer miracle of their being joined in a common purpose at all.

They ranged from guerrilla fighters, Judas and Simon, covertly working towards an armed uprising against Roman occupation, to repentant collaborator, Matthew, who had once extorted taxes on behalf of Roman landlords from people like Judith. Phillip was well-educated and could follow the complex arguments of the Pharisees in contrast to illiterate (and mildly retarded) Tomas, called the twin, because he always shadowed Jesus. Thaddeus and Bartholomew, both Greek proselytes, had the zeal of the newly converted, while some of the disciples, born to their religion, were ignorant of the finer points of the law. Which brings me to our four local fishermen, prosperous enough but only a cut above the landless *Am-ha-arez* in the eyes of the Pharisees: Peter and his brother Andrew, James and John, also known as the Thunder Brothers, because everything they did was loud, from laughing at a crude joke to belching after a good meal. The House of Israel was never monolithic, and Jesus wanted all his people at the feast, not this faction or that—every last lost sheep with dung hanging from its behind.

The invitation, as far as I could tell, still only extended to Jews. Since I refused to convert or call myself a disciple, I remained an anomaly—the proverbial elephant in the living room that no one wanted to talk about. Mary B was a different matter; she made no bones about being a disciple. You might think that the Twelve would have been even more resistant to her, but her years of living with men stood her in good stead. She drew no attention to her femaleness. Her priestly lineage and scholarly ambitions were more of a stumbling block, but she found a champion in Philip.

As for me, no matter how simply I dressed, no matter how adept I was at roughing it, some tendril of fiery hair escaped any head covering I wore, and I could not help the sensual joy I took in my body, not just because I was near my beloved, but because I had always been at home in my skin.

The men's responses to my presence varied. Sometimes I bantered with Andrew, which drove Peter crazy. But then I was, in general, a terrible trial to Peter, for reasons I have made clear. The Thunder Brothers were easy to handle, boisterous, open, and uncomplicated. Tomas was terribly jealous at first and glowered at me fiercely, but in time he seemed to accept me (whether I liked it or not) as an extension of Jesus and would follow me around if Jesus weren't there.

Simon and Judas, the hill fighters, would have no truck with Mary or me for a time. They wanted the Twelve to be lean, stripped down, ready for action, and foresaw complications in the inclusion of women. When Simon realized that we could keep up, he dropped his quarrel. Judas, however, kept his distance. I sensed that he was watching, biding his time. He was the only one of the Twelve who never called Jesus master, the one most likely to challenge him. At times I felt a wary kinship with him, the kind of attraction that mutual antagonism can generate.

We were the core of a community that waxed and waned, not unlike Temple Magdalen's population, and in many ways the wandering band operated on the same principles: welcome the stranger, love your neighbor, break bread with your enemy. But there was something bothering me that I couldn't name until a visit from John's disciples brought my hidden quandary into the open.

We had spent the night out in the hills, as we often did to escape the crowds, and we were just breaking camp when three of John's disciples approached us. We lived rough, but John's disciples eschewed grooming altogether, and so it was easy to recognize them as followers of the wild ascetic.

"You are welcome, companions of my cousin and teacher," said Jesus, and then he called to me, "Maeve."

The men registered my presence with marked disapproval. A prophet with a camp follower? Then one of them recognized me as the Dipper's demon-possessed assailant.

"Why, you...she's the one who—"

"It's all right," Jesus assured them. "I married her."

What was he saying? I wasn't dangerous anymore; he'd tamed me, as if I were a pet lioness or boa constrictor?

"Will you get some food for our guests?" he asked me.

Well, I was his wife, so what else was I there for, right? I tell you: it was one thing for him to go on about how the master must be the servant of all, but it's another thing to have your servitude taken for granted. Though I didn't say anything, as I fetched a loaf and some cheese, I couldn't resist sending a knife spinning through the air (a trick I'd learned from my warrior-witch mothers) so that it landed upright and quivering in the cheese. My point, whatever it was, was taken. I went to fetch a wineskin, and then I plunked myself down beside the visitors.

"So how is John?" I inquired. "Is he still going on at Herod about his sex life?"

Jesus gave me a look. You might say *the* look. If I had been a fig tree (we'll get to that part later) I might have withered, but I am of extremely hardy stock.

"Our Master is still in prison." The man, blushing painfully, addressed himself to Jesus, as if he had asked the question. "But the king fears him; he knows he is a holy man who speaks the truth."

There was an awkward silence as Jesus waited for them to state the purpose of their visit, and the three men waited, presumably for him to dismiss me. I wasn't taking hints; if Jesus wanted me to go he'd have to say so directly. He ignored me, and I became slightly less conspicuous as Mary and the other disciples gathered around. At last the oldest, scruffiest looking locust eater spoke.

"Our Master has sent us to you with a question. He bids us ask you this: Are you the One who is to come or are we to expect someone else?"

That question again, the same one John had asked me at the Jordan River. How anguished he had been, even then, with the multitudes attending on his words, hoping and believing in him as their prophet and deliverer. I had evaded the question then. I didn't know the answer, and what's more didn't like any of the answers the question might have had. I wondered what answer John wanted or dreaded now, sitting there in prison waiting for Herod to work up the nerve to kill him or let him go. Would it comfort him or torture him to believe his feckless cousin was the One? I glanced across the circle at Mary B. It was plain enough to see what she wanted. She gazed at Jesus with rapt attention, her lips slightly parted, heart beating hard under her scrawny bosom.

"Go back and tell John what you have seen and heard." Jesus spoke at last in that voice, low and resonant, that carried without effort or strain into huge crowds, so that each person felt he spoke to them alone. "The blind see, the lame walk, the lepers are cleansed, the deaf hear, the dead are raised to life, the good news is proclaimed to the poor, and blessed is anyone who does not find me a cause of falling."

I looked at John's disciples, who kept their faces carefully blank. Yet it seemed to me as if his words had touched them like a wind, and if they had been trees, it would have torn loose their leaves, left them barer, more exposed. When it was clear that Jesus had no more to say, John's disciples rose and walked away without another word.

Wait! I wanted to call after them. Did he really answer your question? What are you going to tell John? I glanced at Mary B, and saw that, unlike me, she was more than satisfied with his response. Her eyes shone, and she was reciting scripture under her breath. She and John's disciples knew the passages from Isaiah Jesus had quoted, as I did not. Even if Mary tutored me, the story of "The One Who Is to Come," was not the story I was telling myself, as the old druid Nissyen might have said. I had no part in that story—unless, unwittingly, I had a place among the ones who found him a cause for falling. I had fallen for him, all right, at my first sight of him in the well of wisdom of Tir na mban. I had plunged into the water trying to find him. Isis knew, I was in pretty deep now, over my head, head over heels. Fallen in love. Fallen.

All day I felt troubled. Soon after John's disciples left, the crowds found out our camp, and Jesus began to preach. Well, you can call it preaching if you want. To me it sounded more like a tirade. Clearly the delegation from John had upset him, and he was taking it out on the crowd, railing at them about how John was Elijah come again, righteous and fasting, and yet rejected as a madman while he, Jesus (a.k.a. the Son of Man), was rejected as a glutton and a drunkard by this terrible generation. Then he started in on the lake towns where he had done so many miraculous healings—Bethsaida, Chorazin, Capernaum—ranting about their lack of repentance, consigning them to hell. (Note that notorious lake town Magdala was not on the list.)

In my opinion, he was coming unhinged. He had whipped himself into a frenzy—fire flashing from his tongue and his eyes, burning him up, consuming him. That fire needed to go somewhere—under a cooking pot, into the cool earth, through his hands to give the blind their sight, to heal the lame. Or how about into our lovemaking, into life making. For though I harbored a small hope that I was pregnant, I could feel my womb beginning to contract, getting ready for my monthly flow. After awhile, I walked away from the preaching and spent the day feeding people and tending the sick desperate enough to accept care from someone who wasn't Jesus. And so I directed my own fire and kept it from raging out of control for the time being. I knew there was a spark with Jesus's name on it smoldering in me, ready to burst into a full-blown conflagration when the time was right—or maybe wrong. I couldn't hold back forever.

Jesus went on for most of the day, and then towards sunset he did his disappearing act. I swear he practiced the shape-shifting techniques he learned from the druids. Solitude was essential to him, but today I felt resentful. I decided I would go for a stroll myself. Someone else could stir the pot where I'd made lentil stew. If no one tended to it, it would burn. I didn't care. But as I began to stalk away, I overheard raised voices, one of them a woman's. I paused in the shelter of a terebinth tree.

"I tell you," Peter's voice was almost shrill. "He's not seeing anyone else today. Come back tomorrow."

"I will wait," said the woman.

"What!" Peter exploded. "All night?"

"If need be, yes."

"We don't allow women at the camp," a third person spoke; it was Judas.

How dare he! The question of whether or not women could accompany Jesus had been settled, whether Judas liked it or not. I almost interrupted, but decided to wait and see how far Judas would go.

"I saw two women at the camp this morning," she countered.

"Oh them," Peter dismissed us. "They're not really women, they're just—"

I never got a chance to hear how Peter would explain Mary and me away. Judas abruptly took a different tack.

"You came with John's disciples," he stated.

"I followed them," she answered. "I did not come with them."

"I have seen you before." Judas made it sound like an accusation.

"I don't think so," the woman answered nervously.

"Who are you?" Judas demanded.

When the woman didn't answer, Judas grabbed her, pulled off her head covering and yanked her head back by the hair. I could feel it in my own scalp. "Who are you!" my father had demanded when he caught me trespassing in the sacred grove, and he had forced my head back just the same way.

"Judas!" Peter protested. "No rough stuff. You know the Master doesn't allow it."

"You are from Herod's court. In fact, you are his steward's wife," Judas stated, still keeping a grip on her. "You followed John's disciples from there."

The woman stayed silent.

"Judas," said Peter, "let go of her."

"Why are you here?" Judas released her, but I could sense the tension coiled in him, aching for release in action.

"I told you already. I want to see Jesus."

"If you have a message for him or a warning, spit it out."

"Why should I tell you anything?" She was defiant. "I have come to see him."

"If you don't state your business," said Judas, "I will assume you are Herod's spy and deal with you accordingly."

"Judas," Peter objected again. "She's just a woman."

I didn't know which man I found more infuriating—Judas with his bullying or Peter with his condescension. I decided it was time to intervene.

"Is there some problem here?" I stepped out from the tree's shadow.

The woman turned to me with visible relief. I took a closer look at her. She was middle-aged, handsome, simply but well dressed, just past childbearing years when a wife could begin to relax and enjoy her status as matriarch of her household. I could not help wondering what would make her bold or desperate enough to follow John's messengers to this rough camp.

"You are one of the women I saw this morning," she said with a note of triumph in her voice. "One of his disciples."

"No!" said Peter.

"No!" said Judas.

"No!" I said.

The woman looked understandably confused, but she composed herself and spoke directly to me. "I am Joanna, wife of Chuzza, King Herod's steward. May I ask who you are, *domina*?" She used the Roman word for lady, though she spoke in Aramaic.

"She's—" Judas and Peter both started to answer.

"I'll speak for myself," I cut them off. "I am Maeve of Magdala, priestess of Isis." I paused then forced the words out, "and wife of Jesus. You are welcome at our camp, Joanna, and welcome at our feast."

The authority in my voice startled us all. The woman looked at me curiously, and Peter and Judas both took a step back.

"Such as it is," I said lightly. "Lentils again. Come on, all of you. Let's go eat."

"I'm so tired, Maeve," said Jesus that night as he flung himself on our bedroll. "Don't ask me."

"Don't ask you what?"

I sat apart from him, plucking bits of dried grass, already scorched by the sun, seeing if I could toss them into the fire to burn all the way up. It was late, and the others had already drawn apart, some still talking softly, others snoring. Mary B had made provision for Joanna.

"Whatever you were going to ask me."

"You make a lot of assumptions," I said. But he was right; there was plenty I wanted to ask him. No, not ask him, tell him. I didn't even know where to begin, so maybe it was best to let it be. Especially right now when I was so angry, angry and sad.

"Come to bed, *cariad*," he said softly, but I was not softened.

"I just started bleeding."

He groaned.

"Hey, you're the one with the *geis*." I used the Celtic word for ritual prohibition.

"All right," he sat up, "talk to me."

"You just told me not to." I decided to be difficult; I was having cramps, ok?

"You're holding something back. Neither of us will sleep until you give it up."

He joined me in tossing grass and watching it glow and curl before it disappeared.

"Here it is, then," I said. "I am wondering how you're even going to live long enough to have your terrible, awful fate."

"I'm not a Greek, Maeve. I don't believe in fate."

"No, of course you don't. That would be way too uncomplicated for you and your jealous, delusional god, who communicates his utterly confusing will by infesting his chosen messengers with his spirit till they froth at the mouth and spew convoluted, contradictory prophecies. And if that's not bad enough, someone writes the ravings down and calls them Holy Scriptures. Then you all argue over them for hundreds and hundreds of years, interpreting and reinterpreting them to suit your own purposes."

"Maeve, you're getting a little frothy yourself. What are you talking about?"

I turned and looked at him, waiting till he met my gaze.

"Are you the One, are you the One, are you the One who is to Come?"

Needless to say, he did not answer the question.

"Is that what's bothering you, Maeve?"

"It's bothering you, too. You went on a rant for six hours after that."

"Not six, surely."

"I'm a Celt. I'm entitled to exaggerate, but in this case, I don't think I am."

"Tell me what bothers you about the prophecies."

I tossed a big clump into the fire; it sizzled satisfactorily.

"I think they're going to your head," I said. "It's the One business. Everyone crying and clamoring for you. Only you. Only you can heal them.

Only you can save them. Now John is asking are you the One who is to come. Come and do what? Save the people? Save all of Israel?"

Jesus didn't answer. So I went on.

"And you must believe it. You are exhausting yourself. Your so-called disciples are little more than bouncers and bodyguards. Some of them a bit overzealous." I stopped short of telling him about Judas and Peter's treatment of the woman Joanna. It would be a bad idea to get into the habit of tattling on the Twelve. "As for me, I'm hardly more than a camp follower, like any whore trotting after an army, cooking and doing the wash, fetching and carrying for visiting dignitaries."

"You're my wife, Maeve," he said. "I meant no disrespect to you."

"I am also a priestess and a healer. Have you forgotten how the fire of the stars flowed through my hands into your crown?"

I had run out of grass to fling. In my agitation, I got up, just to pace, but he must have thought I was walking away.

"I remember, Maeve. I remember."

There was such an ache in his voice, such sadness and longing, I stopped mid-step and sat down next to him as close as I could without touching him. We were both silent for awhile.

"What can I do?" he said at length. "What would you do, if everyone turned to you, looked to you. If the Most High himself—" He broke off.

I turned to look at him, and all my anger burned away like the dry grass I'd tossed into the fire. He was so naked in his anguish, so open. I felt my whole body flush. My desire for him suddenly so intense, I didn't know how I could bear not to touch him, but I would not be the one to break his *geis*. I breathed the heat between my thighs all the way up my body till it burst in my crown.

"You could open them all to the fire of the stars," I answered slowly. "That's what I would do. The woman Joanna wants to be a healer. You once healed her, she said, and her hands have been burning ever since. You could teach her, you could teach the Twelve. Teach them the way you touch people. The way you love people."

I paused, remembering the change that had come over the paralyzed man that day in Peter's house. Jesus hadn't even touched him, just looked at him, known him.

"You could teach us to love." I took a deep breath. "You could teach me."

"As you are teaching me, Maeve." He reached out and held his hand just next to my cheek, the way you might hold your hand just over a flame. I closed my eyes, and felt the caress in my whole being. "As you are teaching me."

CHAPTER FIFTY-SEVEN

ON A MISSION

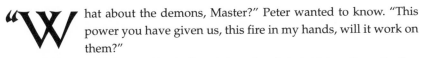

"What about the demons, Master?" Peter wanted to know. "This power you have given us, this fire in my hands, will it work on them?"

As flock after flock of birds flew across the sky to winter places further south, the Twelve, Mary B, Joanna, Jesus and I had made a temporary retreat deep in the hills away from the crowds; Peter was pacing as he spoke, gazing in awe at his hands, touching things—an infected hangnail of Tomas's, a blister on Matthew's foot. Then he made for John, who had chronic troubles with his knees.

"Get away from me, Peter." John gave him a shove. "You're no better than the rest of us here. Save it for the lepers."

"Lepers!" James yelped. "You expect us to touch lepers, Master? You can't be serious."

Jesus answered with an eloquent silence that filled his disciples with uneasiness. They all knew that Jesus had touched lepers, women with female troubles, and even dead people in utter disregard of the laws of purity.

"About the demons," Peter broke the silence and diverted everyone from more fearsome prospects. "Can we command them? Will they recognize the power in us as they do in you?'

I admit I was curious, too, especially since the rumor persisted that I had been possessed by seven demons. It had become part of the mythology surrounding me. Yet I still didn't grasp the nature of demons. My alleged infestation notwithstanding, had I ever encountered a demon?

For a moment the chatter of the Twelve receded and I stared through the Galilean hills to another world where there was always wind and the sound and smell of the sea, except in the depths of the dark grove. I saw my father's face again, so disturbingly like my face but with pure hatred looking out from his eyes. Hatred that had nothing to do with me and yet that drove him to try to destroy me, and, failing that, himself. Was that hatred a demon?

"Maeve," my beloved called me back to the present. And I looked at him, startled afresh by the love in his eyes, fathomless and mysterious. "Will you answer Peter's question?"

"Me?"

"Her?" the Twelve chorused.

"Well, she ought to know," Judas muttered. "She was ridden with them."

"You don't even believe in demons, Judas," Simon rebuked him.

"Maeve?" Jesus prompted.

"Um," I managed. What had become of my native eloquence? "Could you repeat the question?"

"Does the fire of the stars, as you call it, give someone the power to command demons?"

"Well," I decided to answer; what the hell, I'd make it up as I went along. "That all depends on the demon. Some are more biddable than others."

I caught Jesus's eye. He was grinning. Was I being set up? Probably.

"But they always obey the Master," Peter asserted. "You don't deny that, do you, Mary? Yours did. Didn't they?" he added a trifle dubiously.

"Jesus!" I lost my patience. "Will you tell your friends once and for all that you didn't cast even one demon out of me, let alone seven?"

"Your mean she's still possessed?" Several people jumped to that conclusion.

"But it makes a good story." Jesus had me on that one, and he knew it. "Aren't you the one who told me a story is true if it is well told?"

"It was my mothers who said that, not me. You're the one who told me there's one truth. In my case, I found that out the hard way."

I had believed my mothers' story that my father was the shape-shifting god of the sea. I had believed every one of their dozens of tales of my miraculous conception. And then I had found out the truth, the one truth of who he was. And yet, in the end, that truth had come to encompass all the stories. In the end, the truth was a mystery.

"I remember, Maeve. Do you?"

I looked around at the disciples, Joanna and Mary B now among them. Even the slowest sensed some secret history between their beloved Rabbi and me. Jesus was asking me—not to reveal it, perhaps, but to draw from it, to offer it in some way.

"Remember," he charged me.

I closed my eyes and saw my father's face again; the haunted look, the hatred that would overcome him, and yes, possess him. Possessed by that demon, he had entered me by force, driven my soul right out of my body. Then one night Jesus, the boy the druids called Esus, had come to me. He had held his fiery hands just over my body, moving them from my crown until he came to my feet. He had taken hold of my feet, held them in his hands, rooted me again in the earth, in my body, in life.

"It's not what you cast out of me that I remember, Rabbi. It's what you called back to me—the part of me that had been wandering and lost. You restored me to myself; you restored my soul."

"But what about the demons," Tomas fretted. "Where do they go?"

"Master," Peter jumped in, "did you not tell us that when an unclean spirit is cast out of someone it wanders through a waterless country looking for a place to rest? When it cannot find one, it says, 'I will return to the home I came from.' When it finds the home unoccupied and swept and tidied, it goes out and collects seven other spirits—"

"One, two, three, four, five six, seven," counted Tomas, who was obsessed not with the esoteric meaning of numbers but with their very existence.

"Yes, Tomas, eight all together," Peter said kindly. "And they all set up housekeeping. So then what do we do? Where does it end?"

Jesus didn't speak, merely gestured: the field was wide open.

"Any housewife can tell you that you must clean everyday," said Joanna. "Or the house becomes dirty again."

"No, Joanna," said Mary B, discomfited perhaps by the domestic imagery. "The problem isn't that the house was dirty. For the Rabbi said it was swept and tidied. It's that it was empty, unoccupied. Someone has to live there—or else the demons take over. Isn't that what you meant, Mary? By saying the Master restored you to yourself."

I could hardly believe that she was appealing to me instead of Jesus. I turned to him. Demons are your department, I wanted to say. But he just stroked his beard and chewed his cheek lightly, waiting to see what I would do.

"I don't know," I said to Mary. "That might be what I meant. To tell you the truth, I'm still not certain what demons are, but I'm wondering: if they are cast out, then maybe they are like other outcasts—lepers, beggars, whores, the *am-ha-arez*. You can send them away, but they are still there. If people are hungry, they will steal food. If they are reviled, they will seek revenge. Maybe the thing to do is not to cast out demons, but to find a way to bring them in, give them something useful to do?"

Everyone seemed nonplussed, even Jesus. I didn't know if I was making any sense. Could my father's demon have been fed and tamed, given a useful household task? Who was my father when he had been at home? I hardly knew; I had seen only the public man and the private horror. No one had been able to call him back to himself as Jesus had called me. Though I had tried. Manannan Mac Lir, I had called him, father, my father. I had wanted to love him; I did love him. He had almost come back, but then the demon took over again and tried to kill me.

"I don't really know what I'm talking about," I admitted.

"Don't you?" said Jesus. "I wonder. A woman who once abused you as her slave has become your friend and benefactress."

"Oh, you mean Paulina? But I didn't drive any demons out of her."

"No, you gave them quarter!" Judas almost spat. "Isn't that what you just said? Invite the demons in. And you," he rounded on Jesus. "You commend her for consorting with these foreigners occupying our soil, a woman whose husband built a pleasure city on the bones of our ancestors. I don't understand you at all."

"Judas! Don't speak to our Master that way." Peter was on his feet in an instant.

"Sit down, Peter," said Jesus.

"Not that I understand either," Peter added.

"Have I not said to you: Love your enemies; pray for those who persecute you, that you may be the children of God. For God makes the sun shine on the good and the evil and sends rain on the righteous and the unrighteous."

"Are we to make no distinctions then?"

Judas spoke quietly, but I could hear the fury. I wished I could find a way to tell him: I understand your passion for sovereignty. I am the daughter of warrior witches, named for a warrior queen; my father was a military strategist for kings. I might have befriended a Roman woman, but I still see Rome as the enemy. Even if I never set foot on the Holy Isles again, I want my *combrogos* to repel the Romans from their shores. But Judas had always refused to engage in direct conversation with me. My lineage would not impress him; in his eyes I was hopelessly compromised. And he was a disturbing enigma to me. Peter put down his nets for blind bewildered love of Jesus. Why had Judas cast aside his sword? What did he hope to gain?

"God will judge," said Jesus, his voice strangely sad.

In the silence that followed, a flock of birds lifted from a stand of live oaks and spread over the sky. A moment later the wind called *qadim* began to blow. It came from the east bringing clear, cold air. The stars would be brilliant tonight, but we would have to sleep in a huddle if we were not to freeze. My people called this season song time, for the wandering bards would be seeking a hearth and the roving warrior bands would also find a place to roost and tell their tale.

"Maeve," Jesus again called me back. "You still haven't answered Peter's question. Can the fire of the stars command demons?"

"Master, surely you can tell us yourself!" Peter took the words out of my mouth.

Jesus said nothing; he wasn't going to let me off the hook. Well, I still wasn't certain about the demons, but the fire of the stars had claimed me long ago.

"Peter," I turned to the big, red-faced fisherman. "Here's all I know: when the fire of the stars comes, you just love the person in front of you, even if it's only for that moment, even if you don't much like him. You love that one as if she were your best beloved, as if he were god in disguise. As to power over demons, I don't think we command them, it's the fire of the stars that commands us, that wants to come through us to touch the one who needs healing, however she needs it, whether he's leprous or demon-ridden."

Peter usually avoided my eyes, but now he looked at me, and I looked back, and something changed between us, whether we liked it or not. He nodded slowly, and then embarrassment caught up with him, and he lowered his eyes. I turned to Jesus. Satisfied? I wanted to say. He did look immensely pleased—with himself. All at once, I figured it out. He had me; he had us all. He had listened to my criticisms and answered my objections. The disciples were no longer mere followers and hangers on. They now had the authority to go forth on their own to preach and heal and bring the good news of the Kingdom of Heaven. And I was no longer an outsider, along for the ride as his wife. I might not call myself a disciple; I might not care a fig (I use that term deliberately) for scriptures and messianic prophecy. But I was with them now, one of the posse, on a mission with the Son of Man.

Gentle as a dove, clever as a serpent. That was our Jesus. Damn.

And so we went forth in twos and sometimes threes with the authority to do whatever it is you do with demons and the power to heal the sick. We took no haversacks, no coins, no extra tunic, just wandered, accepting hospitality where it was offered and, where it wasn't, shaking the dust of the unwelcoming place from our feet. In fact, this dispersed ministry was a practical way to spend the colder months when camping out wasn't as comfortable, and no one household (except Temple Magdalen where the Twelve feared to tread) could accommodate and feed so many.

We agreed to meet again near the end of Adar in time to get drunk together on Purim. (I know it doesn't tell you that in the Bible—but why else are you listening to this story, if not to get the juicy bits that the Bible leaves out?)

And speaking of juicy bits, contrary to the instructions recorded in the Gospel of Matthew, where Jesus allegedly enjoins the disciples to avoid gentile territory, especially Samaritan towns, we did make a foray into Samaria—as you know from non-synoptic John, author of what I call the Commuter Gospel; there is so much traipsing back and forth between Judea and Galilee.

But the contradictions among his chroniclers are not the point, or my point anyway, which is: that you don't know the whole story of the woman at the well. Not by a long shot.

CHAPTER FIFTY-EIGHT

WOMEN AT THE WELL

Yes, of course, I am going to tell you my version, though I wasn't there at Jacob's famous well, but in town with Mary B buying provisions with the coins Jesus had admonished his disciples not to carry. (We were on our way back from visiting Martha and Lazarus in Bethany, and they insisted on giving us a purse.)

But to get back to the story: have you ever noticed that the encounter between Jesus and the Samaritan woman crackles with erotic energy? It was scandalous enough to begin with, a Jewish man asking a Samaritan woman to give him a drink of water, as she pointed out. Then Jesus made his enigmatic offer of living water. Now imagine the woman answering back in a Mae West voice, a hand resting on an out-thrust hip, a glance through cosmetically thickened eyelashes: "Why don't you give me some of that living water, big boy, so that I may never thirst again?" And Jesus (yes, my husband) flirted back. Why else do you suppose his response was to tease her about her five ex-husbands and her current paramour? All right, so supposedly they go on to talk about worshipping their mutual god in spirit and truth. But that's not what gives the scene its sizzle.

How do I know she was hitting on him, since I admit I wasn't present at their meeting? Here comes the part you don't know: that woman followed us for a day and a night, sizing up the situation and apparently deciding that Jesus had the beginnings of a harem and another concubine would not come amiss.

We were near the border of Samaria and had decided to camp for the night rather than seek shelter in a town where our welcome would be uncertain. And when I woke the next morning, I found her curled up on the other side of Jesus. She was snoring softly, but even then I could tell she was sexy. Not pretty—she had a wide, bruised-looking mouth, bad teeth, a crooked nose that had probably been broken, lank hair. But I recognized at once the tough, tenacious sensuality that I had seen in many a street whore.

Jesus remained sound asleep, too, so I passed my hand lightly over the woman's face, grazing her charcoaled eyelashes until she opened her eyes and stared up at me, at which point I clapped one hand tightly over her mouth. I wanted to deal with the woman alone without rousing Jesus or Mary B. I gestured for her to get up and come with me, and I must have looked ferocious enough that she complied. Or else she was savvy enough to understand that if she wanted to get to Jesus, she'd have to get past me. I dragged her some distance away, and then I confronted her.

"Who are you, and what do you want?"

"Who wants to know?" She tossed her head, doing her best to brazen it out.

"Maeve of Magdala," I said out of long habit.

She sneered eloquently: like that's supposed to impress me?

"Let me put it another way: what were you doing in bed with my husband?"

"Your *husband*!"

I had succeeded in throwing her off-balance, and in a perverse way, I have to admit I was pleased that I did not look like this woman's idea of a wife.

"Yes, I'm afraid he is."

She recovered herself enough to shrug, but I sensed the desperation beneath the bravado. I also noticed that her mouth didn't just look bruised; it was bruised, and so was her eye.

"You're hurt." My hand reached out of its own accord; she flinched and pushed me away.

"I don't need your help."

"I think maybe you do," I disagreed gently.

"Shit," she said, an expression of defeat and defiance in one. I grudgingly admired her economy of language.

"Sit down and tell me what happened."

And so she told me her version of the meeting at the well, which is not so different from John's account—except that she kept repeating: "No man has ever spoken to me that way, no man has ever looked at me that way." To put it simply: she had felt seen by Jesus, known by him, *loved* by him and it overwhelmed her. And just as John says, she went and told everyone in town—including her sugar daddy, who jumped to the conclusion that she was whoring after a filthy Jew. It wasn't the first time he beat her up.

"But I swear it's the last," she concluded. "That man over there you say is your husband, he said he could give me living water, so that I would never thirst. I don't know what the hell he means, but whatever it is, I want it, and I don't have anything to give him in return but my body."

"Who says you have to give him anything?" I countered sharply.

I might as well have said: who says you have anything to give him, anything he needs? For she looked away suddenly as if I had struck her a blow, and I felt acutely the pain of her poverty, of being confronted with a love that asks nothing of you but your pride. How hard such love could be.

"I still don't know your name," I said. "Will you tell me?"

"Susanna." She turned to face me again; her eyes had turned into deep pools; I thought of the well of wisdom on Tir na mBan and the spring rising at Temple Magdalen, of the Nile flooding and receding, leaving fertility in its wake.

"Listen, Susanna," I said. "All water is living, that's what I believe. All water is holy, including the water you gave Jesus to drink from Jacob's well. Maybe you've already given him more than you know."

"But he, he might be, he is...the Savior."

Another one clamoring for the One. I sighed. Well, let her be Jesus's problem then.

Some of you may not want to hear what I have to tell you next—those of you who need to believe that Jesus was always calm, compassionate, full of certainty, in command of every situation. In short, not human. But mine is the Gospel of pillow talk and marital wrangles. So pull up a chair, press your ear against the door (that night we slept in a barn with a stall) and listen.

"Maeve, there's got to be some limit." My beloved had hidden his consternation all day as Susanna continued to follow us, but now that we were alone, he was flat out panicked. "We can't take everyone with us. And this woman is a Samaritan—"

"Like the man who saved your life and delivered you to my gates."

"And she's, well, she's not married and a—"

"Whore? Are you trying to say whore?" I was spoiling for a fight.

"She's not a whore, is she?" He appealed to my expertise.

"She's not a professional. Wasn't trained. I gather she was widowed young and ended up taking care of herself by becoming the unofficial town slut, going from one man to the next. But why am I telling you?" I said angrily. "She says you know everything about her, her whole life story. Damn it, she's in love with you."

Jesus didn't answer right away. In the dark, I could hear him thinking, that is, chewing his cheek.

"Maeve, do you remember what you said to Peter about loving the person in front of you as if he were your best beloved? As if he were God in disguise?"

"And your point?" Tricky bastard, quoting me to myself.

"Well, that's what happens. That's what I did when I encountered that woman at the well. When people say I see them, know them, it's because for a moment I do see with God's eyes, love with God's love. The trouble is, I don't always know what to do after that moment."

"What you usually do is disappear." I decided to be merciless.

"But I don't want people to want *me*. I don't want people to love me. I want them to love God. Don't you see?"

"Oh, I see, all right. You're the one who doesn't see. People, all people, your people, too, are hungering for a god they can see, a god they can touch, a god who can be their lover. Or a goddess," I added fiercely. "That's what a priestess is at Temple Magdalen—a way for the goddess to become flesh."

There was a silence as thick and dark as night in the stable.

"Maeve, you can't mean I should be a male, well, there's no word for it."

"I'd rather not mean that, but I suppose to be consistent, I must." It was all so confused and confusing, this mediating and muddling between the human and the divine.

"But we're married now?" he said hopefully, desperately.

"I don't know that marriage solves anything," I sighed. "'You are lovers, but not just of each other. You are the lovers of the world,'" I quoted the prophetess Dwynwyn for the umpteenth time.

"I always said you took her too literally," Jesus groaned. "Anyway, I'm not going to sleep with Susanna, that's out."

I was glad it was dark, and he could not see how relieved I felt.

"Whatever," I said. "All I meant was: you created this situation, deal with it."

"But how? As you have reminded me, I owe my life to a Samaritan, and I prophesied to this woman that there will be an end to our people's rivalries— but how do I explain to the Twelve that we will be traveling with a Samaritan woman? You have to understand: to a Jew, a Samaritan woman is the uncleanest of the unclean."

"Why do you have to explain anything to them?" I countered. "And by the way, aren't you already traveling with a gentile whore? I thought *I* was the uncleanest!"

"You're my wife, Maeve."

"How you do harp on that."

"Well, it makes a difference. The men have to accept you."

"That's where you're wrong," I argued. "They don't have to accept me—they have to tolerate me, because you insist on it, and some of them have a hard time doing that much."

"What do you mean?"

"Haven't you noticed that Judas won't even look at me, much less speak to me?"

"Oh, well, Judas," he said too quickly, too dismissively.

"Why did you call him to be a disciple?" I asked suddenly. "What is it that makes you call one person and not another?"

"Don't you understand yet?" He was a little testy. "It's not what *I* want. I am listening, always listening for what the Most High is asking of me—even when I don't understand it, especially then."

"So, if your god had left it up to you, you wouldn't have chosen Judas?"

"I didn't say that, Maeve. Don't put words in my mouth. Judas has valuable knowledge to offer and passionate conviction. Israel is a divided house. Pharisees, Sadducees, zealots, rich, poor, educated, ignorant. I am called, no, *we* are called, to bring the people together, at one table, at the feast of the Most High. How else will the Kingdom come?"

"*Cariad.*" I rolled over, not quite closing the space between us but coming close enough to feel the heat of his body, the heat our bodies made together. "I thought paradise was already here, in our midst. I thought that's what we were telling people, showing people. I thought that was our good news."

"Maeve." He rolled towards me. "Beloved, you said *we.*"

Then he kissed me, and we went on kissing, remembering what lips and tongues are for and forgetting everything else, everyone else. But when he entered me, I began to see faces, Judas's, Peter's, faces of men I knew and didn't know. Just as I had received all men before as if they were my beloved, now I received him as if he were all men. I thought of Susanna, too, and tried to make my pleasure a prayer for her. At last I went beyond thought, and all the faces faded in the fierceness of our fire.

"Jesus," I said when we lay spent together afterwards. "Do you remember how you told me, after I calmed the storm, that I didn't need to keep rescuing you. You could handle everything yourself?"

"What a dolt I was!"

"Well, I have an idea about what to do with Susanna, if you don't."

"Thank Adonai!"

"No, thank Isis. Listen, Temple Magdalen might be the perfect place for her. I'd like to go visit for a few days when we get back to Galilee. I've already invited Mary."

"Mary of Bethany? In a pagan whorehouse!"

"She's unconventional and curious. You of all people should know that. Joanna might meet us there; she wants to see how we set up the clinic."

"Is this a female conspiracy?"

"If you'd like to think so. Anyway, why don't you go reconnoiter with the guys in Capernaum before we all get together again."

"What would I do without you?" He pulled me even closer; I could feel his heart beating; I noticed that we breathed in and out at the same time.

"You would be in deep shit."

"Amen."

And so Jesus's women (did I just say that?) had a holiday of sorts among the whores, though we all worked in various ways. Judith was in ecstasies over Mary B—at last, a Torah teacher at Temple Magdalen! All the children and many of the adults took instruction with Mary while we were there. Joanna joined us after wintering with her family at Herod's court where, she reported, John still ranted and languished in prison. She and I made ourselves useful in the clinic, while Susanna agreed to undertake training as a whore-priestess with Dido and Berta. We all helped Timothy with the early planting. Paulina came often to visit with her children, including a new baby, her first son, and Reginus and I spent several lazy afternoons together, confiding in each other about our lives and loves.

Perhaps you would like to hear more about that time, those of you who have grown attached to Temple Magdalen and its inhabitants. Others of you may wonder how I could have willingly left his side for a moment, with his vision of death hanging over us. Maybe this separation was my way of denying impending disaster, pretending we had all the time in the world. Maybe I just needed the comfort of old friendships to strengthen me for what was to come. Anyway, I will have to leave all the smaller, sweeter moments to your imagination. This story must gather force now and begin to narrow like the funnel of a whirlwind. I must keep a clear focus, as if my eye were the eye of a storm.

Soon Jesus sent word for us to join him and the others at one of our meeting places in the hills near Bethsaida. Us, presumably, meant Mary B, Joanna, and me. I thought I had solved the problem of Susanna. Dido and Berta had told me they were pleased with her progress, and she seemed content. At dawn on the day we were to leave, I encountered her at Temple Magdalen's spring. She was sitting and gazing into it.

"Living water," she spoke to my reflection. "You are right about that."

"I'm glad you're happy here," I said.

She looked much better; she'd put on a little weight; Dido and Berta had taught her a thing or two about make-up, mainly that less is more. And her hair had some luster. She had also lost the craven, calculating look of a stray creature that has to beg and dodge blows just to survive. In short, whatever her religion, she was shaping up as a Temple Magdalen priestess.

"Oh, I am," she acknowledged. "Too bad I can't stay."

"What do you mean?"

"I'm going with you."

She turned from the spring and looked straight at me.

"Susanna," I sighed. "It won't work. Jesus may not be prejudiced against Samaritans, but his disciples are. If you love him, you won't put him in that position."

"I didn't say anything about him. I said I'm going with *you*."

"Me?"

"Yes, you, priestess of Isis. I am going to follow you."

I stared at her, not taking in the full implication.

I found myself speechless as the birds started to sing. Susanna's gaze returned to the spring. She was disturbingly serene. I sat down next to her, and stared into the water myself. It gave back only empty sky. No visions, not even enigmatic ones, to clue me about how to handle this predicament.

"Susanna, how can you follow me? I'm not leading anyone anywhere. I don't even know where I'm going."

But that wasn't true. I was going with him, wherever he went, I, who refused to call myself a follower.

"That doesn't matter," she shrugged.

"But why would you want to follow me? Who do you think I am?"

Jesus, I was starting to sound like him.

"Listen, priestess—"

"Please call me Maeve." She said the word priestess the way a cab driver might say lady, with a certain exasperated disrespect.

"If you don't know who you are yet, I'm not the one to tell you. You'll have to figure it out. All you have to do right now is say yes or no, ok?"

"Here's the deal," I said. "I don't want a follower. If you come with me, you come as a companion. And by the way, that means no screwing my husband behind my back."

"I'll be sure to do it in front of your face," she said deadpan, then she cracked a grin—full of crooked and missing teeth—and I knew I had a friend.

And so Mary B (who surprised me by making no objection to Susanna; the spirit of Temple Magdalen must have come upon her) Joanna, Susanna and I went off to meet Jesus and the Twelve.

"What is *she* doing here?" Jesus whispered as we went apart to embrace. "I thought you were going to settle her at Temple Magdalen."

"She's with me," I tried to explain.

"What do you mean?"

"Don't ask. I'll take care of any problems with her, all right? Just kiss me."

Surely the best way to shut him up and get him to stop asking awkward questions.

"Jamie, Johnnie!" I heard the bellowing of a woman's voice, the kind of voice that could make itself heard in a crowded marketplace. "Where did you put that load of dried fish?"

"Who's that?" I asked.

"Salome, the mother of the Thunder Brothers," Jesus spoke into my ear. "She was recently widowed. I'm not sure whether they're looking after her or she's looking after them, but she's attached herself."

"There, there," I soothed him. "At least she's not *your* mother."

"Bite your tongue."

Over Jesus's shoulder, I caught a glimpse of Judas looking like a thundercloud about to burst. I wondered: why did he persist with Jesus? Why didn't he throw up his hands over this unruly operation and walk away in disgust?

"Come, *cariad*, we better join the others."

We celebrated Purim and our reunion with drunken feasting, singing, dancing, and storytelling as jolly as a Temple Magdalen Shabbat. Salome clasped me to her bosom at once—it was the kind of bosom you could use as a small table, and she did, propping her arms against it and deftly slicing vegetables in midair. She had a broad face, permanently reddened cheeks, and looked exactly like the fishwife she had been. Although she is famous for lobbying on her sons' behalf for preferred seats in heaven, she was the sort of woman who mothers everyone, and she called us all by an endless string of inventive endearments.

So now you have met all the women Luke mentions; well, he forgot about Mary B. But then people have confused us—not to mention merged our identities—for centuries. It was a rough life, so we women never did get our numbers up to twelve.

Then, too, as I have indicated, it was not always clear who was following whom.

CHAPTER FIFTY-NINE

DINNER FOR FIVE THOUSAND

Our happy retreat in the hills didn't last long. We were still sleeping off our hangovers when John the Dipper's disciples caught up with us, and we had to lift our aching heads to hear the horrible news.

The story of John the Baptist's end has been the stuff of lurid tales from the medieval passion plays to Hollywood melodrama. Ruthless Herodias, Herod's illicit wife and the object of John's moral ire, tricks out her nubile daughter to perform the seductive dance of the seven veils for the king's birthday. When the delighted king says: name your reward, the well-trained daughter answers: thanks, step-daddy, but all I want is your prophet's head on a platter.

Imagine hearing that story for the first time in the company of Jesus, who had followed his cousin into the wilderness, lived as his disciple in the harsh, heady simplicity of the desert, gone down into the cold muddy waters under the force of John's hands, John who had finally driven Jesus forth to face himself and find his own vision.

"We buried his body," John's disciple concluded with that eerie lack of affect that so often marks the recounting of horrors. "But not his head; Herodias kept it."

Then the man started to tremble, and he turned his head aside and retched.

"Look to him and the others," Jesus said to us, and then he took off alone.

Together we tended John's bereaved followers who had not slept or eaten for days. Whether or not John had instructed them to go to Jesus in the event of his death or whether they simply didn't know what else to do was not clear to us. We gave the exhausted men as much unwatered wine as we had left, and as much food as they would eat, and bedded them down as comfortably as we could. Then we sat around staring at each other and worrying about Jesus, wanting to talk about John and his death, but feeling constrained. It was Judas who finally broke the silence, speaking in low tones, so as not to wake John's disciples.

"You know what this means, don't you?"

No one answered, since obviously Judas intended to tell us.

"There is no one else." He couldn't quite keep the excitement out of his voice, though I believe he tried, out of deference to the dead prophet. "Sure there are plenty of preachers and wonder workers and prophetic ranters, but no one since the Maccabees, except John and Jesus, has ever had the power to gather the people into one force, and John wasted his."

"Hush, Judas, the prophet is not cold in his grave," Peter said nervously. "I don't think the Master would like us to speak of him that way."

"It is only the truth, and John knew it himself at the end," insisted Judas.

"What do you mean John wasted his power?" Mary B challenged Judas, and I wondered if he would be provoked into actually speaking to her.

"I think Judas means that John lost touch with the people," Simon spoke for his comrade. "He got so caught up in the fine points of the Law. To people who have been driven off their land, people who are starving, what does it matter who the king takes to his bed. John got sidetracked, obsessed."

Judas grunted his assent and avoided looking at Mary. I tended to agree with Judas and Simon on this one, but I could see that Mary was getting worked up. Then I remembered that she must have known John during her time with the Essenes.

"You're missing the point, Simon. Herod is a Jewish king, at least in name, and he is flagrantly disregarding the Law of Moses. Don't you get it? It's not about sex." Mary B seemed to have lost her virginal reticence. "It's about the people, Israel, our forgetting who we are, violating our Covenant with the Most High, becoming like our oppressors, like the Romans. That's what John fought against—to the death. What's the use of your going on and on about The People, defending The People, liberating The People, if there *is* no People. What makes us a People? Answer me that!"

"The L-Law and the p-p-prophets!" answered pale, scholarly Philip, who had grown quite pink; he had a terrible crush on Mary, and he always stuttered when excited. "The M-master said: I come not to abolish the Law and the Prophets but to fulfill them." He spoke more clearly when quoting Jesus. "Not one jot or tittle is to disappear."

Judas stood up; he did not look directly at Mary but swept us all with a challenging look that bordered on contemptuous. "I refuse to be drawn into arguments about the Law. That's not my area of expertise; that's not why Jesus chose me to be part of this mission. I'm only stating the obvious, what you would see, too, if you weren't so busy contemplating your navels and splitting hairs. John's death will stir up the people, throw them into turmoil. The time has come to act. They need a leader. Now."

In the silence that followed, I looked at Judas, standing against the backdrop of the stony hills, hills where he had lived in the rough for years, where he knew every vantage point and hideout. His skin was sallow and pockmarked, his expression never far from angry. No, angry is too broad a stroke, too simple a description of some emotion far more complex. Again I had that nagging feeling, like knowing a word but not being able to call it up. I almost had it—what was wrong with this picture, what was dangerous.

"I am no expert on anything." Joanna broke the silence, and, like Judas, got to her feet to command our attention, "nor am I certain why or even if I have been chosen by the Master, but I must warn you all of something, and warn Jesus. I know Herod; I have lived in his court since I was married. The king did not want to kill John; he was terribly afraid of him, more than that, afraid of the spirit of God in him. Herod will be haunted now, dreading revenge from beyond the grave. If our Master appears to step into John's place, guilt and terror will drive Herod to hunt him down. I say we lay low for a while."

As if either of them—or any of us—had any control over what Jesus would do. It's not that he didn't care for us all. But what we wanted didn't matter in the end—nor even what Jesus wanted. It was all about the will of his plaguing Father in Heaven. Well, I had thought my father was a god, too, and look where it had gotten me. Not that I wanted to be anywhere else but in these hills with my beloved between earth and sky.

"I can't face the crowds today," said Jesus. "Peter, is the boat handy?"

When he returned from wherever he'd gone to be alone, Jesus had spent some time with John's disciples after they woke. Now they had dispersed (inevitably spreading the word of John's death) and Jesus was tense and restless.

"Yes, Master, it's in a cove not far from here."

"But Jesus," protested Judas, "the people—"

"I said not today," Jesus answered sharply. "Let's go to the boat."

But as we made for the cove, someone spotted us (a group our size is hard to hide) and people from all the nearby towns soon came and gathered on the shore. Jesus had one foot in the boat when he changed his mind and took pity on the people. For, as Mark says, "they were like sheep without a shepherd." And as I say, Jesus just wasn't predictable. In that way, I have to admit, he did resemble "the Father."

On the surface, the day unfolded like countless other days with Jesus—healing the sick, preaching, debating. Though the disciples had spent the winter ministering to the people on their own, when Jesus was present, they (or I should say we) were once again reduced to the status of handmaidens, ushers, and bodyguards, attempting to keep control of a crowd that kept growing all day. Were there really five thousand or is that just a Biblical figure of speech? I don't know; I didn't count. I left that to Tomas who had an idiot savant way with numbers. But in the late afternoon, I did climb the hill to scan the crowd, try to read its mood.

As I surveyed the horde, I began to see colors and patterns, places where the crowd's collective energy flowed or tangled. There was an undercurrent of expectation, agitation: a miracle could happen—or a riot. I shifted my vision again and focused on the people themselves. Over there I saw a bunch of fierce looking men, trying to stand aloof, hands hovering over hidden weapons. There were several contingents of Pharisees in full regalia, phylacteries strapped to their foreheads, and as always, the *Am-ha-arez*, waiting more patiently than anyone else—not wasting breath on debate, often with sick children in their laps.

"Halloo, lovey duck!" Salome, puffing and mopping her brow, bellowed to me from partway down the hill, clearly unwilling to climb one step further than necessary. "Hubby wants you."

(To the best of my knowledge, in the entire history of the world, only Salome has ever referred to the Son of Man as "hubby," which is why, I suppose, he was careful never to ask: who do *women* say I am?).

When we reached Jesus, he was conferring with his disciples or perhaps it was the other way around. He was sitting cross-legged with his eyes half-closed, as he often did when he couldn't retreat any other way.

"The sooner we disperse this crowd the better," Andrew was saying. "A hungry crowd is a dangerous crowd, and we're out in the middle of nowhere. Send them off to the towns where they can find something to eat."

"Then we can get to the boat," Peter added. "And—"

"And abandon the people," Judas jumped in. "Leave them with nothing."

"What do you mean with nothing!" Mary B took Judas on again; there was a terrible animosity between them. Perhaps they should work it out in bed. "The Rabbi's been here all day, preaching and healing."

"And he's worn out, poor lamb." Salome, of course.

I could hear Judas swearing or counting under his breath, trying not to lose his cool and sabotage his case. I felt a twinge of sympathy for him—all these bloody (sometimes literally) interfering women. But not enough sympathy to keep me quiet.

"Judas is right," I attempted diplomacy, probably a bad idea. "Everyone is waiting for you to do or say something now that John is dead, but from what I can see, whatever you do, people will fight over it." Probably the most prophetic statement I ever made.

"Every possible contentious faction is here," agreed Mary B.

Jesus opened his eyes, and looked at each one of us.

"The whole house of Israel?" Jesus asked.

"Yes," Judas answered with impressive restraint.

"Maeve," Jesus turned to me. "If you had this crowd at Temple Magdalen—"

"They wouldn't fit in the courtyard," I tried to resist.

"Forget the numbers," he dismissed my objection. "If you had a house full of people who couldn't stand each other—yet they were your guests—what would you do?"

This question was a trap; I knew it. Just as he was getting a second wind, my sails sagged. I was too tired to outmaneuver him, as if I could anyway.

"I'd tell them to sit down, shut up, and eat," I answered truthfully.

He beamed at me, as if I were the best student in class. I glared back, but he took no notice.

"Then that's what we'll do."

"What?" asked Peter. "What are we doing?"

"We're going to tell them to sit down and eat. 'Paradise is here,'" he said looking straight at me. "'My feast is laid. Go gather the guests, go gather my people.'"

I recognized the words, of course. The words his god (or, as I had always suspected, my goddess) had spoken to him in the desert. There was no arguing with a vision, but the beleaguered disciples didn't know that yet.

"What feast? What's he talking about? Is this, like, a parable or something?" they asked each other under their breath.

"But Master," Andrew took it upon himself to speak for everyone. "We don't have enough food for so many and if we were to go buy provisions, it would cost over 200 *denarii*!"

"How much food do we have?" asked Jesus.

"After last night's carrying on and what with feeding John's men, Master dear, we only have five loaves and two dried fish," said Salome. "Hardly enough to feed ourselves."

"Maeve, beloved, will you bring the loaves and fishes to me? The rest of you, go among the people, invite them to the feast, tell them to sit down together."

"Don't forget the shut up part," I added.

"Yes, tell them to be quiet until I've finished the blessing."

The Twelve gaped at him. Really, they should be used to impossible situations by now—possessed pigs leaping over cliffs, people rising from the dead. You never knew what was going to happen around Jesus.

"Move it," said Jesus to the disciples.

What was I thinking as I went to fetch our meager supplies—all of which fit in one basket that we'd stowed under a shade tree? To tell the truth, I was not thinking at all. I was noticing: the slant of the light, the shadows cast by stones and tufts of grass, how people's faces looked softer and more open in this last glow. I felt the earth under my bare feet, and the shifting temperature as the sun's warmth began to steal away and the ground gave up its stored heat. When I picked up the basket, I noted the bread still smelled fresh, the dried fish, spicy. I balanced the basket between my breast and hip as if it were a baby and walked back to my beloved.

When he saw me, he looked awed, as if he had not just asked me, moments ago, to get the food. I gazed back at him, seeking the dark scrying pools of his eyes, and then I saw it, what he saw. Light pulsed around me, as if the fire of the stars had overflowed its bounds. Yes, I knew what he saw, more: *who* he saw. With her hands I gave him the bread and fish; with her lips I kissed him.

The crowd hushed, and he began to pray in Hebrew: *Baruch Ata Adonai Elohenu*...In my mother tongue, I prayed with him: Blessed is she, queen of earth and heaven, of dust and stars, who feeds us with her body, whose womb leaps with fish, whose breast is a field of wheat.

There was enough. More than enough. As the story goes, there were twelve (notice the number) baskets of leftovers. Was it a miracle, loaves and fishes magically reproducing right and left? Was it a miracle, a bunch of cantankerous human beings forgetting their feuds for a moment and turning to share whatever they had with each other?

If you've listened to my story this far, you should know by now that I'm not going to explain the miracle, but I will tell you this much. Whatever miracles are, they unfold in the realm of what the Greeks call *Kairos*, god's time or timelessness. Then *Chronos* (who is a Greek god, too, just to confuse matters) begins again, and all hell breaks loose.

"Master!" Judas was exultant, practically glowing in the dark.

I was instantly alarmed; Judas had never to my knowledge called Jesus "Master."

"I don't know how you did it, and I don't care. It was a brilliant move. The men of Israel are united at last. They mean to make you their king. You must speak to them now; they will do anything you say. You have them eating out of the palm of your hand."

"Literally," Simon laughed.

Jesus made no answer. It was night now, and the hill was lit with torches—as if an army had massed. By flame light, Jesus's brown, weathered face looked unusually pale.

"Beloved," I said. "Are you all right?"

He gave me a look of bewilderment that took me back to that night long ago when he had been a young man lashed to a tree in a druid grove, not sure how he had come to be there, afraid he had made a terrible mistake.

"What is it, *cariad*?" I whispered. But there was no way to speak privately with him now. The twelve men and the other four women all waited, all of them uncertain and a little frightened, except for Judas.

"If you don't go to them, if you don't take command, they will take you by force." Judas's tone was urgent. "All you have to do is speak, fill them with a sense of hope and purpose that we can once more be a sovereign people, have a united Israel as we have not since King Solomon. There are twelve of us to carry out your will, to organize, form coalitions as strong as the twelve tribes of Israel. Tonight the people worship you; they are crying out for you. Go to them."

Suddenly I saw it, and wondered how I could have been so blind. Judas had a vision; he knew what the people needed, or believed he did. He had passionate conviction, but what he lacked was charisma—that elusive gift, so unfairly doled out by the gods. Jesus had charisma in spades, and Judas knew it. It would be too simple to say that Judas merely wanted to use Jesus. He was drawn to Jesus, too, even moved by him—the way a musician might admire a perfect instrument and long to sound it, to bring out its full range and power.

"My time is not yet come," Jesus spoke in a low voice, the same words he had spoken to his mother at our wedding.

"If not now, when?" Judas, too, spoke softly, leaning close to him.

In that moment, something terribly charged and intimate was happening between them. They might have been lovers; they might have been King Bran and his opponent in the grove, falling in love as they fought to the death.

"The one who feeds them, leads them," Judas went on. "You have given them bread, will you deny them yourself?"

"Man does not live by bread alone, but by every word that proceeds from the mouth of God."

I closed my eyes, and I saw where my beloved was: back in the desert, being offered the powers of Rome. Ah, my poor love. He had thought he was fulfilling his charge to gather his people for the feast, and now Judas was telling him he had impressed them with a trick no different from turning stones to bread. Everything that had happened in the desert had been a trial run. The real temptation was here, now.

"The people need more than words, they need a king, a true king—not some corrupt Roman puppet—a king they can fight for!"

"My kingdom is not the kind of kingdom you mean. It is not of this world."

"Jesus," said Judas, his voice harsh. "There is nowhere else. There is only this earth. The land. The people—" A sob tore from him, and he scrambled to his feet.

I thought then, and I have thought since, that Jesus should have let Judas go, acknowledged that their differences were irreconcilable, that the faith Judas had placed in Jesus could only be betrayed. Yes, betrayed. For I swear Judas felt betrayed that night, and Jesus could not bear to know it.

"Judas." Jesus spoke his name as a lover might have or a mother, and it stopped Judas in his tracks. "If you love me, stay."

That is the only time I ever saw my beloved abuse his power, his power to call love forth from depths people didn't even know existed. Better he had said, I love you, Judas, go in peace. We all paid dearly for that moment, and no one dearer than Judas.

"Go ahead in the boat, all of you," Jesus commanded. "I will deal with the crowd. Then I need to pray. Alone."

None of us saw how Jesus actually got the people to disperse, a miracle that makes feeding five thousand look like a piece of cake. We went on ahead, some of his chroniclers say to Capernaum, some say to Bethsaida. It doesn't matter. Here's the truth: we made straight for the nearest tavern and got a keg of wine. (Considering the day we'd had, can you blame us?) By the time we saw Jesus walking towards us on the waves, we were all three sheets to the wind. Figuratively and literally. One of those sudden lake squalls had hit, and we were a mess. It was Peter who spotted him first.

"It'sh the Mashter!" shouted Peter. "He'sh walking on water. Do you shee that? He's freakin' walkin'. On the water. Didn't I tell you, he's the messh—"

"Oh, shut up, Peter!" snapped Andrew. "I don't care if you're seeing pink elephants or flying camels, we've got to take in the sails now and row or we're sunk."

"I'm jusht showing my faith. I'm the onliesht one around here with any faith. Mashter!" Peter shouted and he lurched to his feet, not a smart thing to do in his condition or the boat's. "Mashter! Ish that you? Command me to come to you and I shwear I will. I believe—"

And Peter jumped out of the boat where he quickly lost faith that he could swim, much less walk on water.

"Help!" he spluttered, as the waves smacked him about. "Save me."

"Maeve! Calm the wind already," Jesus snapped at me as he reached the boat. "Can't you see that Susanna and Matthew are throwing up all over the nets? What the hell kind of weather witch are you? Do I have to do everything myself?"

I sobered up enough to deal with the squall, and the disciples hauled Peter out of the drink.

"Master," Peter spluttered but no longer slurred. "How can you walk on water, and I can't, how come!"

"Ah, Peter," sighed Jesus. "You have so little faith."

"No, no," Peter protested. "I do have faith, I do, I do! You're the God-damned Son of God. Everybody, you better bow down to him."

And they all did, even Judas who was drunker than I'd ever seen him. All but me. I don't think I've ever been *that* drunk. Jesus looked at me over their heads, with a mixture of amusement and despair.

"They don't get it," he said. "Even after the loaves and fishes."

"Frankly, *cariad*," I admitted. "Neither do I."

CHAPTER SIXTY

WHAT DOES HE WANT?

B ut what about the showdown between Jesus and Judas, you ask, aren't you going to tell us more? Only this for now: because it was not resolved, the conflict went underground. Or maybe a better way to say it is, what remained unspoken between them became a subtle toxin in the atmosphere. You couldn't see it or even smell it, but you breathed it, and it did its damage quietly.

To tell the truth, there were plenty of tensions among us all, and I generated my share, usually just by being myself. Peter and I still clashed frequently, but we had our better moments, too. Here is one for the record.

Not long after the feeding frenzy (as I call that miracle) we were in the town of Gennesaret where Jesus had been challenged to debate the Law with some important Pharisees from Jerusalem. Of course the place was mobbed, and I decided to give the debate a miss. It was so much more Mary B's element, and if anything exciting happened, she would explain it to me.

Somehow, in a town crowded with people clamoring for Jesus, I found what looked like a deserted alley, but as I turned a corner I heard a man sobbing. Even in a time and place where men shed tears more openly, a grown man weeping can be heartrending. I went to see if I could help, and to my surprise I found Peter crouching, crying his eyes out. I knelt beside him, and touched his shoulder. You might suppose he would have pushed me away or told me to leave him the hell alone; what he did instead astonished me.

"Oh, Mary," he wept, burying his face in my breasts. "How can he love me?"

I had often asked myself the same question, but for the first time, I acknowledged the answer: Peter put his whole heart into whatever he felt or did, however foolish.

"Peter, why wouldn't he love you?"

"I bring shame on him."

What now? I thought, but I didn't say it.

"I overheard the men, the learned doctors, talking about the Master. 'Have you seen his disciples?' they said. 'What bumpkins! They don't even wash their hands before they eat!' And I knew they meant me. I'm, I know I'm just a fisherman. I never learned the right way to do things, I never…"

Peter started to sob again. I patted and soothed and let him get the front of my tunic soggy. Thanks to my professional training, I am not squeamish about bodily fluids.

"Listen, Peter," I finally said. "The spite on those men's tongues is a lot filthier than any dirt on your hands. I can't pretend that I've ever understood the Law, but it seems to me that it's not what goes into your mouth that makes you unclean. That's going to pass through your stomach and end up in the shit hole anyway. It's what comes out of your mouth."

"Hey, that's pithy!"

Peter and I were both startled. Jesus, in that disconcerting way of his, had appeared without warning.

"Master!" Peter cried, scrambling to his feet so fast that he knocked me off balance in a most ungentlemanly fashion. For Christ's sake (excuse the anachronism) he acted as if Jesus had caught us having a quickie.

"Help the lady up," said Jesus.

Peter extended a hand gingerly as if reaching into a nest of snakes. There was gratitude for you, and me with his snot still smeared on my breast.

"Come on, you two, I'm about to go lambaste some hypocrites. Maeve, can I borrow what you just said?"

He was in a good mood; he enjoyed this sort of rapid-fire debate. He loved thinking on his feet, shooting from the hip. That's the trouble with writing down his words, and trying to make them into moral absolutes. No one I've ever known was so alive in the moment. Whether he was healing or arguing, he was responding to a particular person in front of him, not to an abstraction.

"It's all yours," I said. "But if you don't mind, I'm going to give the lambasting a miss. I thought I'd go to Temple Magdalen and arrange for some supplies."

"Why don't we all meet you there for Shabbat?" Jesus said casually, as if he and the disciples hung out there all the time. "Then we'll head north together."

"But Master!" protested Peter. "You can't mean for us to eat there! Surely, surely not *sleep* there. What will people say about us, about you? I mean—"

"Get over it, Peter," said Jesus, and he gave the Rock on Which the Church is Founded a playful punch in the arm. "Don't worry, Peter, the whores don't work on Shabbat."

We had a jolly Shabbat together in true Temple Magdalen style: feasting, telling stories, singing and dancing. Everyone enjoyed it, even Peter and Judas, who again drank heavily. It was a relief to all of us to relax and let loose in one of the few places the crowds wouldn't follow us. We were not the only guests that night. Joseph made a surprise visit in the company of the Samaritan merchant who had rescued Jesus. The two men had met through a business transaction in Tyre and, discovering what (and whom) they had in common, had decided to travel south together and stop at Magdala. The next day Jesus spent some time alone with his rescuer, and I caught up with Joseph.

"So how's married life?" Joseph's tone was light, but I could feel his tension as we sat, arms and shoulders touching, with our backs against a huge olive tree. Perhaps, as a married woman, I shouldn't have been so cozy with someone who was once (and might still wish to be) my lover. "Is it what you expected?"

"I never expected to be married, so I wouldn't know. I am glad to be with him…." I hesitated.

"I hear a 'but' coming."

"There's no 'but,'" I insisted. "It's hard sometimes, that's all."

"What's hard?" Joseph prodded. "The crowds, the disciples, the wandering, him?"

I didn't know the answer, and it bothered me. Or my mind didn't. I leaned my head against the tree and closed my eyes. I could sense the slow, unhurried life of the tree, hundreds of years of deepening roots. It seemed as though the tree felt my presence, too, and that it held me as if I were a child.

"I want to have a child with him," I heard myself saying.

And I turned and buried my face in Joseph's shoulder, acknowledging something I'd kept hidden from myself. Not only did I want our child, but I knew in that moment that I harbored a belief that if I got pregnant, I could shift the pattern, change the story.

"Ah, Maeve, Maeve." He stroked my hair and managed not to murmur false platitudes, like "you're young yet" (I wasn't) or "you will in time" (for how much time did we have?). It seemed to me that Joseph had become wiser, less Greek, more, well, Jewish, for lack of a better word. He had learned reason and philosophy have their limits.

"My dear," he said after a time, "you do know that Jesus is in danger."

"So, what else is new?"

"I'm serious, Maeve. Jesus is Herod's new nightmare, now that John is dead, *because* John is dead."

"Joanna—she's the wife of Herod's steward—she predicted as much," I said.

"I know for a fact, never mind how, that Herod has sent out spies to track him. And it's not just Herod who's keeping an eye on him. Word has spread about whatever happened on the hillside that night—no, I don't want to hear about any more miracles; it makes me queasy. Anyway, it doesn't matter. The powers that be, Roman and Jewish, know he could raise an army. If he chose."

"But he doesn't want an army," I said. "He refused to marshal people that way."

"What does he want, Maeve? What does he think he's doing?"

"He, he wants to…" and I realized with a shock, I couldn't answer

"Well, couldn't you talk your husband into keeping a low profile for awhile?"

"Sure, and while I'm at it, I'll ask him to reverse the sun's direction and have the mountains change places with the sea."

"It's like that, is it?" said Joseph.

"It's like that."

We were silent for a time, and I rested against Joseph, enjoying a respite from the sense of urgency that increasingly charged the very air around my beloved.

"We are going to go north to the region of Tyre," I said at length. "I don't know why, and I'm not sure he does either. I suppose Herod's spies will follow."

"At least it's in the opposite direction from Jerusalem and out of the Tetrarchy of Herod altogether. Maeve, I know he has gifts. I sensed greatness in him when he was a green boy out of his mind with guilt and grief. But I still don't understand: why can't he just live? The great Rabbi Hillel taught mercy and truth and yet kept a roof over the head of his wife and children. Why Jesus can't just get down on his knees and thank the Most High for the most beautiful—I'm sorry," he stopped himself. "I'm getting carried away."

"Don't apologize, Joseph. I've asked myself the same question a thousand times."

"Ah, but have you asked him?"

Had I? Had I ever said, Jesus, give it a rest! Let's settle down, keep house, and make babies?

"Our bed is the greensward," I recited from our marriage song, *"The beams of our house are cedar trees.* No, Joseph. No, I haven't."

Nor did I that night. Jesus and I had the tower roof to ourselves, and we made love wordlessly deep into the night, as we had a year ago, before his feet had called him to the road, before he had asked me to walk beside him.

Later that night, in the coldest hour, I woke with no memory of what I had been dreaming. My beloved slept so quietly, I put my hand over his heart, to feel it beating, to be soothed by the slow sea swells of his breath. I curled up next to him, hoping to drowse in his warmth, but I only grew more wakeful. In the stillness, the spring sounded louder than usual, as if it were not a steady trickle but a mighty water rising, moving through the reeds of the riverbanks.

I left my beloved asleep and went down to sit by the spring, sacred water, the connecting thread through all my worlds from the well of wisdom on Tir na mBan, where I had first glimpsed him, to the Jordan flowing through the lake, the waters of this spring joining it on its way to a dead end in the Dead Sea. But there could not be an end; even there the water would rise to the clouds, drift over Jerusalem, fill the pools of the Temple, water the gardens where Anna sat with the doves. Become the dew of a fragrant dawn.

I must have fallen asleep by the spring for when I woke again, the sky was just beginning to pale and the stars to soften. Jesus stood on the tower, gazing to the east. Isis, I prayed, O Isis, and there were no other words to my prayer until I found myself singing a song from the *Isia*, singing to my beloved:

> *Look how the sky's doors open to your beauty*
> *Look how the goddess waits to receive you*
> *This is death. This is the life beyond life.*

> *Look how the day is breaking in the east*
> *Look how the goddess awakens you. Listen*
> *to us singing to you, there among the stars.*

And then I buried my face in my hands and wept.

CHAPTER SIXTY-ONE

ON THE ROAD AGAIN

Hear the wail of a blues harmonica or the long keening sound of a freight train's whistle. I know we're not twentieth century hoboes. But that was the mood: as we kept moving, just moving, watching the clouds shift, watching the birds make paths in the sky, sitting by the fire at night, footsore and stupefied by the stars. Too bad someone didn't have a harmonica or a banjo. A silence had come over us, and it wasn't a comfortable one; or one any of us had chosen. It emanated from Jesus. What burden was he carrying, that made his step drag so? What yoke oppressed him? He who had told us his yoke was easy and his burden light. No one questioned him, not even me, until one day he went too far.

It was late in the afternoon; we had just left a village and were climbing into the hills again when I became aware that someone was following, clearly trying to catch us up. I turned and saw that it was a woman alone.

"Lord, Son of David!" she cried as loud as she could in her breathless state. "Take pity on me. My daughter is tormented by a devil."

The woman increased her pace and her volume; Jesus kept walking as if he hadn't heard.

"Lord, Son of David," she implored him; from her accent and her form of address I guessed she was a gentile. "I beg you, heal my daughter."

Still Jesus didn't turn, though by now some of the disciples had stopped, uncertain of what to do about the importunate woman.

"Lord, Son of David," the woman was wailing now.

"Jesus, you better say something to shut her up," Judas advised. "She's making such a ruckus, she'll rouse the whole countryside and we'll be mobbed again."

"Son of David, save my daughter."

Save my daughter; I stood still as the woman came near me. She was about my age, and she was desperate to save her daughter—as desperate as I had once been.

"Let me help you." I reached out, and touched the woman's arm.

"Yes, oh yes." She seized my hand and pulled me forward, thinking I had offered to intercede for her with the famous healer—never guessing that I had offered myself.

"Jesus, Son of David!" she cried as we caught up. "Have mercy on my daughter."

At last he stopped and turned around, and the woman threw herself at his feet.

"Lord, help me!" she whispered now. "My daughter—"

"I was sent only for the lost sheep of the house of Israel," he said, regretfully but as if he spoke from some great distance.

I didn't know whether I was furious or frightened. Who *was* this man?

"It is not fair to take the children's food," he added, "and toss it to the little dogs."

I started shaking; I was going to slap him, and if he turned the other cheek, I would hit him again. But the Canaanite woman was quicker.

"Yes, Lord," she said, "but even the little dogs eat the scraps from the master's table."

Then I saw him come back from whatever strange, cold place he had been. He looked at her and saw her, really saw her in that way he had. I could tell that he was moved by her fierce humility. She would take anything—blows, insults, scraps—anything but no for an answer. He reached out his hands and raised her to her feet.

"You have great faith," he said. "Go home happy. Your daughter is healed."

The woman kissed both his hands and was gone. Jesus walked on, without a word to me or anyone else. I dropped behind, troubled and heartsick, not yet ready to speak, rehearsing in my mind what I wanted to say to him, most of it obvious: what is wrong with you lately! How could you refuse to help that woman just because she's a gentile? How dare you call her a dog? What does that make me? Don't answer that!

But after awhile my unspoken diatribe spent itself and a great cold silence of my own welled up. I sat in it throughout the evening, avoiding even eye contact with Jesus. If I could have slept alone without the others kibitzing about our falling out, I would have.

(It's not easy being married in the midst of a walking commune. Celibacy might be a more practical practice. The trouble is, human beings aren't practical, and practice of celibacy, or other forms of abstinence, more often makes pretzels than perfection.)

As it was, I crawled into our sleeping roll and simply turned my back to him. He did not so much as ask me what was wrong, so that I could have the satisfaction of snarling at him. So much for his being a prophet and a miracle worker. He couldn't even read his own wife's mind. Or wouldn't. Then he committed the quintessential marital sin; he went straight to sleep, while I seethed, wide-awake.

When I thought everyone else was out for the count, I got up and sat by the campfire, poking at the embers, watching the sparks fly. Inspired by the flames, I decided I'd had enough of cold and silence. It was time to stir things up, so I returned to my husband and kicked him—not very hard, just enough to wake him. He sat bolt upright and stared at me, as if he did not know me, as if I were some wrathful angel or demon visiting his dreams. And well he might.

"You," I spoke in a low voice, knowing that the hiss of a whisper is louder. "Come with me."

He obeyed me—that's the only way to say it. I led him away from the circle of sleepers and the warmth of the fire. A waning moon was on the rise, so there was enough light for us to see. When we'd gone far enough to be alone, I stopped and turned to face him. Without warning, I dropped to my knees in front of him.

"*Adonai!*" I used deliberately a name I had never called him before. "Lord, help me. I have a daughter—"

My voice broke, and no more words came out. I bent over, my head on my knees, near enough to him to feel his legs trembling. Then he knelt down beside me. He felt for my hands and lifted them to his lips, kissing them as the Canaanite woman had kissed his, as disciples always kissed the hands of their teachers. Then he held my hands against his wet cheeks.

"*Domina*," he said. "Lady, forgive me."

And I did.

We stayed awake much of the night, holding each other and talking.

"I am so small," he kept saying. "And what the Most High asks of me seems so big. I keep trying to cut it down to size, but it only gets bigger. But I am still small."

"Small as a hazelnut, small as a mustard seed," I murmured, stroking his cheek.

"Do you really think so, Maeve? Do you even know what you're saying?"

"Anna the Prophetess said it," I reminded him. "Of course, it's my people who know about hazelnuts; they hold all the wisdom of the world inside, but if you roast them, they pop. And you're the one who said the kingdom of heaven is like a mustard seed—so small yet growing into a wild bush that is so profuse, a sheltering place for birds. Why don't you talk about the Kingdom of Heaven anymore?"

"Don't I?" he seemed surprised.

"Nor for awhile. Not since John's death, at least," I said.

"The day of the feeding," he added. "The day Judas tried to persuade me to give in to the crowd's demand for a king."

"Jesus, I've been wondering." I hesitated; he had only just opened to me again.

"Wondering what, *cariad*?" he prompted but he sounded wary.

All right, I'd just say it; I hated having to be so careful with him.

"Why didn't you tell Judas to leave that night? Why don't you let him go?"

He didn't answer right away; my heart sank as I felt his guard go up.

"You've always disliked Judas," he almost accused me.

I was appalled that he could suppose I would be so petty. I didn't know how to defend myself, and I see now that is where I made my fatal mistake—in defending myself at all, allowing him to deflect the attention from himself.

"I don't dislike Judas," I protested, and it was true. My feelings were way more complicated than that. "Judas dislikes *me*."

"So *that's* what's bothering you."

"Jesus! Do you honestly think I care whether your disciples like me or not? Sweet Isis, if I gave a rat's ass about any of their opinions, I wouldn't be here."

"Shush, Maeve!" He kissed me. "You'll wake them. I don't want to deal with any of them right now. I want to be with you. I don't want to fight with you. I want to go in unto you." He used that sexy Hebrew phrase. "The Kingdom of Heaven is within."

Have I told you yet that I'm a sucker—not to mention an easy lay? Not that Jesus was trying to deceive me. No, he was deceiving himself. And I allowed myself to be sidetracked way too easily. It was only a few days past the full moon. If we made love right now, I still might conceive.

"Oh my goddess," I moaned. "Did you say you were small? Small you are *not*!"

(So, in case you were wondering, now you know.)

Afterwards, we lay curled together riding the same slow current into sleep. Just before we slipped over the curve of consciousness into the deep, he spoke again.

"There are so many stories, Maeve, so many. I thought there was only one. I don't know which one I'm in. I don't know who I am. I only know how it ends, Maeve. I only know how it ends."

"Ssh, *cariad*," I shushed my own dread as well as his. "Sleep now. Whatever happens, I'll be with you."

He burrowed deeper into my arms, his head resting on my breasts.

If Jesus had his illusions about Judas, about being able to force a peace with him, through the force of his personality, I had illusions all my own: that the heaven and haven of my arms should be enough—enough shelter, enough comfort, enough reason to live. Though Jesus was less silent and distant for a time, and all of us had some good times together, he continued to go off alone to pray when he could—or, as I suspected, brood.

We made a trip back to Galilee: more healing, more debating, and the added danger of being watched and tracked by Herod's men and possibly others. Judas and Simon did prove useful at spotting spies and knowing how to make quick, ingenious escapes. After a second mass gathering, just barely kept under control, everyone agreed we should make another trip north. This time even Judas was in favor of a strategic retreat. In order to reconcile himself to Jesus, Judas had, I realized, told himself a story: that Jesus was right not to give in to the demands of an incoherent mob full of disputing factions. He needed to think everything out, chart a course of action. Jesus, I noticed, did nothing to encourage or discourage Judas's hope for a coherent plan.

As we headed due north along the Jordan towards Caesarea Philippi, I did my best just to enjoy the journey, the relative relief from crowds, and the terrain that was both green and rugged. We were coming into the mountainous country, the source of various streams that became the Jordan. Above all other mountains rose Mount Hermon, its peak still snowy, an awesome, awful mountain. From its height, Jesus told us, you could see all the way to Jerusalem. He didn't need to say more than that. I knew the mountain was calling him. I also felt its pull; its enormous weight balanced on itself that could crush you if it chose.

When we were about half a day's journey from Caesarea Philippi, we stopped for a midday rest, as was our custom. We'd found a pleasant spot with flat rocks perfect for sunning ourselves after a bracing dip in a stream whose icy waters must have had their rise in the mountains. We'd eaten our fill of bread, wine, and cheese, and Mary B, Susanna, Salome, and I were taking turns going through each other's hair—infestations were a hazard of life on the road, and we had our ways of coping. (Joanna, in case you're wondering, had gone back to her family after the news of John's death and acted as our eyes and ears in Herod's court.) I know I haven't mentioned the women much lately, but we had become comfortable together and relied on each other in many small wordless ways. There are few things as soothing as a fellow creature attentively grooming you—as most mammals do—and we were all looking forward to a siesta. Some of the men were already lying on the rocks and snoozing. Even Jesus seemed content, still reclining after his meal and allowing Tomas to rest his head against his shoulder.

Then, without warning, Jesus appeared to change his mind about resting. Brushing Tomas aside, he sat up cross-legged, his spine straight. Everyone else shifted position, too, and the sleepers woke up. Jesus's change of mood affected us all like a gust of wind in a grove, moving from tree to tree. He rose to his feet and began to pace among us, back and forth, like a caged animal. Everyone watched and waited for some signal from him, some clue as to what he wanted—which really got on my nerves. So I decided to ignore him, and I turned my attention back to Mary B's tangled black hair.

"Who do men say I am?" he broke the silence, and sat down again, looking around at us with the kind of aggressive glare some teachers have that insures only the smartest students will answer. Sure enough, Mary B's hand shot up.

"Some say you are Elijah returned at last," Mary spoke, her voice low and fierce with intensity, almost a growl.

"They say you are a prophet, like the prophets of old, Isaiah and Jeremiah," added Philip, "speaking with the voice of the Lord, leading the people into the paths of righteousness."

"Many say you are a man of the people who could lead us in battle against our enemies," Judas made his point, "the like of which has not been seen since the time of the Maccabees."

"More say you are the new Moses," put in Matthew, "come to fulfill the Law."

Almost everyone said something except for me. So many stories, my beloved had said. I did not want to tell any of mine—the god Esus hanging from a tree, Osiris drifting in pieces in the river. And there were other fragmented images that I dreaded to remember: of a dead tree, of cracked lips against a shattering sky. I kept my silence as if by silence I could take the story back inside the dreaming cave and re-shape it.

Finally the answers subsided, and the stream sounded louder; you could hear each small encounter of water and rock, of resistance and its overcoming.

"But you," Jesus spoke again, so quietly that we all leaned towards him. "Who do you say I am?"

My hands were deep in Mary's hair, and I swear I could feel the hairs rise on her neck, just as mine did. Who would dare to answer him this time?

Peter sprang to his feet. "You are the Christ," he said, "the anointed one."

His ruddy face was pale, sweat beaded on his lip; he looked as if he was going to be sick, all unmistakable signs of the second sight.

"And you!" To his own horror and amazement, Peter turned toward me, pointing so that there could be no doubt which one of us he meant. "You are the one who will anoint him."

Then his knees gave way and he fell to the ground sobbing.

Jesus went to him and with great tenderness touched his neck and his back.

"It's all right, Peter. You have spoken the words the Most High gave you to speak. I say to you, Peter: live up to your name, be a rock, a shelter for those who remain. Be a rock, a stronghold in the time that is coming."

At least that is how I remember what Jesus said to Peter.

No one could rest after Peter's prophecy, so in unspoken accord, we got up and walked on. Jesus took the lead, setting a breathless pace, but he could not outstrip his strange mood. At unpredictable intervals, he'd stop and turn and we'd all stumble to a halt like children playing red light, green light. He'd point at us, make a dire pronouncement, like: "The Son of Man is destined to suffer greatly at the hands of the authorities, even onto death."

Then he'd turn on his heel and take off, and we'd trot after him until he'd whirl around again:

"He who goes into the earth will rise again in three days."

And off he'd go. I don't know about you, but it makes me nervous when someone talks about himself in the third person. I was plain old grateful to the Rock when he girded up his loins and told Jesus to cut it out. Or words to that effect.

"Get back, Satan." Jesus shook off Peter rather violently. "You are not thinking as God thinks but as man thinks."

Personally, I had never cared much for the way his god thought, his god who had called Abraham to a mountain to sacrifice his only son (never mind that at the end he said just kidding); his god who had called Moses up a mountain and weighed him down with stone tablets inscribed with thou shalt nots.

I looked up at Mount Hermon, and I felt uneasy. Was his god calling him to this mountain for some unreasonable reason?

"Listen!" Jesus turned around again. "Anyone who wants to follow me had better be prepared to suffer."

Well, we were all following him at the moment, even me. And we all knew he could get himself and anyone near him into trouble. So what was his point?

"I say to you," he turned again after only a few paces, "if you want to save your life, you will lose it. If you lose it, for my sake, you will save it."

Well, I consoled myself, at least he was speaking in the first person again.

"What is it worth to win the whole world if you lose your life? What could anyone offer in exchange for your life?"

No one answered. We might be following on his heels, but following his train of thought was getting more difficult.

"Listen, anyone who is ashamed of me and my words, the Son of Man will be ashamed of him when he comes into the glory of his Father."

He walked on, and then he turned and looked at us with both tenderness and confusion, as if he had just waked from a bad dream.

"But some of you will not taste death before you see the Kingdom of God come with power." And he began to weep soundlessly in just the way his mother did.

"*Cariad*." I went to him and put my arms around him. "There is enough trouble for each day. Remember when you said that? Practice what you preach."

For a moment he tensed as if he wanted to shake me off as he had Peter. Then he relaxed against me. He felt feverish.

"We are all tired," I said. "We're stopping here for the night."

"All right, *domina*," he said,

With my cheek pressed against his, I could feel him smile.

CHAPTER SIXTY-TWO

TRANSFIGURATION

When I woke the next morning at dawn, the first thing I saw was Mount Hermon. Well, it was hard not to if you were looking north; it took up most of the sky. Clouds drifted past its peak, and when the first red rays touched it, the snow turned rosy, softening the mountain's aspect, making it look like a great breast. I felt more kindly towards it. I had heard there were many temples on Mount Hermon's southern slopes. Mountains tended to be god-infested places; the question was: which gods and what did they want?

I snuggled closer to Jesus's human warmth; we had been sleeping spooned with my back against his front, his arms around me. Though he had not moved or changed his breathing, I could feel that he was awake, too, and like me, contemplating the mountain.

"I'm going up, Maeve," he said. "That's where I'll be able to hear his voice."

"What if that mountain belongs to the heathen gods or goddesses?" I suggested. "Baal maybe or Asherah. How will you know his voice from theirs?"

"Maeve." His tone said it all.

"Oh, yeah. How could I forget, there is only one god."

"You told me yourself long ago; there is no place where he is not. Remember?"

I had indeed, in one gut-wrenching oracular moment, told him not to worry about his initiation rite at the Mound of the Dark Grove; even there, his god would be with him.

"Then why go up the mountain?" I countered.

"It's just something I need to do."

And I knew that was all he would say.

"All right then," I said. "I'll go with you."

"No," he said.

"Yes," I insisted. "You're not going up a mountain like that alone. What is your god's problem? Is he afraid that if other people hear him they'll figure out he's not making any sense?"

"Drop it, Maeve," he said more sharply than usual. "I'll take Peter with me and maybe James and John."

I was too hurt and proud to ask why not me? (Given my attitude, I suppose it isn't hard to guess.) But I wasn't going to accept his refusal either.

"You can't tell me what to do," I informed him. "I can go to the mountain if I want to."

"I *could* tell you what to do if you had any notion of the obedience a proper wife owes a husband." His tone was affectionate now. "But I won't, because you have all these barbaric notions about sovereignty."

"Sovereignty, a barbaric notion? Isn't sovereignty what the Jews have been pining for since the Exile? If your people would make the connection between a woman's sovereignty and the sovereignty of the land, maybe then their sacrifices in the Temple would mean something, maybe then you could be a different kind of king—"

I stopped, aware that I did not want to come to my own conclusion. I did not want to talk about sacrificial kings shedding their blood to renew the goddess of sovereignty.

"Forget it," I said as lightly as I could.

For a while we just lay quietly staring up at the mountain, each of us trying to find a way out of our impasse.

"I won't tell you to stay," he said at length. "What if I asked you?"

"This is a trick," I accused.

"Maeve, please stay with the others, keep them together. Go to Caesarea Philippi and do what we always do: heal the sick, preach—"

"I don't preach."

"Well, tell them stories about Queen Maeve of Connacht."

"I just might."

"Tell them about the Kingdom of Heaven."

"No kingdoms. Paradise, the Shining Isles, the Isle of Apples."

"Fine." He turned me towards him and kissed me.

"I love you, Maeve. Let me go. I'll come back for you. Don't worry."

So according to his wishes (he always seemed to get his way) he went to the mountain with Peter and the Thunder Brothers, and the rest of us headed for town. Rumors that Jesus was in the neighborhood had preceded us, and the sick, the poor, the censorious and the merely curious flocked to us, hoping for a glimpse of the infamous rabbi. We ministered to the people as best we could, laying hands on the sick, casting out demons (I left that to the others). Brave Mary B did her best to preach and teach, and actually managed to engage someone in scholarly debate, albeit the debate centered on whether or not women should be allowed to debate the Law in public.

By midday the crowds had thinned out. Some of the men had been invited to people's homes for a meal, and none of them had the grace to ask that we be included in the invitation. People tended to be warier of the women traveling with Jesus. Although Mary B was an avowed disciple, Salome the mother of grown sons, and I a wife, people tended to regard us all as camp followers. Well, ok, I admit Susanna still had the insolent sexiness of a streetwalker. So perhaps it was not surprising that we were left on our own.

By unspoken consensus, we wandered to the edge of town. Just outside the gates we found a shade tree and sat down to share some bread and wine, all of us gazing toward the mountain. In the valley, the day was mild, even warm, but there was a strange feeling in the air, a stillness that felt like some huge breath being held. Anything and everything could change any moment, especially on the mountain where there could be snow squalls while people sweated in the fields below.

"Master'll be all right, dearies," Salome spoke to our unvoiced apprehensions. "That's why he took my boys with him. They can handle anything—thugs, thieves, Romans, Herod's scum—"

"Earthquake, fire, landslide, flood?" added Susanna.

"Of course, my love," Salome assured her, not catching Susanna's teasing tone. "That's why when the Master comes into his glory, one of 'em is going to be at his right hand and one at the left. You'll see."

No one bothered to reply. Prophecies of her sons' preferment were habitual with Salome and had become a running joke among the rest of us. We all began to drowse, and then the air shifted ever so slightly, the breeze lifting the hair on my arms. I opened my eyes and saw clouds moving towards the mountains.

"I wish we could know what's happening up there," sighed Mary B.

"There are many things to know on the mountain."

All four of us startled at the stranger's voice, a woman's voice. We had not noticed her approach. Now she stood before us, an ordinary looking woman, neither young nor old, in a plain linen tunic. She might have been any woman coming from the fields or going to the well, except for the odd way she had spoken and the intent way she looked at us. I rose to greet her, priestess to priestess.

"Will you come with me?" she asked.

"That she will not," answered Salome, hoisting herself up and assuming her mantle of maternal authority.

"Salome!" protested Susanna also getting up. "The woman may be in need."

"Well, let her say so then."

"How can we help you, good woman?" Mary B also rose. "We are the companions of Jesus of Nazareth. We have been given the power to heal in his name."

I could have argued with her about the name bit, but now was clearly not the time.

"Will you come with me, priestess of Isis?" the woman spoke to me alone. "I am bid by She of the Grove to ask you to come with me."

Salome sucked air through her teeth, something she did on the rare occasion that words failed her.

"Come where?" I asked, sure that I would go but understanding my friends' fears.

"To her temple. It's not far."

"Wait just a minute, duckie." Salome found her tongue again. "How do we know this is not a trap? This She of yours, what's her ailment? Bloody issue? Sores? Demons?"

"Will you come?" the woman asked me again.

I'm not sure why I felt so compelled, why I did not question her further. Maybe because I had been raised by witches and had lived most of my life among priestesses, I expected enigmatic women to turn up with inexplicable requests. The woman had asked her question three times now (at some subliminal level I'd kept count) and I knew I had to answer or miss whatever mystery might open to me.

"Yes, I will."

The priestess turned in the direction of the mountain and started walking.

"Mary of Magdala," shouted Mary B as I turned to follow, "Jesus told us to stay in town. What could be more important than his will?"

"*My* will," I said. "Sorry, Mary, I have to go. It's a priestess thing."

And I started walking.

"Lamb chop!" bellowed Salome. "You are not going off to Lord-knows-where with some strange woman alone."

"I'll go with her," said Susanna catching up with me.

"No, stop, wait. We'll all go." Salome, seeing no other way to retain her authority, abruptly changed tactics.

"But Jesus said to stay here," Mary B held out.

"Master won't be back for hours and hours." Salome dismissed him. "Come on, Mary. You know he'd want us to stick together. And what would we say to him if we let his silly wife wander off by herself and get into trouble?"

Mary B succumbed to this unflattering argument and fell into line.

"Not far" turned out to be about a mile cross-country through cultivated fields to the base of the mountain where a footpath led us uphill into forest— huge vallonia oaks and terebinth with their strong resinous scent. I knew a sacred grove when I entered one: the filtered light, and the eerie peripheral sense of being watched by the trees themselves. After we had climbed for a while, we came to a partial clearing, where level ground was ringed with massive trees, each one distinct, a presence. Here our guide stopped. Birds in the branches above quieted. A sudden wind lifted the leaves, revealing their silver undersides, and then the air, too, was still. Somewhere nearby a stream flowed.

"Where is this temple?" demanded Salome.

Though she stood beside me, Salome's voice sounded far away. Then I saw it. We were in the same clearing, but it was filled with wooden pillars, carved in many shapes, some like women's bodies: heavy breasted and wide-hipped, arms raised to hold up an arbor roof made of thick, luxuriant vines. Other pillars depicted birds and animals or blossoms and fruit. From somewhere—or everywhere—came a fragrance, spicy and sweet, that I could not name, that reminded me of something I longed to remember. I turned to question the priestess, and I saw that she, too, had changed. A skirt the color of flame darted and flickered around her legs. Her breasts were bare and so was her head, except for a crown shaped like a cow's horns. In the curve of the horns rested a dove, and snakes climbed her upraised arms.

"Whom do you seek?" the goddess asked me, for so she was.

"I seek my beloved who was slain," I heard myself answer.

"If you would find your beloved, you must serve in my temple."

"Then I will serve."

Ages passed: days, nights, moons, seasons, years, as I served the goddess in her temple, the mountain temple with its carved pillars and leafy roof that was all at once the Vine and Fig Tree in Rome and Temple Magdalen on the inland sea. I caught glimpses of the orchard on Tir na mBan, and of a chamber overlooking a narrow street, the walls expanding with the scenes I painted there. In all times and places, I gave myself again and again, opening and closing like a rose, flooding and receding like the Nile, until I knew my beloved in everything.

"Now!" the goddess commanded.

The sweet, spicy fragrance grew stronger, leading me to the central pillar of the mountain temple, the pillar called The Tree, and it was a tree, a huge tree rooted deep in earth, stars in its branches, and its great trunk grew around a wound, a hollow that held his suffering body, not in a coffin, but fixed to the stark, dead tree of my terrible visions.

"He will be scattered," the goddess said. "He will be torn to pieces. You must gather the lost pieces and make him whole. You must wash his wounds with your tears and give him life. Do you understand your task?"

I wanted to say, "No! Help me. Don't let it happen," but I had no voice, so I just clung to the tree and wept as the fragrance became a golden cloud that covered us. At last the cloud lifted, and all the gold was in the leaves. The tree was seamless. Then I saw him, standing beneath the tree, whole and radiant.

"Beloved!" my voice rang out over the mountain. "This is the Beloved!"

Then he was gone again.

"So where is this She of the Grove?" Salome grumbled. "And what *are* you doing to that tree!"

I turned towards my friends. Their mouths dropped open. Salome covered her eyes. Susanna wept, and Mary B held herself very still. I could see the movement of her neck as she swallowed. Then I felt the snakes spiraling on my arms. Out of the corner of my eye I caught the flash of the dove's wings. I gazed at my friends, and even Salome finally peeked, then dropped her hands and beamed at me. Each woman was so bright, so beautiful, I felt as if I were seeing her for the first time.

"Beloved," I said more quietly, this time. "You are the beloved. All of us, the beloved."

I went to my friends, and all four of us took hands, shyly, as if we were little girls, and began to walk back down the path. Once I looked back over my shoulder, and saw the priestess, in her plain tunic again, making a sign of blessing with her hands.

CHAPTER SIXTY-THREE

FALL OUT

Those of you who know his story will remember what happened to Jesus on the same mountain—or his official chroniclers' version of it—how he appears to Peter, John, and James in garments brilliantly white (whiter than any earthly bleacher could make them, Mark would have us know). Next Moses and Elijah show up to confer with Jesus, inspiring Peter to suggest building tabernacles to enshrine the three. But then comes that cloud. Remember the cloud? And the voice crying out: "This is the Beloved!" I will leave you to decide if I am blaspheming, tampering shamelessly with a sacred story for my own purposes, or if it is true, as the priestess said to us: "There are many things to know on the mountain." Many ways to know, I would add, and to be known.

Although we felt as though we had been away for a long time, when we got back to town it was only late afternoon. In the central market square where we'd been healing that morning, we found a huge crowd gathered. Not a noisy crowd but a nervous one, intent on some escalating dispute. We could hear raised voices, angrily interrupting each other. The four of us only had to exchange glances to come to an understanding. We all knew that if there was trouble, our gang was likely at the heart of it. We dropped hands the better to duck and weave our way through the onlookers.

Even when we got to the front and could see, it took us some time to figure out what was going on. Matthew and Philip appeared to be fending off some Pharisees who were shouting and pointing past them to Andrew and Simon who were more or less taking turns exhorting a boy of eleven or twelve.

Thaddeus and Bartholomew had hold of the boy's arms, while another man, presumably the boys' father, stood by wringing his hands and calling on Adonai for help.

"Come out of him!" commanded Andrew. "I said come out!"

"By what authority do you heal!" shrieked one of the Pharisees.

"Those aren't the right words," said Simon. "Let me try. In Jesus's name—"

"Whose name?" roared another Pharisee. "Who is your rabbi?"

The same words kept flying, circling like carrion crows over a battlefield. I began to filter out the noise, my focus narrowing to the boy, who stood there frozen, as if he were trying to disappear inside himself. Apparently the disciples were attempting to drive a demon out of the poor child, who was not wailing, gnashing, or writhing or any of the usual dramatic displays. He was barely moving at all. Yet I could see a disturbance in the air around him, a flickering light, arrhythmic as a guttering flame. For a moment that light flared in my own eyes. As my vision cleared, I knew that I had seen what the boy was seeing. The erratic light flashed a warning that he could not voice.

The fire of the stars flowed into my hands, and I moved towards the boy, skirting the disciples who were still loudly pleading with his demon. If only I could touch him, the fire would tell me where to put my hands, how to calm the chaos brewing like a storm behind his eyes, but before I could reach the child, someone yanked my arm so hard I felt it pull out of the socket. I careened backwards, losing my balance, and falling on my other arm. I glanced up just in time to see Judas give me a look of naked hatred before he turned away. For a moment I thought I would swoon, not from the pain, which hadn't registered yet, but from the memory of another man's hate.

"Holy Moses!" Susanna and Salome ran to me and knelt beside me; Mary B had gone to help Matthew and Philip. "I think your shoulder is dislocated. Can you stand?"

They put their arms around me.

"There's a duck. Up you get now," said Salome, "or you'll be trampled for sure."

With their help, I got to my feet, just as the crowd suddenly hushed and turned as one like a flock of birds. Then the shouting began.

"Jesus, son of David!"

"Jesus of Nazareth! Make way! Make way!"

The Pharisees looked grim but also pleased. Who wanted to quibble with disciples when they could have at the Master? But their expressions changed to awe when they actually saw him approach. I turned and looked, too, and then I didn't pay attention to anyone else. No one did.

He was terrifying—and beautiful—the way a natural force is: a black sky split with lightning, a towering wave about to break, a lion ready to spring. It struck me that he had gone to the mountain and absorbed its essence, returning as a god, dominating the sky, wearing the clouds as a mantle. Somehow the father of the possessed boy found the courage to run to Jesus and fall at his feet.

"Master, I have brought my son to you. There is a spirit of dumbness in him, and when it takes hold of him it throws him to the ground and he foams at the mouth and grinds his teeth and goes rigid. Your disciples can't cast it out."

"Faithless generation!" Jesus growled. "How long must I put up with you?"

Andrew and Simon looked stricken, but I hardly had time to think of them. The lights around the boy churned, and his eyes rolled up in his head.

"Look to the child!" I cried out.

Jesus met my eyes for a brief moment, and then he went to the boy who immediately collapsed in seizures at his feet. Jesus and the father both knelt beside him, and had some exchange that I could not hear. Then Jesus raised his voice.

"Are you asking *if* I can help him? Everything is possible for one who has faith."

And the father cried out. "I have faith! Help my lack of faith." Words that have reverberated ever since.

His chroniclers will tell you that Jesus rebuked the unclean spirit, commanded it to come out and never enter the boy again. But here is what I saw. Jesus placed his hands on either side of the child's head, and the fire of the stars flowed through him, changing the disturbed patterns I had seen, and the lights around the boy grew calm and steady. The boy grew so still at Jesus's touch that someone screamed, "He's dead."

In answer, Jesus took the child by the hand, and helped him stand up. In a moment the boy was in his father's arms, and Jesus again turned to me, ignoring the cacophony of the Pharisees behind him. He still had the look of the mountain about him, not its fearsomeness now, but how ancient it was, as if he had stood still through seasons and storms, shaped by the inexorable forces. As he gazed at me, I felt the snakes on my arms and saw the blur of wings. Just before the light of day faded, I caught a glimpse of gold, a current running between us.

That was all we said—or rather did not say—about what happened to us on the mountain. According to his chroniclers, Jesus gave his three witnesses strict orders not to tell anyone what they had seen. As for my companions, even if they'd had the inclination to talk about what had happened in the sacred grove, I doubt they would have had the words. They did fuss over me rather tenderly that evening, but I think their attentions were because of my injured shoulder, not because I had appeared to them (fleetingly) as a pagan goddess. None of us mentioned Judas's assault either. It had happened so quickly, I wasn't even sure the others had seen what he did.

The man whose son Jesus had healed had taken us home with him and given us some peace and privacy in his back courtyard. We reclined after our meal, more tired and subdued than usual. In fact, the disciples were downright glum.

"Master, why were we unable to drive the demon out?" Andrew finally asked the question he had been brooding over for hours.

"That is the kind that can only be driven out by prayer," said Jesus without any reproach in his voice, all the anger that had provoked his public rebuke gone or spent.

Everyone waited for Jesus to expand on his answer, but he said nothing more. The silence deepened. Such a deep silence I felt we could all fall into it, the endless blackness of it, and never be seen again, the earth closing over us, our forms dissolving.

Except that I could not get comfortable enough to dissolve. I tried this position, then that, and finally got up and went to a corner where I could sit with my back supported by the wall. Eventually I dozed until someone touched my shoulder and I woke with a cry.

"What happened to you?" Jesus asked me.

"I don't know," I said, groggy with sleep and distracted by pain.

Gently (and yet with great force) he put my shoulder back in place and then held his hands there, hands so hot I felt my bones begin to glow. Then it felt as though water, sky-colored water, flowed through my shoulder, washing away any trace of pain.

"Better?"

In answer I turned to him and put my arms around him, my face in his neck where I could feel his blood coursing. He lifted me and carried me to our bedroll where we held onto each other wordlessly.

What stopped me from saying: "Listen, honey, your boy Judas attacked me. And what's more, the person he's really furious with is you. He just doesn't know it yet." Some mistaken code of honor? You don't rat on a comrade, however much of a shit he is? Pride? A refusal to admit that I couldn't handle Judas on my own?

And why didn't Jesus press me to tell him more? I think we both shrank from anything that might cause a rift. We were each other's shelter between earth and sky. So we did not talk about Judas, nor did we reveal our separate encounters with divinity, what his god—and my goddess—had revealed on the mountain, the terrible mysteries to come that neither of us understood yet. I did not even tell him I had gone to the grove temple, though I sensed he knew. The knowledge lay unacknowledged between us.

We held each other close, as if we could obliterate any difference between us. For a time, we did. We unmade the map of him and me and created a new world, dense and green, vast and blue all at once. Afterwards we rested, our scent, breath, and sweat all mingled in the darkness between us.

"*Cariad*, let's go home for a while," I said.

"Home?"

"Home to Temple Magdalen for the harvest."

I saw us laughing together, dancing on the grapes, our feet stained purple. I tasted the rich bitterness of fresh olives. I smelled the Temple Magdalen smell of roses and fish, saw the wind feathering the lake. It was all so vivid in my mind's eye, I believed that he must see it, too, long for it, as I did.

"It's time to go to Jerusalem," he said instead. "Will you come?"

I rolled over and looked up at the summer sky, a warm deep black, crowded with stars that made me think of seeds cast blindly, abundantly into the wind. I gazed at the sky for a while, almost forgetting his question, how as usual he had shifted everything.

"Maeve, come with me. I need you there."

Could I have said, I need you, too? I need you to feast with me in paradise. Will *you* come? Will you come with *me*? If I could have, I didn't. I rolled toward him again, and put my arms around him and spoke the words that came to me.

"Wherever you are, I am."

THE VINE
AND
THE FIG TREE

CHAPTER SIXTY-FOUR

THE ROAD TO JERUSALEM

I thought I had lost control of my life before—when I was cast out to sea by the druids, my lover gone, my child stolen from my arms. When I was sold into slavery and prostitution and sold again to a spoiled, unhappy woman. When I searched all those years and could not find my beloved. When he left me again, after such a brief reunion, to go off on his ministry. When I succumbed to his crazy notion that we should marry. In the company of Jesus, I had seen miracles and riots, but nothing—not even my recurrent visions and premonitions—could prepare me for the loss of control that was coming.

There are two ways to go from Galilee to Judea. Last winter Jesus, Mary B and I had gone to and fro via Samaria, where we had encountered Susanna, the same road Reginus and I had traveled more than ten years ago. For this trip, Jesus chose the other route down the Jordan River Valley, and then from Jericho across the rugged mountain passes to Jerusalem. He gave no explanation for his choice, the less comfortable one in late summer, but I knew this path would take us to the former site of John's camp—where Jesus had been baptized and the dove (a.k.a. *moi*) had descended. Not far from there, he and Mary B had once lived with the Essenes. To get to Jerusalem we would pass through the hills where he had fasted and prayed and found his vision. We would walk on the very road where the Samaritan merchant had discovered him naked and near death. This time no one would re-route him to a holy whorehouse in Magdala. And the whore-priestess, who had received him there two years ago, was now his wife.

Like my mother-in-law before me, I "pondered all these things in my heart," because I rarely got the chance to speak alone with Jesus these days. You might think of the Judean wilderness as a vast and empty space. Indeed, I was thankful for the abundance of sky and the starkness of hills, because the river valley itself was heavily trafficked. And our number was rapidly swelling from a small band to what people who didn't much care for Jesus (and there were plenty) might call a rabble—the landless *am-ha-arez*, penitent pilgrims, curiosity seekers, zealots, outlaws and outcasts, even lepers. There was plenty about Jesus and company to alarm the prosperous, the politically well-placed, the pious, the priestly, anyone who liked order.

You can be sure that his decision to pass through (or lay claim to) John's terrain did not go unmarked by various authorities. John had been bad enough, ranting about repentance and the end of the world, creating his own home-made rites, thumbing his nose at the Temple hierarchy. But then he had narrowed his attack to Herod Antipas and gotten himself conveniently offed. Jesus was wilder and wider in his scope, a loose cannon—teacher, preacher, prophet, healer, miracle worker, the people's king. No one was safe from his challenge. And he was drawing nearer every day (like an army or a plague) to the heart of all Israel: Jerusalem.

This journey was no mere hike in which we tried to cover a certain number of miles every day. People clamoring for healing were always rushing us, and we were also met along the way by delegations of Pharisees who wanted a debate. Jesus had a reputation for surprise tactics, and people who prided themselves on their skill, not to mention their superior knowledge of the Law, were eager to best him. Near the site of his dipping—and mine—we met such a party. I did not always pay attention to these contests--it's like watching a sport; you need to know the rules and understand the objective to get anything out of it—but this one caught my attention.

"So what about divorce, Rabbi?" one of the men challenged him. "Is it against the Law for a man to divorce his wife on any pretext?"

As Jesus's wife, and as someone who still didn't have a good grasp of the subject of marriage, let alone divorce, I pricked up my ears and positioned myself next to Mary B, my walking Law library.

"Have you not read that the Creator from the beginning 'made them male and female.'"

"He's quoting from Genesis," Mary B whispered to me.

"And God said: 'This is why a man leaves his father and mother and becomes attached to his wife, and the two become one flesh.' So you see, they are no longer two but one flesh. So then, what God has united, human beings must not divide."

I tried out this theory: Our one flesh, therefore, was debating Law and probably would for the next three hours, while our other one flesh got sunburned. But then (as I'd always suspected) perhaps his god had not united us—which could explain why I had an insufficient appreciation of the Law, and he did not appreciate the terrible effect a desert climate could have on a redhead.

"Well then, esteemed Rabbi!" said another Pharisee in a tone that I can only describe as sneering. "Why did Moses command that a writ of dismissal should be given in cases of divorce?"

"Deuteronomy, chapter 24, verse 1," murmured Mary B. She was one of those avid fans who would rather be on the playing field and eased her frustration with running commentary. "But the Pharisee is quoting out of context. The passage pertains to a case where a man divorces his wife in writing, and she marries someone else. If the second man divorces her, the first cannot take her back—"

"He might not want her back if he divorced her in the first place," I interrupted. "But if he does want her, and she wants to go back, why shouldn't she?"

"Because she is now unclean," Mary said as if it should be obvious (at least to someone who wasn't stupid or hopelessly ignorant).

"But why?"

"She's been with another man. Don't you get it? Listen, Mary, if you want to follow this debate, you have to understand, men have all the rights when it comes to divorce. A woman can't divorce a man for any reason; a man can make a writ any time he feels like it—the problem is he can't reverse it. Ssh, now pay attention. Jesus is speaking again."

"Because you are so hard-hearted," Jesus answered, getting up close and personal as he had a tendency to do. "That is why Moses allowed you to divorce your wives. But it was not like this in the beginning. Now I say this to you..." He paused for a moment as if to let the indignation rise.

Mary B anxiously clutched my arm.

"What did he just do?" I asked.

"He's coming perilously close to putting himself above Moses, or laying himself open to their accusation that he is."

"Anyone who divorces his wife—and I am not talking here of an illicit marriage—and marries another is guilty of adultery."

There was such an outcry at this pronouncement, with everyone speaking at once, that even Mary B had trouble following the argument and kept hushing me though I hadn't said anything. It wasn't till the uproar was over, and the angrily pointed fingers had become hands thrown up in helplessness and disgust that I got to ask Mary the question I was stuck on. (I didn't consider trying to ask Jesus. I wouldn't see him till he flung his exhausted self beside me and plummeted into sleep.)

"What *is* an illicit marriage, anyway?"

"There are two possibilities," Mary B began, as we walked away from the crowd, she abstractedly and I deliberately, with the Jordan flowing muddily beside us. "One is the wrong degree of kinship. Families might have been unaware of some blood tie that later comes to light. The other reason would be that the marriage has been defiled."

"Defiled how?" My mind ran to things like dancing around graven images, something that seemed to upset Moses terribly.

"Adultery, of course," she answered calmly. "Almost always the woman's adultery. A man isn't guilty of adultery unless he takes another man's wife or a virgin."

"You mean it's all right, according to your Law, for a married man to sleep with a whore? No wonder dear old Joseph has always considered brothels a sound investment."

"A man can also sleep with a widow." Mary B liked to be precise. "Which is why widows have to be extremely careful of their reputations. Unless they're old and ugly and have plenty of sons to protect them."

"Wait. So did Jesus just say it's all right to divorce a wife because of adultery?"

"*Only* for adultery," Mary B corrected. "Not on a whim, not because he doesn't like her cooking, not because of barrenness, not because he's found someone prettier or wealthier. That's what our Rabbi is saying. He's seen what happens to women left destitute by divorce. They end up begging or being a burden to their families—or worse."

I thought I knew what she meant by "worse."

"But what about the adulteresses?" I asked. "Aren't they destitute, too?"

"I suppose they are," she said after a moment. "If they survive."

"What do you mean?" I had a sick feeling in the pit of my stomach. I remembered the provision in Roman law that allowed a father to strangle his daughter for adultery; nor could I ever forget the massacre occasioned by Paulina's adultery with Decius Mundus.

"If a woman is accused of adultery, she has a trial," Mary explained. "She's forced to drink a foul-tasting potion mixed with dirt from the Temple floor. If she gags or vomits, her husband *must* repudiate her. And if a woman is caught in the act of adultery, there's no question: the penalty is death by stoning."

"No wonder you never wanted to get married!" I exclaimed.

"That's not the reason I didn't marry," she objected.

"You have to admit it's a good one. Aren't men held responsible at all?"

"Only if they're caught with someone's wife. Don't you see? That's why those men are so upset with him. Jesus doesn't want to let them off the hook. Remember when he said anyone who *looks* at another woman with lust in his heart is guilty of adultery? He's not contradicting the Law of Moses; he's challenging people to take it seriously."

We walked along, kicking at loose scree (it was a *very* stony country, which perhaps explained the favored form of execution) when I had one of those moments, not quite of second sight, for it wasn't a vision—just a sense of heaviness, almost weariness.

"It's going to cause trouble, Mary."

"What is?"

"What he said about divorce and adultery."

"Well, obviously. It already has. You saw how those men stalked off; they're on their way back to Jerusalem even now to report him."

"It's worse than that," I said.

"What do you mean?"

But I found myself at a rare loss for words. How to express my foreboding that his words would remain and become set in stone, become stones to be picked up and cast at people, while the tender, angry, passionate man who spoke them was forgotten?

That passionate man who had not made love to me since we'd begun our journey south. Not surprising perhaps. We were both so exposed: to the crowds, to the elements. Despite keeping myself covered, I felt all the moisture had been sucked out of me, that my skin looked like the cracked earth, where only the hardiest goats managed to forage. I was so tired after a day of feeding and tending to people, I didn't have the energy to object if he preferred oblivion to me. But I missed him, and I was worried about him.

So when I woke one night at the waning moon's rise to find him gone, I got up to look for him. The Judean wilderness is most beautiful at night. The air is so clear, the stars bristle, and the dusty landscape reflects moonlight the way snow does. I saw his shadow before I saw him, because his cloak was the same color as earth. He was following a steep goat path that climbed into the hills near our camp. I am sure-footed and have good night vision, but I did find myself wishing, as the path led to a ridge, that he hadn't chosen to walk a knife-edge. Perhaps he was taking the Adversary's word for it, that if he fell from a precipice, the angels would swoop to his rescue. At last his pace slowed, and I was able to gain on him, though I didn't want to call out for fear of startling him. Then he turned around so abruptly that I nearly lost my balance.

"Who's following me!" he demanded.

"I am not following you," I argued, perhaps unreasonably. "I am trying to catch up with you."

"Oh, it's you," he said, his voice flat. "Leave me, Maeve, I need to be alone."

I suppose a good wife would have obeyed wordlessly, but if he'd wanted one of those, he shouldn't have married me.

"*I* need to be with you," I countered.

Whose need takes precedence? No doubt there was a Law that covers this circumstance, and no doubt it rules in the husband's favor. Well, let him debate me. I was not going to make it easy for him. And so we faced each other in the stony moonlit desert. Then he turned and walked on. I considered picking up a piece of Judea and throwing it at him; instead I just picked up my step until I was walking beside him on the narrow path. One false move and one of us would be lost to history.

"Maeve," he turned to me at last. "I need to be alone to hear *him*."

"*Cariad*." I stepped closer to him, so that we could feel each other's heat in contrast to the cool night air. "You *are* alone. We are one flesh, remember? Your god says so. In the Book of Genesis," I added for good measure. "Though I've had to take it on faith lately."

He neither answered nor embraced me; without thinking I took a step back, and he had the grace to grab hold of my arm when I came too close to the edge.

"Or do you think our marriage is illicit?" I challenged him. "Because I was defiled from the beginning. If that's so, then why did you marry me? I wasn't a wife or a virgin. I was a whore. You could have just fucked me!"

"Maeve!" he grabbed my other arm, not gently. "Will you just please shut up! You are proving my point."

"Oh? I don't recall your having made a point."

"That I can't hear unless I'm alone."

He did have a point. I stopped talking, but when he turned to go, I continued to walk with him silently. When he stopped again, I braced myself, thinking he was going to tell me again to get lost. Instead he started to shake and covered his eyes with his hands.

"It's not just what I hear," he whispered. "It's what I see!" He covered his eyes. "Oh, Maeve, what I see." Blindly, he reached out one hand for me.

"Beloved, let me watch with you. Let me listen with you. Please."

He nodded, and loosing my hand, sat down cross-legged on the path. I sat down next to him in the same position, close but not touching, our knees an inch or two apart. He closed his eyes, but I kept mine open, and I gazed over the valley, finding the moonlit thread of river snaking its way through the desert. The night was so still I could hear the water flowing over rocks, through reeds, gathering silt and salt to take to the Dead Sea. For a time I forgot everything, my anger, my desire, him, me, our story that kept getting away from me.

"What I see." His voice seemed to come to me from far away, as far as the stars. "What I see is the end of the world. The Temple. The Temple will fall. There will be wars, famines, earthquakes. And in Jerusalem. Oh, Jerusalem." Here his voice broke, and he covered his eyes again even though they were closed. "The people will flee to these hills, these caves. Oh, Jerusalem, Jerusalem, you who kill all your prophets!"

My stomach clenched, and I felt sudden stabbing pain in my side that made it hard to breathe, and yet it suddenly seemed important to do just that. To breathe out all the way to the stars, to breathe in their fire.

"I don't understand." He spoke in a low, intense voice, and I knew he was not speaking to me. His god was here: I could feel it, I could almost smell it the way you can smell scorched air when lightning strikes close. "I don't understand. Must the end come before your Kingdom comes? Must it be as your prophets of old have foretold—the earth rent, the people driven from their city, nations warring—before your rule can begin? Or is the end coming, because no one sees it: that the Kingdom is here, the feast set forth. I thought you wanted me to call your people to feast. The people come, more every day, but not to feast—to argue, to beg, to urge me to lead them in battle. Then you show me these terrible things. Oh, father, father, forgive me. I do not know what I am doing."

Then he stopped speaking, in order to listen, and my longstanding resentment of his god suddenly seemed ungenerous. Though Jesus was required by the Law of Moses to revile my goddess, he had never been rude about it. He had slept in my arms in the inner chamber of her Temple. Maybe it was time I came to terms with my beloved's god.

Adonai, I spoke to him silently, I am ready to listen to you for the sake of him my soul loves. You know I love him. Does anything else matter? Talk to me.

I listened, but I heard only the sound of the river, of our breath. I closed my eyes and rested on the sound. At first I saw nothing, and then I saw: nothing. Empty space, a void, defined by a shaft of light entering a stone chamber containing nothing, nothing at all. In the distance I heard shouting, lamenting, swords clashing, vessels shattering. And yet only the light penetrated the emptiness. In time the din faded, the emptiness darkened. I was enclosed in it now; I could feel the cold walls, smell some bitter perfume....

"He will send me a sign."

My beloved's voice called me out of my strange, tactile visions. Or maybe I had simply fallen asleep and begun to dream.

"What?" I opened my eyes to the huge night, the fresh, dry air. Where had I been?

"He will tell me when it's time to act."

"But he's not there!" I blurted out.

"What?" he asked in turn.

"Your god's not there. There's…there's this nothingness. It's…I think it's a tomb, but he's not there."

"*Cariad*," he said to me, and at last he put his arm around me. Did anything else matter? "You're not making sense."

"I know," I said sadly.

Jesus pulled me closer and wrapped me in his cloak, and the warm, living darkness almost banished the impression of the cold walls, the strange bitter scent.

We continued to make erratic progress, slowed by huge crowds. On the eve of Yom Kippur, or The Great Day, as everyone called it, we left Jericho, hoping to be in Jerusalem by nightfall. We might have covered the twenty miles if we had been a small, hardy group accustomed to walking. But the road to Jerusalem is steep, rising from below sea level into the mountains, and we were now a large company. So in the late afternoon, we made camp in a sheltered spot where a trickle of a spring still ran in this dry season before the winter rains. We refreshed ourselves before the fast that would begin at sundown. Jesus, I noticed, ate and drank almost nothing; I guessed that he meant to stay awake all night, praying.

Just before sunset, Jesus called Peter, James, John, Mary B, and me, and asked us if we would walk further into the mountains with him. Then he summoned Judas to put him in charge of the camp.

"Don't you think it's time you and the Twelve of us held a counsel?" Judas challenged him. "We have all these people with us, and we still don't have a plan. Have you given any thought to the matter we discussed?"

He clearly did not want to say more in front of Mary and me.

"Judas, it is not in our hands alone. We will be given a sign."

"Has it ever occurred to you that *we* are the ones to make the sign? That the Most High has entrusted us to act on his behalf?"

Jesus was silent for a moment.

"Judas, I am thinking about what you have said. But tonight is a night for watching and praying. Will you keep watch over the people tonight?"

I noticed my beloved's careful phrasing. Watch over the people. Judas could not refuse, and he didn't.

With Tomas attaching himself at the last minute, Jesus led us further into the mountains. The moon of Tishri, now ten days old, slowly rode down the western sky in the sun's wake. We climbed up and up, as if trying to reach the moon, until we crested a high hill and stopped. We could see her in the distance, see the torches blazing on the Temple heights.

Jerusalem, Jerusalem.

Everyone wept. I wept with them, without knowing why. I loved my companions, and Jerusalem was their holy city. I did not know the city held a meaning for me, because I couldn't name it yet. If I could, I might have called Jerusalem the terrible city, the beautiful city, the place of reckoning.

Jesus said the evening prayers, and then we all sat down to keep watch through the night, leaning our backs against each other for warmth and support. We kept vigil all the next day as well, praying, singing, or sitting in silence, watching the smoke of sacrifice blacken the sky. When the wind was right, we could catch a whiff of incense and charred flesh and hear the blast of the shofar. As the afternoon wore on, I confess I dozed. Into my dreams came the sound of bells and a goat bleating.

"Mary," said Mary B shaking me, "wake up! The Azazel goat is coming."

I was disoriented but got to my feet and went with Mary to join with the others in gazing across a ravine. On the other side, a man dressed in priestly robes led a goat up a steep hill toward a precipice. The goat had a blood red sash decorating its horns.

"What is the priest doing with the zaza goat?" I whispered to Mary.

"The Azazel goat. On the Great Day there are two goats brought to the High Priest in the Temple. The High Priest draws lots. One goat is sacrificed to the Most High. The other goat is driven out into the wilderness and sacrificed to Azazel."

"Who the hell is Azazel? I thought you only believed in one god."

"Azazel is not a god!" She was indignant. "He's a demon or a fallen angel. We give him the sin goat, the scapegoat."

"How can a goat sin?" I was perplexed.

"The goat takes on the sins of the people and carries them away."

"One little goat? Wouldn't you need a whole herd?" I thought of the two thousand demon-ridden pigs jumping over the cliff into the Sea of Galilee.

"It's symbolic, Mary," she said impatiently. "Now, hush. Watch!"

The priest tethered the goat to a stake in the ground. Then he untied the sash. With one precise motion, he tore the cloth in two. One half he placed at the edge of the cliff, weighting it down with rocks. The other he tied again on the goat's horns. I have never seen a goat so still. Maybe the druids were not the only ones who drugged their sacrifices, for surely this sin-laden little goat was about to meet some doom. It was the form that took me by surprise. With the goat adorned again, the priest untied it. Before it could even think of trying to escape, the priest lifted the goat in his arms and hurled it into the ravine. I prayed silently that the goat die at once, not be left crippled to die of exposure or be eaten alive. Jesus prayed aloud.

"Thy holy tribe, thy people, the House of Israel. Before the Lord, ye shall be clean. Ye shall be clean."

The others gazed at him, awed, afraid, knowing, as I did not, that he spoke the words reserved for the High Priest. Then all of them knelt or prostrated themselves. All but me. I walked to the edge of the ravine and looked down. The goat lay inert.

Jesus had said he was waiting for a sign. I prayed to Isis that this was not the one.

CHAPTER SIXTY-FIVE

WOMEN ON THE VERGE

Martha was on the verge of a nervous breakdown and who could blame her? Sukkoth, the feast of the booths, was three days away, and she had close to a hundred people camped out in her courtyards, orchards, and vineyards. During Sukkoth most would de-camp to the streets of Jerusalem, where they'd slap together the booths of palm and willow branches that gave the festival its name. The temporary shelters were supposed to remind good Jews of their nomadic origins, but truth be told, Sukkoth was a good old-fashioned, heathen harvest festival. People drank, sang and partied for eight nights and days, and the crowd at Bethany was already in the holiday spirit. A crowd that included not only Jesus and company but an assortment of Martha's relatives from out of town and overseas. To top it off, Miriam of Nazareth had just arrived (without advance notice) with Jesus's brothers in tow.

This was a bigger gathering than I'd ever had within the walls of Temple Magdalen, and it made the wedding at Cana look like a small, tasteful affair. But when I suggested to Martha that we send word to Joseph for help, she wouldn't hear of it. She was determined (if it killed her) to be the perfect hostess, gracious and unflappable, able to meet any demand.

It wasn't working.

Matters weren't helped by the fact that the sick and the destitute kept coming, seeking healings and handouts. We needed miracles: multiplying loaves and fishes, water into wine, self-cleaning latrines, peace, quiet—at the very least, as Judas kept saying, a plan. My beloved wasn't much use. He responded to whoever or whatever was immediately in front of him, but his vision didn't extend to the kitchens, the storerooms, or the processing of sewage. His chief miracle was to disappear completely from time to time. When he did, no one could find him. Except, I suspect, Lazarus, who had an extraordinary ability to go calmly about his business, and who never blew Jesus's cover.

Whenever they weren't gathered around Jesus, the Twelve—or thirteen, including Mary B—stood around in secretive huddles holding hushed discussions. Salome, Susanna, and I did our best to help Martha, and she did her best to appear grateful and to hide her horror of our uncleanness and uncouthness, sending us on errands out of the house as much as possible. One of the biggest strains on Martha was Miriam, whom Martha treated with a sort of desperate deference. Miriam was useless at household tasks, but instead of staying put in one place, she had a tendency to wander and come to an abstracted halt wherever she would be most in Martha's way. Her daughter Leah, Miriam's usual keeper, had stayed at home to mind the house in Nazareth, leaving guess who as her nearest kinswoman.

"She's *your* mother-in-law!" Martha cornered me on the day before Sukkoth; it sounded like an accusation. "*You* take charge of her."

"How?" I wanted to be helpful, but ordering Miriam around seemed beyond me.

"Haven't you ever heard the story of Naomi and Ruth?" Martha snapped. "Ruth was a Moabite, a heathen, just like you, but she cleaved onto her mother-in-law."

"I know the story," I admitted, shuddering at the thought of myself as a pious widowed daughter-in-law trailing after Miriam, gathering the gleanings of grain, while Ma became a matchmaking yenta and found me a nice, new Jewish husband. I'd have to have a word with Jesus and tell him straight out: Don't even *think* about leaving me.

"So cleave already," said Martha, and she stalked off.

"Let's go for a walk, Miriam," I said when I found her standing still in the middle of the courtyard with people flowing around her as if she were a boulder in a stream.

"Yes." She was surprisingly acquiescent. And I wondered if she, too, was glad of an excuse to get away from the chaos that surrounded her son.

Having been only fourteen when she gave birth to Jesus, Miriam was not terribly old or feeble—though women over forty who'd had half a dozen children tended to look old in those days. She took my arm and leaned on me lightly, not from infirmity, but so that she wouldn't have to pay attention to where we were going or watch her footing. She could drift and dream as usual, with me as her link to earth, but after awhile, there was a shift, and it seemed she was leading me. Soon I was sure of it, as she pulled me from the road, crowded with pilgrims and vendors, and wordlessly led me up a hill dotted with ancient, dusty olive trees.

Have I mentioned that I love olive trees? If the druids had lived in Palestine, surely they would have taught in these groves. Each olive tree is distinct from all the others, the way mature oaks are. Olive trees grow in complexity rather than height—widening, curving, twining. They can live for a thousand years, and their pocked, gnarled bark is porous with witness. Miriam led me to a tree near the top of a hill, and she sat down in its lap, the above-ground roots arranged in comfortable hollows. I found one near hers, and we sat companionably leaning our backs against the tree.

It was a hot, dry afternoon, and sitting in the shade of the tree was almost like drinking water through our skin. Nor was I surprised when a breeze that left the other trees untouched stirred in the branches above us. Though we had an excellent view across the Kedron Valley to the Temple, I tilted back my head and gazed at the sinuous branches, the dark leaves with the sky bright beyond them. Somewhere a mourning dove began to call, and I found myself wishing there were no Temple, no Jerusalem, only trees.

"When the sun rises, they shine." Miriam's voice was soft, mysterious like the breezes she called out of nowhere.

"The trees shine," I answered, as if we were singing a call and response.

"The gates shine," she clarified, and went on in a rhythm. "The Beautiful Gates, the Golden Gates that open to the dawn, that welcome the morning. See them shine. No, don't look." She broke her rhythm, and covered my eyes with her hands. "See!"

But I had already seen. "Tell me what you see!" Mary B had commanded me, when I had come out with her at dawn to this same hill. I had seen the gates turn gold, and I had seen them open, open onto nothing. Nothing.

"One day the Messiah will enter Jerusalem through the Beautiful Gates," proclaimed Miriam, just as Mary B had.

"No!" I cried out.

"Don't, Miriam," said a sharp voice on the other side of me.

Miriam's hand fell away, and I turned and saw Anna, looking small, wizened, impossibly old, her skin textured like the bark of the tree.

"Why not?" Miriam was cross. I could feel the current between the two women, old rivalry, old trust.

"She's not ready. All times may be one to you, Miriam of Nazareth," Anna went on scolding, "but this little dove must move through time. It is her burden and her gift. Visions may come to her, but you must not force them."

It was both irritating and comforting to have older women quarrelling over me as if I were not there. Nothing else so sharply recalled my childhood.

"*You* prophesy." The Blessed Virgin came close to pouting. "Why shouldn't I?"

"Are you called Anna the Prophetess? Prophecy is my burden and my gift."

"What about my burden and my gift?" Miriam countered.

"You have borne yours."

"The Lord God has dealt bitterly with me," Miriam remarked, almost lightly as if it was a response in a litany.

"It is even so," answered Anna, confirming my impression.

Both were silent for a moment, so I decided to jump in.

"I don't understand all this business about the Beautiful Gates and the Messiah." I realized I sounded petulant, even whiny. I was definitely regressing. "And frankly—"

"It gives you gas," Anna finished my sentence.

I was nonplussed, but now that she mentioned it, I did notice some cramping in my lower intestine as well as bloating. All familiar and unwelcome signs that I would bleed again soon.

"I only want to have a baby," I almost pleaded with them, as if they had the power to grant my wish or withhold it from me.

"Poor little Mary of Magdala," my mother-in-law sang. "Magdala, Magdala. Filled and empty, empty and filled, like a sea cave by the tide." Then she stopped singing and spoke. "Did you really think the Lord God would deal sweetly with you?"

"Fuck your Lord God!" I was suddenly enraged.

Neither holy woman was ruffled in the least.

"Yes," agreed Anna. "You do."

It took me a moment to catch her drift.

"He's a man!" I almost shouted. "*My* man. Why can't you all leave him alone!"

"We can't leave him alone," said Anna sadly, "though he is alone, terribly alone. Nor can we leave you alone, though you will be alone, terribly alone. For he is heaven, born on earth, borne on earth, and the way between the worlds is between your thighs," she chanted. "Honey and oil, honey and oil, you will anoint him, hands of fire dipped in the well, the holy well."

All at once, I remembered the second part of Peter's prophecy in the shadow of Mount Hermon: that I would be the one to anoint Jesus. *Anoint him for what?* And I felt as sick as Peter had looked.

"Don't force her, Anna," my mother-in-law cut her off. "I'll tell her when the time comes. That's *my* burden and *my* gift. Not yours."

The silence settled again, and I let it be. There was clearly no point in asking for useful information from these two, whose rivalry appeared to center on who could be the most annoying and obscure. I closed my eyes and concentrated on settling my stomach.

"Mary of Magdala," Miriam said at length. "We must go back to Bethany now. There's trouble. You're needed. The matter could be settled once and for all if anyone would listen to you. They won't, but never mind. Are you coming with us, Anna?"

The only answer was the cooing of the mourning doves. Anna had vanished.

"Harumph!" said Miriam as I helped her to her feet. "Well, at least I had the last word this time, didn't I, Mary of Magdala? Even death can't shut some people up."

"Death?" I queried. "Anna's dead?"

But Miriam would say nothing more.

When we walked into the courtyard of Martha's house, the air was as charged as the moment before a thunderclap when the wind has stilled and everything holds its breath. Martha stood, confronting Jesus in the center of a seated crowd. Her chest was heaving, and she was clearly struggling to control herself. On the ground in front of her was a platter she must have dropped (or hurled?). Bread, olive paste, cheese, and grapes lay scattered among bits of broken crockery. Mary B, sitting nearest Jesus, (yes, you could say at his feet) was the first to unfreeze. She got on her knees and started gathering up the shards, but Martha paid no attention.

"Lord!" Martha said through clenched teeth; she was trying to keep her voice low, but of course everyone was straining to hear. "Do you not care that my sister is leaving me to do all the serving myself? Tell her to help me!"

According to my beloved's chroniclers, Martha says "please," I suppose because they did not like to depict a woman giving the Master a direct order. But, in fact, she did.

Jesus regarded Martha for an awfully long time before he answered. He knew he was in a tight spot, and enigmatic silence (a talent of his rivaled only by his gift for sounding off) is a good delaying tactic. If he told Mary B to get off her ass and serve, he would be denying her discipleship, denying the right of women to be disciples. Keep that in mind, those of you who hate what he said next.

"Martha, Martha, you worry and fret about so many things, yet few are needed, indeed only one. Mary has chosen her place"—(I swear he did not say "the better part" or I would have smacked him)—"and it shall not be taken from her."

So there it is: the dilemma of millennia. If you defend a woman's right to be a doctor, lawyer, disciple, leader, do you inevitably denigrate the woman (or the slave or, in your time, the illegal immigrant) who is cooking, washing dishes, changing diapers, and wiping noses? If no one did that work, where would any of us be? Some people may apologize for Jesus and say that Martha is the self-important, make-work part of ourselves. But I think that's the easy way out. I will leave Jesus impaled on the horns of the dilemma. In fact, in that moment, I did not want to deal with him at all.

"You raised him," I prodded my mother-in-law. "You do something."

But Miriam had closed her eyes and started to sway and hum, which added to the tension in the courtyard. Her only response was to give me a not-so-gentle nudge. I looked at Martha, her face mottled, about to burst into tears. I glanced at Mary, still fumbling with the crockery, looking not only sorry but absolutely stricken. And then it happened. As the prophets say, the spirit of (well, all right) the Lord came upon me.

Just as Martha was about to bolt, I stepped through the crowd and took her hand. With my other hand, I reached for Mary B and pulled her to her feet. And if I do say so myself, it's a goddamned shame no one wrote down what I did next.

"Anyone who wants to be great among you," I began, my druid-trained memory standing me in good stead, "must be your servant, and anyone who wants to be first among you must be a slave to all. For the Son of Man himself..." I cast a baleful glance at my husband, who looked just like his mother, at the moment, swaying with his eyes closed. "I *said* the Son of Man himself, came not to be served but to serve."

There was a stunned silence followed by a lot of gasping and sputtering: the nerve of this gentile hussy (whom the Master had married as some inscrutable act of mercy or in a moment of temporary insanity) daring to rebuke him in public and with his own words. The Lord smite her, turn her into a pillar of salt or something, the wicked woman, or better yet the earth should gape and swallow her altogether.

Jesus opened one eye and looked straight at me. It wasn't a wink exactly, but I took it as an admission: You got me. I decided to push my luck.

"Man may not live by bread alone, but I've noticed you all like to eat. What is more, doesn't our, um," I hesitated, wondering how to refer to Jesus because I could not choke out the word Master, "doesn't our Bridegroom teach us that eating together is holy? Doesn't he invite us all to the wedding feast? Well, who's going to cook it and serve it? You? Me? Her? Him? And aren't we all guests at the feast? The beggars, the sinners, the servants?"

"Tell it, sister!" called out Susanna and she caught the rhythm of my speech and started clapping it; soon the other women joined in, and some got up and started to tap it with their feet. And then before I knew what was happening, I went into a kind of trance and started to chant, singing out line after line in time to the clapping.

> And aren't we the salt
> that gives the feast its savor?
>
> *Come to the feast, last and first,*
> *come serve and be served.*
>
> And isn't it held in the mustard seed
> flavored with the speech of birds?
>
> *Come to the feast, last and first,*
> *come serve and be served.*
>
> And isn't it in the garlic cloves
> the sweet rose and its bitter fruit?
>
> *Come to the feast, last and first,*
> *come serve and be served.*
>
> And isn't it in the fish that leaps
> the bright fish who feeds on hazelnuts?
>
> *Come to the feast, last and first,*
> *come serve and be served.*
>
> Feed among the lilies with my beloved
> with the roes and the hinds.
>
> *Come to the feast, last and first,*
> *come serve and be served.*
>
> And the radiance shall sweeten our tongues
> and sing in our bellies.
>
> *Come to the feast, last and first,*
> *come serve and be served.*

And milk shall flow from our breasts
into the sweet hungry mouth of life.

Come to the feast, last and first,
come serve and be served.

For our mother carries the starry host in her womb
and we are held in the radiance.

Come to the feast, last and first,
come serve and be served.

And so it went on and on, with more and more people joining in the refrain. Then others took over and made up their own verses. I wasn't leading anymore. I had just been the opening for the song that had flowed into our midst. All the women and even some of the men were dancing now. And I closed my eyes and let the sound and the rhythm carry me. When the song finally ended, I opened my eyes and saw Jesus still standing in the same place, still swaying slightly to some music we could not hear. Beside him, Peter, who had surrendered to the dance, looked sweaty and sheepish.

I was sweating, too, and I suddenly felt very exposed. I stared down at the remains of the food still scattered on the ground until I felt my beloved's gaze on me. How to explain that sensation—heat, cold, intensity. I raised my eyes to meet his and saw there nothing I could name—not love, not anger, not laughter, not sadness. Whatever was, or wasn't, there, it frightened me. Then he looked away.

"Mary of Magdala has spoken truly."

I should have felt affirmed, but I did not. His voice was flat and joyless, and he had called me by a kind of title. Perhaps it was a gesture of respect, acknowledgment of my right to teach. But I would much rather he had called me Maeve or even "my wife."

"We must all serve," he said, and he bent down and began to clean up, while Mary B and others close by followed suit.

Martha was horrified.

"No, Lord, no! Stop. It is my honor to serve. You mustn't."

Jesus had the good sense to get up and take Martha in his arms, holding her while she finally gave way and wept.

Meanwhile poor Mary B had collected a pile of debris and was looking at it helplessly.

"Come on, Mary," I said. "Let's go find a broom."

CHAPTER SIXTY-SIX

RIOT

I f I have regrets, and I do, one is that I did not confront the estrangement between us that began that day. Or at least that was the first day I acknowledged to myself that something was wrong, though our conflict may have been germinating for some time, underground where I did not have to see it. Till now I had been able to explain away any tensions as circumstantial—the importunate crowds, the general uproar all around us, Judas's growing restlessness. It had nothing to do with him and me. Sure we might not have much time together, but we were connected, one flesh, as his god put it.

"He is alone, terribly alone," Anna's words haunted me. "And you will be alone, terribly alone." In the days that followed, he seemed determined to fulfill her prophecy. At least he cut himself off from me. Of course, it didn't help that I was "menstruous" again, and therefore untouchable. But it was more than the blood *geis* that kept us apart. I knew that much, but I couldn't fathom what had happened.

Some of you may think that for a smart (or smart-ass) broad I'm pretty dumb. I had challenged him in front of everyone. I had preached to his followers. What did I expect? Yet if it had been a battle of egos only, we could have fought it out and ended up in bed (once I was "clean" again), our lovemaking all the spicier. No, the rift between us ran deeper. My rebuke hadn't caused it, nor had my momentary swaying of the crowd. I think now it was the song itself that did it. And if you don't understand why the song troubled him so, I'll leave you in suspense, because at that time, I didn't understand it, either. And I had no idea what to do.

Since Jesus was clearly avoiding me, I began to avoid him back. But I could not avoid the pain of knowing that I was no longer a source of comfort to him. When he needed a refuge, he turned to Lazarus. If it had been anybody else, I would have been eaten up with jealousy, but I could not resent kind, unassuming Lazarus. He was the only person who did not want something from Jesus. If there had been corncob pipes in those days, the pair would have sat together smoking silently. If they talked at all, it would only be of crops, flocks, fishing, weather. What a relief from his disciples with all their strategy meetings—meetings from which I was excluded.

I did not know just how out of the loop I was until the day you call Palm Sunday. (I know you're used to thinking of that day as the beginning of Passion Week just before Passover, but Jerusalem was decorated with festival palms for Sukkoth.) As I had many mornings recently, I woke on the rooftop alone and cold, my husband already gone. I found him in the courtyard, sitting on a low stool surrounded by some of the inner circle, as I had come to think of them (though Judas and Simon were absent). Jesus was dressed in a clean white tunic. *Very* clean and *very* white. Mary B, the early bird, was not combing his hair exactly—the man had dreads—but oiling it and arranging it, and Jesus was allowing this intimacy.

Mary was the first to notice me; she blushed and had the grace to look guilty—not because she was touching my husband in a way only a wife might be expected to. I knew Mary B better than that. No, Mary's sallow face turned red, because she had let me down. She knew what was going on, and she knew that no one had told me. *She* hadn't told me. I looked at her coldly until, almost against my will, I looked at Jesus.

I couldn't read him. If Mary's face was like a child's primer—big letters, simple words—Jesus's gaze was a cold, stone tablet inscribed with words in a language no one living knew. Still I struggled to translate: This is a mystery. You cannot understand it. This is my story now, not ours. That was as close as I could come. Then Jesus turned as Philip and Bartholomew entered the gate, leading a young donkey.

"We found it, Master," Philip greeted him. "Just as you said we would."

And so we come to my beloved's famous ride to Jerusalem. I had a sense of foreboding as I stood back and watched him mount the donkey. The last time I'd seen him go anywhere except on foot was the day he'd flung himself onto a horse and galloped across the Menai Straits, fleeing for his life, an escaped human sacrifice. The memory was so vivid, I barely registered Mary B's attempt to make amends.

"He's riding a donkey to fulfill a scripture from Isaiah," she was explaining. "'Look your king comes to you; he is humble, riding on a donkey.'"

"My king?" I repeated abstractedly.

"Pay attention. I'm quoting the scripture, so you'll understand what's happening."

"But I don't understand." I turned to her, remembering that I was angry with her. "I thought Jesus told Judas he didn't want to be king. Has there been a change of plan that no one's bothered to tell me about?"

"Not that kind of king," Mary said, gently for her. "Look, he's going now. Let's keep up or we'll lose sight of him in the crowd. Come on Susanna, Salome. Hurry."

So the four of us ran after him, leaving Martha to hold the fort and only Miriam to drive her crazy in the relative peace and quiet.

The throng kept growing as we crossed the Kedron Valley and began our climb toward the city. I tried to get caught up in the spirit, to sing the responses to the psalms or give the odd shout of praise, but I was distracted by the Beautiful Gates, flashing gold in the morning light—the beautiful, terrible gates, hungry for a Messiah. For what was this procession about if not those wretched prophecies?

I was so relieved when Jesus took a right fork and headed instead for the gate below the Antonia fortress, for a moment I let myself believe that we were like any other pilgrims going to Jerusalem for the harvest festivities. Everything would be all right. We'd drink new wine and dance, watch the public celebrations at the Temple, be tourists.

Then we entered Jerusalem.

The street that ran under the fortress was wider than most in the city, and it was lined on both sides with people waiting for the white-robed man on a donkey. As soon as Jesus came in sight, they lifted their arms, making the street a forest of waving palm and willow branches. I felt dizzied by the moving, striated patterns of light and shadow, as if a huge, erratic wind tossed the leaves about. And the shouting was like a storm wind or high surf, so deafening it took me some time to distinguish the words:

> *Hosanna to the Son of David*
> *Blessings on him who comes in the name of the Lord*
> *Hosanna in the highest!*

I felt something land on my head, something wet and nasty. Someone had spit from above. I looked up and saw the soldiers, mounted on the fortress heights at precise intervals, spears poised, muscles taut, ready to move into action. I knew that Roman soldiers considered Jerusalem a hardship post—an oriental city without Roman amenities, full of excitable people who took their weird religion way, way too seriously. Now here was this crazy, unshaven prophet, riding a common beast of burden, for Mithras's sake, causing a hullabaloo. What next?

As we turned a corner, I caught sight of Judas and Simon; they seemed to be alternately parting the crowd and pulling it along. Then I realized Peter and the Thunder Brothers were weaving in and out of the crowd, keeping the chant going.

> *Hosanna to the Son of David*
> *Blessings on him who comes in the name of the Lord*
> *Hosanna in the highest*

So now I knew: all the hushed meetings had been planning sessions for Jesus's dramatic entrance into the City of David. Judas and company must have gone ahead as the advance team to assemble and prime the crowd. Yet the wild response was not simply a matter of clever orchestration and good press. The people's longing for a king was palpable. I couldn't help but feel it. Their cheers caught in my own throat. Their tears pressed behind my own eyes. Now I knew what kind of king Mary meant—a king from a story, a lover king, a poet king, a cocky shepherd boy from ordinary folk, who could slay a giant with a slingshot. A savior king. A king you could worship and adore.

As your beloved.

Suddenly I stopped; the thought hit me with such force. Mary B had been right: he was the Bridegroom of Israel. Not my bridegroom. He was married to his people, not to me. I was not even one of them, not even a good Jewish wife, to comfort and shore him up.

"What are you doing!" Susanna grabbed me. "You're going to get trampled."

She was right; I couldn't stop here, I couldn't turn around. So I let myself be carried along with the crowd to the vast southern steps of the Temple where Jesus dismounted from the donkey and began his ascent.

But I knew I was alone, terribly alone.

People are still arguing about what happened in the Temple—was it planned, was it spontaneous? Was he deliberately trying to fulfill a prophecy from Zechariah in order to bring about the Day of the Lord that would follow certain catastrophic events? I can only tell you what I saw. My source of scriptural analysis had gone to the women's baths with Salome, preparatory to entering the Court of Women where Susanna and I were not allowed. Mary B assumed that Jesus also would cleanse himself for prayer in the Court of Israelites before he went anywhere else. We agreed to meet again in the porticoes where Jesus would surely go to teach.

The Court of Gentiles, where the moneychangers and the animal vendors had their booths, was always a hubbub, but during festivals it was mobbed, and Susanna and I soon lost sight of each other. Jews on pilgrimage from foreign places had to change their money into Temple currency (of course there was a charge). The vendors of doves and goats and other sacrificial animals also did a brisk trade. Only an animal without blemish made an acceptable offering, and only priests got to rule on what a blemish was. You could say it was a racket—or a way of raising revenue for one of the wonders of the world, still under construction. Either way, a lot of money changed hands, and peasants, short on cash, who brought their own animals to sacrifice, often got shafted.

In my opinion, that's what started the riot.

I was milling about listlessly, yes, feeling sorry for myself, when, out of the corner of my eye, I glimpsed an old woman in a purple shawl among the bird vendors. Doves perched on her shoulder and fluttered about her head. Anna! I thought. Never mind that Miriam said she was dead. Who has not pushed their way through a crowd, sure that somehow a friend or lover, mother or father, has somehow come back? But when I reached the woman, a vendor stood in my way, blocking my view of her face.

"Hey you, old Mother," the vendor said. "Where did you get the birds? Where are you going with them?"

Sacrificial birds bought from vendors were caged, so clearly the old woman's doves had not been purchased—they were home-grown or stolen.

"These doves belongs to the Most High," declared the old woman, not Anna's voice, a Galilean accent. "I am giving them to the Lord."

I maneuvered around the man, and saw that she was indeed a peasant woman, weathered, poor, almost toothless, her shawl black not purple. My eyes had tricked me.

"Not if you didn't buy them here on Temple ground, you're not. Not until a priest inspects 'em for blemishes. You Galileans ought to know better by now. Don't you fear to offend the Most High?"

The woman's face fell. I couldn't stand by and watch her being bullied.

"I don't see any blemishes on these birds," I declared, though in fact the birds that had flashed so white against the purple shawl, now looked mottled and dingy, more like common pigeons than doves.

"Oh, and you'd know better than a priest, lady?" he sneered, looking me up and down. My simple, matronly (dis)guise never seemed to help much. The man's eyes said "gentile whore" as clearly as if he'd spoken.

"I'm as qualified as you!" I shot back. "Her birds are cleaner than yours, all squashed in their cages, sitting in their own shit, pecking at each other."

Crowds have a nose like a hound for confrontation. Buyers, sellers, sightseers, had reconfigured with amazing speed into an audience, spoiling for a fight.

"You watch your filthy mouth! These birds has been inspected. And if the priest says they're unblemished, they're unblemished, see? You want to do the old beggar woman a favor, you buy her some of these here birds, certified clean."

"My birds belong to my God," the old woman whimpered in confusion. "I raised them for Adonai from the egg."

"I told you, old Mother, them birds is good for nothing but the cooking pot, if you have one, and if you can manage to chew the old stringy buzzards with your two teeth."

Some of the onlookers laughed at the man's sorry wit; others looked uncomfortable, unsure of whether to come to the old woman's aid or slink away. I was way past that point; I could feel my rage rising like a mighty wind. Suddenly fear scudded across the man's face. For a moment I took pleasure in thinking it was fear of me. And then I heard the Voice.

"And it is written, 'In the Temple of Yahweh the very cooking pots will be as fine as sprinkling bowls at the altar!'"

Jesus (who else) pushed past me and got right up in the vendor's face.

"'And every cooking pot in Jerusalem and Judah shall be sacred to Yahweh Sabaoth.'"

I had no idea what he was talking about, but he was terrifying. Even though it was not directed at me, I could feel his anger whipping the marrow of my own bones into frothy whitecaps.

"'And all who want to sacrifice will come and help themselves from their cooking. AND THERE WILL BE NO MORE TRADERS IN THE TEMPLE WHEN THAT DAY COMES!'"

With a sudden swift motion, Jesus picked up the vendor's stool and hurled it; people ducked and began to run in panic.

"And moreover does not scripture say, 'My house shall be called a house of prayer for ALL people.' You!" He whirled around, pointing his finger in all directions. "You have made it a DEN OF THIEVES!"

And with that he upended one of the moneychangers' tables. And that was all it took, the pent-up rage of the people was released and—for that moment—directed against the Temple's marketplace. Jesus and his disciples turned over table after table. Fist fights broke out between peasants and vendors. Priests came running. It was chaos.

I stood still with the old woman, as if in the eye of the storm.

"Go to God, little ones," I heard the old woman croon, and the birds, their wings blinding white, fluttered into the sky.

"Anna!" I almost accused her. And for an instant, she was.

"Quick, little dove. Open the cages!"

And so while the people rioted, bashing heads and bloodying noses, and Jesus and the disciples chased out the moneychangers with whips (albeit, willow whips) I opened cage after cage, releasing the sacrificial doves, the shadows of their wings making a silent pattern over the pandemonium, wishing I could fly with them beyond all the noise and smoke. When the last cage was empty, I gazed up and flung my longing after them, willing myself to shapeshift.

"Not this time, little dove," whispered Anna.

When I looked around for her, she had disappeared.

CHAPTER SIXTY-SEVEN

FIG TREE

Back at Bethany that night, the mood of the disciples was congratulatory, even elated. Somehow everyone had managed to get away, if not unscathed (there were quite a few black eyes and split lips) at least without being arrested by the Roman guard or by the Temple authorities. This clean getaway seemed a miracle in itself, a sure sign of the Most High's favor. There were no secretive huddles that evening. After dinner everyone sat in the courtyard around the fire, reliving the events of the day, talking all at once, interrupting each other excitedly. No one seemed to notice Jesus's silence. Except me.

"So what do we do next, Master?" Peter asked Jesus.

"It's obvious," Judas broke in when Jesus said nothing. "Strike while the iron's hot, while the crowds are still here for the festival. We occupy the Temple, put the Romans on notice that there will be no more collaboration!"

"But not as a violent mob!" protested Mary B, who could be relied upon to object to whatever Judas proposed.

"It may not be wise to return too soon," said Matthew. "The Temple police will be on the alert."

"They wouldn't dare touch him," the Thunder brothers spoke at once. "Just let 'em try. It'll make what happened today look like a mere scuffle."

"That's right, Master dear," said Salome.

"The people love you, Rabbi," said Philip. "The priests must have seen that. They won't openly risk the anger of the people. They know they have to negotiate."

"We don't want to negotiate," objected Judas. "That's why we must act quickly."

"The people are with us," said Andrew. "No one can stop us now!"

"A Roman legion could," countered Simon bluntly. "Easily. Look, if the Temple hierarchy collaborates, it's for a reason. Let's not fool ourselves about what we're up against. Things got out of our control today. We were lucky, and we had the advantage of surprise. Next time we won't. Before we make a move again, we need weapons; we need training."

"David only had a slingshot!" said Peter. "Moses only had a staff. I tell you the Lord is with us."

As Peter went on and on in this vein, I kept waiting for Jesus to speak; the pressure built up in me until I realized I was the one who wanted to say something.

"But what exactly are you trying to do?" I said loudly.

Peter finally stopped talking and a silence followed. I felt everyone's eyes on me, some resentful, some relieved, some just plain confused. Only Jesus did not turn to me.

"Are you ousting the priests? Or just challenging their corrupt practices? Are you openly declaring war on Rome or just seeking to undermine the occupation? Or are you doing none of those things? What is the message? Repent? Feast? Fight? Pray? Why are you here in Jerusalem? Why?"

It wasn't till I finished speaking that I realized I that I had started seated, speaking to everyone, and ended up on my feet almost shouting at Jesus. At last he looked at me.

"I do the will of the One who sent me."

"You," I said. "*You* do the will of this One. What about the rest of us?" I made sure to include myself this time. "Why are *we* here? What does your god want?"

"He is *our* God!" Peter burst out. "The God of Israel."

"You can't play it both ways, Mary of Magdala," Judas spoke to me directly for the first time. "You are with us or against us. You can't say *you* then change it to *us*."

"Well, I just did," I pointed out. "So I guess I can."

"Of course she's with us!" Mary B took on her adversary.

"She's the Master's wife!" said Susanna, nervously, for her status was less secure than mine.

"Is she?" said Judas quietly.

Was he implying that our marriage was illicit? I turned to Jesus; only he could answer that question. He acted as if he had not heard it.

"Maeve, I cannot stop what is coming." He spoke in a low, urgent tone as if we were alone, as if only I would know what he meant. "I cannot, Maeve. I cannot."

"Cannot or will not?" I asked.

He didn't answer me. Instead he rose and at last addressed the whole company.

"Listen, all of you. What I do, I will do openly. I will not fight again with the moneychangers. I will not hide in crowds. What I say, I will say. What I am, I will be."

And with that, he went off to be alone.

He was still gone when I went to the roof to spread out our bedroll. I was exhausted, as who would not be after such a day, but I willed myself to stay awake. I needed to talk to him. I wanted an answer to Judas' question. I wanted to say to him: if you are a king, who am I? What do you want from *me*?

But when he finally came to bed, it was not so easy. He lay down quietly, so that no part of his body touched mine. I told myself he just thought I was asleep and did not want to disturb me.

"I'm awake," I said.

When he didn't answer, I moved closer to him and put my hand over his heart.

"Are you still *menstruous*?" he asked.

"No." I felt hopeful. Maybe we would make love; it was always easier to talk afterwards. "I stopped bleeding the day before yesterday."

"Then we still have to wait. Remember?"

How could I forget? Seven days after cessation of bleeding until a man could safely go in unto his wife. This from a man who broke Sabbath rules like fingernails.

"*You* have to wait," I said bitterly. "So *I* have to wait. There's no 'we' about it. Judas got that right."

But Jesus was already asleep—or pretending to be.

I almost stayed in Bethany with Ma, Martha and the other women the next day. Salome's hips were hurting from walking on paving stones instead of good old Galilean dirt. When the four of us were together at the well, drawing water for the household's needs, Susanna announced that she'd had enough of the Temple of Jerusalem for awhile.

"But he's going to be teaching in the porticoes!" said Mary B.

Like none of us had ever heard him before.

"Lazarus is going to be shearing," said Susanna. "I said I'd help." And she shut her mouth abruptly and blushed as Mary B gave her a sharp look.

"Maybe I'll stay, too." A day with the sheep might be just what I needed. So much stress, no wonder I couldn't conceive a child.

"No, Mary, you have to come," said Mary B; she put down her jug the better to gesticulate. "Especially after what Judas implied last night about you not being one of us, you *have* to."

"Oh, who cares what Judas said!" said Susanna.

"The old sourpuss," put in Salome.

"I do," said Mary B. "I care. Please, Mary, I don't want to be the only woman."

Now it was her turn to blush for admitting such a weakness.

"Oh, all right," I gave in.

Though we set out for Jerusalem early in the morning, the day quickly grew warm. Everyone was tired from yesterday, but also keyed up, waiting to see what would happen next. It was a bad combination, and tempers were short. We had left the shade of the olive groves and were in the depths of the valley, the sun beating down on the backs of our necks, when Jesus saw a fig tree ahead and suggested we stop and eat some fruit before starting the steep climb, but when we got to the tree, we found it wasn't bearing.

According to my beloved's chroniclers, this encounter with the fig tree happened in the spring when it would have been unreasonable to expect fruit, but in fact it was the harvest season. Very likely the tree had been stripped of its fruit by other Sukkoth pilgrims; or perhaps it had not yet reached maturity. But for whatever reason, this fig tree wasn't putting out, and the Son of Man was extraordinarily put out about it. To put it bluntly, he had a tantrum. He began to curse the tree for barrenness, and he went on cursing for quite awhile, a long, bitter blast of curses (which his chroniclers edited), denigrating the tree's ancestry back to Eden, ending with the most dreadful one of all:

"And may you never bear fruit again!"

When he stopped, it was very quiet in the Kedron Valley. You could hear sounds from a great distance away, goat bells on the hill, voices in the Temple. The disciples stood awkwardly, looking at their feet or the sky, like school children when the teacher has thrown a fit and broken all the chalk, or children when their mother, after cooking all day, flies into a rage and dumps dinner on the floor. But I looked straight at Jesus, my own fury growing in me as I watched his die, spent now on the tree.

"Look!" Peter broke the silence. "What happened to the tree? It's withered!"

And it was, right down to the root, its branches, which had provided shade at least, now dead and leafless. I started to shake and sweat; I thought I would be sick.

Then it got worse.

"I tell you solemnly," Jesus addressed his followers, "if you have faith and do not doubt at all, not only will you be able to do what I have done to this fig tree but even if you say to this mountain, 'Get up and throw yourself into the sea, it will be done.'" He turned and began to walk as he talked, his disciples trailing after him. "And if you have faith, everything you ask for in prayer, you shall receive."

I could hear his voice going on and on as he and the disciples climbed toward the city, but soon I could no longer hear the words. I remained by the dead tree.

"Bastard!" I shouted after him. "Spoiled Brat of the Father!"

Only Mary B looked back, gesturing for me to hurry up, but she did not stop. The Master was teaching, and she didn't want to miss anything.

"You call this faith!" I screamed, my voice breaking.

Then I couldn't see them anymore, either, I was crying so hard. I turned blindly to the dead tree and put my arms around it, pressing my cheek against its shriveled bark. He had killed a tree, blasphemy to a Celt. He had killed a fig tree sacred to Isis for its fruit that looked like a woman's vulva. He had killed this tree, because it was barren.

Barren. Like me.

I slowly sank to the ground. My arms still around the tree, I cried for the loss of my mothers and the woman-shaped island of Tir na mBan that I might never see again. I cried for the loss of my people, for King Bran and Branwen. I cried with homesickness for Temple Magdalen and my sister whores. I cried for my baby, stolen from me. And I cried for the loss of the boy I had loved almost all my life. I did not know this man, whose god withered trees at his command.

When my tears finally ebbed I became aware of the fire of the stars beginning to course through me, as if my grief had cleared out all channels and there was nothing to impede its flow through my hands, through my very pores into the tree. Fire? Say rather days and years of sun's circling, of the moon's changing, fire turned to cool and sweet rain, deep rivers, fire turned to rich, fertile loam.

When I came to myself again, I was kneeling in the shade of a mature fig tree with lustrous leaves, branches heavy with ripe fruit, ready to fall into my hand. I picked an abundance of figs; then I took off my head covering, made it into a sack to carry the fruit, and set out for the Temple.

"I tell you truly, tax collectors and prostitutes are making their way into the Kingdom before you," Jesus was saying as I elbowed my way past scribes and Pharisees to the teaching porticoes. I knew that tone of voice; he was on a rant. "For John came to you, showing the way of uprightness, but you did not believe him, yet the prostitutes and tax collectors did. Even after seeing that—"

He broke off abruptly as a woman with bright red uncovered hair walked straight up to him.

"Talking of prostitutes!" the crowd began to titter.

"Stop, Mary, what are you doing," some of the disciples hissed.

I ignored them all.

"The gifts of the goddess!"

I flung my headscarf at his feet, and ripe figs spilled out in all directions. Then I turned and walked away through a crowd that parted as swiftly and miraculously as the Red Sea.

"Maeve," Jesus called after me, with that voice of his, low but resonant. "Maeve, forgive me."

I did not acknowledge that I heard him. I never looked back. That is the sin I own, not what happened after that. I refused him forgiveness; I, who insisted he was a man, broken and mistaken as the rest of us. I would not turn around—which is what repent means: to turn. I kept walking as fast as I could, away from the Temple, out of his life.

I wandered in the crowded, festival city with no more will or direction than a stick tossed on the rapids. I let the flow of traffic carry me, and eventually I found myself in the poorest section of the lower city with all the other lost people—beggars, cripples, thieves, the *am-ha-arez* washed in with the tide of holiday pilgrims, thinking to find temporary work or to glean the scraps of holiday feasting. There I finally came to a halt and just stood, lost, with nothing to my name, no food, no haversack, no coins, no people, not even a head covering.

"How much?" said someone in my ear, his breath reeking of sour wine.

As I turned to the man, a flash of white caught my eye. I gazed up and saw a dove fluttering in a tiny alley across the street. She rose to perch on an upper story windowsill.

"I said, how much?" the man repeated.

I finally looked at him, a rough man, maybe a laborer from the country, who had heard about the sinful pleasures of the city. There was something about my stare that must have intimidated him; maybe I looked insane; maybe I was. He began to edge away.

"One *as*," I heard myself naming the lowest coin in existence. "Come."

I led him into the alley where I had seen the dove. I braced myself against the wall, lifted my tunic and took him inside.

Jesus, I cried silently, *Jesus.*

It was over quickly. The man pressed the coin in my hand and fled.

CHAPTER SIXTY-EIGHT

TEMPLE OF THE DOVE

So began one of the strangest periods of my life. I used that first coin—
worth roughly two pennies (I had at last become a two-bit whore)—to
send word to Bethany that I was all right, but I was not coming back. No
one should try to find me. Did I secretly hope and believe that Jesus would not
rest until he had searched for me everywhere? The answer to that question is
neither yes nor no. For I did not believe that he *could* find me, even if he wanted
to; I had gone somewhere he could not follow. And if he should happen to discover my whereabouts, I would remain unreachable. I had crossed a line into
another world. I had dissolved our bond.

In a curious way I felt free, freer than I had ever been since I had first seen
him in the well on Tir na mBan and decided that we were each other's destiny.
I didn't believe in destiny anymore. I found I did not believe in anything. Least
of all myself. When people asked my name or where I was from, I just shook
my head and refused to speak. As Sukkoth ended and the pilgrims went home,
I gradually became known to the other slum dwellers as the crazy whore; they
accepted my existence with a shrug and kept their distance. A reputation for
derangement can be a great protection. Eventually I gained a kinder epithet—
the dove woman or just the Dove, because everywhere I went doves seemed to
follow. Not that I went very far. In the days following Sukkoth I lived and did
business in the alley.

One day the Roman slumlord, who owned the building in whose shadow I dwelled, came to check on his property. He kept the flimsy, makeshift upper room unoccupied, so that he could rent it out at exorbitant prices during
the festivals. On discovering me in the alley and after enjoying my services, he

gave me squatter's rights in exchange for my cleaning and repainting the room, patching the roof if it leaked during the winter rains.

I set to work cleaning the place, which had seen hard use during the festival and was full of debris, even excrement left in chamber pots. It took days before I had cleared it out enough to whitewash the walls. When I was done, I went out to the steps, unsure of what to do with the leftover wash, when I felt the fire of the stars begin to flow in my hands. I looked up and down the alley to see if there was someone in need, but it was deserted of all life—not even so much as a rat. Then a dove landed over the low, narrow door to the upper room. I reached to touch its breast, but at once it rose and flew away.

Without really knowing what I intended, I set down the bucket, dipped my hand into the wash and over the doorway, on the crude, mud walls I began to fashion the likeness of the dove. And the fire of the stars flowed through my hands into form.

After that, the crazy whore became even crazier, obsessed with making images. Jerusalem was not a city friendly to the art of painting, which the pious considered a pagan abomination, but there were some decorative arts, designs of plants or flowers painted on pottery; some people decorated their walls with menorahs or other symbols. I took my spare coins to the artisans' quarter and bought paint.

When I painted, always with my hands, my mind emptied out, my heart stopped aching. A fig tree appeared on one side of the door, and a grape vine on the other. Only after I had finished, did I register that I had painted an approximation of the fresco that decorated the brothel in Rome. Next I painted cats in various poses, and when I had painted everywhere I could reach outside my door, I moved inside where I painted in the semi-darkness. I never asked myself what I was painting or why. I just did it. I was neither happy nor unhappy. I was scarcely aware of myself at all. I was a nameless body who ate and shat, fucked and finger-painted. That was enough.

Then one day, when I was out buying paints, someone called out to me.

"*Domina*," he said, and at first I didn't know he was speaking to me, it was such a respectful greeting for someone about to proposition a whore. "Forgive me, *domina*, I don't remember your name. You are Joseph of Arimathea's friend."

At that I turned and saw the maverick Pharisee who had welcomed Joseph's scandalous entourage into his home without turning one of his white, woolly hairs.

"My name is Nicodemus," he reminded me, "and I believe you are now the wife of our notorious young Rabbi Jesus. What a mind, what a wit! It is a joy to hear him in the Temple, a tonic, but I am afraid he takes terrible risks. Men like us need wives to keep us in line."

I panicked. I did not want to be visible. I could not bear to be called wife to a man I could never touch again.

"I am sorry, sir," I said in Greek, pretending I did not speak Aramaic. "I am afraid you have mistaken me for someone else." And I turned and fled.

But the damage was done, my perfect self-protective bubble burst. I had done my best to obliterate myself, but there was no ignoring Jesus's existence. His name was on everyone's lips. My neighbors, the honest poor and the thugs, the sick and the destitute, began to praise him. They worked up their nerve to go and see him at the Temple. Some were healed of their infirmities; some repented their crimes and found new purpose in their lives. Their joy made them brave and generous enough to talk to the crazy whore about Jesus of Nazareth, savior of sinners, champion of the poor. They urged me to go and see him for myself.

"He has a soft spot for whores," a fellow streetwalker assured me.

"I heard he married a whore," said a young girl, whose widowed mother was trying desperately to preserve her virginity.

"Hush now, that's just a nasty rumor," said the widow. "What she means to say is he forgives their sins."

"Well, I think the story could be true," said a sweeper. "The Galilean does what he pleases; he don't care what nobody says. He breaks the Law something terrible. Healing on the Sabbath, they say."

"That's different. That's a mercy to sick folks, but as for marrying a whore—"

The debate became heated, and no one paid attention when I slipped away.

That night I could not sleep—not that I ever slept very long at a stretch. Men came and went from my bed. When the last one was gone, I got up and painted in the dark for the rest of the night, I hardly knew what. Forests, stars, rivers, anything to make the world less narrow, to give myself a way out. The next morning I went to the widow and asked if I could borrow a black headscarf and cloak. When I had covered all but my eyes, I started out for the Temple.

In those days, it was never hard to find him: follow the adoring masses, the cries of outrage from his critics; follow the magnetic pull that drew followers and foes alike. I stopped at the edge of the crowd and leaned against a pillar. He was in the middle of a story, and the sound of his voice seemed to come from the stones under my feet and go right up my spine.

"Then he said to the servants, 'The wedding is ready, but as those who were invited proved to be unworthy, go to the crossroads in the town and invite everyone you can find to the wedding.'"

I closed my eyes, and tears slipped from my eyes, as I wept as effortlessly and helplessly as Miriam of Nazareth. But no angels spoke to me. No comfort came to me as I remembered our wedding feast, and knew that I had exiled myself from paradise. If there were any angels hovering near me, they held flaming swords, barring my way back.

How long I wept blindly, I don't know. When I left the Temple and wound my way through the city to my alley, I sensed someone was following me. But every time I turned to look, hoping against hope that it might be my shape-shifting beloved come, against all odds, to find me, I saw no one. I climbed my stairs, wanting only to curl up and sleep for as long as I could. Before my eyes adjusted to the dim light, I knew someone was there, waiting for me in the room.

"Maeve!"

"Joseph?" I turned and saw him standing in one corner of the room. "What are you doing here?"

"That is an extremely stupid question!" He was furious with me the way only someone who has been worried sick can be. "I am not answering any questions until you answer some first. I haven't been able to get a coherent story out of anyone. Mary says you came storming into the Temple porticoes while your husband was teaching, threw figs at him, and disappeared."

"Did she tell you what happened before that?"

"What! About the blasted fig tree? You're both insane. Fighting over fig trees! What were you thinking, running off like that? What are you doing? Nicodemus says you denied your identity. He assumed he had indeed made a mistake until he heard you were missing. That's when he sent word to me. I've been tracking you down ever since. I asked everyone in Jerusalem about a gentile woman with red hair. 'You mean the crazy whore? The one with the dove over her door?'" He stopped and ran his hand over his brow; the room was stuffy, and he'd worked up a sweat. "I'm afraid it wasn't that hard to find you. Maeve, please, tell me it isn't true."

"It is true, Joseph." I made myself meet his eyes. "I am a crazy, two-bit whore."

"But why, Maeve, why? It's so...so wrong. Even at the Vine and Fig Tree, you were never a common streetwalker. And at Temple Magdalen, you were a priestess!"

"Joseph, a whore is a whore. Priestess, courtesan, those are just fancy words."

"What about the word wife, then? Does that have no meaning to you? You're married, Maeve. You have a husband."

"No."

"What do you mean, no?"

"Oh, Joseph, surely even you know that much of the Law of Moses. I'm defiled. I was always defiled. Our marriage was illicit from the beginning."

"Do you really believe that, Maeve?"

I lowered my eyes and fought back tears. No, I wanted to say. I don't believe that. *My beloved is mine, and I am his; our bed is the greensward; the beams of our house are cedar trees. His left arm is under my head, his right embraces me, and the banner over us is love, love as strong as death, passion as relentless as Sheol.*

"It doesn't matter what I believe, Joseph. The person I was no longer exists."

He looked at me, shaking his head, and then he crossed the room to the half-open window shutters and flung them wide, letting in the noonday glare.

"You have a lot of faults. But I never thought self-deception was one of them. Look!" he commanded with a gesture that swept the whole room. "Look!"

When I saw—and understood—what had come through my hands onto the walls, I cried out and covered my eyes. Joseph came to me and not so gently pulled my hands from my face. Then he stood behind me, holding my arms to my side.

All over the walls in a mixed up jumble were scenes from the story—of Isis and Osiris, of Maeve and Jesus. I had splashed my whole life on the walls in crude but searing images. There were two in particular that made my hands shake and sweat break out on my brow: A tree with my beloved at its core, his arms stretching into the branches, his feet merging with the roots. On the wall directly opposite I had made a sketch of the temple walls, with the window shutters as the Beautiful Gates opening onto sheer air.

"I didn't know," I whispered.

"What do you mean you didn't know?" Joseph was incredulous. "It's true, you have no technique, no sophistication, but you've turned this squalid room into something like a pagan temple. It's extraordinary. You must have meant something by it."

I shook my head. "I can't explain it, except to say I've been out of my head. Maybe I *am* possessed by unclean spirits."

"Nonsense!" said Joseph uneasily. "But if you think so, it's all the more reason to go back to your husband, the exorcist."

"I told you, I can't."

"Why? Because the Law says you're defiled? Since when did you abide by the Law of Moses?"

"Never. And I still don't. But *he* does. He has to. He's in enough trouble as it is."

Joseph was silent for a moment.

"What you say of him is true," Joseph conceded. "I should know; that's why I'm in Jerusalem. The Sanhedrin is in an uproar about the man. People either love him or hate him, and everybody's afraid of how the Romans might react to a leader so popular, and, well, unpredictable. I won't lie to you, Maeve; you are not exactly an asset as a wife. But whether or not you go back to him, you can't stay here in this rat-infested, stinking slum. You're coming with me. I'll take you anywhere, anywhere in the world you want to go."

"Oh, Joseph." I turned to him and touched his cheek. "You are the dearest friend."

"It's settled then?" His voice was full of yearning.

"Joseph, I'm so sorry, no."

"Then at least go to back to Magdala," he said stiffly. "I'll arrange an escort."

"I can't."

And I realized it was true. I could not go near Jesus, but I could not go away from him either. Just flat out physically could not.

"What I am supposed to do, Maeve?" Joseph asked miserably. "How can I leave you here? I know of the man who owns this building; he's little better than a Roman sewer rat. And what do you expect me to say to people? You can't just disappear."

"But I can. I have."

"You're deceiving yourself again, Maeve. If I can find you, other people can."

I felt such a mix of elation and panic that I knew it was true.

"Joseph," I said to him. "I've made a terrible mess of my life, and I don't know how to get out of it. I don't have any right to ask you anything, but I'm going to. Please just give me a couple of days to think what to do. Don't say anything to anyone. I promise I'll send word to you somehow when I decide where to go next."

"But will you think?" Joseph was clearly not happy. "I mean *think*! With your mind? Are you capable of thinking clearly?"

"I don't know, Joseph. Please, I love you. Leave me now."

"Two days, Maeve. I am staying with Nicodemus. I want word in two days."

And Joseph left me alone in my makeshift mystery temple, shortly to be the site of my arrest.

I see now that the whole thing was a setup. Morning was usually a time of respite from business. But that morning a man came to my door at about the second hour (eight o'clock your time). I took him in, because it was easier than sending him away. While the man heaved and grunted, I stared at the ceiling, wondering what I might paint there. The streets below were always noisy, so I did not hear the men stealthily mounting my stairs, till they burst into the room.

"Adultery! Caught in the act!" they shouted. "You are under arrest."

My customer leapt off me, and pushed past the intruders. They let him go—another sign of a setup. To buy time to think, I slowly, casually pulled on my tunic, as if their presence were a mere annoyance. Then I faced my accusers: three Levites, two Pharisees, and a Sadducee, Temple bigwigs all. Who had tipped them off? For one horrible moment, I thought of Nicodemus or, worse, Joseph. Who else knew where I lived? Then I remembered: I had gone to the Temple yesterday, and someone *had* followed me here.

Someone who knew me and wanted to use me to get at Jesus.

"What the hell do you mean, barging in and scaring off my trade!" I tried to throw them off by going on the offensive. "What's all this jabbering about adultery? Don't you know a gentile whore when you see one? You have no authority over me. Get out!"

"You are married to a Jew, and therefore subject to our Law."

"Who told you that?" I covered alarm with scorn. "How drunk was he?"

The Temple officials weren't there to debate with me. I stood my ground, thinking they would be afraid to touch me for fear of defiling themselves. But they had that all figured out, and as soon as I showed signs of putting up a fight, they called in their backup, a couple of off-duty Roman soldiers, happy to manhandle a whore for a few pieces of silver. I made quite a bit of noise as they dragged me out of the alley. My neighbors peered out their windows, but nobody was about to interfere with a Temple delegation and an armed guard. Yet I was not utterly deserted. As they hauled me away, I saw the shadows of doves' wings on the rubbish-strewn street.

It wasn't long before I knew they were taking me to the Temple. Don't let him be there, I prayed. Let him be far away. Don't let him be shamed because of me. Don't let him suffer because of me. Don't let him be there. Isis, Adonai, have mercy.

I kept my eyes on the ground as we crossed the Court of the Gentiles, but I sensed that people were standing back, hushing in anticipation of a spectacle.

My accusers led me to the teaching porticoes, and when we came to a halt, there was complete silence. The soldiers released me, their job done. I couldn't run now. I was in the middle of the crowd that surrounded Jesus. I could feel his eyes on me. I lifted my head just enough to look at his feet, his beautiful, brown feet, clean from the ritual baths but travel-worn, like his old sandals. I did not look at his face. If he had to repudiate me, I did not want to make it harder for him.

"Rabbi," said one of the Pharisees who had arrested me. "This woman was caught in the very act of committing adultery. And in the Law, Moses has commanded us to stone women of this kind. What have you got to say?"

For a moment I felt confused. Didn't they know I was his wife? Why else had they bothered with me? Then I got it. Of course, they knew. By demanding his opinion on the Law, they were setting a cruel trap for him with me as bait. If he did not condemn me, he would look weak and hypocritical. If he did, he would appear harsh and unfeeling. Either way, he would lose face before the people.

I continued to gaze at his feet, shutting out the growing agitation of the crowd. Dear feet, I spoke to them silently, I have held you in my hands; I have pressed the arches of my feet against yours. You have walked beside me in green places and in desert places. You have walked through my dreams. Dear feet, forgive me for running away from you. Forgive me.

"Your answer, Rabbi!" the Levite pressed him. "The people are waiting. Speak!"

But Jesus would not be rushed. He bent down and began to draw in the dust with his finger. His concentration was so absolute that everyone was pulled inside it, as if they were the ground and his finger lightly traced some secret hidden deep in their body's memory. When he stood again, I saw what he had scratched in the dust. An inscription in *ogham*, the druid script that only I could decipher: Maeve.

"Let the one among you who is guiltless be the first to cast a stone at her."

That was all he said. He waited a beat, and then he bent and continued writing in the dust. The silence was so profound that I could hear his fingernail scraping the stone. Doves perched on the porticoes made low liquid sounds. Then came another sound: footsteps at the edges of the crowd moving away. Someone else followed and another and another, more and more.

At last only Jesus and I remained. He stood up, and I saw that he had inscribed his own name next to mine.

"Woman."

I lifted my eyes and looked at him; it is the hardest thing I have ever done. Stones would have been softer than what I saw in his face. A terrible emptiness, not void of love or anger or grief, but so vast they had disappeared.

"Has no one condemned you?"

"No one, Rabbi." I called him by his title.

Our names lay discarded in the dust.

"Neither do I condemn you. Go. Be free from sin. Be free."

Before I could move or speak, he turned and was gone.

CHAPTER SIXTY-NINE

HOW TO WASH FEET

I don't know how long I stood in the porticoes after Jesus had gone—it may have been seconds or hours. But when I moved again, I ran as frantically and erratically as the day I left him, only now I was trying to find him. I had no idea what I would say or do when I did. I had no expectations of him, least of all that he would take me back as a wife. I only knew I had to be with him again. "Be free" had no other meaning for me.

I accosted people at every turn, always with the same question, "Have you seen Jesus of Nazareth?" Everyone knew the name, but no one could tell me where he was. I tried the Pool of Siloam where he taught and healed when he was not in the Temple; I checked inside his favorite taverns. After I had searched every nook and cranny of the city, it dawned on me that he must have gone back to Bethany. So for the first time since our parting, I left the city walls and struck out across the Kedron Valley.

I vaguely registered that it must be afternoon, for the sun shone on the back of my head from the west. I stumbled down the steep slope, faint and no doubt in shock. In the depths of the valley a cool breeze met me, and I heard the sound of flowing water.

"You must stop and drink," a voice inside me spoke.

Only then did I see the fig tree, and the spring that rose near its roots, becoming a stream running through the valley.

"Drink deep," the voice said.

I threw myself on the ground beside the spring and drank the sweetest, purest water I have ever tasted.

"Eat," said the voice.

I rose and picked a fig, the first food I had eaten that day. It tasted like the water given form. It tasted like mercy. Greatly restored, I ran on up the Mount of Olives, not stopping till I reached the house at Bethany.

The courtyard was deserted, and there were no traces remaining of the huge Sukkoth encampment. Clearly Jesus was not here, but I ventured into the house to see if I could find someone who might know where he had gone.

"Martha," I called. "Mary. Lazarus."

A servant peeped out at me from the kitchen courtyard, then turned and ran. A moment later Martha appeared, looking at me with cold fury.

"I know I have no right," I acknowledged. "But please, I beg you, tell me where he is."

"You!" Martha gained enough control of herself to speak. "You will not trouble him anymore. Stoning is too good for you. Go back where you came from. Whore," she spat. "You have abandoned him, dishonored him, endangered him, betrayed him—"

"Martha, enough!" Lazarus entered the room and put a staying hand on Martha's shoulder. "It is not for us to accuse her."

"Why not!" She shook him off. "Who else will do it? *He* won't."

"That is my point," he said quietly.

"Please," I asked again. "Please tell me where he is."

"You will not tell her." Martha rounded on her brother. "You will not."

Then she burst into tears.

"There, there," said Lazarus, patting her awkwardly and looking utterly miserable. "Can't the woman at least wait here? He may want to see her."

"Well then, he needs to be protected from his own foolishness. I will not have her under this roof. I will not—"

At that moment, brother and sister were distracted by Miriam of Nazareth (who had apparently decided to stay on indefinitely, though her other sons had long since decamped). She drifted in from the courtyard like a ground mist, humming to herself. Though she appeared to take no notice of my presence, she did list in my direction.

"Mary, Mary, quite contrary." (It may not rhyme in Aramaic but that was the gist of her greeting.) "My son is at the house of Simon the Pharisee who pretends to admire him. My son knows better, but he can't resist a contest of wits. Who raised him that way?" she lamented. "He must get it from his father's side."

"Miriam!" Martha protested. "Don't let this gentile slut bother Jesus. Order her to leave him alone! She is unworthy of him. She has disgraced your son and your house!"

Miriam ignored Martha and turned to me.

"Go! It's *beshert*." (Yes, she did say it in Yiddish; she's the Blessed Virgin Mary and she can do whatever she wants.) "It's meant. The angels told me. So who asked you? I said to them. They didn't bother to answer; they are always interfering. They told me to give you this."

From the folds of her robe, she pulled out an alabaster jar and placed it in my hands. It looked exactly like the one Aemiliana had sent from Rome as a wedding gift.

"It is." Miriam answered my thought. "I knew the kind of life you'd be leading with my son, so I kept it safe for you."

"But," I suddenly broke into a cold sweat, remembering Peter's prophecy that I would be the one to anoint Jesus, "Aemiliana said to save it—"

"It is not for his head, not tonight, Mary of Magdala." Her voice was gentler than I had ever heard it, as if she pitied me. "Only his feet. Then you will bring the jar back to me for safekeeping until his time is come."

My time is not yet come, he had said to his mother at our wedding. What did he mean by that? What did she mean?

"Lazarus, tell her where to find the house."

"But—" Martha made one last attempt.

"She must go." Miriam cut her off. "Now."

If you are wondering how I was going to gain entrance to the house of a prominent Pharisee, the answer is I didn't have to. When debate of the Law was on the menu, the erudite host served dinner in a courtyard that opened onto the street. Onlookers were welcome to watch and listen. The meal was private, but the debate was public entertainment.

Coerced by Miriam, Martha had provided me with more modest attire than I'd arrived in, and I managed to work my way to the front of the crowd without drawing much attention to myself. Most of the Twelve were there, as well as Mary B, Susanna, and Salome. They were too intent on the debate to notice me, which is just as well, as they were likely as furious with me as Martha was. I crept closer and closer until I could just glimpse his feet, which were still caked with the dust of the road.

How could Simon the Pharisee have failed to direct his servants to offer him a footbath? It was the first rule of hospitality. The neglect had to be deliberate, an insult, a subtle way of announcing to the world: I have allowed this upstart rabbi to debate, but he is here on sufferance. He is not one of us.

As I gazed at my beloved's feet for the second time that day, all my pent-up grief and longing overflowed. If I had been thinking clearly, I would have held back; all he needed was a gentile whore or a defiled wife—take your pick—making a spectacle of him. But I didn't think. I only knew I had to get to his feet, the feet I had loved in every god-bearing stranger I had received at Temple Magdalen.

The next thing I knew I was kneeling over his feet, my tears forming gullies and rivulets in the dust, like a flash flood in the desert. My hair came undone and made a curtain, and behind that fiery veil, I kissed his feet all over, each toe, the arches and the tendons, the raised blue veins, the heels. An appalled silence had fallen over the room, all the more obvious for titters and whispers.

"If he's such a prophet as all that, you would think he'd know what sort of woman is touching him."

"How can he allow it?"

"He's even crazier than I thought."

But I could not stop myself. When his feet were clean from tears and kisses, dried from my hair, I pulled the alabaster jar from my tunic pocket. As I sat back on my heels and opened it, the sharp, musky scent of spikenard filled the air. While I rubbed the ointment into his feet, he began to speak, dreamily, almost sensually.

"Simon, I have something to say to you."

"Say on, Master." There was no mistaking the sarcasm in the Pharisee's voice.

"There was once a creditor who had two men in his debt. One owed him five *denarii*, the other fifty. They were unable to pay, so he let them both off. Which one will love him more?"

"The one who was let off more, I suppose," said Simon grudgingly, no doubt regretting that he had ever invited Jesus to debate.

"You are right."

Until that moment I had kept my attention wholly on Jesus's feet. Then I felt his hand graze the top of my head. I looked up and met his eyes, and could hardly believe what I saw, the tenderness, the fullness. He had come back to me; he had come back.

"You see this woman?" He spoke to the Pharisee but he kept his gaze on me. "I came to your house, but you poured no water on my feet, but she has poured her tears over my feet and wiped them away with her hair. You gave me no kiss, but she has been covering my feet with kisses. You did not anoint my head with oil, but she has anointed my feet with ointment."

His voice broke, and he waited for a moment. I became aware of other people's breathing as their own longing caught in their throats.

"For this reason, I tell you her sins, *many* as they are," here he paused and smiled at me, "have been forgiven her from her mother's womb, from the time before time, in all the worlds. And so she loves greatly, holding nothing back. And so she loves."

That is how I remember what he said, though his words are recorded differently, and people have argued for millennia over what he meant. Some say he forgave the woman (a.k.a. *moi*), because she loved much; some say he meant the opposite: that she loved greatly because she was forgiven so much, like the man who owed the fifty *denarii*. I say forgiveness is always a mystery and a grace, surpassing all miracles.

"Who is this man?" people asked each other. "Forgiving sins as if he were God!"

"Beloved," he spoke to me alone. "Your faith has saved us. Go in peace, and I will come to you. Wait for me. Don't let the others drive you away."

Before that night I thought I knew all there was to know about lovemaking. I believe now that I knew nothing. Despite the years of loss and longing, the joy of our reunion, the consummation of our wedding, I must have kept some part of myself untouched and apart. After that night, whatever I had held back was gone. Or if not gone, then utterly changed. Where does the water go when the dam bursts and the river flows free? Where is the scent of an open rose? Where does a storm wind come to rest? Until that night I was a virgin.

Afterwards it was strange to feel our bodies become distinct again. We nestled close to each other, and I felt such peace and containment, as if we floated together in the womb, lovers before we were born, like Isis and Osiris.

"*Cariad*," Jesus called me back to the world of words and air. "I need to ask your forgiveness."

"Don't you know?" I murmured. "You are forgiven from your mother's womb, from the time before time, in all the worlds. Besides, I have nothing to forgive you—"

"The fig tree," he began.

"Hush." I kissed him. "The fig tree is fine."

"I know. And I know that you restored it, Maeve. I stopped there every day on my way to and from Jerusalem and drank from the spring and ate of the figs. The tree was my only comfort. I told myself, if the fig tree was alive, you must be all right, even if I never saw you again—" He broke off and pressed me tightly against him; I could feel his tears on my cheeks. "I want to tell you I am sorry about blasting the tree, and even sorrier for how I hurt you."

"I hurt you, too," I said. "On purpose. I heard you call out to me in the Temple. I could have turned around then, and I didn't. I chose to cut myself off from you. I wanted to destroy our marriage. And I did, at least according to the Law."

"But then you returned to me."

"I was dragged back to you as an adulteress."

"You returned to me," he said. "You turned again to me."

I knew then what he meant.

"And you turned again to me," I answered.

Turn, return, turn back, repent. Why must people make such a grim business of repentance? It can be both sweet and sexy. My beloved and I turned again to each other and repented—most fervently.

"Maeve," he said still breathing hard. "I wasn't even done confessing."

"Maybe I don't want to know this part," I suggested, thinking he had found solace with Susanna. I would not blame him, but I didn't need details.

"I don't suppose you do, but I need to tell you. It affects you, me, all of us."

"All right. Just remember your sins, *many* as they are, have been forgiven."

"It's just that the fig tree wasn't the only thing I blasted. I don't know how much you've heard, but you must have sensed where things are heading. You were there when I drove out the moneychangers. You saw the kind of mood I was in the day I cursed the tree, even if you didn't hear me preach. And you saw how they tried to trap me today—"

"That was my fault," I broke in.

"Beloved, the Temple authorities would not have tracked you down, if I hadn't baited them."

It occurred to me to wonder again who had told them where to find me.

"Jesus, listen, I was at the Temple the day before I was arrested. Someone followed me when I left; it must have been someone who knew me, and who else would know I am your wife but one of the—"

"It could have been anyone," he cut me off abruptly.

So. There were things we still couldn't talk about; things he didn't want to know.

"I've made a lot of people very angry," he went on before I could say more. "I've told parables that were extremely pointed at the expense of the powerful. I've told parables that upset everyone, even the companions. I denounced the entire Temple hierarchy as well as the most prominent Pharisees. I called them names, whited sepulchers, pristine on the outside, and full of death and rot on the inside, and that was just the start."

"You got a little carried away," I understated.

"I made the old prophets look like paragons of diplomacy and restraint."

"Have mercy!" I exclaimed, still trying to make light.

"Actually, I didn't make much mention of mercy. I predicted, oh, Maeve, terrible things. Visions would overwhelm me. You remember that time on Mona when I said the Menai Straits would run with blood and the Groves would burn? It was like that. I felt sick, but I couldn't stop myself. I declared that the Temple would be destroyed, not a stone left on stone. Even worse, I said things about myself that I still don't understand, about my coming again in glory to judge the world at the end."

"Oh, my love." There didn't seem to be anything else to say, so I just held him. He moved his head, so that it lay against my heart.

"Our friend Joseph of Arimathea came to talk to me in Bethany. He said the Sanhedrin has been meeting about me. They fear that I am stirring up the people to revolt, and that Rome will retaliate against the Temple. Well, it's no secret that the Emperor Tiberius would welcome an excuse to revoke the rights Augustus gave the Temple. No other conquered people has such rights.

"Joseph told me something the High Priest Caiaphas said that haunts me: 'It may be to our advantage that one man should die for the people, rather than the whole nation perish.' That's not the strange part; offering the Romans a ringleader could simply be a matter of bargaining, compromise, nothing new. Just as everyone was taking up the point for debate, Caiaphas stood up and cried out in a loud voice: 'Not for the nation only but for the scattered children of God.' Then, according to Joseph, Caiaphas collapsed, and the meeting was suspended."

We were silent for a moment and though Jesus held me close, I felt cold.

"What do you think he meant?" I finally asked.

"I don't know, but I believe he was prophesying, without meaning or wanting to. I keep thinking about the words I heard in the desert: 'My feast is laid. Go gather the guests, go gather my people.' Who am I gathering if not the scattered children of God? And, well, I have been thinking, maybe that is how I am to do it; I must *be* the feast, the sacrifice. Even the druids saw me as a sacrifice all those years ago."

I felt my whole body stiffen. Here was my rival, not his god, not his disciples, but this death that called to him.

"Beloved, your people gave up human sacrifice long ago. Your god despises it. As for the druids, they had no right to your life; they rigged the lots; they chose you because it was expedient."

Even as I spoke, I knew reason was no use. He drew me closer, and I relaxed my tensed muscles. Bracing myself could not protect me against whatever pain might come.

"Maeve, my dove, you may be right. And I may be clinging to the idea of prophecy to justify myself. Because I've already said and done enough that the Temple authorities could arrest me on some charge or another and turn me over to the Romans. It is only a matter of time, or of timing, really.

"Here is my sin, Maeve. All the things I've been saying, the horror I've been prophesying, I may have spoken the truth, but it's not the whole truth; it never was. I let myself forget this." He touched my breast. "And this." He kissed me softly. "I forgot the beauty of a desert night full of stars, the taste of wine and fresh bread, the smell of the earth after it rains, Peter's face when he finally gets a joke. That's why you were so angry with me, isn't it? I forgot the Kingdom of Heaven. I betrayed it. How could I be calling people to the feast when I was blasting fig trees? It's crazy. I've been crazy. Will you forgive me?"

"From before time," I told him. "And beyond."

"Oh, Maeve." He clung to me and wept. "I don't want to die. Not without loving it all more. Maeve, what have I done? Was I made for this death or did I make it for myself? I don't know. I don't know."

"We are alive now, *cariad*," I whispered. "That's all that matters."

And at last we fell asleep in each other's arms.

CHAPTER SEVENTY

THE PLACE BETWEEN

You may be wondering how the other companions felt about my return into their midst. It can be harder to forgive an offense against someone you love than a wrong done to yourself. I understood their predicament and didn't expect much quarter from them. That Jesus forgave me and obviously delighted in me only made matters worse. His friends had been outraged on his behalf at my behavior (and some of them had enjoyed it). Now their righteous indignation had no outlet, for they felt they could not express it openly. So it turned into resentment. A resentment shared by everyone but Susanna, who made no judgment of me, and Salome, who had relieved her feelings by slapping me in the face, and then immediately clasping me to her bosom.

I think it was hardest for Mary B. Not only had I betrayed Jesus, but I had betrayed her. She had stood up for me in front of Judas, and what had I done but to prove Judas right; for if our marriage hadn't been illicit before, surely it was now. I had been saved from stoning only by Jesus's formidable presence—and presence of mind. And according to the Law, he should have divorced me on the spot. How strange that Mary B, the most devoted to the Law of all the disciples, should be the one to resolve the underground conflict that could have torn us all apart.

The companions were still staying at the house in Bethany, though Jesus and I had made a bower for ourselves out in the vineyards. A couple of days after my return, when Jesus was off in the fields with Lazarus, I came around a corner and overheard angry voices in the back courtyard.

"I just don't understand how he can take her back," Peter was saying, no doubt for the zillionth time.

"Over and over she has jeopardized our cause," said Judas. "Now she has very likely destroyed it."

"Who will listen to him anymore?" lamented Andrew. "Cuckolded by a whore."

"I tell you, that's why he hasn't gone back to the Temple," said Judas.

"If he goes back, he'll likely be arrested," put in Simon.

"And yet he prefers her to us all," moaned Peter.

"He likes her best," echoed Tomas. "He likes her best."

"Well, she is his wife," said John.

"She shouldn't be," countered James. "Even the Master said divorce should be allowed in such cases."

"Allowed doesn't mean he has to," Susanna spoke up.

"According to the Law it does," said Philip.

"The Law doesn't rule love!" declared Susanna. "Listen, he's loved her since he was a boy—"

"How can he?" Peter held his head and rocked back and forth. "*We* are the ones who truly love him. She is faithless; we are faithful. *We* know who he is. We have done his bidding in all things. We—"

"You say you love him, Peter." Mary B, who had been sitting quietly with her head resting on her knees, suddenly looked up, her eyes bright and fierce. "Have you paid any attention at all to his parables?"

"Of course I have!" Peter blustered. "I know them by heart."

"So you know by heart the story of the overseer who paid the same wages to laborers who came late as the ones who had worked all day? You can recite the tale of the son who squandered his inheritance and yet when he returned penniless and starving, his father ran to meet him with an embrace?"

Peter looked down at his big fisherman's hands and said nothing.

"Listen, all of you. Love has nothing whatsoever to do with deserving. We may not like it, and I don't much, but that is what our Rabbi teaches. If we are disciples, that is the discipline we must practice."

In the uncomfortable silence that followed, I came into the open. I went straight to Mary B and knelt before her. Then I took her hand and kissed it, the mark of respect a disciple shows a teacher.

At that, dear, brave Mary B burst into tears and forgave me more than my recent sins—she forgave me the original sin of existing at all.

When Jesus did go back to the Temple to teach, we all agreed that I should not go with him—for his safety and my own. So I stayed with Martha and Miriam, who had ensconced herself in Bethany for the winter. I was doing my best to be useful and Martha had grudgingly allowed me to do some wool carding—I'm afraid I hadn't much skill or experience at the other fiber arts. I was sitting more or less contentedly in a bit of wan sunshine when Miriam wandered out to join me, spinning with a drop spindle and humming. Having settled us both (as if we were difficult toddlers who needed a playpen), Martha had taken herself off to the markets. We sat companionably for a while; there was never any need to make small talk, something I had come to appreciate about Miriam. Then, without breaking the rhythm of her spinning, Miriam spoke.

"Start packing, Mary of Magdala."

I was taken aback; everyone else, even Martha, had become reconciled to my presence, and Miriam had made no objection to my return in the first place.

"I'm not leaving your son again," I said firmly. "Ever."

"Did I say anything about your leaving him?" she said crossly as if I were annoyingly slow. "I said start packing; you're all going to be leaving in a hurry."

The angels must have given her a hot tip. As if in confirmation, a flock of small birds lifted from the courtyard trees and flung themselves into the curve of the sky where they wheeled and flew away. I felt a sudden burst of exhilaration. We were going to get the hell out of Jerusalem. Be free. Live.

"I didn't say that either," my mother-in-law snapped. "Take it a day at a time, Mary of Magdala. Come on. I'll help you pack. It'll be simpler without Martha."

There wasn't all that much to organize, a few extra blankets because it was winter, some flatbread, cheeses, full wineskins; the companions always traveled light. We made a small bundle for each person. Just as we were finishing, we heard horse's hooves headed in our direction at a full gallop—an unusual and alarming sound, for only Romans rode horses. Then the horse thundered through the gate with a grim-faced Joseph and a thoroughly rakish looking Jesus clinging to its back.

"Maeve," Jesus waved to me, "we're going on a holiday."

It was too early in the morning for Jesus to be drunk, but he was so loose and slaphappy he seemed as though he must be. He slid haphazardly off the horse, while Joseph dismounted more cautiously, and then handed the reins to Jesus.

"Find someone to see to the horse, Jesus," Joseph said tersely. "I beg leave to have a few words with your wife."

Leaving Jesus laughing maniacally while his mother hummed in much the same manner, Joseph and I went apart to talk.

"What's going on, Joseph? I thought he was going to the Temple, not the tavern."

"He went to the Temple, all right," said Joseph. "And he was immediately confronted by a delegation of Temple officials. They asked him point blank if he was claiming to be the Messiah."

"What did he say to them?"

"'If you'd been paying attention, you'd know.' That was the gist of it. They didn't like his tone, Maeve, and they charged him with blasphemy and wanted to stone him immediately. Nicodemus began to argue that he had to have a formal trial in front of the Sanhedrin. That gave us the time to give them the slip. Fortunately I have a friend among the soldiers at the Antonin fortress. He lent us a horse."

"Where are the others?"

"Following discreetly. They'll catch up, but you and Jesus need to leave now."

"Where are we going?" I was beginning to see why Jesus was giddy.

"If Jesus had any sense, you'd be coming with me to Joppa and taking the next ship to Alexandria. But your stiff-necked husband has agreed only to cross the Jordan. At least you'll be out of the reach of Herod Antipas and the Roman procurator, if only technically. I suppose he means to carry on his crazy mission from there."

"Yes, I suppose he does."

Take it a day at a time, Maeve of Magdala, I said to myself.

"There's something I want to tell you, Maeve, and then you've got to get out of here. I hope you never come back to Jerusalem, either of you. But I want you to know that I bought the building where you were living."

"Why would you do that, Joseph?" I was baffled; he had seemed so horrified by what he called a rat-infested slum.

"Your paintings, Maeve. I can't explain why, but I wanted to keep them. Nicodemus is going to keep an eye on the place for me. So for what it's worth, you have a bolt hole in the city, if you ever need it."

I decided not to remind Joseph that I had already been arrested at that address.

"I don't know what to say," I began. "How can I thank you—"

"You can't." I had never seen Joseph so upset and angry. "Just shut up and get out of here. That's all I ask."

"Forgive me, Joseph!" I flung my arms around him. "Forgive us."

That winter in the desert was the happiest time in my life, all the more so, because I had no illusions that it could last. Our tent city became a sort of makeshift Temple Magdalen, with lots of singing, dancing, storytelling, as well as preaching (at which Mary B and others so inclined took their turn) and as always the healing of the sick. We shared whatever food we had with whoever showed up. Whether it was a few crusts of bread or a fresh catch of eels, there was always enough. Peter and some of the others received visits from wives and children. To my great joy, Dido, Berta, and Reginus came for a sojourn. Paulina hired camels for them and loaded them with lavish gifts.

Only Simon and Judas left camp for any length of time, presumably to make contact with various factions in the hills. If they reported back to Jesus or carried messages from him, I was not privy to it.

Towards the end of the winter came two days of heavy rain, followed by one of the most exhilarating sights—and scents and sounds—in the world: sudden desert spring. Dry earth was veined with green; anemones and acacia burst into brief, ecstatic bloom, migrating birds stopped to feed in the temporary marshes. Even as I reveled in the fleeting lushness, I felt a sense of foreboding. Spring is a restless season, the end of stasis, everything raw, open, and new. Demanding of action. Till, plant. Change, move. Begin again. Our holiday, as Jesus had called it, was about to end.

We were all sitting around the fire one evening when messengers arrived from Bethany.

"It's your brother," said a man I recognized as one of Lazarus's shepherds. "He is gravely ill, near death. You are to come at once, and your sister begs you to bring the Rabbi with you."

Mary B was already on her feet, gathering her things. Jesus hadn't moved or spoken. He just sat gazing at the flames.

"Of course you can't go, Master," Peter spoke up. "I am sure you understand, Mary. He could be arrested; he could be killed."

If anything could have gotten Jesus moving, it would be a challenge like that one. But he remained silent.

"Then we go armed!" declared Judas, who had returned to camp a couple of days before. "It's about time we stopped hiding and skulking in the wilderness. Give me twelve hours and I can have the advance guard of an army marching with you—and more where that came from in a day or two."

"Shut up, Judas. Shut up, all of you!" Mary B burst out; then she turned to Jesus. "You are coming, Rabbi?"

I was so sure he would go, I'd started packing, too, but when I looked again, he still hadn't moved.

"Jesus!" Mary's voice broke. "Please, Lazarus needs you."

At last Jesus rose, went to Mary and gathered her in his arms.

"Go now, Mary," he said. "I tell you this sickness will not end in death. Not Lazarus's death. I will come soon, when the Most High tells me it is time for God's glory to be revealed."

Mary looked so confused and bereft that I was poised on the brink of being angry with him, but instead of confronting him I took a leap and landed somewhere else altogether.

"I'll go with you, Mary," I heard myself saying.

Then in the next moment, I felt the wrench. How could I leave Jesus; I had said I would never leave him again. I did not have time or the heart to second-guess myself. Jesus reached for me and pulled me into his embrace.

"Go now, beloved," he said to both of us. "I will come soon. Trust me."

And I found that I did. That trust was the new ground under my feet.

By the time we got to Bethany, Lazarus was in a coma. Martha was so distraught that she had forgotten my offenses and clung to me the same way Mary did, as if through me they could touch Jesus. Salome, who had stayed behind when we went to the wilderness, had taken over running the household. Mary, Martha, Miriam and I took up vigil. The two sisters held the sick man's hands. I cupped his head, the fire of the stars flowing from my hands gently, without urgency. Miriam sat in a corner spinning and humming. The quality of her voice was soothing now, a drone like bees in an orchard. We all rested on the sound.

It was just before dawn, the day after we'd arrived, that I became aware of being in two places at once: the room where I sat with the other women, their tired faces lit by the low-burning lamp—and a river where I floated on a barge with Lazarus. In both places, my hands cradled his head. On the river we were moving east with the current towards a brightening sky. We came to a bend in the river where a crowd stood on the shore. Though he lay still in the chamber, the Lazarus on the barge sat up and began pointing excitedly, telling me the names of the people waiting for him, but before we could get there, our boat ran aground on a shoal.

"Push on!" cried Lazarus. "Tell the oarsman to push on!"

Then I saw her: she was as big as the sky; she was the sky with the morning star as her crown. No, she was just a girl, a slim young girl swimming in the river. Now she rose up, huge again, a cow with dark eyes and swollen udders; she wore the horns of the moon and the sun bloomed like a many-petaled flower between them.

"Look, Lazarus!" I cried out.

Then my vision shifted, and I saw through his eyes, a man rising from the river holding one moment a staff, the next a serpent.

"Moses!" whispered Lazarus, and he began to chant, "*Shema Yisrael: Adonai Elohenu, Adonai Echod.*"

I heard Martha and Mary weeping, and at the same time the river man spoke.

"Wait," he said to Lazarus. "Wait here until your name is called."

"I have to wait," Lazarus sighed. "Moses has commanded it. Will you wait with me, since my friend Jesus has not yet come?"

"I will wait with you," I assured him.

The Lazarus on the barge lay back down with his head in my hands.

That's when Martha and Mary began to wail; the river scene receded to the edges of my vision, I turned my attention to the sisters.

"What is it?" I asked.

"He's dead!" Martha shrieked. "Can't you see he's dead? Our brother is dead!"

I looked at Lazarus in the bedchamber at Bethany. I felt for the pulse in his neck, and then I laid my cheek against his mouth. I couldn't feel anything, and yet I could see light flickering all around him. He wasn't dead yet. He was waiting on the shoal.

"He's not dead," I tried to make myself heard over their keening. "Mary, Martha! He's not dead."

They stared at me, and then looked at Lazarus and started wailing again.

"I tell you, he's not dead. Moses told him he must wait."

"The woman's mad," Martha moaned. "My brother dead, the man who could have saved him far away. How could he? Lazarus loved him so, he would do anything for him. How could Jesus send his crazy— "

"Hush," sniffled Mary. "She means well, Martha."

"Ma," I appealed to my mother-in-law. "Tell them he's not dead. Tell them Jesus is coming."

Miriam just kept humming as she helped to gather oils and spices for anointing the body for the grave.

"You're not going to bury him alive!" I protested.

"Mary of Magdala!" Martha rounded on me. "My brother is dead. If you won't help us prepare his body for burial, then leave! Go away now, anyway. It is not right for you to see his nakedness. You are not part of the family."

"Wife of my friend," I heard Lazarus calling me, and I could see the bright sky of the other world and smell the river. "Don't argue with my sisters. They'll do as they please. They always have. Come and wait with me."

So I let Martha shoo me away. I took a skin of watered wine and some bread and cheese and went to sit outside the cave that would be Lazarus's tomb. Maybe there was still something I could do to prevent this gruesome mistake. I scanned the distance, straining for a glimpse of Jesus, wondering if I should try to find him, hurry him.

"Wife of my friend," I heard Lazarus's voice again. "Just wait with me; that is all that is required. You know where, you know how."

And then again, I was in two places at once, outside the cave, still able to hear the wailing from the house, and on the pebbled shoal with Lazarus, the river flowing around us, over the stones, through the reeds.

Just before sunset I saw the funeral party processing toward the tomb, bearing Lazarus on a bier. There were so many Temple dignitaries in the procession, it was just as well that Jesus was not there.

But where *was* he, and what was I to do? Throw myself in front of the bier?

"No," Lazarus spoke to me from world of the river. "Just keep waiting with me."

"But they're about to entomb you alive!"

"If I die, I die." Lazarus was not worried. "Someone will call me when it's time."

"But—"

"Just wait with me, dear friend of my dear friend. There is something here for you, too."

And so I waited. In time the mourners went away, and it was quiet again. Night came with stars and cold and then the dawn. At the river it was always dawn, and a warm breeze touched my face and played in my hair. Lazarus, his head in my lap, talked about how the lambing season had gone with someone I could not see. Then *she* spoke to me, the one whose voice whispered in the river reeds.

"Do you know the way now, little sister?"

"To where?"

"To the place between."

"Am I there?"

"You are. Do you know the task now?"

"To wait?"

"This time. In the time that is coming, there is a greater task."

"Will you tell me what it is, my sister, my mother?"

"Listen. Watch."

I heard the sound of wailing again, and became aware of my rocky surroundings and the heat of the midmorning sun. I had forgotten where I was.

"You can get up now," said Lazarus, his voice faint and far away.

I rose and saw my beloved striding across the fields, flanked by Mary and Martha and trailed by the disciples. As he drew nearer, I could see that his face was wet with tears. He stopped in front of the tomb and stood quietly for a moment. Everyone waited fearfully to see what this unpredictable, grief-crazed man would do.

"Roll away the stone!" he commanded.

"Master, no!" Martha was horrified. "It's the fourth day since he died. He'll smell!"

"Have I not told you that if you believe, you will see the glory of God?"

"Do as you will." Martha threw up her hands.

Some of the men rolled away the stone and everybody stepped back, covering their noses and their mouths with their sleeves. Everyone but Jesus.

"Lazarus, Lazarus," Jesus half-spoke, half sang his friend's name. "Lazarus, come forth. Lazarus! Lazarus!"

And Lazarus did, stumbling in his grave swaddling toward the sound of Jesus's voice while people screamed or fainted. At last there was silence again.

"Unbind him and let him go free," Jesus commanded.

Free, I wondered, would Lazarus ever again be free? He had longed so for the other shore. What had he given up for his friend Jesus! How would Lazarus ever live down his rising from the dead?

Mary and Martha, beside themselves with joy and terror, managed to unbind him, though they were both trembling. At once they fell into their brother's arms and held him tight, until he gently shook them off and went to embrace Jesus.

Over Lazarus's shoulder, Jesus caught my eye where I stood apart from the rest. We exchanged a long look. Then almost imperceptibly, he nodded in full acknowledgment. He knew.

CHAPTER SEVENTY-ONE
HOLDING NOTHING BACK

It was plain that we had to leave at once. When word got out that Jesus of Nazareth—miracle healer, rabble-rouser, son of David, son of man—had returned from exile to raise a man from the dead, nothing would stop the crowds. Whether they loved him or hated him didn't make much difference. So I left the others and went to the house to throw some supplies into a satchel.

"Mary of Magdala."

I whirled around and saw Miriam standing in the doorway to the storeroom.

"Daughter of my heart."

The endearment shook me. She had taken the angels' word for it that I had a part to play in her son's life; now and then she had seemed to pity me, but I did not expect affection.

"Take this."

Although the light was dim, I knew it must be the alabaster jar that I had returned to her for safekeeping after I had anointed Jesus' feet. Inadvertently I shook my head and took a step back, but there was nowhere to go; she had me cornered. Life had me cornered.

"It is time, time to pour it out," she said in a sing-song voice, "pour it to the last drop, to the last drop, holding nothing back, nothing back."

She came to me and pressed the jar into my hand.

"You know," she said. "Mary of Magdala, you know who he is."

I shook my head again and bit my lip. He is my beloved, I wanted to say. He is your son, you crazy old woman. I want no part of this…whatever it is.

"You must anoint him."

"Why?" I cried out. "Why must I?"

"Because," said Miriam. "You are She."

With that, she turned and left the storeroom, while the onions I'd been holding slipped through my fingers and arranged themselves around my feet.

If you need to hide out for a while, the best place to go is to the house of a leper. Simon was in fact a former leper, Jesus having healed him. But people tend to be cautious where leprosy is concerned, and Simon enjoyed his recovery in the solitude to which he had become accustomed. He took the onslaught of unexpected guests with good grace and served us goat cheese and his own honey-wine; for Simon was a beekeeper.

There was not a lot of conversation at the meal. What do you say when one of the guests has just raised another from the dead? Lazarus had come with us, a fugitive from curiosity seekers, while Martha, Ma, and Salome had remained at the house under the protection of Joseph and the armed guard he had brought with him. Lazarus, always quiet, was even more subdued than usual. Though Mary B and Susanna hovered near Lazarus and coaxed him with food, he ate little. Now and then he'd catch my eye, his unspoken query plain in his eyes: Do you remember that place? Was it real? I would nod and for a time he would seem reassured.

Jesus was silent, too, and appeared lost in his own thoughts. The companions kept glancing at him nervously. 'What would Jesus do?' is a question people have been asking from the start. It was no idle question for the companions whose lives and fortunes depended on the answer. With the Passover beginning in two weeks, the stakes were high. Pilgrims would be pouring into the city, along with extra Roman troops and Roman procurator Pontius Pilate himself. Passover was the most volatile of the three major festivals. It was a celebration of the people's escape from the yoke of slavery. What better time for an uprising against the Roman oppression? What better time for the Messiah to walk through the Beautiful Gates and lay claim to the holy city?

I did not bother to speculate; I already knew in my bones that we wouldn't be going back to our desert encampment. Some reckoning was at hand; I wished I knew how to shift it, the way I could shift the wind on Lake Gennesaret, or the way a sailor could angle into that wind, shift the rudder just a few degrees and avoid some peril. As I reclined at the meal, I found I was half asleep, worn out from watching and waiting in two worlds. That other world was still close by. Now and then I could hear the wind and the water in the reeds. I could hear her voice. Some things you can change—by the tilt of your head, by the blink of an eye—but the great rhythms go on: moon, tide, life, death.

I must have fallen all the way asleep, for I came suddenly awake as I fell forward and narrowly missed a plate of cheese. I decided to get up and go outside to empty my bladder and clear my head. I walked out alone, breathing the sweet, spicy smell of cooling earth. At the new moon, the stars were bright, their thin light spilled across the sky. Still gazing up, I squatted to relieve myself and I felt the alabaster jar in my pocket pressing against my thigh. When I was done, I wandered into the garden where Simon kept his hives. I took out the jar and held it in my hands. What if I just hurled the jar away? What if I refused my part as the one who anointed him?

The answer did not come in words but sensation, as if my cells were honeycomb, alive with bees. It was like the fire of the stars, not in my hands only, but in every pore, not entering through my crown only, but through my feet, earth-fire, burning and sweet. The jar became heavy, so heavy, as if it contained mountains, seas, winds, all wanting to be released, poured out. Unbound, set free.

I walked back into the courtyard, the alabaster jar cradled in my hands. I paused and looked at Jesus, reclining between Peter and Tomas. He looked up at me and smiled, his eyes as bright and fathomless as the night sky. I could hear his thoughts as plainly as if he spoke them.

I am ready.

I moved around the circle till I came to stand behind him, then I knelt so that his head was level with my breasts and I broke open the jar. The scent of spikenard filled the night as I poured the ointment on his head. My fingers flowing with spice and fire, I worked the scented oil into his dark, wild hair.

For a time no one moved or spoke, just stared at my hands on his head, their own senses dazed by the powerful, disturbing scent. Then the muttering began, rising until one voice became distinct, accusatory.

"What does she think she is doing? Ointment like this costs the earth. It could have been sold for over three hundred *denarii* to feed the poor."

"Hush, Judas," Peter's voice shook. "Don't you see? She's anointing him."

"Extravagance, waste."

Jesus leaned his scented head against my breasts for a moment; then he sat up.

"Your quarrel is not with her, Judas. What she has done for me is well done. The poor will be with you always, and you must care for them. Me, only a little while. When she poured this ointment on me, she prepared me for burial. In truth, whenever anyone tells my story, what she has done will be told as well in remembrance of her."

No one spoke after that pronouncement, though some wept. Soon we all went off to sleep. Just before I went to spread our bedroll, I discovered I was *mentruous* again. So I made a separate bed for myself far from the others, out near the hives where Jesus found me crying so hard I that could not speak. No more of those soundless, effortless tears that had come now and then as a gift. These sobs tore from me; my whole body ached with them. It took Jesus some time to get anything coherent out of me, but when he understood at last, he gathered me in his arms and held me steadily while I tried to push him away. Finally I wore myself out and leaned against him.

"Anoint me, my beloved," he whispered.

Before I could ask him what he meant, he released me and took off his tunic. Then he lifted mine and pulled it over my head. We knelt facing each other, naked.

"Anoint me."

And he took my hand and guided it to the source of all life. In wonder, I dipped my fingers into my blood and anointed his head, his brow, his lips, his throat, his heart, his belly, his sex, his hands, his feet. Then he anointed me in the same places. When we were done, we gazed at each other in the moonless night, until the air turned warm as day and the bees woke and hummed around us. Then we made love, again and again, until we fell asleep joined.

CHAPTER SEVENTY-TWO

WHORE'S TEARS

Having a vision or intuition of what is to come is not the same as knowing how it will happen, when or what it will mean. Jesus was living on radical trust that he would know what to do when the time came, that his god would guide him—which frustrated some of his followers terribly. When the hubbub over Lazarus rising from the dead died down (forgive the pun) and the curiosity seekers lost interest, Jesus moved us to a cave in Gethsemane on the Mount of Olives where there was an ancient olive press that had fallen into disuse. The cave offered some shelter and privacy, and a little further up the hill, there was a sweeping view of Jerusalem. Each dawn, Jesus went to watch the terrible Beautiful Gates as the sun turned them gold.

All day long, Jesus received whoever managed to seek him out; these included not only those in need of healing, but Pharisees friendly to what they saw as his cause to reform the Temple, who wished to warn and advise him. He listened to all of them, but gave no indication of what he would do. Hill fighters, comrades of Judas and Simon, also came to see Jesus, urging him to help mobilize the masses who would come to Jerusalem for Passover. To these men, he also listened but gave no answer.

Mary B and Susanna, who had become adept at making sure they were not followed, went back and forth between our camp and Mary's house, bringing supplies and carrying messages. Lazarus had gone home, and Joseph continued to stay at the house with a guard he had hired to protect the Bethany family. One day, Mary B came with a message for me.

"That Roman woman, Paulina, is at our house, asking to see you. I didn't want to bring her here. Too many people know about the cave already, but I told her I'd see if I could find you. You'd better come. Martha is practically breaking out in hives at having to entertain her."

I looked at Jesus, sitting a few feet away, with some of the disciples, not to ask his permission, which I had never done, but because every small parting was hard. He felt my gaze and turned to me, smiling tenderly. He gave a little flick of his eyes, which I understood to mean: "Go on. Get out of here. It'll be all right."

I found Paulina reclining in a shady part of the courtyard, drinking wine and eating dried figs. She actually bestirred herself to get up and meet me with an embrace.

"Bona Dea!" she exclaimed, stepping back to take a look at me. "You have become such a peasant, Red. Don't you worry about your complexion at all? You're going to look like parchment in five years' time. You skin is crying out for a good long soak in asses' milk."

"Your complexion is a testimonial to the benefits of spa treatments," I laughed and kissed her smooth, soft cheek. "You look like you're still eighteen and you a Roman matron with three children. But what are you doing in Judea?"

"Sit down with me and have some wine, and I'll tell you." When she'd settled us, she went on. "Pontius Pilate called Lucius here to consult about a new building project for Jerusalem—a theatre and a circus for gladiatorial games and races. I believe Lucius is going to try to discourage him; he says it can only cause trouble to introduce Roman sports and pastimes in a city full of religious fanatics. So I decided to come with him—although it's an awful time to be in Jerusalem, so crowded, raw sewage in the streets. Pilate ought to ask Lucius to redesign the city's plumbing instead, if you ask me. And, my dear, the smoke and stink of slaughtered animals. Frankly, when I want city life, I much prefer Alexandria."

"So why are you here?" I asked again when she'd run out of breath.

"To see you, of course!" She paused for a beat. "To warn you, if you want to know the truth."

"It's probably no use," I said. "But go on."

"I'm sure you know that there are always extra troops in the city at the festivals, just as a precaution. But Lucius says there is now a rumor among the military higher ups that there is going to be a Jewish uprising during Passover, an attempted coup. Of course, it can't succeed. Various people have been identified as leaders or instigators. One of them is your husband."

I shrugged; Paulina's news was old to me.

"It really doesn't do to go raising the dead," she scolded. "Or whatever it was that really happened. Pontius—who, between us, is not a nice man;

ruthless and ambitious and terribly worried about his status at home in Rome—he might not take what he considers oriental parlor tricks very seriously, but that ass Herod Antipas does. I'm sure you know Herod is obsessed with your husband, thinks Jesus is his old nemesis—what's-his-name who wore the smelly camel skins—risen from the dead. Quite tedious on the subject. No one in our set invites Herod to dinner anymore.

"Anyway, Pontius thinks it's to his advantage to join forces with Herod against Jesus or any other rebels coming out of Galilee. Lucius has heard that there's a warrant out for Jesus's arrest. And Joseph—who's around here some-where; I asked him to let us have some time alone first—Joseph thinks there's a deal in the making between Herod and Pilate and what's-his-name, your high priest."

"He's not my high priest." I split hairs in a desperate attempt to distract myself.

"Whatever." Paulina had patience only for her own tangents. "The point is, get your husband out of here now."

"I don't think I can."

"What on earth do you mean?"

"If Jesus doesn't want to go, he won't go."

"But what difference does it make what he wants or what he thinks he wants?" Paulina was honestly baffled. "He's a man. You're a woman. You are, or were, a professional, for Isis's sake. Surely what your husband wants is up to you!"

I started to laugh, I did laugh, but somehow I ended up crying instead. With more tact than I would have credited her for, Paulina shut up and came closer to comfort me. But instead of putting her arms around me, she began gently, and with great concentration, to scrape my cheeks.

"What on earth—"

"Whore's tears, honey," she said. "Cure anything. I'm glad you turned on the water works, Red. I almost forgot I was supposed to give this to you."

I watched her carefully slide my tear from the tiny scalpel into the vial I had last seen on the altar at Temple Magdalen.

"Berta and Dido sent it. They decided you ought to have it with you. Old Nona gave it to you, after all."

Paulina lifted the vial on its string and placed it around my neck. Then we held each other for a long moment. All our strange history, begun so long ago in a Roman bath, pressed between us, its essence extraordinarily sweet.

"You know," Paulina said. "Your other half isn't the only one who can raise people from the dead. You gave me my life, Red. Don't think I'll ever forget."

Now it was my turn to harvest tears.

"I'm not a whore, Red," Paulina sniffled. "Don't dilute the potency."

"The hell you aren't! Honey, you've always been a whore at heart."

"Thank you, Red," she said receiving the designation as the honor it was.

A little while later, Joseph joined us. We all drank quite a bit of wine and there were more hugs and tears and drunken joking about whether or not Joseph should be considered an honorary whore whose tears ought to be added to the mix. Then Joseph got serious.

"I know a lot of people, including some of your husband's followers, look at me as a collaborator, because I do business with the Romans; I'm even a Roman citizen. Well, I will make no excuses for myself. But, Maeve, for Jesus's sake, you need to understand how things look from Caiaphas's point of view. He represents the Temple, the living heart of Israel, but Judea is occupied. Caiaphas has to appease the Romans; it's his job. The wholesale slaughter of men, women, and children during the Roman siege of Jerusalem is within living memory. If there is a rebellion, the people will be massacred again, and the Temple will be shut down. Caiaphas will have failed in his first duty. Frankly, Maeve, Jesus is a threat to a most precarious peace."

"You make a persuasive argument against him," I said coldly. "Tell me, Joseph, have you convinced yourself? Do you believe Jesus should die for the *pax Romana*?" I almost spat. "So that we can have business and worship as usual? Is that what you want?"

I saw the pain in his face, and for one horrible moment, I didn't care, I was in so much pain myself. Then he bent his head to hide his hurt, and I felt stricken.

"I'm sorry, Joseph." I touched his hand, and he looked up again.

"Do you want to know what I want, Maeve?"

I nodded.

"I want you and your Yeshua to live a long life beneath your own vine and fig tree in peace and unafraid. I want you both to die of old age surrounded by your children and grandchildren."

This time I did not unstop the vial; there were too many tears, too many tears to be contained.

We parted near dusk with mutual promises; they would help in any way they could—preferably with plans for exile. For my part, I agreed to repeat their warnings to Jesus. I already knew it would do no good, but they were my friends, and I owed them at least that much.

It was nightfall by the time I reached our camp. I found Jesus, alone for a rare instance, leaning against an ancient olive tree, gazing toward Jerusalem, its watch towers alight with torches but otherwise a huge shadow against the stars. I kept my promise to Paulina and Joseph and told him everything they had said.

He listened and received. I sat so close to him, I could feel him absorb the words, their meaning, the love that prompted them. When I was done, I fell silent. There was no need to press any case. It was not a matter anymore of argument.

The silence lengthened and deepened—a well full of water and stars.

"I want to celebrate Passover at the Temple in Jerusalem," he spoke at last. "But I don't want harm to come to anyone on account of me. I want to be able to say, 'I have not lost any one of these you gave me.'"

He paused for the length of a heartbeat.

"I don't know what to do, Maeve."

I didn't answer, but as I waited for words to come I remembered the upper room, a temple of the mysteries, Joseph had called it, the room that Joseph had taken care to preserve.

"Beloved," I said. "Does it have to be *the* Temple of Jerusalem or can it be *a* temple in Jerusalem?"

"What do you mean?"

"That is for me to know and for you to discover in good time. If you will trust me. Will you?"

Another heartbeat.

"I will."

CHAPTER SEVENTY-THREE

THE LAST PARTY

My version of the preparation for the Passover Feast, a.k.a. The Last Supper, differs drastically from the one told by his official chroniclers. Well, try to imagine any of the Evangelists saying: we celebrated Passover in the upper room where the Master's wife used to turn tricks, that is, when she wasn't finger-painting pagan images on the walls. It just isn't plausible.

If you agree, you are not alone.

The next morning I revisited my scandalous refuge with Mary B and Susanna, telling them only that Jesus had consented to let me prepare a chamber in the city for the Passover feast. I sensed their growing alarm as we mounted the steps to the painted doorway, the vine and the fig tree framing it, the dove flying over it, and the cats lolling on either side. When we went in, I flung open the shutters to let in as much light as possible, and I watched my two friends stand and take in the scenes on the walls. Susanna trembled and wept. Mary clenched her jaw, and then slowly, deliberately closed her eyes.

"What have you done!" she said. Opening her eyes again, she turned to confront me. "What have you done? What have you done?"

"I don't know," I answered truthfully. "I don't think I did it, not exactly. I mostly painted in the dark. The pictures wanted to be there."

"Why is the Master in the tree?" asked Susanna. "And is that you in the boat? What do the pictures mean?"

"I don't know," I said again. "It's a kind of a story. The story of Isis and Osiris—only it's not. It's his story, my story, our story. But…I don't know what it means either."

I listened to myself with dismay: I, who had once been a bard in training, the daughter of poets and storytellers. Had my dabbling with images robbed me of my verbal prowess? Had one of those ubiquitous demons struck me dumb?

"I'm sorry," I said, feeling dumb in more than one sense. "I don't know what I was thinking. We can't possibly have Passover among a bunch of idolatrous pictures. Let's go find Nicodemus; he may know of a place where we can keep the feast."

"No." Mary B straightened her spine and turned around to look at the walls again. "The paintings are idolatrous, and yet there is something true here."

All three of us just stood for a moment, gazing at the images. Then Susanna turned to me.

"Mary and I know who you are," she said quietly. "We saw you that day on Mount Hermon when you became.... when you became *Her*. We know."

Now I felt shaken. Don't! I wanted to say. I wanted to make the case against myself. Who am I, after all? A gentile barbarian, a whore, an adulteress. Very likely I have a recurrent case of demon-infestation. Don't give me any power. Don't look to me for anything. I'm not Her or, as Ma had expressed it more grammatically, She. Shit.

"So what do we do?" I handed the decision over to them.

Mary B shrugged and gave me one of those: you-are-so-stupid looks that made me feel much better.

"We start making preparations for the feast."

"It'll be all right," Susanna reassured me. "But maybe we could bring in some hanging plants."

"And," added Mary B, "we'll want to keep the lighting very low."

All the women helped—Mary B, Susanna, Martha, Salome, Joanna who had rejoined us, Miriam, and when Paulina heard about the preparations from Joseph, she came to direct everyone, which upset the pecking order until she and Martha discovered their common passion for bargain hunting. They procured everything from the requisite foods and a place nearby to prepare them, to couches, tables, and oil lamps. Mary B, I am grateful to report, took charge of people's reactions to the paintings, leaving me free to arrange plants with Susanna, so that the room resembled an overgrown garden more than anything else. Ma, as always, stood directly in everyone's path, humming.

I was close to content in those last few days before Passover, in the midst of the women by day, in Jesus's arms all night. The company of the women comforted me—the increasingly ribald jokes, the bustle, even the arguments.

I know I preached a sermon about how everyone ought to serve, men, too, but by unspoken agreement we left the men out of the preparations. In any case, women were much less noticeable, coming and going, fetching and carrying amidst the holiday throngs than a band of rough-looking Galilean men would have been, what with soldiers everywhere on the alert for rebels.

Because it was so dangerous for Jesus to enter the city, especially in a group, on the feast day, the men split up and entered alone or in pairs through several different gates. At each entrance, one of the women passed by carrying a water jug on her head. Some people have found significance in Jesus instructing his disciples to follow a water bearer, speculating that this enigmatic figure signifies the Age of Aquarius. Our reasons for meeting the men with water jugs on our heads were in fact quite practical. We needed the water for washing, and in a crowded street it was easier for the men to keep the raised jug in sight. Because a woman carrying water was such a commonplace sight, we hoped that no one would notice that we were leading the notorious Rabbi and his closest followers to a gathering place inside the volatile, festival city.

Jesus entered Jerusalem last, and as a concession to us all, he kept his face hidden in the shadow of his cloak. He followed a modestly draped woman, her fiery hair tamped all the way down, through the maze of streets till we turned into the alley where I had seen the flash of the doves' wings. I climbed the stairs first, and then paused at the top to wait for him. At first I wondered if he even saw the paintings around the door, his gaze was so intent on me. When he came to stand before me on the threshold, his face broke open into a huge smile.

"I am the Vine," he said. "You are the Fig Tree."

He paused to give me a lingering kiss.

"Priestess, will you take me inside the Temple of the Dove?"

When Jesus stepped into the room, all commotion ceased. The men, who had been avoiding the images or gaping at them in horror, while Mary B behaved like a docent giving an art lecture, all turned to study Jesus's reaction. The only sound you could hear in the upper room was Martha pouring water into basins for foot washing. It is hard to describe what I saw on Jesus's face. It wasn't an emotion I could name; more a sense that he was not only taking the images in but also entering into them—as if they were not crude paintings but another world that only needed his seeing in order to come to life.

At last he turned to me and bowed his head. When he looked up again, I saw in his face an odd mixture of anguish and relief. I wished I could ask him what he had seen in these pictures I hadn't meant to paint, but the bustle had begun again, with Martha trying to corral everyone so that she could begin washing feet.

"Let me, Martha," Jesus commanded.

Ignoring Martha's protests, he took her towel, and stripping to his tunic, wrapped it around his waist. Motioning for everyone to sit on the couches and stools scattered about the room, he reached for a basin and went to work. At first the men were too shocked to speak. What was the Master thinking, kneeling before them, doing the work of women and slaves? Tomas whimpered, Matthew squirmed, Andrew turned red. Peter, further down the line, grew increasingly agitated as Jesus got closer and closer to his own huge slabs—especially dirty and callused because of his fallen arches.

"Lord!" Peter burst out when his turn came. "Are you going to wash *my* feet?"

"At the moment, you do not know what I am doing," said Jesus. "Later you will understand."

But Peter wasn't listening.

"Never!" he declared. "You shall *never* wash my feet!"

And he tucked them under his body out of Jesus's reach.

"Oh, Peter, Peter," Jesus said with the mingled affection and exasperation he especially reserved for Peter. "If I do not wash you, you can have no share with me."

Peter gaped at him, still not getting it; then he took a flying leap of faith.

"Then wash all of me! Hands, head, feet!"

Peter got to his feet and started to strip, and everyone laughed, breaking the tension created by Jesus's strange behavior.

"Peter," said Jesus. "Just sit down and let me have your feet."

Peter lumbered back down and let his beloved Master bathe his feet while his own tears washed his face.

At last Jesus came to Judas. I had been so intent on Jesus that I only noticed the others when he neared them. As soon I glanced at Judas, I saw that something was horribly, fatally wrong. The air around him churned in turmoil; his face was pale, almost greenish. His fists opened and closed, and his breathing was uneven.

"Yes," said Judas as Jesus knelt before him with the pitcher and basin. "It is fitting that you should wash my feet, wash all our feet. You," his voice broke, "you we have called Master, you I have followed all these miles and months and years, trusting you, trusting you to be our new Moses, you have become a slave. A slave in Egypt. Worse than the slaves in Egypt. They at least cried out and groaned under their oppression, while you, you choose it! You revel in it!"

His eyes swept the room, the paintings of Isis and Osiris not quite concealed behind the plants.

"You are enslaved to *her*!" Judas pointed at me. "Her and her Egyptian goddess, her rich Roman friends, and that collaborator from Arimathea she screws on the side—"

"Peace!" Jesus's deep voice cut through Judas's high-pitched tirade. He reached for Judas' foot.

"No!" Judas shook him off, and stood up, knocking the basin over. "No peace! 'I bring not peace but a sword.' Remember when you said that? Where is your sword? You let people believe you are the Messiah. But you do nothing, nothing to free the people."

The others were on their feet, ready for a brawl. Slowly Jesus stood up.

"Peace."

The sound of his voice resonated in the silence that fell. Then Judas walked toward the door where he turned to face Jesus.

"I will follow you no longer," he said. "You have betrayed your forefathers. You have betrayed your people. You have betrayed *me*."

He rushed to the door, and we heard him clattering down the steps.

"Judas!" I ran out, catching sight of him as he fled down the alley. "Come back!"

"Let him go, Maeve," Jesus came to stand beside me. "He must do what he must do."

I turned to him, stricken, asking wordlessly: Is it true? Have I turned you from your people? Your purpose?

"He speaks as much truth as he is able to speak," he answered.

The rest he said, or I heard, silently: The truth when it is naked, stripped of all illusion, is beautiful, and terrible, too terrible and beautiful to bear. He took my hand and we went back to the others.

"I will never leave you, Master!" Peter clambered to his side. "I would die first."

"Peter," said Jesus gently, "before the cock crows, you will deny me three times."

I shivered; a chill breeze blew through the open windows, and I went to close the shutters. Then we all stood awkwardly. No one knew what to do. Except Ma.

"Eat!" she said. "You think the first Passover feast was any easier? Come, we have a feast before us. Yeshua! What are you waiting for? Give the blessing!"

And so began the Last Party.

"Listen, my beloved companions, and remember," Jesus said, as we passed the unleavened bread and drank the first cup of wine. "Whenever you break bread together or share a cup of wine, I'll be with you, in your midst. Haven't we always feasted together? Hasn't there always been enough and more than enough? I tell you, whenever two or three gather together to share what they have, there I am. There is life. There is the Kingdom of Heaven. Remember. Remember me then."

"But why do we have to remember you?" Peter burst out. "Where are you going!"

"Where I am going now, you can't follow. Not yet. But you will in time."

"But how will we find you if we don't know where you're going?" Tomas fretted. "How will we know the way?"

"I am the way," Jesus said quietly.

That is all he said. Or that is all I remember. If the Last Party was indeed an evening of esoteric teaching, only those words remain with me. The words and how he looked at each of us in turn, letting us understand him in whatever way we could.

When he turned to me, I saw the path the rising moon makes across the water. I saw paths made by wild goats in mountain passes. I saw how a flower tracks the path of the sun, how waves part for a ship's prow; I saw myself opening all my ways to him.

After the second cup of wine, we loosened up and began to sing somewhat irreverent ditties about the plagues of Egypt and then more dramatic ones about the parting of the Red Sea. With the third cup of wine, we sang the ecstatic victory song of Moses's sister, Miriam. Then all the women took up tambourines (we always had those at a feast) and danced. Soon the men got up and danced in their own circle. And we all sang, songs with no words, the women ululating.

At last a hush fell. We stood bright-eyed and flushed, glistening with sweat, wild with love for each other, as we had been that last night at the Wedding of Cana. Jesus went and flung open the door, in case Elijah should be waiting to come in. Still on our feet, we drank the fourth cup of wine. Then Jesus set down the cup and crossed the room to me. He took my hand and kissed it, the kiss of a suppliant to his priestess. When he released my hand, I took his and kissed it, the kiss of a disciple to her teacher. Then we stood facing each other, not touching, as the companions made a circle around us. In one movement, we came together and kissed each other on the lips.

"Beloved." Jesus put his arms around me and spoke softly in my ear. "Thank you for this temple. Thank you for this feast. I am going back to

Gethsemane now with the men. Spend the night here with the women and come and find me in the morning."

Every muscle in my body tensed. I knew what he was saying—and not saying.

"I am going with you!" I whispered fiercely.

"No, Maeve, I am asking you to stay here with my mother and Martha. It's too late for them to go back to Bethany tonight. Stay and make sure they are safe."

"They'll be all right without me," I pleaded. "They can go to Nicodemus if they need anything. Don't ask this of me. Please don't."

He held me closer, but he did not relent.

"I am asking it of you, Maeve. You are the priestess of this Temple. Tend it. Keep watch here."

I bent my head and spoke into the hollow of his throat.

"Not as I will, then. But as you will."

"I love you, Maeve."

And before I could speak, he released me and made for the door.

After the men left, we set about cleaning up, storing the food that would keep and sharing the rest with people on the street. We were still sweeping and tidying when the soldiers burst into the room, swords at the ready, eyes darting into every corner. We all stopped what we were doing and drew together.

"Bunch of women!" one of the soldiers shouted out the door to others apparently waiting outside, in case anyone tried to bolt.

"Interrogate them, *stultus*!" came the answering shout.

"Have you come to do homage to our goddess?" I asked, stepping forward.

"What?!"

"Our Lady." I gestured to an image of the goddess in her boat.

"Where is he!" One of the soldiers advanced on me.

"There are no men here!" I declared. "Except yourselves. We are a sisterhood in sacred service to the goddess. This is our temple. And you are perilously close to violating it and invoking her wrath. What is your business with our Lady?"

The soldiers began to look nervous.

"Jesus! Jesus of Nazareth. We know he was here. Where is he?"

The other women got into the act.

"A man," they tittered in shocked tones, making signs for warding off evil. "A man here in the Temple!"

"Seems like some kind of weird cult, Captain," the soldier called out the door. "No men allowed."

"Mithras!" cursed the captain, who clambered up the stairs.

"Desecration!" the women shrieked. "They must leave at once."

"No, sisters," I gestured for them to be quiet. "Let's not be so hasty. It may be that the goddess has sent these men to us as dedicates."

"Ooo! Dedicates. Oh well, then, that's different."

"What the hell are you on about?" said the captain "Tell us where this Jesus is."

"Jesus? Is he a dedicate?" I wondered. "Perhaps he lost his nerve. Some men do. You see, this is the time of year that our goddess welcomes the sacrifice of the manly parts." I picked up a paring knife. "So few men have the courage these days. But really it's not that bad. We give you plenty to drink first, and it doesn't hurt much. A quick stroke of a well-sharpened blade and then…" I gestured to the charcoal brazier. "She likes them roasted—with rosemary and garlic. We prefer them that way ourselves."

I had been steadily advancing and the men steadily backing away.

"Forget it!" the captain barked. "He's not here."

And they tripped over each other in their hurry to get away.

We started to shake and held onto each other, choking on silent laughter until we cried. Then abruptly, we sobered up.

"Quickly, Mary," Ma said to me in a low voice. "Go and warn him."

"He told me to stay here and take care of you," I felt obliged to say.

"The danger to us is past," she pronounced. "Besides, my son may think he's the Messiah; he may think his father is God, but I'm the Mother, and I'm pulling rank. Go."

I didn't need telling twice; I was on my way.

"But the precious dove can't go alone!" protested Salome.

"I'll go with her," said several voices at once.

"Just the two Marys," decided Ma. "Now go."

CHAPTER SEVENTY-FOUR

WHAT IS TRUTH?

W hile Mary B and I wind our way through the streets, keeping to the shadows, slipping through the Antonin gate just before it is closed for the night, running across the moonlit Kedron Valley, I want to tell you something. We are coming to a part of the story that no one knows firsthand. None of us witnessed Jesus's interrogation by Caiaphas, Herod, or anything but a bit of public drama with Pilate. Yet here is where people begin casting blame, first on Judas, then on the Jews. Here at the tragic heart of his story, a greater tragedy begins: centuries of persecutions, inquisitions, pogroms, holocausts.

All along I've had differences with my beloved's chroniclers—mostly because they edited me out. In what comes next, you will find more serious discrepancies. Believe whom you will. For what is truth? A story well told, as my mothers maintained? The historical facts, such as they are? The truth is, a story can have a life of its own. And the most factual accounts have a point of view (admitted or not, depending on the truthfulness of the narrator). Those who first wrote my beloved's story had their reasons for the slant they chose—like sucking up to the Romans who had destroyed the Temple of Jerusalem and scattered the Jews over the face of the earth—but if the Evangelists (especially John) could have foreseen the consequences of the blame they cast on the Jews, they might have run mad and hanged themselves as Judas did.

For what it is worth, here is my witness.

That anyone was at our camp was not immediately evident. We'd been doing without torches and fires since we took up residence to make it harder for anyone to find us. Mary and I concealed ourselves in the shadow of a big olive tree and scanned the garden. We wanted to be certain no one had followed us before we tried to find Jesus. When my eyes adjusted to the disorienting patterns of moonlight and shadow, I saw him across the grove, leaning against another tree with branches high and sparse enough that the moonlight touched his face.

For an instant, it seemed as if the painting in the upper room had come to life, and then still another image transposed itself: the boy Esus lashed to a tree in a druid grove. Had someone captured and bound him here? Then I saw that he was moving his arms, gesturing, speaking to someone I could not see. I couldn't make out the words, only the anguish. All at once, he threw himself on the ground. I started to go to him, but Mary B clutched my arm and held me back.

"Wait!" she whispered. "Someone's coming."

Then I heard it, too, the sound of running feet and ragged breath. We turned and Judas hurtled towards us, naked except for a makeshift loincloth he had wound clumsily around his private parts. His face and arms were a mass of cuts and bruises, and it looked as though his right arm might have been broken. I didn't need to see his back to guess that it was covered with bleeding welts.

"Judas!" I called softly; he stopped and looked around. "Over here!" "Where is he?" Judas demanded when he recognized us. "I've got to warn him."

"What happened to you?" said Mary B

"I was picked up by the Romans. They're looking for him. They interrogated me about him. I played dumb, so they stripped me and beat me. When I still wouldn't talk, they tossed me out into the street."

"I wonder why you didn't tell them?" said Mary coldly. "You said he betrayed you. Why didn't you betray him? That would be one way to be rid of him."

Judas stared at her, his face working as if he were about to be sick.

"Mary," I put my hand on her arm. "This is no time to fight among ourselves."

"I wouldn't turn my worst enemy over to *them*," Judas choked the words out. "How can you think...I never meant to...."

What Judas meant or didn't mean, what he told or didn't tell, I will never know. Just then Judas caught sight of Jesus as he pulled himself up from the ground.

"No!" I cried, sensing in a flash what was about to happen. "Judas, stop! They're using you."

But it was too late. Judas was already running out into the open, making straight for Jesus. He fell to his knees before him and kissed Jesus's hand.

In an instant, Judas, Jesus and the stupefied disciples were surrounded by a mixed contingent of Temple guards and Roman soldiers.

I strained forward, but Mary B held onto me fiercely with both hands.

"Mary of Magdala, keep your head!" she commanded in a whisper. "If we are going to be any use at all, we mustn't be seen. Hush! Listen."

"Who are you looking for?"

Jesus's voice was clear and commanding. The soldiers stopped advancing but kept their weapons drawn.

"Jesus of Nazareth," the chief Temple guard answered.

"I am he."

The timbre of his voice raised the hair on the back of my neck. The soldiers took a step back from him. Emboldened, Peter and the Thunder brothers drew swords. Immediately the soldiers moved on them.

"Who are you looking for?" Jesus asked again, stepping forward and stopping the soldiers in their tracks.

"Jesus the Nazarene."

"I told you, I am he. I am the one you are looking for. Let these others go."

As the guards and soldiers moved towards him, Peter struck blindly and lopped off the ear of a Temple servant. Jesus calmly bent, picked up the ear, and restored it, further terrifying everyone.

"Put away your sword, Peter," he said. "Am I not to drink the cup my father has given me?" He looked across the clearing to the tree where Mary and I were hiding, and I swear he knew I was there. "The cup I was born to drink from before and beyond time, in all the worlds."

Then as if he were some wild and unpredictable animal, the guards and soldiers rushed Jesus and bound him as the terrified disciples scattered. All except Judas who stood gaping, transfixed with horror and helplessness.

"Take that one, too!" shouted one of the Temple guards. "I know him. He instigated a riot at Sukkoth."

As one of the soldiers lunged at him, Judas found his legs again and dodged him. The soldier managed to catch hold of Judas's loincloth, but it was so loosely wound that Judas slipped free of it and ran away naked into the night.

"Let the vermin go. We've got the one they want."

Though Jesus offered no resistance, the soldiers jerked at the rope erratically, forcing him to stumble and fall every few feet. Whenever he fell, they'd drag him as he struggled to get up.

I still don't know how I kept from hurling myself on the soldiers in full *beansidhe* cry. There is intense shame in powerless witness of anyone's humiliation, let alone if he is your soul's beloved, your heart's heart. Mary had told me to keep my head, but I know I wasn't thinking clearly. When the thing you've dreaded most comes to pass, it's hard to take in that it's happening. Yet your senses become bizarrely heightened. You notice everything—a loose clump of earth or fresh sheep's dung under your feet, the grating quality of someone's laugh. At the same time nothing seems real at all. Somehow you keep going, even if you think you can't. You take the next step and the next, the next breath and the next. If you are lucky, you hold tightly to the hand of someone who is as frightened and lost as you are.

In just this way, Mary and I crossed the Kedron Valley, keeping just out of range of the guards' torchlight. Gradually we became aware that some of the men were following, too. It was still dark when the soldiers reached the Antonin gate and called to the watch to open it. Most of the men held back under the cover of a rock or tree or a dip in the land. Mary B and I pressed ourselves close to the wall; in a moment, we spotted Peter creeping towards us on his belly. Then he, too, was pressed against the wall. I looked up and saw that by blind (literally) luck, we were in a spot that could not be seen from the watchtower. Edging our way along the wall, we managed to slip inside the gate and duck into an alley before the watch bolted it again.

From our hiding place we listened to the sound of the soldiers' feet, marching in time, all business now, no more fun and games with the prisoner.

"It sounds like they've turned right," whispered Mary B. "We can catch up if we cut through the alley."

Mary's sense of direction proved to be accurate, and we trailed the guard through the streets of the upper city and into the outer courtyard of a small palace. The soldiers and Jesus were admitted to the house at once, and the door closed behind them, shutting us out. We turned and clung to each other, all of us shaking.

"This is the High Priest's house," said Mary, her teeth chattering.

"What does that mean?" I asked. "Is the Sanhedrin in there, waiting to try him?"

"They wouldn't meet here," Mary was certain. "There's a chamber at the Temple where the Sanhedrin deliberates."

"Then what—?"

But I didn't finish my sentence. I thought I knew. Caiaphas had to see him; Jesus haunted him, this man he had prophesied would perish not for the people only but for the scattered children of God. He had to see him face to face before—

"No!" I said out loud.

"What?" Mary and Peter were both alarmed.

"There's still a chance. I'm going to get Joseph. He kept Passover with Nicodemus instead of us, in case anything happened. He'll still be there. He and Nicodemus can talk to Caiaphas; they can reason with him."

"Maeve," Mary put her hand on my arm. "Caiaphas can't do anything if Pilate—"

"I've got to go," I shook her off. "You'd better go tell the other women."

"All right," she agreed.

"I'll go with Mary," Peter said.

I stopped in my tracks.

"No, Peter, no! You wait in the courtyard and keep watch in case they move him."

"But the High Priest's household is waking up," protested Peter as a maidservant came out to tend a fire in a charcoal brazier. "What if someone—"

"Stay," I commanded him as if he were a big, whimpering dog, and I ran as fast as I could to Nicodemus' house.

Nicodemus' long-suffering wife opened the door.

"So it's happened" was all she said, and she went to fetch the two men.

In what seemed an impossibly long time to me but must only have been a few minutes, the three of us were half-walking, half-running through the grey, dawn streets, wasting no breath on words. When we got to the courtyard of the High Priest's house we found Peter still there, huddled just inside the gate, sobbing.

"Peter! What's happened?" I crouched beside him.

"He said, he said I would deny him, deny him three times before the cock crowed, and I did. I did, I did."

He began to wail again.

"Peter!" I hugged him, and then I shook him hard. "Get over it. Is he still inside?"

Before Peter could answer, the door opened, and the guard emerged with Jesus still bound. For a moment, I saw only Jesus. He caught my eye and didn't smile exactly but he conveyed a sense of lightness and ease that both confounded me and reassured me. Then all the other players came back into focus and the action started again.

"The High Priest has come out!" whispered Nicodemus.

Caiaphas stood in the courtyard facing Jesus. I had glimpsed the High Priest before and had always thought of him as a man in his prime, confident to the point of arrogance. Now despite his full priestly regalia, he looked frail, bowed, as if his robes and office were too big and heavy for him. He called for a servant to bring him a basin of water. Slowly, thoroughly, never taking his eyes from Jesus, he washed his hands.

(I know you have always been told it was Pilate who washed his hands of the innocent blood, but the custom is Jewish. Trust me, Romans did not concern themselves with a little blood on their hands, especially not the blood of Jewish troublemakers.)

"*Shema Yisrael: Adonai Elohenu, Adonai Echod.*" Caiaphas began to weep as the sun spilled into the city. "Israel, Jerusalem, hear me. Yahweh Sabaoth, hear the words of your servant, you alone know my heart. My hands are clean of this man's blood."

With that the High Priest turned and walked back into his house, and the guard marched Jesus out of his courtyard.

Time began to warp as it does after a sleepless night when there is nothing you can do anymore but wait. Joined by the other Companions, we followed Jesus and his guard to Pilate's headquarters, then to Herod's Jerusalem digs, as they batted him back and forth, the way two cats will amuse themselves with a mouse.

Word spread quickly that Jesus of Nazareth had been taken into custody. A crowd had gathered by the time Jesus staggered out from Herod's palace into the street, naked except for a purple rag thrown over his shoulders and a crown of thorns on his head. Though he looked the worse for wear with blood and bruises on his cheek, he managed to wear the crown almost rakishly. When he smiled, the people wept and cheered for him, until the soldiers beat them back with swords and whips. Still, many followed as the armed guard dragged Jesus back to Pilate again.

Then there was more waiting and waiting on The Pavement, the only place where Pilate ever appeared before the people in Jerusalem. The soldiers ranged along the walls of the Antonin fortress could keep watch over the crowd from above. Soldiers also guarded the raised platform where he would sit. At the first sign of a disturbance, Pilate could retreat into the fastness of the fortress, and through a series of secret passages exit from Jerusalem altogether, if necessary. As the sun climbed in a glaring sky, those huge flat paving stones soaked up heat. Though it was only mid-morning, our throats were parched; none of us could bear to speak. I felt sweat trickle between my breasts and down the back of my knees. Only Martha's insistence kept us from severe dehydration as she made us drink from a skin of well-watered wine.

At last Pilate came out and took his seat on the platform, and the crowd stirred, hackles rising, a low growl in its throat. Pilate was playing a dangerous game; what he did in this precarious moment could spark or quell a rebellion.

I could see that he knew it, and even relished it. Here was another chance to send a not-so-subtle message: you people are dangerous and *out* of control. Rome is dangerous and *in* control. Now who do you suppose will win? I looked at this man who held my beloved's life and death in his hands, as he took his time getting comfortable, pointedly ignoring the crowd, as he arranged himself in his chair. There was nothing remarkable about him; I had seen hundreds like him pass through the doors of the Vine and Fig Tree in Rome. He was not obsessed with Jesus like Herod or torn by self-doubt like Caiaphas. The job of ruling an unruly outpost of the empire could be tedious; today he hoped to be amused. That was all.

Finally Pilate gave a curt nod; a few moments later, Jesus was dragged out, still wearing the tattered purple and the thorns, but it was clear that Pilate had had him severely beaten; he could barely stand, and he eyes were dazed by the sudden light. A cry went up from the crowd that was more like the moan of a wounded beast than an angry roar. I swear Pilate could smell fear, though not a muscle moved in his face.

"Silence!" Pilate said just as the sound died away, as if he had commanded it.

"Behold the man." He gestured to Jesus. "Your king." The contempt in his tone was unmistakable. "The King of the Jews. Yes?"

If the crowd hailed him as king, they could all be slaughtered on the spot; they kept an uneasy silence.

"Lord Procurator," said one of the Temple Elders. "Begging your pardon, I believe you may be under a misapprehension. This man may say he is king, but as you know the Jews have no king in Judea."

"No king?" Pilate arched an eyebrow. "No king at all?"

"No king but Caesar, that is." The Temple elder got the gist.

"That is most gratifying to hear," said Pilate, "but I am afraid that is not what my friend King Herod Antipas tells me. He says that you people want a new king, a new King David. He says you have chosen this man. Are you going to deny him to his face when he stands here in his robe and crown?"

Pilate mocked, but Jesus did look like a king; his eyes had adjusted to the light and looked clear and unafraid. Though he had been dragged out of his cell, he was now standing by himself. His breathing was slow and deep. Another cry went up from the crowd, perilously close to a cheer, but no one took Pilate's bait.

"Very well, then," said Pilate. "Since no one will answer me, I will ask the man himself."

As he motioned for the soldiers to bring Jesus closer to him. Pilate shifted sideways in his chair, so that Jesus could look at him without turning his

back to the crowd. This was theatre, and if he was going to humiliate the Galilean, he wanted everyone to see the man's face.

"I am going to ask you a simple question," Pilate spoke to Jesus the way
men of his class always spoke to peasants, as if Jesus were slow-witted. "And I
want a simple answer. Do you or do you not claim to be king of the Jews?"

Jesus gave him the simplest answer of all: silence.

Pilate waited for a moment, and signaled to one of the soldiers who
came forward and struck Jesus a blow across the face. He staggered but did not
fall. As soon as he had regained his balance, he slowly, deliberately—so that no
one could miss the gesture—offered the soldier his other cheek. The soldier
was unnerved and took a step back.

"Again," Pilate said softly, but everyone heard him.

The soldier obeyed, but without much force. Pilate waved him away.

"You will answer my question," Pilate said, almost mildly, as if it were a
mere point of information. "Do you call yourself a king?"

"My kingdom does not belong to Rome," Jesus answered at last. "It is
not a kingdom you know how to find. For it is much vaster than any empire
and yet it is small, small as a mustard seed, small as a hazelnut."

Then Jesus turned from Pilate and looked straight at me. As our eyes
met, I felt the fire of the stars flowing between us, a great, golden, invisible
river.

"So you admit that you style yourself king!" Pilate said. "And of a great
empire no less."

Pilate's attempt at sarcasm failed; for the man before him, however
bruised and bloody, looked so undiminished that his claim seemed simply
true. There was the vast sky over him and beneath the paving stones the depth
and mystery of the earth. Jesus seemed as immeasurable as both, whereas
Pilate looked like the petty official he was.

"King is your word," answered Jesus, as if the two were discussing the
complexities of translation. "I can only tell you this: for this I was born."

He paused and in that moment I saw him walking beside the Sea of
Galilee the day he set forth from Temple Magdalen with those very words
singing in him: for this I was born, for this I was born.

"For this I came into the world," he went on. "To bear witness to the
truth. And all who are on the side of truth listen to my voice."

A timid cheer went up from the crowd again, but my heart sank. I could
see it in Pilate's face, his jaw clamped, his teeth gritted. He was done playing.
Jesus was trying to make a fool of him, and he clearly had the power to sway
the people. He had to go.

"Truth," Pilate spoke in a low voice to Jesus alone, but I was near enough to hear him. "What is truth?"

Then he addressed the crowd.

"I find this man guilty of conspiracy against the lawful rule of the Roman Empire. Anyone found to have consorted with this man in furtherance of his cause shall be charged with the same crime and punished accordingly, that is, put to death.

"Take him away," he said to the soldiers flanking Jesus. "Take him away and crucify him. The rest of you disperse this crowd. We are done here."

CHAPTER SEVENTY-FIVE

THE COUNTRY OF LIFE

I njustice was swift in those days. No waiting for years on death row in the hope that an appeal might succeed, or new evidence be found, or a pardon granted. The Romans' preferred method of execution was ingenious but crude. No need for elaborate preparation: just a heavy crossbeam to be carried by the condemned man himself. The upright beams were already in place on Golgotha, a hill beyond the city walls.

Because of Pilate's pronouncement about guilt by association, the Galilean men had made themselves scarce. Only Lazarus, Joseph and Nicodemus, whose connections would likely protect them, waited with the women at the dungeon gate of the fortress.

"But where is Miriam?" I asked Mary B, taking in for the first time that she wasn't with us. "Wasn't she there at the Upper Room with the others?"

"She was there," Mary said. "I told her he'd been arrested, but I don't know how much she took in. She refused to come with us. She kept insisting there was something she had to do. I suppose one of us better go find her now."

"Oh, the poor dear lamb!" Salome was stricken. "Of course. I will go to her. A mother needs another mother at a time like this. And when I find my two sons and finish knocking their two heads together, I will see that they care for Miriam as if she had carried them in her own womb."

Salome hurried off just as Jesus was led out, exhausted, bleeding, but still on his feet. I forgot everyone else. Without thinking, I went to him. The next thing I knew I was on the ground, where a soldier had flung me.

"We've got to stay calm," said Mary B as she and Susanna helped me up. "For his sake. It'll only make it harder for him to see us getting beaten up."

The soldiers hoisted the crossbeam on his shoulders and gave him a shove to get him moving. He reeled under its weight.

"Please," I begged the soldiers. "Let us carry it for him."

The men just laughed.

"Prisoner seems to be popular with the ladies."

"Looks like he's got a whole damn brothel following him."

To drown out the lewd comments, Mary B began to sing in a clear, strong voice.

> *Hosanna to the son of David*
> *Blessings on him who comes in the name of the Lord*
> *Hosanna in the highest*

"Stop your caterwauling, you crazy bitch!" shouted one of the soldiers.

But she kept singing and we all sang with her, and the soldiers gave up trying to silence us. Who knows why? Maybe because it broke up the monotony of their day, maybe because it strengthened their prisoner and helped him move more quickly. We sang and sang, making as much of a circle around Jesus as we could on the narrow street, surrounding him with our voices. We kept singing all the way through the city.

When we stepped outside the gate, something stopped us. Maybe the sky was too big, the grade of hill too steep. In the silence, Jesus stumbled and one of the soldiers commandeered a passerby to carry his cross the rest of the way. We walked as close to Jesus as we could get. I kept my eyes on our feet, and as we walked the stony terrain, I had an odd sense that I had lived this moment before. *The country of life makes me weep. The stones here are so hard.* Yet I had chosen it, to walk on this earth with him. *The country of life makes me weep.* Blades of new grass pushed past the stones and pierced my heart; the anemones bloomed here and there, bright as blood.

We kept our eyes on the ground for as long as we could; for Golgotha was a grisly sight. A dozen men already hung from crosses in various stages of dying. Two more condemned men brought up the rear of our own procession. While the soldiers set to work, binding the crossbeams for the three new prisoners to the uprights, Jesus had a brief moment of respite. He stood still, his eyes closed, letting the wind wash over him. Dust coated his open wounds and stuck to the sweat on his face. Martha tried to give him a drink from the wineskin, but the soldiers wouldn't let us touch him. Then his cross was ready. I opened my mouth, but no sound came out.

"Jesus!" Mary B spoke, her voice amazingly strong. "Jesus, we are here with you, praying. We will not leave you."

Jesus nodded, and opened his eyes, taking in each of us, looking last of all at me.

And then it began.

We held tightly to each other to keep from screaming as the soldiers hammered nails through his forearms—not the hands, as you may have been told, for the weight of a strong man could tear his hands loose. In the arm, the nails rip the flesh and then get caught fast in the bones of the wrist. Then the soldiers bent his legs and drove a long iron spike through both his heels. On the upright beam was a wooden slat, just large enough for the victim to half-sit on. It was not meant for comfort, but to prolong the agony of death by suffocation. Jesus seemed half-suffocated already, holding his breath to keep from crying out.

The soldiers carried out the mechanics of execution as if they were any workmen doing any job, all in a day's work, and that made it even more dreadful. When Jesus was fixed to the cross, they nailed a placard over his head. In Latin, Greek, and Hebrew it read: King of the Jews. Then the men sat down to while away the dull hours of his dying with a dice game.

I looked at my beloved stretched out on the bare, dead wood, the empty sky behind him. Then I gazed only at his face, his eyes closed, his lips parched and cracked. These were the cracked lips I had seen over and over in nightmare visions all my life. The moment was happening now.

All at once I remembered; there was another part of the vision. I was not helpless. I knew what to do.

Esus. I called to him silently, the name I had first called him, the name of the god suspended from a tree, the name of a boy I had once unbound from a tree. *Esus.*

My beloved opened his eyes and looked at me from the cross, just looked.

No. I heard him speak in my mind. *No, Maeve, I can bear the pain.*

Do not argue with me, I answered sternly.

No, Maeve, no. This suffering is mine.

You are wrong, Esus ab Miriam. Remember your vision inside the druid mound. You know the suffering is mine, too.

No.

Yes. For my sake. For love's sake.

Then my beloved cried aloud, and I was there on the cross with him. I became him. I became pain so absolute that whose it was seemed meaningless. Lacerated flesh, torn muscle, wracked bone, pounding head. Words can't say it. There was no place of ease by which to identify this pain. There was nothing to hold onto. Then I found some floating scrap of will (whose I don't know) and

I grasped it, praying in and out, in and out, O love O love O love. My prayer became heartbeat, breath, a tiny coracle moon resting in a sky of pain, drifting on a sea of pain, and I rode it on and on. For minutes, for hours, I don't know. O love O love O love.

Maeve of Tir na mBan, a voice commanded. *Mary of Magdala. Come back. Come back to yourself.*

It was not my beloved's voice; I did not want to know whose it was.

No.

Yes.

And I was back on the hill standing before the cross in an eerie half-light. The soldiers cursed and people moaned in terror; I looked at the sky and saw a shadow over the sun. Night had come in the middle of the day. People cried out to the helpless man on the cross to save himself, to save them all.

"Mary of Magdala." I turned and saw Miriam standing beside me. "There is something else you must do now."

Her voice was hard as the stones of Jerusalem, as the nails that pierced her son. And I knew she was the one who had called me back.

"I thirst," my beloved cried out, his voice like a desert; the wind still blew hot and dry, unrelieved by the noon night. "I thirst."

In the dim light, I saw Miriam take out a sponge she had soaked in a jar. She stuck it on the end of a hyssop stick and handed it to me.

"Give him to drink," Miriam commanded.

"*Eli, Eli,*" he cried out. "*Lama sabachthani!*"

"Beloved, hear me," I spoke with my own voice and more than mine. "I will never forsake you before or beyond time, in all the worlds."

The soldiers made no made no attempt to stop me as I put the soaked sponge to his cracked lips. I felt his mouth open and his tongue probing the sponge, savoring the moisture as if it were a kiss.

"O love," he whispered; then in a louder voice he cried, "It is finished."

His head fell forward.

For a moment there was a silence more absolute than any I have ever known, as if the world had not yet come to be. Then the birds began to sing at once, flock after flock flinging themselves into the sky as the shadow fled and the light returned.

And Miriam began a high keening chant:

> *I am Miriam*
> *my name means bitterness*
> *and I will mourn*
> *mourn and not be comforted*

for the Lord God has dealt bitterly
with his handmaiden.
Once I said yes yes
be it unto me according to your will
I am Miriam
my name means rebellion
and now I say no
the holy one will not win
what the holy one wills
he shall not have
For I am the mother
and I say my son shall sleep
sleep in my womb
sleep until he rises
rises with the sun.
I am Miriam
my name means bitter rebellion
the angels are round about me
And you shall not have him
terrible one, you shall not
you shall not have
my son.

Miriam sang on and on. Even those who wanted to comfort her had to stand back; repelled by a force field around her—invisible but bright and hard as a shield. After she sang her fierce lament for the third time, it dawned on me. She wasn't mad with grief; she had a plan, a brilliant, audacious plan. I picked up the jar that had held the sponge and sniffed it, confirming my suspicions. When no one had known where she was that morning, she had been gathering herbs, bitter herbs, sweet herbs, saving herbs. Then I looked at my beloved, seemingly dead, and saw the lights flickering around him, just as they had around Lazarus. When I closed my eyes, I could hear it: the sound of the river.

Joseph came to me then and put his arms around me.

"Maeve, I'm so sorry," his voice broke. "I'm so sorry."

"Joseph, listen," I said. "We've got to get him down off the cross. Please make the soldiers take him down."

Joseph gave me an odd look, but did not question me. He approached the soldiers, who had lost no time returning to their dice game, now that it was apparent that the end of the world wasn't at hand. I heard the clink of coins as

Joseph tried to bribe them. He argued for a while, and then returned to me, shaking his head.

"It's no use. They're terrified to disobey orders. They're allowed to cut the Jews down an hour before sunset out of respect for the Sabbath, but they won't budge till then."

"Joseph!" Another fear dawned on me. "They won't take his body, will they? We can't let them!"

"I haven't been much use, Maeve, but that much I can do for him, for you. I own a tomb near here. I have already petitioned the proper authorities and they will let me have the body."

I kissed his cheek and went to sit with the other women weeping at the foot of the cross. But I did not weep; I held fast to his foot and listened to the sound of the river while Miriam's song hushed to a sigh like the wind in the reeds. Strange as it may seem to you, I even fell asleep for a while. In my dream, I saw our feet again. *All the worlds are here,* I heard a voice say. I could see the golden spray around the island of Tir na mBan in the Otherworld and the cold stream in the country of the dead. But the country of life held all the worlds. *Here the stones are so hard; here the earth is so sweet. The country of life makes me weep.*

"This one is already dead."

I woke suddenly to see two soldiers standing over us.

"Out of the way, you sorry-ass whores."

We scrambled to our feet and waited for the soldiers to take him down from the cross. I held my breath. Miriam's plan was going to work.

"Best to be sure," one said to the other. "Lot of strange goings on today."

Before any of us knew what was happening, the soldier took his spear and gave a swift thrust up under the ribs straight into Jesus's heart.

Blood and water poured from his side, as if he contained the whole ocean and the last rays of the dying sun. Someone screamed. For a long time there was nothing but sound. When it finally stopped, I saw Miriam cradling her son in her arms.

He was dead.

CHAPTER SEVENTY-SIX

TIR NAN OG

The tomb—a man-made cave really, hollowed out from a hillside—was spacious and clean. There was an antechamber and two rooms, each with two stone slabs built into the wall. You could easily live in the tomb, let alone be dead there. We brought in oil lamps and incense and covered the slab reserved for Jesus with thick, woven cloths, strewn with flowers and aromatic herbs. None of us could bear to think of his naked body resting on the bare stone. When we were ready, Joseph and Lazarus lifted Jesus and laid him out, as if helping him to bed, and then left the women alone to prepare his body.

As we set to work washing away the dust and the blood, we saw that scarcely an inch of him had not been lashed, pierced, and bruised. And yet it was his body still. The body that had touched us, held us, healed us. From this body had come the voice we loved: teasing, ranting, arguing, telling jokes and stories. This was the body Miriam had once carried inside her womb. This was the body I had taken inside mine, till inside and outside had no meaning anymore. Some people say that at the very moment of death, the person is gone, the body just inert matter, matter that does not matter anymore. I do not find that to be so. As I washed and anointed him, I still knew him in his body. I still loved him for having taken on this dear, particular flesh. While I tended his body with the other women who loved him, I felt almost at peace. There was no other place to be. There was nothing else to do.

When we had finished washing him, we rubbed his whole body with fragrant oils, aloe, myrrh, and spikenard. Then we loosely wrapped him in linen; we would wrap him more securely in fresh linens before the tomb was finally sealed.

"Well," said Martha after we had all stood gazing at him for some time. "We have done all that is needful here. We must go now and keep the Sabbath, as he would have wished us to do. We will come back the morning after."

Weeping softly, the women touched him, each in her particular way, before they filed out of the tomb.

"Come, Mary," Martha spoke to me as she waited at the door. "There is nothing more for you to do here now."

"I am going to stay with him," I heard myself say, "until you come back."

"There is no need," objected Martha. "Joseph has arranged for guards to keep watch. They will be here soon."

"I'm staying."

"But it's not seemly, a woman alone all night in a tomb."

"I will be with my husband."

"But it is not our custom."

"It is my custom."

"Martha." Miriam appeared in the doorway. "Let Mary of Magdala be."

Ma's voice was weary, flat, horribly ordinary, bereft of angelic whispers and fragrant breezes. I felt a sudden sharp sense of loss. Stay with me, I almost said. But she was already gone. Martha shrugged, set down her lamp, and followed.

And I was alone with my dead beloved in the tomb. I sat down near his feet, just sat and waited for the tears to come, for grief to claim me. But all I felt was tired and maybe a little envious. Death looked so restful.

When I heard voices outside, I thought nothing of it, assuming it was the guard Joseph had posted. Other sounds followed, grunting and scraping. I got up and went into the antechamber just in time to see the last sliver of dusky light disappear.

The tomb was sealed.

I cried out. Of course I did. But if anyone heard me, no one answered. It occurred to me briefly that I ought to be frightened. But I didn't have the energy for it. The others knew I was there; they intended to come back in two days. I could manage without food or water for that long. The lamp Martha had left would burn for a while yet, perhaps all night. I picked it up and went back to the chamber where Jesus lay.

In his grave swaddling he could have been any dead body—not the body of my beloved. Martha was not here to scold me; there was no one to offend, so I unwound the linens and gazed at him again, intent on every detail, going over and over him, as if committing a poem to memory, the place where his eyebrows almost met, the hollow under his cheek bone, the hair that still smelled like gorse and wild thyme, the narrow valley between the muscles of his chest, the thrust of hip bone, his penis curled in the nest of thick dark hair, his legs, each muscle standing out, and his feet, pierced through the tendons at the heel, still beautiful, brown as new-turned earth, tough, but each strong bone delicately defined.

I gazed and gazed until my eyes ached. The pressure built in my tear ducts, in my throat, in my heart, and still I could not weep, for how do you weep the sea? My grief felt that immense. Then I remembered that if my own tears wouldn't flow, I had tears with me, hanging on a cord around my neck in a little vial that rested against my breasts.

Whore's tears. Cure anything.

I lifted the cord over my head and took the vial in my hands. Unstopping it, I held the tiny scalpel, and dropped the tear beaded there onto his wrist, where the nail had been driven in. Then I bathed the other wrist with a tear, and as I washed each wound again, from the tiniest laceration, to the death wound in his side, I began to sing aloud, my voice resounding in the stone chamber. Over and over I sang:

> *Set me like a seal on your heart,*
> *like a seal on your arm.*
> *For love is strong as death,*
> *passion as relentless as Sheol.*
> *The flash of it is a flash of fire*
> *a flame of Yahweh himself.*
> *Love no flood can quench*
> *no torrents drown.*

Then the song began to change or another song wove in and out.

> *For the river that flows from my heart is a flame*
> *that will carry me over the seas*
> *and I will unbind you from the tree*
> *from the tamarisk tree and the oak*
> *yes I will unbind you from the tree*
> *the bare tree and the leafless one.*
>
> *For love is as strong as death*
> *passion relentless as Sheol.*
>
> *No flood can quench my love*
> *For I am the queen of all rivers*
> *who makes the waters rise and recede*
> *and I will seek you among the reeds*

I will find you forever
For mine is the power to remember
and I will re-member you.

I will kiss you with the kisses of my mouth
I will fill you with the breath of life.

Set me as a seal on your heart
like a seal on your arm
For love is as strong as death
passion as relentless as Sheol.
The flash of love is the flash of your fire
and you shall rise with the sun
a flame of Yahweh himself.

And I sang and sang until the vial was empty of its last tear. And then my own tears rose like the Nile in flood, and I washed him all over again. At last I lay down beside him, and when the flame in the lamp burned out, I gave his cold body my own fire, and I kissed him with the kisses of my mouth and breathed into him the breath of life, until I felt his warm living arms surround me, till he rose in me and we loved again with the river singing in the reeds all around us.

That is all I remember until the earthquake. The ground rose and roared and shook itself. Then just as suddenly it was quiet again, until the birds began to sing, cautiously at first, then madly, joyously. I got up and followed the sound, stepping from the dark chamber into the antechamber that was filled with dawn light.

The stone had rolled away.

I stepped out of the tomb into a garden, fragrant with spice. Drops of dew caught the early light and hung distinct on every petal and leaf. Flocks of birds tossed themselves into the air, spiraled, and then lit in the branches of a huge tree, a golden tree that shed its own light.

Then I saw a man, tending the tree, perhaps pruning it. The tree was so bright I could not see him clearly. I thought he must be the gardener of whatever this place was. Where was I? I turned and saw the tomb, gaping behind me. I must have fallen asleep beside Jesus's body, for I'd had such a beautiful dream… Then all the hairs stood up on my neck as it finally registered: I had woken alone. Jesus's body was gone. I whirled around and there was the shadowy gardener still busily pruning the golden tree.

"What in the three worlds is going on around here?" I demanded.

The gardener turned toward me.

"Love is as strong as death," he remarked in an offhand tone, as if he were saying, lovely morning, isn't it? "Oh and passion as relentless as Sheol, of course."

I gaped at him, his features still not coming into focus, the tree blinding me.

"Maeve, my dove."

It was his voice, his voice.

"Sweet holy fucking Isis!" I breathed.

"Yes," he agreed.

And then I saw him clearly: standing naked under the tree, laughing, beautiful. His wounds still showed, and yet at the same time they were healed.

"Jesus!"

I wanted to rush straight into his arms, but something held me back.

"I know," he acknowledged. "This body takes some getting used to. It's the same as when a butterfly is first unfolding its wings. You can't touch it yet. But *cariad*, you can come and stand with me, stand with me beneath the tree."

I walked across the garden to the tree, my feet bare on the damp, sweet earth. I saw that, like him, I was also naked, naked and as radiant as the morning rising all around us. And so we stood together under the tree, not touching but taking each other in more deeply than we ever had before, taking in the whole singing radiance of the world, and giving it back to each other, giving it back to the world.

"Beloved," Jesus said after at least one eternity. "Will you go tell the others?"

"What shall I tell them?"

"Tell them, it's all right. Everything is all right. I'm going ahead to Galilee. I'll meet them there."

"Why can't *you* tell them?"

"They wouldn't be able to see me or hear me. Not yet."

"What makes you think they'd believe me?" I objected. "Hey, just because you died and rose again, does that mean I get all the hard jobs now?"

He burst out laughing. (There is no sound more beautiful in all the worlds than that man's laugh.)

"Maeve, do you know how much I love you? Listen, *cariad*, I can't explain everything. Explanations are not a good idea anyway. Remember that. Will you just do this for me? Bring everyone back to Galilee? To Temple Magdalen, if you can. Everyone could use a holiday."

"Can't you go with us?" I asked wistfully.

"Not this time," he said gently. "Not in the way you mean. But I am with you. You know that, don't you? I am with you always."

Slowly, almost involuntarily, I nodded.

"I will see you in Galilee then, Maeve, my heart."

"By the way," I stalled him. "Did you know that you're naked?"

"Yes, I know. It's not really a problem for me, though."

"I get it," I said. "It's a god thing, right?"

"Something like that." He seemed uncomfortable. "But you know, Maeve, I'm still Jewish." We both looked down; he definitely was. "And there is only one God—"

"So much for the god-making death, then," I said almost lightly.

"By the way," he changed the subject. "You're naked, too. You might want to put something on before you go find the others. To keep from dazzling people too much."

"Jesus," I said. "Will you just please tell me one thing before you go?"

He looked at me with such tenderness; I thought I would burst into new leaf on the spot for the sheer joy of it.

"Yes, beloved."

I drank in the sight of him standing under the tree that shed its own light. The garden was still cool and spicy even as a warm fragrant breeze touched us lightly.

"Where are we? What is this place?"

"Maeve, *cariad*. Don't you know?"

I shook my head.

"Tir nan Og," he whispered the name of that Shining Isle where time reverses like a tidal river. "Tir nan Og."

Then he was gone.

I was alone in the garden. I looked down at my naked body, golden with the light of that place. It seemed a shame to cover such glory. But he had asked me to tell the others. It was time to go. I went back to the empty tomb to look for my tunic, which would be filthy. On the empty bed, I found instead vestments of fine gold cloth, just like the ones in which we robed Isis on high holidays. Beside the robe lay a crown of fresh, wild roses, the kind that grew at Temple Magdalen. There was an ankh for my right hand, and a sistrum for my left.

You will excuse me for not being more surprised.

As I vested myself, I heard him singing—from a great way off, from inside my heart—one of the morning hymns we sang at Temple Magdalen:

Because of Isis, there is a heaven
Because of Isis, there is an earth

Because of Isis, winds blow in the desert
Because of Isis, the sweet sun shines

Because of Isis, the river floods in spring
Because of Isis, plants bear fruit

Because of Isis, we live and grow strong
Because of Isis, we have breath to give thanks

When I was all dressed and about to leave the tomb, I spied the empty vial on the bed and the tiny scalpel. I picked them up and went out into the garden. Before the sun could draw it up, I harvested the dew of Tir nan Og.

CHAPTER SEVENTY-SEVEN

WHAT HAPPENED AFTER

I am not going to say much about how the good news, so to speak, was received. You can guess. I met the women on their way to the tomb. (In case you are wondering, my gold vestments became invisible once I left Tir nan Og but there is no explaining how my tunic and cloak were so fresh and clean.) Miriam merely smiled a secretive smile; she already knew. Mary B, Salome, and Susanna, who had been with me on Mount Hermon, embraced the mystery and me at once. Only Martha was a little balky—until Mary B reminded her that, after all, their brother had walked out of a tomb alive.

"But that was different!" objected Martha. "The Master called him forth. Who on earth could have called Jesus back from the dead?"

"Explanations are not always a good idea," I said hastily, quoting my beloved.

And Martha, being eminently practical, let the matter go.

I don't think any of the men believed me at all. Grief-stricken, terrified, and exhausted, they heard only one part of the message:

Go home, home to Galilee, home to the Gennesaret, to the smell of fish, to the always-changing light and wind on the water. Go home.

So we all got ready to go, except for poor Judas. Whether he hanged himself to avoid further torture at the hands of the Romans, or out of guilt for whatever part he played, willingly or not, in Jesus's arrest, or out of despair at what must have seemed to him his utterly lost cause, I do not claim to know. But I believe the thirty pieces of silver story is a crock. I reckon my beloved's chroniclers included it, because the thirty pieces of silver makes a neat correlation with a passage from the prophet Zechariah. (11:12-13, if you want to look it up). That is one way to tell a story, but it is not mine.

And forget Potter's Field. Kindhearted Lazarus for once disregarded his strong-minded sisters and buried Judas in his own erstwhile tomb.

Then all of us, including Joseph and the Bethany family, set forth for Galilee, this time through the mountains of Samaria where wildflowers bloomed in profusion. Once on the shore of the Gennesaret, the women, even Martha, decided to stay at Temple Magdalen, and the men, except for Joseph and Lazarus, went with Peter to Capernaum. Jesus's brothers and sister also joined us and sorted themselves accordingly—the men with the men, Jesus's sister with us.

There, I said to my invisible beloved, as I stood on the tower of Temple Magdalen at dawn, having stayed up all night with Dido, Berta, and Reginus, salting the dew of Tir nan Og with fresh whores' tears. *There, cariad, I have done my part; the rest is up to you.*

Did I doubt my own story in the days that followed? No, I was too much at peace. Yes, I missed him in his body. But the very wind and light, water and earth seemed to have taken on new, shining qualities. I would turn my head or blink my eyes and see that I was still in Tir nan Og.

The hardest part about that time was how confused and dispirited the men continued to be, how un-comfortable, literally. Then, after driving Priscilla out of her mind and out of the house (she came to stay with us), the men did the only thing they could think to do (besides going on a permanent drunk): They went fishing.

That's when it happened.

He showed up at Temple Magdalen just before dawn one day, looking just like himself, only more so, wearing ordinary clothes, though they were no-ticeably cleaner than usual. I watched from the tower as Mary B came into the courtyard and saw him standing next to the spring. She ran straight into his arms. He was quite touchable now, able to weather innumerable hugs and kiss-es as the whole Temple Magdalen household woke and rushed to greet him. I am happy to report that he embraced his mother tenderly.

As I came down from the tower into the courtyard, he was still holding Ma. When he finally released her, she looked all of about fourteen years old.

And then it was my turn.

His kiss was spicy and sweet as the garden.

"I won't be long in this form," he whispered in my ear. "But you know time isn't what we think it is."

"I know," I said, though I didn't really.

Then, taking my hand, Jesus turned to the whole crowd at Temple Magdalen and said two words:

"Beach party!"

While the morning stars melted into light, we got a keg of wine, and went down to the shore to get the fire going. As the sun rose, Jesus scanned the water.

"There!" he said, with such gladness in his voice. "That's Peter's boat!"

And so it was, drifting off shore about a hundred yards away.

"Hey, my friends!" he called. "How's the fishing? Caught anything yet?"

"No!" they hollered back. "We've been out for hours. Nothing!"

"Throw the net out to starboard, and you'll find something," Jesus said.

We saw the men fling the net up and out; for an instant it caught the light and turned as golden as the tree, the mesh as intricate and beautiful as its branches. Then they hauled the net through the water. We could tell by the way they bent and strained that the catch must be huge.

Then one of the Thunder Brothers turned and recognized Jesus.

"Peter! Look. It's him! It's the Master."

Peter did not need telling twice; he quickly tied his outer garment around his otherwise naked self, and took a flying leap into the water where he landed with a huge splash.

"Poor Peter!" Jesus was laughing so hard, I thought his wounds would split open. "He still hasn't figured out how to put the right spin on it."

Peter flailed towards us, his progress ungainly. But his joy made him beautiful. Jesus held out his arms to Peter, and the other men, shouting with excitement, rowed hard, towing the teeming net behind them.

"Bring some of the fish you caught," said Jesus, all wet now from Peter's embrace.

The men hauled in the nets, gutted some fish, and we fried them fresh over the charcoal fire. We spent the morning eating and drinking, laughing and crying. Now and then we plunged into the water and splashed each other like children. In the afternoon, we retreated to the shade of the olive orchard, our heads resting against each other's shoulders or in each other's laps, so that we were all intertwined and connected like the roots of the trees.

"Peter," said Jesus as we drowsed together. "Do you love me?"

"Yes, Lord, you know I love you."

"Feed my lambs."

"Peter," Jesus asked again a moment later, "do you love me?"

"Yes, Lord, you know I love you."

"Peter?"

"What!" Peter was bewildered and a little anxious.

"Do you love me?"

"How can you ask me that? You know I love you."

"Then feed my sheep."

We were all silent for a moment, and it dawned on me that by asking Peter to avow his love three times, Jesus had given him a chance to heal the shame of his three denials. Jesus gave us all chances, as many as we needed. All we had to do was love him and—oh, the horror—each other, I suppose, and even ourselves in all our perversity and innocence. Get down and dirty in the singing radiant muck of it all.

"All right," said Peter dubiously. "But you know, Lord, I've always been a fisherman. So maybe you could tell me. What do sheep eat? Besides grass, I mean."

Jesus threw back his head and laughed.

(And if you want to extrapolate from this exchange that Jesus had just founded his church and put Peter in charge of it, well, that's your affair.)

Jesus was with us often in the next few weeks, usually showing up whenever it was time to eat. Or, equally, it became time to feast whenever he was with us. The Companions became almost accustomed to his unannounced comings and goings—insofar as anyone can ever get used to a miracle.

One night he appeared beside me on the tower at Temple Magdalen. We watched the full moon cast its light on the water. (I smiled a secret smile at the moon's round face, knowing that I had not bled at the last dark of the moon.) It had been a month since I had washed his cold body with tears, and felt him rise warm and alive again inside me. Now as we stood close together, I sensed a difference in his presence. His warmth was less solid, more like warmth itself—as if I stood next to a fire or in a patch of sunlight.

I began to tremble.

"Maeve," he spoke to my thoughts. "It's almost time."

I didn't have to ask him time for what.

"Will you take everyone back to Jerusalem?"

"I don't want to go there."

It was not so much an objection as a simple statement of truth. I didn't want to go back into time, into turmoil, to the place of so much suffering, to the place of his death.

"I know, cariad," he acknowledged. "But you know I need to go there."

"Do I?" I turned to look at him.

"There's another part of the story. You know it. You painted it yourself in the upper room, in your temple."

I closed my eyes and saw the Beautiful Gates, so wrongly named. They were the Dreadful Gates, the Terrible Gates.

"Can't we skip that part of the story?" I whispered to myself, to him, to anything that was listening.

"Forgive me, my dove," was all he said.

We all trekked back to Judea, Jesus sometimes walking beside us and sometimes not. We reached Bethany a few days before the festival of Shovuos, the celebration of the first harvest of the barley that was planted in the winter. The companions were a little apprehensive about entering Jerusalem again, but Shovuos was a small, tame festival compared to Passover. Pontius Pilate was back in Caesarea, and the remnant of the militant factions that had been persecuted and subdued during the last feast had retreated to the hills to prepare to fight again another day.

We got up when it was still dark, and by dawn we crested the Mount of Olives and began walking down into the Kedron Valley towards the Beautiful Gates. Jesus was waiting for us beside the once-blasted fig tree that now graciously bore figs in and out of season.

"I am going on alone now," he said. "One day you'll all come. And you'll know that I am there. And you'll know that I am here. There is nothing to fear. Love is as strong as death."

He paused and looked at each person, coming at last to me.

"If you need to remember, ask her. Maeve of Magdala knows."

He seemed about to say more; he searched my face as if he would find the words there. Then he turned and walked alone towards the Beautiful Gates.

I followed him with my eyes, and then with my wings. I could see the white whir of them at the edge of my vision; I could hear them beating the air. I rose up with the sun and rode on the ray that struck the gates, turning them as golden as the tree of Tir nan Og.

The beautiful terrible gates swung open, and my beloved walked into the Temple.

Sea, sun, rock, wind. Nothing. Everything.

Then I heard a voice singing:

> *Look how the sky's doors open to your beauty*
> *Look how the goddess waits to receive you*
> *This is death. This is the life beyond life.*

> *Look how the day is breaking in the east*
> *Look how the goddess awakens you. Listen*
> *to us singing to you, there among the stars.*

It was my voice.

I was standing again under the fig tree. I turned and looked at my companions who were gaping at me with something approaching awe. In the Book of Acts it says two men in white appeared to the disciples.

I am here to tell you: it was a woman dressed in gold.

"Why are you Galileans standing here staring into the sky?" I asked.

"The Master," said Peter. "The Master. Where did he go?"

Slowly I turned and looked all around me. The sun was pouring into the valley now, every drop of dew shining. Overhead a flock of birds wheeled and turned.

"He's here." With my hands I swept the sky, the valley, all of us, until I brought them to rest on my heart. "He's here."

Suddenly I felt so hungry I thought I might faint. I reached up my hand and picked a fig.

I am the Vine, you are the Fig Tree.

"Come on," I said. "Let's eat."

ACKNOWLEDGMENT OF SOURCES

W riting a novel is like going on a journey. When I begin, I have some idea of where I want to go, places where I want to stop along the way, but very little idea what will happen when I get there, or even how I will get there. On this journey books and their authors can be helpful guides. The works I mention below are more than reference books; they became companions on the way.

The Roman Story

Roman Women: Their History and Habits, by J.P.V.D. Balsdon (first published in 1901) more than lived up to its title and told me what I wanted to know about everything from nomenclature to hairstyles, political intrigue to religious piety and scandal—in short, all the juiciest gossip from every period of Rome's long history. In this work of lively scholarship, I first encountered the story of Paulina and Decius Mundus, the author's account derived from those of Roman historians, including Tacitus and Suetonius.

Nickie Roberts' *Whores in History: Prostitution in Western Society* has excellent material on the origins of sacred prostitution as well as a wealth of historical detail on the extraordinary variety of prostitution practiced in imperial Rome and the working conditions whores faced. I owe the backstory of Domitia Tertia to Roberts who noted that women of the Senatorial class sometimes registered as prostitutes to escape forced marriages in which they had little autonomy and could be punished harshly (exiled or put to death) for adultery.

To Sarah B. Pomeroy, author of *Goddesses, Whores, Wives, and Slaves: Women in Classical Antiquity*, I am grateful for the chapter "The Role of Women in the Religion of the Romans" with its extensive section on Isis worship and why this goddess appealed to women of all classes, from Senator's wives to street whores.

To poet and scholar Patricia Monaghan (*see permissions*) I owe thanks for her gorgeous renditions of a hymn to Isis and a hymn from the Egyptian coffin texts, both found in *The Goddess Companion*.

Everything I needed to know about the life of a Roman slave, I found in Keith Bradley's *Slavery and Society at Rome*. From him I learned the endless titles and job descriptions for slaves, such as the *a purpuris*, the slave in charge of purple clothing worn only by those of senatorial rank, and Maeve's title *pedisequa*, one who sits at the feet of or follows on the heels of her owner.

Those who know Sir James George Frazer's classic *The Golden Bough* will recognize the legend of the runaway slave who becomes the King of the Wood—until the next runaway slave tears off a golden branch and challenges the king to fight to the death. Frazer sets this story at Nemi, the site of Paulina's country villa.

The Terrain of the Gospels

My first source is, of course, the Gospels themselves, which I read over and over. Though as an English major I love the language of the King James Version, most of the direct quotations in the novel are from The New Jerusalem Bible. I also studied the non-canonical Gospels of Thomas, Philip, and Mary, and others. All the Gospel scenes in the novel, however, come from Matthew, Mark, Luke, or John.

I never tired of reading books about the life of Jesus and found all of them moving and helpful in some way. I mention below the ones that gave me particular information used in the novel.

I owe great thanks to The Reverend Bruce Chilton, not only for his brilliant and original *Rabbi Jesus: An Intimate Biography* but for his previous works on Jesus's life and times. He has also kindly met with me in person and answered my questions as well as encouraging me to seek my own answers by introducing me to the *Mishnayoth*. I am particularly indebted to Bruce Chilton for the way he brings the disciples to life through Jesus's playful nicknames for them, and I saw no reason to depart from his characterizations. Finally, I thank Bruce Chilton for giving me a more precise understanding of why Jesus drove the money changers from The Temple. His knowledge of the many forms of Judaism practiced in the first century, and how they sometimes clashed, is unequaled.

A.N. Wilson's book *Jesus, A Life* provided insight into the Feeding of the Five Thousand, how it was a miracle in more ways than one, and why it was a pivotal moment in Jesus's ministry.

Russell Shorto's *Gospel Truth: The New Image of Jesus Emerging from Science and History, and Why it Matters* offered a refreshing and succinct survey of the current writing and thinking about Jesus. I particularly relished Shorto's nickname for John the Baptist, The Dipper and I refused an editorial suggestion that I use a seemlier term in my novel.

I am grateful to The Reverend Cathy Surgenor for introducing me to Kenneth E. Baily's *Poet & Peasant and Through Peasant Eyes: A Literary-Cultural Approach to the Parables in Luke*. To him I owe my understanding of both the setting and the social nuances in the story of the woman who washed Jesus's feet with her tears.

Hayyim Schuass's *The Jewish Festivals, History and Observance* was an invaluable guide, and helped me to understand and set the scene for all the celebrations from Temple Magdalen's (extremely unorthodox) Shabbat to "The Last Party."

My most constant companion in the terrain of the Gospels was Henri Daniel-Rops and his book *Daily Life in the Time of Jesus*. He probably did not know that his book is a novelist's dream, for it details exactly how it would feel to be alive in first century Palestine—weather, birds, plants, food, clothing sounds, scents, smells all lovingly described.

To all these writers, scholars, historians, storytellers and fellow travelers I give my gratitude and respect.

A Note on Onsite Research

I was fortunate to be able to make two trips during the writing of *The Passion of Mary Magdalen*, one to Italy and one to Israel. I have visited all the sites named in the novel with the exception of Mount Hermon and Bethany. Geography makes its own contribution to the story or as one map I purchased in Israel says: "Five Gospels record the life of Jesus. Four you will find in books, and one you will find in the land…"

A special thank you to Orly, the guide of my tour in Israel, and a riveting storyteller.

One of my strongest, happiest memories remains a trip by boat from what would have been the site of Magdala to Capernaum where Peter lived—a very short ride. In that moment, the whole story snapped into place, became, in some bone-deep sense, true.

For more on my travels, research, and reading group guide, visit:
www.passionofmarymagdalen.com

PERSONAL ACKNOWLEDGMENTS

T hank you to Deirdre Mullane, the fiercest, most loyal agent any writer could have, and a gifted editor with a sure touch. Thank you to Paul Cohen of Monkfish Publishing for taking the leap and landing with both feet—and for reading the novel more times than anyone else. Thank you to Georgia Dent for the cover, gorgeous beyond my wildest dreams. Thank you to my husband Douglas Smyth for enduring love and partnership.

And finally, thank you to my *combrogos*, my companions, so many to name and so wonderful and various in your gifts that I will have to trust you to know who you are. (If in doubt, ask me. I will thank you profusely and in person.) I could never have kept faith all these years without you.

The Maeve Chronicles

~ forthcoming ~

PREQUEL
DAUGHTER OF THE SHINING ISLES

In this Celtic wonder tale, young Maeve and Jesus, brimming with youthful charm and arrogance, find each other and fall in love, forging a bond that is stronger than death. Born to eight warrior-witches on a magical isle, Maeve heads for druid college with high hopes of meeting the Mysterious Other she has glimpsed only in visions and dream.

From the start, Maeve and Esus, as the druids call him, are sparring partners, by turns delighting and outraging each other with their opposing views on just about everything. Their pleasure is overshadowed by a brilliant but unbalanced druid who knows a perilous secret about Maeve's past. He also becomes obsessed with Esus as a perfect victim for the most sacred druid rite.

In a daring scheme, Maeve risks everything to save the life of the one she loves.

SEQUEL
BRIGHT DARK MADONNA

In this poignant and picaresque novel, Maeve navigates the dizzying world of the early church. Determined to found a movement in his name, Jesus's disciples have many disputes, but all agree on one point: Maeve, an unconverted gentile with a disreputable background, is an unfit mother for the scion of the Savior.

With Jesus's mother in tow, Maeve hides out for a time in the mountains of Galatia, raising her daughter in lonely peace, till one day a man, half-dead from stoning, is brought to her for healing. Enter Paul of Tarsus, who immediately sets about trying to convert Maeve—to Christianity!

Before she finds peace, Maeve's midlife adventures will take her to Ephesus for a final showdown with Paul, to a hermit cave in Southern France, and at last to the British Isles where long-unfinished business awaits her.